A Café on the Nile

Bartle Bull

Carroll & Graf Publishers, Inc.
New York

First Carroll & Graf cloth edition 1998
First Carroll & Graf trade paper edition 1999
Fourth printing September 2000

Carroll & Graf Publishers, Inc.
A Division of Avalon Publishing Group
19 West 21st Street
New York, NY 10010-6805

Library of Congress Cataloging-in-Publication data is available.
ISBN: 0-7867-0675-9

Manufactured in the United States of America

For Grandpa

On Honeymoon, 1909

— *Acknowledgments* —

A Café on the Nile demanded a diversity of expertise beyond the knowledge of its author.

Richard F. Pedersen, former president of the American University in Cairo, assisted me generously with his expertise, advice, and introductions. John Rodenbeck of Cairo, Haut Languedoc and the Oriental Club, whose implacable scholarship is as broad as it is deep, ruthlessly edited several editions of the manuscript to assist the author's struggle to be faithful to the details of Cairene life and culture. Less grueling to work with were the deceased journalists of Cairo's daily English-language newspaper, *The Egyptian Gazette.* Reading three years of their work (1934–1936) introduced this writer to the daily life of Egypt and gave a sense of how the 1930s inexorably rushed into World War II. Also helpful in developing a sense of time and place were Captain John Plant and several members of the Khayyatt and Wissa families, particularly Gertrude Wissa, who was also very kind to my father during the war when he was in hospital in Cairo recuperating from a severe wound.

Other friends who generously provided specialized assistance were: Robin Hurt, the "hunter's hunter," and Terry Mathews, the distinguished sculptor, on wildlife and Africana; Andrew Carduner on automotive matters; Jim Hare and the other veteran pilots of the Rhinebeck Aerodrome; Alan Delynn and Douglas Fairbanks, Jr., on period films; Valmore J. Forgett of the Navy Arms Company; and Peter Horn and R. L. Wilson, the pre-eminent American scholar of fine guns, on Italian weaponry.

I also owe debts of inspiration and information to many of the war correspondents and historians who covered the Italo-Ethiopian conflict, and to the helpful and hospitable people of Ethiopia, particularly Teodros Ashenafi and Ephraim Negori.

At the critical and creative level, my thanks to Constance Roosevelt, Winfield P. Jones, Dimitri Sevastopoulo, my son, Bartle B. Bull, my agent, Carl D. Brandt, and my editor, Kent Carroll, all sharp-eyed readers who made *A Café on the Nile* a better book.

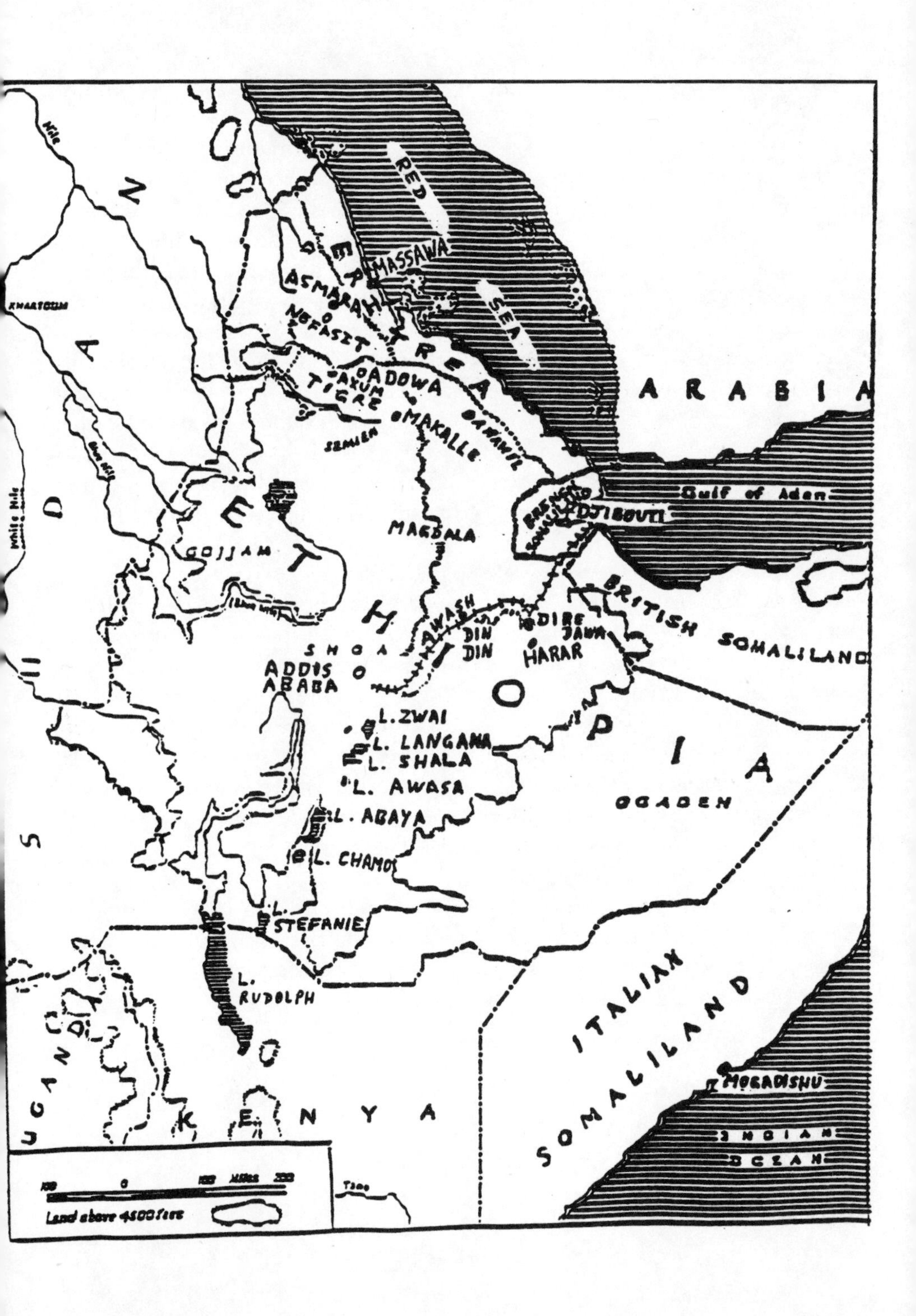

SUDAN
KHARTOUM
Nile
White Nile
RED SEA
MASSAWA
ASMARAH
NEFASIT
ERITREA
ADOWA
AXUM
TIGRE
SEMIEN
MAKALLE
DANAKIL
ARABIA
Gulf of Aden
FRENCH SOMALILAND
DJIBOUTI
MAGDALA
GOJJAM
ETHIOPIA
AWASH
DIN DIN
DIRE DAWA
HARAR
BRITISH SOMALILAND
SHOA
ADDIS ABABA
L. ZWAI
L. LANGANA
L. SHALA
L. AWASA
L. ABAYA
L. CHAMO
L. STEFANIE
L. RUDOLPH
OGADEN
ITALIAN SOMALILAND
MOGADISHU
INDIAN OCEAN
UGANDA
KENYA
100 0 100 MILES 200
Land above 4500 feet

— *The Characters* —

Olivio Fonseca Alavedo *A dwarf, the Goan proprietor of the Cataract Café in Cairo*
Clove Alavedo *The oldest child of Olivio and Kina Alavedo*
Abd al-Azim Pasha *The Royal Chamberlain of the Abdine Palace in Cairo*
Musa Bey Halaib *The Undersecretary of Public Works in Cairo*
Charles Crow *An American artist, on safari in Abyssinia with his fiancée, Bernadette*
Ernst von Decken *A German soldier of fortune and friend of Anton Rider.*
Diwani *A Wakamba, Anton Rider's gunbearer*
Anunciata Fonseca *A woman from Portuguese East Africa, a former lover of Anton Rider, now living in Djibouti*
Colonel Lorenzo Grimaldi *An officer in the Italian air force, the lover of Gwenn Rider*
Dr. August Hänger *A German specialist in dwarfism*
Kimathi *A Kikuyu, Anton Rider's head safari man and former tracker*
Ilsa 'Knuckles' Koch *Dr. Hänger's nurse*
Wellington Llewelyn *The first son of Gwenn Rider*
Bernadette and Harriet Mills *American twins on safari with Charles Crow and Anton Rider*
Lord Penfold *An elderly Englishman, resident in Kenya*
Anton Rider *A professional safari hunter based in Kenya, as a boy raised by gypsies in England*
Denby Rider *The son of Gwenn and Anton Rider*
Gwenn Rider *A Welsh woman at medical school in Cairo, the separated wife of Anton Rider*
Tariq and Haqim *Nubian brothers from the Sudan, employed by Olivio Alavedo*
Theodorus *The abbot of a Coptic island monastery in Abyssinia*
Captain Uzielli *An officer in the* Bersaglieri *regiment of the Italian army*

A Café on the Nile

— 1 —

The Cataract Café rocked gently in the wake of a police launch, the lavish hemp coils of her port bumpers protecting the broad barge from the cracked stonework of her fashionable mooring on the Nile.

Proud of his sea legs, Olivio Fonseca Alavedo extended his short arms and balanced himself neatly while he climbed the steps to his shelf behind the bar. His toes tightened and curled like little snails in his slippers while he waited for the swells to ease and merge into the slow current of the river. Soon would come Assumption Day, the fifteenth of August, 1935, his fiftieth birthday. A remarkably advanced age for a dwarf, and there was much for which to be grateful. Born in a hovel in Goa, the natural grandson of the Portuguese archbishop, he now possessed respect, and friends, and children, though no son. He was rich, though never rich enough, and this Depression provided a feast of opportunity. But he could not anticipate many more birthdays. Whatever he was to do, he must do now.

Gazing out the porthole at the domes and minarets that rose above the flat roofs of the city, he reviewed his schemes for the day. He was certain of one thing: war was coming to Africa. Why else had the Italians bought enough of his light long-staple cotton for forty thousand uniforms? He thought of the cotton bourse in Alexandria, the most dangerous casino in Africa. Through the mauve morning haze he watched the river slip past like some immense dark creature. He thought of the distant rapids and waterfalls, all the rushing cataracts that gave life to the river and their name to his Café. He breathed in the warm dusty scent of Cairo, the dry thin air of the desert mixing with the smells of the aromatic trees that lined the banks of the Nile and the sweet rotting fruit that washed against the piers. As he reflected, he heard the busy scratching of the river rats scuttling along the side of the barge. If war was coming, an honest man must be prepared.

When the barge steadied, Olivio lowered his arms and let his fingers dally in a tray of orange-yellow mangoes. He sniffed each oval fruit near the base of the stem, first with one nostril then the other, hunting for the flowery aroma of perfect ripeness. He held each mango between his palms, pressing it gently as he made his choices. Selecting six, he drew a cutthroat razor from a shelf beneath the bar. Peeling off the leathery skins, he dropped the bleeding fruit into a coarse strainer resting in a pottery bowl. Then he cut each one into two equal cheeks before ripping out the nubbly pits. With vigorous twists of his wrist, he mashed the exposed fruit through the strainer. Gnawing on the best pit with the grating energy of a beaver, he inhaled the dense fragrance of the pulpy juice while he reflected on his many blessings. He put the bare pit to one side and seized the bowl with both hands. Lowering his face to the frothy nectar, he gulped down the thick juice in one long draft.

Already he had acquired many acres of the richest land on earth: farms and plantations in the delta of the River Nile. In that floodplain, millennia of accumulated sediment had built a fertility even greater than his wife's. The dwarf licked the orange froth from his lips and wiped his sticky domed head with a bar towel as he thought of the vast flatlands covered in dense white cotton buds that made his other farms in Kenya and Portugal, Goa and Brazil seem hazardous and barren.

Best of all, Olivio had six daughters. Girls of uneven appearance, to be sure, the blood of India and Africa and Iberia mixing in their veins like the turbulent headwaters of the Nile. Some were tall and olive-skinned like the Fonsecas of Portugal, others dark and broad like their Kikuyu maternal ancestors, but all fine limbed and adoring of their father. As yet only one or two carried modest traces of his deformity. All, he feared, were hot beneath the skin. Already deeply voluptuous, the two eldest had been confined for staring after men with their wandering brown eyes. Would their mother, Kina, a woman without the gift of speech, but with glistening ebony skin and breasts like ocean waves, ever bear him a boy?

Only the eldest child, Clove, was truly like him: short and brilliant, with insight brighter than a torch. He thought again of his wife, and, with equal spirit, of the woman who now waited belowdecks on the soft divan. Soon the rising light would sparkle on the silver paint that covered her nipples and upper eyelids. Throughout the lower Nile, Jamila was celebrated for her ability to bend thin gold coins in her navel. She was not one of the heavy-hipped buxom dancers who performed, when young, at smart supper clubs and weddings, and, grown older and softer, at hotel bars and Egyptian musical cafés. Nor was she one of the conventional but select belly dancers who entertained occasionally at the palace, or at small private parties of the rich. Jamila was a lady. Blessed, Olivio thought, was any gold dinar that was introduced into such a navel: at once soft as an angel's breath, yet in motion powerful as the gears of a locomotive.

Olivio stepped down the narrow stair behind the bar. He moved along the starboard wall of the saloon, adjusting the brown rattan blinds to admit more air, for soon the furious heat of the day would be upon them. The dwarf peered out through one of the heart-shaped openings of the sandalwood window screen and noted the dark high-water mark on the stones of the quay.

He became suddenly alert as a new sound caught his ear: a once familiar rhythm, one for which he had been waiting. A cane tapped firmly down the gangway that led from the sidewalk promenade to the barge. It was the sound of friendship.

But how did he look? To avoid seeing himself, the dwarf had forbidden mirrors in the Café.

Olivio nipped into the pantry and examined himself with his one eye in the lustrous rear surface of the silver punch ladle. Distorted but clear. How appropriate, he thought. The little man started at the top, taking a scarlet tarbush from a peg on the wall and setting the flat-topped conical hat on his smooth head. He adjusted the silk tassel that fell to the left. He turned his head to one side. How well these Turkish hats suited him, like an informal crown, bringing the gifts of height and dignity. Reason enough for his move to Egypt from East Africa a decade or more ago.

His eye passed quickly over the reflected round face with the prominent forehead, not seeing the white and pink ridges of old scar tissue from the fire that had destroyed his home in Kenya. He did not notice the ears hanging in empty loops like the handles of a vase, the thin red lips, the nose flat and smooth as a baby's. The false eye was properly centered. He adjusted the neck and shoulders of his *gallabiyyah.* Pearl grey, it matched his eye. He was prepared.

"Ahoy!" Adam Penfold descended one step to the deck and tapped his cane twice against the rail. "I say, ahoy!"

Olivio stepped from the saloon bar into the bright daylight of the deck café. He bowed as deeply as his contorted back permitted, his heart alive with joy and pride. How rare to be host to a man he loved, especially one who had been his master.

The dwarf held out his arms and looked up with his mouth open as the smiling Englishman hurried to him. Two lean porters in shabby robes waited behind on the embankment, lifting a large packing case from a donkey cart by means of two poles that rested on their shoulders. What could this be? the dwarf wondered.

"Happy birthday, my dear Olivio, though a bit early." Lord Penfold's faded blue eyes smiled down from the drawn craggy face as the laugh lines at their outer corners deepened into wrinkles. His white and grey eyebrows reached forward like bushes on the edge of a cliff. He rested his hands on Olivio's shoulders.

"Oh, how we've missed you! Kenya's not the same without you." Penfold shook the dwarf with delight in his eyes. There was so much they knew of each other. "Brought you a present so you won't forget us."

"Never, my lord." Olivio wagged a forefinger in reproach and peeked around the tall slender man at the wooden case. He gestured impatiently to the Egyptians to set it down. He recalled the lessons of hospitality once provided by his English master, and for the moment he suppressed his curiosity.

"How may I refresh you, sir? A cool drink? A juice, perhaps a small gin?"

"Bit late for one, too early for the other." Penfold wiped his lined forehead with a wrinkled handkerchief. "Could you spare a glass of stout? Damned hard duty rushing about in this heat, beating off these Gypie beggars."

"A Bull Dog for his lordship." The dwarf clapped his hands sharply. When the dark drink was brought, he presented it himself. Then he looked back at the case with a sparkling eye. "May we open this now?"

"Course, but do you mind if I rest my leg and take a sip while you're about it?" Penfold collapsed with a groan into a high-backed wicker chair beside one of the round marble-topped tables.

Olivio reached up and gripped the polished mahogany rails. Dismissing the pain in his lower spine, trying not to waddle from side to side like a common midget, he climbed the sloping gangplank to the quay with small swift steps. Above his head the tassels of the curved yellow canopy swung gently from side to side as he advanced up the oriental carpet that ran its length. At the top he ignored a filthy importuning urchin, already taller than Olivio himself, who was collecting cigarette ends in a small sack hanging from his waist. Beggars were to Cairo what rain was to London and heat to Goa.

The dwarf stalked around the crate, touching it here and there with his fingertips, trying not to skip and caper. On the far side he found the words, stencilled in black: SENDER- ZIMMERMAN, NAIROBI, KENYA. The finest taxidermist in all Africa! His palms, never burned by the fire, began to sweat.

"Open it, idiots!" Olivio ordered the Egyptians, knowing how Lord Penfold disliked his harshness with servants, but confident his former employer, like all English gentlemen, spoke no language but his own.

"Must you wait for your mother to give birth to another ass?" He could put anger in his words, but not his tone. "Open it!"

One porter drew a rough thick blade from his rope belt and began to prize up the lid. Passersby paused and gathered to observe, clucking and whispering with anticipation.

"Careful, you fools!" Olivio said in a gentle voice as the first board splintered free. "One slip and I'll drown your children like kittens!"

The man levered up the long nails, palming them with cunning and concealing them in a fold of his robe for later sale in the iron market. The other porter hauled out the straw that topped up the crate. When the lid was off, the two cleaned out the remainder of the packing and looked to the dwarf for instructions. An old man scrambled to gather the discarded boards.

Olivio advanced to the side of the crate. Rising on his toes, he gripped the splintery edge and stared inside. He sniffed. He could smell the red dust of East Africa. Proud of his sense of smell, the dwarf pressed his face into two small handfuls of straw. He snuffled and sneezed and cast down the straw. Then he studied the large parcel inside the crate.

What might this be? An object, over a yard long, shaped like a barrel but with a sharp prow, and tightly swaddled in thick burlap. Olivio looked up, incensed to see a score of Arab boys pressing forward on the other side of the crate, struggling for positions of advantage as they sought to look inside. Where was his fierce Nubian servant with the lash?

"Lift this treasure out and bring it to my Café," the dwarf called to the porters, disgusted by their bare feet and filthy hands. He crossed onto the barge and pointed at the largest table.

Determined to honor his friend's gift, Olivio shrilled instructions as the two men bent over the edge of the case. Groaning deeply, no doubt exaggerating the strain of his effort, the larger porter sought to raise one end of the object. Unable to dislodge it, the man raised his red face and pressed both hands to his back. Both men stared at the dwarf and shook their heads.

"Do as I say!" Olivio snapped. "Raise it out!" Only Lord Penfold's presence prevented him from revealing the harsh edge of his impatience.

The men turned back to the case. Behind them a large grey motorcar slowed as it approached along the busy avenue, making its way through a swarm of over-burdened bicycles, horse-drawn gharries, open lorries and motorcars. Donkeys tottered by under baskets of figs and charcoal. The Daimler pressed through the confusion of the curbside traffic, its silver grille gleaming like the armored prow of a royal barge sailing through a throng of small craft. Nearby, herded tight together by running boys with long waving whips, a pack of mangy camels trotted to the butcher.

The driver's door opened and an immense man emerged with a horsehair switch in one hand. His face black as a moonless night in the Sudan, the Nubian chauffeur opened the rear door.

Like a jack popping from its box, a young girl jumped to the curb, two belted schoolbooks swinging from one hand. Perhaps fourteen, shortish, with a smooth oval face, heavy shiny lips, large black eyes and a single long pigtail, she was dark and exceptionally shapely. Her breasts pressed against her green school pinafore like melons in a sling.

"Papa!" she called with a full smile. Seeing nothing but him, not touching the railings, she skipped down the gangplank to bend over her father and greet him with two kisses.

"I present my oldest daughter, Clove. Lord Penfold." The dwarf spoke slowly with the air of a man raising the lid of his treasure chest. "You knew her as a child."

"What a fortunate father." Penfold greeted the girl with a crinkly smile as she curtsied.

"Aren't you my godfather?" The girl turned her large black eyes on the Englishman. "You and Mr. Rider?"

"Yes, child, Anton Rider and I are your two delinquents," Penfold confessed, embarrassed he had brought no present. "We were just opening a surprise for your father."

Clove walked to the chest and peered inside, ignoring the pressing boys as the Nubian chauffeur flicked his lash and pushed aside the swarming youths. The two porters returned to their struggle. One end of the heavy object began to rise, then slammed back down.

"Ah!" the smaller porter cried, his fingers caught between the cargo and the splintery wall of the container. "Allah save me! My hands!"

"Tariq," said Clove calmly, pointing at the wooden retaining plank that had been nailed to one wall of the case to secure the present inside. "Rip out that board first."

The Nubian reached in and seized the long narrow board in both hands. At the other end of the chest the Egyptian screamed and struggled to free his fingers.

Tariq tightened his grip and wrenched with both hands. The eight nails whined as they were bent and torn free from the wall of the chest. The watching youths gasped and stepped back with respect as Tariq tossed the plank onto the sidewalk and lifted out the object. The freed man shook his hands like mop ends and sat down on the curb, wailing and rocking from side to side. Clove bent over him briefly.

"You'll be fine," she said in Arabic before returning to her father.

Tariq, expressionless, set down the parcel on the largest table of the Café.

"Sturdy chap," Penfold said to Olivio.

"I myself will unwrap this, my lord," said the dwarf, proud of his servant's display, once again finding utility in the physical abilities he himself had been denied and was obliged to procure.

Adam Penfold wiped his face and nodded with a smile. He replaced the handkerchief in his left cuff and gave each porter ten piastres. "Thank you," he said to the men as they departed.

Olivio drew back the binding strip by strip as if unwrapping a mummy. The thing on the table began to take shape. Could it be? Impossible! Yes! A horn. Two horns, front and behind. Quickly the dwarf unwrapped the final swathes. The mounted head of a white rhinoceros, two glass eyes shining under hard grey lids. He looked more closely, admiring the immense square upper lip and the occasional thorn-like lashes. But what was he to do with this monstrous perissodactyl?

"Magnificent! My lord, bless you. This noble beast is more than I deserve!" Olivio feared what this tribute must have cost. He glanced at Penfold, trying not to catch his eye, not wishing to be seen noticing the frayed cuffs and missing button of his unpressed suit. His noble friend had a taste for generosity but not the means.

"Daddy!" Clove touched her father's shoulder with one hand, the tip of the front horn with the other. "He'd be lovely over the bar!"

"Brilliant, my treasure!" exclaimed the dwarf, reaching up to pinch her ear, then turning to Penfold. "Always your animal will live in honor above the bar. The Cataract Café shall be his home."

"Nothing at all, old boy," mumbled Penfold. "Just something to remind you of the old days. I say, is it time for that stiffener? Dash of Indian tonic with the gin, if you will. Protects one against this fearful heat."

"Please follow me." Olivio held open the beaded curtain. Penfold limped into the saloon. The Englishman sat in a high chair at one end of the bar and watched the dwarf climb his ladder to prepare the drink. He thought he detected pain in the movements of his little friend. The older man remembered without bitterness the day when he had seemed rich, and Olivio poor.

"Drink, my lord, and then I shall tell you why I invited you to Cairo." The dwarf's right eye twinkled as he set the gin on the bar. For a moment he paused and gazed at his daughter as she opened the French primer on the counter beside him and carefully pressed each page flat as she turned it. "In truth, it was not for my birthday, though I am so honored that you should come for that."

"Not at all. But if it's some sort of mischief, I'm past it." As Penfold drank, he regarded Olivio more closely. "May I ask how your new eye is getting on?"

Not ashamed of this artifact, the dwarf spoke plainly.

"The eye is cold in the mornings and warm as a boiled egg by the evening," he said from his shelf, recalling the curious pleasures Jamila had invented in bed while she toyed with the smooth object, warming and moistening it most intimately. "Although it was fitted at the German clinic in Alexandria, the finest and most expensive in all Egypt, yet I think it is not perfect."

"Il me plaît, Papa," said Clove in a cheerful voice as she rested one hand on her father's hunched shoulder and cupped her other hand.

Speechless with pride, Olivio stared with his good eye at his former master. Had Lord Penfold noticed that his daughter spoke French? French?

With one thumb the dwarf pulled up the hairless lid of his left eye. The ivory sphere popped from the socket and fell into his daughter's palm.

Clove wiped the eye on her short puffed sleeve and rolled it along the surface of the bar towards her father's friend.

"Nous aimons, vous aimez, ils aiment," she said softly. *"Je t'aime,"* the girl added, kissing her father's cheek.

Olivio enjoyed the crazy stare of the iris and pupil as the eye spun along the polished leadwood.

"She does seem a bit soft." Adam Penfold squeezed the eye between his fingers. "Rather like the billiard balls in a bad club. Very likely one of those Sudanese elies, used to an easy life wallowing about in the swamps. You'd be better off with proper Kenya ivory from the highlands, old boy. Or maybe a hippo tooth. They're harder, but a trifle yellow, of course. Might make you look a little jaundiced, if you know what I mean."

Lord Penfold passed back the ivory ball and studied the dwarf's right eye. "Though perhaps we could ask Anton Rider to hunt up a hippopotamus that'd make a handsome match."

Next they'll be fitting me with crocodile teeth, thought the little Goan as he counted the change in the money drawer. As it is, I'm the only man in the world with one eye from India and one from Africa.

"Heaven knows the dear lad needs some business," Penfold continued. "There's no money in safari hunting these days."

"Mr. Anton's problem is in Cairo, not the bush," said the dwarf.

"Eh?" said Penfold with interest. "Haven't seen either of 'em home in Kenya for a long bit."

"Miss Gwenn finds no comfort in his wandering life, my lord, and is still here completing her study of medicine." The dwarf hesitated. "And living under indelicate circumstances, I fear."

"You don't say," said Penfold, concerned about his friends' marriage, but not wishing to inquire directly.

"Miss Gwenn and the boys are living in the house of a diplomat, an Italian officer, one Colonel Grimaldi."

"How very peculiar."

"Life is not easy," said Olivio, completing his tally of the bar money. "Not much cash last evening, my lord."

"Hard times at home, as well." Penfold swung his game leg. "How are things in Cairo?"

"Busy as an anthill, and so fashionable," said Olivio. "And with a wife, most costly. The tailors are only Armenians, but the styles are French. The gentlemen's shoes are English, not too pointed. The Greeks are waiters, cigarette makers, even lawyers. The beggars, too, understand their business, though they are children to one who knows Bombay."

Penfold wiped his spectacles and peered at *The Egyptian Gazette* with watery eyes while the little man recorded the tally in the bar ledger. As he picked out headlines, the Englishman craned his head closer and closer to the newspaper, like a chicken picking seeds and scraps amidst the dirt.

"Look at this, will you? ITALIANS PROVOKE BORDER INCIDENT WITH ETHIOPIA. SEVEN ABYSSINIAN SOLDIERS KILLED AT WAL WAL. ETHIOPIA MOBILIZES AND PROTESTS TO LEAGUE OF NATIONS. ITALIAN MOUNTAIN TROOPS SAIL FOR ERITREA." Penfold looked up from the paper, his jutting eyebrows raised with concern.

"What business have those Eyeties down there, I ask you? Not the sort of type one wants in Africa. Don't set a good example." Indignant, he slapped the paper on the table. "They're already banging about next door in Libya. Someone's going to have to stop 'em before it all goes too far."

"War is in the air, my lord, and we must have our house in order."

As if not hearing, Penfold continued. "HITLER ADDRESSES TORCHLIGHT RALLY. GERMAN YOUTHS DRILL WITH SHOVELS. Here comes Fritz again," he grumbled. "Should've finished 'im off last time. TWO MILLION ON RELIEF IN NEW YORK." Penfold groaned and folded the paper before continuing.

"Will this Depression never end? All the farms in Kenya are bust, including mine, or what's left of it. In London the soup queues run on for blocks. Seems even the Yanks are poor these days. 'Bout time. But doing a bit better since they chucked out the engineer and elected that chatty Dutch chap with the bad legs."

"Here we are fortunate, my lord. There is nourishment, and life is not too dear." The little man nodded respectfully, waiting for the right moment to unveil his scheme while his old master carried on. Recalling the night when Penfold had saved his life, he considered how gentle and deferential his old friend appeared, almost timid in his manner, yet how courageous and active he could be when that was needed.

"Plenty of mischief about in the world, Olivio, and some of it getting closer. Old Mars stirring about again and all that. These Italians bullying Abyssinia, or Ethiopia, or whatever they're calling the place now. Seems that Mussoloni . . ."

"Mussolini," Clove said in a quiet voice, exchanging a glance with her father after she spoke.

"Yes, quite," said Penfold, pausing to look at the girl, astonished by her knowledge. "Seems this Mussolini fellow wants to gobble up a bit more of Africa, like the rest of us used to, I suppose. Only they're starting a bit late, and Abyssinia's 'bout all there is left. Hordes of his Eyeties been passing through Suez for months. Now he's unloading those fancy new armored cars in Somaliland."

"If war comes, we must be prepared to do our part," said the dwarf. His lordship hadn't changed, Olivio observed. His mind still wandered hopelessly, unable to concentrate on business and self-interest. He knew Adam Penfold would scorn the prospect of profiteering if his country were at war.

"Last World War ended in Africa," Penfold mused, finishing his new drink and sighing. "Shouldn't be surprised if the next one begins out here. Lord knows where it will end. Not sure poor old England can stand another one just yet."

"If war comes, my lord, England will need friends to provide her with food and clothing."

"Mmm." Penfold looked at the little man with care.

"Here in Egypt, cotton and sugar are the answer. Your English warriors will need uniforms, and last time cane sugar was like gold."

"I see your point."

The dwarf considered how to present his proposal with dignity for his friend. "In Cairo, these are days of opportunity. It is the time to buy. It is about this that I have invited you to Egypt." He leaned forward and pinched the open loops of his ears. "All that is required is money and friends."

"I wish you good fortune, Olivio," Penfold said awkwardly.

"It will be our good fortune, ours, for I require your help, as a partner. I wish to buy more estates in the Delta, rice and cane and cotton, dowries for my daughters and wealth for my old age."

Penfold shifted in his seat. "Sounds a bit risky, should've thought, in times like this."

"It is the best time. The banks are failing! The most powerful European firms are locking their doors! Even the rich Copts are selling their villas in Alexandria!" responded the dwarf with enthusiasm, drumming both his hands on the bar. "For the first time in generations the cotton farms of the Delta are available to a man with money in his hands."

Olivio's grey eye stared at his friend, as if hypnotizing the older man. "The soil is sixty feet deep!" Leaning forward across the bar, he held both hands up beside his own face, the fingers spread like a spider's web and the small smooth palms facing Penfold. "Sixty feet! This is our chance, my lord." He paused, then continued more slowly without blinking.

"But in Cairo everything depends on how a man is seen. What is his appearance? Who does he know in the ministries? Is he respected by the clerks? Will they remember his gifts? Do they feel they can cheat him at the land registries? Who will get the water in a dry year? Who will not have too much when it floods?" The dwarf wagged one forefinger and continued, speaking slowly, as if instructing a child.

"An honest man needs powerful patrons and allies, my lord, protectors. With an English gentleman like yourself, these Egyptian scum will never trifle. They will not know who you know and who you do not know, where your influence begins and where it ends." His eye shone. "If you and I are partners, my lord, at no cost to you, we will make each other rich."

Tempted despite himself, Adam Penfold frowned and sighed slowly before speaking. "I'd hate to bring you my bad luck, old boy, and perhaps I'm a bit tired for such affairs."

"Money will refresh you, my lord! Pounds and shillings, guineas and pence make a man young, especially in the eyes of the ladies. Ha! Have you ever seen a beautiful young woman with a poor old man?"

The dwarf licked both lips with his thick tongue and shook his head from side to side. "You will see. Oh, yes. All we need is the name: Penfold Partners Estates."

— 2 —

Raven-dark against the dim grey light, the immense black leopard stood over Anton. Their two bodies were identical in length and weight. The hanging belly of the animal almost touched his own. Blood fell on him from the wounded cat and mixed with his. The leopard's stout legs rose from the four corners of the hospital bed like the columns of a four-poster. The thick heat of its breath bathed his face like a lover. The animal lowered its mouth to Anton's left shoulder. He felt the long stiff whiskers brush his cheek before the leopard's teeth pierced his skin and ground against his collarbone.

The sensation of pain brought Anton to life again, cutting through the dreamy shield of the morphine. Alternately feverish and chilled, he felt the cool dawn mist of Abyssinia's Din Din forest mix with the humid heat of Djibouti's Hôpital Français.

Raising its wet muzzle, the night hunter looked down at Anton Rider. The oval yellow eyes glared like miners' lamps. The leopard raised its left forepaw, hesitating, waving it slowly to left and right as if searching for the man's old wounds. Anton dreaded the hooked yellow dewclaw set high above the creature's ankle. Finding his wounds, the cat extended its claws and stroked him. The four talons reopened Anton's upper arm as the pain and the memory drove him back into the insensibility of his fever.

He was back in the fly camp in the Din Din, on a recce for his next clients. It was the sort of safari he truly favored, opening up new country, his personal problems almost forgotten, travelling light with Kimathi, his headman and longtime tracker, and an Ethiopian camp boy, Josef, shooting only to eat, with none of the fuss and trophy madness and distraction of looking after people who didn't belong where they were. Unpaid for months, Kimathi followed him from habit. The three had detrained at Awash Station in central Abyssinia. After a fine lunch at the old Greek hotel, for two days they'd climbed with a pack mule until they reached the forest at seven thousand feet.

"Shall we camp here, Kimathi?" Anton said quietly, speaking for the first time since they'd entered the cool dark canopy of the woods, enjoying the change from Kenya. A thin stream ran through the oval glade beside him. He set down his pack and bolt action .375, pausing for Josef and the mule to catch up, pleased to feel fatigue in his legs for the first time in many months.

"Not yet, *Tlaga,*" said Kimathi, still appearing fresh, his eyes sharp and alert under the broad wrinkled forehead and tight grey curls. "If we camp higher up, near the moorland, we will not need to move again." The heavy-shouldered Kikuyu glanced up through the poles of podo carpus that rose sixty or seventy feet above his head. "It's like the Aberdares," he pointed out, thinking about the dark damp forest in the mountains of central Kenya.

"But higher, more remote." Anton knelt to study a chaos of old prints in the soft earth by the stream. Forest antelope, wild pig, leopard, antbear. "And the canopy's even denser."

He'd passed by the Din Din on previous hunts in Ethiopia, smelling its cool freshness as he journeyed by, always regretting he hadn't the time to pause and follow the winding game trails that tunnelled into the darkness of the high-altitude rain forest. In the Aberdares the game tended to be darker and more elusive than their siblings in Kenya's lower brighter regions, and here in the Din Din, the animals were said to be yet more wary and melanistic. Anton wondered what these dark creatures must be like.

He traced the most recent tracks with his fingertips and studied the small dark moist beads nearby.

"Serval cats, a female with a litter." Anton stood and took a few more steps along the narrow game trail, careful not to tread on crisp leaves or fallen branches. Then he crouched in silence and stared between the trees.

Off to one side in a small clearing was a shamble of moss-covered rocks. Playing on a bed of porcupine quills before a crevice in the rocks were three serval kittens. Already slender and long legged, two had dark stripes developing on their pale yellow shoulders and backs. The stripes faded into spots along their flanks. The third kitten was pure black. His yellow-green eyes shone like pale emeralds set in coal. Dominant, the young black cat tussled on his back as he cuffed the others about and nipped the large oval ear of a sibling. Never had Anton seen a serval like this highland cat.

A fierce high-pitched cry came from the far edge of the clearing. *"How-how-how."* Perhaps a foot and a half at the shoulder, a spotted buff-colored female sped to her litter and batted the young servals into the abandoned porcupine burrow. Then she turned and faced Anton. Her back arched like a bow. The hair along her spine stood erect.

Taking his eyes from the cat, trying to diminish her alarm, Anton backed quietly away, hoping not to induce her to abandon her home. He found Josef sitting beneath the head of the mule, tired and nervous in the unfamiliar country. The lead rope hung over his shoulder.

"Too far," the slender young man muttered in Amharic while he picked at his feet.

Ignoring the Abyssinian, Kimathi stood. "Let's march."

"I'll lead the mule," Anton said, slapping the animal into motion.

After another hour, Kimathi paused in a high glade in the forest and spoke quietly. "Here we should camp, *Tlaga.*" He leaned his shotgun against the crook of a tree. "The moorland is nearby."

The three men made camp, flushing green pigeons as they moved. Anton and Kimathi stood on the two sides of the mule and unpacked the carefully balanced load. The damp straight poles of the podo carpus surrounded them like giant prison bars. The white fungus of Old Man's Beard hung like ghostly wet sails from the spars of the mahogany trees. The tangled roots and branches of wild fig trees wrestled with each other.

Anton unfolded an old army canvas, preferring an open shelter to the confinement of a tent. He stripped a three-foot branch with his knife and jammed it into the ground. The other tip of the branch he set into a tin tea mug placed upside-down under the center of the canvas to prevent the stick from tearing the fabric. He took the cords that were attached to each corner and tied them to roots and a stake. While he worked, Josef gathered wood and Kimathi started a fire and chopped up herbs and wild onions to help cook the sausages.

The three hungry men ate in silence. Josef, close to the fire, stared into the forest and nervously rubbed the worn silver cross that hung from his neck. Darkness fell swiftly. Occasionally they heard monkeys swinging and chattering in the high branches above them.

"Your Ethiopian is already scared," said Kimathi as he sucked his fingertips, ill-humored because there was not more food. "They are all girls. Next time we'll bring his sister. At least then . . ."

"They say they make fine soldiers," Anton said, also in Kikuyu. He passed the last bits of goat cheese to his companions. "Perhaps the Italians will find out. Every Abyssinian over ten carries a sword or rifle."

Kimathi, unimpressed, ate his share quickly, then spat and began to clean his teeth with a wedge of bark.

"And their slave-raiding parties are still feared in your country," Anton added. "Been stealing Kenyan girls for years. He's probably your cousin." Anton squinted across the fire. "Looks a bit like you, only younger."

Careful not to smile, Kimathi stood and belched and relieved himself at the edge of the forest. "Time to dream of meat and women," he said, setting out his coarse khaki blankets under the canvas.

Anton, chilled by the rapidly dropping temperature, dragged more wood to the fire. "We'll be up early to spot the nyala and bag something for the pot." He clapped Josef on one shoulder. "Get some sleep."

"That warrior you brought will stay awake to keep us safe," Kimathi said with a grunt as he lay down, his gun beside him.

In minutes Anton and Kimathi were asleep under the canvas.

They made the camp their base for nearly a week. With each day in the field Anton's senses and instinct heightened.

They found the Din Din to be a storied forest from the brothers Grimm, haunted by sleek black creatures that existed nowhere else on earth. On early cold mornings the breath of the animals fogged when they exhaled. The damp and the darkness of their forest seemed to be inside them. Like the young serval, the genets, normally tan and grey, were black as aces in the Din Din. The animals' shadows and their bodies blended into a single swift-moving darkness as they fled from human sound or smell. Like the forest elephants of central Africa, some of these creatures were smaller than their fellows of the open bush or savannah. A few, particularly some carnivores, seemed larger.

Anton had promised his American clients a large antelope unique to Abyssinia: mountain nyala. It would be hard hunting, and Anton reckoned to make it easier by selecting his campsites and shooting roosts before bringing in his clients, two American sisters and an artist friend who would not be hunting.

Elusive as bongo, over four feet at the shoulder with wide spiral horns, the mountain nyala could either be tracked interminably in the forest itself and shot at close range, if at all, or hunted at the edges of the alpine moorland that rose above the forest. There the shy males lost themselves in the giant grey heather that rose six feet or more and waved and rolled and curled in the wind like ocean swells.

He knew it would be a matter of climbing the rocky hills above the moorland and glassing down to spot the nyala, praying for a shot at two or three hundred yards. He'd heard that often one was obliged to fire across a precipitous gorge to the opposing valley wall. Sometimes the animal would tumble to the bottom or lodge in the jagged rocks after the shot, requiring the hunters to climb down and up fifteen hundred feet to recover the carcass. Not the sort of thing for rich young ladies from Lexington, Kentucky.

At last he found a perfect spot, a spiny jutting ridge near the forest, with a downward view to three sides over the moorland. Returning to the Din

Din with Kimathi, knowing the Africans craved camp meat, Anton hesitated as he set his desert boot on the game trail that led to camp. His eyes widened in the dim forest light.

Fifty yards inside the forest, directly before him, ink black as the robe of a priest guarding a cathedral door, stood perhaps the most splendid of all antelope: a Menelik bushbuck.

The handsome male twitched its large pointed ears, barked once and turned to bolt. In the same instant Anton raised his rifle and fired. The bushbuck collapsed across the trail. Anton ran to the animal as Kimathi cut a stout limb from which to suspend the carcass for the walk to camp.

"Finally *Tlaga,* the Watchful One, is feeding his African followers," Kimathi said reverentially as he lifted his end of the burden.

Carrying the rifle in his free hand, the weight of the pole was heavy on Anton's left shoulder as they made their way back to camp. How appropriate, he thought, that this regal antelope should be named for the Abyssinian emperor who had slaughtered an Italian army so many years ago. Before Anton stepped into the glade, he heard a wild stamping and the shrill scream of the mule. The warning struck him like a shot.

"Josef!" Anton called, instantly dropping the pole and chambering a round without looking at his weapon. He glimpsed flashes of dark green and crimson feathers and heard the turacos cawing noisily in the branches as he entered the clearing.

Still hobbled, the mule bucked and kicked near the stream. Its face was torn in deep parallel lines, one eye ripped out, its upper lip flapping loose over its teeth.

The young African lay on the trail at the far side of the clearing. Anton knelt by the body and gently turned it over to face him. He undid his kerchief and rinsed it in the stream before cleaning the face of his companion. Josef's neck and shoulders were savaged by teeth marks. His carotid artery was open and leaking like a torn garden hose. The silver cross had been ripped from his neck. His heavy panga, the long blade bloodied, was in his right fist. The man's body was still warm, his own blood not yet lost in the leafy ground.

"Leopard," Anton said, looking up at Kimathi. "Looks like Josef got one good hack at him."

"Ndio, Tlaga," said Kimathi, more impressed by the dead man's wounds. *"Chui."*

"A big male." Anton rinsed his scarf and tied it around his neck.

"A female would reach up and scratch him with her dewclaws," Kimathi said, as if instructing Anton. "But this bastard was big. He knocked Josef down and chewed him." The Kikuyu pointed to one large pad print and measured it with his spread fingers.

Anton saw drops of blood leading along the other track from camp.

For tuppence he'd bury the lad and let the leopard go. He'd already found the perfect spot for his upcoming safari. But Josef and Kimathi, and even the leopard and he himself, would expect something different. The animal was wounded, and there was an account to settle for one of his men. He had no choice.

"Get me the .450. You take the twelve gauge. Double-aught buckshot." Anton dusted his fingers over a cluster of footprints. "We must've scared him off. If we can't find him now, we'll build a hide down the trail and leave the bushbuck for him. He should be back. Didn't have time to feed."

"Ndio," said Kimathi evenly, knowing Rider would not leave a score unsettled.

Anton checked both weapons before they set off. He was glad to have Kimathi at his back.

The two men walked slowly in silence until they came to a smaller glade on the trail. On the downwind verge of the clearing they worked together without speaking while they fashioned a blind of branches and bark, woven grass and leaves. While Anton checked the firing positions inside the hide, Kimathi added a thorn branch or dead leaf here and there to integrate the outside with the bushes on both sides. Then they examined the trees on the upwind side of the glade, searching for a place to hang the bait.

They ignored a magnificent wild fig, knowing that leopard disliked the milky sap that ran from a fig tree when it was clawed or cut. Both nearby mahoganies were undesirable, bearing the mark of man, cuts in their trunks made by honey hunters who had chopped out the wild hives of the large forest bees. Finally Kimathi pointed to a mature acacia. Anton studied its branches and nodded.

After carving out steaks from the bushbuck's back strap, they hung the carcass from a horizontal branch of the acacia. While Anton hauled on a rope that lifted the carcass to a branch, Kimathi lashed each foot of the Menelik separately to the thick limb to prevent the leopard from making off with the bait in the night. Hanging upside down twelve feet above the ground, the bushbuck offered a clear broadside shot from the two peep-holes of the hide forty yards away. The men blocked each peep-hole with a plug of tangled leaves and branches.

Later in the evening Kimathi and Anton buried the Abyssinian, careful to leave the cross between his folded hands, honoring Josef's Coptic faith. Afterwards Anton did his best to clean the wounds of the mule. Then they feasted quietly on the tenderloins. Rarely had Anton eaten better meat or enjoyed it less.

"To Josef," Anton said, pouring Metaxas into his coffee and drinking before he passed the mug to Kimathi.

"Your Ethiopian has left us a fine job," said Kimathi dryly. He drained the mug and passed it to Anton for more brandy. "This black demon is not good luck. A wounded leopard is like an abandoned woman. Angry to the death."

"You don't have to come, old man," Anton said, knowing better. He rose and tied the mule to a heavy log near the fire, lest another predator drive it off.

"What am I to do if the leopard kills you?" Kimathi said simply. Then he shrugged. "He won't be our first cat."

Anton nodded.

For several hours they lay down in turns. From time to time Anton heard colubus monkeys swinging through the canopy, unusually restless behavior for these diurnal creatures. He knew the goat-like bleating of their alarm calls would warn him if the leopard returned to their camp to feed on its kill.

During his watch, Anton's mind drifted to his two boys at school in Cairo, and to the woman he had lost. He thought of Gwenn's green eyes and slender figure and perfect skin, of the proud fresh way she had about her. Unsupported by him, she was making her own way. Safari clients were scarce as unicorns during the Depression, and he'd sent Gwenn only a few quid now and again. Soon she'd be a doctor, with her own life and work. Then she wouldn't need him, if she ever had. Already he'd heard she'd taken some sort of lover, a count, Spanish or Italian or whatever. He wondered if part of her still loved him. He was proud of her but more sad than he could admit. He had the sensation that his family was passing him by.

At what age, he mused, did regrets begin to outweigh hopes? He was not certain when his carefree mood and life had turned from promising to troubled, but he knew his failure with Gwenn was at the heart of it. He longed for her and the boys, both his own son, Denby, and his stepson, Wellington, but he seemed an outsider in their world, a nomad best cared for from a distance. Now he feared they might never come home to Kenya.

He felt guilty after a year and a half away. But despite the boys, and several old friends he hoped to see, Anton was dreading Cairo, knowing the visit must bring his failures to vivid life. It would be awkward enough to be badly dressed and scrimping, holding back on tips and meals, without proper presents for the boys and Gwenn, unable to take her and his clients to Cairo's elegant clubs and restaurants. He knew he would find himself resenting the success of other men, the way even attractive women resented the fresh beauty of younger misses.

At first, as a white hunter, he'd made far more than most young men, but now, with clients scarce and many contemporaries enjoying more secure lives, the world had turned upside-down. For years he'd thought his childhood with the gypsies in England and his life with his hunting clients in Africa, tycoons and grandees from a dozen countries, had made him at home anywhere, at ease with anyone, and in ways it had, but now, in a deeper way, he felt an outsider everywhere he went. Only in the bush was he truly relaxed and at home, expansive instead of restrained.

In the bush, or at cards, he never felt poor, and occasionally, with a drink or a girl, one could put things aside, but in the city, money became essential, and being a husband or a father carried costs he could not pay. His pockets were still empty, his profession, if it were one, every day less promising as he grew older and the Depression lingered on. In time, the rich safari life of his youth might not be a life at all, but it was the only life he knew. He hadn't managed to provide for his safari boys, let alone Gwenn and Denby and Wellington. How could he ask Gwenn to be his wife again? And every day her life was more her own, his sons older and more distant, as he himself had been, without a father.

When Anton had first come out to Africa, the Romany lessons of his boyhood, hunting and cards and boxing, trick shooting and horse coping, even reading fortunes in camp fire ashes and tea leaves, had seemed advantages, each a modest mastery that helped him to get on. But now they seemed a curse, preparing him for a life that served only his youth. Worse, too often he found himself slipping, as if by frequent accident, into violence and gambling. How could an unemployed hunter who'd never been to school support a wife and family? What could he do next year, and in five or ten?

One successful safari now would make a difference. Anton was certain war was coming to Africa, and he was desperate to squeeze in these next American clients before the Italians invaded Ethiopia. Already Mussolini's troops were massing in the Italian colonies to the east and south, and Italian patrols with native scouts were testing the borders along Eritrea and the Ogaden.

He'd meet these American clients in Cairo and sail with them back to Djibouti before taking the train into the interior and starting the safari in Abyssinia. Already he'd spent the advance the Americans had wired him, using every farthing to pay his debts and hold his safari staff together in Kenya. Where would he be without credit and sleight of hand? Now he needed the balance of the safari money. If he couldn't help Gwenn with the school fees, how was he ever to claim her back?

Anton rose to his feet and stretched when the night began to brighten. "Our leopard is waiting," he whispered, shaking his friend by the shoulder. "If you want to come, stay behind me with the shotgun."

Kimathi rose and the two returned to the hide. In the early morning, a chilling damp wind gusted towards them from across the glade. After an hour of sitting silently, Anton moved into position by the peep-hole. He checked his load and took two long soft-nosed .450's from the spares in his pocket and slipped them into the cartridge loops of his shirt. That was all one could use. If you couldn't stop a leopard with four shots, he'd have you anyway.

Anton settled comfortably, his old Holland & Holland across his knees. He carefully drew the plugs and set his right eye to the peep-hole and watched the first light brighten the thick mist. The tall trunks of the podo carpus became the masts of ghostly sailing vessels as the mist floated through the Din Din. At home in Kenya, leopard generally came back to feed between seven and eight, after the first sun had warmed them. Anton prepared himself to discern a spotted form with a small round head and a long tail pause by the pool before climbing to the bait.

The mist thinned and Anton made out the body of the bushbuck. He glanced at Kimathi and tapped his own front teeth and chewed. No longer suspended from the branch, the carcass now lay along the top of the limb, where the cat must have lifted it to feed in the night. Even from the hide, Anton could see that half of the bushbuck or more had been devoured, perhaps thirty or forty pounds of meat.

Kimathi pressed Anton's ankle and pointed.

Nearly flat on the ground at the side of the pool, its body pressed low between its angled legs, an immense creature, well over seven feet long nose to tip, lay with its face at the water's edge. The round head was exceptionally large. But the cat's dense soft coat was even more astonishing than its size. Dead black, the leopard had no spots.

The forest itself seemed silent. Anton was careful not to hold his breath, knowing he must be steady for the shot.

The leopard turned its head, for an instant revealing two glowing yellow eyes, and licked the shallow wound in its right shoulder.

Anton felt his skin prickle and his muscles tighten. These were the moments that made this life worthwhile.

The animal slowly swished its tail from side to side while it drank. Anton waited to raise his rifle until the sounds of the cat climbing into the tree covered any small noise he might make in setting his weapon to the peep-hole. The leopard rose and relieved itself, lifting its tail and scratching the ground with both hind legs. Anton saw no twitching of the small ears, no suggestion of alarm.

Light-moving, loose as a kitten, the cat turned and climbed the acacia with a sudden rush. Anton estimated the black beast at almost two hundred pounds, the weight of a full-grown lioness. It was the largest and most beautiful leopard he had ever seen. It was the devil himself.

The muscles of the animal's shoulders bunched in black ropes when it buried its face in the belly of the bushbuck, pinning the carcass to the branch with its forepaws while it tore at the raw meat and guts with long curved canines.

Anton closed his left eye and sighted the double-barrelled rifle just behind and below the right shoulder. He held his breath.

Just as he squeezed the front trigger, there was a sudden disturbance in the hide beside him. The leopard leapt in the air with one explosive growl.

Trying to keep the beast in his sights, deafened by the shot's echo in the still of the morning, Anton fired the left barrel. Then he turned in the tight space to see Kimathi chopping at a viper with his panga. What blasted luck! he thought angrily. Anton reloaded as he watched, mindful of how his friend dreaded snakes. Everyone was disturbed by different things. As a child Kimathi had been bitten, and nearly killed, by a black mamba.

The leopard vanished into the forest, grunting as it fled.

Near Anton's feet, its flat head split and severed, the thick body of the mountain adder still wriggled and twisted like an eel in a trap. Sweating heavily, bounding about in a crouched position, knocking down the walls of the hide, Kimathi kept after the torn snake, cutting and hacking it into smaller and smaller fragments.

Anton stood and stretched. He must give his friend a chance to settle down. After years in the bush, Anton had come to believe in luck and superstition.

He knew he had wounded the great cat, not killed it. Most likely a smashed shoulder, enough to enrage the leopard but not stop it. Whether the animal had moved first at the sound from the hide, or whether he himself had been distracted, he was not certain. But now he had a wounded leopard to follow.

He recalled the words of old man von Decken, who'd taken him on his first hunt when Anton was a boy in Tanganyika. "Wound a lion, *Engländer,* and he may skulk off to die. But hit a leopard," the silver-haired German planter had warned, wagging his cigar, "and you are his till he dies. He will go for you. Always."

Taking their time, giving the animal a chance to bleed and weaken, Kimathi and Anton broke up the hide and checked the ground by the pool and under the bushbuck. "There is much blood," said Kimathi sourly, "but not enough."

"And it's thick as treacle." Anton touched some with his fingers, smelling it and rubbing the blood between two fingertips. He didn't like what he saw. It promised a serious but not immediately fatal wound. Bright red and bubbly would have meant a vital hit.

Anton stayed in front as they followed the wet trail, climbing deeper into the forest, crossing narrow game tracks and small dark glades. After a time he crouched to enter a tunnel-like game trail, probably the path of a bush pig or red river hog. He felt his senses sharpen with tension. The leopard, he knew, would not warn him with the threatening growl of a lion. Concerned he would not have time or space to shoulder and aim his Holland for an accurate rifle shot, Anton turned back to face Kimathi.

He put one finger to his lips, then took Kimathi's shotgun in his right hand and exchanged weapons. He gestured for Kimathi to stay back. Although it wouldn't have the stopping power of a large soft-nosed bullet, with the shotgun he'd be able to get off two fast shots that shouldn't miss.

The uneven trail of blood and prints led them to the high edge of the forest. Fingers of moorland reached into the thinning woods. The tall heather was still damp and sparkling in the morning light. Anton felt a gust of warmer air and smelled the aromatic scent of the rocky moorland replace the chill moisture of the woods.

As they stepped from the cover of the forest, avoiding steep clefts in the ground, a troop of black and white colobus monkeys howled and leapt from tree to tree in the canopy above the verge of the moorland. Anton heard a single musical call from the sky and glanced up.

He saw a crowned eagle tighten its wings. The white and reddish-black bird dived between two trees and caught a colubus in mid flight. Flapping furiously, laboring, perhaps a yard long from bill to tail, the massive long-tailed eagle rose slowly as the monkey struggled in the bird's yellow talons. The primate's furry white mantle and long tail tuft dangled helplessly as it rose in the air. The rest of the troop scattered down into the lower canopy, catapulting from bough to bough, bleating hysterically and landing feet first among the thicker foliage.

A single grunt rose from the heather several yards ahead. Before Anton could shoulder the gun, there was a violent rush at his feet. In the distraction with the eagle, he had disregarded his deadly adversary. He fired a snap shot at the black streak, missing as the giant leopard tore through the heather and sprang towards his face.

Filling the sky like a black cloud, the cat struck his left shoulder and knocked Anton down as he fired the left barrel. Stunned by the force and ferocity of the charge, he felt the animal open his flesh and cut his bone. For an instant it seemed the injury was not his but some remote misadventure. Then he heard Kimathi holler as the African fell out of sight to one side.

On his back, his gun lost, he sought desperately to kick the heavy animal off him with his legs. Anton raised his left arm to protect his throat while drawing his knife from his belt with his right. He felt every muscle and tooth and claw of the cat fighting frantically to kill him. He was overwhelmed by the sensation of the driving will of his attacker.

The leopard seized his left arm in its teeth. At last Anton felt the startling shock of pain. A few inches away, the animal's blazing eyes stared directly into his as if the creature knew him. Anton smelled the stench of its breath and saw where the buckshot had punched a hole in the cat's back. For an instant he became intently aware of the detail of the leopard's body. Close as a lover, he now saw, in the brighter light of the open moorland, that despite the appearance of its solid color, the leopard bore a pattern of sable rosettes that subtly marked its coat. The dense black coat was not a bluish black, but instead was tinted with a very dark chocolate brown.

Fighting back like an animal, yelling he knew not what, Anton plunged his knife into the leopard's neck. Then he twisted it free and stabbed again. With a furious shrill roar the animal released his arm and madly clawed his other shoulder. Its blood splashed Anton's face as the cat pulled back its head with the knife still lodged in its throat.

Kimathi climbed from the gully where he had fallen and knelt beside the struggling thrashing pair. He wanted to shoot but was afraid to kill his friend. Finally Kimathi lunged forward, pressing the .450 into the leopard's chest as he fired.

Screaming, the raging animal fell from Anton onto its back, all four feet clawing wildly in the air, the great talons extending and retracting in its agony.

Anton rose unsteadily to his knees, his chest ripped open and both collarbones running blood. In a blood-rimmed daze he saw Kimathi fire again from two or three feet, taking the cat in the top of the head behind the eyes. Bone and blood splashed over all three. Anton stood and staggered, looking for his gun. As he collapsed, he saw Kimathi lunge towards him.

"Tlaga!" the African yelled as he caught Anton between his arms.

"Why are you not singing?" Anton asked a few moments later, briefly conscious while Kimathi bathed his wounds by the stream, the shock still greater than the pain. "We must sing as we always do to honor the great leopard we have killed," he said slowly to his friend in a failing voice before his eyes closed.

Kimathi filled Anton's wounds with disinfectant and bound them with his own shirt. As he worked, he sang the song of a Kikuyu hunter in a deep powerful voice that echoed through the Din Din.

For two days Anton had passed in and out of consciousness, always aware of Kimathi beside him as the African tied Anton to the wounded mule, flogged the animal back to Awash Station, bundled him onto a pallet for the train ride to Djibouti and carried him across his arms into the Hôpital Français.

Anton had lain in the hospital for over two weeks, giddy with morphine, dreaming of the magnificent creature that had savaged him, wondering at this retribution for all the animals he himself had killed. He rested with each arm suspended in a sling about the wrist and elbow, while the doctor and two elderly nuns treated his thirty cuts and bites. Twice a day for one week, like the leopard in his dream, they had reopened the cuts in his arms and shoulder to flush them with antiseptic and purge them of infection.

One evening, dreaming of Gwenn but assuming it was the night sister come to bring him water, unable to use his arms, Anton had not opened his eyes when a hand raised his head and held the cup to his lips. Then he had smelled the rare perfume.

He knew at once who it must be: his first woman, Anunciata, who had introduced him to lovemaking in the *donga* in Kenya so many years before. "Outdoors is best," she had said, and he had found it so.

"Blue Eyes," the Portuguese lady said as she set the empty cup on the bedside table. "You must not move. Let me take care of you."

— 3 —

"Water, Abd al-Azim, water," Count Grimaldi said to the Royal Chamberlain as he sorted through the sepia photographs presented by a court procuror. Young boys and girls, awkward in their costumes, gazed into the camera with hopeful startled eyes. The Italian examined one closely and stroked his grey mustache.

"Too young, even for the palace, but remarkable for her age." Lorenzo Grimaldi slipped the picture into the breast pocket of his white air force uniform, careful not to disturb the rows of medals. "Remarkable."

As Italy's air attaché to Egypt, he had many obligations. At present he was preparing for the visit of Vittorio and Bruno Mussolini, the Duce's sons, both aviators in the *Disperata* squadron of the *Regia Aeronautica,* now magnificently equipped with the tri-engined Caproni bomber. Soon, he thought with satisfaction, these Roman eagles would be hunting in the skies over Abyssinia.

"Tell me, your excellency," said the Egyptian, "is your country bringing war to Africa? Was Libya not enough?"

Grimaldi kept contempt from his voice when he replied. "We Italians are a peaceful nation, Pasha, but we must protect our borders." In fact, he knew well that Italy intended to build its own empire, and he was certain it would not be easy. For the second time the Mediterranean would be the *Mare Romano,* the *Mare Nostro.* At last there would be the *Africa Orientale Italiana* long promised by Benito Mussolini. The costly pacification and colonization of Libya was only the beginning.

"Of course." The Chamberlain waved one hand, his tone increasingly patronizing. "But our friends at Saïd and Suez report that twenty-five thousand Italian soldiers a month have been passing through the Canal this year. Surely so many Roman warriors are not needed to defend Italian Somaliland and Eritrea against a few wild *shifta*?"

"You will have to ask the army," Enzo said stiffly, preparing to redirect the conversation. "I am an aviator." He placed his white leather gloves on the small table beside him while his host continued.

"Or is it, perhaps, that your country has come too late to the colonial ball? Already, France and England and Germany, even Portugal and Belgium, have taken all the African brides." The Egyptian rubbed his hands and smiled. "Abyssinia is the only virgin left, and she doesn't want to dance with you."

Insulted, the Italian raised a decanter of water from the copper tray resting on the inlaid desk of Abd al-Azim Pasha. His hand steady, Enzo poured drops onto the desk until a small pool formed.

The Pasha stared at Grimaldi without speaking. The court official was above this outrage. He was an Old Boy of Victoria College in Alexandria. There the schoolboy jokes had taught him what to expect from an Italian.

"With a single bucket of water, Abdu, I can kill you or save your life. Too much, too little, makes your estate rich or poor, a desert or a garden or a swamp . . ." Enzo tapped his forefinger in the water, waiting for his host to betray annoyance.

"You need not instruct an Egyptian on the value of water." Annoyed at this insolent use of the familiar form of his name, the Chamberlain stiffened in his chair and squeezed an amber worry bead as it passed through his fingers. He was habituated to the presumption of the British, the arrogance of the French. What could this Italian teach him? He smiled and continued, first glancing up at the long slow blades of the ceiling fan.

"We are not children, Colonel Grimaldi. We are not Negroes. Even your Napoleon had to come here to learn what water means, and to study our civilization, though he was too stupid to build the canal, foolishly believing the Mediterranean and the Red Sea were different heights . . ."

"Do not blame us for the French, Abdu."

"You Europeans come and go," continued the Egyptian dismissively, ignoring the interruption, waving one hand from side to side, taking pleasure in deflecting his guest's line of thought. "Greeks. Romans. French. English. But for four hundred years Egypt was an Ottoman province. In terms of civilization, Constantinople is our capital, not London or Rome or Paris."

Grimaldi set down the decanter and resumed in a calm voice.

"Here in Egypt, only one twentieth of your land is habitable and fertile. One *feddan,* one acre, in twenty. Which acre depends on where the Nile flows and floods. And in the Delta the Nile is controlled by the Great

Barrage north of Cairo. And who, Abdu, controls the dams of the Barrage, who decides which gate shall be opened, and which sluice shall be tight and dry as an old woman? Who determines which lands shall have one harvest, and which two, even three?"

"King Fuad decides where the waters go, your excellency, like his father and grandfather before him. One seventh of Egypt's farmland is his." The Chamberlain turned and gestured at one of the two framed photographs on the wall behind him. "One day His Majesty's son, Prince Farûq, will have this royal power."

The handsome youth, fifteen, his face open and smoothly rounded, looked down on them with calm pale eyes. His soft chin rested on the high collar of a dark military frock coat, adorned with golden epaulets, braid and medals. A tall tarbush crossed his brow, set low over his right eye, reminding observers that, despite military school in England, Farûq was above all an Ottoman prince, a lord of the East, although the founder of his house had been Albanian.

Before continuing, Abd al-Azim Pasha looked down and selected a powdery confection from a platter on the desk.

"As a practical matter, of course, such things are determined by the Minister of Public Works, and, in the case of matters pertaining to irrigation, by the Undersecretary, my dear cousin, Musa Bey Halaib. He determines whether a canal is to be filled with weeds or with water."

Grimaldi recognized the invitation. "Is your cousin a practical man, Abdu?"

"Musa Bey is a man of the world." His tone friendlier, the Pasha sucked the honey and fine sugar from his fingers. "But there are many who would whisper in his ear, and bring him suitable favors."

Grimaldi was aware of Abd al-Azim Pasha's resentment of the palace Italians, the court officers and servants who had insinuated themselves into the royal household. Enzo saw it would be necessary to join the pasha's interests more closely with his own. Already they had shared one discreet and profitable adventure: a cotton contract for Italy's new African campaign. Now those winnings were committed to a new project, buying land that the new irrigation scheme would transform from desert to lush fertility. Today Grimaldi was speaking for a consortium of important Italian investors.

"Is anyone else playing our game, Abdu? Are we early enough?"

"If we buy too early, the scheme may change. Too late, and it will be too dear." The Chamberlain enjoyed the opportunity to lecture his arrogant guest. Like many Egyptians of his education, he had learned to exploit, more than resent, the misguided condescension of the Europeans. If Caesar and Napoleon had not managed here, how could these men? The pleasure came in playing one against the other.

"But, as our new guests the British would say, there are one or two others who seem to be bowling at the same wicket."

"I do not play cricket," said the Italian.

"In particular, there seems to be one troublesome buyer in our path, shrewd, with plenty of money. But as yet his new purchases are not joined into one estate, and some he may have bought in error. Here in Egypt, investors require more than money. The irrigation scheme is not yet complete, and of course we enjoy certain advantages."

"Is our rival an Egyptian or a European?" Grimaldi could tell that his host would not reveal the name, preferring the power of secrecy to the generosity of disclosure.

"No, not Egyptian," Abd al-Azim said slowly, "yet not exactly European either. A curious man, and cunning."

The Italian glanced at the wall to his side. Nile scenes, drawings and watercolors and photographs, covered the space. Grimaldi understood the fascination. Lateen-sailed feluccas crossed the green waters above the Aswan dam. Columns of trudging laborers shouldered baskets of rock towards the rising towers of the Great Barrage. A woman labored at an Archimedes screw. Grimaldi looked back at his Egyptian host and took a long sip of mint tea before he spoke.

"If we know where the water will go, Pasha, you and I will know which farms to buy. And if the water stops, a farmer must sell." Enzo formed small watery trails on the desk with the tip of his finger.

"With the Nile, those have been fatal games, your excellency. In the time of the pharaohs, princes killed for such favors. And in the days of Alexander, and Cleopatra, and the Caesars. Legions marched if one dike was built without authority. Have you forgotten that the valley of the Nile was the granary of ancient Rome?"

The Italian aviator did not reply. Sometimes this Egyptian surprised him.

The Chamberlain turned in his seat and tapped the map of the Delta that covered the wall beside the photograph of young Farûq. With Cairo at its southern base, the inverted pyramid of the Delta extended north to the Mediterranean, with Alexandria just beyond its western corner, and Port Saäd to the east. Just above Cairo, at the site of the Great Barrage, the river divided into two main channels. From both of these a maze of tributaries and canals extended to all sides. "There are limits, your excellency, even in Egypt. Even in this household."

Grimaldi raised his eyebrows and considered what was transpiring in the royal apartments nearby.

"Limits?" he said. With five hundred rooms, a gilt theater and a two-hundred-car garage and alabaster hallways with life-size mosaics of naked *houris,* the Abdine palace had a place for everything. Even the prince's sisters were not spared, sucking their nourishment until unnatural ages from the breasts of two-hundred-and-fifty-pound nurses.

"Limits?" Grimaldi said again, picking up his gloves and standing. He looked down at the Egyptian and smiled without humor. "In Cairo?"

The Chamberlain paused and returned the smile.

"Are you off to the aerodrome, Colonel?" he asked, informed earlier that the Italian's flight coat and goggles were in his automobile.

"I admire Egypt from the air," said Grimaldi, "and I'm keen to test our new Breda." Italy's latest fighter was awaiting him in its civilian colors. He wondered how long it would be before Italy would be fighting for Egypt itself.

Gwenn Rider was the only woman in the ring of students in the circular gallery. She rested her arms on the railing and stared down into one of the two new operating theaters of the King Fuad Hospital at Qasr al-Ayni. With farming impossible in Kenya during the Depression, and no medical school in British East, she'd moved to Cairo with the boys in 1929, the second year the Faculty of Medicine admitted women.

Cairo had been good to her, although the stiffer English ladies would not receive her now, or welcome her children to play with their own, knowing her to be a double sinner, separated from an English husband and living with an Italian. Some of the grander Egyptians and diplomats seemed to share that sensibility. Seeing her shunned one day at the Café, the dwarf had approached Gwenn with his best bow. "In Cairo," he said to his old friend, giving her the finest corner table, "hypocrisy is always in fashion. They say the French brought it from Paris, with Napoleon's savants, I believe."

Fortunately, convention and license often dined together in Cairo, and Gwenn had found as many friends as she had time for. As Olivio reassured her another evening, "In Cairo there is a camel for every rider."

Gwenn watched the amputation with dispassion. Long ago she'd become inured to the medical realitites, even to suffering. Now it was only brutality she could not accept. She had seen what machine guns and wire and gas and explosives had done to men's bodies in the Great War, and she dreaded what modern weapons would do in the next one. At least the League of Nations had outlawed the use of poison gas.

The surgeon-in-chief spoke aloud in careful English as he worked. The students beside Gwenn took notes. Since the founding of the school in 1827, instruction had been carried out successively in French, Italian, German and Arabic. Now, thank heaven, all the teaching was in English.

Tired, perspiring from the heat, she glanced at the wall clock. Complicated operations were always a race: while you patched up one or two things, the rest of the body began to protest and run down. It was like the incision:

bigger was better for working on the damaged organ, but worse in terms of complications and healing. It was nearly four o'clock. The boys would be home from school any minute. Fortunately Sana, the housekeeper, would be waiting for them.

"There! Your turn, Doctor." The voice of the surgeon-in-chief rang through the theatre. Gwenn watched the handsome grey-haired man step to one side, flexing the tension from his fingers in his slippery wet red gloves as a younger doctor advanced to the table with a long-toothed surgical saw.

She would soon become a doctor, and in two more years, a surgeon. Then perhaps back to Kenya, practising medicine and starting up the farm again once she'd made some money. But what about the boys, and Lorenzo, and what about Anton? Could things ever really work with him? She wondered if Anton was on safari, and, if not, what woman he was with. It was about time for him to come to Cairo to see the boys. Now she both missed him and dreaded seeing him. In town he was always so on edge. For him, the bush, safari life, had become a refuge instead of a profession. The truth was, Anton had always been too young for her. Or was she too old? It was difficult enough that she'd always been more serious and practical.

She watched two orderlies place the leg in a pan on the floor. Three other cases waited on trolleys by the door. It reminded her of being a girl in Wales, mufflered against the cold, gripping her sister's hand in the crowd of praying families while the accident whistle howled and cages of broken miners clattered to the surface. Soon she'd be able to help, but in Abyssinia, not in Wales. Yesterday, she had almost committed herself to going to Ethiopia with the Egyptian medical team.

The class was dismissed and Gwenn hurried down the stairs, relieved to find Omar, her regular driver, asleep in his Citroën near the entrance. Fortunately this sort of luxury was cheap in Cairo.

"Afternoon, Omar," she said, tapping on his window and smiling. "Home, please."

A lottery ticket rolled behind his left ear for good luck, leaning on the taxi's horn, braking and swerving like a polo pony, Omar swung through the crowded streets, knowing she hated this sort of driving but convinced it was his manly duty. Directly before them a sack of rice fell from a donkey cart and burst when it struck the road. Gwenn braced herself against the front seat as Omar braked, barely missing several women who dashed into the street to scoop the rice into the long skirts of their robes.

"Well done, Omar," she said when he drew up outside the house. "We made it."

Feeling late and guilty, Gwenn dropped her medical books on the hall table and hurried into the kitchen, wishing she had time to run upstairs and take a bath and put up her feet. Tired, knowing Lorenzo liked to find her looking her best when he stopped by, Gwenn was conscious of being less strong than she used to be.

"Hello, boys," she said brightly, comforted to find them at the large kitchen table having their tea. Wellington was helping his younger brother punch air holes in the tin lid of a large bottle containing a green tree frog Denby had caught in the garden.

"You can go home now, Sana," Gwenn said. "Sorry I'm late again." She touched the older woman's arm as Sana removed the apron that covered her black dress and drew a shawl over her shoulders. The woman gathered some leftovers into her string bag and departed with a wave to the boys.

"How was school?" Gwenn stroked the top of Wellington's red head. It made her sad to feel him bridle slightly when she touched him. She moved behind Denby's chair and rested her hands comfortably on the younger boy's shoulders.

"Yes, Mum," Wellie said, briefly glancing up before turning to his plate of almond cookies and green and red ices. He was big and solid for fourteen.

"Where's your homework?" Annoyed he had not answered her question, she tried not to sound sharp, but she knew he wasn't doing well this term.

"I forgot it at school." The boy looked up but avoided her eyes. "Sorry. I'll catch up tomorrow. Promise."

Denby pulled his schoolbook close to his plate and opened it while his mother pursued Wellie.

"Tomorrow there'll be more homework," she said impatiently, trying not to be annoyed at Wellington because of the wasted school fees. The money wasn't his fault. All the same, she didn't know how she'd manage if Lorenzo wasn't paying the bills.

Gwenn bent over and kissed Denby's soft cheek. "How're you, darling?"

"Have you got a pencil?" Denby said, wiping both hands on his shorts.

Gwenn rummaged on a shelf crowded with medical texts, photographs and airplane models with Italian markings. She handed her son a pencil and put a kettle on the stove.

Denby took the pencil and looked up at her with his father's clear blue eyes. "Mummy," he said with hesitation.

She squeezed his shoulder, sensing he had something hard to say. "Yes, sweetheart?"

"They asked us at school today if our fathers would be here for Field Day," Denby said in a hurried voice. "There's going to be a tug-of-war, you know, boys against the dads."

"I'm not sure," Gwenn said, looking out the window, wondering when Lorenzo would be coming by.

"We usually win, because there aren't enough fathers, but if . . ." He stopped, feeling his mother was distracted.

Gwenn knew what Denby was thinking: his father was strong enough to outpull all the boys. She was aware how much her sons wanted Anton home. And sometimes, she did, too.

"I'll try to let you know, dear," she said. At that moment she saw Lorenzo's long black Bugatti draw up before the larger house next door. She stepped back into the hallway and looked at herself in the mirror before hurrying upstairs. She had difficult things to discuss with Lorenzo, but it never seemed to be the right time.

When she came down she heard Lorenzo and Wellington laughing in the kitchen.

"Amore," Lorenzo said warmly, his lined intelligent face breaking with a smile. He rose and took one of her hands as he kissed her. After several years of barren marriage with Anton, she had welcomed Lorenzo's gift for making her feel like a woman once again. In bed he generally substituted sophistication for vigor, with a skillful sensitivity that often pleased her. She had come to appreciate his touch, even the scratchy feeling of his mustache, but she was still uncomfortable with his affection before the boys, though only Denby sometimes seemed to mind. Also, at first, she had welcomed Lorenzo's maturity, his sense of authority, his taking charge, but now she found that too controlling, limiting instead of comforting. Soon she might not need him.

Wellington turned and looked up at his mother with excited eyes. "Colonel Grimaldi says he'll take me flying on Sunday."

For an instant, her hand still in Lorenzo's, she thought of their first meeting, and their first morning, when he had taken her flying at dawn. It was then that she had decided to take Lorenzo as her lover. They had flown in low towards the Western Desert with the sun rising swiftly behind them, sharing a flask of coffee as the blood-red face of the Sphinx rushed to meet them, floating above the darker desert like a gory ghost.

"If you've done all your homework, Wellie," Gwenn said, freeing her hand to go to the stove. She had too much homework of her own. How easy it seemed to buy a child's favor, she realized. For a moment she considered uneasily how the thought applied to her.

"Tea?" she asked Lorenzo, noticing that Denby was playing happily with pieces of a new model airplane that were spread across the table. The instructions on the lid of the box were in Italian. Already Denby had learned a few words of Enzo's language. "You mustn't spoil the boys so."

"Oh, Mum," Wellie groaned.

Sometimes Gwenn felt that she was on one side and these three men on another but she knew that none of them felt that way.

"You English don't know how to love your children," Lorenzo said, but with a clever lightness, as if without accusation.

Annoyed that there was more to the comment, that it related also to her feelings for him, Gwenn started to reply but changed her mind.

"The water's nearly boiling," she said instead. "Tea?"

"Coffee," her lover said, unbuttoning his trim uniform jacket and sitting down. "You English are so strict with children. Denby and I were just starting on a magnificent new fighter, a Macchi. With it we will sweep the skies." He lifted the model's light wooden fuselage and took it through a dive at Denby. "Rat-tat-tat!"

"I wish you'd stop teaching the boys about planes and bombs and killing people," she said reproachfully, pausing before continuing in a more gentle voice. "You and I can have a cup on the terrace while the boys do some reading. There's something I should talk to you about."

She detected a wariness in Lorenzo's eyes. It warned her of the hard shrewdness that lay behind his graceful manner.

"It's just about an idea I have," she added, turning away and setting out the cups, just as pleased to put it off, disturbed by the coolness growing between them, but now willing to take advantage of it. "Something they've suggested to me at medical school."

"Could we do it later? I have a bit of work to do next door before we go to dinner," he said, absently bending over to help Denby sort out pieces of the wings and tail. "I'll just have a little coffee first while you take tea with the boys."

Gwenn sat silently, sipping her tea, studying Lorenzo, strangely detached, wondering what she should do if she was still with him when Anton came to Cairo. Lorenzo'd been an angel, caring for her and the boys, and occasionally she felt she really loved him, but mostly she wasn't sure, hating his work, certain he was helping to plan a new war in Africa. With luck, she thought sadly, glancing at her sons, by the time Anton arrived she might already be in Abyssinia herself, and away from all of them.

"Look, Mummy," said Denby, holding up the Macchi, "she's almost ready to fly!"

— 4 —

"Let's meet at the Cataract Café for drinks," Anton had told his clients, ringing them in their rooms at Shepheard's the moment he arrived at his pension in Cairo, but he had not expected the scene that greeted him now on the embankment. Tomorrow he'd get in touch with Gwenn and arrange to meet his sons, but first he was counting on his old friend Olivio to give him the painful news, where she was living and with whom.

He wondered what these Americans would be like. He was relieved they'd hunted before, though not in Africa. First timers were always a risk, often finding themselves too far from home. Anton hated nothing like an unhappy camp fire. Even experienced hunters found Africa a different world, and Anton never credited a client's claims until he saw him in the field. One of this lot was an artist, and these Yanks had insisted on an unusual adventure. Abyssinia should provide it, he thought, lightly rubbing his wounded shoulder, thinking of the black leopard. It was his second week without bandages or a sling.

The din grew louder as he approached along the pocked limestone embankment near the Pont des Anglais. Could all this be coming from Olivio's café? Arriving under the eucalyptus trees, Anton shouldered his way through the growing throng of passersby and beggars. A sherbet peddler offered him brightly colored drinks. A lottery vendor pressed a flier into his hand. Anton glanced at it. *Moassat Lottery: 1st Prize Five Thousand Pounds Egyptian. Happiness! Fortune! Ease! Guaranteed by the National Bank of Egypt.* "I could certainly use it right now," he muttered.

"Libb! Sudani! Tirmis!" cried the hawkers, moving through the crowd, selling dried seeds and nuts in rolled paper cones and cigarettes from

wooden trays hanging from their shoulders. Others sold newspapers and pictures of the king and prince. Tumblers and fire-eaters and jugglers struggled for space to perform. A line of motorcars waited to unload at the head of the gangway. Paper lanterns brightened the trees along the quay. A carpet seller draped his wares over nearby branches. An incense vendor wove through the crowd like a genie, aromatic smoke rising from his round copper tray when he lit one tiny cone. Musicians lined the dockside, competing with wooden flutes and painted leather drums, cymbals and bagpipes.

At the end of the gangplank four Nubian retainers held back the crowd. Tariq, their leader, glowering and raven black under his broad white turban, armed with a *qurbash* ending in a horsetail lash, flicked the rhinoceros hide whip at the darting street boys, then bowed to the guests as they emerged from their vehicles. Surprised by the formality of their dress, Anton felt self-conscious in his worn linen jacket and old twills. Thankful the faithful garments had been sponged and pressed at his pension, he adjusted the red scarf knotted about his neck as he approached the top of the gangplank. Too tight in the arms, chafing his shoulders, the tan jacket hung unbuttoned.

Anton permitted a Cairene beauty and her Egyptian escorts to precede him. Raising her long dress with both hands as she approached the gangway, her high-collared silk cloak almost brushing Anton, the woman gave him a brief smile as she passed. Flourishing walking sticks, well-groomed, sleek and plump as stout grey pigeons, the men wore dark English suits, diamond stickpins and expensive tarbushes. Anton smelled the thick odors of incense and strong tobacco rising from the crowded deck below.

Behind him a woman screamed.

"Ow! Help! He stole my purse!"

Anton spun about to see a young red-haired woman clutching for a broken purse strap as an Egyptian youth stumbled beside her and sought to break away. Before anyone could move she seized the loose collar of the young man's *gallabiyyah.*

"How dare you!" she yelled in a broad American accent, releasing the strap and clawing furiously at the man's throat.

"Damn you! I'll kill you!" She pulled violently and the *gallabiyyah* ripped. Her nails tore lines in the man's neck as she kept after him like a wounded leopard. Twisting away from her, the thief tripped against the gangway and fell fifteen feet into the water with the woman on top of him.

Anton took two steps to the edge of the embankment, stared down as the two entangled figures broke the surface of the river, and dived after them. He heard the din of the crowd behind him as he fell, then felt the slap of cool water on his face before his head struck the side of the houseboat and he lost consciousness.

* * *

When Anton opened his eyes the round face of the dwarf was staring down at him, framed against the arabesque design of the painted ceiling, like a fat-bodied spider in its web.

"Welcome to Cairo, Mr. Anton!" Olivio still held Anton's right hand in both of his. Through the deck above there came the roar of guests and music, laughter and dancing. "We are in my private offices here in the hold of the Cataract Café."

Anton glanced about, his head aching, a hard lump swollen over one ear. "More like a Turkish bordello, I'd say."

Rich hangings, decorated chests, Turkish carpets and massive standing candleholders were scattered about the long dark chamber which stretched the length of the boat. Everywhere Anton saw varied creatures combining the body of a lion and the head of a man, versions of the Sphinx: small stone statuettes in vitrines on the walls; one, lying on the floor and carved in wood the size of a lion, with a cobra on its brow and a beard at its chin, and a leather cavalry saddle askew on its back; and, painted floor to ceiling the length of one wall, the Great Sphinx itself, in the exact color and worn form of the original at Giza. A padlocked cabinet hung on the opposing wall.

Glancing down, Anton was horrified to find himself wearing a brocade dressing gown and lying on a soft velvet divan that reeked of old perfumes. "What've you done to me, you little rascal?"

"While your clothes dry, we have dressed you in something from the armoires." And added a little something, the dwarf said to himself. Dismayed to find his friend had barely three pounds in his pockets, Olivio had crumpled and soaked a few banknotes of his own and slipped them into the shabby garments. Finding no charm in moderation, he took pleasure in alternating between the extremes of greed and generosity. "Soon your own things will be dry, Mr. Anton." One of the cooks was now pressing his guest's jacket on a hot plate.

"Can you spare me a brandy while I'm waiting?" his friend asked.

"It will be brought to you. Now you must forgive me while I join my guests." Dreading the climb, Olivio walked to the stair and bowed. He recalled the youthful enthusiasms that had complicated the hunter's marriage, his affairs with clients that had not remained secrets of the camp. "Indiscretions must be discreet, Mr. Anton," he had said once to his young friend. Rider had smiled, but not obeyed.

The dwarf spoke again before climbing the stair. "Here in Cairo you must permit me to arrange your entertainments."

A warm female laugh came from a chaise longue in a corner of the hold behind Anton.

"Thanks for trying to help," said the cheerful American voice. "But you shouldn't dive if you can't swim."

"I can swim." Anton turned his head, unable to keep the irritation from his voice.

"If I hadn't held up your head, you would've drowned in that sewer." The woman stepped over with a glass in her hand and sat on a high tasselled cushion beside the divan. She wrinkled her nose. "My, you smell sweet."

"It's the couch," Anton said gruffly.

He noticed the bright scarlet lipstick on the glass and examined the lady while she drank. Her short wet hair was combed back like a boy's. Anton's *diklo,* his red gypsy kerchief, was knotted across the top of her head. She seemed at home in her loose paisley silk robe. She raised Anton's chin with cool fingertips and held the brandy to his lips.

"I hope you're better in the jungle than you are in town."

"Does it matter?" As soon as he spoke, Anton realized who she must be.

"You bet it does! I'm Harry Mills, Harriet. You're meant to be our divine white hunter."

"Excuse me." Anton smiled and tried to sit up, then closed his eyes with dizziness. This was not the way a professional hunter was supposed to meet his clients.

"I'm sorry, I didn't know who you were."

"My sister Bernadette and her fiancé invited me on their safari," she said, her eyes studying his face and body with care. "They're dying to meet you. They hear you're the best shot in Africa. But they won't be happy to see you like this."

"No, they won't." Anton sat up and closed his eyes. He recognized the tone, and the type: spoiled, smart, well educated in their own sense, more assertive than any European girl, a rich attractive American woman used to getting her way. One or two had already got their way with him.

Harriet examined two torn nails on her right hand.

"Clawing these filthy thieves is no good for a girl's nails." She flicked one forefinger and frowned as she picked out a piece of dark skin from under the clear lacquered nail. "Ick." Then she looked up and studied Anton carefully before she spoke again. She admired his long fingers when he rubbed his blue eyes.

"I helped that weird little man undress you. What do you suppose he does down here? The strangest clothes and whatnot in that closet." Harriet ran one hand through her hair and shook her head to loosen her curls. "Looks like everyone stays here, from the Pope to Catherine the Great."

"Olivio has interesting friends." Anton smiled despite himself. How like the dwarf to have his client undress him. His little friend had not changed.

Her eyes glittered with interest. "I gather you're one of them. I asked him where all your lovely scars came from, front and back, all the strangest places. Some of the prettiest ones look brand new." Harriet sipped the brandy, sliding the tip of her tongue along the rim of the glass. "I hate to think where you've been."

He noticed her overly generous, pouty lips, with no angles on top, just a high full curve, very nearly the mouth of a beautiful black woman, somehow too lavish for this girl's slender looks.

"I love this one." She reached to trace the bump on his ribs with two fingernails. His stomach shivered and tightened. One side of her robe fell open.

"What did my friend tell you?" Anton said, careful not to shift his eyes to her small high breast and rosy pointed nipple. Upstairs the bagpipes began to keen. He changed his mind and stared at her shamelessly, assessing how she'd react.

"Wouldn't tell me, just said you'd taken a lot of swims." Carelessly she moved one hand to close her robe a bit.

"Harry, Harry!" another American voice called from the stair. A pair of stilettoes landed unsteadily on the cabin floor.

"Harry! What's going on down here? Oh, my!" An identical redhead waved at Anton, spilling champagne from her glass. "Shame on you, sister."

"He's our Tarzan," said Harriet. "This is our famous white hunter, Mr. Anton Rider."

Her sister gazed at her appraisingly. "Well, behave yourself, Harry. He's only half yours, you know." The second girl paused to drink. "Does he always dress like that?"

"Good evening," Anton said, finding himself admiring her legs. Why did American girls always have the best legs?

"Hi, I'm Berny Mills, Bernadette. Thanks for looking after my sister. I hope you'll try to save me one day. Isn't she lucky you can't swim?"

"I can swim," Anton said, pleased to be interrupted by a roar of cheering from the deck above. Not quite himself, for an instant he was not certain which girl was which. He wondered if they always repeated each other.

"Hurry up you two!" Bernadette said. "And come on upstairs. They're about to sing 'Happy Birthday.' " Anton followed Bernadette's legs as she climbed the steps.

"Don't forget, my twin sister is engaged," Harriet whispered sharply, helping Anton to his feet.

"Excuse me while I change," he said. Carrying his own damp freshly-pressed clothes, he walked to a dark corner of the cabin and quickly changed, feeling her eyes examining him while she stood smoking by the foot of the stair. Already exposed to the feline competition of the twins, he speculated what this might mean on safari.

* * *

"Dear boy!" Adam Penfold called to Anton, waving his cane above the crowd, grey and lean and distinguished as a secretary bird. Anton steadied himself against the doorway to the saloon and returned the greeting.

Inside, the bar was crowded with jostling European men raising their hands to get the attention of the besieged barmen. Uneven colored light shone from enamelled glass lamps hanging from a painted beam in the ceiling. Anton noticed the enormous mounted head of a white rhino hanging on the wall behind the bar between a flag of Goa and a photograph of King Fuad. Dressed in naval uniform, the Egyptian monarch stood stiffly on the deck of the immense royal yacht, the *Mahroussa.*

Adam Penfold limped over and shook Anton's hand. Anton noticed his friend's waistcoat was buttoned incorrectly, and he grinned at the detail, pleased to know one man who would never change. Could it be he did these things on purpose?

"Let me get you a drink," Penfold said, regarding his friend with concern. "You're not looking in top form. I hear you found your clients."

"They found me." Anton's head was still pounding.

A drum began to thunder at the other end of the Café. Bagpipes wailed, then ceased. Cries of "Quiet, please," cut the din. People stepped aside as a young girl, perhaps twelve, honey-colored and well formed, made her way forward carrying a large chocolate cake forested with candles. She had in her step some of the high skip of an excited schoolgirl yet she carried her body with the knowing confidence of an experienced young woman. Friendly voices called out to her. "Well done, Ginger!"

Taller, darker, full-bodied, another girl followed: Anton's godchild, Clove. He went on his toes and waved to her but was not seen. Her dark eyes sparkling, she smiled and waved at Lord Penfold as she passed, carrying a two-year-old in her arms. "Hullo, Clove! Good show!" called a guest. Behind Clove came three more girls, all dressed in the matching long green socks, pleated skirts and blazers of their European school.

All five girls gathered about the cake on a narrow platform on the starboard side. A radiant black lady stood to their left in a white French evening dress and long white gloves, striking and voluptuous as an opera diva, with gold at her wrists and pearls a vivid white at her throat. The wide welt of a pink burn scar crossed one collarbone and disappeared over her shoulder. The woman took the hand of the youngest standing child. The girl, perhaps four, shiny black as her mother, pressed her other hand into the side of the cake and smiled up with huge brown eyes.

"Happy birthday to you!" the crowd sang.

Tariq placed his hands under the dwarf's arms and lifted his master like a puppy. With great care the burly servant set the little man down on the bulwark behind his children.

"For he's a jolly good fellow!"

Olivio Fonseca Alavedo gripped the railing behind him with his left hand. He straightened his shoulders as best he could and looked down on his guests, intensely conscious of the scene. How often his own life amazed him. But there would not be many more candles. The dwarf knew his own birthdays were numbered. He could expect, he would hazard, about as many as an Egyptian goose, three or four, perhaps five, each more painful than the last. Already the afflictions common to little people were gaining on him. Even he could not escape the cost of his body's distortions.

Olivio acknowledged an individual here and there. He held up his right hand. For a moment there was near silence.

"Thank you." The dwarf bowed, raising his tarbush with both hands. His head was perfectly round and smooth. Once embarrassed by his bizarre physicality, he had learned to exploit it, as a great beauty might her legs or breasts. His right eye shone. "Thank you, my friends." Some were, he thought, some were not. With most of Cairene society in Alex for the season, many of his government acquaintances and friends and clients among the Muslim secular elite were absent from the party.

The pipes howled. Drums beat. Two torches flared on the flat roof of the saloon. The guests gazed up. Between the torches a woman appeared, wrapped in a veil and cloak. In the moving shadows behind her, Olivio's pigeons fluttered nervously and retreated to the darkest corners of their coops.

The dancer opened her cloak. Murmurs and exclamations rose from the guests. Two cymbals crashed. The woman, glistening with almond oil, hurled her cloak down into the crowd. A wizened Frenchman grabbed it and pressed it to his nose. "Jamila!" the man cried. "Jamila!"

As Olivio gazed up at her, he recalled how he and this dancer had passed his birthday afternoon only a few hours earlier. It had been a gruelling and yet refeshing interlude. Shortly before tea-time, he had rewarded Jamila's generosity with one of his own special gifts: the ability to insinuate his entire hand, the left and smaller one, properly oiled with cashew liqueur, inside her. Instantly growing still, her body waited like a bomb with a glowing fuse. He did the same, holding his nail-less fingers tightly together like the wings of a trussed pigeon. In this moment they knew each other. Their breathing at last in perfect harmony, he opened his slippery hand inside her like a night flower blossoming in darkness. Jamila had shivered and cried out, her body twitching and jumping like a trout on a stream bank, electrified as his tiny nimble fingers rioted inside her. Unable to please women with the common gifts of charm or appearance, the dwarf had grown adept at his own rare skills.

Naked save for a short beaded skirt, two tassels and a row of small gold coins suspended across her belly, the dancer clicked golden finger cymbals behind her head and closed her eyes. She arched her back and cocked her belly. The coins rippled and shimmered. The guests roared. The Frenchman waved her cloak.

Standing beneath Jamila in the doorway to the bar, Anton looked across the deck into the upturned faces of the other guests. Kina caught his eye and answered his wave with a rich smile. Except for Penfold and the twins, all the rest were strangers. Anton had heard guests conversing in Russian and German, Turkish and Greek and French and Italian. Never, not even among the gypsies as a boy, had he seen such an exotic gathering, a circus of silk and sharkskin suits and colored *gallabiyyas,* tunics and robes, military caps and tarbushes. There were Africans dressed as Europeans, and Europeans clothed like Moors.

Only the soldiers seemed to share a common ethic: smart well-fitted uniforms, polished leather, decorations, Spartans among the partying Athenians. With a growing sense of war and crisis, the military were back in fashion. Their varied caps were arrayed on a side table at the foot of the gangway.

Anton noticed three young Egyptian officers seated together, all captains, proud and erect, sipping lemon juice and not speaking, as if present to observe and not participate, perhaps reflecting the new nationalist spirit said to be sweeping the officer corps. England and France were reported to be their unstated enemies. The three stood when a German officer joined their table. Standing behind them, Harriet beckoned to Anton and raised her glass. "Must do your duty," Anton mumbled to himself.

Anton made his way towards the smiling American girl, excusing himself as he struggled forward.

"Isn't it grand?" Harriet said when he joined her, raising her glass to the crowd. She took his arm firmly and led him to a table where Bernadette sat drinking with a thin young man. Frowning, he was sketching on an artist's pad with the concentration of one alone in his studio.

"Charlie," Bernadette said to her blond companion, who remained absorbed in his work. She poked him. "Charlie, wake up! Our hunter's here. Meet Anton Rider."

The man stood and greeted Anton eye to eye with an open friendly smile. "Charles Crow." He set his pencil behind one ear and sought to match Anton's handshake. "Join us, please. There's so much we want to hear."

Anton looked about for a chair. Harriet clung to him like a wait-a-bit thornbush. He was glancing past the gangway when he felt his heart stop.

"Excuse me," he said huskily, stepping away from Harriet.

A striking couple hesitated at the top of the gangway. Grey-haired, not tall but impressive and distinguished in a white uniform with medals and gold wings above the breast pockets, an Italian colonel stroked his silver mustache while he stood aside to let his lady descend first.

Perfectly erect, her neck straight and her chin high, the woman walked forward. She was a tall slender woman in a quiet fitted linen suit, with tawny wavy hair and a lightly tanned, sculpted face with strong but rounded cheekbones and full but finely shaped lips. The only woman Anton had ever loved. The green eyes caught his. Gwenn. His wife.

Anton walked directly to her.

"Anton . . ." Gwenn began, shock in her voice and eyes.

"Excuse me, won't you," Anton said without looking at the officer, "while I speak with my wife." Before the man could reply, Anton took Gwenn firmly by one elbow and led her to the far edge of the boat. He was aware of his clients staring after him through the crowd.

"Anton, please, you can't behave like this," Gwenn said, pulling herself free, annoyed she had let him take control. "You're embarrassing me. Where do you think you are?"

"I am your husband," he said quietly after a pause, attempting to gentle himself. "You look lovely tonight."

She stiffened when he leaned to kiss her cheek.

"Things have changed," she said more softly, looking him in the eye, an appeal for understanding in her tone.

"Who's your Spanish bandleader?"

Anton saw her hands clench.

"He is not Spanish," she said with irritation. "He's an Italian officer."

"Really?" Anton stared across the deck, assessing the enemy.

"You must apologize to him." For a moment she touched Anton's hand. "Please," she added, still cupping his hand.

"I'll apologize to you," he said, meaning it, moved by her touch. "I'm sorry."

"He's been very good to us," she said, fearing Anton would resent it but needing to explain. "Very generous to the boys and me."

"How good?" Anton said with bitterness, regretting it at once, knowing he was spoiling things. He felt her pull away. "How generous?"

Without blinking or speaking, firm again, Gwenn looked back at Anton and raised her chin, her lips thin and tight. She began to move off. She'd been afraid it would be like this.

"How are you and the boys?" he said, trying not to lose her.

"They're wonderful," she said as Anton forced his way alongside her through the noisy crowd. "We're all fine, thanks, getting on."

"Can I see them tomorrow?"

"Of course," she said, speaking over her shoulder, furiously calculating Lorenzo's schedule. "The best time would be first thing, a bit before eight, just before they leave for school. You could go with them, if you'd like."

Gwenn looked ahead towards the gangway. Her escort stood staring grimly as she approached.

"Lorenzo," Gwenn said, controlling her voice to a normal sociable tone, "this is Anton Rider, Count Grimaldi."

"Good evening," said Enzo crisply, bowing slightly but not offering his hand.

"While I'm in Cairo," said Anton before turning on his heel, wishing the man would give him some excuse for violence, "please let me know, Count, how much I owe you for tending to my wife and children."

No more said, the eyes of the two men met like animals in the bush.

— 5 —

Gwenn leaned against a column by the door and watched her sons walk towards the automobile. Still upset with the way he had caught her off guard last night, she watched Anton waiting by the car to accompany them to school. Behind him, Lorenzo's driver, Kamil, flicked dust from the Bugatti's crystal hood ornament with a long feather duster.

Tall and solid for fourteen, Wellie pulled his younger brother by the hand. Both boys wore stout brown shoes, long grey socks, grey flannel shorts and the maroon blazers and caps of Prince Albert College. Denby, nine, swung his new hockey stick in his other hand. He dragged behind his half-brother, pulling free and flailing at a locust resting on the edge of the walk. He was so like his father, Gwenn thought. The giant grasshopper, perfect as a hieroglyphic, rose in the air on the smooth edge of the stick and took flight.

Anton had arrived on foot. He loved to walk, but she doubted that was the reason. Gwenn was certain he had no money. Tan and almost boyish for a man of thirty-four, even from a distance she could tell he was better suited for East Africa and the bush than for Cairo and the Gezira Club. She knew he never had liked Cairo. The elegance and squalor whose contrast excited other visitors were to him equally distasteful, and part of her agreed with him. She looked at Anton again, more carefully.

Tall and rangy when they'd first met, now he seemed bigger and harder, perhaps a little less loose when he moved and spoke, but he still had the honest eyes and open tanned face and the bump on the bridge of his prominent nose. The women must love him, especially his safari clients, who always saw him at his best. Eight years older than Anton when they met, now Gwenn felt older still. Her stomach tightened and she pressed her lips together. Perhaps their ages mattered after all, and more to her than him.

Gwenn remembered how things had been at first, on safari in the hills, working together at the farm, making love under the sky. She had been astonished by his experience, by his physical understanding. "Outdoors is best," he had told her one afternoon. What a shame it could not last. All she'd wanted then was to build a family on land of their own. She still had the farm, but by now it must be back to virgin bush. Kenya seemed so far away, so long ago.

She saw Anton squat on his heels as the boys came to him. Wellington released his young half-brother and stepped forward first. He pulled off his cap and held out his hand. Anton grinned and took Wellie's hand and ruffled his red hair. With the boy's own dad long dead, for years Anton had been Wellington's only father.

Denby hesitated. Anton opened his arms and enfolded his son. The boy buried his face in his father's neck. Gwenn, touched, put a hand to her mouth. She knew this was what mattered. She pressed her lips together as her eyes moistened and her stomach tightened. She knew how Denby had waited for this time, and Wellie, too. Part of her felt the same. The boys were at an age when Anton would appear all a father should be: strong and brave, adventurous, a hunter like no other. But she knew the other Anton: absent, impractical, improvident about tomorrow, dependable only in a crisis. Unfaithful. Sustained intimacy and responsibility seemed strangers to him, yet to her, and others, he represented the wild manly side of what many women wanted.

Anton remained low on his heels, one hand on each of Denby's shoulders. Then he unbuckled his wristwatch and handed it to Denby. The boy held the watch, turned it over in both hands and looked up at his father, his face wide with wonder. Anton took back the watch and removed a penknife from his pocket. He cut two holes in the strap with the tip of his knife and secured the watch around his son's left wrist. Gwenn clenched her jaw and tried not to cry. She saw Anton close the knife and give it to Wellie. He must have nothing else to give them.

Kamil held open the door of the Bugatti. The small Italian flag on the mast was shrouded in a black leather hood. The boys climbed in. Anton hesitated, then turned and looked back at Gwenn. He waved to her. She could feel his uncertainty, and his longing. Gwenn lifted one hand and tried to smile. Anton climbed in and the automobile pulled away. Soon the car would be bringing him back. She stared after them, then turned quickly and went inside.

* * *

"May I come in?" Anton's voice called hesitantly from the front door before she was prepared.

"Of course. Come in the kitchen and have a cup of tea." Nervous, Gwenn combed her fingers through her hair and led the way, wondering if he would try to kiss her. She was both relieved and faintly downcast when he did not.

He sat on the edge of Sana's seat at the kitchen table and watched Gwenn fix the tea, enjoying the sight of her as he recognized her ways. The shelves behind her were crowded with medical books and photographs of the boys, but none of him, he noticed, jealous that the house and its details were not his. He wondered if she had put away photos of her lover for this visit.

"You've done a wonderful job with the boys," he said, noticing with distaste the bottle of Amaretto and the sack of Italian coffee on the tea shelf. "Denby's just like you." Determined and independent, he thought.

"It's China tea," she said, preparing to dilute his cup with hot water from the second pot. "Lemon?"

He held out one hand to protect his cup. "I'll have mine dark, with milk, please. Plenty of sug."

"It's China. It's not meant to be strong." Why do I always tell him what to do? Gwenn thought as she spoke. "Milk spoils it."

Anton ground his teeth. "Please give it to me the way you think I should have it," he said in a controlled neutral voice, reminded of how things used to be.

Appreciating the humor of this small submission, she looked at him and began to smile while she downed the pot and poured the milk.

"Did you like the school?" she said.

"Seemed a bit strict, but I haven't much to compare it to," he replied easily, thinking to disarm her. One shelf of Dickens had been his school, nailed above the low door of the *vardo,* the gypsy wagon he'd shared with his mother and her Romany lover. He understood why Gwenn wanted the boys to do better.

"They said I arrived too late to meet the masters."

"The boys love it. Wellie might be head boy in a couple of years, if he can get through Latin and his sums."

"Latin?" he said, feeling sorry for the boys.

"Of course."

She was determined to keep their talk on the boys, he saw. He decided there was no way to proceed but by being blunt.

"Gwenn, at the end of term, or when you finish your studies, I was hoping you'll all come home."

"Home?" She didn't bother to keep the bitterness from her voice. "How much time did you ever spend at home?" Stiffening, she turned aside sharply and began to fuss with things on a shelf, her back to him.

"You know I was working," he said reasonably. "Safaris are my job. We couldn't live off that hopeless farm." This was usually the moment when she brought up his infidelities, he thought, strangely pleased that now she had lost that edge.

Deciding he had little to lose, Anton did what he had been wanting to do. He stepped closer to Gwenn and placed his hands to her sides and kissed the corner of her neck and shoulder. She did not pull away, but inclined her head towards his, naturally, as if tickled but not put off by his touch. For a moment her cheek rested against his.

"*Makwa,* Missy, laundry," said Sana from the doorway, a pile of linen in her hands. She had been nearby, as Gwenn had instructed her.

"Hello, Sana," Gwenn said, moving apart and turning around, her emotions confused. "This is Mr. Rider, Denby's father."

"Good morning," Anton nodded briefly, not deterred, but feeling the intimacy slipping away.

"Gwennie, you're my wife. The boys are my sons. You know . . ."

"When were you last my husband?" she said bitterly, closing herself, her cheeks hollow as she stared at him with anger.

"Were you ever my husband for more than a few weeks at a time?"

"I'm not going to let this Italian of yours buy my sons."

"Sons, husband?" she snapped. Her face scarlet, her fists clenched, Gwenn turned away, then spoke slowly over her shoulder, meaning to hurt him. "The boys and I can't even remember what you're like."

For a moment well pleased with herself, she listened to his steps as he left her.

Enzo Grimaldi set down the coded message. All his life, he reflected, had been a preparation for this time. On his twelfth birthday his father had taken him into the gun room and unlocked the cabinet containing the box of his own father's things from the Abyssinian campaign of 1896. Apart from his grandfather's sabre, there was not much. Spurs, two medals, a small leather diary, a field telescope, a belt buckle and brass buttons engraved with the she-wolf of Rome. Exactly six years later, Enzo and his father toasted the old soldier with spumanti, and the box became his.

A cavalryman, Count Grimaldi had commanded the Eritrean Brigade of native infantry at the battle of Adowa, the greatest defeat ever suffered by a European colonial army. Four thousand Italians died that day in the rocky valleys and mountain passes that looked down on the five Christian churches of the town. They were more fortunate than their surviving Eritrean brothers-in-arms, regarded by their former ruler, Menelik, the emperor of Abyssinia, as traitors to their blood. Enemies deserved defeat, traitors something more memorable. The captured Eritreans understood this code.

As he sat against a juniper tree with his sabre beside him, slowly dying of his wounds, treated with consideration by the victors, the count and another Italian officer watched as one thousand men he had recruited and trained and led were lined up in six parallel rows. A dark-robed Tigrean blade-sharpener sat in the shade of the tree behind theirs with his thick oval stone set between his feet. At the man's side a stack of *sayfs* waited in their tooled leather scabbards. The two Italians heard the steady scraping of steel against stone as the old man held each long curved sword to the whetstone before testing it on the nails of his left hand.

In front of each column of prisoners was a log. Beside the logs waited the eager Galla swordsmen, red-cloaked, tall and dark and lean-faced, dismounted horsemen being rewarded for their loyalty. The *negaret,* a large copper war drum adorned with threadbare lion skins, beat slowly. Chatting and jesting with each other, the Gallas collected their sharpened swords, each man examining his with care. Then the ritual began. In the distance, in the center of Adowa, the long ceremonial horns of the white-robed priests invited the Christian celebrants to mass.

The first Eritrean prisoner had his right arm held across the log. His hand was cut off with a single blow at the wrist. A roar rose from the watching Galla fighters. Hundreds more rushed over and gathered around on foot and horseback, chanting, entranced, long curved swords waving wildly in the air. The prisoner's left foot was held across the log. After a time the weary swordsmen slipped in pools of blood. The maimed bled and died. Some dragged themselves through the chanting Gallas and sheltered under bushes, moaning and binding their stumps with fragments of their robes. The logs were dragged to dry ground. Fresh soldiers set to work.

Count Grimaldi, almost delirious, struggled to stand with the help of his sabre. Unable, he called to an Abyssinian captain. The man walked over and inclined his head with respect. Gesturing his wish, the count demanded the same treatment as his men. Understanding, the captain gently lifted the count in his arms and carried the wounded Italian to the head of one line. The captain set Grimaldi down. Instantly a frenzied Galla raised his sword and cut through boot and bone. The count died before the second blow.

Two years later the second Italian officer had visited the Grimaldis at their villa in Lombardy to pay his respects and deliver the count's possessions. After lunch, Enzo's father led the soldier into the library and left him with a bottle of grappa and a tablet of paper, requesting him to write of the late count's final days. Later the sheets were bound, a single word and the year engraved on the cover: *L'Abissinia, 1896.*

Enzo turned and ran his fingers along the curved blade of the sabre mounted on the wall behind his desk. How many times had he sneaked into the library, taken down the slim leather volume and sat on the floor behind his father's desk reading that account? By the age of thirteen, Lorenzo Grimaldi knew each word of those eighteen pages, every detail of that mortal African ceremony. As a boy, Enzo was aware that for generations the mutilated Eritrean survivors, wandering mendicants, recognizable by their wounds, reminded Abyssinians of the price of supporting Italy's adventure.

To one side of the sabre was a signed portrait of *Il Duce,* the block-like Roman countenance solid and determined. On the other was a detailed map of the horn of Africa, from the Sudan to Kenya. On the short wall to the side were six drawings of the flying machines designed by Leonardo da Vinci. The wall opposite carried photographs of Enzo in his trainer at flight school in Calabria, in the open cockpit of his Fiat CR-1 during the war in Libya in 1927, and standing before three bi-winged Breda 19's with his brother pilots of the aerobatic squadron. He had always enjoyed the technology of warfare.

Enzo read the message again and crumpled it and set it on a copper tray. Then he lit it on fire. He stepped to the embassy window and gazed across the Nile to the Manyal Palace.

His duties had grown as the invasion of Abyssinia approached. No longer was it a matter of securing intelligence of British intentions and calming his Egyptian counterparts while Italian troops and laborers and supplies poured south through the Suez Canal.

One of the few senior Italian pilots with experience in Africa, he had assisted with the operational preparations of the *Regia Aeronautica.* On the first day of warfare, four hundred Italian aircraft would be committed to the battle. And now, it seemed, he would have the honor of being called on to join his brother aviators in Italian Somaliland or Eritrea. His personal interests in Cairo must be put aside.

The war itself did not daunt him, nor the need to simplify his life and leave so much behind. But there was one assignment he hoped would not be his: determining, on behalf of the air force, the military advisability of using poison gas in Abyssinia, a delicate question since it had been banned from warfare by the League of Nations under the Geneva Convention of 1925.

Already, in Sicily, he had participated in secret testing of the airborne canisters. If needed, fifty new aircraft were ready for the work. He prayed the war would be quick and easy. A long and ugly conflict, especially with poison gas, could provoke an oil embargo against Italy and the closing of the Canal to Italian shipping. Without fuel, the army would die in Africa. Even Adowa would be forgotten in the vastness of such a catastrophe. Lorenzo Grimaldi did not wish to represent his family in a second Italian disaster.

Instead of flying, perhaps he should entrain to Port Saäd, or drive to Suez, and catch one of the better troopships south. Four transatlantic liners, including the splendid *Giulio Cesare,* were about to sail from Naples with thirteen hundred skilled laborers and five thousand Blackshirts. Other passenger vessels were being purchased from Canada and Germany. He picked up *Il Giornale d'Oriente* to check the sailings.

The first page of one of Cairo's Italian newspapers carried a photograph of Benito Mussolini standing on the gun carriage of an ancient cannon in the harbor at Genova, his right fist raised, addressing men of the *Valpusteria Alpini,* invoking the Augustin past as he celebrated the 2,688th birthday of the city of Rome.

"You will avenge Adowa!" the Duce roared to the departing soldiers. "All Italy stands behind her sons leaving for Africa, who prefer a heroic life to a purposeless existence. We Italians are the protagonists of a great historic development. Our future lies to the east and south, in Asia and Africa. The entire world must recognize the value of the Fascist spirit."

Enzo's orderly entered with a second cable. The count tore open the telegram from Rome. "You will embark at Suez," it concluded. The decision had been made for him.

He picked up the snapshot of the English girl, taken at the aerodrome after their first flight together. His white scarf was knotted around her neck. A pair of his goggles was in her hand. Her smile was bright and excited as a schoolgirl's. Even now, her beauty and her spirit still refreshed him. He would miss her, and even her sons. He had been teaching the boys to ride and fence, and Wellington how to shoot.

He thought with anger of how she had treated him at the Café, the public insult of it. Finally she had remained at his side, almost trembling. Cold and speechless after her Englishman stalked off, later she had given Enzo an apology but no affection. Someone must pay for this humiliation. It was embarrassing enough conducting such an affair in Cairo, not to speak of the expense. He had learned that the more generous he was, the more thankless she became, unable sometimes not to reveal the resentment common to recipients of largesse.

Tonight they would be dining at Groppi's, their favorite restaurant when they were alone. After that, if things went well, perhaps a dance at the Mena Lido.

Grimaldi rose and walked out to his waiting Bugatti, reminding himself that, despite last night, he must be generous and be careful to leave her feeling affectionate and well disposed. Anything else would drive her back to Rider.

"You have not been yourself since your Englishman arrived yesterday," Enzo said after dinner when Gwenn declined to take his hand. "Do you still love him?"

"Oh, I don't know. Perhaps in a way, sometimes," she said slowly, trying not to shrink away. "But it's not the same."

The Bugatti pressed them together as it turned left into Garden City. Gwenn kissed Lorenzo lightly on the cheek. Dinner had not been the usual gay evening. For the first time in almost a year and a half there had been silence between them, not the easy comfortable silence that could be better than talk, but the distant unsympathetic sort she had always promised herself not to endure with any man. She knew it was her fault, but tonight Lorenzo also seemed preoccupied. She had told him she was too tired to go dancing.

"Will you come to Suez Friday and see me off?" he said, annoyed that he had to ask, but knowing she would never offer on her own.

"I'd love to, Lorenzo, but you know I've got the boys to look after." And an examination at medical school, Gwenn added to herself. She touched his hand fleetingly. She and her children were still guests in his house, and he was going to war. If only he could leave before their relationship turned nasty.

"I'll miss you," she said after a moment, thinking that at times she would. "Why must you go now?"

"*Il Duce's* sons are sailing from Naples on the *Saturnia,* and I'm ordered to board at Suez and sail with them to Eritrea. There'll be special trains from Cairo to greet them at Port Saïd."

"Why are you all going?" she said, knowing she was provoking him, perhaps hoping it would distance them. "Is this war of yours really necessary?" She knew he was tired of defending Italy's ambitions.

"It's not a war," Lorenzo said, speaking carefully, as if to a child. "We are just protecting Italian territory. These Ethiopians cross the border every night, killing people, stealing cattle. They kidnap children for their slave trade, you know. Savages."

Her lips tightened before she spoke. "Please, Lorenzo, we both know that's not what this is about. The Emperor has promised to end slavery."

"Why do you all make such darlings of the Abyssinians?" he persisted. "They treat each other like animals. They're the last country in the world still buying and selling human beings."

"Mussolini wants to enslave the whole country," she said, hearing the anger in her own voice. "Isn't that what all your planes and men are for? Why can't you be honest with me, Lorenzo?"

"Honest? You wish the truth?"

"You know I do," she said through thin lips, feeling her face tighten.

"Ethiopia is the only country in Africa not yet colonized, apart from Liberia, and it already borders two Italian territories. And we have a history there, one that honor requires us to pursue. It's high and cool, healthy, good farmland, perfect to settle our unemployed population. Already it is one half Christian." He paused and looked at her. "Haven't your own people colonized one quarter of the earth?"

"Thank you, Lorenzo, for telling me the truth at last, or at least part of it."

For a moment neither spoke.

"You didn't ask me what I'll be doing while you're away," she said quietly in the silence.

"Forgive me, *cara,*" he said, taking a deep breath, his tone softer. "Please tell me." He stroked her hand with his.

"I've been asked to go to Abyssinia myself."

"You?" he said, laughing nervously, his hand stiffening.

"At the hospital they're asking for volunteers to sign up for Ethiopia," she said, trying to keep her voice neutral, aware that this political issue was widening fissures between them that both had long ignored.

"The Egyptian Red Cross, actually the Red Crescent Society, they're sending out two ambulance teams as soon as possible. They need eighty or ninety people. They know I drove an ambulance in France during the war. They want doctors, nurses, orderlies, drivers, mechanics, especially with wartime experience . . ."

"What for?" Lorenzo said too sharply, shrugging both shoulders.

Gwenn turned her head and looked at his profile in the darkness. What did he take her for? A nit?

"What for?" she snapped. "To help people after your Italian invasion." She withdrew her hand.

"There is no Italian invasion," he said with indignation. "I've told you all that before. Haile Selassie and his Abbos are attacking our outposts, occupying our water holes, lying to the League about the frontier lines. He gives Italy no choice."

"Lorenzo, please. You're not talking to the newspapers. You and I know that's all nonsense. Your Duce just wants a new Roman empire. He says so every day."

Gwenn saw Enzo turn his face away again. Under the intelligent charm, there was an anger that she feared. She must not let him upset her. But if he needed to hear the rest of the truth, she would tell him.

"Mussolini even wants Egypt and the Sudan, to link up with Libya and Ethiopia and Eritrea and Italian Somaliland. You know it. You're part of it all. Please don't lie to me anymore, Lorenzo. I'm tired of it. If he starts this war, the whole world could get involved."

"Don't you British have an empire? Why shouldn't we? Egypt and Britain were provinces of Rome before the time of Christ. Why should Egypt be part of the British empire today? Look at a map. The Mediterranean should be our sea, not yours. Egyptian students, the Blue Shirts, are demonstrating against you British every day."

"That's not the point. There'll be innocent casualties who'll get no care if we don't go." Gwenn stared out the side window into the darkness as she spoke.

"Then you've already decided to go?"

"I'm thinking about it. I wanted to talk to you." Her hands clenched. "But I see that's not possible." She knew she must move out. But where would she and the boys go?

"You know I love you," he said, too late, "and you know what I must do."

And now I know what I must do, she thought as the car pulled up outside Lorenzo's house.

"I'll just run next door and check on the boys," Gwenn said, knowing he still expected to sleep with her, and dreading the intimate evasion that lay ahead. She was uncertain whether to acquiesce or resist, knowing she would find compliance or withdrawal almost equally distasteful. Perhaps a cowardly alternative would be best, sending Sana over with some message of excuse.

"I'll probably see you upstairs in a minute," she said quickly.

Entering the house, exhausted, Gwenn closed the door behind her with relief. Confused by her conflicting feelings, still so angry at Anton that she was considering sleeping with Lorenzo from spite, but also from past affection, she closed her eyes and leaned back against the door with a sigh.

— 6 —

The dwarf sat in his leather saddle bestride the wooden sphinx. With the Café always busy, the hold had become Olivio's favored sanctuary for reflection. His apricot nectar, untouched, rested on the broad lip of the tall ecclesiastical candleholder that stood on the floor beside him. The river's dawn dampness, penetrating the sides of the boat, was deep in his joints and spine, hardening his very lymph and marrow, reminding him of the medical report still clenched in his right fist, and the remorseless progression of his deformities.

Olivio glanced to his left with a tired eye. The doors were open on the camphorwood cabinet that hung on the long wall. The padlock dangled from its small chain. Centered on the first shelf was a Middle Kingdom clay statue of the god Bes. The Egyptian deity of dwarfism stood on short bowed legs. His belly hung forward. The wide low-set navel was framed by the hands that rested on his hips. His thick tongue protruded from a prominent triangular head.

The fragment of a twenty-first dynasty papyrus rested to the right of Bes. Images of the dwarf god mingled with depictions of the sacred dung beetle, the scarab Khepri. The related composite creatures, half dwarf, half insect, shared large rounded trunks and short curved limbs. All were surrounded by a circle of flames, symbolizing triumph over enemies, and the relationship of the sacred scarab to the burning disk of the morning sun god. How well these ancients had understood Olivio's condition, and its distinction.

His eye turned upwards to study one of his favorites: the tracing of a sarcophagus papyrus from the Egyptian Museum at Turin. A naked singer is bent gracefully over the frame of a chariot. Her perfect raised flanks, Olivio's favorite detail, extend just past the end of the vehicle. Behind her a priest stands on tiptoes. His mouth is slightly open as he penetrates the singer with his enlarged phallus while she turns her face backwards to regard him over her shoulder with dark oval eyes set under angled brows. Two slender girls are drawing the chariot. A long-tailed monkey with widespread toes stands on the traces, playing with the reins. Below the monkey walks a dwarf carrying a satchel in his right hand. With the other hand the little man seeks unsuccessfully to capture the attention of the two girls, towards whom his immense rigid phallus is extended upwards. He, too, is on his toes, though not for the same reason as the priest, Olivio was certain. For the depicted dwarf, the cause would be *talipes equinus,* a congenital deformity of the foot, that compels a man to walk with his soles flexed. Olivio's stubby toes toyed with the stirrups as he savored the details. How alive it all was for him. How much these ancient Egyptians understood.

A bronze statuette of a later period stood next to this magical paper. A kilted humpbacked dwarf with the tail of a crocodile, he held a baton of authority in his right hand. His club feet rested on the shoulders of two swine to evidence the dwarf god's mastery over malignant forces.

At least, thought Olivio, they appreciated the peculiar qualities a small figure could possess, particularly the dwarf god's five attributes, one celebratory, the sponsorship of wine and music and dancing, and four protective: the protection of warfare and the dead, and of sleep and women, particularly during childbirth. Olivio thought of Kina. Yesterday evening she had discussed her pregnancy. It would be their last. Would his son be born this winter? If he were, would he be what other men considered normal, or would he share his father's life?

The dwarf spread the two pages of the medical report before him on the shoulders of the sphinx. The clinic in Alexandria held no answers, merely confirmation of his decline. Perhaps it was time to journey to the Dolder Institute near Zürich, the home of achondroplasiology, the study of dwarfism in its most common forms. The Swiss, it seemed, had a price even for dwarves.

He knew he should make the pilgrimage to Zürich. There he would suffer a Himalaya of expense and indignity, but he would learn what he must know: the prospective progression of his maladies, the extent of time remaining, and the prospects for his children. The cost he could dismiss. Bad news he could accept, perhaps. But the humiliation of presenting himself naked before cold-eyed Swiss doctors and attendants while they discussed him in German, measuring him and writing notes, this was beyond the frontier of his endurance.

What sort of men and women must be drawn to such work? Their magnet must be different than mere science or compassion. Were they nourishing a taste for horror?

These doctors would not examine him with the matter-of-fact comfortable acceptance with which his farmers picked at a cotton worm, knowing the repellant creature to be a normal part of nature.

Their professional demeanor could never conceal the repulsion and curiosity with which they would observe him. First they would measure him from crown to pubis, and from pubis to heel, determining the segment ratios by which his proportions deviated from the normal. They would grade his abnormalities with careful figures. Perhaps one doctor or, worse, a nurse, would hold a tape to his naked body, calling out each millimeter while another repeated and recorded the evil numbers.

Then they would proceed limb by limb and organ by organ, starting with a study of his head, assessing the ossification of the cartilagous bones, noting the expanded cranial vault and the diminutive facial features, the depressed nasal bridge and the protruding jawbones common to dwarfism. They would be disappointed by relatively normal conditions, and entranced, even charmed by the extremity of deformity. The worse he was, the greater their relish. For them he would be a feast. Must he feed this appetite?

When the dissection was complete, he would be presented to Dr. August Hänger himself, like an exotic dish served to a gourmet. First the specialist would regard him with sterile assessing eyes. Doubtless the great physician would slowly open a folder on his desk with meticulous pale fingers, glancing down with a brief encouraging movement of his lips as he requested Olivio to drop his clinical robe and reveal himself. At least of one feature they would all be jealous.

Olivio Fonseca Alavedo knew how he would react. His intelligence would be aflame with anger and resentment, the fury of his pride burning hotter than the molten center of the earth. Later, at night, in luxury at the Dolder Grand Hotel, alone, with his porcelain chamber pot waiting in the cabinet of the bed table beside him, his worst enemy, self-pity, the goblin of the night, would devour him.

Most manifestations Olivio had held at bay. His bandy legs and modest talipes were not intolerable. As to all his limbs, the progression of disturbance had not been severe. Although he constantly fought against his waddling gait, there were many men who got about with greater hardship. He took pride in his nimble fingers and his extraordinary sense of smell. His large head fortified his appearance. His body's folds of excess soft tissue were concealed by his garments. His mental development, his brain, normal in most dwarves, in him gleamed like a dazzling lighthouse on a black and rocky shore.

His spine was his fear, and he had studied it. The spinal cord did not fall straight from his *foramen magnum,* the hole in the base of his skull, as in most men. Instead, it twisted like a serpent. Its compression and distortion were inexorably increasing. His lordosis had progressed without relent, the lower spine gradually curving inward more and more. This was the cruel enemy against whom Olivio required succour. But must he go to Zürich?

The dwarf considered how instead he might bring the Alps to Cairo, the Swiss mountain to Mohammed.

Was Dr. Hänger aware that Egypt was home to more dwarf remains than was the rest of the world? That due to the regard in which they were held in ancient Egypt, dwarves were mummified and preserved as nowhere else, that the dry air of the desert had protected even those skeletons that had not been saved by man's hand? That the child's size of dwarves' caskets had misled grave robbers as to their importance, thereby preserving not only their bodies, but the accompanying jewelry, cosmetics and even the statuary models of their servants? That the first dynasty tomb of King Semerkhet at Abydos had yielded two complete dwarves, their tibiae well bowed, their mid-facial depressions evident beneath the enlarged vaults of the tiny skulls? That another dwarf's skeleton, of the Badarian period, was over six thousand years old, that its uneven clavicles and distorted vertebrae awaited Dr. Hänger's personal examination? That on the Nile, dwarves had been gods? Gods!

Olivio felt himself tremble. His skin perspired where it could, reminding him of the hellish fire that had consumed his cottage in Kenya many years before. Trussed up in bed, costumed in the lacey garments of a privileged English infant, entertaining Kina, he almost had been burned alive. Smelling smoke, Lord Penfold had dashed out of his own bungalow, covered himself in a soaking blanket, and burst into the flaming cottage with a panga in one hand. Slashing the cords that bound Olivio, Penfold had lifted the gasping dwarf and held him to his chest like a child beneath the blanket as he chopped his way out through one of the weakened burning walls. A third of his body scorched, one eye charred, his skin and flesh blistered with black bubbles, his fingernails forever lost, the dwarf had not thought it possible to suffer so and live. Miss Gwenn had nursed him through the agony. Anton Rider had helped to avenge him. Without those three, his present life would not be his. Even today, fire was the dread of his life.

Reflecting on his condition, Olivio folded the report from the Alexandrine clinic. He shook his feet from the stirrups and slowly descended from the sphinx. In a few moments the dwarf stepped out onto the deck of the Café. He stared at the river and turned the matter in his mind, considering what lure would be required for a Swiss doctor devoted to achondroplasia. One informant had advised Olivio that the specialist was in fact a German, an expatriate, a severe balding man with somewhat uneven features. He must learn more about this doctor, and make him his.

He would send to Zürich a letter, a parcel and a banker's draft. How many men had received a suitable gift thousands of years old, and money, and such an invitation?

"I prefer to go by motor rather than by the crowded steamers of the *Compagnie des Bateaux-Omnibus,*" said the dwarf as the three motorcars joined the early northbound traffic on Shari Qasr al-Ali. "I suspect you are pleased to be leaving the city, Mr. Anton."

"Very," said Anton from the driver's seat, brooding over the thought of his sour interview with Gwenn the previous day, reflecting on what he should have said. "Where are you taking us?"

Olivio sat on the elevated passenger seat of the open Sunbeam Alpine, enjoying the smell of the smooth Connolly leather. He wiggled to fit his cushion into the deep arch of his back.

"Just follow the first Rover, Mr. Anton. This way lies the city of Alexandria, the Nile Delta, and the richest lands on earth."

The dwarf turned his head as far as he could and studied Anton through one of the thick round brown lenses of his driving goggles. In many ways he thought of Anton Rider as his second half. How complete they could have been as one! He himself was exquisitely cerebral and indirect, his mind more fecund than the schemes of all the Curia, but his physical self was hobbled and shameful. He could weave like a spider but he had not the legs to range his web. Anton was as candid as a child, more direct than an eagle's dive, but nimble and long-muscled as a cheetah.

"How far is your farm?" Anton asked. Olivio, he knew, was a townsman, and he was surprised the dwarf took such interest in his rural properties. He suspected, with affection, that the little man wished to show off his success. He only wished he could do the same.

"The first is but eighteen miles forward. There we will take lunch in the shade of giant palms and voyage on to the next estate by *felucca.* Perhaps you will kill numerous birds for our supper. We have brought fine guns and many cartouches."

"I'm not a great hand with a shotgun, Olivio." Just then Anton swerved to avoid a donkey cart. The small grey animal trotted furiously with its head down while its master slept with his chin on his chest. Save for scraps of red onion skins, the bouncing cart was empty. "Rifle's more my line."

"Ah, but the meat of the river ducks is so very dark and sweet, though they are not now so plentiful." Olivio moistened his lips one by one. "With them we will fry tart yellow apples from my orchards and prepare rice from my fields."

"Faster, Daddy," Denby called from the jump seat, beating the floor with his hockey stick, feeling in charge with his big half-brother absent. Wellie was back in Cairo, in a soccer match, battling the hated tadpoles of the Lycée Française. Gwenn was at the hospital. Anton was disappointed but not surprised she had not made time to join them.

"Faster!" Denby cried.

"I shall direct the driving, thank you." Olivio spoke sharply without turning his head. Faced with certain physical limitations, the dwarf had learned long ago the necessity of controlling what might happen around him. Venturing out always carried risk, the hazard of ridicule or incapacity in some unexpected situation.

"Before we lunch, Mr. Anton, I will show you the true secret of Egypt." Olivio was anxious to divert his young friend. The dwarf regretted that the harmony of life eluded him. "Its treasure does not lie buried inside the hidden chambers of a pyramid, as most think, or marked on the Rosetta stone, or secreted in the belly of the Sphinx. No." He shook his head.

As they left Garden City behind and turned inland to circumvent the British Consulate-General, the second Rover pulled alongside, its Arab driver erect and haughty, his hawk nose close to the windscreen. In the seat beside the driver Harriet encouraged the man on. She gestured gaily towards the Sunbeam, blowing a kiss, demanding some response as her automobile pulled ahead. Anton lifted one hand from the large steering wheel and squeezed the twin air horns. That should do, he thought. From the corner of his eye he saw Bernadette and Charles kissing in the back seat against the fleeting backdrop of the railway station.

"Why are they doing that, Daddy?" Denby pressed his windblown blond head forward between the front seats.

Anton was happy to feel the boy's hand on his shoulder. He still ached from missing him. "I think your Uncle Olivio would be better at explaining such things, young man," he said dryly.

"Why do they not follow in line, Mr. Anton?" The dwarf clicked his heels together in annoyance as they motored up Shari Shubrah. "I shall have that driver walk home without his sandals."

After another hour or more, without warning the road turned from pavement to packed dirt. The small oval brake lights of the Rover ahead were suddenly enveloped by the tunnel of fine brown dust into which the Sunbeam pursued the first car. Coughing, Anton slowed sharply and turned on his lamps. Denby tumbled into the front of the car.

"Back to your seat!" Olivio scolded, drawing a long silk handkerchief from a pocket and tying it about his mouth and nose. Children, in his experience, were like big dogs. Too large and active for their intelligence, unrestrained, potentially demeaning to him, they tended to accentuate his own condition.

The first car braked abruptly and pulled off the edge of the road. As Anton followed suit, a battered green police bus rumbled past. The crescent flag of Egypt was painted on the door. Anton saw young men in coarse thick uniforms staring out like rows of aging schoolboys. He pulled off the road, following the Rover until it parked among a cluster of palm trees. The dwarf removed his goggles and bandana.

"Now, Mr. Anton, I will show you the source of life and death."

Curious what the dwarf had in store, Anton stepped from the car and walked around to the left side to assist Olivio. As he opened the door, the dwarf looked up at him with the countenance of a baby owl. The round hairless head was now entirely brown, the color of the road, save for white circles around his eyes and the beak-like lightness of his little nose and mouth. Anton held out his hand and his small friend stepped down. Denby clambered out, scraping the side of the car with his hockey stick.

"Idiot child!" the dwarf cried. "You have scratched my machine!"

Anton winked at Denby.

The others emerged from the closed Rovers, clean and unscathed by the filth of the journey. Bent and stiff, Adam Penfold climbed out slowly from the third car amidst a swarm of girls. He stood uncertainly until Clove came up to him. Each time she saw him they were better friends.

"Let me help you, Uncle Adam," Clove said, taking Penfold by the hand and slowly leading him with care. Pepper and Marjoram hurried after them. Through the palms ahead there rose a sound like heavy surf on a beach.

Tariq, the driver of the third car, came to Olivio for instructions. Anton could not hear what the dwarf said, only the angry tone as he snapped instructions to the Nubian. Tariq approached the Arab driver of the Americans' car and spoke a few words. The man turned aside without acknowledgment, confident in the superiority of an Egyptian chauffeur to a black servant. Tariq placed his left hand on the man's shoulder and turned him around as if he were a clothes hanger. Without speaking further or changing expression, the massive Nubian lifted his right arm and with a slow movement slapped the man once across the face. The driver staggered back, then began to clean the vehicles, cursing the *afrangi* woman who had instructed him to pass his master.

Aided by Tariq, Olivio led his companions forward among the palms. Before them rose the Great Barrage: a massive wall of red brick, nearly a mile wide, divided into two sections by a lush green promontory near its center. Fascinated, Denby stared at the crenellated ramparts and towers that fortified either end of each section of the dam. Scores of vertical gates received the rushing river as it hurried smoothly through the broad openings in the wall. Some gates were entirely closed, the water held back by black steel plates. Others were open to varied extents.

Long-legged herons and snowy egrets circled and dived over the swirling pools and reed beds along the margins of the river. Above the riverbank nearby, rows of burial mounds were set into the slopes near the palms. Penfold paused with Clove to catch his breath.

"The air is so fresh and sweet," he said as the girl smiled up at him patiently.

"Reminds me of the highlands, child."

"Do you mean in Scotland, Uncle?"

"Heavens, no, dear. Nanyuki, in British East. Where your papa and I used to live."

Tariq lifted Olivio and set him on the flat stump of a palm. Penfold joined him, resting awkwardly on the edge of the dead plant. Encouraged by Clove, two of Olivio's younger daughters, Rosemary and Cinnamon, passed small glasses in copper holders and served sugared lime juice and dates to his guests. With the Nile behind him, balancing himself with a hand on Penfold's shoulder, the dwarf raised one arm and gestured towards the dam like a priest at mass. He waited to begin until all were listening.

"She took much blood and fifty-five years to complete." He gestured towards the Barrage. "Here were lost some scores of the laborers who died during the work, crushed, drowned, stricken with exhaustion like slaves of the pharaoh laboring in the red eye of the sun."

Olivio paused and looked down. He wished to make this a day his children and his guests would remember after he was gone.

"There, at the Gazirat al-Shir, the island in the center of the Barrage, the Nile divides into two great rivers, the Rosetta and the Damietta, and each river into a thousand canals that nourish the lands that feed Africa and clothe Europe." And make some men rich, he thought, catching Penfold's eye as a twinkle came into his own.

"Soon, to the west, a new canal will be built, bringing water and life into the edge of the Western Desert." He stepped down, adding to Penfold in a quiet voice, "You will see. It is there we will build our first new farm."

"Splendid," said Penfold, distracted by the sight of Denby and Anton walking off.

"Come on, lad, let's go explore the dam," Anton said to Denby.

"It's a castle," the boy cried, following eagerly as his father walked along the bank towards the dam past scattered parties of day-trippers and picnickers.

To their right, twenty feet above the river, fields of vivid green clover alternated with small nursery patches of tight rows of seedlings for ornamental plants and hedges. To their left the bank fell steeply to the riverside, where fish hung from wooden racks and women slapped wet clothes against the stones.

"Can we climb one of the towers, Daddy?" Denby said with wide blue eyes.

In response, Anton held out his hand and smiled. His son hurried to take it as they approached the open paved courtyard before the first pair of towers. These were connected to two more towers by a double drawbridge that topped the shipping lock built into the end of the dam.

Anton felt his son's excitement as they crossed the drawbridge. At last they were sharing an adventure.

"I reckon this is the tower where they keep the prisoners," Anton said in a loud whisper. Above their heads, massive stone counterweights were set into the hinged steel frame that served to raise the two sides of the bridge. "Perhaps we'll hear them screaming from the dungeon."

Uncertain if his father was serious, the boy glanced up at him as they crossed.

"Watch out for the guards," Anton said.

"What will we do if they see us?" Denby said, caught up in the game.

"Use your sword," Anton said, feeling Denby's grip tighten.

"Oh," Denby said after a pause. "But they'll have pikes."

"Shh," said Anton.

They climbed the circular staircase set inside one of the towers. Denby paused to look down through each of the narrow pointed windows that pierced the thick tower wall. Six stories up, they smelled the cool air of the Nile as they stepped out onto the open crenellated roof of the tower. Anton admired the magnificent gardens that extended from the far side of the Barrage. Denby ignored Clove when she waved and cried out to them from the riverbank. "Maybe they'll capture those girls," he said. "Then we could save them, perhaps."

Denby stared down at one of three mobile cranes as it rolled slowly towards them along the railroad tracks set atop the upstream side of the dam wall. "What are they doing?" he said. "What's that?"

"It's a siege machine," Anton said.

"That's what I thought," said Denby, staring down. "They're going to throw stones at us."

Under the direction of a European engineer, the crane gang positioned the heavy crane car directly above the nearest dam gate before setting brakes to lock the wheels of the car in place.

Thick steel plates were suspended by pairs of heavy chains across the opening of each gate. Anton and Denby watched several Egyptians secure the chains at either end of one plate to the two winch drums set at both ends of the crane car. Two other men stood waiting at the long handle of each winch.

"Steady, lads, together now!" the engineer yelled in a Scottish accent. "Pull! Go!" He clapped his hands together.

The teeth of the gears were engaged to the winches. The men leaned into the handles. The chains tightened. Slowly one massive plate began to rise.

"Time to go," Anton said. "Adam's waving at us to join them."

Denby followed his father down the stairs, dragging behind at each window until they emerged at the base of the tower.

They suddenly heard the fierce grating sound of steel against steel. Men screamed as Anton and Denby stepped out onto the Barrage. Anton saw one end of a chain snap free over the edge of its drum. Lashing violently like the end of a whip, the chain slapped the top of the dam, then disappeared between the tracks under the crane car.

"Daddy!" Denby cried, scared, grasping his father around the waist. He watched the Scottish engineer run over and berate the agitated workmen.

Anton placed one arm around Denby's shoulders. "Just a little accident, lad," he said as he led the boy off.

They found the dwarf waiting for them, again standing on the stump, his hands clasped behind his back, patient, unusually silent, thoughtful as he watched the violent incident conclude. Anton and Denby each took one of his hands and helped him down. Together the three walked back to the waiting motorcars.

After a short drive, they descended near a lagoon set back from the Nile.

"Perhaps, Mr. Anton, while the servants prepare lunch, you will shoot geese and ducks?" Olivio nodded to the Nubian. Tariq set down two cartridge bags and unstrapped a leather guncase.

Denby stood nearby. Fascinated, he watched his father inspect and assemble one of the two shotguns with sure swift hands. Pleased by his son's attention, Anton became conscious of the boy's admiring stare.

"Mantons," Anton said, impressed. "Joseph Manton was the father of every modern gunsmith," he said to the boy. Then he checked the blued well-oiled barrels, closing the gun and swinging it through the flight of a passing goose as Denby stared up with his mouth open. "Fine guns."

"Made in Calcutta. The favored firearms of the gentlemen of Goa," Olivio added with pride. He sat at the center of a large spread of colored straw mats under an open-sided canvas tent. He fanned himself with a heart-shaped straw fan. "My punt-boys will pole through the reeds like water snakes and roust up the birds for you."

"Why not let Charles or one of the ladies have a go?" said Anton, glancing over at them in invitation, always keen to learn how new clients handled a weapon.

"I don't shoot." Charles glanced up from his sketch pad and studied the pigeon tower centered in the lagoon before them. "But the twins will kill anything. They're from Kentucky, you know."

"Let's go," said Harriet eagerly.

Rising from a foundation of dried mud, a five-story brown pyramid was an elaborate fifteen-foot dollhouse for birds, topped with domes, crenellations, minarets and nesting alcoves, all faintly round-cornered and decaying. Covered in droppings, the clay and mud tower was home to several hundred fat grey pigeons. Two pigeon keepers, their white *gallabiyyahs* pulled high between their legs, stood in the shallow brown water with nets. A third keeper sat cross-legged on the shore, clutching a struggling pigeon in his lap and clipping its wings with long shears.

Anton stood on the bank watching an older man, lean-limbed as a heron, wade around the sides of the island castle, a wicker basket in one hand, a trowel in the other. With the care of a dentist or a man gathering caviar from the belly of a sturgeon, he scraped and scoured the paste-like grey droppings from each cranny and battlement and deposited them in the bucket. Completing his work under the eyes of his master's guests, he waded slowly ashore with the bucket held before him in both hands. The man's thin legs were covered in puckered folds of wrinkled skin, like some ancient amphibian rarely ashore.

Anton looked carefully at their left hands as he gave each of the twins a gun, hoping to find a way to distinguish between them.

"Checking for an engagement ring?" said Harriet as she inspected her weapon. "Berny left hers in Lexington so it would be safe, and I've always given mine back."

Bernadette and Harriet began to follow Tariq down the riverbank.

"Do you want to come with us, Denby?" Anton said, extending one hand back towards his son, "or stay here with the others?"

"Can I carry the bullets?" Denby said, running to join them.

"Always be careful with guns and ammunition." Anton handed him a cartridge case before they set off after the twins.

"Whilst they hunt, you and I can tour my estate," said the dwarf to Penfold. He waved a summons and a *fellah* brought forward a narrow pony cart with a donkey harnessed in the traces. The peasant led the recalcitrant animal by the head. "Can you drive a cart, my lord?"

"Should hope so." Penfold recalled the tall-wheeled gig he and his mother used to drive in the summertime in Wiltshire. Both he and Olivio climbed up with difficulty. Penfold flapped the reins on the donkey's shoulder, but the animal remained still. He flicked the whip sharply, catching the beast on the inside of the ear. The donkey eased forward with dignity.

"One moment, please," said Olivio after they had gone a few yards. "It is my duty to be vigilant."

Penfold stopped the cart. Both men watched as the elderly pigeon keeper knelt between two long rows of pomegranates, groaning like a rusty hinge while he lowered himself. A barefoot young boy stood behind him. Moving the basket slowly before him, the man spread the excrement evenly around each plant as he advanced on his knees. Muttering and grumbling with each movement, he mixed it into the soil with the edge of his trowel. The child followed, retrieving any wasted material and patting down the earth around each plant with the palms of both hands.

Olivio nodded with satisfaction. Adam Penfold, keen for a drink, slapped the reins against the donkey. He was impressed with what he saw. "Never got the hang of farming, myself," he grumbled. "Failed at it in two countries. Hopeless, really." Penfold was confident the dwarf would make a splendid partner, but the very devil of a boss. "Must say, old boy," he said with admiration, "looks mighty fertile."

"True," said the dwarf, trying to be patient with his teaching, "but that is not what makes our Delta so valuable. It is alluvial, you see, which makes it nearly flat as a piece of baked *aysh baladi,* so easy to till and irrigate once the landowner has levelled it correctly."

"Aha," said Penfold.

"Now bear left, if you would, my lord, between the avocadoes there and this forest of mangoes." Olivio closed his eyes and gripped the seat of the cart as the donkey entered an aggressive jouncing gait and the cart bumped along the rough track between the varied plantings. His spine was on fire. He tried to speak in an easy voice. "Though most fields are now under water, I will show you how we farm in the Delta."

In the heat of the late afternoon, weary after shooting and touring and eating, most of the party dozed as Olivio's *felucca* sailed slowly up the Nile. Anton, pleased with his clients' shooting, slept like a dead man, well nourished with grilled shish kabab and duck, fava beans and rabbit stewed with Jews' mallow and rice, and a number of Olivio's tiny fat-breasted pigeons stuffed with cracked wheat mixed with oil and garlic and the birds' own chopped livers, hearts and gizzards. Charles Crow, a light eater, sat sketching beside him. Harriet fanned herself with her straw hat while she looked at the sleeping hunter.

"We are here, Mr. Anton." Olivio tapped Anton's foot with a walking stick. "Mr. Anton, it is now time to disembowel."

"What?" said Anton, lulled by the gliding motion of the shallow broad-beamed vessel, images of the cool East African highlands still filling his dreamy head. Far above him, a wooden pulley block knocked rhythmically against the tall mast. He saw his son messing with the ropes. Denby looked over to see if his father was watching. Anton smiled, then leaned over the side and splashed his face. He could not imagine a nicer day.

"I mean it is time to disembark, Mr. Anton. Here the river becomes a new canal. We are near the edge of the Western Desert. To our right, the richest land on earth. Some yards to our left, rocky burial grounds, wasteland, barren desert without end."

Groggy, Anton rose and helped Adam Penfold to his feet. Then he jumped onto the swampy bank and reached up to help the ladies descend. Harriet took her walking shoes in one hand and raised her long khaki skirt with the other. Without warning, she leapt into Anton's arms. They fell together onto the soft damp shore. Their cheeks touched. He felt her lean body against his. Blushing, Anton jumped up quickly, wondering what Denby must be thinking. Nearby, Tariq was carrying Olivio ashore.

"Harry, you hussy!" yelled Bernadette. "Shame on you! When will you two stop throwing yourselves in that river?"

The dwarf was waiting for his guests on an earthen parapet that separated two square emerald-green fields of young rice. For a moment he stared down at their perfect richness. To him, each grain was a blessing.

Two camel carts waited on the strip of higher ground between the flooded fields, fitted with canopies, cushions and straw mats. The surly beasts chewed slowly and batted their cynical eyes. The camel drivers struck their wrinkled knees with long staves. The animals rocked to their feet as the travellers climbed into the carts.

Olivio was aware of the head *makadam,* or camel-man, observing him with wary eyes as his master inspected each animal himself. Doubtless, the dwarf suspected, the surly rogue had been using the beasts for his own purposes. With Tariq at hand, the man kept all impertinence from his expression.

Olivio looked at the beasts with rare admiration. Of all animals, the camel was one of only two with whom he felt a kinship. Ugly and awkward to the ignorant eye, yet curiously gifted: sage, enduring and self-contained and, best of all, blessed with an aptitude for vengeance. Abuse a camel once, and, in five years, as you strode past, he would nip you savagely with long yellow incisors, or splash you with his pungent long-held urine.

First the dwarf verified that the brands on their necks were his own. Enjoying their peculiar odor, he examined each camel for signs of abuse, particularly the open harness sores that would draw first flies, and then maggots, and finally sharp-beaked birds that would pick out maggots and flesh together, leaving ugly running pits until the camel had lost all value. He was pleased to see that the humps of his camels were fat and erect. When they arrived at his new farm, he must remember to examine the manner of their kneeling, for unless a camel knelt by bending fore and hind legs at once, it was not in full health.

Reserving comment, Olivio climbed into the lead cart and they set off.

After a few hundred yards they came to a line of bamboo surveyor's stakes set into the sand or piles of rocks. The land became drier and harder as they advanced, broken only by occasional short palms and tufts of hardy grasses. Sprinkled with rocks, the hard sandy slopes receded into the distance like ocean waves.

Tire tracks preceded them, Anton noticed, and then he heard a commotion up ahead.

He recognized the battered police bus before they came to it. It was the one that had passed them on the road. The carts stopped behind the bus. Everyone except Olivio stepped down.

Two knots of policemen struggled in their direction. Armed with heavy batons, their ill-fitting green uniforms dusty and rumpled, the young men sweated and cursed as they dragged two barefoot villagers towards the bus. Anton saw one officer with a sidearm.

In the background stood the mud buildings of a small village centered around a single well. Women in long gowns clutched their children and wailed. The *fellahin* ran here and there, trying to impede the policemen, who were raking up vegetable plots and punching holes in the mud walls of houses with sledges and heavy poles. Three policemen were beating a white-bearded man who sought to block the path to a well.

"This is my land!" Olivio cried in a cracked voice. "This is my village! These are my people!" The little man began to tremble. Clove rushed to his side and clutched his arm to support him. "Help me, Tariq, lift me down. We must stop this deviltry."

"Stay here," Anton said to Denby and the others. "Clove, keep the children by the carts. I'll try to help Olivio." He joined Tariq and Olivio as they hurried towards the village. Not deterred, Penfold limped after them, determined to support his friends.

"Master!" The old *fellah* by the well threw himself at Olivio's feet.

"Thank Allah you are come! They say the land is not yours. That our village will be flooded by the new canals. They are forcing us to leave. They threaten to poison our well and fill it with stones!"

"*Khanzîr*!" yelled a policeman, clubbing the man across the back with a baton as the two others came between him and Olivio. The dwarf, furious with impotence, his face mottled red and white, raised his hands.

"Idiots!" he screamed. "Idiots!"

One policemen swung back an arm to belt Olivio with his open hand.

Anton grabbed the man's arm and wrenched it behind his back harder than he meant to. He heard the shoulder crack like a dry branch. The other policeman struck Anton with his baton.

Tariq lifted one man by the waist and swung him until his head banged the stone well. Other policemen ran to join the fight.

Storing his rage, his tiny fists tight, struggling to suppress the shaking of his body, Olivio stood by the side of the well cursing the police. There were tears in his eye. He felt dizzy. Not used to such activity, the dwarf's body had become a furnace. His poreless burned skin was unable to sweat and adjust to the temperature.

Penfold limped over to Olivio. He raised his walking stick to protect his friend and was himself knocked to the ground by another policeman.

Two shots rang out. Tariq bellowed.

"The next man is dead!" The Egyptian officer aimed his revolver at Anton. Noticing the blood running down Tariq's upper arm, Anton considered trying to disarm the Egyptian but instead stepped back with both palms raised, knowing the children were nearby. The fighting ceased.

"Captain Thabet, Special Police," the officer introduced himself in careful English. "Who are you?"

"Are you speaking to me, young man?" Adam Penfold said calmly as he brushed the dust from his suit.

"Who are you?" Thabet raised his voice.

"I am Lord Penfold. You are assaulting British subjects."

The officer hesitated, then gestured at Olivio. "And what is this creature?"

"I am Olivio Fonseca Alavedo. You are thieves. You are destroying my property," the dwarf said in a slow cold voice, staring up, his face now entirely white. Containing a gasp of pain as he bent over, he lifted his dented tarbush from the ground and set it on his head with both hands.

"I will not forget you, Captain Thabet. Nor this dog who tried to strike me. Today you lost your pension."

Thabet hesitated, then his face hardened and he spoke in a firm tone. "We are acting with the authority of the palace. The transfer of this land was not properly recorded. You are all under arrest."

"You have no authority to arrest foreign nationals, or to steal their property," Penfold said in a reasonable voice, his dignity tangible. "Under the Egyptian Capitulations, you know. You would be making a most serious mistake, sir."

"This is Egypt. I am doing my duty." The captain spoke rapidly to several men, then addressed one more comment to the foreigners. "There is one way to settle this."

The policemen began hurling rocks and the dark legs of a donkey carcass into the well. One man lifted the animal's head. Large black flies rose from the open veins and the flapping skin at the base of the head and clouded after the man as he carried it to the well. Villagers screamed and wailed.

"No!" cried Olivio. "Captain Thabet, stop that man."

The officer did not respond.

Anton stepped forward and grabbed the policeman as the man dumped the donkey's head into the well.

"I will shoot!" the officer yelled, raising his revolver.

"Excuse me, Captain," said a loud American voice. "Give your pistol to Lord Penfold or I'll make an awful mess."

Startled by a woman's voice, Captain Thabet turned to see Harriet just behind him with a levelled shotgun.

"Now!" she said.

Thabet laughed and turned his back to her.

Harriet clicked off the safety and fired one shot into the right front tire of the police bus. The vehicle slumped unevenly like a wounded animal. Anton saw that Harriet held two extra shells between the fingers of her left hand.

Thabet looked back at the American woman and also noticed the cartridges.

"Don't be silly," Harriet said.

Thabet handed the pistol to Penfold.

"Enough," Olivio said quietly, directing his guests to their carts. "It is time to journey home."

As they drove to Cairo in the evening, Denby slept with his head on his father's lap. The dwarf lay on the backseat, his head on a cushion, scheming in the darkness. Never since the fire had his body brought him such pain. His mind toiled as he sought to determine who could be the source of this mischief.

"In the past," muttered the dwarf after a time, not caring whether Anton listened or not, "government minions, tax collectors, minor functionaries and the like have been interfering with my properties."

"Sounds like Kenya," Anton added uselessly. Preoccupied, he was concerned that Gwenn would be upset that he had become involved in violence with Denby and the girls nearby.

"Seen alone," continued Olivio impatiently, "each incident may seem part of the chaos of Egyptian administration, but together I see a pattern, a design of obstruction and disturbance."

"Doesn't sound good," Anton offered, trying to show interest.

"Not at all. Not at all, Mr. Anton," said Olivio Alavedo to his naive friend, wagging his head from side to side on the cushion as he turned the problem in his mind, studying it like the planes and angles of a gemstone.

"Rather it confirms the wisdom of my program, if I may say so. Someone else, someone powerful who must know the plans for the canals, covets my land."

At home with indirection, the dwarf scented the trail of a secret rival, some well-advised scoundrel he must identify and thwart.

— 7 —

Anton leaned against the Nile parapet, his fists in the baggy pockets of his bush jacket, waiting for Gwenn to come out of the King Fuad Hospital. Every time the hospital door opened, he stood forward from the wall, trying not to show his eagerness, but it was never Gwenn. He reminded himself that medical students did not have predictable hours. He reviewed again what he planned to say.

Hungry, faintly hungover after a night of frantic fox-trots with the twins at Groppi's Rotunda and the Kursaal, Anton remembered what an island Gwenn had been for him in his wanderings. Coming home to her had always been the best. Especially early in the morning, unsaddling his horse under their baobab near the Ewaso Ngiro, stripping off his shirt and washing his dusty face in the chill water and gathering a few small riverstones to toss at her window until she awoke and realized who it must be. Waiting outside until she ran out to him, hugging him and rolling in the dew-cold grass while he felt her warmth.

But he'd never taken to the life. The endless dreary toil of the farm, always short of help, fighting the weavils and locusts and caterpillars that stunted the coffee and spoiled the wheat, and the worms and parasites that sickened the cattle and killed the sheep. All the magic vitality of Africa that made him love the bush instead was turned against them on the farm, showing itself as a thousand inhospitable enemies trying to drive them and their crops and animals from the land. But Gwenn never gave up. She was never bitter with the failures and the debts, saying Kenya was better than the mining life in Wales. She was unrelenting and determined to build a family and a life on this very bit of land, and irritated and disappointed every time he left on safari.

Finally each return and each departure became too painful for both of them, and they knew it could not work. Even when things seemed at their best, he knew she'd felt him pulling loose. In a place like Cairo, or even Nairobi, there was enough to sustain a lonely spouse, friends and clubs and entertainment, but in the bush a marriage had to nourish itself, and she'd seen that he could never do it. And that was without his other foolishness, mistakes a woman could not forget, even when Gwenn, for a time, cared enough to blame it on his youth. At last he'd come home, three weeks late from a hard safari in the Karamojo, knowing in his belly he would find them gone.

The boys made it so much worse. He wanted his sons but now he could not be part of their world. Already he was fed up with Cairo. "You're just not a sociable animal," Gwenn had told him once long ago. "You're a wild animal."

Anton couldn't bear to pass on to the boys his own father-less emptiness. He tried not to think of the dream he'd had last night. In it he was young, standing with his own father, so close to him that he could not see the face of the father he had never known. "When you were wounded," he asked, looking up, "was it very painful?" "Yes," his father said. "Yes." Anton hugged him, pressing the side of his face against his father's body and trying to wrap the tall man in his arms. When Anton began to cry, his father cupped the back of his son's head with one hand, then put his strong arms around Anton, and asked, "Why are you crying, boy?" "For us, Daddy," he had answered.

The hospital door opened and Gwenn stepped out. The sight of her still moved him. She looked tired, older, but he knew her age would never bother him. She was surprised to see him but didn't seem annoyed. He smiled when she approached, admiring the way she carried herself. Even her stride seemed trim and forthright. When she came close to him, he noticed the lines about her eyes and mouth. They made him hate the time they'd lost.

"I came to apologize for the other day," he said, looking Gwenn in the eye, not touching her. "I didn't mean to be that way."

"Oh, that's all right," she said, smiling briefly, recognizing his habit of directness, appreciating the contrast with Lorenzo. "I wasn't so nice either."

They kissed each other lightly on the cheek.

"Denby said he had a lovely day," Gwenn said, standing back a bit. "He was exhausted, but he wouldn't stop talking about that castle on the river and your battle with the police. I'm afraid he enjoyed it."

"I . . ."

"But the boys can't grow up like that. I won't let them be all rough and wild. They can't grow up the way you . . ."

"I'd like to see more of Denby," Anton said too urgently, knowing he was pressing. "And you and Wellie, too," he added quietly.

"Would you like to walk a little?" she said, collecting herself, hating the pressure, not wishing to respond. "After duty I always walk along the river to clean away the hospital."

They fell into stride together and walked slowly with the river. Anton thought of long evening walks along the Ewaso Ngiro, holding hands, or, with the boys, stopping to toss in a stick, then pitching stones after it as it bobbed along and disappeared like a small animal jinking through the bush.

"That mischief with the police doesn't sound good," she said in a stiffer voice, turning to look at him. "In Cairo one doesn't want that sort of problem."

"I couldn't help it," he said, annoyed at justifying himself. "I know you assume I made things worse, but Olivio was in the thick of it, and even Adam got messed about. They needed my help."

"I'm sure that's right," she said, knowing she was making trouble, "but somehow you always seem to find the roughest way to handle things."

"Do you think Adam and Olivio were looking for a brawl?"

"I didn't say they were." She quickened her pace.

Anton felt himself grow angry but reminded himself what he had to do. Arguing with her wouldn't help. For a moment neither of them spoke.

"This probably isn't the right time, Gwenn, but I have to ask you." He felt her stiffen and thought she began to walk less close. "I'm sorry I haven't been able to help more," he said. "I want to, and I will."

"I understand." She turned her head briefly and regarded him. "We're managing."

"I'd do anything to have you and the boys back."

"Back?" A shadow of bitterness entered her voice. "Back where?"

"Home, of course. Kenya, where the boys belong. They'd love it there."

"How would we live?" she exclaimed, her voice rising. "Every day you told me Cairn Farm could never work." She rolled one hand in the air before her. "Things are going along here. I'll be a doctor soon. The boys are in school, a good school. They need to stay in one place. The world is changing. Who knows what's going to happen? They need a real education, a future. I won't raise them like . . . like . . . you know . . ."

"I need them, Gwenn," he said, pausing in his walk and turning to face her.

"They have friends here, so do I," she said, walking more briskly. "I'm comfortable with our life. It's taken me a long time to build it."

"The boys need a father," he interrupted. "Denby . . ."

"The boys are fine, thank you," she said quickly, although she knew he was right. "They understand."

"Understand what?" Anton said, rushing on. "Do you love him?"

"Who?" she said, disgusted by her own cowardice.

"You know who I mean," he said aggressively. "Your Italian. Do you love him?"

She felt her stomach tense. Then she spoke slowly when she replied.

"When you've got no money and you're on your own, and someone's good to you and your children, you get confused."

Anton stared at her and raised his voice.

"Gwenn, leave him. The children don't belong in his house."

"Where would we go?"

"Gwenn . . ."

"Please." She stopped and faced him, touching his arm as if to soften the rejection. "I can't, not now, Anton, not yet, at least." Unable not to justify herself, she continued, suspecting she was punishing him because she'd missed him, saying something she should've said years ago, not now.

"You can't expect us to change our lives each time you surprise us and appear."

Feeling cold, alone again, he paused before replying. "I promise I'll do better." He almost stopped, then continued bitterly.

"Maybe it's my fault, but it's disgusting, the three of you living off him there like that." He spoke angrily, remembering all the times Gwenn had upbraided him for infidelity.

"Aren't you embarrassed?"

"Embarrassed?" she hissed, furious.

"What must he think of you?"

"He loves me," she said in a slow hard voice, holding up one arm to stop a taxi. "He cares for me and for the boys and you never really have." She stepped to the car, hearing the excess in her words as she spoke.

"What do you expect us to do? Live like beggars because of you?"

Silent, empty, Anton held the door as she climbed in.

When the taxi pulled away, Gwenn turned and looked back at him through the rear window, making no gesture as tears filled her eyes. His face was bleak as he watched her pull away. It was always impossible with Anton, she thought, but he could still tear her heart as Lorenzo never could.

It was just past Anton's time of day. He sat on the deck of the Cataract Café and watched the Nile brighten from west to east. Soon a scattering of insects, warmed from their night-time hibernations, would stir and rise, drawing the fish to the surface, and the waterbirds to the fish. He recalled tickling trout as a boy in England, well trained by the gypsies, poaching in the bitter-fresh damp air, lying on his belly at the streamsides at dawn, fishing with cold bare hands, ready to flip the silverbellies on the bank and fall on them.

"I present you coffee, Mr. Anton." Olivio wore an open striped twill vest over his *gallabiyyah* against the morning coolness. "Kenya coffee, of course, but prepared for you in the rich Turkish manner." The dwarf set the copper tray on a table and seated himself beside his friend.

"I have something to reveal to you," Olivio said after a moment. He tapped a chamois sack that rested on the table beside the tray. Only with old friends was he not embarrassed by the smooth tips of his short fingers, by the naked roundness of his fingerbones, mottled with the raised pink and white poreless skin the doctors called "proud flesh."

Olivio loosened the drawstring at the bag's throat and withdrew the treasure: a closed oval vase of smooth graywacke. The lid was fashioned in the form of the head of a sphinx, a long-bearded sphinx with a spitting cobra between its temples, a sphinx not of Giza, but of the Valley of the Kings. Remnants of bright paint lit the face here and there, a luminous cast of coloring, it seemed to him, with the innocent clarity of watercolors, but also the rich patina of enamel or glazed oils. The serene stone creature seemed to regard the dwarf and his friend with assurance.

"This, Mr. Anton, is older than any artifact in all of Europe. It is a canopic jar. Inside the lords of Egypt had their brains and viscera preserved after death. Here was the human core of the afterlife."

Anton watched Olivio remove the smoothly fitted lid with delicate care.

"This jar contained the organs of a child, a prince." Or perhaps, thought Olivio, an honored dwarf, even a god.

"How did it come into your possession?"

"Ah. It was brought to my attention, shall we say, and I kept it from the wrong hands." The dwarf peered inside, then sniffed it. His eyelids closed, he was able to savor the private odor of a distant time.

"The preservation of human remains is a work for masters. Only in this do science and religion come together, Mr. Anton."

"Mmm. Never thought of it that way." His interest waning, Anton glanced across the Nile. "Have you always been onto this sort of thing?"

"In Old Goa, we possess a great wonder, the mummified body of St. Francis Xavier himself . . ."

"I see," Anton said, forcing himself to follow.

"In 1452 this saint arrived in India, bringing Christ. Later he carried the cross to the Chinese, but in death he was buried as he had asked, in the Basilica of Bom Jesus in Goa."

Olivio recalled his adventure as a tiny youth of ten, making his way between the rice paddies inland to the ancient disease-ridden capital of Goa, rooting about among the abandoned Portuguese colonial ruins to find the basilica, dropping a modest coin into the filthy palm of the barefoot guardian, and standing on a prayer stool to peer through the thick shadowy glass at the exquisite unravaged face of the sainted Jesuit.

"And what are your plans for this pot?" said Anton, impatient for a drink. It was time to address a different subject.

"In this canopic vase, my ashes will return to Goa. There this sculpted vessel will be set behind an engraved tablet in the chapel at the College of St. Paul." Already the four-hundred-year-old chapel, where once, crouching beneath a pew, he had observed Father Santiago looting the poorbox, had been restored through the munificence of Olivio Fonseca Alavedo himself.

"We must all think of the future," Olivio said, coming to the point. He prayed his friend would heed this message.

"Tell me, Olivio, where would one go for a spot of gambling?" For once Anton had a few quid in his pocket. Dollars, actually, the final payment from the Americans. He would have to risk them to rebuild his life. "At least," he said, thinking grimly of Gwenn's remarks, "there are still a few things I know how to do."

Obliging his friend, Olivio switched subjects gracefully. "Muslims are forbidden to gamble, Mr. Anton, but Cairo is a casino." The dwarf pinched his thumbs and forefingers together as if rubbing banknotes. He sensed his friend's desperation as he continued.

"The poorest *fellah* wagers his hard-won milliemes on the lottery. Already young Prince Farûq is drawn to bezique and chemin-de-fer. For some British officers, and Arabs, Turks and Greeks in the coffee houses, it is backgammon. There are cards and cockfights and roulette salons, horse races at the Sporting Club, bridge and poker at the Automobile Club, dice at the bars, street games of thrown sticks and wooden boards with round stones. Some gamble for money or camels, others for girls along Wagh al-Birkat and Clot Bey, a few for children or land."

"Cards," said Anton keenly. "Cards."

"A place for gentlemen?"

"Perhaps something in between."

"For hearts and spades, Mr. Anton, clubs and diamonds, it depends on whom you wish to play with, and how much you have to lose."

"I must make money." If he could ever manage it, he would pay the debt on Gwenn's farm, nearly eleven hundred quid. But, on the other hand, if he lost this money, there could be no safari.

"Then I would go to the desert on a Wednesday. Tonight, if you like. Go left past Mena House and the pyramids, beyond the Great Sphinx, on the high dunes at the desert's edge. There rich men have erected party tents for entertainment." The dwarf paused and extended his arms to the sides, opening the gates to a different world.

"There on warm evenings ambassadors give cocktails. Fine ladies dressed in the silks of Paris present supper parties and speak of Monte Carlo with jealous friends while they watch the lights of Cairo sparkle along the Nile."

Olivio leaned close to Anton. His grey eye opened wide, like a night bird in the halflight. He wagged two fingers and continued.

"Past all these tents, at the very end, at the edge of the wilderness, there are two, I am told, two tents where at midweek, rich men gamble and divert themselves, wagering on a card the gold of a pharoah's tomb." He held up one finger. "The last tent, with the black and white stripes of a bedouin prince, is renowned for high wagers. Ali Baba's, they call it."

"Sounds perfect. I'll go tonight."

"Tell them you are a friend of the Cataract Café, and they will welcome you," said Olivio. At that moment it occurred to him how he might help his friend to extend his winnings. "And you must do me the service, Mr. Anton, of permitting me to add my money to yours. Whatever you take, I will send the same. I shall back you."

Anton's face brightened but he added caution for his friend. "Hate to see you lose with me."

"We will share the winnings, and the loss. And if you win, perhaps you will invest with me in new lands in the Delta," the dwarf said in his quiet voice, as if conspiring. "But I have one suggestion."

"Yes?"

"Go twice. The first time enjoy yourself and lose. Let your demeanor be untroubled by your losses. The second evening every table will be open to you. How the ladies will smile when you enter!"

Anton nodded appreciatively. "Very sound."

"And permit me one other thought."

"Of course, Olivio." Anton recalled the delight the little man took in the perfection of arrangements. There was no detail too fine, no artifice beneath attention.

"You may wish to invite Lord Penfold to accompany you."

"My pleasure," Anton said, though he was unsure this would be a good idea.

"Yes, yes, of course, but not for that." The dwarf tried not to sound impatient, but how could this hardy friend be so naive? Why was he so difficult to help?

"As a cloak, Mr. Anton, as your mask. His lordship will add a gentler tone, a different sense of purpose to your visit. He will be trusted."

"I understand," said Anton.

"And one final thing. If you are to win, at evening's end you will do well not to leave this tent unaccompanied. Even you. In the souk they say that what the Greek loses inside the tent, he recovers outside. I will send you in a motorcar, with Tariq as your driver, and perhaps his brother for an escort. I have secured Haqim's release from prison and he needs employment."

— 8 —

"You were not yourself last night." Enzo spoke quietly and reached for Gwenn's hand across the breakfast table. Hers remained rigid under his touch. She hated these small endearments when she did not feel right. Each one was a test she could not pass. It was nearly a week since they had last shared breakfast, normally a favorite part of their routine.

"You've been so different since he came to town," Enzo persisted, irritated to see new round tins of Ovaltine and Scott's Porage Oats, the sort of vile details of English daily life that travelled the world with their swollen empire.

"There's something I have to tell you before you leave, Lorenzo," Gwenn said, choosing the less personal of two unpleasant subjects.

"You can tell me anything, *cara*." He squeezed her hand. "You know that."

How distinguished he looked, she thought, in his summer uniform. Men were so confusing. For a year she and Lorenzo had been almost happy. Now she knew he was excited to be leaving. In a few minutes the Bugatti would be back to take him to Suez.

"I'll be leaving soon myself," she said, trying to speak in a calm unprovocative voice, knowing it was hopeless. "For Ethiopia."

"I thought we'd already settled that nonsense," he said harshly, making no effort at respect. "It's impossible. You would embarrass me." He waved both hands dismissively. "Aren't there enough wretches for you to help here in Cairo?"

"Lorenzo, this is something I have to do, for myself," she said, noticing how much older he looked when he was angry. "Why can't you try to understand?"

"I am an Italian officer, Gwenn. My country is on the edge of great things. Yesterday thirty thousand people met *Il Duce's* sons at the quay in Port Saïd. Tonight I will sail with them from Suez for Italian Somaliland and Eritrea." He spoke with pride, slowly, lecturing. His voice was hard, but his eyes were sad.

"Soon these savages you wish to serve will be my enemies. They will try to kill me. They mutilated my grandfather. How can you do this to me?"

"I'm not doing anything to you. It's people like you who are making us go."

"Stay home, Gwenn." He leaned forward with his face close to hers. "Stay home. Look after your children. You have no business there."

"Business there?" Her hands clenched the edge of the table. "What business does the Italian air force have there? It's the middle of Africa."

His voice became still more severe and biting as he moved from the political to the personal. "And who invited you to Africa? Your penniless gypsy?"

For the first time Lorenzo was revealing his jealousy of Anton. He was trying to hurt her. She knew people often unconsciously created conflict before they parted. It was self-protection, of course, to reduce the pain of separation. But this was more than that.

"I came to Africa by myself." She rose and looked down at Lorenzo before continuing. "And my husband is not a gypsy. He was partly raised by gypsies." Her cheeks were white and tight. It irritated her to be justifying Anton, and herself.

"And what about me? Don't you owe me anything?" Enzo said, now openly hostile. "Don't you owe me more than you owe the Ethiopians? And shouldn't you be looking after your children?"

"Don't use the boys. I always look after my children, thank you. They'll be fine. They'll be staying with Mr. Alavedo."

"That disgusting midget! How can you leave them with him? He's the joke of Cairo."

"Those who know Olivio do not think so. And he is not a midget. We will be moving there at once."

"Will you be sleeping with him as well?" Grimaldi said, hurrying on before she could reply, his voice rising, talking himself into a rage. He leaned forward with his face close to hers.

"My friends were right, of course," he added, as if to himself, his tone contemptuous. "I should never have associated myself with the daughter of a coal miner. What could one expect?"

Gwenn made no reply as she felt her shoulders tighten and her spirit grow more contained. She turned and walked from the room as if she had never known him.

The sphinx rose before Anton like an immense lion in the moonlight. At the end of the macadam, Tariq stopped the Rover and stepped down to release air from the tires, helping the automobile to move across the sand.

To his right Anton saw the dark entrance to the layered catacombs of the necropolis, a warren of the dead mostly younger than the pharoahs but older than the Caesars. Several low uneven openings were black against the greys of the steeply rising hillside. It was impossible to tell where the work of man began and ended from these cave-like entrances to the collapsing chambers and narrow twisting passageways.

Although the man had not spoken, Anton could feel the presence of Haqim in the seat before him, filling his position like a block of obsidian. In his coarse dark grey *gallabiyyah,* Haqim had been invisible in the night. As robust and substantial as his brother, but shorter, thicker, flat-faced and at least as black. It was as if Tariq had been bound and pressed down in a vise, compacted, formed into a denser mold. Once or twice Anton had detected humor in Tariq, even gentleness when he helped with the girls, or lifted his master in his hands. But in Haqim he found only a stolid menace. One sentiment the man did seem to possess: loyalty, in gratitude to the dwarf for having procured his freedom.

Anton turned to speak to Lord Penfold, but saw that his friend still dozed.

Tariq started the car and drove slowly across the packed stony sand to the left of the sphinx. The orange taillights of a Daimler preceded them. To their left was Cairo and the Nile. They passed the first tents, higher on the dunes to their right. Some were darkened and not in use. Others glowed like giant lanterns on the rim of the desert. Lights showed through their sides and cast halos into the blue-black night. Shadows danced across one canvas like cutouts in a light show, moving together to a tune he recognized, "In the Mountain Greenery."

Anton recalled his first evening at the gambling tent one week before: dressed in his only suit, giving his name and introduction to a doorkeeper from the Arabian Nights. The night outside contrasted with the vitality within, the swift card-handling of the table hosts, and the overwhelming sense of richness.

After a lifetime under canvas, he had not imagined he would ever see such opulence in a tent. Even the poles were swathed in colored piping and topped with rose-like crowns of red satin. Silent waiters in pointed slippers passed trays of champagne and canapés. Elegant women, British and European and Egyptian, laughed and chatted with men in white and black dinner jackets. Beneath it all, the machinery of gambling carried on. Dice rolled. Decks were cut and shuffled. Cards were dealt. Balls spun and clicked. Chips and plaques were stacked and tossed. Men signed notes and wrote checks.

The main gaming tent had led on to two others, smaller, less brightly lit. In the first, food was arranged on low copper tables. A violinist in a worn tailcoat, some sort of frayed expatriate, most likely Hungarian or Austrian, played romantic airs with his eyes closed and his head bent over his instrument. Men and women lounged on outsize cushions and divans. In the other tent, water pipes bubbled and a belly dancer churned behind veils of incense. Her flat gold slippers and bare shoulders were stationary as her stomach rippled and the golden tassels of her low girdle flashed out from her hips.

Anton had taken his fill of drink, feeling bitter and sad after his row with Gwenn. He'd played poker and *vingt-et-un* and *chemin-de-fer,* winning at times, but losing more, enjoying the distraction of the women, especially one blond siren from France with compelling milky decolletage, disturbingly reminiscent of an old flame. Finally he'd left on his own with two hundred pounds less in his pocket, tipping handsomely as he rose and took his leave. Tonight, he would do better.

Tariq stopped the car near the foot of the long ridge of the dune.

"Adam, wake up," Anton said in a gentle voice, touching his friend's arm, "we're there."

"What?" said Penfold, rubbing his forehead, trying to remember where he was. "Oh, right you are, on parade."

They descended and walked the last thirty yards. Anton glanced back. Tariq had turned the car around and was sweeping it with a feather duster. Anton could not see Haqim. Penfold took Anton's arm and leaned on his cane as they climbed to the striped tent. This time Anton was wearing his first dinner jacket, black and double breasted, hurriedly put together by Olivio's tailor with guidance from Adam on the details.

"Messieurs," the doorkeeper bowed. Anton smelled incense as they walked through the short tunnel-like corridor formed by the entrance to the tent. They paused inside. The Greek host came forward to greet them, inclining his head as he extended a smooth hand. Tasselled amber beads swung from the other.

"Welcome back to Ali Baba's! A friend of Mr. Alavedo, I recall? Mr. Reader, do I have it not?"

"Rider, thank you. Lord Penfold, may I present Mr. Kotsilibis, our host."

Penfold nodded. His tie was uneven, like the wings of a broken butterfly. One wide grosgrain lapel was marred by the tiny burn holes of cigar ash. A long-link gold chain drooped between the pockets of his black vest. Anton was proud of him, erect, white-browed and distinguished as an old hawk surveying his kingdom from a barren treetop. There could be no mistaking what he was and whence he came. But Anton knew Adam would not hear clearly in the crowd of voices.

"Much welcome to you, your lordship." The Greek bowed. "Champagne? Scotland whisky?"

Penfold gazed past the Greek to the bar with watery eyes. His hands were jammed into his jacket pockets with only the thumbs sticking out. Anton could see the Levantine was impressed to be ignored, mistaking bad hearing for aristocratic disdain.

They drank. Anton looked about at the tables, pausing to watch a game here and there. He was concerned about Adam, aware of his habits of improvidence and misfortune, and knowing he carried fifty or sixty precious pounds, an advance from Olivio on money Penfold expected from England. Still, his gaming might be helpful and distracting.

"No need to play nanny, thanks, old boy," Penfold said cheerfully to Anton as he joined a low stakes *chemin-de-fer* table. "Always been able to lose a few guineas on me own."

Anton drifted into the buffet tent for a nibble, then wandered into the second small tent. No dancer was at work. Instead of cymbals, Anton heard the thunder of a snoring red-faced Scot, prostrate across a mound of cushions. Only the man's toes touched the ground. His kilt hung down like a lampshade beneath the tight black dinner jacket.

"Engländer!" roared a voice with real joy.

Anton stared into the shadowy corner, recognizing with astonishment the voice of Ernst von Decken. There he saw the heavily built, hard-set German, seated behind a copper table with a slender dark woman in an immaculate white cotton robe. Somali, Anton judged, always finding them the most beautiful. Erect, her head back, laughing quietly, she touched glasses with her companion as Ernst cried out again. The stern-faced man had one hand picking through a dish of pickles, the other under the table. Ernst had never had a taste for thin-lipped virgins, Anton thought as he hurried over with a smile.

"Schnapps, aquavit!" Ernst hollered at a turbanned barman as he rose to his feet. *"Pesi, pesi!"*

"Ernst von Decken!" Anton grinned like a boy, smelling the drink and sweat while his friend grappled Anton to him with strong arms.

"This is Gretel. Will you excuse us, *Schätzche*? My English friend and I must speak of business."

The lady rose gracefully. She shook Anton's hand with cool thin fingers and left the tent, her robe hanging neatly like folds on a Greek statue. Only her high pointed breasts interrupted the line of the garment. Anton remembered that Ernst avoided native names for his women.

"Your hair's gone all white, von Decken," said Anton. "Something must've scared you."

"Not white," protested Ernst, running one hand through his thick wavy hair, his cold blue-grey eyes brightening in a smile. "The ladies say it's silver."

Anton sat and the two men shared drinks and cigarettes.

"How's your father?" Anton said, hoping Ernst wouldn't ask him about Gwenn.

"Dead, a broken heart. After you English won the war and stole our farm in Tanganyika, the life left him."

"I'm very sorry, Ernst." For an instant Anton recalled his first day at Gepard Farm, stalking topi with the old man, feasting in the early evening on fresh meat and fried German apples, drinking on the verandah at nightfall as Herr von Decken smoked and told tales of the early days before the Great War. "When Africa was wild," he used to say, "before so many white men came and ruined it." His stories had made Anton want to be a hunter.

"So I still haven't got my piece of Africa." Ernst pulled a wrinkled map from his breast pocket.

"Who has?" Anton shrugged.

Von Decken ignored the question and continued. "But I have found a man to help me buy back the farm." He spread the map on the table, securing two corners with plates of pickles and olives.

"Who's going to pay for it?" Anton said, remembering the von Deckens' fields of flowering sisal and the fragrance of the orchard below Kilimanjaro.

"Ein Katzlmacher." Ernst's cheek was swollen with pickles. "Benito Mussolini."

"Why would the Italians pay for it?" said Anton, thinking he saw the French blonde regarding him from the entrance to the tent.

"Pay attention." Ernst banged a coin onto the table. "Do you know what that is, boy?"

Anton lifted the heavy silver coin. He admired the full-chested lady wearing a crown and a low bodice. "Probably fifty years old, Austrian, a Maria Theresa silver dollar. They still use them all over Abyssinia and Somaliland, for everything: doweries, cattle, slaves, as jewelry. Call 'em thalers. Don't make them anymore." Before he finished, Ernst was already shaking his head.

"Wrong. The original dies are in Rome. Never been used since 1896. That toad Mussolini has just minted a million fresh ones, to buy his way in Ethiopia, bribe the princes, corrupt the priests, spread mischief. Last year he bought Pope Pius, this year it'll be the Ethiopian bishops. All the same tarts. The coins're on the way out now, bound for Eritrea." Ernst lowered his voice before continuing. "But once they start shunting them around Africa, they'll be harder to keep in hand than clouds or quicksilver. I only need a few thousand."

"I didn't know you were a highwayman," said Anton, interested despite himself. He couldn't remember Ernst talking so much.

"I'm whatever the lord requires. At present, a purchasing agent for the Abyssinian military. That's why I'm here. They're trying to buy modern weapons to fight the Italians, but some countries won't sell to them because they're still slavers. My master down there's a shifty black devil in high-laced boots and striped red pantaloons, young Ras Gugsa, the prince of Tigre, a general, he says, but the Eyeties are trying to switch him before the war starts. Be cheaper to buy the bloated whore than fight him." Von Decken coughed deeply and took another of Anton's cigarettes before continuing.

"There should be some money chests moving about. With any luck, Ras Gugsa will ask me to escort his lot. He can't trust his own chaps. The silver coins're in small wooden crates, five thousand to a chest. I'm having a few boxes made myself. Identical, they are. Once they're screwed shut, even a cardinal wouldn't know which are which." He winked at Anton and drained his drink. "Should be useful." Ernst continued before Anton could reply. "Thought you'd be interested. Could mean some fine bush bashing, slipping out across rough country, type of thing you were good at when you were young."

"Not my sort of line, old man, but I wish you luck," said Anton. Borrowing and gambling were bad enough. He still drew the line at thieving.

Ernst hadn't changed. He ignored Anton and carried on. He dragged one end of a pimply pickle across the map, leaving a moist snail-like trail.

"I'm planning a couple of different routes out of Ethiopia, depending on where we grab it and who's hunting us. But the best way could be to head in deeper, instead of making for the coast, away from the Eyeties, not into them. Run west to the Rift lakes, then south to Kenya, down your way."

"Sorry." Anton shook his head, though he was calculating how it might be done. He noticed the Somali lady waiting by the entrance to the tent, graciously turning away the attentions of two admirers. Doubtless Gretel knew how von Decken would react to such distractions.

"It wouldn't be like stealing," Ernst said, wiping one hand against the other. "Consider it patriotism. When the war comes, the Italians'll be the enemy. You *Engländers* might even be in it. Only be a matter of you and me getting our share first. Look on it as just another safari. I'll do the nasty stuff first, then hire you to see we make it out." The German tapped the map with the butt of the pickle, then popped the briny cucumber into his mouth. "We could hook up somewhere around Lake Zwai, here, south of Addis."

" 'Fraid I'm already spoken for, Ernst. I'm on my way to Abyssinia myself with some American clients."

"Still an English schoolboy," said the German, shaking his head. "But in Africa anything can happen." He beckoned to Gretel.

Jealous of Ernst's romantic pleasure, Anton left them together.

Returning to the gaming tent, he spotted the French lady, her figure even more lavish than he remembered as she leaned over some lucky chaps seated in a corner. Still upset about Gwenn, tired of rephrasing their arguments in his mind, he stood behind Penfold with a gin and watched the woman while his friend lost modestly at *chemin-de-fer.*

The French lady turned and wandered closer, her sculpted grey silk dress shimmering feverishly when she moved. He grinned as she approached.

"Good evening," said Anton.

"Who is your big brutish friend?" she said, pausing. "Is he German?"

"Very," said Anton, distracted by her perfume as the woman stepped closer, her breasts nearly touching him.

"Looks like he'd be useful in a fight," she said admiringly.

"He is," said Anton, trying to hold her interest. "I owe him a lot."

"What sort of thing?" she said, raising her eyebrows.

"Oh, a lift in the bush, some hospitality on a farm in German East Africa, watching my back in a bar fight," said Anton, waving one hand, not joking, remembering the hunting and the mining and the brawls. "And perhaps a little gold dust." That seemed to get her attention.

"Do you like to gamble? Doubles?" She offered Anton a Sobranie from a shiny silver case with blue enamel stripes. "Perhaps I can help?"

"Thank you." He took one and a passing waiter lit their cigarettes. "Help what?"

"The other evening I believe I saw you lose, *monsieur.*"

"I usually do," Anton said, smiling warmly, regarding her with more respect. "That's why I'm always welcome."

"Join us, please." She gestured to a far corner of the busy tent. "Otherwise my friends'll just talk business. And I need a partner, playing bezique. I believe you Americans call it pinochle."

"I'm not American. I'm from Kenya, but I think I remember the game." He looked at her thoughtfully. "Isn't that the one where you try and score a lot of points over several hands?"

"Bravo! Quelle innocence!" she exclaimed with humor. "Didn't I see you at Shepheard's with some leggy American girls? I remember your blue eyes." She took Anton's arm and led him slowly through the crowd, ignoring the

acknowledgments of other men, for the moment treating him as if he were the only man in Egypt. It was a sensation he had forgotten and enjoyed.

"What's this?" she said, feeling the sheath strapped to the inside of his right forearm.

"Something an old friend gave me." For years the slender gypsy knife had accompanied Anton. More recently he only carried the *choori* on special occasions, sometimes for luck.

"What do you do?" she said, looking up at him.

"About what?" He felt her chest against his arm and pressed closer.

"Dans la vie," she said with a shrug. "In life."

"I hunt."

"Mmm," she murmured. "How dangerous."

She led him to a small square table in a corner of the tent. A soda siphon, an open bottle of brandy and piles of house chips rested on the green tablecloth. Two men rose to greet them, a European and a short heavy Egyptian in tight English evening clothes with a red flower in his lapel.

"Enchanté," said the pale jowly Frenchman, expansive and jovial in his double-breasted white dinner jacket, a rosette in the buttonhole. "*Un bon pigeon,* Cerise?"

"Je l'espère." She smiled and cracked two new packs of forty-eight cards each. "We'll see."

A waiter came over and set a hookah beside the Egyptian. The perfectly prepared coals glowed brightly at the center of the water pipe.

Cerise leaned forward towards Anton and passed him the deck to cut.

"Would you like to play with me?" she said with innocence, her eyes witty and inviting.

"Of course."

"Doubles?"

"Better play no partners," Anton said. "You wouldn't want to go down with me."

"The game is one thousand points," announced the Frenchman genially. "Usual scoring, high points for aces and royal melds, each hand's winner adds value of his cards to the cards taken in the winning tricks. *Roulez.*"

If he was going to make his money, Anton knew this would have to be the game. He couldn't afford to lose a second time.

They played for an hour or more and drank and smoked, chatting while the cards came evenly and demanded little concentration as Anton's card memory kept track. He reckoned he and the girl were both several pounds ahead. In the brighter light that hung above the table he realized she was older than he'd thought, and older than he was, probably nearly forty, maybe even more. If he wasn't careful, older women would become a habit. They would make him lazy.

"A gift from Ali Baba for Mr. Alavedo's friend," said a table steward to Anton, presenting a bottle of iced champagne and glasses. Anton saw the dark eyes of the Egyptian tighten as he regarded Anton more closely. Two fresh decks waited on the corner of the table.

"Let's do something more interesting." Cerise, seated opposite Anton, lifted a glass to her lips. She wiggled down a bit in her seat and rested her stocking foot between Anton's legs beneath the tablecloth.

"We'll deal four cards at a time," she said. "I'll go first, yes?" Her toes worked like lobster claws exploring the seabed. "All right, Monsieur Musa Bey?"

The Egyptian nodded, his cheeks hollowed, his lips not leaving the mouthpiece of the hookah. Cerise dealt them each four cards at a time. Anton caressed her foot while she dealt, rubbing the arch and squeezing the toes. Cerise made no expression while she turned the cards. Though impressed by her card handling, and with her unrevealing face, Anton returned his concentration to the threat of cheating.

Once would be enough, he knew, with the four-card deal. It always came when it was the victim's turn to deal. Then one cheater would cut the cards to him, probably stripping four of the eight aces or royals to the top of the deck so that the second cheater would be dealt the aces by the victim.

Anton knew more about card cheats than most. He recalled the young gypsies being trained at cards in the evening, sitting cross-legged in the sheltering circle of the *vardos* while the dogs cracked bones in their teeth and dozed under the wagons. The children turned the large colorful cards onto scarves laid out by the camp fire, the girls learning to tell fortunes, the boys to gamble, playing casino and kalabrias and cribbage, poker and pinochle. In time each twelve-year-old lad could remember two decks in sequence, and could peel and palm and strip and stack and crimp and read marks and signal and double deal like a magician.

Ernst von Decken came up behind Anton and rested a heavy hand on his friend's shoulder.

Uneasy, Anton waited for the sting as the opposing players bid each other up. Each time the losing bidder was required to match the entire kitty. He himself would have to win the hand before the pot reached the point where they would cheat. He prayed for bezique, the high-scoring combination of the queen of spades and jack of diamonds, a particularly appropriate pair he thought. Bidding and raising on weak hands, failing to make their bids, the players repeatedly anted up to match the growing kitty as the game circled the table. The pot grew to two hundred, three hundred, four hundred and twenty pounds. Anton was rapidly reaching his limit. Cerise seemed to have lost something of her carefree manner.

Anton inclined his head and Ernst bent over him. "Can you spare fifty quid?" Anton whispered. The German stood straight and laughed aloud, clapping his hand up and down on Anton's shoulder.

"I came over to steal your blonde," Ernst whispered in Anton's ear. "Not to be your bank."

Feeling his own arousal, Anton wondered if the German was aware of Cerise's mischief under the table.

After another round, the pot was something over twelve hundred pounds. Anton could feel his body tensing like a drawn bow. His pockets were almost empty, the entire safari advance and Olivio's stake both on the table. His small friend could afford it, but he could not. Thank God for his gypsy education: the more desperate the gamble, the more calm the demeanor. He loosened his face with a smile.

" 'Fraid I'm getting a bit weary, old chap." Penfold leaned over beside Anton and spoke into his ear. "I'm up a few guineas. You carry on doing the Lord's work. I'll just step out and catch a bit of kip in the motor."

Anton nodded, watching the Frenchman shuffle the deck on his right.

Ernst saluted Penfold with rare respect. "Lord Penfold, sir!" He clicked his heels and snapped down his chin. *"Kapitän Ernst von Decken, Schutztruppe."*

"Good Lord!" said Penfold amiably, shaking hands. "The German." The two men chatted for a moment before Penfold left the tent.

"Jolly nice Hun," Penfold mumbled to himself as he squinted into the crisp starlight of the desert, "but sometimes 'e forgets who lost the Kaiser's war."

Sensing the sting was on, his own hands damp, Anton took a cigarette and casually positioned the lady's smooth silver case on the table to his left. He lifted the cut deck and served four cards to the Egyptian. In the case he saw the reflected corners of two kings and two queens, all hearts, cross the silver between the blue enamel stripes. Double marriage, a winner. He looked up and saw the strain in the soft face of the Egyptian. With his right hand, the man played with the flower in his buttonhole, distractedly plucking the tiny red petals, then rolling and crushing them between his fingers.

Knowing he must interrupt the play, his manner still relaxed, Anton dealt to Cerise. He recalled that professionals, dreading notoriety, always avoided calling attention to trouble at their tables, thereby giving an experienced opponent an advantage. As Anton's right hand flipped Cerise her cards, he rocked her champagne glass. The wine sloshed out, splashing her cards.

"Mon Dieu!" Cerise moved one hand quickly to steady the glass, spilling more wine onto the table. *"Zut!"* Cerise turned up the soaked cards and squirmed, twitching her foot and clenching her toes in his crotch as drops of champagne trickled over the edge of the table into her lap.

"Pardon me!" Anton said, passing her his handkerchief. "I'm afraid we'll have to put aside those cards. They're spoiled now."

"Eh, alors!" said the Frenchman with exasperation, but restraining himself, adding nothing more as he exchanged looks of recognition with the Egyptian.

Anton opened a fresh deck and handed it to the Frenchman to cut. Now they would need another hand or two to rearrange the cards. Anton dealt. The other players watched his hands with heightened concentration.

His own cards, no aces but all royals, might be enough to win. The Egyptian, his cards clenched tight, paused and searched Anton's face with small hard eyes. The man bid three hundred and fifty points, then the others offered three sixty, three ninety. The game was still for a thousand points, with six hundred already made. Everything Anton wanted to accomplish this night was now within his grasp.

"Four hundred points," Anton bid, taking the large risk in order to win the raise. Around the table, no one spoke as the others watched him. Anton showed his own cards first, knowing from the other faces that he had won. One by one, they all showed and dropped their cards, giving him the hand and the pot, roughly six times his original stake, he reckoned.

The knot in his belly relaxed as Anton drew the pot towards him with both hands. Small red fragments of the bey's flower were mixed with the banknotes, chips and plaques. Now he'd just play another hand or two to make the leaving easy. Meanwhile, they'd have to start building the kitty again. He cut the deck for the Egyptian. Cerise's toes, even more active and skillful since Anton's victory, again aroused his attention. The Bey dealt.

A commotion at the entrance interrupted Anton's concentration. He lowered his cards and looked up.

Tariq filled the entryway. His dark eyes flicked around the smoky tent. It was as if some wild animal had wandered into a drawing room. Two waiters sought to block his path. One touched his sleeve. Like a stallion resisting the bridle, Tariq shook himself irritably and raised his hands. The men stepped back as if they had been burned.

"Excuse me, please." Anton threw in his cards and anted in to match the small pot before rising and hurrying to Tariq.

"This gentleman's with me," he said to the circling staff.

"The lord, *effendi,*" Tariq said. "He is hurt. Come now."

Anton saw there was no time for explanations. He returned to the table and excused himself again.

"Damn me," he said to Ernst. "Olivio warned me it was dangerous to leave this place alone."

"Your dwarf's in Cairo?" Ernst said.

"Very much so." Anton gathered up his fortune of cash and chips.

"Where are you staying in Cairo?" the blonde asked as Anton left.

"The Pension Agamemnon," he said hastily, appreciating her disappointment, doubting she would come to call.

Anton and Tariq and Ernst hurried to the car, slipping and scuffing down the steep dark side of the dune. Gretel followed more slowly.

Penfold sat in the backseat, pressing a discolored handkerchief to his head. The side of his shirt collar was dark with blood. His monocle was cracked.

"Sorry to interrupt your game. Rascals gave me a nasty thumping. Three of 'em. Don't mind the money, always losing that, but they pinched my father's half-hunter and chain."

Anton took the handkerchief and examined the bleeding gash that ran from Penfold's right ear to eyebrow.

"Rather nasty. Might need a stitch or two," Anton said. "Where's Haqim?"

"Straight ahead," said Penfold wearily. "Towards the old catacombs."

"Be right back." Anton removed his jacket and tucked it around his friend's chest. "Stay with his lordship, Tariq."

"Let me join you," said Ernst with eagerness. "It would be a pleasure. This is no work for a nice English boy."

"No, you look after Adam. They might come this way." Anton handed Ernst the handkerchief. "Please see if you can clean up that cut and stop the bleeding."

"Good hunting," said the German with a grin, passing the handkerchief to Gretel.

Angry with himself for thinking of money instead of his friend, Anton trotted off into the near darkness. The moon, dimmed by patches of haze, was higher now and smaller.

Anton came to the first entrance, two low stone columns, rough and unfinished, seemingly cut from the rocky hillside itself. He stood still and listened. He discerned a cluster of dim figures seated cross-legged near some coals a bit farther along the slope. They seemed from a different world. Anton knew better than to ask their help.

He heard the rush of feet and a cry of pain from the catacomb. He bent and stepped inside, holding his slender knife in his right hand, his matches waiting in the other. His hands met a rough wall, then a corner with a sharp turning. He turned the corner and found a dim glow rising from the next chamber.

He stumbled and looked down. A prone figure blocked the passage, illuminated by a small oil lamp burning from a long wick set in an open bowl. Anton knelt.

The dead man wore one sandal. His severed right hand, the fingers spread, lay in a pool of blood by his side. Punishment for theft, Anton guessed, thinking of Haqim. A long dagger, snapped in two, lay near the body. Two leather charms, the usual protection against syphilis and tapeworms, were tied to a thong that circled his broken neck. A leather purse was at his waist. Anton opened the purse and found Lord Penfold's gold chain, but not his watch. He stepped over the corpse as sounds of violence echoed towards him.

Anton picked up the lamp and, bent low, entered the next chamber.

Haqim, his left arm apparently paralyzed, raging and cursing as he fought, was grappling with two men. One turned to face Anton.

"Afrangi!" the man cried, lunging at Anton with a short curved knife.

Anton hurled the oil. The fuel flared in the darkness, spreading like a cloak over the shoulders of Anton's assailant. The man's *gallabiyyah* blazed like a giant torch, his face haloed by the rising light. Flames climbed his neck. Shadows darted about the ceiling and walls of the chamber. The man screamed and dropped his knife. He dashed past Anton, throwing himself down in the passage, rolling in the dirt and beating at himself to extinguish the flames, then rising and running off until his cries grew faint. Anton crouched in the darkness, holding his blade before him, hearing only grunts and curses as Haqim and his last enemy fought.

Suddenly there was silence in the dark chamber. Then Anton heard a footstep shuffle on the stone floor.

"Haqim?" Anton called into one cupped hand, trying to throw his voice, moving swiftly to one side as he spoke.

A blow grazed his shoulder. Sparks flew when a heavy stone slammed the wall where he had stood. Anton swung the choori in a wide upward arc. He heard the blade tear cloth, then felt resistance as he finished the stroke and swung again. A man cried out and fell against him. Anton stepped back until he felt a wall behind him. He stood still and heard a man collapse to the floor, choking and spitting like an animal drowning in its own blood.

Anton lit a match, the knife ready in his right hand. His shirt-front was sticky with the blood of his attacker. Hakim lay nearby, still breathing, his head bloodied, apparently knocked senseless by a blow from the stone. The match winked and went out. Anton lit another and held it high.

Ten feet across the room an Egyptian lay in a growing pool of blood. His eyes were open and still. The fingers of his right hand were thrust inside a long wound that ran from collarbone to chin.

Anton searched the body. He found a small roll of English banknotes and one gaming chip, but no watch. He wiped the knife on the man's robe. With no belt, thinking he wasn't properly dressed for this sort of work, Anton put the knife in his teeth. He knelt beside Haqim and lifted the man on his shoulders. Groaning with the effort, his wounded shoulder throbbing, Anton was certain he had never lifted a heavier burden. Haqim's body was dense as stone. Awkwardly Anton struck another match and, stooping, made his way along the first passage.

The distant figures by the fire watched him without moving as he stepped out into the night with Haqim.

Not a moment too soon, Anton thought, staggering in the sand as he saw the lights of the Rover blink twice.

"Good Lord!" He heard Adam exclaim at the sight of him in his bloody dinner clothes with a knife in his teeth and the immense Nubian across his shoulders. Tariq ran to meet them and took his brother from Anton's back.

"This was the best we could do." Anton handed the gold chain and cash to Penfold and collapsed onto the running board of the automobile.

"You would have done better with your German friend along," Ernst said with his hands on his hips.

"What happened to the other chaps?" Penfold said eagerly.

"One needs some wet tea leaves. Be good for his burns. He must be the sod who's got the watch," said Anton, ignoring Ernst while he wiped his face and hands with a cloth from the glove box.

"Shouldn't be surprised if the other two turn up on the teaching table at Gwenn's medical school. I'll ask her to give them a couple of extra incisions for old Haqim here."

"Glad to see my *Engländer* still enjoys a brawl," growled Ernst, thinking how useful his friend could be after the heist. "I'll catch up with you at the Agamemnon. Perhaps we can share a boat to East Africa."

— 9 —

"Clove seems to have a way with those pigeons," said Adam Penfold, staring up to the flat roof above the bar where his goddaughter was feeding the caged birds from a basket. "What's she serving 'em? Getting a little peckish meself."

"Corn, my lord," said Olivio Alavedo. "And perhaps tamarind seeds for her favorites." He was annoyed by his friend's distracting wandering mind but pleased by any attention to his favorite child. His Clove did love these columbines. Unlike several of her sisters, however, she never lamented that some birds were destined for the pot. Like her father, Clove had an instinct for the laws of life. Her favorite birds were the dark-winged couriers secured in a special cage above the others, pigeons whose enemy was not the knife but the hawk.

"It seems they may have us up before the Mixed Courts, Mr. Anton." The dwarf said after a moment, setting a dish of hot vegetable *samosas* on the table, each stuffed with spiced mashed peas and chopped baby onions from his farm. "The Special Police we encountered on my land, that dog Captain Thabet, were working for the palace, or someone close to it."

As other men had an instinct for polo or the piano, an aptitude for painting or philosophy, so Olivio Alavedo possessed a gift for detecting the malign. Like a ferret after a mole, once on the scent he found no tunnel too dark or deep or twisting.

He knew this incident at the farm had a darker source than incompetence. With other acquisitions, he had found himself frustrated, as if the bank or ministry that denied him had been turned away by some competing hand. He suspected some enemy he had not yet detected, a rival for these properties, someone whose cunning schemes were not unlike his own. Already he had been approached by the agent for some unknown buyer. Were they trying to scare him off, to deter him from acquiring and developing the new estates he had determined to pursue?

Olivio wondered what might happen to a man like himself in an Egyptian prison or, worse, in a work gang digging silt out of the canals. Years ago, he had learned to discipline his imagination, except on suitably intimate occasions. Unrestrained, it could transport him to excess. One image, however, now refused to be suppressed. He remembered once seeing the hands of a *fellah* who years before had served in the penal quarry at Tura.

Nearly blind from the white limestone dust and reflected sunlight, the man bore the hands that always identified a survivor of the quarry. Broken-fingered, stiff like two warped boards, coarsened and calloused beyond any other mark of toil, they were the extremities of some strange animal. What could hell provide after Tura?

Olivio steadied himself. After all, this was Egypt. Special arrangements were always available for a price.

"The Mixed Courts?" said Anton. Parched and dusty after a morning gallop with his twin clients by the pyramids, he finished his second drink. These Kentucky girls could ride.

"The mixed tribunals are part of the Capitulations we worked out in the old days with the Turks, who used to rule this lot," said Penfold, brightening. He sipped his gin and tonic whilst he struggled to recall his history. He saw Olivio and Anton waiting for further explanation. Olivio seemed unusually attentive. It was rare these days to have someone pay attention, and he continued cheerfully.

"Came from the old Consular Courts. Means no foreigner is subject to Gypie laws or courts or taxation, can only be tried in courts made up of mostly foreign judges."

The frothy red orange juice was the best Anton had ever tasted. A modest hangover made it better still. One always drank too much in the city, and an evening with his clients at the Semiramis didn't help. He dipped one corner of a *samosa* in the chutney. Another week of this and he'd be soft and idle. He groaned to himself and looked at Adam critically as the old gent smeared his *samosa* with pasty Marmite.

"Better than rough native justice, young man," said Penfold, confused by Anton's expression. "Some of the old Ottoman punishments were rather unpleasant. Came between you and your grandchildren."

Penfold paused and winked at Olivio. "You're looking a little off, old boy. Better join me in a drink. We're lucky, really. It's only going to get worse. The young Egyptian officers, the patriotic associations, the students and all that, are clamoring for an end to the Capitulations, even want our troops sent home. Madness, really. They reckon it's their Egypt and all that sort of rubbish. Never was theirs, of course. Turks had it for four hundred years." Pleased with his account, Penfold brushed thin flakes of pastry from his jacket.

"Sounds like I'd best get my clients on the boat before all this gets underway." It was like when he was a boy, Anton thought, the gypsies breaking camp at night whenever there was trouble, knowing better than to hang about for worse to come. In twenty minutes their caravans would be hitched and underway. But now he was sad to be leaving his boys.

"Probably would be to the good," said the dwarf, concerned also about the messy result of his friends' evening gambling near the pyramids. "And it wouldn't hurt for old Haqim to have a little holiday."

"We can take the train to Suez tomorrow and just catch the steamer for Somaliland," Anton said. At least he wouldn't be put to the expense of taking the twins tea dancing at Shepheard's, he thought, shaking his head. They liked champagne.

Colonel Grimaldi tapped on the glass with his knuckles, and Kamil pulled the Bugatti over to the edge of the corrugated pitted roadway. Enzo stepped down, stretched and breathed deeply. Here, in the Eastern Desert, between the Nile and the Canal, the forms of the sand were softer, more beach-like, less rocky and more susceptible to the winds. Broad dunes rose before him as far as he could see. The count relieved himself and lit a cigarette. Kamil did the same on the other side of the road. Grimaldi smelled the warm dusty air as the Khamseen gusted up from the south. The car's Italian flag flapped. Clumps of camel thorn bounced and tumbled as they blew across the road.

The grey prow of a ship emerged in profile between two dunes to the north, as if sailing through the sand, then disappeared behind the distant tan hills before revealing its complete superstructure as it moved to his right past a lower stretch of the sandy horizon. Only the thin column of black smoke remained steady as the vessel came and went between the soft-shouldered dunes like the silhouette in a shadow game. Probably one of ours, Enzo judged.

Over a hundred and fifty Italian ships had passed through Suez so far this year with men and supplies for East Africa. Four had passed in 1934. For each man, the French leeches who ran the Suez Canal Company were charging Italy seven francs, for each ton of freight, twenty-five francs. The French were selling Abyssinia. Perhaps one day they would sell each other, Grimaldi thought irritably.

He would soon be at the Canal. Enzo wished Gwenn were there to see him off. She had been packing when he left, preparing to move the boys to the villa of that disgusting midget before she herself left for Ethiopia. Enzo was experienced enough to know how he would miss her. He doubted if she realized it, but he was aware of whence the problem came. It wasn't her work, or his, or the coming war, or all the things they'd said, or hadn't said. It had to be the Englishman. Everything had changed when Rider arrived in Cairo.

"One day I will make him pay," Enzo said quietly as he stared across the desert.

Yet in a way it wasn't even Rider, but rather Gwenn's stubborn sense of how things ought to be. Rider and this coming campaign had brought it all together.

"It's not you, Lorenzo, and it's not him," she'd said finally, looking up from her packing while he stood angry in the doorway. "It's me, or the way I want to be."

Grimaldi lit a second cigarette and thought about her words. He remembered the evening when things were better between them, when she'd told him about her mother's pathetic life in a mining village in Wales. It was more than he'd wanted to hear.

"At least my mother had a few important things," Gwenn told him, speaking as if she knew he would never understand. "She carried on her life the way it was meant to be, with one man, her children and a place that was always hers."

Enzo flicked the cigarette into the desert and walked quickly to the waiting Bugatti.

"Be sure and stop just before Suez and wipe down the car," he ordered as Kamil held the door for him. Even the Lalique falcon at the front of the bonnet was covered in dark sand.

In less than an hour they were at Suez. British and Egyptian flags flew side by side at a chain of military posts. But Grimaldi knew it was not the flags that mattered. The immense brick barracks at the edge of town were British. Something between a fort and one of those nightmare British textile mills. In front of the walls a crowd of soldiers with bagpipes cheered a football match between two Scottish regiments. Enzo felt resentment swelling inside him.

Flag flying, the gleaming Bugatti pulled up at the main dock past the end of the Canal at the Gulf of Suez. A crowd of five or six hundred Italians waited. Fascist *squadristi* in black hats moved amongst them, handing out leaflets and giving instructions. Young men carried Fascist pennants and the royal flag of Italy. A small band played the marching songs of the Blackshirts. Cries of *"Du-ce! Du-ce! Du-ce!"* rose from the crowd as they recognized the embassy car. The religion of *ducismo* was already alive in Africa.

"Good afternoon, *Colonnello.*" A consular officer saluted Grimaldi. "The *Saturnia* will be here in one hour, sir." Enzo smelled the harbor-side odors of oil and refuse, always a reminder of the first time he had sailed from Genova for North Africa.

He walked through the bazaar into the town and took a drink in a dusty café. Everywhere Enzo saw Italian soldiers, briefly ashore from the troopship *Quirinale.* They would help to form a crowd for the reception of the Duce's sons. The soldiers, mostly farm boys and children of the slums, seemed incredibly young and excited. Many wore straw military topees purchased from hawkers who worked the street. Most were lads for whom a trip to Rome or Venice would have been an incredible adventure. Now they were being asked to conquer Africa.

He saw the common soldiers make way for a party of *Bersaglieri,* elegant in the trim dark kit and black leather hats of the elite mountain regiment celebrated for running on parade. Proud, robust, the *Bersaglieri* laughed loudly as they swaggered past with their long cock's feathers waving from their hats in the breeze. Enzo had always been annoyed by the arrogance of the army's special units, preferring the sense of fraternity that bound his country's aviators. He asked himself what must be the background of these men that a few rooster feathers should give them such a sense of rank.

Colonel Grimaldi saw their troopship lying well off the dock to make way for the *Saturnia.* Her decks were lined with hundreds of black mules tied to the railings. He wondered how these European animals would take to the mountains of Africa. Lashed to the deck behind the mules he recognized a squadron of *Autoblinda* 611's, Italy's magnificent new seven-ton armored cars. One was equipped with a 37mm cannon, the others with twin 8mm machine guns. Built with the lessons of the Libyan campaign in mind, each had four driving wheels at the rear. Their spare wheels were secured to the sides amidships, slung low and free-wheeling to prevent the vehicles from bottoming out in uneven terrain.

Enzo paid for his drink and walked to the *Saturnia.* His kit was already on board. He was immediately requested to report to Air Marshal Italo Balbo.

In the passageway leading to the marshal's cabin, he was obliged to pass a younger officer. Forced close together in the narrow corridor, the soldier assessed Grimaldi with prominent, almost popping eyes. He was a *Bersaglieri* captain, Enzo realized, stocky with muscular calves and thick thighs that gave him the look of a man who could march forever. The soldier gave Colonel Grimaldi a perfunctory salute but barely moved aside to allow Enzo to pass. Compelled to turn sideways as he approached the door, Grimaldi smelled the man's sweat and noticed he wore a shoulder badge Enzo had not seen before.

"Join me in my cabin, Grimaldi," Italy's first air marshal called from his seat, fatigue heavy in his deep voice. "There are delicate things we must discuss, and one or two officers I wish you to meet."

The cabin of the old vessel smelled of cigarettes and fresh paint. The paint reminded Enzo of the extraordinary effort his country was making on every front. Three leather bags were piled by the door. Through the portholes came the sounds of boat whistles, the band and wild cheering from Italian soldiers and sailors and civilians.

"Vittorio! Vittorio! Bruno!"

Grimaldi saluted crisply, excited to be meeting Europe's greatest aviator, the "second Columbus," the first man to have led a massed formation of aircraft across the Atlantic. He remembered gathering around a radio with his brother pilots at the base outside Tripoli, cheering wildly, some men in tears, as the report came in of Balbo's squadron of twelve flying boats landing in the harbor at Buenos Aires. Thousands of Italians lined the docks and beaches, drinking and cheering and waving Italian flags, one of many such receptions the squadron received as it toured North and South America in triumph. In 1933 Balbo had done it again, this time as Italy's new Minister of Aviation, leading a flight of twenty-four twin-hulled seaplanes across the Atlantic. Landing in Lake Michigan to visit the Chicago World's Fair, the airmen were received by a crowd of one hundred thousand waving Italian flags. Later Balbo had been given a ticker tape parade in New York and had lunched with President Roosevelt at the White House.

Enzo and Balbo sat at a small table. The naval pilot stroked his short copper-colored beard, then poured two *grappas.*

"I'll be leaving you here, Colonel. I'm off to Tripoli as the new Governor General of Libya. So you can have my cabin." He coughed and lit a cigarette. "And my responsibilities." He looked at Grimaldi with experienced assessing eyes. Enzo was saddened to see the marshal's exhaustion. He seemed too old for Africa.

"The Duce's boys are only twenty-one and seventeen," Balbo said. "And the world is watching them. You will look after them as your own sons. But they must be seen to fly and to lead. And I need not tell you that they must come home. If they don't, you won't."

"Can they fly?" Enzo asked, aware that the marshall, though an ardent Fascist and one of three leaders of the march on Rome, was rumored to hold reservations about the Duce.

"They can fly, but this is war. You will soon see what I mean. Bruno is the youngest pilot in Italy. His training was a trifle hurried. You will not confuse him with Mars, but he is obliged to set an example for these peasant boys." The marshal waved his cigarette towards the dock. "With your help, he will be bombing savages in the mountains in Africa while his schoolmates are pinching tourists and sitting for their examinations. Do you understand me?"

"Yes, sir."

"When appropriate, you yourself will fly with the *Disperata* squadron, Colonel Grimaldi." Balbo filled both glasses. "Sometimes it may be you who will actually fly their aircraft and drop the bombs."

"As you say, Marshal," Enzo replied crisply, dreading the distraction of this assignment.

"And there is one more matter, also involving fine judgment and iron discretion. If things go badly on the ground, the generals will be clamoring for poison gas. They are all veterans of the World War. They know gas works, if the enemy has no masks." Marshal Balbo coughed and crushed out his cigarette.

"The Abyssinians have no masks. Italy lost half a million dead in that war, less than twenty years ago, and *Il Duce* will not permit that to happen again. They say he was there, as a sergeant in the trenches against the Austrians."

"I understand," Enzo said, understanding too well. Of course, gas was really no worse than any other weapon, but the politics of it was something he despised and feared. In every campaign some soldiers were sacrificed to politics. Did an Ethiopian peasant care which way he died? Why must his own career be threatened by such nonsense?

"Officially, we have no gas," Balbo continued wearily. "The League says it's a crime. But as you know, the canisters are already ashore in Massawa and Mogadishu. For ten years we've been building our supplies down there. Over two hundred tons, and more on the way. In Rome, they'll will be awaiting your recommendation, Colonel." He paused, waiting for Grimaldi's acknowledgment.

"Yes, sir."

"Of course, the Grand Council of Fascism, which is to say *Il Duce* himself, will make the final decision."

Enzo understood why the marshal was pleased with his new post. Balbo continued.

"And if the gas is used, Colonel Grimaldi, pray that it does the job." There was silence between them while the two officers listened to cheering from the dock. "If not, some say the Duce is prepared to turn to bacterial warfare. Then our country will truly be alone."

The old pilot stood and walked to the porthole. For a moment he stood staring out, shoulders hunched, arms crossed over his belly. Finally he turned and faced Grimaldi, raising his voice above the cheering of the crowd.

"Italy cannot lose another war in Africa. Today we are building the largest expeditionary force ever assembled for a colonial campaign, and the *Regia Aeronautica* must see that it does not perish." Balbo paused to finish his drink before adding, "Open the door, would you, Grimaldi, and ask that officer outside to join us."

"Colonel," Balbo said after the man entered, "this is Captain Uzielli of a new test unit of the *Bersaglieri,* a paratroop company, designed for special operations. You may have heard of him. He was a celebrated football player for Bologna, center half, I believe, Uzielli?"

"Fullback, sir," said Uzielli with the thick accent of that city.

"I don't recall," said Grimaldi, not wanting to become familiar with the man. He saw now that the captain's shoulder flash was designed in the white outline of a parachute.

"Uzielli is aware of the gas program, Colonel," said Balbo. "If action is needed on the ground, gathering information, recovering canisters, questioning prisoners, dealing with witnesses, whatever, he and his men will be doing the job. If we use the gas, you should expect to be working together."

"Is this your first time in Africa, Captain?" said Grimaldi, studying the man more closely, noticing the thick neck and large ears. The broad scar on his left cheek was almost lost in the dark deeply-lined face of a Romagnan peasant. Enzo rarely enjoyed working directly with the army, and he hoped he would not see this surly man again.

"I served in Libya, sir, in twenty-nine, Somaliland in thirty-one and thirty-two," said Uzielli in a proud harsh voice.

The two senior officers sipped their drinks, offering him nothing. The marshal cleared his throat before speaking again.

"Before he had to leave Libya," said Balbo, coughing, "Captain Uzielli developed a useful but unpopular specialty, hunting down and eliminating the rebels responsible for the sort of atrocities that give war a bad name. In each case, he caught them, and a few more besides, although once his men killed the wrong lot. Where was that nasty one, Captain?"

"Do you mean Sarir, sir?" said Uzielli, pleased with the recognition.

"That was it, Sarir. Although, with any luck, even there the guilty may've died with the innocent." The air marshal drank and looked at Grimaldi. "Sometimes these things can't be helped, you know."

"Quite, sir," said the colonel.

"That will be all, Captain," said Balbo, waiting to speak again until the cabin door was closed.

"You must understand, Grimaldi, that both the Mussolini boys and the gas are delicate discreet missions for which you can never be honored. There could be promotion, but no medals." Marshal Balbo rose and took Enzo's salute. "All this may not help your career, Colonel, but if you fail, it will destroy it. *Buona fortuna.*"

Before Grimaldi could reply, there was a knock on the metal door of the cabin.

"Enter!" called Marshal Balbo. "Enter, please."

The door opened and three young men in uniforms of the *Regia Aeronautica* crowded into the cabin.

"Welcome, gentlemen," said Balbo, his voice invigorated, rising smartly to his feet and ackowledging their salute. "Colonel Grimaldi, I present Lieutenant Mussolini, Captain Ciano, Lieutenant Mussolini."

The men exchanged salutes, the three young officers stiff in their tall polished boots, baggy jodhpurs and tightly buttoned tunics. The marshal's tone became more personal.

"I wish I could be flying with you all. Vittorio and Bruno are with the Fourteenth Bomber Squadron, *La Disperata,*" said the old pilot, clapping the younger brother on one shoulder. "Capronis, magnificent. And Galeazzo has just taken command of the Fifteenth."

Balbo turned and gestured towards Grimaldi. "The Colonel is an old hand at campaigning in Africa, and his grandfather died leading our native infantry at Adowa." The three young men looked at Enzo with respect while Balbo filled their glasses. Grimaldi was astonished by their youthfulness. Only Count Ciano, married to the Duce's elder daughter, seemed at ease, more than a boy, perhaps ready for war. Vittorio, heavy-faced, like his father, presented a bouncy cocky manner. The cinema was said to be his deepest interest. Bruno, dark and nervous, appeared even less than seventeen. Grimaldi saw at once that he must speak privately with their flight crews.

"You all have much to fly for," said Marshal Balbo as he clicked his heels and raised his glass.

"To *Africa Orientale Italiana!*" The five men drank.

"Remember one thing: where you are going, the main thing is to stay in the air!" Balbo smiled like a boy. "And now it is my duty to leave you, gentlemen. But you have much to discuss," said the marshal with enthusiasm, holding open the cabin door.

"Africa awaits you."

"My parents asked me to welcome you to our house," Clove Alavedo said with a warm smile, exchanging kisses with Gwenn at the center of the curving driveway that led to her father's villa on the Nile embankment. Cuban royal palms bordered the property along the street. Four gardeners toiled on their knees among the red-flowering bushes and Brazilian pepper trees that surrounded the three-story house. Two girls sat on a swing beneath an immense banyan tree centered on the lawn. The red fruit of the shade tree carpeted the grass around them.

"My father promised he'd be home soon," Clove said as she led Gwenn to the front steps. "And my sisters can't wait to have your boys here." Tariq stepped around Clove with two house servants and began to unload baggage from the Rovers.

"I'll carry that one," said Denby, jumping down from the second motor-car and blocking one of the servants from removing a wicker cage from the seat beside the driver.

Clove's younger sisters gathered at the top of the steps and watched Wellington and Denby advance towards the house.

"What's in that?" Cinnamon said to Rosemary, seated beside her on the swing, pointing at the cage. "I'm sure it's something horrid."

"I hope you and your parents won't mind, Clove, but I asked Dr. Fergus from the hospital to come by this afternoon for tea," Gwenn said as Clove led her up the steps.

"Of course not," Clove smiled. "How lovely."

When she came down from her room an hour later, Gwenn found her host and Malcolm Fergus already sharing tea. Trim and cool in his tan linen suit, always attentive to others, his eyes sparkling through his spectacles, the frail-looking Scottish physician seemed to be getting on with Olivio.

"Welcome, Miss Gwenn, welcome to our house!" cried the dwarf with true delight, worried only by what might transpire between Wellington and his precocious daughters. "This eminent physician, Dr. Fergus, advises me that in three days you leave for Ethiopia. How we will miss you here in Garden City. Though with the boys here, I know your heart will be with us, too."

"Our lorries and ambulances and supplies have already been loaded at Port Saïd," said the elderly Scottish surgeon, rising to greet Gwenn. "It'll be our turn at Suez."

"I do not understand such haste," said the dwarf, wagging his head from side to side, thinking that actually it was the benevolence of the mission that exceeded his comprehension. His assessment of the Scotsman was not satisfactory. "As yet there is no war. How do we know you will even be needed?"

"Already there is skirmishing along the borders," said Fergus, accepting more tea from Clove, growing increasingly animated and youthful as he spoke. "This war will be terrible. Tanks and planes against barefoot soldiers and civilians. They will need us, Mr. Alavedo, very soon."

"Malcolm's right, Olivio," Gwenn added, touching the dwarf's arm. "This is why we're doctors."

"Yes, of course," said the little man, recalling how Gwenn's nursing had saved him after he himself was burned. "I see."

"And we are all most grateful for your generous contribution to our Abyssinian Relief Fund, Mr. Alavedo," said Fergus. "One of our ambulances is yours."

"Nothing, nothing," said the dwarf, inclining his head with modesty while his favorite daughter beamed with pride. Generosity was rare enough, and over the years he had learned to make the most of it, especially his own. Too vain and showy a presentation, however, and the gift was resented. But totally anonymous, unrecognized, it lost much of its value. Best to begin as if anonymous, then to enjoy the modesty of disclosure by another.

Olivio leaned forward. His single eye did not blink while he spoke to the doctor in a different tone, cold and serious.

"I rely on you, Dr. Malcolm Fergus, for one thing: you will look after Miss Gwenn." He paused.

"My gift is not for Ethiopia. It is for her."

"I will do my best," said the doctor. Astonished by the little man's intensity, he tried not to blink as he looked the dwarf in the eye. "You may rely on it."

"Now we understand each other," said Olivio Alavedo more quietly, sitting back against his cushion. "More tea?"

Surprised to learn of Olivio's largesse, embarrassed by his words, Gwenn spoke for herself.

"We have to go and do what we can," she said, thinking how she hated to be leaving her sons. Tonight she would have to tell them. She recalled their distress, and her own confused emotions when Anton had stopped by to say good-bye, surprising her with a generous envelope for the boys' expenses. Gwenn had welcomed him to Cairo with reluctance, now she was sad to have him leave. She was confident that Wellie would take the news of her departure as well as could be hoped, but she dreaded Denby looking up at her with tight trembling lips as his eyes filled. Desolate already with her own sense of loss, she spoke again, as if explaining things to her sons.

"The Abyssinians won't have any other medical help, and we want to be there when we're needed."

— 10 —

"Why is that young English fairy staring at the girls?" said Ernst von Decken, spilling a few drops as he helped himself to more turtle soup. He spoke to the turbanned waiter slowly and firmly. "Just leave the tureen on the table, boy, that'll do. Right there."

"Not so loud. Dr. Pointer'll hear you. And he's not a pansy," said Bernadette as the ship's clock chimed across the small dining saloon of the *R.M.S. Otranto.* "He's a very distinguished South African physician, and he's in love with my lovely sister, Harry." Bernadette smiled brightly at her twin. "He follows Harry around the deck like a hungry puppy. Sometimes he even wags his tail."

"Dr. Pointer's just confused," said Harriet, turning her head to look Anton in the eye as she spoke. "He thinks I'm Berny. They always do," she added, filling Anton's glass with white wine. "Why is our handsome hunter so quiet?" she said, knowing this would irritate Anton's burly German friend.

"He's dreaming about the bush," said Ernst, looking at Harriet with excessive interest, it seemed to Anton. "These English boys love animals. It's all they think about."

"Sorry," said Anton, trying to smile, tired of worrying about his arguments with Gwenn. He noticed that Ernst had shaved and washed with unusual care. His rugged face shone. His bristly grizzled hair was parted in the center and combed back. He wore one of Anton's red kerchiefs around his neck like a cravat.

"By the way, isn't old von Decken looking awfully smart this evening?"

Anton observed admiringly. "Never seen him so slicked up and splendid. Well done, Ernst."

Ernst gave Anton a cold look and helped himself to more soup.

"And what about you?" said Harriet, her own bowl finished, leaning towards Ernst for a light. She examined the German's experienced face, touching his hard hand with hers while she shielded the flame against the breeze of the ceiling fan. "What do you think about, Mr. von Decken?"

"Sex," said Ernst at once, looking her directly in the eye with no trace of a smile. "Sex. Professor Freud has taught us Germans always about sex to think. But it is something about which I have no experience."

The crafty old bastard must have noticed Harriet reading one of her psychology books, Anton realized with irritation. Some game was afoot here. He saw Harriet's eyes sparkle when she broke into laughter.

"How's your friend, Gretel?" Anton said to Ernst in a loud voice. "Shame she couldn't join us for dinner."

The German ignored him and finished his soup.

"Dr. Pointer invited me to play poker with some friends tomorrow evening," Charles Crow said in the silence, putting his hand on Bernadette's. "Probably wants to ask me about your sister."

"He's rich, you know," Bernadette said, smiling at her fiancé. "From a diamond family in the Rand. He's on his way home to Port Elizabeth."

"I'd be careful, if I were you, Charlie," said Anton to the young artist. "Some of these sharps work the steamships."

When dessert was finished, Ernst excused himself. "I must take a tray to the cabin," he said. "My friend does not feel well at sea." Anton was not certain whether Gretel was a bad sailor, or whether Ernst was avoiding the awkwardness of bringing his African lover to the dining room.

"Gute Nacht," the German said to all, bowing his head with a smile. Harriet's eyes followed him as he left.

After dinner the others drank brandy and smoked and chatted on the starboard passenger deck, eager for a sight of the coast. From time to time they made out the lights of other ships in the distance. The tips of a hazy yellow crescent moon pointed south to Africa.

Even more than the reassuring clacking wheels of a train, the steady throbbing of the ship's engines reminded Anton of what it had been like to be young and on his way. Sixteen years ago, lean and optimistic, he'd worked his way out from Portsmouth to Mombasa on the old *Garth Castle.* If only he could start again.

"Good night," he said, standing when the ladies rose. "They'll bring you early tea in your cabins." By then, he thought, the warm westerly wind would wash over them as they entered the Indian Ocean. Morning would bring them the dusty scent of Africa south of the Sahara. Home.

* * *

Asleep with the evening's wine and brandy too rich on his tongue, Anton was awakened by a quiet knocking on his cabin door.

He opened his eyes. The moon, higher and smaller and whiter, hung at the top of the porthole. By now, he thought, lying on the edge of sleep, Gwenn, too, would be on her way to Abyssinia.

The banging on the metal door grew louder.

"Who is it?" he said heavily.

"It's me, Harry. I can't sleep." Bang. Bang. "Open up."

Anton wrapped a striped Orient Line towel around his waist and stepped to the door. He smelled her perfume as she brushed past him and entered the small cabin. He reached for the light switch.

"Don't. It's lovely with just the moon. I've been walking around on deck and it's so perfect I couldn't bear it." Slightly scared but proud of her boldness, she sat on the edge of the one small chair. "I brought most of the bottle, but I've only got one glass."

Anton held out his toothbrush glass and she poured some champagne. He knew he must behave himself. He had learned it was best to defer these things until the very end of the safari, in case it was disaster, and always to let the client make the first overture. On the other hand, he thought in a flash of anger, if Gwenn could carry on so shamelessly, why shouldn't he?

The American girl stepped to the porthole and rose on her toes. Her trim figure was outlined in the slinky silk dress. Sometimes he understood the signals of a woman's choice of clothes. This was going to be difficult. Although he could barely see Harriet's, he thought about her shapely slender legs. Speculating for a moment, not much caring about the answer, he wondered whether Harriet had come to him because she knew Ernst was busy.

"Ooh, come and look!" she exclaimed. "The sea's shining like a golden plate!"

"It's the phosphorescence and the moon. Never like this up north." Anton stepped towards her and looked over her shoulder. For a moment neither spoke. A necklace of lights grew on the horizon. Three or more ships were steaming south in formation.

"Italian troopships heading for Massawa and Mogadishu," he said. "I wonder if all those men will make it back home."

"You haven't." She turned her head to the side and spoke over her shoulder in a softer voice, not the usual brassy Harriet. "Why did you first come to Africa?"

"Oh, I was young, eighteen. I came looking for adventure, and one or two other things." Mostly things he hadn't found or kept: his fortune and a family.

"Me too."

She turned around and leaned her lower body against his. She held her head back and drank her champagne, studying his face in the light of the moon. He sensed she was eager but not desperate. Now he knew she must feel him through the towel. He could not see her shadowed face. She placed her left hand on his chest, bending her fingers so the tips of her nails touched his skin. He made out the dark red highlights on the edges of her head's silhouette. She ran her hand down his naked back along his spine and settled her fingers on the top of his towel. He liked her touch.

She finished her champagne and cast her glass out the porthole. She held out her hand for Anton to finish his. When he did, she threw his after hers.

"We'll have to drink the rest from the bottle later on." She took his hands and wrapped them around her back, then guided them down until he clasped her buttocks. Tight and high, with faint hollows in the cheeks, like a young Kikuyu, and a sharp indentation at the top of each leg.

"I'm told that's my best feature. What do you think?"

"It's too soon to tell," he said as she raised her face to kiss him. Giving up, excited, he squeezed her hard in both hands and pulled her against his lower body until he felt the bone of her pelvis. "We'll see."

"Busy place." Adam Penfold looked around at the knots of men waiting in the long high-ceilinged anteroom at the Ministry of Public Works. Already they had passed through dim crowded halls lined with alcoves where surly lethargic clerks sipped tea and ignored the sweating supplicants who stood in lines and bunches before their desks. Stacks of dusty grey folders tied with brown ribbons overwhelmed the desks and floors and windowsills. "What do all these people want?"

"Water, my lord," Olivio informed him, admiring his friend's new double-breasted white linen suit. Just the thing to impress old Musa Bey Halaib. The Undersecretary in charge of irrigation was a man who understood. He would appreciate the blue-striped tie, frayed and stained as it was.

"Water. Some want more, others less," the dwarf continued. "In Egypt, so little changes. I will show you hieroglyphics where lines of petitioners, bearing presents, crave an audience with officials of the pharoah."

Penfold preferred poverty to supplication, but perhaps this would be something in between. He had learned to understand the words of Gibbon: "It is better to be humbled than ruined." And after all, this new suit wasn't bad for four days' work. The buttons were proper bone, and with his sloppy habits it would soon appear worn enough. Then it would be his. At least his shoes, old Joseph Box's work, were ancient as an elephant, the brown leather almost black with age and wear and polish, all but the gleaming toe caps covered in the veins of a thousand fine cracks.

Olivio lowered his voice, pleased to show his friend how much he was at home. "That large group whispering in the corner is the deputation of notables from Upper Egypt, here to protest the new plans to lower the river by flooding certain basins. This would drown their *sefi,* the summer crop of cotton, before it can be gathered." Olivio smiled. "That, you see, would make other cotton farmers rich by reducing the crop and raising the price."

"And who's that noisy mob on the other side?" Penfold drew a handkerchief from his left cuff and dried his face.

"Ah, they are here every day. These are the big rice farmers from Dakhlia Province. They will not have come empty-handed, and today they may be admitted to submit their plea. Already some have brought lawsuits. Of course, those men must present the largest gifts. For the rice to grow, they require the flooding of their fields. They demand that the gates in the banks be opened and the waters set free."

Near the entrance two men unrolled large sheets of engineering drawings. Their three companions, one English, were disputing some details on the renderings.

"And those men, my lord, are up to even costlier mischief. They are tendering for the contract to strengthen the Assiut Barrage, a dam completed before our time, south of Cairo. Five years ago they lost to the French in their bidding to raise the height of the Aswan dam. It is said the French spent more on the minister's villa in Alexandria than on the dam. Ha! Ha! This time the British firm undertakes to use Egyptian cement in their work."

"Who makes the cement?"

Perhaps his lordship was learning. "A number of gentlemen. Working with interested friends at the palace, we have volunteered to assist the nation with this patriotic enterprise."

A door opened. A stern-faced young clerk appeared, immaculate in black shoes and European dress. Silence fell over the hall.

The clerk advanced to Olivio and bowed. "Musa Bey will receive you now, effendi."

Olivio stood with a small square parcel in one hand, handsomely bound with a pink silk bow. He and Penfold followed the Egyptian through two smaller, more formal waiting rooms. The tapping of Penfold's cane punctuated their passage. The clerk held open a heavy polished door. They entered a large office furnished in the English manner.

"How I salute you, Mr. Alavedo!" Smiling warmly, the Egyptian strode around his desk and clasped Olivio's free hand in both of his. Tightly packed into a fitted dark suit, with a red carnation at his lapel, he was a short heavy man whom only Olivio made appear tall.

"I bring you a modest gift, Undersecretary, for your exquisite daughter,

Yasmin, on her wedding. The sort of trifle elegant young ladies enjoy wearing on their wrist." Olivio recalled the fifteen-year-old child, the image of her father: squat, well dressed, a shadow of mustache above her thin lips. As an ornament, the jewelled bracelet would be hideously wasted. As commerce, it would find its own reward.

Olivio inclined his head towards the Englishman. "And may I present to you my esteemed partner, Baron Penfold. The lord jouneys now in Africa, visiting his estates in Egypt and British East Africa."

"Welcome to Egypt, your grace." Musa Bey Halaib bowed and shook hands. "Whatever I may do to make your stay enjoyable, that will be my pleasure."

"Thank you," Penfold said. These people would never understand proper address. Why must they try?

A servant entered and set a tray on a low table. Three cups surrounded a small brazier. The steaming odor of rich coffee clouded up from a copper pot.

Musa Bey Halaib offered seats around the table.

Penfold looked at the man more carefully. Couldn't think where, but damned if he hadn't seen the chap somewhere before. Still, all these jumped-up types looked so much alike, and worked so hard to please. How was one to know?

The Undersecretary brought a wooden box from his desk.

Penfold accepted a cigar and looked about the room. He declined the cutter and instead pinched and cracked one end between his long fingers. His knuckles seemed stiffer and thicker every day. And in a few minutes he'd have to go back to that filthy loo.

The wall facing the windows was covered in a mural depicting the stages in the building of the Suez Canal. On the extreme left men and donkeys and camels and machines toiled in the sand. At the other end stood a high-bosomed lady in a lavish hoopskirted gown.

The Bey noticed Penfold studying the painted wall. "A great work," he said. "Our canal. Could not have been done without the *corvée,* 'forced labor' I fear you English would consider it. One hundred thousand laborers died for Egypt."

"Mmm, thousand a mile. Seems a bit costly, all the same. Rather like the pyramids, eh?" Penfold squinted through his monocle. "All planned by a Frenchie, of course. Wouldn't want to work for one of 'em meself."

Concentrating with a frown, Penfold turned his cigar against the soft coals in the brazier that his host held up for him. He looked up and puffed gently. "May I ask the name of the lady on the wall?"

"This woman is the Empress Eugénie of the French, opening the canal in 1869. Like so many women, most expensive. The Khedive built an opera house for her reception in Cairo, to be opened with the first performance of *Aida.* Of course, this Verdi, being an Italian music man, was late with *Aida.* So he gave us *Rigoletto* instead, and the Italians have been with us ever since." Musa Bey Halaib rolled his eyes, knowing how these British felt about the Latins.

Olivio, afraid that Lord Penfold would never let the conversation turn to business, coughed and addressed the Undersecretary.

"How are the rains in Abyssinia?"

"I am told the rains continue every day and every night. Soon they will be here."

Penfold blew smoke with satisfaction. "I thought it never rained in Egypt."

"It does not. The Blue Nile will bring the rains of Abyssinia to us. And the White Nile too. Already the Nilometers are rising at Malakal and Rossieris. At Khartoum the river stands at over sixteen meters. If it reaches eighteen, in three weeks the sewers will overflow in Cairo and there will be water in this office and malaria for the poor. Above Aswan, already villages are flooded and bodies float from their graves."

"Can nothing be done?" said Penfold.

The Bey drew himself up and gripped the heavy gold chain of his watch.

"All is being done, lord. In every village the men labor on the banks and the women build mud fences before their houses." He spoke with pride.

"The sheiks and the *omda* are fined if they do not see the work is done. My cousin, the Minister of Communications, has laid telephone lines on the embankments with phones to notify of any breach. I myself sail tomorrow on the steamer *Dandara* to inspect the reinforcement works with the Inspector General of Lower Egypt Irrigation and the *mudirs* of the provinces."

"How fortunate is Egypt to have Musa Bey Halaib governing the floods," Olivio put in. He sipped his coffee and assessed his host's mood, surprised to find him with so much time.

"I imagine your grace was at school with Sir Miles?" said the Bey in a different voice. At last we are at business, thought Olivio. The rogue wants to see if his lordship possesses influence with the High Commissioner. At least the British still have some power in this ill-governed land.

"Bit after my time." Penfold puffed at his dead cigar, thinking of school. "Big chap. Too big, really. Broke my nephew's shoulder at the Wall. Lunching with 'im tomorrow."

Whatever was that wall? Olivio wondered in frustration. But Mussa Bey Halaib nodded warmly and seemed to take the point. The dwarf heard the murmur of voices gathering outside the door. A hint?

"So how may I be of service?" said the Egyptian.

Olivio set down his cup. "Nothing at all." He had made it his business to learn the peculiar tastes of his host, and he knew he must lure the Bey bit by bit. "I wanted to invite you to the Café for one of our quiet private evenings."

A rare brightness came into the Egyptian's brown eyes. For an instant he revealed himself. "This would be an honor, not to say a pleasure."

"Just one point of information," the dwarf said absently. "Have you a chart of the new canals running off the Rosetta?"

"A chart?" Musa Bey Halaib was instantly official, remote again. He steepled his fingers and paused to reflect. "A chart, you ask? Not really. At least, nothing definite drawn by this ministry. I would not wish to mislead you."

Or give us a numbered map with your ministry's name on it, thought the dwarf, lest one day it prove embarrassing in the wrong hands. He was grateful that the Bey's final sentence had put him on guard.

At that moment Olivio saw a long cigar ash fall onto Lord Penfold's suit. His lordship seemed unaware of the catastrophe as the ash rolled down his magnificent broad lapel, losing mass and breaking in two, leaving dusty grey trails before it fell to the floor. The dwarf detected that the tragedy had also caught the notice of the Undersecretary, who doubtless mistook his lordship's unawareness for grand indifference.

"But in confidence, between gentlemen, I could provide you with early drawings of the new canals from the Ministry of Engineering. You must conceal them like a secret passage to the pharoah's tomb, and destroy them the day they are not required."

The Bey removed a folded paper from his pocket and passed it to the dwarf.

"I hope you will find these sketches trustworthy. But I must warn you, the chamberlain, my cousin Abd al-Azim Pasha, says the palace itself takes an interest in this matter. Naturally, sometimes he speaks for the palace, sometimes for himself."

"Of course." Olivio rose. "Do present my respects to your wife. And my blessings on lovely Yasmin and her fortunate groom for one hundred years of happiness and wealth." The dwarf bowed and smiled before giving the traditional bridal toast of Goa.

"Saúde, amor, dinheiro e tempo para gastolos."

— 11 —

Anton rose and dressed, disappointed that last night's visitor to his cabin had not returned. For a time Harriet had made him carefree. He stepped into the corridor and climbed the companionway to the passenger lounge and promenade deck, thinking he might come across Ernst, who had taken dinner in his cabin.

Not finding the German, Anton took a gin from the night bar, signed a chit and strolled along the starboard rail. He brooded for a moment over Ernst's last words before he'd gone below.

"Remember, *Engländer,*" said his friend, already slightly drunk, "how my papa used to complain about the end of his unspoiled Africa?" The German stopped and nodded slowly to himself before continuing. "Well, if this war's a big one, maybe it'll be the end of our Africa."

Lights shone through the windows of the card room. Anton glanced inside and was surprised to see six men still at cards, some in evening dress. One was Bernadette's fiancé. Charlie looked tired, more than tired. He had his jacket off, his shirt cuffs turned up over his thin arms. He was pouring a whisky while another man dealt.

Anton swished the gin about in his mouth and spat over the side. He watched the dark coast of the Sudan slip past. Here and there lights sparkled from the shore. He was ready for his bunk, but he'd better check on Charlie. He wasn't yet responsible for his clients in the parental way he would be in the bush, when every thorn would be his doing, but already they were in his care. He turned and strolled into the card room.

"Care to join us?" Charles coughed and waved aside a cloud of cigar smoke. Anton noticed his face was sweating. Half-empty bottles of whisky and gin and brandy were scattered on the table.

"Be a pleasure," Anton said. The worst part of being a white hunter was having to please the clients, night and day. At least now he had a little money in his pocket. Putting aside his irritation with her romance, he'd been able to give Gwenn quite a few quid for school fees. "Gambling money?" she had said, knowing him too well. "Cleaner than what you've been using," he'd replied, hating himself as soon as he'd said it. Then he'd given most of the rest to Olivio to invest in the dwarf's new farm scheme. Olivio, nervous for once, had warned him it could be an all-or-nothing roll. But they both knew Anton was used to gambling.

He lit a cigar and sat down. "What's the game?"

"Poker, they tell me," said Dr. Pointer, smiling. The handsome curly-haired South African pulled more cash from his pockets, sterling and dollars, and dropped the banknotes on the table. "Low hand stud, ace low."

The other men introduced themselves without standing: two Belgian bridge engineers en route to Eritrea to help the Italians extend their roads into the interior, an American journalist from the Hearst organization trying to reach Addis Ababa before the war broke, astonished that no one recognized his name, and a Glasgow trader sailing home to Berbera.

"They tell me you're a hunter," said one of the engineers, Maurice, a solid coarse-featured man with a broad nose and a smooth scar under one eye. Anton knew the type: part of the itinerant underworld of roaming specialists who contracted out to country after country. Maurice spoke English easily with a thick off-French accent.

Disliking the skeptical tone of the remark, Anton decided not to treat it as a question. He said nothing.

"We're calling it an even five dollars a pound. No time for money changers," the Belgian continued, looking down at his cards and pushing two quid into the middle of the table with the back of a large hand. "How's the shooting near Asmara?"

"Not bad, but you're better off further up country. Past Adi Quala probably's best. Mountain nyala, bushbuck, good lion." Confident these two would skin him if he let them, Anton took his time checking his cards. Pair of eights. He hesitated, then threw in ten dollars. "Do you hunt?"

Maurice cracked the thick scarred knuckles of his right hand. "Mostly ivory, when we were working in the Congo."

"In Leo they used to call Maurie *Boucher de la Nuit.*" The second Belgian chuckled. "He got most of his ivory dozing in our truck at the waterholes, usually with a drunken black bitch in his lap, waiting to blind the stupid elephants with the headlights before he shot 'em. Pretty good at it. Saved a lot of running about. Do you hunt like that in Kenya?"

"Not without losing your license and getting chucked on a boat." Anton felt himself grow hot. "We call it 'Mozambique style,' Portuguese hunting. I don't shoot elephants, myself."

"Too big for you?" Maurice said without smiling. He cut the deck for the Belgian on his left to deal. There was a slight bend on one edge of the card at the top of the cut.

"That's the second time you've done that, Maurice." Pointer said, his voice shaky. He reddened and tossed his cards on the table. "You're crimping, creasing a card so you can control the cut."

Maurice squinted through the smoke at the South African doctor before he spoke. "If you're not happy, Pointer, we'll settle it outside." Maurice stood and removed his jacket. He spoke to his companion. "Watch my money, Jules. I'll be right back."

Dr. Pointer walked unsteadily to the door. The other players watched through the cabin window as Pointer waited, fists clenched, stretching and setting his slender shoulders, shuffling his feet on the wooden deck. Maurice followed him outside. Without pausing, Maurice crouched and turned swiftly in one motion, hooking, punching Pointer in the stomach with all his body behind the blow. Pointer collapsed against the window.

"Mistake," said Jules without looking outside. "Maurie used to be a middleweight."

Pointer leaned forward, free of the window, rocking slightly. He raised his hands to defend himself. Maurice shook his shoulders, loosening his muscles, then swung and hit Pointer even more forcefully in the same place. As Pointer cried out and doubled over, Maurice spun him around by one arm and slammed his face against the window. Pointer's eyes were closed, his nose bleeding. His body slid down, smearing blood on the glass. Maurice brushed his knuckles across his mouth and spat towards the fallen figure.

"Hold on there!" Charlie jumped up and dashed through the door. Anton hurried after him. Jules followed.

"Stay out of it, boy," Jules ordered Charlie, blocking his path.

Charlie tried to push Jules aside, pressing the flat of one hand against the Belgian's chest and at the same time trying to shoulder past Maurice to Pointer.

"Easy there," said Anton, too late, stepping forward just as Jules and Maurice punched Charlie at the same time. Charlie went down, vomiting on himself and lying still.

The two men looked at Anton. He could see they'd done this before. Slow down, he told himself, one at a time. Not the way Charlie did it.

"No need to carry this too far," said Jules, the bigger of the two. His face was flushed with drink and excitement, but Anton saw he was still in full control.

Jules straightened his bow tie and looked Anton in the eye. "Don't be stupid. Maurie's a professional."

"So was I."

Anton recalled the beatings he'd taken as a young fairground boxer, shilling for the gypsy gamblers, barehanded, fighting any farmboy of his weight, one after another, until finally he met one who could keep him down.

Anton knelt down and wiped Charlie's face with his handkerchief before lifting his client and settling him in a deck chair. Anton pulled back Charlie's lower lip. He examined his mouth carefully. He took a deck blanket from the next chair and covered the groggy American. They hadn't even got to East Africa, and already Anton had broken the first rule of every professional hunter: protect your client. Now, he warned himself, it was probably best just to take Charlie to bed and let the rest of it go. Then he heard laughter behind him.

"You fellows owe my friend two teeth," Anton said over his shoulder. As he straightened he took off his jacket.

"Shall we make it one tooth each," Anton said, pointing first at one man, then the other, "or can one of you chaps spare two?" He handed the jacket to Jules.

Confused, Jules took Anton's coat in both hands.

Anton spun and hit Maurice in the belly with all his force.

Grunting loudly and turning red, Maurice crashed sideways, stumbling into chairs and a small table. He fell heavily, collapsing on his face, then slowly gathered himself onto his hands and knees.

Ignoring Maurice, Anton faced Jules and swung lightly at the Belgian's stomach with his left. The big man dropped the coat and lowered his hands to defend his belly. Anton's right caught him in the mouth.

Jules fell against the railing spitting a broken front tooth. Gasping, he leaned against the rail facing Anton, his mouth open and bloody. A second tooth hung sideways from his upper gum.

Trying to control himself, Anton stepped towards the railing. His right hand was bleeding. He was within an ace of pitching Jules into the Red Sea. He heard Maurice scrambling up behind him.

Anton looked at Jules. "We're not quite finished," he said quickly. He slapped Jules across the face, hard, first with one open hand, then the other. Left, right. The second tooth fell on the deck. Then Anton turned to face Maurice.

The man stood by the door, breathing deeply, fists low at his sides, looking solid and ready but not threatening. He wasn't going to be easy. If it went any further, Anton would hit him across the face with the table. No need to hurt his hands any more.

Only a few feet away, Pointer struggled to his feet. Charlie was still in his chair.

"All square, gentlemen," Anton said calmly. "Good night to you both." He turned and helped Pointer inside. He had learned not to finish everything.

The American journalist, who hadn't left his seat, smiled at them, drink in hand. All the money was stacked in neat piles, probably by the Scotsman, Anton reckoned. He took his and Charlie's, then stepped back on deck and picked up his client in his arms.

"Hope the war'll be this much fun," said the writer, holding the door. "They should've noticed you had a broken nose."

"Why is it, Olivio, that both the heron and the flying boat fly downstream in the morning and upstream in the evening?" Adam Penfold mused, folding yesterday's *Egyptian Gazette* in his lap and struggling to keep his left foot steady against the energetic pressures of the grizzled bootblack.

Penfold wondered if his friend was well. The dwarf seemed flushed, a trifle disarrayed, and there'd been a fearful row belowdecks just before the old boy came up. One of his cheeks looked a bit torn, and his mind seemed elsewhere. Sometimes it wasn't easy conversing with the little man. It was as if they were having different conversations. "What do you think, eh?"

"These are not matters on which I inform myself." Exhausted by the turmoil of his delights in the hold, Olivio now was trying to concentrate on more practical matters: the distribution and rotation of crops on the new farm at Sa al-Hagar, bearing in mind world market considerations, irrigation needs, his Lisbon bankers, feeding the wretched *fellahin,* harvesting schedules, export controls and a reserve for bribery requirements. Not to mention his latest enemy: the pink boll-worm.

Olivio had learned to study his enemies. He now understood how these little creatures worked. No one knew better than he that size did not determine menace.

A single female cotton moth laid two thousand eggs in a night. Once he had waited for the larvae to hatch. Sitting on a fine rush mat under a parasol in the cotton field, holding an ivory-handled magnifying glass to his eye, he had watched this evil fertility yield its fruit within four days.

The morning sun dried off the last of the dew and the small ripe eggs began to warm and bake and burst. An infinity of tiny pink worms wiggled and struggled against each other, finally tearing the filmy elastic sheath that had bound the eggs together. Preferring the shade, the larvae immediately began to feed on the under surface of the leaves. At first, like children, they were gregarious and fed together. But after a day or two they sought their own leaves, dispersing and fastening on his cotton buds. After ten days, swollen and heavy, the larvae fell to ground in the warmth of the day, slithering up later to feed at dusk. In two more weeks the boll-worms built cells in the earth and became pupae, concentrating and storing their vitality, emerging ten days later as moths, ready to fly over his fields and lay another generation of eggs, by the thousands, the millions. Seven times a year. In some of the fields, only bare stalks remained. In others, a few high leaves survived, with an occasional cotton bole left here and there. Did his cotton rivals in Russia, America and India battle such foes? It reminded Olivio of Miss Gwenn's struggles with her farm in Kenya. He heard his lordship wander on.

"Still, seems extraordinary, the more you think about it. Both of 'em, bird and aircraft, even lean back a trifle and advance their legs when they land on the Nile, then tuck in against the bank for the night. Imperial Airway ties up to the float dock there. The heron settles in among the reeds. What do you make of it, eh?"

Penfold set his monocle and squinted down as the bootblack tapped his left shoe. He checked the progress and exchanged it for his right foot. Always lead with your left, his father had taught him.

"I suspect, my lord, that both these creatures are driven by self-interest." It was like speaking to a child, so he might as well make this a useful lesson.

"Self-interest." Olivio raised one forefinger. "The heron, I surmise he is concerned by the reflection of light on the water, and the casting of his own shadow, for he must see his prey, the fish, without their becoming aware of him. The great seaplane, on the other hand, wishes the river to speed it when it ascends, and slow it when it lands." The dwarf wagged his forefinger.

"We must contrive to think as they do, my lord. Self-interest, the iron law of self-interest, that is the point, sir."

"Both take on fuel in the morning," Penfold noted wryly as he dropped a coin into the cupped hands of the bootblack, then another, aware his friend would think he was overdoing it again, but knowing this trifle of largesse meant more to this old Gypie than it did to him. In addition, it made him feel just a bit grand, and, for the moment, not poor.

Olivio followed the small transaction with care. Still overtipping. His lordship would never learn.

The boy packed his rags and brushes and bottles and polishes into an ornate chest of carved wood and copper. He grunted quick thanks and darted up the gangway.

"Poverty, my lord, is the daughter of generosity," Olivio noted as he spread a map on the table between them.

"Speaking of that, I've been thinking about this partnership scheme of yours, Olivio." Penfold finished his tea and picked up the *Gazette.* "Far too generous of you, really."

The dwarf look startled. What nonsense was this?

"Can't have you pitching in all the cash if we're to be true partners, you see." Penfold admired an overloaded *qayyasa* as it glided past the Café. The gunwales of the rivercraft were but inches above the smooth-flowing river.

What was the lord planning, to sell his new suits? This costly grey nail-head was already a mess.

"I'll flog off a few more scraps of Wiltshire. Nothing left in the green-houses, anyway, but rotting weeds the size of sunflowers. The old stables haven't seen a hunter in years. Still, I don't know, my dear wife cables me she insists on keeping a few stalls, just in case."

Perfect place for Sissy Penfold, Olivio thought. Distaste washed through the dwarf like bile. He recalled the hideous indecencies Lady Penfold had required of him before Olivio had become his master's friend.

"Oh," said Penfold, wiping his new monocle on his soiled school tie, "something finally came to me whilst I was tossing about last night. Those flowers, you know. Never liked to wear carnations, meself. Belong in a dentist's office, really."

"What's that, my lord?"

"Remembered where I'd seen that Musa Bey of yours before we called at his office, the Undersecretary. He was out at Ali Baba's the night young Anton and I had some fun and those chaps robbed me."

The dwarf stiffened in his seat, his senses heightened. Did he smell a scoundrel?

"He was playing bezique or some such with Anton. Bit too clever with the cards, I understand. In league with some Frenchie. Wearing a red carna-tion. Same chap, dead sure. Would've come to me sooner if I hadn't been so knocked about that night."

"No doubt, my lord, no doubt." Olivio craned forward and almost patted Penfold's arm. "Musa Bey Halaib, was it? How very interesting."

"I must say, by the way, seems a bit bad form of us to pinch a government map, don't you think?"

"The government itself gave us this map." The dwarf shrugged, feeling a rush of pain from the small movement. Was this the moment to talk to his lordship about life itself: their investment in the Delta? Things were getting complicated, and more costly. Their rivals were beginning to disclose their hand. It would mean ruin or riches.

"Still, hardly the way to learn where to buy one's land."

"The map didn't teach us where to buy land. It showed us where not to buy." Olivio pointed at the line of the proposed canal indicated on the chart. "The map was prepared to mislead us, to waste our substance, to induce us to buy what others wish us to buy. By no accident was it waiting in the Undersecretary's pocket."

"How do you know?" Penfold said, his watery eyes wide and innocent as a baby's with astonishment.

"This map tells us the new farm we visited will always be a desert. Why then would they send a busload of Special Police to seize it?" He knew his lordship would not answer.

"You see," the dwarf continued, "they were trying to warn us off, sir, to deter us from increasing our estates. The devils are trying everything. First, violence. Now, deceit. What is an honest man to do?"

"Looks like things're hotting up down south," said Penfold, wandering again, not wishing to continue with this tiresome subject. He wiped his monocle and mumbled the headlines to Olivio, an old habit he had revived when he came by the Café each morning. "ETHIOPIAN WAR INEVITABLE. ITALY PRESENTS IMPOSSIBLE DEMANDS. WANTS RAILWAY AND ITALIAN ADVISERS. ABYSSINIAN EMPEROR REFUSES. Dear, dear."

"Yes, my lord," the dwarf said patiently. He feared his friend was more and more out of touch, part of a gracious world that was slipping away, that would be gone like a candle burning down. "Yes, indeed." Olivio nodded.

"And Abyssinia's just the beginning. The Fritzes'll be even worse than these Eyeties. Always are. Down in Tanganyika, what we used to call German East Africa, those old bush Huns, planters and what not, are getting lustier every day. Holding rallies in Arusha. Running up new flags. All sorts of mischief. Damned if they don't want the whole place back, sisal and all, mind you. They forget who lost the Kaiser's War. Seem to be getting switched on by that little screaming chap with the black mustache back home."

"As a dead Frenchman said, my lord, in times like these, we must cultivate our own garden." The dwarf rose to attend to some details of his establishment. "Excuse me."

"Not at all." Penfold sighed and squinted at the *Gazette.* His tea was cold. There was so much going on: inventions, the Depression, war, the cinema. Thank God he wasn't a young man and had to do something about it all.

So far Cairo was quite an agreeable escape. Sissy was in England, though sometimes it seemed he could still hear her voice, shrill and clear as a jay with a broken wing. "It's time I thought about myself for a change," he heard her say, usually after some moment of exquisitely selfish behavior. The dunning notices from the Nairobi bankers still had not caught up with him. But at night he would lie awake in his splendid room at Olivio's villa and fret about his failures. He prayed Olivio's speculation would see them all through. Even if you trimmed all the corners, holding things together was expensive, though for him it was just a matter of staggering along. For Anton, he knew, it was a deal more serious, what with Gwenn and the boys still in play. But the lad had a chance. At least he was the very best at what he did.

"Good news, godfather?" said Clove, kissing his cheek, at his side with a fresh pot of Lapsang and a plate of *petits fours.* She was aware how he enjoyed this morning ritual.

"Scarcely, my dear," he said, smiling on her and picking up another edition of the *Gazette.* "Just look at this, will you: HITLER ADDRESSES 500,000 PEASANTS AT HARVEST FESTIVAL. A Hun's idea of a romantic picnic, no doubt. KEY WEST HURRICANE BLOWS TRAIN INTO SEA. MUSSOLINI DENIES THREAT TO NILE AFTER INVASION OF ABYSSINIA. There's no end to it all. HUEY LONG SHOT. FIFTY ITALIAN SUBS IN RED SEA TO BLOCK JAP SUPPLIES TO ETHIOPIA." Shaking his head, Penfold took one of the small frosted cakes in his fingers.

"My goodness," said Clove with concern.

"Here's a nice one. FRENCH TANKS FOR ITALIAN ARMY. RENAULT TO DELIVER 325. Just what one would expect. Can't turn one's back on those Wogs for an instant."

The *petit fours* carried the faint taste of apricots. Penfold sucked his fingertips and sighed, knowing no one really cared what he said, but glad Clove was listening. "The wretched League better sort out this Ethiopian mess. If it doesn't, the whole last war will've been for naught and we'll have another one before you know it. Mark my words, child. This old world of ours will never be the same."

"May I ask you a question, godfather?" Clove said, a trace of the coquette in her movement as she shifted her position in the chair.

"Of course, my dear," Penfold said gently, noticing how very unlike a child she now appeared.

"You know Wellie, don't you? Wellington, Mrs. Rider's boy?"

"Indeed I do. He, too, is my godchild."

"What do you think he's like?"

"Fine young lad, should've thought. Known 'im since he was a nipper."

"Do you think he's too young for me?"

"Well," said Penfold awkwardly, groping for another cake, sad that he himself was too old. "These things are hard to say, you see, Clove. Not really sort of thing I'm good at. Might be best to ask your father." He nodded eagerly, relieved at the thought. "That'd be the thing, really. He understands all that sort of business."

— 12 —

"Do you think women do it more than men?" Harriet removed her eyeglasses and looked up from her book. Biting her fleshy lower lip, she frowned, so intent on her question that she ignored the busy scene in the harbor of Massawa.

"Do what?" Bernadette raised an eyebrow. "Harry only thinks about one thing," she said to no one in particular. "Do what, Harry?"

Anton began to pay attention. He sat between the twins on the fan deck of the *Otranto,* sweating under the tan canvas awning that stretched from port to starboard, drinking Pimm's with his clients. Harriet had been reading *The Development of Personality,* underlining passages and, he could see, writing quarrelsome notes in the margins.

"What Jung says, Berny, I told you. Projection, transferring to the object of our affections the fantasy of our idealized romantic mate, what he calls here the *anima.* That's why you start out madly in love. Soon we're disappointed, of course, and try to change the other person to make him fit our idea." Harriet paused, annoyed to see Bernadette rolling her eyes at Anton, as if her sister were mad.

"Pay attention, Berny. Then we feel destroyed when it breaks up, as if we've lost our emotional core, when all we've really lost is the useless dummy we've been mixed up with. Don't you see? It's perfect. It's always like that. He's right."

"What could Carl Jung know about love? He was Swiss." Bernadette spoke with certitude. "But of course they do it more, men. That's why all they want is the outside. All the rest of us is in their heads, they make it up, until we teach them what a mistake they've made, that we're not the way we look."

Dear God, Anton thought, were American women all the same? All this fierce chatter, as if they were always on the verge of some private war.

"But Charlie understands us, don't you Charlie?" Bernadette poked Charlie's shoulder. Silent, Charles sat with his back to her, his shirt dark and wet in the fetid heat, sharpening a pencil with a penknife as he studied the frenzied port set against the flat barren coastline of Eritrea. His sketchbook was clipped to the bandleader's music stand he employed as a portable easel. Three-legged, wonderfully light and stable, it would be perfect in the field.

"The town looks so exciting!" Bernadette said. "All those lovely Italian soldiers! We'd better go ashore. Remember how we learned a little Italian in Florence, Harry?" She raised one eyebrow at her sister. "It's the only way to learn, really."

"You'll have to behave yourself here, Berny," Harriet said as if she meant it.

"Engländer!" Ernst called, beckoning to Anton from the head of the sloping gangway that led to the motor launch. Tired of Jung, Anton rose and joined him.

"Massawa's worse than the Vatican." Ernst gestured with both hands towards the shore. "Crawling with Italians. *Katzlmachere* everywhere. Did you notice all the ships standing off the harbor waiting to unload?"

"I counted forty, most with home ports like Naples, two thousand miles away or more," said Anton thoughtfully. "The captain says those ships from Calcutta and Jakarta are full of cotton for uniforms and fodder for mules and tobacco for the men." He looked over the side at the smaller Italian seagoing vessels moored to one side of the main dock, stern first to conserve space.

"What did I tell you?" said the German bitterly, shaking his head. "The day's over for old dogs like us, Rider." He took Anton's last cigarette. "Our Africa's finished."

"Not quite," said Anton to the older man. "There's still time for a few more safaris."

Ernst watched the deckhands load his baggage into the launch. "There's more white men right here than you and I've seen in all our years in Africa. And it won't be long before this thing starts." The German's look hardened. "I've got to pick up my empty chests and truck, then Gretel and I are off this afternoon to start hunting up my silver coins." He gave Anton a jarring clap on the shoulder. "You know the way I'll be running."

"You won't see us," said Anton, declining the offer for a final time, "but if things get nasty, the Rift lakes'll be your best way out."

"Something else," said Ernst, lowering his voice. "Are they rich?"

"Who?"

"The twins, idiot. Most American women have too much money."

Anton tried never to talk about his clients. "Not sure who's got it, but Charlie paid me for the safari. Back in Cairo, thank God."

"I think these girls're rich," Ernst said. "Otherwise they'd have to be nicer."

"Maybe," said Anton, trying to see where the German was leading. "But being a beautiful woman is like being a millionaire. You can always get someone to do what you want."

"For a time, anyway," Ernst concluded, flicking his butt into the sea. He pressed his hand on Anton's shoulder. "We'll meet you at Toselli's for a quick drink before we leave." Ignoring the steward who hovered nearby for his tip, Ernst and Gretel joined the queue for the small boat.

Except for the two Belgian engineers, the Massawa passengers paused and waved cheerful good-byes as they stepped down the gangway and climbed into the launch. On the deck behind them booms swung out from the masts and lowered nets of cargo onto the decks of waiting lighters.

Left on his own, Anton wiped his old field glasses and raised them to study the busy port.

A hundred yards inshore, the stone quays were a chaos of struggling shiny black navvies stripped to the waist, white-robed Arab merchants and turbanned seamen, Italian soldiers and sailors, transport lorries, mules and camels. Behind it all stood two immense three-story stone buildings facing the waterfront, each with broad terraces running the entire length of every floor, crowned with elaborate curving ironwork facades. The ground-floor terraces formed a busy streetside arcade, crowded with men and women carrying umbrellas and parasols against the pressing heat of the sun. The structures were fitting centers for Italian commerce and industry: substantial and practical, if not elegant. The sandy grey of the local stone blended with the mountains that rose behind them in the heat haze. Patriotic flags hung limply in the thick humid air from the railings of each building.

The largest wharf was entirely covered with several hundred new Chevrolet trucks parked wheel to wheel. Italian mechanics were connecting batteries and topping up oil. Barefoot black boys squeezed in and out, drawing finger designs in the thick dust that covered every vehicle. A squadron of fifteen Fiat light tanks waited on wooden pallets, toy-like with their low silhouettes and boxy cabins. Gunners clambered over the tanks, checking their pairs of linked machine guns. Sentries stood guard over piles of war materiel while bands of black urchins stared at their weapons and waited for a moment of inattention to steal past.

At the other side of the harbor, crowds of Italian peasants, perhaps a thousand or more, lounged on packs and bundles, or leaned on pick-axes and long-handled shovels smoking and talking. Anton had read in the Cairo papers that these men, unemployed at home and sent to Africa on time contracts, were being organized into labor companies for road gangs, with men from the same village kept together for morale. Now he saw *squadristi* moving slowly among them, wiping their sweating necks with black bandanas. Bawling orders and pointing, the Fascist leaders seemed to be directing the men to a column of dusty trucks.

Through the din of the port, Anton heard the tired drums and cymbals of a Blackshirt band welcoming thousands of their countrymen ashore from the transport *Conte Biancamano.* The men were loading directly into lorries for the climb to the healthier climate of Asmara, fifty miles distant on a new stone road, eight thousand feet up on the Eritrean plateau and just thirty miles from the Abyssinian border, and thirty more from the old battlefield of Adowa.

Overwhelmed by the artistic opportunities before him, Charlie flipped another page on his pad and began sketching the *Biancamano.*

Along her entire length, the sides of the three upper decks of the old passenger liner were plastered with posters of Benito Mussolino's head in profile, each ten times life-size, bearing the basin-like field helmet and wide chin strap of the modern Italian army. Anchored nearby were three water tankers, one converted to an ice-maker, and the gleaming-white hospital ships *Urania* and *California.*

For the first time Anton felt war was truly at hand. He was astonished by the scale of the Italian preparations. In Cairo the war talk had been just another distant daily topic, like county cricket or the London shares market. Regimental football and polo at the Gezira Club were far more urgent. No one took the Italians seriously, except his wife, he remembered. Laughing British officers, veterans of the Great War, said the Eyeties were more dangerous as allies than enemies. But they hadn't seen Massawa.

He set down the binoculars. If his clients were to spend their safari in Abyssinia, they'd better hurry.

Anton watched the *Otranto*'s launch tie up at the stone quay of the customs office. The two Belgians spoke to a white-uniformed port officer and then walked to a waterfront hotel.

"Hope we've seen the last of that lot," Anton said to Charlie, alluding to the night of cards but not getting his client's attention. Anton's eyes followed the two engineers until they were out of sight.

The launch wove its way back across the oily water past the floating docks and between the ocean-going dhows and tall-funnelled tugboats, hordes of small craft and a few rusty coastal freighters, their open decks piled with wooden barrels and canvas sacks.

"Care to go ashore, gentlemen, ladies?" The deck steward wiped his forehead. "Launch is ready. We'll be sailing for Djibouti and Berbera at midnight."

"Good idea!" Bernadette gently kissed Charles's swollen mouth, proud of him for the poker fight. "While Charlie goes to the dentist, we can do some shopping."

"Is it this hot in Djibouti?" Harriet asked the steward. Her short red hair was curling wildly in the humidity.

"In Djibouti, ma'am, the Frenchies pray for cool days like this. Even the mosquitoes can't take it down there."

Harriet frowned sulkily and wiped her brow with a napkin.

Charles packed his drawing materials and they walked to the gangway. Harriet waited her turn at the rail. Anton admired the way the twins looked in their long pleated khaki skirts, entirely appropriate yet saucy in a fresh schoolgirl sort of way. Last in line, he moved close behind Harriet at the top of the steps. His lower body touched her perfect tight buttocks. That was one thing she was right about. They were her best feature. He felt her warmth and held himself against her. She did not move away. He spoke quietly.

"Do you always throw your champagne glass into the sea before you get underway?" he asked.

Harriet turned around sharply. "Pardon me?"

"Do you always toss your champagne glass into the sea before . . ."

"What are you talking about?" Harriet said with indignation, stepping onto the gangway. She paused and turned to look him in the eye. "You must have the wrong girl, Mr. Rider."

Anton blushed. Dear God, it must have been Bernadette, pretending she was Harriet. Instead of looking after his client, in two days Anton had seen Charles beaten and cuckolded. He looked at her closely, but now he wasn't sure. Perhaps it had been Harriet after all, and now she was just playing with him, trying to make him embarrass himself with Bernadette?

"Hurry up, you two," called Bernadette from the launch. "And please do try not to throw yourselves in the water."

They stepped ashore and a port official checked their passports. The man accepted a tip and arranged for Charles to visit the Italian military dentist on the *California.* Charles returned to the launch, waving at the twins as the small craft headed for the hospital ship.

Anton was pleased, already feeling more at home than he had been in Cairo. He and the girls paused before a bronze monument to the Italians who had fallen fighting the Abyssinians near Massawa in 1885. Wilting flowers and Fascist garlands covered its stone base. While the twins struggled to translate the Italian inscriptions, Anton studied a group of Eritrean *askaris* loitering nearby. Harriet came over and took his arm.

"Italian colonial infantry," Anton said, admiring the African soldiers. Tall and dark, flat-bellied and slender-legged, barefoot, they wore green sashes above their baggy khaki trousers and puttees.

"Ooo," Harriet said, "aren't they lovely. I'd adore one of those cummerbunds, and look at the beautiful fat tassels swinging from those red fezzes."

"These chaps remind me of Kenya's King's African Rifles," Anton said. "Good soldiers, I'd wager, fraternal and undemanding and enduring." If these troops were well led, and as loyal to Italy as the K.A.R. were to England, men like these could give the Italians the edge they'd need in Ethiopia. "And they're traditional enemies of the Abyssinians," he added.

He thought of the dwarf and smiled.

"There is no pay, no reward," Olivio had said to him years ago, wagging a forefinger, "more precious than the opportunity to settle old scores. Revenge is our most enduring emotion." And it was true. There always seemed to be some Africans eager to fight alongside whatever Europeans were battling other Africans.

The twins took Anton's arms on either side. They entered a narrow sandy street and set out for the native market. The air was thick with hot dust. They walked through a wall of humidity and heat. A cart loaded with bales of Italian flags trundled past them. At the second corner they passed a whitewashed Banco D'Italia and a mosque with a tall minaret, slender and white as a cigarette. A line of Italian officers lounged at the bank's door, chatting as they waited to get inside, some with the cocked and feathered mountain hats of the *Bersaglieri,* others with the insignia and field caps of the Blackshirts. Several men turned and stared at the twins.

"Ciao, bellezze!" one young officer called after them, bowing deeply and touching his hat. He made a loud wet kissing sound with his lips. Bernadette turned her head with a haughty expression. The men cheered and laughed. *"Ma quanto siete bone voi due!"*

"Are you going to let them insult us like that?" said Harriet with pouted lips.

"How do you know it's an insult?" Bernadette inquired sweetly.

"Do you want me to fight the whole Italian army?" Anton said. Harriet probably did.

Two hours later, they returned to the waterfront, grimy and thirsty as camels. Anton was annoyed to be carrying a large woven basket laden with the twins' purchases: head scarves and riding whips, daggers and native jewelry. They found Ernst and Gretel waiting for them at a table at the harborside café of the Hotel Toselli. Anton noticed how Ernst, stretched out, more relaxed than he had been on board, already had the look of an old hand ashore, comfortable with the dust and heat, his boots and grey shorts and sweaty shirt just right for all that lay ahead.

There were two other European women on the canopied terrace. Middle-aged Italian nurses, plain as turnips but courted by a dozen uniformed men, the women assessed Bernadette and Harriet with curious ungenerous eyes.

"Your Belgian mates are sitting over there," Ernst said to Anton. "Drinking with the enemy. Probably telling 'em what a dangerous swine you are."

Anton tried not to turn and look, but was aware of the Belgians sitting with several Italian officers at the far end of the café. Jules stood and left the table when he noticed Anton's party.

Anton ordered bottles of Italian mineral water and cold Verdicchio. He was keen to have a few moments on his own. Once the safari was underway, he would never be off duty.

"Excuse me for a bit," he said, rising. "I'm going back to that bank and get a little useful currency." He stepped off quickly before anyone could offer to join him.

Strolling back with a pocketful of Maria Theresa silver thalers, he entered an alley to take a shortcut to the hotel.

With a hunter's instinct, Anton sensed something behind him. He turned sharply and looked back. Three men were hurrying after him, apparently Italians, stevedores or laborers, thickset sturdy dark-faced men. One held an axe handle. The biggest carried a boat hook.

He would have to deal with them, he realized, but not where it would make a stir in port. His clients would not be reassured by a third brawl, and the Italian authorities might detain them ashore if there were trouble.

Passing the rear wall of the mosque, Anton found a narrow open door. He entered and removed his desert boots. He found himself in an open-roofed chamber to the rear of the columned prayer hall. Behind him the Italians hesitated, arguing in the doorway.

Anton walked slowly along one wall of the prayer hall, carrying his boots, his head bowed respectfully. Rows of silent white-robed Muslims sat cross-legged on prayer rugs. Anton paused and touched his brow with one hand, enjoying for a moment the refreshing coolness of the shaded room.

Under the open front archway of the mosque, nine or ten Muslims were slipping on their sandals, preparing to leave. Anton spoke to them in Swahili and passed several coins to the man who best understood.

"One silver thaler," he said, holding up the handsome coin and turning it in the sun, "to the man who brings me that Italian's boat hook. You'll find me at Toselli's."

Anton stepped out into the heat, feeling exhilarated by the chase, his senses heightened, as if he were stalking in the bush. Two of the stevedores were hurrying around the corner of the mosque.

"After them!" cried the man Anton had paid. Drawing daggers, the gang of Muslims made for the Italians. As Anton turned to walk back to the café, he heard oaths and the clamor of violence rising behind him.

"Good God! It's a hundred and eighteen here in the shade," Bernadette said as Anton returned. Charles had joined them at the café. Anton glanced at the thermometer mounted on the wall beside a bronze plaque to the hotel's namesake, Major Toselli.

"Who was Toselli?" said Harriet.

"The commander of several thousand Italians who were overwhelmed and butchered by the Abyssinians, in 1895, I think it was," said Anton as the twins drank thirstily. "Up in the mountains somewhere."

"Were the Italian nurses sweet to you, Charlie?" asked Bernadette.

"The nurses were most obliging," Charlie said dryly, unfolding a sheet of paper from his pocket and starting to sketch a harbor scene. "You know how I hate pain, Berny. While the dentist worked away, two Italian beauties held me down to make sure I didn't wiggle."

"Can I do that after we're married?" Bernadette said with big eyes, her mouth open and inviting.

"Meanwhile," said Charlie, already preoccupied with his work, "one of the damn orderlies confiscated my sketchpad."

"Who'd want those old sketches?" asked Harriet, drawing a sharp look from her sister.

"They said the carabinieri would call my harbor drawings espionage and lock us all up," Charlie said, licking his front teeth. "Here, take a look." He pulled back his lower lip and held his head sideways towards the girls, mumbling as he spoke.

"The doc picked two teeth out of a huge cabinet, bonded 'em together and popped them in." He opened his mouth wide. "Worst of it was all these little drawers full of teeth, all colors and sizes, yellow and brown, like a tackle chest stuffed with fishing flies. Hate to think where they came from. Just hope mine'll stay put till we get home."

"My poor Charlie." Bernadette placed one hand on his cheek and stared at the new teeth. "They're a bit long. Must've come from a rabbit stew."

"What was the boat like?" Anton said. "The *California*."

"Converted passenger ship," Charles said. "They're sure getting ready for a party. Seven hundred beds. Bacteriological labs, saloons turned into operating theatres, air-conditioned wards where the holds used to be, most of them already full."

"Full?" Harriet said. "They haven't even started fighting."

Charlie nodded. "Malaria. Some of 'em looked half dead. Thin and amber yellow, with their eyes dripping goo. What a smell. Hope we don't catch it. Mustn't forget our quinine."

"What on earth does that silly man want?" Bernadette interrupted. "The one with the torn robe." She pointed at an Arab standing at the edge of the terrace. "Looks like he's trying to get our attention. His forehead's bleeding and he's waving that big hook at us."

Anton stood up and reached into his pocket.

The Arab came over and presented the long pole to Anton. *"Effendi,"* he said, bowing his head. The tip of the hook was wet and shiny. Anton was aware of the Belgians watching him from their table as he gave the man a coin and shook his hand.

"Asanti, sana." Anton, smiling, turned and handed the pole to Ernst. "You'll probably be needing something like this."

Ernst rose to say good-bye. "By the way," he said to Anton, "those native troops looked better than their officers. I wouldn't want them chasing me in the mountains."

"Good luck," Anton said, worried about his own safari. He noticed Gretel watching calmly, her chin high, as Harriet gave Ernst a long hug and a kiss on the lips.

Astonished by their embrace, Anton considered whether he had missed something on the boat.

"Charlie," Anton said after Gretel and Ernst had left, "there's something I must ask you all one more time. It's going to get messy in Abyssinia. Why don't we do the safari in Somaliland, British Somaliland for preference? Get off the boat at Berbera. There's fine lion and beautiful people and villages and hump-shouldered cattle to draw. You'd love it." He saw both twins waiting for Charlie to reply. It's his money, Anton thought.

"Nope. It'll be fine," said Charles, shaking his head without looking up. "There's nowhere like Ethiopia, and we'll be way out in the country sketching Coptic churches and old monasteries." He drew in another giant portrait of Mussolini.

"And shooting," added Harriet.

"They've been squabbling here for years," said Bernadette dismissively, a spoiled tone in her voice, "and there hasn't been a war. The League of Nations wouldn't stand for it."

"Well," said Anton with resignation, "it's your safari. Luckily it's a big country, 'bout ten times the size of England. There should be room for everyone to get lost, perhaps even this Italian army."

"It's time I did something useful. Don't quite know what, but perhaps I should be moving on," Adam Penfold muttered to his friend. "Chap grows stale lounging about like Cleopatra."

"But I need your help here in Cairo, my lordship. I need your influence." Olivio watched his partner dust cigar ash from the perfect peaked lapel of the new sharkskin suit. One tiny spark still glowed among the grey ashes. This handsome garment would never be the same. He must try to explain what mattered.

"Aware now of your lordship's participation, and of your acquaintance with the High Commissioner, the ministries are respecting my claims and applicaions." The dwarf sniffed the cool river air and leaned forward with his palms extended.

"Their hands are open to our friendship, and to other things, of course. Soon the crisis will be upon us! Next week the new irrigation scheme may be confirmed. Already unknown buyers seek to force the sale of our new estates. They covet our share of Egypt's future. Even our cotton worms are not safe in their eggs!"

"What seems to be the matter?" Penfold said absently, keen to broaden his friend's interest in the world. He returned his eyes to the *Gazette.*

"Look at this, will you. GERMANY TO REQUIRE CERTIFICATES OF MARRIAGE WORTHINESS. HESS SIGNS BILL. SEXUAL HISTORY MUST BE DISCLOSED. HAS THE CANDIDATE ANY NON-GERMAN BLOOD? Hmm. Should've asked my dear Sissy to satisfy something like that. ITALY SENDS CRACK UNITS OFF TO ERITREA. LANCERS OF SAVOY LED BY ROMAN ARISTOCRACY. That should bring 'em to their knees, or worse. Seems this Abyssinian business is getting messier. Border incidents. Italians threatening on two fronts. League dithering." Penfold looked up, his eyes large and pale blue, staring as he opened them wide to let his monocle drop. "What's to be done?"

Burdened by respect, praying his lordship would weary of this distracting nonsense, the dwarf restrained himself from responding.

"Time for a drink, old boy," Penfold said, pausing. "Any chance of a Stella?"

Olivio tapped his foot twice on the deck and a *suffragi* shuffled over and took the order with a bow. The little man watched his friend indicate a photograph in the *Gazette* with his monocle.

"Only look at this poppycock, will you," Penfold continued with rare energy in his voice. "Seems this Mussolino fellow has installed huge marble maps on the new Avenue of Empire in Rome. Here he is, posing against a map showing Trajan's empire stretching from Britain clear to Asia Minor and Egypt."

That sounds a little more serious, Olivio thought. With difficulty he moved forward in his seat to observe the photograph. It was true. Wearing a new steel helmet, Mussolini appeared by the map of ancient empire, chin jutting forward, eyes possessed. Statues of the Caesars were arrayed behind him, waiting to march.

His homage rendered, the dwarf returned at last to business.

"My lord, my lord! While we sleep and chatter, evil is hunting us like bats in the night. Our enemies scheme to claim our land. Others connive to change the course of the canals. The devils are busy, bribing, stealing, corrupting. They whisper we are not Egyptians, not entitled to the newly irrigated lands! Who are these people?" The dwarf spread his fingers and stared at his friend in outrage.

"This Farûq himself is only Albanian. Albanian! Most of these people are really Turks. My young daughters were born on the River Nile. Our application is in their name. Are my Clove and Cinnamon and Cayenne less Egyptian than Nefertiti?"

Olivio's shoulders pained him as he extended his short arms to both sides. "Our little desert could become a garden. Sand and scorpions will be replaced by the blossoms of cotton and mountains of mangoes! But I require the appearance of your lordship's influence." A tear glistened in Olivio's eye. "Please." It was a word he rarely employed.

"Money isn't everything, old boy."

Olivio looked at his friend as if he had slapped the dwarf across the face. The baron had learned nothing. A world war, global Depression, personal ruin had passed through him like a bowl of spiced beans. In England his estates were all but gone. In Kenya, his farm had returned to virgin bush. His hotel lay empty and rotting, only the red termites still boldly at work. Even in good times the guests never paid their bills. In the old days, when he himself had presided as barman and major domo at the White Rhino, it was Olivio's fierce vigilance that had deferred bankruptcy and kept the hyenas at bay. Today he must find a way to induce this Englishman to do what was required.

Olivio knew he could never change Lord Penfold's attitude, but he might modify his conduct. If not an appeal to self-interest, perhaps a call to duty; a remarkable inversion.

"We have an obligation to Mr. Anton," the dwarf said with weight. He knew Lord Penfold cared for Anton like the son he had not had. "Every penny he owns, and those he does not, are invested in our care. He has trusted us, you and me, with his life. If we fail, our friend is destroyed." He saw Lord Penfold's brow begin to crinkle.

"Mr. Anton is not a practical man. We must do for him what he cannot do for himself." The dwarf understood too well. Anton always considered himself an outsider, but with money that might not matter.

"Dear, oh dear," the Englishman said quietly, understanding fully how his little friend was using him. "Well, if anything should ever happen to me, do see that my share of this investment nonsense passes along to Rider, won't you?"

"Of course." How could such a man still miss the point? The dwarf tried again. "But if we help Mr. Anton prosper now, so much will follow. Then he can rebuild Cairn Farm for Miss Gwenn. His love will return to him. His sons will be his. Without them his heart is dead."

"I thought he looked rather well. Seemed busy enough with those twin girls from the States, though I must say he was a bit fraught at your birthday."

"A man has only one heart, my lord." Englishmen never understood romance.

— 13 —

"Is she dry, Paolo?" Enzo Grimaldi asked his personal mechanic and batman, keen to be up before full sunrise lit Eritrea. His long flight coat hung open, the tall collar raised. Lined in Libyan sheepskin, the coat was an old friend that brought him luck. The brown leather was dry and cracked like the cheeks of an old Calabrian peasant. Enzo's sidearm, regularly cleaned and checked by the faithful Paolo, hung on its belt over his left shoulder.

"One hour, Colonel, just a little sun," advised Paolo firmly, coughing before he spoke. A veteran of the Great War, Paolo had been gassed on the Austrian front as a boy of seventeen.

Wrapped heavily against the dawn chill, the white-haired mechanic held his head beside the Fiat CR-20 and sniffed the paint. For a week the colonel had kept him experimenting with various paints to adapt the spirited aircraft to the colors of East Africa. Now the engine cowling was painted a silver-grey and the fuselage and wings a pale brown with two green stripes near the tail. The tail itself had three vertical bars of green and white and red, the white stripe brightened by the crossed red shield and golden crown of King Victor Emmanuel. Centered on the fuselage was the rondel of Fascist Italy, a bundle of rods with a projecting axe blade, the fasces, the emblem of authority in ancient Rome.

Grimaldi touched the front edge of the lower wing. He felt only the faintest tackiness. No paint adhered to his fingers. Satisfied, he buttoned his coat and belted the Beretta over it. Enzo enjoyed the balance and smooth action of the 9mm short-round service automatic, fresh from Pietro Beretta's plant in Gardone, one of the new weapons commissioned by the Duce for the campaigns that lay ahead. The short barrel barely projected past the slide, making it more compact than Germany's long-barrelled Lugers and more elegant than the American .45's.

"Fire her up, Paolo."

Enzo grasped a strut, rested his left boot on the footplate and swung his right leg over the edge of the cockpit as if mounting a horse. It was a moment that always made him feel young and excited, rather like a cavalier setting out from his castle.

Paolo drove the charger truck up to the nose of the airplane and connected the starting shaft of the truck to the propeller hub of the twelve-cylinder engine. Then Enzo switched on the magnetos and Paolo turned on the truck engine to engage the starter shaft and turn the propeller. The Fiat stuttered and caught with a kick. Flames flared from the exhausts and the aircraft shook. Impatiently, though he knew better, Enzo revved a bit fast.

Paolo shook his head without looking up. Enzo smiled and eased up. He studied a map and sipped coffee from his flask while the engine warmed to a steady throaty roar. He listened to its changing tone as he would to a newly tuned piano.

He loved even the smells: the bitter coffee, the plume of exhaust, and the sharp morning air of Africa. It would be a cold flight in the open cockpit after he left the Nefasit aerodrome. He pulled the leather flight cap down over his ears, wiped his goggles on his scarf and drew on his gloves. Beneath him, Paolo circled the plane once more, checking the wheels and the tension on the struts, wiggling the ailerons with both hands.

This would be the colonel's first flight over Abyssinia. He glanced down fondly at Paolo. He always felt that the old man was aloft with him. The mechanic had been with Enzo since his first flight over Libya in '31.

Enzo increased the revs. Instead of shaking unsteadily, the aircraft now trembled evenly as it strained against the chocks and brake pedals like a young thoroughbred at the gate.

Paolo removed the chocks from the wheels. Grimaldi crossed himself and taxied downwind past the double line of crude open hangars, the smaller ones with rush sides and thatched roofs, the best of them with wooden walls and corrugated tin roofs. Eighteen giant Capronis waited like knights' chargers in their stalls. Nearly thirteen feet high, with a wingspan of sixty-five feet, each could carry over a thousand pounds of bombs.

The day before, in the presence of a gathering of Eritrean notables, all the Capronis had been rolled out to have their engines tested. The Eritreans, respecting position more than accomplishment, were more excited to meet the sons of Benito Mussolini than to meet the veteran officers. They were astonished to find the Mussolinis and Ciano standing in line with their fellow pilots of the *Disperata* squadron.

Each flight crew stood at attention beneath the nose of their aircraft, raising their right fists and stamping in the Fascist salute as the deputation passed. One by one the mechanics fired up each plane's three nine-cylinder Alfa Romeo engines, each capable of two hundred and seventy horsepower. Fifty-three engines shook the ground as the aircraft strained against their chocks, overwhelming the visitors with dust and thunder.

Foreigners sometimes ridiculed the Italian air force, but Colonel Grimaldi was proud the *Regia Aeronautica* had pioneered heavy bombers. The new Caproni six-engine bomber was the largest land-plane in the world. In the next Abyssinian war, he was confident, Italy would recover what she had lost in the last.

Past the hangars Enzo saw two sentries, Italians, pacing along the wall of the low cement building that housed the canisters. Their job was too important to be trusted to Africans. If the British did decide to close the Canal, stranding the Italian army without fuel, poison gas could be the savior.

Grimaldi made a turn at the end of the hard dirt strip and faced down the length of the runway with the wind in his face. He revved the engine and raced down the airstrip. Paolo waved as the colonel pulled back the stick. The elevators angled and the fighter left the earth.

He felt free and excited. His favorite time was just before the end of the first climb, with the engine stretching and the sense of exhilaration still fresh before he settled into the flight and began to think of other things.

The air grew thin and cold. Enzo levelled off at eight thousand feet. The Nefasit aerodrome was lost in the glowing orange arc of the rising sun behind him. He saw the dark ridge of the western horizon retreating over the rim of the earth. Enzo banked thirty degrees to the southwest, making for the Eritrean-Abyssinian border at about a hundred and thirty miles an hour.

It was the best time for reconnaissance. The light was perfect, before the haze gathered. His adversaries would be asleep in their camps. Anyone hearing his engine and looking towards his flight line would be blinded by the rising sun. He was aware that the Abyssinians possessed a small air corps of diverse craft flown by a motley band of international adventurers, mostly Swedes and Belgians, but including one American Negro and several exotic aristocrats. From a technical standpoint, he was interested to see how they would perform, particularly if flying Fokkers or the Bleriot-Spad 51, but today he did not anticipate being tested.

The land beneath him grew higher and harder as he flew over what he thought must be the frontier and the Abyssinian province of Tigre. Ascending plateaus, each higher and rockier than the last, led on to the west past occasional villages, clusters of round thatched huts with pointed roofs and small herds of animals enclosed by rough walls of rocks and thorn branches.

He searched for the chain of steep ravines that would guide him to Adowa. He found a deep gorge, as yet untouched by sunlight, and dropped down between its lips. Air currents gusted and buffeted the Fiat CR-20 as he tried to maintain the height of the ridge lines on his wings.

The plane handled well. He thought of the old gentleman who had designed this aircraft, and given it his initials, Celestino Rosatelli. When Enzo was a cadet, Signor Rosatelli had visited flight school, flying in himself in an earlier model, the CR-1.

"You are living the dreams of da Vinci," Rosatelli told the young pilots, his forefinger raised high and shaking with emphasis, his thick white eyebrows flaring like wings. "Wherever you fly and fight in my planes, da Vinci and Rosatelli will be aloft with you."

Enzo followed the rocky maze as the sun reached into the steep twisting ravines and the deep valleys that joined them from the sides. He was astounded by the sheer jagged face of each ascending cliffside, many two thousand, three thousand feet or more. Militarily, it was the harshest landscape he had ever seen.

He recalled sitting on the floor of his father's library after school, his imagination dazzled by the detailed engravings of Britain's punitive Abyssinian campaign of 1868: Emperor Theodore's men dragging cannon up to his mountain fastness at Magdala, a thousand of them hauling on ropes bound to the massive wooden wheels of Sebastopol, the giant mortar thought by the Ethiopian monarch to be his ultimate defense; and the British, 32,000 strong, laying their own railway from the coast as they advanced to the foot of the mountains, then packing dismantled artillery onto the backs of elephants brought from India, finally storming Magdala as the emperor killed himself, and in due course departing to the coast, taking up their iron rails as they withdrew. As a boy, he had thought the British stupid for bringing elephants to Africa, not realizing how much easier the smaller Indian elephants are to train.

Sunlight struck the white dome of a church, and Enzo recognized the town of Adowa rising before him. His mind turned to his grandfather.

"I have a family debt to honor," he murmured.

Enzo banked north up the next gorge, climbing, missing the town to his left, climbing higher, searching for the wide valley where he'd been told the army of Ras Seyum, the commander of the province of Tigre, should be gathered. It was September 28, a special day, he knew, for the fierce Christians of Abyssinia.

Today was the celebration of Masqal, stolen from the pagans, the day to celebrate the end of the rains and the beginning of spring, the universal time for launching military campaigns, and, in Abyssinia, the Feast of the Cross, still the start of the slave-raiding season. Enzo smiled to himself. Even chains brought blessings: the international arms embargo designed to compel Abyssinia to abandon slavery had left her virtually defenceless.

He rose over a ridge. The hosts of Ras Seyum lay before him: a vast disorderly assembly of tents and lean-tos, cooking fires, mounds of equipment, thousands of tethered horses and mules and camels and scores of thorn-branch enclosures filled with goats and cattle. Tonight, to celebrate the holiday, the men would be feasting on raw beef. Here and there pennants flew from long staffs set in the ground. A large circular clearing had a tall cross at its center. There were several clusters of vehicles. He counted ten or twelve antiquated artillery pieces and at least four modern trucks, possibly French, carrying pairs of heavy machine guns trained on the sky. Hundreds of figures scrambled from tents as he approached, darting about and brandishing rifles.

He would have time for just one or two passes, he calculated. He swept by the camp, climbing fast before banking and circling back. He dived to gain speed, trying to concentrate on identifying and counting the heavy equipment. As he fell, the camp became a chaos of running men and bolting animals. Sheep trampled through camp fires. Men reached for their weapons. Many fired rifles into the air. One bullet struck his tail where it joined the fuselage. Not disturbed, always fatalistic in the air, Enzo flew on steadily.

Twice he made a longer slower sweep past the edge of the encampment, leaving the Fiat to fly itself at nine thousand feet above sea level, perhaps two thousand above the camp. He leaned out and studied the frantic scene with his field glasses, amazed by the numbers of men and camp followers and animals. But it was not, he thought, an army.

He considered what these savages would face: modern armor and aircraft, perhaps poison gas. Since the beginning of the year, over two hundred thousand Italians had debarked at Massawa and Mogadishu, arriving by sea like Agamemnon's army before the siege of Troy. More were on the way. Ten divisions, five regular army and five Blackshirt, were prepared for the offensive, though the latter did not impress him. As a professional soldier, Colonel Grimaldi had limited faith in the Blackshirts. Fine, he thought, in Rome, to crowd the Piazza Venezia for roaring demonstrations, but for mountains like this, Mussolini's street Fascisti would never be prepared. No matter what the Duce claimed, these were not the Romans of the Caesars.

Returning to more immediate concerns, he checked his gauges. With a range of under five hundred miles, it was time to fly home. Enzo dropped down and followed the ravines, finally emerging above the first plateaux.

The air was thicker and warmer. He was so low he could practically smell the bush. Like an animal in the late morning sun, his aircraft had forgotten the stiffness of the night cold. The machine was warmed and at its best. Grateful to Paolo, he flew a steeplechase, testing himself and his equipment.

Using the pedals and joystick, constantly adjusting his altitude, Enzo flew over trees and huts, banking along the walls of ridge lines, diving into valleys and rising easily on the warming air. He loved this sort of flying. He would have looped, but was too low. Concerned about the propensity of the CR-20 to stall, instead he performed a slow barrel. This was not the time to be on foot in Africa. He followed a narrow stream west towards Eritrea.

Climbing once, Enzo saw the drier landscape running off into the scrub desert to the southeast, towards the great waste of the Danakil. A dark line moved across the pale ground: a camel train, progressing northwest from the direction of French Somaliland, probably bearing supplies to trade with the Abyssinians. Help for the enemy, Enzo thought harshly. He veered south and dived for the camels, not firing his two machine guns, but enjoying the engine's scream as the needle trembled and touched a hundred and sixty-five miles an hour. Camels panicked and scattered, galloping off in all directions. Several riders fell. Packs and bundles broke free and split open when they hit the ground. Excited as a boy, Enzo levelled off at sixty feet and waggled his wings. It reminded him of the war in Libya. Had his grandfather felt like this when he rode into Africa?

Enzo turned in a long arc, climbing slightly and returning north over the ragged column. Too late, he saw a cloaked figure lying on his back among a cluster of stones. The long barrel of an ancient rifle followed his line of flight, leading him like a bird. There was one puff of smoke. A heavy bullet passed through the lower wing just beside the cockpit to his left. Fine shooting, he thought, feeling a shadow of fear. Enzo considered swinging back and using his guns. But today his mission was reconnaissance, not war. That would come soon enough.

Shortly before he found his stream, Enzo spotted two giraffe browsing on trees near the edge of the desert. He followed the stream again, but took less pleasure in flying low, his concentration now disturbed. Scanning the ground ahead, he saw a group of lions lying in the shade around a carcass. He reduced his air speed and dropped down. He thought of Ethiopia's tiny black emperor, Haile Selassie, in his conceit calling himself "the King of Kings, the Negus Negesti, the Lion of Judah," the two hundred and twenty-fifth consecutive monarch to have claimed the title founded by Solomon the First, the son of David.

The pride rose to their feet as Grimaldi came in. A lioness crouched with some cubs, covering one with her forepaws. Two lions, smaller females, began to run. An immense black-maned lion rose from behind a thornbush and stared without flinching at the incoming plane. Enzo saw his mane stand out like a medieval collar and his dark tail rise straight in the air. Defiant, angry, the lion opened his mouth in a roar Enzo could not hear as the Fiat flashed overhead. He came around, dropped to fifty or sixty feet and pursued the lion as the animal began to run from him. With his own speed at about ninety miles an hour, Enzo estimated the lion must be doing over thirty.

Enzo circled. As he returned to the tiring beast, the lion stopped running and turned to face his pursuer. His tail stood straight in the air like a rod. Enzo saw the rage in the animal's face as he depressed the trigger button. The aircraft bucked as both guns fired. Two lines of bullets tore up the dust before they crossed the lion's chest and shoulders. Enzo dipped his wings in respect and made for the base at Nefasit.

"Finished!" Gwenn exclaimed, completing the white circle around the large red cross she had painted on the roof of the Morris ambulance. "Now they can't bomb us."

The seven ambulances and two Bedford lorries had been delivered with crosses painted on their sides but none where they'd be needed, Gwenn had pointed out. "It's not neat," she added, deploring the messy edges of the design, "but I suppose the Italian pilots won't mind that." She winced for a moment, thinking of Lorenzo, but forced herself to shove the thought aside. "At least it should save our lives."

"You must've learned that in the war," said Dr. Fergus, knowing she'd served as a Volunteer Ambulance Driver. His thin arms braced the ladder as Gwenn stepped down with the paint pot and brush.

"That leaves just the Bedfords for tomorrow," Gwenn said wearily, sidestepping any talk about the war in France and Belgium. She paused and wiped sweat and paint from her face with an old rag. Nearby, in the same open-roofed mud-brick warehouse next to the Addis railroad station, other members of the medical team were unpacking chests and counting and sorting supplies. She and Fergus left the warehouse to find one of the mule taxis that waited under the eucalyptus trees outside the station.

"It's only a week now, but I feel I've been trapped here all my life, bickering and intriguing and bribing these Abyssinian officials to let us unload the blasted ambulances off the train cars," Fergus said as they walked. By now Gwenn knew the old doctor was refreshed by indignation, his Scottish nature offended by the waste. "Why're people so damned hard to help?"

"We shan't be here much longer," Gwenn said, "though I'm certain I'll miss the bustle of Addis." What she did not add was that she was excited by what lay ahead. Sometimes she felt guilty to find herself relishing the cruel days that were in store, as if the Africans would be paying for her fulfillment. Their suffering would give value to her calling.

"Meantime the railway Frenchies've been charging us for each day they can't use the flat cars, and now for each day we use their rat-filled warehouse." Fergus did his best to hurry past the clamoring drivers to the head of the line, pleased to see the foremost cart was shaded by a tattered brocade canopy. "So French," he muttered. "Making money off both sides."

Gwenn helped him up as he continued.

"Who knows?" Malcolm shook his head. "Perhaps trying to save lives is too dear in Africa."

"Hotel Splendide, please," Gwenn said carefully as the driver aroused his mule. "Hotel Splen-dide."

On the long ride from the station, they passed intense glimpses of the African vitality that surrounded them like an ocean. There were crowded villages of huts and shacks that lived inwardly on their own within the great city like ethnic quarters in London or Paris. Small processions of Coptic priests paraded serenely in folded white robes like so many fluted Greek columns, marching from ceremony to ceremony beneath tall waving umbrellas and strange complicated crosses and clouding incense. Open markets sold camels and silver, goats and coffee, bananas and swords and ancient rifles. Roiling gangs of children with bare feet and thin legs and perfect oval faces tussled like puppies in the dusty gutters.

"The children are so beautiful," Gwenn said, reminded painfully of her sons. Each day she missed their time together and worried if they were well and getting on at school.

Wherever they journeyed in the immense widely spread city, Gwenn and Malcolm saw soldiers: cowled officers astride mules with lion skins across their shoulders; parading chieftains attended by slaves bearing swords and umbrellas; dancing mountain cavalry bright with tasselled red saddles and plumed manes; Haile Selassie's Imperial Guard, drilled daily in the streets by white officers, each man lean and barefoot, meticuluous and proud with his European uniform, feathered cap and modern rifle.

"Never seen such a lot of soldiers. Seventy different ethnic mobs in this country, and damme if they aren't all coming to town for dinner tonight," said Malcolm. "Why don't they go where the fighting's going to be?"

"Rallying to the emperor is part of the ceremony of warfare out here," Gwenn said, repeating recent knowledge, sensing she was watching the energy of the nation concentrating in the capital like coal being shovelled into a furnace. "They're answering the royal *chitet,* the summons to war."

"Well, jumping about in Addis won't serve 'em this time," said Fergus. "Good Lord!" He turned on the bench seat to look back at a large party of tall sword-bearing men making camp by the roadside. "Those must be the Gofas."

Their faces painted with ochre like Florentine villas, their leader's three lion cubs leashed to an immense planted spear, the Gofa warriors stalked about, brandishing long swords and driving off scattered families of other Ethiopians who had made rough shelters in the open space.

Gwenn was relieved to arrive at the hotel. Feeling hideous, wanting time to herself before the evening's parties, knowing she'd have to wait in line for the filthy hall bathtub, Gwenn had been hoping to return to the Splendide in the early afternoon while the journalists were still busy or sleeping it off. Blessedly situated near the government telegraph office, the decaying Splendide was the trading house for all the information that passed between Abyssinia and the world.

"What ho, nurse!" called out Herb Klein, the war correspondent for the *Chicago Tribune.* Chewing on a cigar, clearly eager for someone to talk at, he looked down from the crumbling tiled terrace of the Splendide as Gwenn and Malcolm slowly climbed the hotel steps. The writer's short-sleeved shirt was dark with sweat.

"You're looking a little stretched, Miss Rider," he added, standing to pull out a chair through a clatter of broken blue and white tiles. The story was that most of the tiles had been stolen on the way up from the coast. When they ran out, the masons plastered down a temporary filler coat of stucco, which soon deteriorated in the rains, leaving the tiles to slip about the terrace like checkers on a board. Gwenn thought she'd seen some just like them at the Dire Dawa station restaurant on their way up from the coast.

"And your doc looks like he could use a few gins," Klein added as he bawled for a glass and pushed a bottle towards the doctor.

"Sound thinking, Klein," said Fergus wearily, collapsing, his energy and complaints exhausted. "Thank God you travel with gin in your spare typewriter case." He nodded appreciatively as Gwenn wiped the new glass before he filled it and lifted it towards Klein. "Any news?"

Knowing it would be a long answer, Gwenn secretly removed her shoes beneath the table. She wiggled her toes and calculated how long she would have to stay before politely excusing herself. She studied Malcolm's drawn face, worrying if his heart would take the altitude and the strain. He seemed to be alternating between being cranky and enthusiastic, between bursts of energy and longer periods of fatigue.

"News? Always news," said Klein keenly, wiping his face on the end of the filthy tablecloth, "Always. We've got a hundred and thirty foreign journalists here spitting up the same rubbish. Our war with the censors goes on without quarter. No prisoners. I spent three hours at the censor's desk next door at the PTO and got three paragraphs through. Didn't matter which ones as the guy didn't speak English. Damn good stuff but three graphs isn't enough for my readers, not even in Chicago. The fellas who didn't bribe him, Swiss and Canadians, that sort, are still in line. Censor'd been to the Addis Lycée. He's some sort of princely family, all puffed up.

Worse than a real frog. Wanted to show off. Very thorough. Did a helluva job on the pieces for the *Figaro* and *France Presse.* Nothing left, really. Stuff came out looking like a crossword puzzle."

Fresh sweat on his face, Klein paused and emptied his glass, glancing down to the other end of the long table where the representative of *Die Zeitung* tapped mercilessly at his Remington. "Of course, Fritz there is fairly new out here and still thinks he has a deadline to meet. Say hello, Fritz." The small German nodded and smiled without looking up. "Hello," Gwenn said quietly, knowing Klein called all Germans "Fritz."

"Any news about the war?" she asked, feeling the long gin revive her.

The American glanced at his notebook. "Seems De Bono's Italians are massing at the eastern border near Adowa and Makalle, lots of 'em. Hundred thousand or more. Imagine trying to feed all those boys in that wilderness. Some skirmishing down on the Somaliland side, near Dolo, most likely Ethiopian irregulars and Italian colonial troops. And your Brits are building up the Mediterranean Fleet, bringing out the *Prince of Wales.* And there's a lot of talk-talk in Geneva."

"Enough of all that. What's on tonight here, in this Paris of Africa?" Fergus said, leaning forward on his elbows, his mood and look improving. The table rocked and the German looked up from his typewriter, his eyes huge and bewildered through their round metal spectacles. He bent down and reset two tiles under the feet of the table.

"Say, Fritz, would you mind doing the whole floor, while you're at it?" called Klein in a loud voice. There was no response when the German's red face rose from under the table.

"Lot of news here, too," Klein resumed, looking at his notes again. "Starting off with cocktails at the Deutsches Haus, thanks to Fritz there, so be nice to him, Miss Rider." Klein persisted in his habit of ignoring Gwenn's wedding ring. "Then on to the Belgian legation for a solid feed before some dance party or other at the Perroquet. Belgians always put out the best food and booze. Comes from trying to compete with the French, you know, been at it for ever."

"Good show, Klein," said Fergus, brightening. The best part was it would all be free. He watched the German clean his typewriter keys with a fine brush. Did the man think he was about to be graded by a professor?

"Sounds lovely." Gwenn rose to go.

"Fritz'll be giving us all a lift," said Klein in a louder voice, tossing a box of matches against the chattering Remington and receiving a crisp nod in confirmation. "He needs my help getting his stories. Seems he got a real car today, part of the new Germany. Right, Fritz?"

The typing continued, steady as a Mauser automatic.

"Excuse me, please," Gwenn said, wondering if the German's name might actually be Fritz. She rose to enter the hotel, praying nothing had been stolen from her room in this light-fingered capital. Tonight she would wear her last pair of stockings.

"Fritzie says we've got to stop at the Fascist Club for a quickie on the way," Klein said later, after they had all climbed into the German's battered Benz. For a moment they sat in quiet support while the native driver struggled to start the machine. Gwenn was pleased to see Malcolm looking better after his rest. She hoped the same was true of her.

"It's near the bazaar, almost on the way," Klein added encouragingly when the engine caught.

"Do you mind if Gwenn and I stay in the car while you two go inside?" Fergus said to Gwenn's relief when they pulled up outside the freshly painted stone building. Fascist flags hung on either side of the entrance. "Could be a bit awkward for us."

Fritz held open the door and said, "Please join us."

Uncomfortable, Gwenn left the car and climbed the steps of the Fascist Club with Malcolm Fergus.

Both reception rooms were crowded. Gwenn's eye was immediately drawn to the Italian minister, Count Vinci-Gigliucci, standing beneath large portraits of King Victor Emmanuel and Benito Mussolini.

"Since the trouble started," whispered Klein to Gwenn too loudly, "the Wops haven't kept an ambassador out here. Just this Luigi."

Gracious and relaxed, the Italian diplomat swung tan leather driving gloves in one hand and bowed to the guests as he welcomed them in four or five languages. A nervous aide stood behind his left elbow, securing names and introducing guests, occasionally whispering details in the minister's ear. A second aide stood to his right, hurrying the guests away with offers of drinks and canapés.

"The guy's enjoying it all," Herb Klein said more quietly as he and Gwenn moved up the line. She smelled the American's cigar when he spoke close to her face. "Not every day you can give a bash in a city just before you invade it."

Gwenn was aware of the minister looking her over as she approached him. An aide whispered in his ear. She wondered if he knew Lorenzo.

"I understand you are a volunteer with the Egyptian Ambulance Brigade," said the Italian in careful English, smiling when Gwenn was presented. "Perhaps one evening soon you will dine with us." He kissed her hand lingeringly, as if certain that would please her.

"Yes," she said, answering only the first remark. An instant suspicion formed that it was Count Vinci-Gigliucci who had arranged the impediments at the railroad station. "I believe other brigades are on the way, from Britain, from Holland and Sweden, perhaps more, we hope."

"What is all this for?" the count said lightly, smiling as if in confusion, his accent and evasion annoying reminders of Lorenzo. "For what do they need ambulances unless Abyssinia intends to start a war?" He shrugged before turning and bowing to the ambassador of Spain.

"If they weren't planning an invasion, why would they mind us being here?" Gwenn whispered to Fergus. Declining drinks, she and Malcolm waited near the entrance for their friends.

An hour later, stuck in a line of motorcars outside the Belgian embassy after they'd stopped for a cocktail at the Deutsches Haus, Gwenn noticed clouds of flies gathered over dark pools in the dirt road. Stepping down in the twilight, she accidentally set one foot in the moisture. Nearby, just across the road, several young boys waved long sticks as they tended a small herd of cattle. "Dinner," Klein said with a laugh.

"Bienvenue à Bruxelles!" said a short but handsome Belgian officer when they entered the embassy.

It was like Brussels, she thought, recalling what she had read of that city on the eve of Waterloo. Then, too, fatalism and excitement had blended with a sense of imminent apocalypse to create a rare exhilaration. The best wines were opened first. The dancing never stopped. Romances of a lifetime blossomed during a single ball. But in Addis, European ladies were scarce as mermaids, and Gwenn was flattered and courted as never before. Had it been Brussels, her dance card could not have been so full. It made her feel young.

"Let me escort your party to the garden," said her admirer eagerly. Gwenn glanced at her feet as they walked down the steps, horrified to see her right shoe was stained with blood.

The Belgian officer presented Gwenn with a glass of champagne under one of the two tents set up in the walled park behind the embassy. She had flirted with the man briefly at a party given by a Czech arms dealer two nights before but could not recall the name.

"Thank you, Captain," Gwenn said. Knowing Malcolm would be disappointed with such a drink, she asked, "Have you any gin or whisky for my friend, Dr. Fergus?"

"Michel, if you please." The young officer bowed, his dark hair sleek and parted in neat lines like Valentino. "Yes, we have whisky, we have gin, everything. The ambassador insists we empty the cellar. He doesn't want Mussolini and the Blackshirts to drink it."

Another officer approached them. "You are the toast of Addis, ma'am," he said to Gwenn, raising his glass with a shaky hand. "To the Nightingale of Shoa!"

"What is the Belgian army up to in Addis, Captain?" said Dr. Fergus genially, accepting his whisky.

"We are training the Imperial Guard, Doctor," replied Michel, reluctantly taking his eyes from Gwenn's but careful to have her hear his report. "Three battalions of them, three thousand men equipped with the finest Belgian rifles, Lebels, plus a handful of cavalry on big Australian horses we've just brought out. We're even teaching the officers to read and write. French, of course. But the emperor insists they go barefoot. Thinks it keeps them tougher on the march."

"I thought the Swedes were training the Guard," said Dr. Fergus.

"No, sir," said the Belgian smartly. "They're only running the Cadet School, and one or two other minor things. Really, they're only trying to peddle their weapons." He turned back to Gwenn and looked her in the eye and smiled.

"Cadet School?" said Gwenn, deciding to be interested.

"Yes, miss," said Michel keenly. "It's nothing much, really, mostly show. Just over a hundred young Ethiopian boys, mostly aristocratic families, many with their own servants."

"How do they look?" asked the doctor, leaning forward, enjoying a fresh drink.

"Not so bad, but they're not ready yet," said the Belgian officer without turning his head. "My Swedish friend says they're smarter than Swedish boys of the same age. No surprise there! But weaker physically, not used to sports, of course, and too many have syphilis."

"Of course," said Fergus.

"Excuse me, miss," said Michel. "I'm not used to speaking with a lady."

"Not at all," said Gwenn, liking him. "Soon I'll be a doctor myself."

Dressed in a dark English suit, his lean face sharp and intelligent, an Ethiopian official joined the circle that was gathering around Gwenn and Dr. Fergus.

"Welcome to Abyssinia," he said. "I believe your ambulance brigade is half Christian and half Muslim, like my nation." The official pointed at the great roasting pit that lay between the two tents.

Bleeding generously, whole carcasses of sheep and oxen were being carried forward on long poles. "These lambs and beefs are from the personal herds of the emperor," he said, spreading his hands and fingers, "freshly butchered at the door of this embassy, a gift to our friends, to give strength to all of you who have come to help our country."

Other Ethiopians, Tigreans and Shoans, soldiers and government officials, princes and *rases* from the ancient cities of Gondar and Axum, were scattered through the party. European traders and diplomats, soldiers and adventurers gathered about a number of slender, perfectly erect, black women with small oval faces and exquisite features, one or two in European dresses, most in graceful cotton *shammas.* Seven or eight elderly Ethiopian notables, lean-faced men with thin beards, loose white jodhpurs and cracked patent-leather shoes, sat arguing on a group of chairs to one side. In the distance she saw a man who reminded her of Anton.

"See that tall black fellow with the white scarf and all the gold braid, charming the Swedish ambassador's wife?" said Michel, leaning close, gently covering one of Gwenn's hands with his own.

"Yes," she said, withdrawing her hand a bit, but not completely.

"That's the famous Black Eagle of Harlem, an American pilot here to fight for Africa," the Belgian said with enthusiasm as he tried to take her hand more tightly. "Yesterday he crashed one of the emperor's planes. That leaves the air force with nine or ten."

A large gold cross held in his clasped hands, a Coptic cleric with tight white curls moved slowly through the crowd, nodding acknowledgments while two retainers struggled to hold a tassled ceremonial umbrella above his head.

"Thank God," said Michel. "At last. The *abba*!"

"What's that?" said Malcolm, tiring.

"The bishop," said the Belgian officer. "Wouldn't do to feast without him."

It was the moment for which the hungry guests had been waiting. Everyone shouldered forward towards the meat as the long-robed cleric approached the charring flesh. Blood dripped into the fire from the freshly slaughtered animals. Flames jumped from blazing fat. Cooking aromas and wood smoke swirled about the bishop like incense when he stretched his arms towards the fire and blessed the pagan feast with sweeping motions of his cross. Astonished at the ritual, Gwenn recalled the cattle and the mess in the street outside.

Sweating servants struggled forward, coughing and spitting in the smoke as they hacked away bits of barely cooked flesh while others turned the spits.

"Won't you sit with us?" an elderly gentleman said to Gwenn. She accepted, hoping she could do so without too much involvement. At once the man advised her that he was a Swiss constitutionalist employed by the emperor.

"Curious, really," he said, pulling out her chair, "I've been hired to review the Abyssinian constitution recently adopted from Japan. You know, the one of 1889."

After that introduction, the Swiss sat silently beside Gwenn, as if exhausted by his labors, while she was courted by a chatty stammering Englishman from the Anti-Slavery Society, dismayed with his failed attempts to induce an immediate end to bondage here in the land of Solomon and Prester John, the oldest Christian kingdon in the world.

"How is it possible," moaned the emancipator, "that the only African country never colonized is the only one still rife with slavery? And did you see that public flogging?"

"Not so loud," said Fergus, "we're eating the emperor's beef."

When the Englishman rose to get her a plate of food, Michel took the man's seat and refilled Gwenn's glass with wine.

"May I show you a photograph of my fiancée?" he said after a moment, removing from the breast of his tunic a coquettish picture of a voluptuous girl with small eyes and long fair braids done up in a crown. The girl was seated on the grass beside a picnic lunch.

"She's lovely," Gwenn said.

"Of course," said Michel, "she's really much prettier than that."

Before Gwenn could reply, an elderly English lady bent over her shoulder.

"May I come by tomorrow and help roll bandages?" said the woman. "I could bring some friends from the Wild-Flower Protection Society. We're dying for something to do. It's so exciting."

"That would be very helpful," Gwenn said.

"You've just come out, haven't you? Have you any news?" the lady asked. "I hear our battle fleet is in the Mediterranean. What will the League do?"

"I really couldn't say," said Gwenn as Michel began speaking to her quietly from the other side.

"Could you possibly have a picnic with me tomorrow?" the Belgian said eagerly. "We could go up into that steep forest just above the town."

She hesitated before replying, tempted by his youthful enthusiasm and her own imminent departure. And there wouldn't be time for too many complications.

"We're all off for the Perroquet," Klein interrupted in a loud voice, pushing back his plate and wiping his mouth as he rose from his seat across the table. "Fritzie!" He banged his spoon on the table to get the attention of his German friend. "Fritzie, better go and call for the car. Fritz, up, you've had enough!"

"May we have a champagne later at my hotel?" whispered Michel as Gwenn stood. "The Imperial, room nine, if I'm not in the billiard room."

"Perhaps," she said, tempted, recalling the advice of an experienced English countess: always arrive with a toothbrush and an open mind. She wondered how often the countess had followed her own advice. "But now I have to dash with my friends."

"Nine!" Michel called after her, holding up as many fingers.

Half asleep and smelling of *tajj,* the driver started slowly but gained spirit as the Benz warmed. Gwenn was squeezed between him and Klein, who leaned out and waved and hollered at other friends crammed into ancient motorcars rushing from party to party across the enormous city.

Losing its way between royal parks and vast slums, the car hurtled along broad unpaved avenues past the crowded shelters and sparkling camp fires of the tribal armies that were swarming in from the provinces. In the streets there was not a man without a weapon. Thousands of ghostly robes crouched around cook fires set in the middle of the roads and foot paths. When the car slowed, Gwenn saw children playing in the night and lean hairless dogs slinking about in the shadows, snarling over scraps. For a moment she thought of Wellie and Denby. Here she was, rushing off to parties and thinking of dashing young officers. Still, she comforted herself with the thought that they were safe and happy at Olivio's, especially with Sana cossetting them with the pastries and affection that Egyptian women always lavished on young boys. Denby would be spoiled and petted by all the girls, and Wellington would soon be old enough to take a different sort of interest.

Lavishly hosted by several arms dealers and concessionaires, roaring feverishly on all three floors of the decaying hotel, the party at the Perroquet had none of the restraints of the diplomatic receptions. A piano, an accordion and a violin played Mozart and Benny Goodman while strangers danced and drank and argued and embraced in the dining room and halls and on the terrace, yelling at each other over the din in languages that often found no comprehension. At another time Gwenn would have been repelled but she found herself sharing the exhilaration, enjoying the excitement of Addis on the brink.

"Will you dance, my dear?" asked Dr. Fergus with a courtly smile, his dour demeanor gone after a few drinks, his face rosy with whisky.

"I'd love to, Malcolm," Gwenn said. They swept out onto the crowded dance floor, the old doctor's steps surprisingly agile and smooth. Suddenly she was chilled by the idea that she might not have a chance to dance again. All around her, even the lovers talked of war. She looked across the dim crowded smoky hall and saw Klein climbing the stairs, led by the hand by a very young African lady in a white *shamma.* His other hand held a bottle by the throat.

Gwenn and Malcolm were squeezed against the piano by another couple. Jealous of their affection, Gwenn watched the girl kiss her companion on the neck. His eyes were shut. "Will they close Suez, sweetie?" the girl asked him.

For hours Gwenn danced with men she did not know and knew she would never see again.

"Breakfast!" Klein said at last, steadying himself when he gripped Gwenn's shoulder after she finished a dance. He leaned over the seated sleeping figure of Malcolm Fergus and slapped him gently across the face. "Time for breakfast, Doc. Fritzie's gone to get the car."

They drove back to the Splendide where the Associated Press was hosting its weekly breakfast party. Guests brought the booze. Everything else was laid on by the Yanks.

Gwenn went upstairs to wash her face and change her shoes and find a pullover, knowing that if she lay down for a moment she would not rise. As she came back downstairs, her feet aching, the odor of strong Ethiopian coffee rose to greet her. Pots steamed in the cool morning air as the sun rose over the busy terrace. One or two men slept with their faces on tables. Others smoked and typed and hollered for food and hot towels while they laughed about the night's adventures. Suddenly starving, Gwenn accepted plates of kippers and eggs and thick native porridge running with honey.

"Where were you?" cried Michel, rushing up, stumbling on the tiles. "I waited all night." He was not quite so handsome in the morning light, she noticed, his eyes red, his tunic stained. Gwenn wondered how she looked.

"We stopped at the Perroquet for a drink," Gwenn said. Looking up, she was alarmed to see Malcolm steadying himself against the terrace railing while he squinted at a paper held between his hands. Bad news? she thought at once.

"Excuse me, please," she said to Michel.

"Of course," said Michel reluctantly, as Gwenn rose and hurried to the doctor. She led Malcolm to a seat.

"I can't find my specs," Fergus said, handing her the document.

"We're off," she said an instant later, no longer tired, waving good-bye to her Belgian as she led Fergus up the steps. "We've been assigned to the Somali front, near Harar. Let's go and pack. I'll help you."

By noon they had left it all behind and motored east towards Harar, to what was expected to become the southern front. Three days of slow driving through the hills and mountains gave them the opportunity to break in the vehicles, reorganize the loads and bemoan the first follies of their Armenian mechanic. Whenever they paused to stretch and eat and service the trucks and ambulances, Gwenn was refreshed by the brisk air that swept the rich fields of wheat and guinea corn and barley that flourished in every valley. Here and there small oxen, singly or in pairs, dragged primitive plows fashioned from two bits of wood tipped with iron. Nowhere did she see a cart or a wheel of any kind. Once Gwenn bent and squeezed the heavy soil between her fingers. She pinched and opened the fat green head of a barley stalk and admired the way the grain grew thickly into every fissure of the surrounding rocks and cliffs.

Back in the ambulance, as they motored on to the old Muslim capital, her mind turned to the Kenya highlands and her own farm. The earth reddened as they climbed towards the city built on trading slaves and coffee.

The governor of Harar had not expected them, but rode out to greet them in princely style after their vehicles had been stopped by guards outside the city's ancient walls. Groves of *gat* grew nearby, the shiny dark green leaves hanging loosely from tall stalks set in neat rows. The old warrior wore a beaded cloak and a lion's mane headdress.

"Here in my province of Harerge," explained the bearded governor from his saddle, addressing them through an interpreter who stood by his stirrup, mimicking each of his master's florid gestures while he spoke, "we will not be attacked from the east, from Eritrea, no, but from what they call Italian Somaliland to the south."

Two mounted attendants carried the governor's ancient silver-banded rifle and his round pointed shield and long sword in its tassled leather scabbard. While he spoke, other servants, bowing, spread a scarlet cloth on the ground and set out presents for the doctors and nurses: oranges, monkey-skin rugs and silver bracelets. Gwenn noticed pale bands of skin around the wrists of one servant. The mark of shackles? she wondered.

"After the war," the governor said, patting his belly, pausing for his interpreter to do the same, "you will be my guests in Harar to feast on macaroni. Macaroni, for there will be Italian officers toiling as chefs in my *gibbi.*"

The governor presented for medical care his wives and children and aged retainers. While others conducted the examinations, Gwenn and Malcolm passed through the crenellated gate and searched the narrow hilly streets for a suitable hospital building. Helping Malcolm toil up and down the steep streets, she wondered why the Scots so often lost themselves in distant charities.

A band of cloaked Harari lepers watched with ghostly eyes as the two Europeans crossed the main square before the Coptic church. Several comely narrow-hipped young women, Adaris, she guessed, bent double, unfastened the long green and yellow sheaves of sugar cane that were lashed to their backs. Arriving at the square in colorful printed robes, each bearer and her stalks appeared like a separate bunch of tall flowers. Smiling and chattering, they cut each seven-foot stalk into short sections suitable for market. Gwenn watched small boys run up and chew on scraps of cane. Just like Denby with a sweet, she thought. A reedy-voiced muezzin began to wail from a minaret. Others joined in from scores of distant mosques.

"There's nothing suitable," the chief surgeon concluded wearily, sitting down on a low wall near the square. "And we need fresh water."

"Let's set up in a grove near that stream a mile or two before the town," Gwenn said. And so they did.

Within two days the field hospital was surrounded by a noisy dependent village of beggars, launderers, petty traders and wood gatherers. When a group of lepers sought to approach the clinic, the children of these new dependents drove them off with stones before Gwenn could intervene. She wondered if these outcasts were patients at Harar's Capuchin leprosarium, celebrated for treating lepers with injections of copper. Across the river a camel market began to gather, responding to the government's call for transport animals.

Each night at Harar, Gwenn lay on her back in the low tent, with the flaps up, gazing out at the vast clear African sky. The longer she watched, the more stars she saw and recognized, the sparkling panoply interrupted only by the slender leaves that hung black against the bright night. She remembered evenings at the farm when Anton had taught her the stars, one of the lessons of his gypsy training.

Waiting for war, the doctors and nurses served the needs of Harar. In the mornings Gwenn rose early and strolled upstream to bathe in the cleaner water, eager to begin the days for which she had long prepared. Each morning the lines lengthened as new patients straggled in from the surrounding Galla villages.

"I'll bring her in, Lieutenant," Colonel Grimaldi said to Bruno Mussolini as they heard the Caproni's port propeller feathering down. The colonel sniffed and smelled the bitter aroma of an electrical fire. "I'd like to see how she handles with two propellers." The seventeen-year-old pilot, his face pale and sweating, was beginning to overcompensate with the flaps and the center and starboard props. The aircraft on their port wing had begun to pull away.

Enzo shut down the stuttering engine just as she began to smoke. With no bombs or payload, he was not concerned about the ability of the two remaining engines to bring her in safely. The rest of the squadron parted and let them come in first. Turning as he banked, coming into the wind, Enzo brought in the big Caproni using barely half the runway. Paolo raced towards them in the rescue truck, standing in the back with two other men and barrels of water equipped with crude pumps. The ground crews waited at the end of the strip to check and service their aircraft. Enzo saw a knot of *Bersaglieri* lounging to one side, watching the Capronis come home.

"All good training, Lieutenant," he said to Bruno, slapping the youngster on the shoulder after he unbuckled. "Nothing serious." Bent low, relieved things had turned out so well, Grimaldi made for the hatch. Not such a bad lad, Enzo thought as he walked away from the aircraft, but dangerous in the air.

"Cinzano and soda," the colonel said a few moments later, enjoying a cigarette, his back against the high bamboo bar set along one side of the combined officers' mess and flight room at the Nefasit aerodrome. He noticed Captain Ciano seated by himself writing in his diaries. The Mussolini boys were smoking and drinking with the other pilots of the *Disperata*. Of the squadron, only Bruno seemed not quite at ease. Next to him one of the men was struggling to repair a radio. The aerial was strung up along a post to the thatched roof. The rear panel of the black Marconi lay on the table as the man checked the tubes and tightened the wires.

Enzo saw Captain Uzielli explaining a map to a *Bersaglieri* lieutenant at one of the rough tables nearby. Grimaldi had to stifle his annoyance, knowing that the paratroopers had to be posted at a forward air base. Already they had complained about being obliged to use the unsuitable Capronis for their practice drops.

Despite his advantage in rank, Enzo was aware that the *Bersaglieri* viewed themselves in a special light, fancying that a lieutenant in their regiment could out-soldier any general in a regular formation. A parachute unit, of course, would presume still more.

"Should be easy," said the young soldier to Uzielli in a loud voice, "if the infantry concentrates here and here and gets good support from the air. It won't be as bad as Libya. These savages'll run like sheep . . ."

"It's never easy in Africa, boy," said Uzielli. "The distances are too great, the land's too bloody hard, and every now and then the *negrettos* fight to the last. In Somaliland we found a snake or scorpion under every stone." He paused and gulped his red wine.

"For the first few weeks, it'll be easy enough. They'll love it in Rome. Thrusting columns, swift violent battles when the enemy concentrates, victories for all these pretty airplanes and machines and modern weapons. But it'll get nasty on the ground. You'll see. It always does."

"But we're going to have half a million men," argued the lieutenant, waving his hands, "soldiers and farmers and road builders . . ."

"They'll disappear." Uzielli waved his hands.

"Disappear?"

"Into these vast highlands." Uzielli raised his voice and banged on the map with his empty glass. "And the occupation's always worse than the battles," he said, pouring from the bottle. "Every barefoot shepherd boy has a spear or rifle. Along the upper Juba, we lost . . ."

"Captain," interrupted Grimaldi as he strode by, obliging Uzielli to stand. "I'd like your men to do one more jump tomorrow."

"We jumped again this morning, sir," said Uzielli. "Another man broke a leg coming down in the rocks, and the trucks were late finding us."

"You and your men are still too slow leaving the planes, Captain. Scatters them all about like leaves in a storm." Grimaldi spoke as if he had not heard the soldier's words, knowing he was embarrassing Uzielli in front of his junior officer. "Man won't have a chance if he's caught out there alone."

"These bombers weren't designed for jumping, Colonel," Uzielli said in a harder voice. "Fuselage too cramped, hatches too small. If you reduced the airspeed, sir, my troopers'd fall tighter." Uzielli crossed his arms. " Each drop we lose a couple of men to injuries. I don't recommend more training jumps."

"Load your men at seven hundred hours tomorrow, Captain," Enzo said, wanting to squash this arrogant *contadino.* "You'll be dropped in easy country nine or ten miles west. No packs, light weapons. Get them out fast this time so we don't have to do it again." In a lighter tone he added, "I'll be right behind you in the CR-20. Do your boys good to run back in."

As Grimaldi walked off, Uzielli saluted, his dark eyes hard and bulbous, wondering if he would see the colonel on the ground in wartime.

"May I join you?" Enzo said pleasantly to the young officers when he came to Bruno Mussolini's table. The radio, he noticed, was almost reassembled.

"Of course, sir," said a pilot. "Fine job bringing her in like that, Bruno," the man added to young Mussolini before turning back to his fellows. "Those damn mechanics better keep us in the air."

Bruno caught Grimaldi's eye, then quickly looked away without speaking.

A burst of wind gusted up from the west and hot grey sand dusted through the mess. Nearby, four signalmen carried one of their comrades past on a makeshift litter.

"What happened to him?" called one of the pilots.

"Snakebit while we were laying telephone cable," grunted one of the bearers. "Worse than Sicily."

"Hurry up with that radio, Massimo," said another flyer, checking his watch. "It's almost time."

Static crackled from the radio as the last tube was screwed back in place.

"Tomorrow make certain your aircraft are in shape, gentlemen. You don't want to come down in the bush," said Grimaldi. "The next morning could be it."

All nodded to him before they lowered their heads. The signal sharpened and Asmara came in clear as a church bell in a village at home.

"Romani!" cried the great voice as the crowd in the Piazza Venezia roared in surges like a storm at sea. Even Colonel Grimaldi could not suppress the prickling thrill that charged his spine.

"We have been patient for forty years!" cried Mussolini over the wireless. Enzo could almost see the Duce's staring eyes and raised fist as the cheering throng drank in his energy. Italy had been promised that the public audience rallying to hear the announcement of war would be the largest gathering in human history: summoned by bells and sirens, over twenty-five million Italians were said to be assembled in every town square and school yard and marketplace from Brindisi to Bergamo. At Enzo's table the hands of the young pilots tensed. Bruno Mussolini sat still as death as his father's voice reached Africa.

"Tomorrow Italy takes her place in the sun!"

— *14* —

"Isn't he the most thrilling man in the world? I can't bear to look at him." The lady closed her eyes and passed the playbill to her friend. "If I were Merle Oberon, I hate to think how I'd behave."

"The Cataract Café and London Films present Douglas Fairbanks," the leaflet read, "in *The Private Life of Don Juan,* directed by Alexander Korda, with a distinguished cast including Merle Oberon. Surprise Short: *Cock o' the Walk.*"

A Nubian attendant sold tickets to arriving guests as they passed down the gangplank onto the deck of the Café. To the left of the gangplank, the pit. Rows of small gold folding chairs waited near the white movie screen that hung against the outside wall of the bar. To the right, the dress circle. The usual round marble tables and comfortable rattan chairs had been pushed back towards the bow of the barge. Rich Copts, senior British officers, important merchants and other elegant Cairenes sipped Veuve Clicquot and nibbled zucchini *sambusak,* or *samosas,* as the Café's Goan proprietor preferred to call them. The serious drinkers, all British, were at work in the bar behind the screen, gathering drinks before the lights went out.

Olivio stood beside the screen, his back to the beaded curtains that covered the doorway to the bar. His hands were folded behind him. He wore his new emerald green tarbush. He snapped quiet instructions to the staff and nodded amiably to his guests of distinction.

"I must raise the prices," the dwarf muttered, disturbed by some of the less suitable clients who were fussing over their seating too near the screen. "Who do they think they are?"

"The Swedes, *effendi!*" said Tariq to his master. "They say they will not sit beside the Japanese or the Italians."

"Very well," said Olivio judiciously, "seat them next to the rail, beside the Argentines."

The seating at these events was more complex and difficult than a coronation. Certain Italians and Germans could not be seated near some other diplomats and soldiers. The threat of war in Abyssinia, and the use of the Canal to supply the prospective invaders, had heightened many little dramas, adding some swagger to Cairo's Italian community and drawing vocal resentment from Italy's critics. The Japanese, despite their discreet ways and almost flawless, if overly tight, English clothes, were still unwelcome neighbors to some due to their brutal invasion of Manchuria, China and Korea. Various lovers needed to be together, or at least nearby; others to be far apart. Enemies, passions, intrigue. It was, as the wise old men in Goa would say, his heart's blood. Olivio massaged one open earlobe. He observed an Egyptian party of government functionaries sipping colored juices and debating politics in intense whispers.

"If only you knew who was toiling belowdecks," he murmured, glancing towards the door to the hold.

The sides of the Café were garlanded with small electric bulbs, alternating pink and white. Olivio noted Clove, a precocious wizard with mechanical things, standing in the bow polishing the lenses of the two Gaumont-British Kalee portable projectors. He trusted his daughter, but he reminded himself to be certain all went smoothly each time she and Tariq changed the reels.

Olivio still marvelled at the process. Of all the modernities that were buffeting his world, he found films and automobiles the most congenial. Each gave him a capacity that nature had denied him, the ability to transport himself with ease, and an opportunity, in darkness, to be like other men and share their pleasures equally. Soon he would purchase the 1936 Hillman, the Minx Magnificent. His would be the first in Cairo. A light machine, but stylish, it would be perfect for the girls.

The great ten-pound reels rested on a chair between his daughter and Lord Penfold. He wished his friend could share his sense of magic, rather than be so averse to all modernity.

"Isn't the cinema marvelous!" Olivio said with excitement. "How our world is changing."

"Can't be helped." Penfold shook his head.

"Think of it, my lord," exclaimed the dwarf while Penfold stirred his gin with his little finger. "An entire world waiting inside eight round silver tins! Each reel prepared to display twenty-four frames per second, ninety feet per minute!" He spread his arms enthusiastically. Penfold raised his white eyebrows with gentle tolerance but said nothing as the dwarf carried on.

"Tonight a magic world of old Spain, created in England, and brought to life on the ancient Nile for the guests of the Cataract Café!"

"Set it here, please, Tariq. Ouch!" said Clove, pinching her finger as she guided the first reel onto the central sprocket of the projector while Tariq held the heavy wheel of film.

The Nubian mounted the first reel, and Clove began to thread the nitrate film, almost a thousand feet of nitro-cellulose, a substance so volatile and flammable that once ignited it would burn even under water. Warned by her father of the horrors of fire, Clove always made certain that the lamp house was clean, the chimney vents clear, and the loops set precisely to prevent jamming and overheating of the film.

Soon both projectors were ready, the first loaded with Walt Disney's *Cock o' the Walk,* the second with the first reel of *Don Juan,* Clove's own suggestion for the evening's main performance.

"Drive off those wretched street boys. They are gathering like rats on the quay," Olivio said to Tariq. "The scoundrels wish to see, without cost, some corner of my screen. Next week, I shall hang a curtain along the port side."

When every table was taken, each chair occupied, Olivio flipped a switch by the door to the bar, off and on and off. Conversation slowed and ceased. Olivio clapped his hands twice in the darkness. To one side, a single watercraft glided past the Café with lanterns glowing fore and aft. To the other, the occasional motor vehicle illuminated the road along the embankment. Overhead were the stars of Africa and a swelling gibbous moon. How he loved this moment!

Clove looked to her father and raised her eyebrows for permission to begin. The dwarf smiled at his child and nodded twice. She switched on the Mazda incandescent lamp. The first machine turned, came up to speed, and *Cock o' the Walk* began the entertainment.

After an unpleasant experience at a film soirée in May, Olivio now declined to show newsreels. Scenes of Chancellor Hitler toasting Air Marshal Goering's lavish marriage to the statuesque film star Emmy Sennemann had brought roars and guffaws from British officers, and furious outrage from the German guests. Followed by his entourage, the German ambassador had stalked from the Café like a pocket battleship leading a fleet through a storm in the North Sea.

Olivio walked to his daughter and stood behind her, just able to peer over her shoulder. He was annoyed that a few regular guests, principally diplomats and bankers and one distinguished emigrée courtesan, a Hungarian celebrated for her lips, were not at their regular tables.

"Why are those tables empty?" Clove asked him.

"They will be seated by the galley when they return," he said. "Our envious rivals have lured them away, probably the Cosmo Cinema and the Diana Palace."

"Oh, dear," Clove said, her expression hardening like her father's.

"What are they exhibiting, my child?" Olivio asked, certain she would know.

"The Cosmo's showing *China Seas* with Harlow and Clark Gable," Clove said, proud of herself, "and the Palace is offering Myrna Loy and Spencer Tracy in *Whipsaw.* They're saying it's in three dimensions."

"Fraud! Nonsense!" said the dwarf. "And who are Tracy and this Gable to Douglas Fairbanks?"

On the screen, pirouetting animated doves satirized the choreography of Busby Berkeley. Laughter warmed the audience. Seeing they were content, Olivio nipped inside and opened the private door to the stairway that led to the hold. Complete darkness. The odors of sweet perfume and incense. Irresistible, he thought. And these were not the natural scents of Musa Bey Halaib. Did Olivio hear the jingle of thin gold coins brushing together? Was Jamila in motion? He stood on the top step and closed the door quietly behind him.

With obligations on deck, and only ten minutes to a reel, Olivio had not time to change into a proper costume. It was not fair. But while his eye adjusted, he removed two objects that hung on the back of the door: a sphinx-head mask and a short black velvet cape. Not enough for the transformation of mood and mind that was the gift of a full costume, but a helpful step towards unleashing the imagination.

He heard a heavy hurried scuttling down below, as if some beast, perhaps a wild hog, were rushing into a thicket. The Undersecretary for Irrigation must be getting closer! he thought with a grin. What a surprise the Bey would find!

The cartoon neared the end. Clove prepared for the projector changeover, her favorite part of the job, one that always reminded her of her private piano lessons with the naughty French music instructor. Embracing, wings and beaks touching, the plump birds circled their tall dovecote in a romantic finale. A few feet above them, Olivio's pigeons hunkered silently in their coop on the roof. Clove rested the toes of her right foot on the changeover pedal that connected the two projectors. Disney's Silly Symphony credits appeared on the screen. She started the motor of the second projector.

Olivio heard the laughter cease. He turned back with reluctance and hung his cape on the back of the door.

The last frame died. Clove hit the pedal. The incandescent lamp on the cartoon projector turned dark. The lamp on the second projector came to life. The sound switched to the active projector in a seamless changeover unnoticed by the audience. Not as critical as later changeovers, but a good test.

Olivio slipped through the beads, pleased by the appreciative murmuring of his guests, proud of his daughter's skill. He stood against a bulkhead staring up at the screen with his lips parted.

Douglas Fairbanks as Don Juan. Evening in Seville. Bouquets tossed to neglected ladies on balconies. Fearful husbands lock up their wives, alarmed the great lover is back in town. But is it Don Juan or an imposter? Douglas Fairbanks, with sword and mustache, impossibly charming, the true but aging Don Juan, is eluding his angry wife, Dolores. His physician recommends a less romantic life: "Don't climb more than one balcony a day. Then slowly reduce that to four balconies a week. In fifteen years, no more balconies."

Two dancers vie for Don Juan's attention. One is deceived and seduced by his imitator. Don Juan courts the other. Riding home at dawn in a cabbage cart, exhausted, Don Juan wonders if women can be worth such effort.

Clove tapped the pedal. Another perfect changeover. As Olivio prepared to slip away, he heard Don Juan address his steward: "Aren't there women who love fat men?" The dwarf paused to hear the reply: "Yes. Very rich, fat men." He hoped Lord Penfold was being attentive.

Olivio returned to the stair. His pointed slippers, deep green silk to match his tarbush, created no sound. He reflected on one of the delights of Egypt: what elsewhere would be regarded as an exaggerated form of dress, even derided as a costume, was seen here as normal fashion. On the other hand, that made dressing in costume even more demanding. Masked and caped, the dwarf descended the stair with infinite care. Was he being too generous to the powerful man at play in the hold?

Raised in Smyrna, where her mother had been a privileged concubine, and her grandmother a slave, Jamila spoke seven languages like a scholar. When it pleased her, during lovemaking she murmured passages of Aretino or Abu Nawas or the *Arabian Nights.* Like farming or soldiering, hers was a family tradition.

Taken by the Russians in Circassia in 1850, Jamila's grandmother had been curly blond, pale and wild, tall and lovely like so many of her Black Sea race. Transported at nine years old, she had been exhibited naked at an auction, turning very slowly in a circle while an attendant twisted one of her hands above her head. An elderly Turkish merchant purchased her for seven pounds sterling, procured from the sale of fine Bokhara rugs. For three years she was trained in his household. Too old to enjoy her fully in any carnal sense, the merchant made her the sensual virgin that delighted his last years. They played backgammon for sexual favors and essayed the arts of arousal with humor and celestial patience. Freed at his death, her lessons learned, she established her own household and provided entertainment for important guests. Her only child, Jamila's mother, caught the governor's eye and bore a daughter and became an enviable figure in the ancient city of Smyrna.

The vizier arranged for his child to have one rare gift: an education in books and languages. And from her mother, Jamila learned the art of dance. With olive skin, full breasts and hips, but slender legs and curly blond hair, altogether somewhat spare and unsubmissive for the Ottoman taste, she was the best of several worlds. When she danced, it was for herself.

From time to time Olivio acted as her protector or personal banker, never asking too much in return. He contrived to be the one man in her experience who seemed interested in her pleasures, not his own. Handicapped in the pursuit of women, the dwarf had learned to be a servant to their private delights, rather than to his own, at least initially. With Jamila he had found a point on the chart of sensuality where her path of satisfaction crossed his. Equally wise and adept, rarely stirred by conventional lovers, they found a droll delight in entertaining each other.

Olivio sat on the lowest step and waited for the betrayal of a sound or a moving scent in the long blackened room. The gentle rhythmic slapping of bare feet upon the wooden floor caught his ear. Then the sibilant shushing of thin gold coins driven by a body's movement. From the opposite wall he heard the grunt of labored breathing: Musa Bey Halaib. There was a rush of movement, a light elusive laugh from another quarter, and Olivio regretted that it was time to climb the stairs. Sometimes he dreaded what the future might hold if the Undersecretary were to expire here on such an evening.

The third reel was well in progress. Here was Don Juan himself. A friend asks the secret of his success with the ladies. "Dull husbands," Fairbanks answers wearily, "and the careful avoidance of intelligent women. They rob a man of his glory." Soon Don Juan's imitator is killed in a duel, charged with being the evil seducer himself. Don Juan determines to take advantage of this confusion to feign his own death. There are possibilities here, Olivio thought, as he watched the great lover attend his own funeral in disguise, surrounded by scores of weeping inconsolable ladies in black, all pretending to have been his lovers. "This is the greatest day of my life," exclaims Don Juan. "I've never seen any of them before." The reel changed. Inspired, Olivio returned to the stairway.

The game also had changed. Now it was a favorite of the dwarf's, a romantic adaptation of Pin-the-Tail-on-the-Donkey.

Three stout candles had been lit in the hold along the length of the vessel. Deep shadows darkened into black circles at the perimeter of each flickering light. Jamila stood in the center of the room, oiled and slippery and shiny-skinned as a freshly picked date, naked save for a little silk and gold. She moved easily, as if exercising and stretching her long firm muscles before a race. From the side, her shoulders and chest and belly and hips moved with the arching rippling smoothness of a snake or wave. Her head and feet were still.

What could the Bey ever provide him in exchange for this? Olivio crossed himself, knowing the answer. Already their conversations had danced around it like butterflies about a blossom: the disturbance with the police at his estate and the threatened trial before the Mixed Courts. The Undersecretary would not provide a fixed conclusion, or suppression of the evidence, or dismissal of a complaint, but instead an intervention that would leave no trace, merely what came naturally in this timeless land: delay, and more delay, a perpetual postponement of any proceeding. That hateful young policeman, Captain Thabet, would be a grandfather before he found his way to court. The danger of this solution, of course, was that so long as the matter lingered on, the obligation to the Undersecretary would require repeated nourishment. Mulling over this dilemma, the dwarf pinched his earlobe until it tingled.

Blindfolded, dressed in a yellow and green Pinocchio suit with three enormous buttons and a wide black patent-leather belt that bound his body like metal hoops around a barrel, the Undersecretary advanced towards the dancer on his hands and knees. Olivio marvelled at how many roles this man could play. Red-tipped and bulbous, the Bey's immensely long costume nose led before him like the armored prow of a slave galley. Whenever Jamila paused and the guiding sound of her movement was lost, the Undersecretary stopped crawling. His breathing, never a pleasant sound, now aggravated by his nose extension, became the only noise in the room. When the music of movement resumed, he advanced. The dwarf knew well to what sacred garden the Egyptian sought to guide his nose. If she was not careful, Pinocchio would do better than he deserved. Despite himself, Olivio felt jealousy rise within him like a cobra from a basket.

Two feet from Jamila when she ceased to dance, the Bey lunged. With the fearless grace of a matador, Jamila lifted one leg. The Undersecretary crashed forward beneath her. Olivio could feel the richness of the man's pain and frustration. The Bey lay on his side on the hard floor, whimpering, his nose bent, the black silk bandana hanging over his eyes. In the shadow behind Musa Bey Halaib the immense painted face of the sphinx bore no expression. There was so little the creature had not seen before. For a moment Olivio admired the flawless image, sixty-three feet long, precisely one third that of the original. Then the woman stepped back and began to dance, faster, with energy. Stirred, his appetite refreshed, her suitor gathered himself for another try.

From upstairs came the shrill sound of whistles, then the thunder of stamping feet. His guests! Something must have happened with the film! Olivio scuttled up the stairs.

Breathless, he hurried past the bar and passed through the beaded curtain to the deck. Catastrophe! His daughter had fallen asleep and missed the changeover, leaving the loose end of the nitrate film to lash wildly around the receiving reel.

"Clove!" he cried as he emerged. In the crisis of the instant, he had neglected to remove his sphinx mask.

"Mother of God!" a woman shrieked in horror when she turned and saw the partly costumed dwarf burst from the hold. He nipped back inside and tucked the mask behind the bar.

"Tariq, quickly," said Olivio, "champagne for the dress circle." Then he walked to Clove and stood quietly behind her, squeezing her shoulders gently.

"Father," she said, turning and looking him in the eye, "I am so sorry."

The dwarf studied his daughter, his eye bright as a torch in the dim light. He spoke quietly, with no anger.

"You and I, child, cannot afford to make mistakes in public. Humiliation always waits close beside us, like a shadow."

Clove nodded and bit her lip. He kissed her cheek by way of encouragement. Embarrassed but calm, she restarted the motor of the second projector. She tapped the pedal.

Douglas Fairbanks filled the screen, distraught at his rejection by a tavern wench who does not believe that the actor is in fact the "dead" Don Juan. He visits the theatre to attend the opening of a play about his own life. He leaps onto the stage and interrupts the spectacle to announce that it is in fact he, Don Juan, not dead, but alive! No one believes him. In desperation, the great lover wanders home. "Marriage is like a beleagured city," he muses. "All those that are out want to get in. Those that are in want to get out." Resigned, as the film ends Don Juan climbs the balcony to seduce his own wife.

An interesting notion, Olivio thought. One day, he wondered, would it come to that? Mercifully, his own dear wife, being Kikuyu, expected him to take younger women from time to time.

Applause and laughter and cries for drinks rose with the lights. Proud of Clove's selection, Olivio passed among his guests, apologizing for the interruption, accepting their appreciation for the entertainment. Tariq helped Clove pack the reels in their silver metal cases. While he stacked them and moved the projector, she decided to precede him to the wooden cabinet where the tins were stored under the stairway in the hold.

Clove walked to the door and opened it, at first hearing no sound from below due to the clamor of the Café. She stepped down into the candle light.

There before her was the Undersecretary for Irrigation. Flat on his back beside the sphinx, his eyes closed, naked save for a long pointed nose, he was touching himself with one hand.

From the bottom step, Clove stared down. Fascinated, her own pubescent fantasies engaged, she did not hurry as she regarded the two appraisingly. She was her father's daughter.

The Bey's feet were bound together by a broad black belt. Several gold coins glittered on the planks nearby amidst the green and yellow tatters of some material. Exhausted, his soft flesh was moist and relaxed, spread outwards around his body like a puddle of damp batter. In the shadows several feet from him stood a naked woman with her back turned, one arm raised as she sponged herself from a basin.

Opening his eyes, the man looked up and met Clove's gaze. Musa Bey twitched violently, then whined some exclamation, struggling to roll on his side while the young lady calmly turned her back and climbed the stair.

— 15 —

"Welcome to Africa, welcome home Bwana Rider!" cried the handsome grey-haired black man as he caught the rope the lighter's boy hurled to the quay in Djibouti's busy harbor. Bernadette thought she detected humor, possibly even mockery in the man's deep voice.

The lighter slowed as it approached the dock. Shallow and low in the water, a smart tricolor snapped at her stern. Small boys with beautiful excited faces swam after her, diving and clamoring for francs and centimes. Others dashed down the worn stone steps of the quay, eager to fend her off and be of service.

Everywhere Bernadette noticed small assertions of Gallic precision and authority against the mass and color of Africa. Coming in, they had passed the burned-out hulk of the luxury liner *Fontainebleau,* the most prominent vessel in the harbor, now serving as a breakwater. Near the quay the tricolor flapped from the harbor-master's tower, reminding visitors that this Somaliland was French.

Anton stepped ashore first and turned to give the twins a hand.

"No, thank you," said Harriet dryly, accepting the strong arm of the African instead. "I don't want to get wet."

Anton let this pass. "This is Kimathi," he said, embracing the man after they were all ashore. "He'll be head man on our safari."

"Will he take us hunting?" Bernadette shook Kimathi's hard hand and raised one eyebrow at her sister.

"Sometimes, if you're good, miss," Anton said, feeling at home again. Lowering the wide brim of his brown bush hat, he squinted into the heat that shimmered above the waterfront. "He saved my life again not so long ago."

"My white master is a child in the bush," said Kimathi with gravity, leading them to a group of five other Africans who were gathered about a large orderly pile of baggage and camp gear. The men brightened and straightened as soon as they spotted Anton Rider. Anton greeted each man slowly, laughing and asking questions, listening to their eager responses in what Bernadette took to be Swahili. All wore similar canvas khaki shorts and dark green shirts, some more faded than others. The initials "A.R.S." were stitched above the shirt pockets. Bernadette noticed that Kimathi and one other man had shirts with cartridge loops instead of pockets.

Anton turned to introduce his clients. "Laboso here can skin an eland before it falls down, and Lapsam cooks so badly he has no teeth." The chef grinned with the round empty mouth of a blowfish.

"This skinny Wakamba gent is Diwani, our old gunbearer," said Anton, putting an arm around the man's slender shoulders. "He's been hammered once or twice by buff and rhino but he's still got the finest eyes in Kenya." Diwani's lean face crinkled as deep dimples cut down across his cheeks and webs of lines made new patterns under his eyes. His earlobes hung in long open loops that housed small ivory containers holding his snuff and charms.

"Miss Bernadette, Miss Harriet, Bwana Crow," Anton said carefully. The men nodded and smiled, each one shaking hands as Anton introduced him by name and job, and always something more. It reminded Harriet of her grandmother returning home to the horse farm in Lexington after a trip to Aiken or Saratoga.

"And this is Haqim," Anton added to the safari staff, knowing the Nubian's reception would be cool. "A new man from Cairo. He'll be helping in camp." The burly Sudanese nodded once but made no further gesture.

"Jambo," said Kimathi as the other men remained silent.

While the rest waited for the luggage to be collected from the boat, Anton went to the *Douane* with two men to get the guns out of bond with some of his recently won riches. Accompanied by Kimathi, the twins strolled about the harbor as the heat rose. Not quite as frantic as Massawa, Djibouti seemed hotter and less European. Each African arrival gave Bernadette the sensation of getting to a costume party just before it ended: still crowded and colorful, noisy and apparently cheerful from the door, but on closer view running down, rough at the edges, with too many needy people close to desperation. Keeping a safe distance from Kimathi, several barefoot boys followed them about, occasionally holding out their hands and pointing at their mouths.

Anton returned and led his clients on a walk up to the columned verandah of the Hôtel des Arcades, a decaying two-story structure set on a hillside at the edge of town. The tables and chairs were the chipped green metal of Tuilleries park furniture. He chose a table in the back row where the roof and crumbling stucco columns prevented the sun from oppressing the guests directly.

"Ouch," said Bernadette, touching the top of one of the front tables as she passed. "It's hot enough to light your cigarette." She thought Anton seemed nervous as he glanced about the terrace.

They breakfasted on fresh warm brioche and small cups of strong coffee on the verandah. As they sipped their second cup, a waiter presented an envelope to Anton on a cracked dinner plate that the white-robed Somali set on the table. The twins could not help reading the two words written on the envelope in a careless elegant hand: "Blue Eyes."

Bernadette felt Harry's curiosity like a weight suspended over the table. Typically unaware, Charlie sketched away on a small pad he kept in a side pocket. Pretending not to watch Anton open the envelope, both girls saw the room key when he began to remove it, then let it fall back inside. Bernadette looked up and caught her sister's eye.

"I'd best go inside to arrange the rooms," Anton said, trying to conceal his excitement. He was not good at it, Bernadette thought, like a boy on Christmas Eve. "We'll be off by rail early in the morning on the sleeper for Dire Dawa and Addis."

The twins were led upstairs to a large white stucco bedroom with a ceiling fan that would not turn. Dark wooden beams crossed the room. Paint chips and bits of stucco were gathered in the corners. A pretty Somali housemaid brought towels and poured buckets of hot water into a big tin basin on the floor. Surprised at the bottom of the basin, scalded, a fat black beetle floated belly up, perfectly preserved as an Egyptian scarab, its two-inch antennae reaching before it on the steaming water. Bernadette poured in a few drops of oil. She left the beetle for Harry.

They began to undress. While Bernadette sat in the tub and soaped herself, Harriet examined her body in the mirrored armoire. To one side she saw a slender green lizard stalking a fly on the wall. Doing the Lord's work, she thought.

Harriet wore a towel around her waist. Frayed but clean, it bore the double M monogram of the *Messageries Maritimes.* She admired her flat belly and touched the baby-smooth clear skin of her shoulder. Turning sideways on one foot, she arched her back to push out her fanny. She pinched her pink nipples several times until they hurt and cupped one hand under each breast, lifting and pressing them towards the center of her body.

"Poor Harry. Don't bother." Bernadette blew perfumed soap bubbles at her. "I've tried everything. Nothing helps. You'll still have a figure like Tom Sawyer."

Harriet glanced at her sister and batted her eyes. "They say girls with small breasts have to be good at something else." She made a round shape with her lips and winked.

Abruptly Harriet put one finger to her mouth. "Shhh, he's in there!" She pressed her ear against the locked door that led to the next room. She heard a woman's laughter, warm and relaxed, then a few teasing words in what she took to be Spanish or Portuguese. Harriet understood the tone if not the language. Gripping the soap, dripping bubbles, Bernadette leapt from the tub and set her eye against the keyhole.

An olive-skinned lady sat on the end of a bed pulling long hairpins from her dark hair. She wore a creamy silk dressing gown. Anton passed in front of the keyhole. The woman slipped her right hand inside her gown and stroked her left breast.

"Shame on you, Anunciata," Bernadette heard Anton say. He blocked Bernadette's view for a moment as he returned to the foot of the bed.

Anton knelt in front of the woman with his back to the door. He said something the twins could not hear and placed one hand on the woman's knee. Bernadette had the sensation she was looking directly into the woman's dark eyes as the lady smiled and reached down and touched Anton's face.

"You always have new scars," the woman said, speaking English in a smooth soft Latin voice while she regarded him with eyes brown as chocolates. She cast up her chin and shook her head slowly from side to side. Thick hair tumbled down about her shoulders. Anton took her hips in his hands and pressed his face into her lap as she parted her knees. She closed her eyes when Anton's head moved against her crotch. Anton's left hand went inside her robe. She reached to her side and freed the sash that held the waist. Anton's hand reached up and found one breast. As he fondled it, Bernadette felt her own small breasts grow warm and tight.

Anton raised his head and held his right hand to the woman's lips. She moistened his thumb and middle finger in her mouth. Bernadette let out a soft gasp.

Harriet struggled to push her sister from the keyhole without making a disturbance. The towel fell from her waist. Red-faced, naked and dripping, Bernadette looked up and punched her sister in the stomach, smearing her with soap. Breathing hard, unable to speak, the twins glared at each other with years of fury.

"We'll take turns," Harriet whispered fiercely. She put one eye to the keyhole.

Naked save for high-heeled white shoes, the woman sat on the bed leaning on one hand. Her head was back and to one side. Long shiny dark hair hung across her face like a velvet curtain. The fingers of her other hand were working through Anton's hair. He was still completely dressed. The woman adjusted herself as Anton's right hand went between her legs and under her buttocks.

Fascinated, jealous, Harriet guessed what he was doing. She remembered his long fingers.

Anton's other hand was stroking and squeezing the woman's left breast. His head was moving slowly between her legs. One shoe fell, then the other. Her legs tensed and flexed. Harriet saw that her free breast was full and heavy, not as high as on a young woman, but still magnificent, slick with sweat, the dark nipple erect. The woman was past her prime, but richly so, perhaps the better for it, Harriet conceded with admiration. For years the sisters had taken the slender woman's delight in observing that a voluptuous rival would not age well. Before them was an alarming exception.

Harriet felt herself become wet. She pulled away from the door and closed her eyes, not bothering to conceal her breathing from her sister. She moved to one side and Bernadette took her place.

The woman rested her legs on Anton's shoulders. Her feet were bent back with tension. Bernadette noticed the scarlet nails as her toes curled tight. Moans came through the crack in the doorway.

Anton stood and removed his clothes. Oh, Lord, Bernadette thought. The woman pulled herself backwards on the bed until her head was on the pillows. She rolled onto her stomach and rose on her knees with her head down. Bernadette observed that the lady had a little too much hip. Anton climbed onto the bed behind her. Neither spoke. Leaning forward on his left hand, Anton reached under her body and took her right breast with his other hand as he knelt behind her. The woman reached back between her legs and guided him. They must have done this before, Bernadette observed. After a time, the woman cried out.

Bernadette leaned back and put her palms on her temples. She stood and stepped into the warm soapy bathwater.

"Thank God that bitch won't be on our safari," Harriet snapped in a low voice.

The twins looked at each other and began to laugh, but not completely. It was like being sixteen again. But today there was more frustration mixed with the excitement.

They dressed and brushed their hair, being careful, without the need to speak of it, to appear as much alike as possible. They opened the door and walked along the dark hallway arm in arm.

Charlie and Anton were waiting for them on the verandah, smoking small dark cigars and chatting over gin and cassis. It was the first time the two men had seemed so relaxed together. The heat had eased, dropping into the nineties, Harriet guessed.

"Did you have a nice bath?" Anton said to the twins. His eyes sparkled, vividly blue, alive. "You must be thirsty."

In the morning a Renault taxicab called for them. The windscreen and trunk door were missing, Bernadette noticed, the tires smooth as balloons. Filthy blankets covered the seats. The one-eared driver rubbed his hands and bowed to Anton. *"Bienvenue, Monsieur Reeder! Aha! Je vous embrasse, patron!"*

"This is Vincent," Anton said. "Vincent has learned two things from the French. Greed and speed."

Charlie spoke for the first time. "Named after van Gogh, I assume."

Bernadette looked at her fiancé with new admiration, kissing him briefly on the lips as he held open the door.

"A *cheval*!" said Vincent as he started up. Off they roared, flinging everyone back against their seats. The taxi gained speed as it hurtled downhill towards the center of Djibouti.

Frantically they rattled through town. A suitcase bounced from the trunk. The Renault spun to one side when Vincent braked. He and Anton leapt out. The case, Harriet's, Bernadette was relieved to see, had burst open. Somalis swarmed about it. Men and boys clutched for cosmetics, undergarments, shoes.

Harriet jumped down and helped Anton and Vincent recover her dusty possessions. "Give me that!" she cried, snatching Jung's *Essays on Analytical Psychology* from a barefoot black child.

"What a horrible town," Harriet said grumpily, flinging herself back into the rear seat when the suitcase was finally restowed.

"Don't be so grouchy, Harry." Bernadette patted her sister's knee, guessing why she was cranky. "It's not as bad as they told us. And here comes the station. Lord, it looks like a circus."

The railroad station was an intense mixture of Napoleonic order and colonial chaos. Black gendarmes with white sun flaps hanging from blue kepis swung truncheons, threatened and hollered "*Allez*!" and blew on silver whistles to keep the traffic moving along the busy curbside. Leprous beggars and European engineers, porters and purveyors of drinks and fruit and nuts crowded the long platform. Steam clouded around them from between the great wheels of the black Swiss locomotive that waited to make the three-day run to Addis Ababa. The coal car and the water tank car waited to serve her, followed by several short wooden goods cars, five grey and one white passenger cars, and a small caboose, all bearing the heraldic scripted CDE of the *Chemin de Fer Djibouti-Ethiopien.* The white carriage was the first-class car.

"You stay with the clients on the platform, Haqim," said Anton, concerned lest the Nubian upset the protocols of the French-trained train crew, "and Kimathi and two of the boys can load the luggage and camp gear. By the way, well done, ladies, on the canvas luggage," Anton added before entering the white car to confirm the arrangements. "Always like clients who follow instructions. Leather would've attracted ants."

He stepped back down to the platform. "Everything's in order. I'll show you to your cabins."

"It's like a yacht," Bernadette said once inside, admiring the upholstered cabins, each one compact but fitted out in wooden panelling and brass. A Somali steward, crisp as a starched linen napkin in his fez, sash and long white robe, dusted the seats and folding table with a feather whisk.

Bernadette walked back alongside the train with Anton while Harry availed herself of the tiny cabin bathroom. In the second baggage car they found one of Anton's boys, a young Kikuyu, guarding their property with his body, stretched out on the khaki canvas tent bags with his eyes closed and his mouth open like an old man at the opera. At the end of the platform, Bernadette noticed, a knot of women were selling fruit and gourds and baskets.

"Afars," Anton said, as Harriet hurried to their side. "The married ladies are the ones wearing black cotton shawls across their faces and shoulders." He paused in his stride and turned to the twins. "The other ones're the virgins." The dark-eyed maidens were bare-breasted, with beautification scars in raised lines on their cheekbones and full shapely lips not unlike the twins' own, he noted.

"Hate to think what they'd make us wear," Bernadette said to her sister.

Bernadette was not pleased, however, by the black volcanic terrain that received them after the train drew out of Djibouti. Not even cactus relieved the desolate prospect. From time to time the train paused at railroad settlements along the arid landscape. Late in the morning, crossing the frontier at Douenle, a green, yellow and red flag welcomed them to the kingdom of Abyssinia. Women in colored cotton robes raised baskets of nuts and dates and oranges to the windows of the first-class car. Natives scrambled on and off the other coaches while the train was being fueled and watered. She heard feet running along the roof of the coach. Then Africa moved past them again, more slowly as the train climbed. The land became browner and greener. The window was painted with dust that sparkled redly in the high sun.

Lunch was served on the covered stone terrace of the track-side *Buffet de Dewele,* a small island of comfort in a vast sea of bush. It was a marvel of frayed white linen, *billi bi* and *gigôt d'agneau,* passion fruit and *port salut* and Tavel.

"The French do things so well," Bernadette said, nibbling a *petit four.*

"I thought you hated the French," Charlie said.

"Everyone hates the French," the twins said together. "But they know how to do things."

During the main course, sensing movement under the table, Bernadette found Harry's empty shoe, then felt the wriggling of her sister's leg. Annoyed, she guessed that Harry's bare foot was exploring Anton. Harry was exceptionally good at it. Both sisters could play marbles with their toes. Bernadette looked at Anton's face, impressed to find him conversing with Charlie in a natural voice. She wondered if he knew whose foot it was.

"This evening," Anton said, speaking a bit more rapidly than usual, "the train will stop for the night on a siding, and in the morning we'll be in Dire Dawa for an early breakfast. That's where our Abyssinian tracker and a few other chaps'll be meeting us."

"I love trains," said Harriet, looking forward to the rest of the ride, pleased she had already pulled the catch on Anton's side of the door that separated their cabins.

"Here's where we get off," said Anton, knocking on Charlie's door early the next morning, trying to sound fresh as the train chugged to a stop at a large ochre-colored station. As always, he found himself excited that the safari was about to begin.

"It's so French," said Bernadette, noting the painted signs as they walked along the Dire Dawa platform: *Commande Centralisée des Mouvements, Facteur Lignes, Inspecteur* and *Chef de Gare.* "Are we really in Africa?"

They met the safari staff halfway down the platform.

"You three chaps unload the kit. Kimathi, you find the other lads and the animals. Then start packing up," Anton said. "Lapsam, off to the market with one of the boys and buy what we need. These ladies like their fresh veggies. Hop to it. Haqim, you watch the baggage. Keep your eyes on those gun cases. We're setting off in two hours."

Anton and his clients struggled between the camel carts and sleeping donkeys to a dusty café across the station square, the Makonnen. There they ate baguettes with thick dark honey from the hills. Charlie, sketching, gave a coin to a gaunt bearded minstrel who sat in the dirt under an orange tree stroking the single string of a square banjo with an arched horsehair bow. A blind boy of nine or ten squatted beside the man, accompanying the minstrel on a short wooden flute. Other children gathered about, touching and leaning on one another, their eyes bold and merry in smooth oval faces.

Bernadette felt her heart pounding from the altitude and strong coffee. "Look!" she said, thrilled, as a hawker of metalwork spread earpicks and rings and crosses on a cloth on the adjoining table.

Anton groaned when the twins rose to inspect the hawker's wares.

"Typical," said Harriet to her sister as they took out their purses. "He doesn't understand shopping."

"What did you expect?" said Bernadette.

Finally the twins bought matching silver Coptic crosses with rings at the top.

He was a different man, Harriet realized, watching Anton organize the camp. She sat in a folding canvas chair with Carl Jung in her lap, a pencil holding the place while she studied her African bird book. Her eyeglasses rested on the tip of her nose.

When the wind brushed her, she inhaled the sage-like scent of the thornbush and the violet-flowering wild herbs beside her. She recognized a bee-eater, square-tailed and sharp-beaked, vivid blue as a sapphire, flitting from bush to bush with short swift flights. The shiny dark leaves of a wild fig tree rustled above her head. The camp was pitched on a rise at the edge of the Chercher hills that joined the great plateau of central Abyssinia, but was set well back from the escarpment to escape the night wind. Behind her she heard the comfortable sounds of mules and donkeys and camels grazing.

Harriet had not appreciated the complexity of a safari. Like an orchestra or hospital, every function had its proud discreet specialists: tent boys and *saises,* trackers and gunbearers, and boys, some of them white-haired, assigned to laundry and latrines, wood gathering and water hauling. Even the mules were specialized: pack mules, sturdy and callused; leaders, sure-footed and experienced; and riding mules, better fed, high-gaited, long-legged and expensive.

Harriet smelled the blue woodsmoke as she watched Anton stride about the camp in his loose khaki shorts, a .375 in one hand. He bent to check the tension on a tent peg, then signaled Kimathi.

"Have this one tightened," he said in a firm friendly voice, switching in and out of English and Swahili. "Put the fires there and there, and the loo behind those bushes, the shower-bath over that branch behind the ladies' tents."

Harriet thought he moved with the easy command of a stage director or a great chef in his kitchen. All the things about him that had seemed a bit off center in Cairo, and even on the boat, his somewhat informal clothes, the restlessness, his weathered tan, his bright moving eyes, his powerful hands, were now just right. His deference had given way to authority, his hesitation to precision and confidence. Noticing the muscles of his legs, she remembered seeing a leopard in a circus cage and thinking how much better the animal would look where it belonged.

She'd noted this in men once or twice before. She had often thought that women, raised to adapt themselves to men, to a man's friends and life and work, even to his name, seemed better at adjusting. Less adaptable, a man's quality seemed more dependent on the right circumstance. Harriet's boyfriends were never comfortable playing games at which they did not excel, particularly if the girl were good at them. Generally, for a woman, the man was the test; for a man, the test was life itself. All the same, there was nothing more exciting, she thought, than seeing a strong man in his element. It hardly mattered what that element was.

Harriet chewed on her lip and pondered the arrangement of the tents. The open-sided dining tent was already up, and it looked as if four sleeping tents were being laid out in a row between the stream and the main fire. Hoping the tents wouldn't be too close together, she thought of what she'd seen at the hotel in Djibouti two days before.

She watched boys dragging in branches and logs and chopping kindling with a hatchet and panga. Others brought water from the stream. Lapsam and his cook boy were at work, nursing a fire between several large flat stones, filling a huge battered black kettle, rolling dough, and setting out the sacks and tins.

About half the men, like Kimathi and Diwani and Lapsam, seemed to be Kenyans, Kikuyu or whatever, part of Anton's regular safari crew. All the rest were Somali, except for another skinner and an Abyssinian tracker. They seemed different from the Kenyans, more slender and elegant, rather handsome, Harriet thought, with dreamy dark brown eyes. It made her remember some of the different looks among the Negroes back home. Strange, she thought, that she had to come to Africa to consider such distinctions.

She saw Anton laying out the gun cases on the folding table in the dining tent. Quickly, Harriet wiped her face with a bandana, and ran both hands through her hair. She left the books on the chair and walked over. She looked at the rifle he had set down and recognized it instantly. It was perhaps the finest all-purpose weapon for heavy game: a double-barrelled Holland & Holland .375, with a long walnut stock worn and rich as a well-loved burl pipe.

"Pretty," she said.

Anton, totally concentrated, spread back the canvas covers and opened the cases one by one. Holding the barrels against the sky, he checked the weapons and wiped each one with an oily rag: a magnificent pair of 12-gauge under-lever Woodward shotguns, a .600 Nitro-Express elephant gun by William Jeffery, two Rigby .303's, one doubled-barrelled, the other with a shortish single barrel, a Gibbs .450, a Colt .45 Peacemaker revolver, and, looking like a child's weapon beside the heavy guns and rifles, a Winchester .22. Green metal ammunition boxes were stacked under the table. Enough for a small war, she thought.

"May I?" She touched the double Rigby.

"Of course." He had learned, whenever possible, never to call either twin by name.

Harriet raised the rifle, turned to face outside the tent, shouldered it, swung and aimed.

"It fits," she said with pleasure.

Anton nodded and unbelted the leather straps on the last case, a battered canvas box with one leather corner missing. He looked at the weapon without touching it. Near the end of the barrel, a pair of long brass-jacketed bullets were secured in two slits cut into the fitted felt mat of the box. "Ever seen one of these?"

Harriet lifted the heavy rifle and turned the double .450 in her hands. She opened it, looked through the barrels and closed it, appreciating the smoothness and balance. She read the inscription on the breech of the well-blued barrel: Gebrüder Merkel.

"This should stop anything," she said. "Where'd you get it?"

"Tanganyika, in the plantation country, near Kilimanjaro, just after the war. From Ernst's father."

"Oh," said Harriet, trying not to let her voice betray too much interest. She had enjoyed the hardy German, and was curious about his life. "What was his father like?"

"German sisal farmer, very old school, gritty as they come," Anton said with affection. "He adopted me for a few months when I first came out. Hugo von Decken, his name was. One of the pioneers. He wouldn't let me leave for Kenya without it."

"How old were you?" she asked, smiling.

"Nineteen."

"Why'd he give it to you?"

"Said he was too old to use it . . ."

"Wasn't Ernst jealous?" she interrupted too eagerly.

Anton noted the odd undertone, but let it pass. "He should've been, but he wasn't."

"What are those two bullets?"

"Uttendoerfer Nitro Express .450's, from before the war. They're the last of the three boxes Mr. von Decken gave me when I started walking."

"Walking?" She tossed her head and ran her fingers through her red curls as she looked at Anton. "How far did you walk?"

"All the way. To the Kenya highlands, north of Nanyuki," he said, pleased to be relating this boyhood adventure. "One evening I'll tell you some of the old man's stories about the early days."

"Tell me one now, please, before everyone comes and bothers us."

Anton looked at her. It was the first time she'd seemed truly interested.

"Well," he said, forming his thought, "he'd hunted with the old elephant hunters, hard eccentric lonely men, when it was still Africa, back around 1900 or before, the 1890s, I reckon. Running all day till the thorns tore the shirts from their backs, hunting the great bulls, a hundred pounds or more of ivory a side. So one evening I asked von Decken what was his best elephant." Anton grinned.

"I can still see him. Standing in the shadows near his verandah, the sisal hanging on the drying racks behind him, his white eyebrows and silver hair standing out against that dark leather face and the black night sky."

"What did he say?" Harriet had not seen Anton so excited. She wished they could have more time alone.

" 'Young man,' he said, 'elephants are like women. The best one is the next one.' "

Anton watched Harriet while she bit her lip thoughtfully and placed the Gebrüder Merkel in its case.

Anton felt a familiar tingle. He knew this was what Gwenn always hated about him, getting so caught up in the present moment. She might be in Ethiopia right now, he realized. He might have seen her from the train window had he looked out at the right time. He frowned, dismissing the thought. They would never meet here, and what if they did? Gwenn had avenged herself on him, and humiliated him in front of the boys with her damn Italian count. Soon she'd be chasing the war, and his safari would be avoiding it. He'd never meet his wife on this trip.

Smiling, catching his eye, Harriet looked at Anton expectantly.

— *16* —

"At this moment the *Bersaglieri* and the *Valpusteria Alpini* are crossing into Abyssinia," said Captain Uzielli as the sharp fiery rim of the sun rose behind him over Nefasit.

"No, no, Captain," said the liaison officer from the 1st Gruppo Blackshirt Battalion of Eritrea. "It is our *Fascisti* legions who are leading the attack."

Jaunty and proud in his baggy trousers, starched black shirt and tasselled hat, the former party *squadriste* almost danced as he stamped his boots to keep warm. His sleeve patch bore the motto of his unit: "The Life of Heroes Begins After Death." He stood back from the large map pinned to one of the two rough walls of the flight room, then leaned forward and slapped it with his leather gloves. "The 29th July Division will be the first to march."

Sipping coffee and smoking at a table near the edge of the thatch-roofed shelter, putting aside bitter thoughts of Cairo and Gwenn Rider, Colonel Grimaldi was amused by the rivalry. He knew who would be first in the air.

"It is soldiers who will fight this war," said Uzielli harshly, stepping closer, his face hardening. With the Duce's sons nearby, gathered with other young officers around the radio, chewing hungrily on square pieces of breakfast pizza, he dare not go too far.

Contemptuous, the Blackshirt did not reply.

Had it been so, too, for the legionnaires of Julius Caesar? Uzielli wondered as he held his tongue. He was not a scholarly man, and he would never be a senior officer, but, like all youths of his generation, he'd been raised during the hardships of the Great War while studying the military exploits of ancient Rome. He liked to see himself not as a commander but as one of those unthanked scarred centurions in the days when the legions marched from Londinium to Alexandria, battling barbarians at the outposts of empire, his short sword rarely dry.

As a young man, and sometimes now, he dreamt of slaughtering barefoot hairy Britons in their fens, storming Masada to kill the Jews, parading in Rome with enemies from a dozen tribes and nations stumbling in their chains before the chariots, the bundled rods and axe of the fasces leading his legion. He was certain that, then as now, the real soldiers never got their due, that their requisite brutality was unfashionable between campaigns. If a legionnaire or a *Bersaglieri* were fortunate, his rewards were plunder and adventure and fraternity, and sometimes a little sex with the locals.

"Where did you serve in Libya, *Centurione*?" Uzielli finally asked in a low voice, employing the Fascist rank.

The man stepped back as if struck in the face.

"Where were you, *Bolognese*," the Blackshirt asked intently, his thin voice rising, "when we were marching on Rome?"

Uzielli opened his mouth but controlled himself and turned away. How could he ridicule the unit named for the Duce's birthday? As he turned, he found himself face to face with Colonel Grimaldi.

"Captain," said Grimaldi easily, knowing the soldier was annoyed to have his dispute witnessed, "make certain your men are prepared."

"Yes, sir," said Uzielli, anger still in his face. "They are ready now."

Grimaldi was relieved that the Italian Air Force was not divided as were the forces on the ground, where proud regular formations like the Savoy Grenadiers and the Gavinana Division were competing for supplies, men and glory with the Blackshirt legions, each one named after a prominent date in Fascist history.

The colonel walked over to Bruno Mussolini, who was standing awkwardly behind a throng of his fellow pilots.

"Have you checked our Caproni, Lieutenant?" Grimaldi said to the young aviator in a cheerful voice, aware that Paolo himself had gone over the aircraft after her regular maintenance was complete.

"Si, Colonnello," said the pilot, straightening, his voice uneasy as he looked around.

"Splendid, Lieutenant," said Enzo, clapping Bruno on the back. "Remember this day: October third, 1935. Once again, Rome is on the march in Africa! Today we will share a flight you will never forget."

The radio crackled and the volume rose with the martial music of the Fascist anthem, the signal for which they had all been waiting. Every man present stood, some at attention, others arm in arm. Together they sang *"Giovinezza,"* the song of youth, while the sun rose over Africa.

"Gentlemen," ordered Colonel Grimaldi, "to your aircraft."

In minutes the men were in their bombers. Engines roaring, the nine planes of the *Disperata* squadron taxied in line down the dusty runway. Turning slowly at the end, each hesitated briefly, fed its engines and accelerated down the airstrip as the ground crews and observers cheered and waved their hats in a cloud of dust that sparkled red and pink in the early light.

"La Disperata!" they hollered.

Airborne, Grimaldi turned and looked back to check the formation. Acting as co-pilot in the three-man crew, he saw that his own aircraft was flying low under Bruno's control. Enzo turned his head and glanced to the right. The dawn sun shone back at him, reflected from the white bellies and underwings of the squadron. He forgot his loneliness as he admired the giant three-engined aircraft.

At nearly four thousand feet, the Capronis sailed forward in three tight flights. Enzo made out the white teeth of the skull and crossbones insignia painted on the side of the nearest plane. Vittorio Mussolini looked down from his cockpit and saluted Colonel Grimaldi, gesturing with his fist and raised thumb. Enzo nodded with satisfaction. The young pilot was playing his part. Through the round port window in the fuselage Enzo saw the bombardier moving about, preparing to start the war. For now the machine gun turret atop the fuselage was empty. In a few minutes the bombers would pass above the marching columns and approach their target: Adowa. After forty years, Italy would be avenged. Grimaldi recalled that Benito Mussolini himself had been an impressionable boy of twelve at the time of Italy's humiliation at Adowa.

On this front alone, from Eritrea a hundred thousand men were advancing into Abyssinia in three columns under the command of old General de Bono, a veteran of Italy's African campaign of 1887. From the south, under Graziani, tens of thousands would be attacking from Italian Somaliland, supported by the great base at Mogadishu. Graziani was a general who knew how to fight in Africa, Enzo thought, recalling his boast of pouring cement into the desert wells of Italy's enemies in Libya.

"Bit faster, Lieutenant," yelled Colonel Grimaldi into the roar of the engines, tapping the airspeed indicator with his knuckles. "We're slipping back." The bomber trembled as Bruno sought to comply too urgently and the three engines lost their beat. "Steady, now, that's it," said Enzo reassuringly, still anxious as to how the young pilot would perform. "Well done."

With envy, Grimaldi made out the smaller aircraft flitting below them in the distance, the Bredas and Fiats that were scouting and strafing ahead of the army.

Before reaching the border the Capronis flew over a squadron of motionless *carro veloce,* Fiat-Ansaldos. Yesterday a fighter pilot had reported that the narrow box-like three-ton tanks had been abandoned by their exhausted crews the day before the invasion, when the temperature inside the steel machines reached one hundred and twenty degrees and the 13mm armor became too hot to touch. Worse than Libya, Grimaldi had thought when he heard the news.

Just beyond the edge of the vast plateau, they passed the engineer brigades, already at work inside the Abyssinian frontier, extending the road that had been built to the border before the war began. Lines of Italian navvies were drawing tools from trucks loaded with picks and shovels. Enzo made out two bulldozers lurching heavily about like elephants with their heads down.

Next they flew over the support columns, bringing forward the mobile kitchens and supplies to sustain the fighting forces. Italy's military doctrine required that every regiment provide three classes of food, one each for enlisted men, non-commissioned officers and officers.

Responding to the requirements of Rome, and to Fascist agents working within each factory, every manufacturer in Italy was marching on this mountain road in Africa. Lancias and Spas, Isotta Fraschinis and Alfa Romeos struggled along in line with diesel-powered three-ton Bianchi Mediolanums and six-wheeled Fiat 621's.

The colonel pointed down, but Bruno seemed unaware of the instruction. "Lower, Lieutenant!" he yelled, tapping the altimeter, concerned that the other bombers seemed to be falling below them. Bruno nodded and dropped a hundred feet to rejoin the squadron. Sharp drafts of cold air whistled through the cabin, and Grimaldi cursed silently.

The Capronis soon came to what he thought must be units of the Fascist militia, moving in good order along the unpaved tracks, no doubt singing their favorite tune, *"Faccetta Nera,"* as they marched in the cooler air of the high country. Their black shirts contrasted with the tan shorts that were the standard issue of Italy's tropical uniform. Advancing before them were the Tuscan regulars of the Gavinana Division, well dispersed along a broader front. The infantry must appreciate the highland climate, Enzo thought. When the Gavinana had arrived at Massawa in June, six men had died of the heat before the division disembarked. It had been one hundred and thirty degrees on deck, and more in the steel holds.

Finally they came to the Eritrean askaris, leading the attack with skirmishers and small scattered groups of a few dozen men, each under an Italian officer. Spotting them, Enzo thought of his grandfather and the native troops he had trained for battle. Below he could see the pop and sparkle of ground fire. It always amazed him how much detail you could see from the air.

There was no heavy action until the mountains near Enticcio, the last town before Adowa. There, below them, the *Disperata* found a flight of CR-20's already engaged, supporting the Eritrean units that were fighting to clear the high passes. The Ethiopian defenders were visible from the air, clustered behind rocks and ledges on the steep hillsides. Perfect job for the *Bersaglieri,* Enzo thought, knowing that what was considered a challenging ravine in their training grounds in the Dolomites was in Ethiopia a dimple. This was a vast rugged landscape, where the gorges were fifty miles wide and cross-hatched with sawtooth peaks and bottomless chasms. The other Capronis began to descend several hundred feet.

As the bombers came in, the three light aircraft climbed and turned to meet them, wagging their wings, their machine guns already empty. One, probably struck by ground fire, trailed a plume of dark smoke. Her pilot waved as if unconcerned. The man's brother pilots took up position on either wing, preparing to escort him home.

"Wouldn't want to be him if he goes down among the Abyssinians," Enzo hollered, uncertain if Bruno heard him, hoping he had not. Enzo noticed the young pilot's stiff bent-forward posture, like an anxious old lady driving a motorcar, and the white-knuckled rigid manner with which the boy clenched the controls.

Below, the colonel spotted a single mass of retreating Abyssinians, perhaps four or five hundred men and numbers of mules and horses crowding together as they fell back through a narrow gorge. Enzo felt his stomach tighten. This was the moment to spur his horse and lower his lance. How he wished he were in his fighter and could dive and do his duty.

Enzo considered what he had been advised about these old enemies. They were not like other black Africans. They had a written language, an intense pride of race and history. Although some claimed that fewer than a dozen Ethiopians could read a map, they were credited with administrative ability, discipline, even a tactical sense. In European terms, they were serious.

Adowa itself they found to be a town of a few two-story stone houses, many mud and thatch hovels, and cattle enclosures, wells, several churches and market squares. Robed figures scrambled for shelter, abandoning their animals and arrays of produce as the three flights of Capronis approached in line at about two thousand feet.

Intelligence from Addis had advised that, anticipating the attack, the enemy forces had already abandoned the town in order to make clear to the League which side was the aggressor. The colonel was annoyed that the *Disperata,* coming in at nearly top speed, a bit over one hundred and twenty miles an hour, was not flying lower.

"Slower and lower would do the job better," he growled to himself beneath the trembling din of the three engines. Recalling Marshal Balbo's orders, however, he did nothing, fearful of the result if a lucky ground shot struck one of the Duce's relatives.

As Adowa rose before them, reminding the colonel of a hill village in

Tuscany, Grimaldi turned in his seat and signalled to the bombardier. He felt a rush of cold air as the man opened the hatch beneath the racks of bombs. Enzo punched Bruno's shoulder and pointed back, thinking the lieutenant would wish to give the first order. But Bruno stared at him through his goggles with no expression. Frightened, he was barely managing to keep control of the plane. Disgusted, Enzo raised his arm and the first bombs fell.

All around them, the explosives tumbled and floated down. Enzo sipped coffee from his thermos and watched distantly, as if in the balcony of a cinema. To help calm down the child, he passed the flask to Bruno.

Across one market square a line of explosions burst open, flashing red, then were covered instantly in dense puffs of grey dust. Camels and donkeys and cows bolted and died. A woman and child disappeared when a bomb hit the stone wall of a well against which they sheltered. Natives ran from the burning town. Bombs exploded in the rocky surrounding fields. Climbing slowly, the Capronis droned ahead and turned for home. Beneath them, the town burned.

Approaching the Nefasit aerodrome, Enzo's mind was with the small planes still diving and strafing in the mountains behind them.

"Well done, Lieutenant!" he hollered after a time, extending his right hand to the young Mussolini. "First blood!"

Ignoring the gesture, Bruno leaned forward and vomited on the instrument panel.

Many pilots had done the same, Grimaldi reflected with good humor, pleased they were almost home.

They were the second plane down. Eager hands helped them from the hatch.

"How was it, Colonel?" said Paolo, his eyes bright, eager as a boy.

"Perfect," said Grimaldi, stripping off his goggles and clapping the old campaigner on both shoulders. "Everything. The attack's on schedule. No bombers lost, no enemy aircraft, and Lieutenant Mussolini here did his duty." He smiled at the young man, now wiping his mouth on his sleeve. "Right on target."

"The bombs!" said Bruno excitedly, animated for the first time. "They were like flowers! Blossoming, all red and yellow. You can't imagine how beautiful."

"Check my Fiat, Paolo," said Grimaldi, quickly changing the subject, "I'm going up as soon as she's ready. And find me some bread and cheese and coffee."

A sense of freedom filled Enzo as he flew back to the front alone. Pleased to be in an open cockpit, he strained the CR-20 as he climbed towards the mountains at nearly a hundred and fifty miles an hour. His fuel and bullets would not last long, but he was determined to make a difference in some part of the engagement.

The road was thick with men and vehicles. Enzo dropped down. Several soldiers waved up as he flew past.

Both sides of the route were littered with scores of broken-down vehicles. Alarmed, Grimaldi saw the legs of soldiers laboring beneath their machines, and the backs of men bent over them, working on the idled ambulances, reconnaissance vehicles, command cars and trucks of all types, American, British, Italian. What would things be like when they got to the interior and the supply lines snaked through hundreds of miles of hostile mountains? He recalled how powerful and overwhelming the Italian forces had seemed when he saw them crowded on shipboard, massed in port at Massawa and lined up at the aerodromes. But from the air, seen against Africa, between the vast horizons, they were ants lost in a brutal landscape.

The front itself had not advanced far. If anything, he thought, banking to starboard, it had widened and grown jagged. He snaked the Fiat along a line of narrow intersecting valleys and gorges, past scattered units of advancing troops. Climbing to turn, he spotted a column of dark smoke. Before him opened a small valley choked with Abyssinians moving south through a mountain village, contained and inviting as a Christmas box of toys. Several huts were burning. Thousands of white-robed warriors were pressing forward, with bands of horsemen and camels and mules scattered amongst them. Rifle fire popped as he flew past.

Breathless, his body stiff with excitement, Enzo banked and came around in a wide circle. At the mouth of the valley he crossed himself and dived. His engine screamed as the plane fell faster and faster. His wings buffeting with the air speed, he dived to two hundred feet and loosed his machine guns. His body seemed to be flying by itself. The gunfire shook the aircraft and marked two lines through the mass of careering men and animals, straight and neat as railroad tracks.

Gasping with exhilaration, Enzo climbed at the end of the valley and returned for a second pass. The smell of blazing thatch thick in his nostrils, he dove through the smoke of the flaming huts and emptied his guns. His blood roaring in his ears, he turned for home without looking back. Only then did he notice that both his wings were punched with bullet holes.

Even for Ernst von Decken, Africa still held surprises. After growing up on the flanks of Kili, stalking lion with Masai playmates and sucking warm blood through straws from the throats of their cattle, after four years on the run with the *Schutztruppe* during the World War, butchering Britishers from Tanga to Kasama, swilling melted hippo fat with his askaris, Ernst thought he had not much to learn.

But Abyssinia was another world, an Africa as different as the Sahara and the Congo. Ernst drained the rest of his warm beer and wiped the froth from his lips with the back of his hand. *Talla,* they called the local barley beer. It was the first word he'd learned in this hellish country. He'd always been brilliant at languages, if you put aside grammar. Africa, however, was like Belgium. Neighbors never talked the same language. In Ethiopia, he'd been assured, they spoke almost a hundred.

Beside him on the terrace of the *gibbi* the Somali girl dropped the dark cloak from her shoulders as the morning changed rapidly from cool to hot. With pleasure he glanced at her smooth elegant face, normally not the attribute that drew him to a woman.

If he were inclined to marry, Gretel could tempt him.

"You're like a boiled egg," he had said to her one morning, enjoying the lovely uncomprehending smile with which she greeted the remark.

"Cool to the eye, hot to the tongue, just like a boiled egg," he had explained while he stroked her thigh. Generally, this was a quality reserved to the best blondes, but this proud *Schwartze* was an exception, dignified yet wild. She would be difficult to replace, unless he was rich, of course. He shifted heavily in his seat and rubbed his red eyes. Down between the carved posts of the terrace he gazed at the spacious courtyard of the modest wooden palace. Like all *gibbis,* this grand house sat proudly on a hilltop.

Today the courtyard was more frantic than ever. Ras Gugsa's Italian allies, or patrons, were expected at any moment, personal representatives of General De Bono himself. They would bear news of the Duce's reward to the only Abyssinian defector worthy of high payment, the prince who had opened one of the gates to his country, the mountain road that led to Addis. Silver coins, Ernst thought, a suitable reward for betrayal in the world's oldest Christian kingdom.

Treachery, of course, was to Italians as congenial as opera. At bottom, von Decken knew, they were all Borgias and Machiavellis, not Caesars. To most Europeans, the silver thalers might seem a bribe for treason. But to an Ethiopian, such payment was a mark of respect, tribute from an admiring ally. When it came to bribery and betrayal, these Wops and kaffirs drank from the same cup.

"Another beer," he said to Gretel. She rose at once, expressionless, while he concentrated on opening two tins of sardines. Anticipating the feast, flies gathered on his wrists. Others swarmed and jostled on the lid of the open tin of peach halves that waited on the table.

In the courtyard below, Ras Gugsa's men milled about, sharpening swords and polishing rifles. Many of the firearms were military issue from the 1890s. Others, carried in leather scabbards or wrapped in cotton like the old women, seemed still more ancient originals, their long barrels bound to the stocks with bands of brass and leather, their splintered shoulder butts carved steeply inwards in deep crescents. Only the Ras's personal guard was properly armed. Ernst acknowledged their captain with a nod and watched the hawk-faced officer arrange his men in uneven lines. Their sandals slapped the packed dirt of the courtyard. The dark khaki uniforms were baggy on their slender bodies. Like most Africans, Ernst was certain, these would fight well if properly led, and their ability to cover ground would be unmatched. He saw a bearded black prisoner chained like a dog to the wall behind them, most likely a Shoan loyalist. The wretch sat on the ground, picking at his bare feet, apparently chewing bits of callus and nail. Probably his last meal.

Gretel returned with his beer just as a motorcycle roared into the courtyard. Spinning artfully, the rider braked in a fury of dust, like a Roman playboy late for a party. The Italian scout pulled off his leather helmet and goggles. He shook his head and spat before setting the stand of his *Moto Guzzi* and pulling off his gloves. Ernst watched with disgust, sipping peach juice from the can. Driving steadily, habituated to the unpaved roads of Africa, he and Gretel had made the journey from Massawa to Makalle without incident or hardship.

It galled Ernst to see Italy, Germany's scorned enemy in the last war, establishing the African empire his own country had lost in 1918. Doubtless the main Italian column was still a few miles back, twisting around the endless cliffside turns, climbing yet another escarpment as rocks were spun off by the wheels of their lorries and dropped hundreds of feet below. In truth, the terrain would be their only challenge. For a moment, he thought of what had been German East Africa, and wondered if his own side would ever get a second chance. Perhaps, he thought, and next time we'll do it right.

Gretel declined the peaches and Ernst gulped down the sweet fruit whole, slippery as oysters. He had been in Africa long enough to ignore the flies that fussed at the corners of his mouth.

Ernst's own truck, a wide short-bodied Fiat, waited in a corner of the courtyard. The wooden slats of the eight replica money chests were nailed down like a second floor of the bed of the truck. In just over an hour, Ernst could pry the boards loose and assemble them with the flat-headed wood screws that were in a tin under the driver's seat. Each chest, like the originals, was designed to hold eight sacks of coins and would weigh fifty-five pounds when loaded, the maximum practical weight for a porter and the optimum for one side of a mule's load. Each set of slats included one board, now facedown, bearing a black stencil identical to that of the royal Italian treasury.

The boards reminded Ernst of how his father had brought the old family hunting lodge from the *Schwarzwald* to Arusha, meticulously disassembled, each German beam and plank clearly numbered on both ends with black oil paint, so the numbers could not be washed away and yet would be hidden once the reassembly was complete. One day these new boards would enable him to buy back the old house.

Ernst offered a slippery brisling to Gretel on the blade of his penknife. Fat flies moved slowly in the oil. She blew them off and took the slender fish neatly in her small white teeth before the flies could resettle.

He finished his beer as a high-wheeled staff car entered the courtyard. He noticed the fresh dents on the Alpha's front fenders where the bent metal was free of dust. One headlamp was broken. Two spare tires were strapped side-by-side at the front of each running board. A lieutenant jumped out of the front seat and opened a rear door. A stocky colonel stepped down shakily, no doubt nauseated by the rough drive. He gathered himself, slapping his cap smartly on one forearm to shake loose the dust. Ras Gugsa's guard snapped to attention. Not bad, by Italian standards. Ernst remembered how his own askaris, barefoot and in rags at the end of the campaign, but razor-lean and brave and loyal as Doberman pinschers, could have drilled any Prussian till his boots cracked.

Ras Gugsa, of course, would think it princely to keep his paymasters waiting. No doubt the soft swine was now peeking out the window and trying on his new Italian uniforms. The ras would make a perfect Fascist officer: vain and corrupt, elusive when the time came for cold steel. All the same, von Decken thought, it would be best to avoid these Italians in order to reduce the chance of complications.

Ernst rose and walked back to his apartment. Gretel followed him. She pulled the heavy embroidered curtain across the doorway and drew off her robe without speaking. He turned and faced her. She rose on tiptoes and bit his upper lip until it bled, hanging on and moving her head from side to side with short sharp movements like a terrier. Her dark nipples were hard and pointed. He tasted the sardine on her tongue. Then he sat on the bed with a groan. *"Danke, Schätzchen,"* he said while Gretel unlaced his boots.

When Ernst finally descended into the courtyard of the *gibbi,* the Italians had already left, rejoining the column that was pressing on south towards Makalle and Addis. Ras Gugsa's aide, Jesus, a man preoccupied with rank, was waiting for him, strutting uncomfortably in his new Italian jodhpurs.

"Here your instructions," Jesus said slowly with some difficulty, apparently uncertain how much respect to accord the German. "And here the Italian letter of transit."

Ernst looked at the papers, relieved to see a warrant for the collection of fifty-five thousand silver thalers, signed by General De Bono himself.

"I escort you to Makalle with a lorry of the prince's guards to take the money chests," the thin very dark man continued. "Your woman is here at the royal *gibbi* until you come with the silver." Ernst had introduced Gretel to Ras Gugsa as his fiancée, both for her own protection and to increase her value to Ernst in the mind of the Ethiopian prince.

The arrangement must seem artful from the Ras's point of view, the German thought as he checked the tins of spare petrol, but it showed little understanding of Ernst von Decken.

Driving south for Makalle, with a dozen of Ras Gugsa's bodyguard asleep in the old Ford truck that followed him, Ernst passed the camps of the Italian baggage train. Beside him, apparently thrilled to be motoring, Jesus sat forward on the edge of the seat as if reviewing the troops.

Hundreds of mules, exhausted by the hurried climb to eight thousand feet, stood tethered to rope lines, the marks of their pack frames sharp on their worn flanks, their heads bent low as they grazed and devoured small piles of straw and grass. Italian muleteers and Eritrean camp followers squatted nearby in separate groups, the Italians boiling water for macaroni, the Eritreans munching flat bread and mealies. A lorry driver, cursing, waving his arms, labored over the steaming engine of his heavy truck. In its open bed, covered by a tarpaulin, rested a small Italian tank, perhaps twelve feet long. Ernst saw the two-man crew lounging against the tarp, smoking and laughing in the sun, doubtless waiting for orders to dismount and lead the assault up the road at the first show of resistance.

Farther along Ernst was forced to slow as he came to the work gangs, filling in holes in the unpaved road and widening it every five hundred yards to let opposing traffic pass. He knew grading and paving parties would follow, making permanent the Roman road from the Red Sea to Addis Ababa. Even in the near desert of the southern front, an Italian officer had boasted to him, the Italians were beating mule tracks into lorry roads as they pushed northwards.

"Every country does two things well," his father had told him one evening in German East Africa while they smoked and watched the laughing boys skin an eland without drawing blood. "What about us," Ernst had asked the old man while they smelled the thick chops grilling, the finest meat in the world. "What are Germans good at?" Old von Decken took the pipe from his yellow teeth. "Marching and giving orders." Ernst wondered what else the Italians could do besides road building.

The Italian commander had already made his forward headquarters at the administrative center in Makalle. Entering the busy town, Ernst drove through a dusty market square carpeted with grey eucalyptus leaves. Sitting cross-legged, men sold stacks of mealies and dried peas and guinea corn from open sacks. He drove on past lanes of small square houses topped by patches of brown grass and scraps of beaten tin. He passed a large circular stone church set in a walled compound.

"Stinking priests," Ernst muttered to himself, despising clerics, resentful that the Orthodox church owned one third of Ethiopia.

Surrendered without a fight, thanks to Ras Gugsa, Makalle opened the imperial road that led on to Addis. At the capital, Ernst had heard, an Ethiopian army of seventy thousand men had trotted past Haile Selassie for four hours on its way to the front. Other armies of native levies, hundreds of thousands strong, were being mobilized to encircle the invaders. On the southern front, after the first Italian victories in the Ogaden, Abyssinian officers accused of cowardice by the emperor were being flogged, bayonetted and shot, *pour encourager les autres.*

Ernst presented his pass to the Italian guards and drove into the headquarters compound, a four-sided cluster of brick and plaster buildings. Jesus descended and rejoined the Ras's guard. During an interminable wait at the quartermaster's office, Ernst listened to bemedalled officers shouting hysterical demands for provisions and armaments.

"What!" bawled one. "No olive oil, no blankets! Do you know where we are? How are my men to eat and sleep?"

Von Decken remembered his commander, von Lettow-Vorbeck, bone thin from malaria, seven times wounded, fighting up and down East Africa year after year, living off the bush and whatever his men could capture. Perhaps, Ernst thought sourly, one day these prancing dandies will learn what soldiering means.

Finally he was permitted to present his warrant for the Maria Theresa thalers. The major raised his eyebrows at the number and the signature, then passed into a private office. "Back your truck into the garage shed behind this building at 0 five thirty tomorrow," the major said quietly when he returned. He looked at Ernst with contempt. "I suppose this bribery is cheaper than paying pensions to Italian widows."

"You'll be doing both soon enough," Ernst replied aggressively.

He left the office and drove his truck to the aerodrome located on a high plateau past the edge of town. A small advance party of the *Regia Aeronautica* was preparing the airport, raising wind socks, stringing out wire for field telephones, and measuring the two grass runways, which crossed each other. Two small tanker trucks with the markings of the Italian air force stood nearby: aircraft fuel. Groups of Eritreans and Tigreans hung about here and there, wary of each other, waiting to see what opportunity they might find with the Italians. Donkeys and goats nibbled freely along the runways, probably the only ones doing useful work, Ernst thought.

Eventually he spied what he had hoped to find. Two old aircraft were parked wing to wing under a crumpled shed at one end of the longer runway. Ernst parked his lorry. He waved a salute to the busy Italians at the far end of the strip and wandered over to the straw hangar.

Potez 25's, he recognized at once, French workhorses, ideal reconnaissance aircraft. They were in mixed service all over Africa. Open twin-seater biplanes, eight or nine years old, but capable of one hundred and thirty or more miles an hour, and able to carry at least a quarter ton of bombs or freight.

The first one bore the black-maned Lion of Judah painted on its sides. Perhaps once part of the Emperor's flight, it was now badly tattered and probably used for mail and for ferrying important passengers between Abyssinia's distant provinces. One wheel strut was broken. The two-bladed wooden propeller rested on the ground beneath one of the lower wings, which were far shorter than the upper wings: built rather like a hartebeest. One blade of the prop was badly split and splintered. Altogether, the aircraft appeared to require too much time and attention.

The second Potez looked a trifle sharper, if not ready for the air. Like her sister, her tail was painted with the green, yellow and red stripes of the ancient Coptic kingdom. An English machine gun was mounted behind the rear seat, pointing backwards through the metal circle of the large aerial gunsight above the ammunition drum. He saw an oil can with a long curved spout resting against one of the two spokeless wheels. The starboard cowling was raised. Someone was at work.

Ernst stepped towards the airplane. He opened the hatch of the baggage compartment set into the fuselage. He groaned when he saw its stingy capacity. Typically French. Then he climbed onto the wooden box that rested by the nose. He removed an oily rag and a long lug wrench and studied the engine. An old hand at mechanical improvisation, this was something the German understood. The twelve-cylinder, Lorraine-Dietrich looked surprisingly clean and almost ready.

Ernst heard a sharp voice below him, speaking as if in a very loud whisper.

"Effendi?" A young thin-faced Abyssinian stared up at him with intelligent eyes. The man was short and barefoot and garbed in the usual rough peasant *shamma,* but his dark hands were shiny and slick with oil. As Ernst stepped off the box, he looked down and noticed the man's feet. They were smooth and uncallused, the right one suffering from a fresh cut on the outside. Not the feet of a man accustomed to going unshod.

"I am not Italian," Ernst said slowly, first in English, then in French. He seized the man's thin right arm. "Are you a mechanic or a pilot?"

The man tried to back away without replying.

Money, force, or persuasion? Ernst considered. He put his free hand on his pistol holster and blocked the man's path. Of the three, he usually preferred the second.

The man hesitated. *"Je suis pilote."*

"Shall we fly to Addis?" Ernst crowded the man towards the back of the shed. "I have much money. I will inspect the engine, you will fly."

For some moments the two spoke quietly in the hangar. Ernst learned that the pilot, Ephraim, had been trained by the Belgian military team in the capital. A Shoan, he was at least three hundred miles from home. To return there, Ephraim would have to pass through many enemies: Tigrean, Italian, and worst of all, the Galla, still celebrated for mutilating their foes, and now known to be seething with rebellion as they saw the power of the Emperor decline. He would be smarter to fly over them all. Ernst arranged to meet Ephraim at dawn.

"Everything must be ready." Von Decken squeezed the pilot's thin arm. "Everything, her fuel tanks full. The better you do, the richer you will be." Ernst cast a surreptitious look about the hangar. "For now, remove the propeller so they see she cannot fly."

— 17 —

Olivio Fonseca Alavedo stared up as the giant flying boat came in line with the river and cast its shadow on the Nile. For an instant he thought of how this great stream connected him to his friends lost in Ethiopia. Each drop that flowed past him had journeyed a thousand miles or more, gathered by Lake Tana in the highlands of Abyssinia, then north through the fens and swamps of the Sudan, past the ghostly ruins of the upper Nile, down the rushing cataracts, and now through Cairo itself, before giving life to his own lands in the Delta.

As the craft touched the water and met its shadow, the dwarf balanced his elbows on the deck table and set the telescope to his eye. Like Dr. Hänger himself, the distinguished scholar of achondroplasiology, this polished instrument was German: precise, far-seeing, unmatched at examining objects small to the eye. Clove stood beside her father's chair, one hand lightly on his shoulder as she followed his line of sight.

The *City of Khartoum* taxied smoothly on its broad scalloped belly and came to rest five minutes ahead of schedule at its dock across the Nile. Nice to Cairo in seventeen hours, twenty-five minutes, with stops at Naples and Athens and Alexandria. The flying boat's three Jupiter engines stilled. The waves of her wake rolled across the river and died against the port side of the Cataract Café. The dwarf adjusted the extension of the three brass cylinders until the Union Jack on the dock came into perfect focus.

He watched the white-uniformed dockmen secure the aircraft to the wooden pontoon decks that extended along her flanks. One worker bungled and dropped a noosed painter into the river.

"Even in spotless fitted uniform," grumbled the dwarf, "a *fellah* is still a *fellah.*"

"Of course, Father."

The wide bow of the plane towered over the dock. A midship door opened from the inside of the aircraft. The roped gangway was run up and hooked to the floor of the door hatch. A steward stepped down and swept the gangway. The silver-whiskered captain emerged, a braided cap tucked under his left arm. Olivio tapped his slippered feet together with impatience.

One by one the passengers descended. Some paused at the head of the gangway to stare at the minarets and domes of Cairo. They were in Africa. Adults and children alike shook hands with the captain, who waited at the bottom, straight as a guardsman. Why must the British always conduct these little drills? No wonder they were ridiculed by all the Europeans, who wished so often to be like them.

Dr. August Hänger stepped from the doorway of the aircraft. It could be no other man. This was the master of his future.

Happy for her father, Clove watched him adjust the telescope. She knew how much he needed this physician. "Is that your guest, Father?"

"It is he," said the dwarf without interrupting his concentration.

Olivio began at his feet. The doctor, an angular short man, wore black wing-tipped shoes, perhaps a trifle too heavy. His suit, somewhat short-jacketed in the continental manner, was pearl grey. "Oh, dear," said the dwarf quietly. A dark grey and white polka-dot tie was knotted beneath the exceptionally high collar of the man's white shirt. The collar was stiff as porcelain. The German must have changed on the aircraft. He wore a wide-brimmed Panama with an overly broad black band. Years with Lord Penfold had taught Olivio the unforgiving ethic of such details. Except for formal waistcoats, his lordship was not comfortable with pearl grey.

Beneath his hat, Olivio knew, the doctor was bald as the Sphinx. Long white sideburns extended forward under his knobby cheekbones. Three deep parallel lines crossed his forehead above the peaked dark eyebrows. His mouth was broad and uneven, his lips thin as eggshells. His nose was heavy and prominent like the beak of a parrot. The two sides of his face seemed strangely out of balance. Olivio studied the man's unchanging expression, still hoping to identify the secrets of Dr. Hänger. Many he had learned already.

The German walked slowly down the ramp without benefit of the gangway ropes. His movements displayed both caution and pride. Only with the most stringent diet and disciplined habits did the doctor keep at bay the paralyzing infirmities of severe arthritis. He began each morning and each lunch with a tumbler of warm water, into which three spoonfuls of vinegar and one of honey had been dissolved. Vegetables and fruit and fish gave him nourishment. Sweets and alcohol and meats stiffened him like *rigor mortis.* Light vegetable and fruit soups were the comforts of his evenings. The cold and damp of Switzerland must be a heavy cross to this man. Tomorrow, of course, was the doctor's seventy-first birthday, and Olivio had prepared a special sort of celebration.

As if knowing he was watched, Hänger paused and raised his face and peered across the river. He flinched as the sun struck his pale shiny countenance. Even at this distance, the dwarf felt the penetrating force of the man's eyes. Dark, too dark to determine their color, a fierce brightness leapt from them.

Olivio took the lens from his eye. This would be a man to test him. The dwarf rubbed one earlobe, then raised the telescope.

Half a dozen baggage handlers scrambled to unload the luggage, driven by their turbanned overseer.

"I wonder if they'll do what Imperial Airways promises," said Clove.

"What is that, child?"

"Have the luggage in the hotel rooms before the guests arrive."

"They will," said the dwarf, admiring the teak launch of Shepheard's Hotel. "What sort of boat is that?" he asked.

"She's Italian, Father," Clove said. "A Riva."

The *Lotus* waited at dockside near the slightly less elegant vessels of other caravanserai, the Semiramis and the Continental-Savoy. Her brass and wood shone. The doctor declined assistance as he stepped aboard. He touched his hat brim, bowed stiffly and seated himself beside an elegant lady. There was a slight commotion nearby as a dock boy caught and coiled a rope, and a lesser speedboat dashed away with the baggage.

Olivio detected a puff of exhaust as the twin engines were engaged. The heavy launch barely trembled. The *Lotus*'s bow rose ever so slightly before she cut across the Nile towards her canopied mooring below the grand hotel. At Shepheard's he'd heard it boasted that at thirty knots you could thread a needle or rest a glass of champagne on her deck without a drop spilling.

Olivio lowered the telescope and rubbed his eye.

"How did you know it was him?" Clove said.

"Though we have been separated by desert and sea and mountain," said the dwarf, as if telling her a child's tale, "your father has studied this man as he would before purchasing an estate in the Delta."

August Hänger stood in the cool hallway with his hands clenched behind his back, his knuckles rigid and painful. The flight had aggravated his condition. Only warmth and a severe massage could repair him, but he had left the nurse in Zürich. He watched the assistant manager turn the long key in the lock of the outer door. The man took one step, opened the inner door and stood aside with a bow. The physician had not been obliged to pause at the desk.

"Mr. Alavedo has completed all the arrangements, Doctor," the manager had said in a voice of quiet discretion as he welcomed the German at dockside. "Later we will require your passport to complete the police card."

A dark wooden fan turned slowly in the vault of the ceiling as Dr. Hänger entered the sitting room of his apartment. He handed the manager his Swiss passport and the man bowed and took his leave. The doctor noted with relief that his two medical cases had been set down in the entry hall. He employed no instruments but his own. Large, steel-cornered, each heavy leather case bore the staff and serpent of Aescelepius painted in a small white circle on the center of the lid.

The doctor looked about the room. There were no flowers. Could this dwarf know he was allergic to certain flowers and herbs? He heard the door click shut behind him. Centered on a round table was an outsize basket of fruit, more perfect than a painting, and, behind the basket, two carafes topped with linen napkins. A black lacquer box lay on the table in front of the basket. There was no card. He guessed what it might be. He had once before received such a box.

He stepped to the table, relishing what lay before him: mangoes and pomagranates and lemons, dates and grapes and avocadoes, each fruit choice and ripe, picked at its prime, each one an antidote to his illness. His dark eyes fixed on the box. He opened the clasp and raised the lid.

Inside was a jewel, set into a shaped velvet fitting: the second of a set of three ivory images from the reign of Pharoah Krakhanaton. Like the first diminutive figure, this too was a naked capering dwarf, his legs hideously bowed, his bare feet resting on a spool of ivory that would fit into one of three holes in a sixteen-inch-long ivory pedestal. The pedestal itself, and the left figure, had arrived in Zürich two months earlier, one part of the inducement that had lured the physician to Egypt.

August Hänger stood in silence and examined with a doctor's eyes the three-thousand-year-old effigy. It seemed to be a statue of the same man: sway-backed, buttocks prominent, the left leg even more warped than the right. The head had broad bat-like ears, hollow cheeks, wide almond-shaped eyes, a beak nose. Yet in this image the dwarf seemed older, his face less lively, his belly lower, the penis slightly smaller. This statue bore no necklace. What had been the life of this small man? Had he suffered the cruel intensities of life so common to dwarves?

The doctor knew the gift of this treasure would be completed when he finished his patient's treatment and received from Herr Alavedo the third and most tortured figure. He could then set the three round ivory spools into their common pedestal, and the small priceless monument would be restored. This ancient toy would give his own life's work a link to ageless civilization. Then he would be able to wind a string around all three spools and make the three dwarves twirl and dance whenever he pulled it. He closed the lid and secured the clasp. How had his new patient acquired this treasure? What must be its worth?

Turning to the basket, Dr. Hänger lifted a carafe containing some ochre fluid and held it to his nostrils. Apricot nectar. He thought he smelled the warmth of the African sun still imprisoned in the fruit as he raised the carafe to his lips and drank the entire infusion. He set the bottle down and tried the second darker drink. The liquorice juice left him with a brown and orange mustache.

Wiping his mouth on a napkin, the doctor chose an apricot from the basket before walking stiffly to the door of the bedroom. He dreaded bending to remove his shoes. He stood in the doorway and bit into the fruit. In front of him was a large bed crowned by a gathered mosquito net suspended from the ceiling. Its drawstring hung down, touching a pillow on which rested the head of the most ravishing woman he had ever seen.

The juice of the apricot, warm and rich as blood, ran from the corners of Dr. Hänger's mouth. He stepped to the bedside. A sweet scent welcomed him. With a groan he raised one foot onto the white linen coverlet at the edge of the bed. The thin gold coins of her earrings tinkled when Jamila leaned forward and undid the double knot of the black shoelace. Her amber skin was a pool of honey against the smooth white linen of the sheets. As she moved, the bedclothes fell from her heavy breasts. Her nipples and upper eyelids were painted silver.

This was no Alpine flower.

Dr. Hänger sat up in bed preparing the petals of the skin of a fig aided by a surgical blade. Three sets of calipers, a measuring tape, and a set of limb and digit charts lay atop the rumpled sheets.

Shrouded by the mosquito net, naked in the dim striped light that entered the room between the slats of the wooden blinds, the old physician cut four perfect lines through the dark soft skin. He wagered that each line was within a degree or two of a ninety degree angle to its fellows. He marvelled that the exterior of a fig's skin could be so dry, the inside such a flood of sweet moisture. Like a pregnant woman, this fig was at a stage in its life when it would have burst open of its own accord, its vitality unconfineable. Purple juice and fine black seeds began to leak through each wound. Released from the tension that had joined them, the tips of the four petals curled back slightly from the top of the fruit, exposing the luscious perfection of the purple meat.

The chatter of finger cymbals distracted the doctor from his work. He looked up and removed his rectangular gold spectacles. Jamila was dancing for him. He peered through the shadow of the netting. Oh, Lord, he thought. Another such dance would kill him. She had already provided him with more pleasure than he could remember or imagine. At midnight, the instant of his birthday, he had achieved orgasm for the first time in nine years. More than that, she had taught him how to bring her to climax. As the first light touched the shutters, Jamila had melted with a single orgasmic cry that must have reached the hotel's kitchens. As a tonic for arthritis, this was better than vinegar.

Although he had measured them himself, repeatedly, the dimensions of this creature were indeed a marvel. Like many physicians, it was Dr. Hänger's dream, and occasional practice, to convert patients into lovers, and lovers into patients. Alas, his peculiar specialty, dwarfism, had combined with his own physical and temperamental disabilities to limit the satisfactions available to him.

For the last two hours, however, instead of measuring and documenting deformities, he had applied the meticulous standards of his science to an appreciation of nature's perfection. Astonished again by the youth she had exhumed within him, he watched Jamila's body begin to ripple to her music. He struggled to regard her with scientific German eyes.

Most remarkable, from the medical standpoint, was the range of her movements. Whereas a dwarf, like many arthritics, typically had twenty or twenty-five percent less range of motion in each limb and joint than did a normal person of similar age, this woman had perhaps thirty percent more. Her spine was limber as a serpent. The doctor thought of the tormented creature in the lacquer box.

Jamila had a command of her muscles such as he had never witnessed nor thought possible. She seemed to break down each complex motion of the body into its separate elements, until each muscle and organ, even the most intimate, was an independent instrument to orchestrate as she chose. While the drums thundered, the violins trembled. Actually her body was more like the choir at Kïln, with each singer, boy or man or woman, able to rise and give voice either separately or together, sometimes slow and delicate, at others able to shake the cathedral walls in joined crescendo.

He watched, not breathing, as the girl opened her mouth and moved her lips while she danced. He placed his knife on the bedside table beside the empty bowl of *Kaltschale,* an earlier treat. Arriving unsolicited at the outer door, the bowl seated in a larger vessel of crushed ice, the chilled fruit soup, a blend of imported plum and cherry, was his very favorite, a specialty of his native Westphalia. How had they known? The dancing girl had spooned the soup into him as if he were her infant, and he had been.

He glanced down at the piece of fruit resting on the folded napkin in his lap. The fig was ready. A few more minutes and the naked stripped fruit would soften and lose its shape. He snapped his fingers, a test of his condition.

"Liebchen," he called to her in a thin voice. His fingers snapped like a gunshot.

Jamila ceased her dance and raised the net. The woman sat naked on the bed, facing him. Her perfume surrounded him, sweet and natural as a high pasture of edelweiss in early spring, when the shaded side of the valley still sleeps under snow and the opposite, sunlit, is painted with vivid Alpine flowers. She raised her legs, one firm limb above each of his shoulders. She shimmied towards him until her painted toes were braced against the white padded headboard behind him. Dr. Hänger wriggled beneath her, struggling to move his body down the bed so as to lower his head.

Leaning back on her hands, her back stretched along his thin pale thighs, her throat turned up with her head cast down between her arms, Jamila tightened her breasts, first one, then the other. The dark nipples stiffened obediently. Her stomach moved in a slow wave-like motion as she approached the fig with her cleft. The odors of the fruit and the woman became indistinguishable when she teased the fig with the trembling walls of her vulva. He folded the golden arms of his spectacles and set them on the bedside table.

"Meine Schätzchen."

Jamila's body gripped the fig and lifted it from the napkin. She rippled her belly and the pinched fig began to split and leak. The doctor lowered his face and nipped at the juicy fleshy fruit as it swayed and bobbed before him.

Nearly overcome, his heart bursting, Hänger drew back and gasped for air, the tiny purple seeds glinting in the juice on his nose and chin. What would they think in Zürich? He plunged his head forward, his mouth slightly open, sucking up and pursuing the disintegrating fruit within the woman.

It was time to work, Dr. Hänger reflected as he studied the Nile through the window of the Daimler. An amateur arborist, devoted to exotics, he admired the trees that lined the embankment and shaded the sidewalks of the grand houses facing the river. He was astonished by their diversity: jacaranda, sausage trees, Chinese mulberry, and, unless he was mistaken, African tulip trees, thread palms, baobab and banyan, even Australian lemon gums and Indian laburnums, all the fruit of empire. As a younger more nimble man, he had taken hiking holidays under the dark canopies of the *Schwarzwald,* relishing the reflective solitude of the forest, especially the early moments of the frequent rains, when the green branches above drummed delicately but the brown needles underfoot were still dry and springy. Occasionally, in high summer, after a rain, the great German forest steamed like a kettle.

On his first such hikes, as a boy, he had searched fearfully for trolls in damp stony corners of the steepest woods, but after a time he learned that their dark presence was one of the spirit, not the flesh. Years later, practising and resident in Switzerland, where his specialized work seemed to provoke less distaste than in Germany, he had resumed these walks in still steeper mountain forests.

But as arthritis seized him like drying cement and the mountain climate punished him, August Hänger had retreated down to Zürich, creating his own small forest, both outdoors on his grounds, and inside in the shelter of his magnificent glass arboretum. There he cultivated small semitropical trees and shrubberies that shared his need for a hot dry atmosphere. Grown stiff, living alone, in the late afternoons he would nap on a blanket set on the sandy soil under his dwarf begonias, dozing while the grumbling iron pipes of the radiators eased him with the parched heat of his own sahara. Above him the yellow funnel-shaped flowers closed for the night and the snow-brushed glass roof grew black as the sky.

Here in Egypt, he had found the climate he had labored to create at home.

Dr. Hänger rapped with his stick on the glass behind the driver. Tariq's head turned on its short thick neck as he looked in the mirror to find the passenger's eyes and learn what he required.

"*Halt!* Stop now!"

Tariq pulled the car to the curb. He stepped down and opened the rear door. The German climbed down and walked back along the embankment using his black cane, his frame cruelly stiff again after his unaccustomed carnal exertions. He stopped under a shade tree and looked up. Imported from India, he guessed.

The handsome deciduous tree flowered above him. Its long horizontal branches spread evenly like an umbrella and rose thirty feet or more above the promenade. He extended a hand and gently cupped one of the jointwood tree's clustered pink and white blossoms. A few pods and many bipannate oval leaves were scattered on the ground around him. The doctor drew a handkerchief from his breast pocket. Clenching his cane, he bent and collected a single cylindrical pod. He wrapped the capsule tightly in his handkerchief, praying it would not trigger his allergy. He walked back to the Daimler, checking that the two medical cases were well secured to the chromium luggage rails at the back of the automobile. They drove on to the Cataract Café.

Now he must earn his welcome.

Dr. Hänger found himself unusually tense with anticipation as he stepped from the car at the head of the ramp leading to the houseboat. Could he now be feeling as his patients did when they approached his clinic?

This patient's final letter had emphasized that he would never be examined in a clinic or other medical facility. A sense of privacy and fierce self-respect were not uncommon in such patients. The doctor understood the humiliation and hostility that often greeted his instruction to disrobe.

A short servant in a white *gallabiyyah* led him down the gangway. Did this dwarf favor diminutive staff in order to enhance his own height?

Tariq followed with the cases. The deck of the Café was empty. The servant led the physician to a table near the doorway to the bar. Dr. Hänger sat down and was offered a glass of apricot nectar. He sipped from the glass and watched Tariq enter the bar and carry the cases through the door to the hold. Frothy, slightly sweet, the fruit drink was the finest in his experience. The doctor felt his joints loosen as he drank it. With such potions he could live forever.

When Hänger was finished, Tariq asked the German to follow him.

Refreshed, August Hänger descended the steps to the hold. The door closed behind him. He placed his feet with care in the dim light. At the bottom of the stair he turned and looked along the immense room, startled by the overwhelming image of the Sphinx. His medical cases rested near its front paws. The far end of the chamber was bright, illuminated by four open portholes on the starboard side of the boat. A square white sheet was spread on the floor within this flood of light.

A dwarf stood naked in the center of the linen sheet, pale yellow, his big belly hard, his scrotum low, the scarred chin raised, fists on his swollen hips, defiant, a veritable troll.

— 18 —

"This is why we're here," Charlie said, looking down from the edge of the massif to a horizon of the Abyssinian highlands. He sat on a rock and opened his small box of watercolors. For a moment no one spoke.

"I've never seen so far or smelled air so clean," said Bernadette, breathing heavily at the high altitude after a short walk from camp.

The rim of the escarpment was split by steep ravines edged with grey thorn bush that clung to the dry rocky land. The bowl immediately below them was dappled with clusters of yellow wildflowers, reminding Bernadette that the September rains had just passed. The sky was clear and luminous, the landscape immensely open, even more so than in the Far West at home. At first her eye failed to notice the middle distance. Then she detected greener patches and occasional round stone dwellings with thatch roofs set near tall clusters of slender trees. Steep slopes bore narrow terraces and neat stripes of cultivation.

"Millet?" asked Harriet, pointing.

"Coffee," Anton said.

"Will we have good coffee on safari?" Bernadette asked. She saw Anton's eyes twinkle.

"We'll try," he said. Then, as an afterthought, "Coffee was invented in Ethiopia, miss."

"I thought they invented coffee in New Orleans." Harriet looked through her binoculars and studied the land that fell away to the northeast. She focused on the rail line that led from Dire Dawa to Addis Ababa.

"All began right here," said Anton. "A shepherd noticed his goats getting jumpy whenever they nibbled some green berries. He tried a few, then took them home and cooked 'em."

Bernadette sat on a rock and took off a boot. She shook out the stone and plucked thorns from her socks. She watched Charlie dilute and mix his watercolors. He released drops of water from the cap of his canteen onto the small panels of paint and stirred in the water with a wooden match, raising the swirling colors, trying to copy the floating lavender haze that hovered where the distant foothills met the sky. Kimathi stood behind her. He held a Rigby and shook his head as he squinted at the unfinished painting. Bernadette guessed he wanted meat for the camp. She smelled the strong odor of his body and wondered how she smelled to Kimathi.

"Memsahib," Kimathi interrupted Bernadette's reflections. "Hartebeest!" He pointed with the rifle to a far slope in a valley below them. "Fine meat."

"Can we get one?" asked Harriet, excited.

"Good idea." Anton took the weapon from Kimathi, pleased to have an opportunity to test the twins' rifle shooting. "One of you ladies come with me."

Harriet and Bernadette stood up and began to follow him.

"I'll toss you, Harry," said Bernadette.

Harriet threw a coin on the ground.

"Tails," said her sister. Both knelt.

"I told you," Bernadette said. "It's tails." She turned and walked after Anton, leaving her sister with Charlie and Kimathi.

"Put these in your pocket," Anton said, giving her a handful of .303's.

A few moments later, Anton stopped and pointed. Bernadette stared. She saw nothing. Anton stood behind Bernadette and pointed over her shoulder. She raised her light field glasses and adjusted the lenses, scanning impatiently from side to side.

At length she saw them. First four, then six, a dozen hartebeest, grazing on the darker patches of grass in the light bush of the slope. They were high-shouldered antelope with broad curled horns, and long, almost ugly faces. Bernadette caught Anton's eye and smiled. For an instant she was reminded of hunting with an old forester along the Bitterroot in Montana.

Anton put one finger to his lips, then brushed the air towards his face with both hands. The wind was with them. Bernadette began to think like a hunter.

Anton handed her the Rigby and started to descend a gentle ravine in the massif. She took two .303's from a pocket, loaded the rifle, checked the safety and followed.

Her cotton khaki leggings served her well as she chose her footing between the sharp rocks and grey thorn bushes. From time to time Anton looked back and waited for her, occasionally helping her over a cut in the rock or up a steep rise. They arrived at an immense boulder standing alone like an abandoned house at one edge of the ravine. They eased forward in its shade. Anton crouched between two broad-eared cactus plants and pointed.

Bernadette raised her glasses. She saw one hartebeest, a young male, brown as a block of cocoa, only his rump a reddish cinnamon. He stood like a sentry on the slope of a huge anthill. He shook his head, twitching long oval ears and testing the wind.

Anton sat still until the young bull began to graze. Then he waved Bernadette forward, moving gradually to the side to outflank the guardian animal. If they went too far across the wind, the young male would take their smell. They advanced slowly from bush to bush and rock to rock. Each time they stopped she felt the drumming of her heart. Finally they lay flat. Bernadette smelled the dust as they crawled up a narrow dry streambed. This was true safari hunting. She knew Harry would be furious.

Bernadette's chin rested on the hard grit of the streambed. Close to her face she saw dark beads round as pearls, probably antelope spoor. Immediately before her eyes she watched a column of ants, red and large as tram cars, marching around the hollow end of a short yellow tusk. Boar or wild pig, she guessed.

Anton rubbed dust on his face and raised his head just above the level of the low grass bordering the streambed. She did the same and counted eleven hartebeest, including three young, perhaps sixty-five or seventy yards off, slightly to the left and below them. Anton moved his head and nodded to the right. Bernadette stopped breathing, trying not to tremble with excitement.

There he was: magnificent, the big bull of the herd, darker than the others, his face and upper legs marked with black lines, his back sloping sharply down to low hindquarters, his double-curving horns wide and heavy. The bull shook his head, chewing as he flicked his black tufted tail. A silvery aura shone across his shoulders, perhaps from the white tips of his hair, Bernadette guessed, like a mature grizzly.

Bernadette pressed the Rigby into her shoulder. She felt a gust of wind as she breathed in and settled for the shot. She saw Anton nodding and gesturing with his trigger finger. She flicked off the safety with her thumb and closed her left eye.

Suddenly from her left came a shrill nasal snort. The sentry. The big bull stiffened. A second snort and the bull tossed his head. Bernadette squeezed the front trigger as the herd moved. The clap of the shot echoed off the rocky slopes.

Anton and Bernadette ran towards the fleeing hartebeest. An animal was on the ground, kicking, its head down, legs in the air. She heard the drumming of split hooves as the others plunged across the bush into thicker country. For an instant she caught their heavy odor on the air.

Anton knelt over the thrashing animal, a young female with small horns.

"Oh, God, I'm sorry," Bernadette said, upset, feeling empty, one hand covering her mouth. She knew what had happened.

"Can't be helped." Anton drew his knife, understanding how she felt. "That shy old bull bolted first, exposing this girl behind him to your shot."

"This happened to me once before." Bernadette rubbed her eyes. "When I was a girl, hunting elk." She put one hand on his bare forearm.

Anton pressed his knee against the hartebeest's shoulder and pulled one horn back with his left hand. The animal resisted weakly, twitching thin legs as her head rose reluctantly. Bernadette saw one enormous brown eye staring helplessly. Anton stretched back the antelope's neck and sliced his knife across her throat.

He cut off the head. Then he ran the tip of his blade from throat to anus, cutting only the skin. Bernadette reloaded the first barrel and set the Rigby against the fork of a small tree. Determined not to appear squeamish, she spread the animal's legs to the sides to help Anton as he cut deeply along his incision and cleaned out the belly and chest cavity.

Anton wiped his blade on the grass inside the animal's stomach. Flies and small dark beetles were already at work on the moist pile of the hartebeest's intestines. A shadow moved past Bernadette's feet, and she looked up. High above her a large grey eagle floated without moving its wings.

Anton seized the carcass by the feet and swung it across his shoulders. Probably about her weight, Bernadette judged, about a hundred and ten. She collected the rifle and followed Anton uphill as the day darkened.

"Bernadette did very well," Anton said later as the camp gathered around. "First blood, a fine Swayne's hartebeest. She's a sort of kongoni." He knelt and counted thirteen prominent rings on the horns of the pale chestnut animal. Anton glanced at Kimathi. "We don't get these down in Kenya. Used to range right up to Palestine. Ancient Egyptians bred 'em for animal sacrifices."

Bernadette grinned proudly as the hungry men smiled and chattered. Charlie put a congratulatory arm around her shoulder. Angry at being left out, trying to conceal a surge of jealousy, Harriet gazed bitterly at the substantial carcass but did not speak. She decided not to bother with her new movie camera.

The skinner sharpened his knife as the cookboy grabbed two feet and dragged the body to the cooking fire. Properly trained to flatter his clients, Anton's staff waved and smiled and bowed towards Bernadette as they examined the hartebeest.

"Aren't you meant to shoot the males?" said Harriet.

"Your sister very nearly got the master bull," Anton said as Bernadette turned angrily to face her. "This lady must've been grazing behind him. Not such a fine trophy, but she'll eat a lot better."

"Good job, sis." Harriet sought to suppress the resentment in her voice, not for Berny's sake, of course, but for everyone else's. Berny would know better. Harriet set the heavy Bell & Howell movie camera back into its snug red felt fittings and snapped shut the two clasps on the black case. After all, it was her camera, and she'd brought it to film her own trophies. If Berny wanted moving pictures, she could have brought her own camera.

"Everyone's starving," Harriet said. "You look like you need a good bath, Berny. Better hurry."

Anton was taking an early whisky by the fire with Charlie as night fell. The twins passed by in slippers and belted cotton bathrobes, carrying soap and towels to the canvas shower stall under the branch of a tall acacia. They were whispering fiercely to each other. Quite a pair, he thought, impressed by Bernadette's steadiness on the hunt.

"How'd the painting go?" Anton said to Charlie, though he was more curious about the giggles that now reached them from the shower.

"There was too much to paint, and I couldn't get the colors right. Everything here's deeper and brighter, more vivid." Charlie drained his drink. "I'm afraid the landscape's better than I am."

Suddenly screams came from the shower. Anton grabbed his revolver belt from the back of the chair and dashed across the darkened camp.

The canvas shelter lay on its side. Warm water trickled from the shower bag lashed to a branch overhead. Both girls were naked.

"Some insect bit Harry," Bernadette said calmly. She snatched up a bathrobe from the wet ground.

"A scorpion! It bit me!" Harriet was doubled over, examining the crease where her right thigh met her belly.

Anton threw the other bathrobe over her shoulders. "Better come over to the light and let me take a look." He led her by the hand towards her tent.

"Do they kill you?" Bernadette hurried after them.

"Not likely," Anton answered over his shoulder. "Depends on what sort it was. Did either of you see it? Was it light or dark? How long were the claws?"

"See it? How could I see it?" Harriet snapped. She turned and faced Anton at the entrance to her tent. Her hair was wet and dark. Her face was flushed, her lips swollen and red. She looked about sixteen, Anton thought, a very mischievous sixteen. People always looked younger when they came out of the shower.

"Do you think I'd let it bite me if I saw it? It must've been hiding in my damp towel. I put the towel around my waist and felt this awful sting. I dropped the towel and it scuttled off. It was as big as your hand, with a tail like a buggy whip."

"It was tiny," Bernadette said, gazing up at the sky. "Heaven's sake. Probably frightened the poor scorpion. Oh, what a lovely moon."

Harriet glanced at her sister with narrow eyes. Her lips were tight.

"Go into your tent and dry off while I get my medical kit," Anton said to Harriet in a quiet voice, trying to be comforting. "If it was one of those killing yellow scorpions, the sort that flourish in Egypt, you'd already be swelling up, and in terrible pain."

He went to the cook fire and washed his hands with hot water. Then he collected his kit and entered Harriet's tent. She sat on her cot with her right leg outstretched and her bathrobe pulled up to reveal the small wound, and exceptionally good legs. Anton knelt by the cot and opened his canvas satchel, aware of Bernadette standing behind him with her arms folded, watching them. An oil lamp hissed on the small table by the head of the cot.

"Please leave me with the doctor," Harriet said to her sister without looking up.

Bernadette turned in the tight space. She left the tent, then raised the flap and stuck her head back inside. "Try to be quick," she said. "I'm starving."

Flattered by the sisters' rivalry, Anton pressed two fingers against the small mound of red swollen flesh. "Does that hurt?"

"Of course, Doctor." Harriet shifted on the cot as he touched her. "But it feels better when you touch it."

He leaned over her, conscious of the fresh smell of her body, and examined the dark point at the center of the wound where the tail of the scorpion had lashed forward and injected the venom.

"Not too bad. Probably just one of those pesky desert scorpions. It'll make less of a lump if you rub it a bit and disperse the venom."

"Won't you kiss it and make it well?"

At the invitation Anton moved one hand down her leg, enjoying the smooth skin and firm long muscle of her calf. He lowered his head and licked the raised flesh. He felt her fingers running through his hair. Her knees parted and he moved his face between her legs. Soon she grew moist and he smelled her sex, reminding him that red-headed women always smelled differently. She groaned and twisted her fingers in his hair as he continued.

"Hurry up, you two!" Bernadette's voice carried from the camp fire. "Come and have some champagne, Harry, best thing for you. Hurry up! You'll spoil my meat."

Their first safari dinner was a feast of fresh baked bread, hartebeest chops and red currant jelly, roast potatoes and gravy, and carrots and onions, with tinned rhubarb and caramel flan for desert. Excessively vivacious, the twins avoided talking directly to each other. Waiters in short white jackets poured red wine from the shadows. Anton told hunting tales and marvelled at how indistinguishable the girls always looked in the evening. It had to be deliberate. Their clothes and jewelry and hair styles were identical. If Bernadette wasn't holding Charlie's hand, he wouldn't know who was who.

A commotion interrupted them from the edge of camp. It was Diwani, who'd been dispatched to the nearest village to winkle out tips on the local game. Out of breath and sweating as if after a race, he hesitated a few yards from the dining table, holding a small grey envelope.

"That's odd." Anton excused himself and rose from his seat. Plucking an ivory container from his earlobe, from which he took a pinch of snuff, Diwani spoke to him in a low excited voice.

Anton put a hand on Diwani's shoulder and talked to him calmly. His back to the dining table, he opened the envelope and read the telegram from the British mission in Djibouti, addressed to him care of the station master at Dire Dawa:

> WAR BEGAN YESTERDAY STOP ITALY INVADED ABYSSINIA TWO FRONTS STOP BOMBED ADOWA AND RAILROAD STOP ADVANCING FROM EAST AND SOUTH STOP HMG ADVISES ALL FOREIGN NATIONALS MUST LEAVE ABYSSINIA AT ONCE STOP SUDAN OR KENYA ONLY WAYS OUT STOP

His mind racing to devise plans, Anton folded the telegram and slipped it into the rear pocket of his trousers. Thank God he'd brought good maps. He squeezed Diwani's shoulder, speaking to the tracker in Swahili.

"Say nothing to the other boys until the morning, Diwani. Nothing, do you understand? Not one word."

"Ndio, bwana." Diwani sneezed and nodded with respect.

"Everything all right?" Charlie said as Anton sat back down.

"Not entirely," Anton said. Just the beginning of the next world war, he thought.

"Seems things are hotting up with the Italians and our hosts, the Abyssinians. Tomorrow I might ride into Dire Dawa and check the news." He rolled his linen napkin and slipped it into a carved wooden ring before standing.

"Best if we all tuck in early. Could be a long day tomorrow if we have to move camp." Anton needed time to think. He'd been too young for the last war. He wondered what the next one would be like.

After the others had gone to their tents, Anton returned to the fire with a cigar, two maps and an enamel mug filled with Fonseca port, his favorite, Bin 27. It always reminded him of Anunciata. For nearly an hour he smoked and drank and studied the well-creased maps. The Italians had a long way to come, with the mountains protecting Abyssinia on the eastern front, and the desert of the Ogaden making a broad barrier to the south. That should give the safari plenty of time to get out of the country safely. But even more than for his clients, he worried about Gwenn. She was certain to find her way to the hottest corner, where she'd be needed most. Whatever else, he admired Gwenn's courage and determination. And, despite himself, she was always with him. Why hadn't he left things better with her?

Of course Kenya was the answer now. Straight south along the Rift Valley lakes, ending up at Lake Stefanie before crossing into the Northern Frontier District. Same way he'd told Ernst to make his run for it. Should be about seven hundred miles to the border, maybe eight or nine if they had to swerve about a lot. But mostly friendly healthy country on the way, plenty of supplies, decent climate. Could still make some sort of safari out of it, but probably best to buy a couple of lorries and push on fast.

Anton rose and strolled around the camp, checking the animals, supplies and tents as he made his round. Normally it was one of his favorite moments of the day. The boys acknowledged him as he passed the cook fire. Charlie was snoring heroically in his tent. Anton caught Diwani's eye and put one finger to his lips before refilling his cup and beckoning to Kimathi.

"*Ndio, Tlaga?*" said the African as Anton put one hand on his thick shoulder. The two men began to walk together about the camp, speaking quietly in Swahili.

"Time to go home," the Kikuyu agreed. "We must outrun them."

After telling Kimathi the news, Anton went to his own tent. He raised the canvas flap and stepped to the lamp, reaching into a pocket for a match.

"Don't," a voice whispered from his cot.

He obeyed but did not reply.

Harriet's come to finish what was interrupted, he thought, sitting in the camp chair to remove his boots. And why not? It might be a long time before any of them had fun again. He dropped his clothes on the chair and stepped naked to the cot.

"I smell something good," the voice whispered.

"Port, Miss Harriet." He guided her raised hand to his mug.

"Mmm."

He climbed into the cot, grateful that his own was extra wide.

She found his face and met his lips, her mouth eager.

"You're scratching my face," she giggled into his ear. Then she bit it sharply, almost making her teeth meet through his lobe, knowing he could not cry out.

Increasingly excited, relishing the feel of her smooth slender body, too eager, Anton rushed on selfishly and soon lay panting inside her, annoyed with himself for not doing better.

"Thank you," she said tartly as they separated on their sides. "Now it's my turn." She took his hands and guided one between her legs. With the other she invited him to stroke her.

Anton caressed her as she worked slowly to arouse him. He ran his fingers over her face. She bit his thumb and he passed the hand down her throat and over her small breasts. She took his ear in her teeth, making his body twitch, careful to nip him again exactly where she had before. He stroked her smoothest skin and felt her body enter a new rhythm. His hand moved across her upper thighs, first one leg, then the other, but found no bump where her wound had been. He searched again.

"Bernadette!" he whispered sharply, recoiling. "You're not Harriet!"

"Shh," she whispered. "Perhaps I am."

— 19 —

The Sheba Palace, once a tin-roofed roadhouse for merchants and rich travellers on their way to Adowa or Gondar, was roaring with drunken Italian officers, their faces flushed and sweating, their tunics open. The Greek proprietor, a year's business already done, seemed surprised to see a European not in uniform.

"Yasoo," he cried to Ernst von Decken, wiping his hands on his filthy apron before he reached across the bar to shake hands with the German.

Ernst forced a place for himself by the wall and consumed two plates of greasy goat stew. For several hours he sat on a stool and smoked and drank beer, watching the soldiers, all so young, play cards and link arms as they sang to an accordion, not patriotic party marches, but sad love songs that made Ernst feel old.

Once his neighbor spoke to him. "What are you doing here?" the Italian captain said in a slow thick voice, his lips dark with encrusted wine.

"I'm a trader," Ernst said sullenly, coughing in the smoke. "Austrian."

There was no further conversation.

Nearby, a few older soldiers were grumbling about the war, recounting tales of stragglers being butchered by villagers, of a column of lorries, crowded with wounded, lost and stuck on a mountain track before being overturned and burned by swarms of Africans. Others speculated what it would be like if the Italian army near Makalle, seventy thousand men and fourteen thousand animals, was forced to retreat through the mountains.

What did these Italians expect when they came to Africa? Ernst asked himself without sympathy. As he drank, he considered his scheme and found his plan was changing. He felt himself growing greedy. Instead of stealing only eight cases of silver and sending Jesus back to Ras Gugsa with many full chests and eight false ones, Ernst had decided to fly off with as many chests as the Potez could carry. He chuckled as he thought of the rigorous afternoon this lackey Jesus would endure in the cellars of his master.

Finally the captain slumped onto the bar. The proprietor stepped over to clear the wasted space. *"Amore, amore,"* the young soldiers sang again.

"I'll take care of him." Ernst put the officer's arm over his shoulder and dragged him through the back door towards the wooden lavatory shack. Outside, the man's feet trailed in the dust. Ernst dropped him behind a thorn bush on the other side of the stinking shed.

"You don't need this," Ernst said, crouching and unbuttoning the captain's field jacket.

Singing a merry Fascist song, an Italian with one arm in a sling appeared at the back door of the roadhouse. As he staggered towards the lavatory with a bottle in his good hand, Ernst lay on his side, feigning sleep. The Italian set the bottle on the ground and swung open the door. He stumbled inside and collapsed belching and singing.

Ernst rose and pulled off the captain's jacket. Folding it inside out, he discovered a crumbling wallet, thick with family photographs and old letters and the usual papers. Ernst dropped the wallet on the ground beside the captain. Then he bent and retrieved it. He removed the pictures. They could be dangerous. He stuffed the photos into the man's trouser pocket and returned the wallet to the jacket under his arm. Before leaving, he snatched the wine bottle. As he walked to his truck through the cold night, he heard the man in the lavatory sob and cry. Ernst took a long drink of Gattinara before starting the engine.

The sky was passing from black to deepest blue when Ernst showed his pass to the weary guard at the compound gate. He was thirty minutes early. He slowed in front of the headquarters building, paused, and put the lorry into reverse. The wine bottle, now filled with sand, rested on the seat beside him. The eight chests were under a tarpaulin in the back of the truck.

He backed around the building and found the guards' truck parked near the entrance to the garage. Nearby, Ras Gugsa's men were beginning to stir at their smoldering fire. Ernst's guardian, Jesus, was not an early riser. Ernst stepped down with the wine bottle. He stopped on the far side of the Ford, then strode to the fire without the bottle. Cursing loudly, he kicked dirt over the fire.

"Up! Up! Get up at once!" he hollered at Jesus. "You and two men guard the entrance to the garage. Order the others to wait by the gate with their weapons." The man rose shakily.

I'd better do it the way they told me, Ernst said to himself, backing the truck into the dark garage. He climbed down and beat on the rear door of the headquarters building. The door was opened by an Italian soldier. The young man blinked and struggled to pull up his suspenders. A row of wooden chests ran along the wall of the dim corridor behind him. Ernst's heart beat faster when he recognized the black stencil of the Roman treasury. Two soldiers were asleep on the floor beside the boxes. Another stood gazing at the door, rifle in hand.

"Quick now, you have orders, signed by old White Beard, General de Bono himself!" Ernst snapped, handing the first man the stamped warrant. The lieutenant pulled on his tunic and buttoned the collar. Suddenly alert, he yelled orders at the soldiers behind him. Two men began to carry the chests to the garage. Ernst examined each case. A third man came out and began loading the boxes into the truck.

Ernst stopped one of the young soldiers after the first few were in the lorry. "They won't all fit. Too damned heavy. Take all the cases that are already in this truck and load them in that old Ford while I check the rest." Ernst walked forward and barked at Jesus.

"Protect these cases with your life. If you lose one coin, the Ras will eat your liver."

At last the boxes were loaded, sixteen in each truck. The eight false chests were in the Ford. The sky was brightening as Ernst signed for the coins at the bottom of the warrant. He turned the key and pressed the starter.

Before he could pull away, Jesus stepped to the offside window of the truck. The Ethiopian opened the door and climbed in. Disturbed by this complication, Ernst turned on the headlights. He was aware of two guardsmen clambering onto the back of his truck. The Ford, with the other men aboard, followed him as he drove slowly forward. He felt the weight of the silver as he drove out through the gate and accelerated.

They would come to the airport turnoff in two miles. Ernst put his elbow out the window with his eye on the cracked rearview mirror, waiting for his plan to unfold. Behind him, the Ford alternately fell behind and gained speed, like an old man stumbling to keep up. Finally it stopped altogether and the driver blasted the horn. Ernst slowed and stopped the truck. The sand from the wine bottle had done its work.

Sitting close to Ernst on the narrow bench seat, Jesus turned and leaned out his window. He looked back down the road and gestured at the Ford. He had one hand on the door handle when Ernst tapped him on the shoulder. Jesus turned to face him. Ernst shot him in the chest, not wanting to splash the cab with the bone and blood of a head shot.

The gun's report sounded like a grenade in the confined space. The Abyssinian jumped and twitched as he was hit, then opened his mouth and stared at the German, groping at his wound with one hand, reaching slowly for Ernst's throat with the other. Ernst shot him again, a bit higher. Jesus collapsed against the door, blood soaking down between his legs.

The two soldiers in the rear leapt down. Ernst reversed sharply, feeling the hard bump against the rear of the truck when their bodies took the blow. The men screamed. One fell under the truck before Ernst braked, shifted into first and drove over him for the second time. The other man raised his rifle as Ernst pulled away. Shifted by the violent bouncing of the truck, Jesus' body slumped against Ernst and fell face down in his lap.

Thank God I didn't train those men, Ernst thought, bending over the wheel, his chin touching Jesus's shoulder while he waited for the gunfire. He shoved Jesus onto the floor as he gained speed, wincing when he heard two wild shots.

He turned sharply onto the airport road and, turning off the headlights, stopped to don the captain's jacket. When he approached the aerodrome, he blinked the lights twice, the signal for Ephraim to prepare to start the aircraft's engine. In order not to arouse the Italians at the airport, he drove slowly past the two tents of the *Regia Aeronautica* that were pitched beside the tanker trucks. One man stood urinating between the tents. Ernst leaned out and waved casually as he drove by. The man ignored him in the near darkness and bent to enter his tent.

The Potez 25 was waiting at the far end of the runway, the chocks braced against her wheels. Ernst accelerated, then braked violently beside the aircraft. He jumped down and grabbed the raised blade of the propeller with both hands to swing start the engine. The black pilot stared down at Ernst through his goggles, nodding as he switched on the magnetos. Ernst swung the blade down, but the engine did not catch.

"Verflixt!" Ernst cursed. He swung the other blade down and the first cylinder sputtered as he leapt aside. Smoke poured from the cowling as all twelve cylinders fired and the propeller turned. While the engine warmed, Ernst loaded the first case into the small hold, then another and another.

"Les Italiens!" The Abyssinian was leaning down, yelling at him. *"Vas-y!"* Barely able to hear over the roaring engine, Ernst knew there must be trouble from the camp. Grunting with the effort, he jammed seven more cases into the hold. He slammed and latched the door. Six left. What a waste. He grabbed one, mounted the pilot's footplate, and dropped it into the man's lap. Surprised, Ephraim gasped under the heavy weight.

As Ernst bent and threw aside the chocks, he saw one of the distant tankers begin to move. The plane trembled, tilting slighty forward while Ephraim toed the brake pedals and raised the engine's revolutions. Ernst grabbed a final chest and clambered awkwardly into his seat, facing backwards, sitting on top of the folded parachute. He shoved the chute down under his feet and grabbed the two handles of the machine gun as he settled in. A Vickers, he confirmed with approval. "I only wish I could see where we're going," he growled. Then he threw off the safety and engaged the ammunition drum.

The ground moved by with deathly slowness as they advanced with the wind. The tail, heavy with the load, scraped along the ground, dragging the tail skid like the blade of a small plow.

When Ernst felt the Potez swing violently from left to right, he twisted around and stared forward. Ephraim, with the chest in his lap, was jockeying back and forth, trying to avoid an oncoming fuel truck that was holding course down the center of the runway, straight at them.

Well over halfway down the airstrip, Ephraim swerved to the left. The tanker roared past, just missing the lower right wing but passing under the main wing itself. A man leaned out of the truck window firing a pistol. Ernst heard the crack of the shots as one struck a forward strut that connected the fuselage to the upper wing.

The aircraft and the tanker pulled away rapidly in opposite directions before the truck braked and turned back to pursue them. As it came broadside, Ernst pulled the trigger and swept the tanker from left to right. He saw the windscreen shatter and sparkle like a handful of diamonds tossed into the rising light. The bullets cut through the driver and drilled a row of holes along the side of the truck.

A vast purple explosion shook the ground. The power and heat of the blast slammed Ernst back against his seat. For a moment his mind went black.

As he blinked his eyes, he knew they hadn't made it.

"Scheissdreck!" he yelled as he smelled the oily fire.

Ephraim turned the overloaded Potez on the rough verge past the end of the runway. Heading into the wind, they taxied back to the end of the bumpy strip. The middle of the airfield was covered by a wall of red and orange flame beneath an immense rising curtain of black smoke. Ephraim rose in his seat and pitched his crate of silver dollars over the side. The case burst open.

"Dumkopf!" Ernst screamed.

They gathered speed down one edge of the runway. Suddenly the second tanker appeared. A man in long white underclothes knelt beside the truck, firing a pistol with both hands. Ernst swung the gun on him. Praise God pilots carry only pistols, he thought grimly. He hesitated, then fired two bursts. He watched the man fall just as he felt the blaze of the fire sear his own shoulders. The gasoline must be all around them, he realized. Was it hot enough for their own tank to explode?

For an instant they were in the furnace. Then they were through. The

Potez gained speed, bouncing heavily, almost aloft, then climbed slowly into the rising sun as the head wind blew the smoke behind them.

The German closed his eyes, then turned to Ephraim and beat him on the shoulder and grinned and gave the thumb's up to his pilot. He didn't bother to tell him that he had thrown out his own reward. Then von Decken settled back and watched the ground recede below.

Flying had never held much charm for Ernst. Still, anything was better than marching across Africa, particularly when burdened by hundreds of pounds of Italian silver. Even a French aircraft was better than nothing. But who could have confidence in their mechanics or dependability, he thought irritably, particularly in a plane maintained by these sharp-faced Abbos? Uncomfortable in his tight flying helmet, Ernst gazed past the rounded corrugated metal of the tail at the vast landscape of the Abyssinian highlands. His bristly face felt pinched and red. Thirsty, disgusted at the thought, he wondered which Abbysinian had last worn this leather helmet.

To his left, the cleft of the Blue Nile was slowly vanishing in the distance, as the river descended north and west towards Lake Tana before rushing on to Khartoum and Cairo. Ernst glanced to his right into the rising sun. In another forty-five minutes they should be sighting the small airfield near Awash, to the east of Addis on the rail line to Djibouti. That should be safer than landing in a besieged capital with a planeload of silver thalers. In Awash they could refuel, or he could buy or steal a truck and escape southwest past the lakes to Kenya.

As Ernst turned his eyes from the sun, he was startled by a faint glitter in the eastern sky.

Another aircraft? He twisted in the narrow seat and struck Ephraim on the shoulder. The fool turned the wrong way, staring at Ernst through his goggles. Ernst pointed east and Ephraim looked back to his left. Then the pilot spun about to face him, babbling, but unable to make himself heard over the chatter of the 450-horsepower engine. The man reached under the control panel and passed Ernst a pair of field glasses, filthy with aircraft grease. But at least they were German.

Ernst slung the strap over his neck and raised the long-barrelled Zeiss binoculars to his eyes. His elbows on the chest of coins, he rested the field glasses atop the Vickers. With one hand he shielded the lenses from the sharp sunlight.

After a moment's searching, he spotted three aircraft in tight military formation. Ernst heard the engine change pitch as Ephraim tried to gain speed and begin a gradual climb, turning away from the unidentified aircraft, to the south towards the Rift lakes. A hundred and thirty-five must be about tops, with a ceiling something over twenty thousand feet, though they couldn't do nearly that without oxygen. He wondered what sort of aircraft these were. If the heavy Potez could go either higher or faster, they might be all right. He'd sooner throw out the pilot than the silver. How Ernst wished he was in a new shark-grey Heinkel 51, a proper killer, the finest biplane fighter in the skies.

Like most men who took pleasure in field sports, Ernst did not enjoy being hunted. He'd had enough of that in the last war. At least these hounds weren't British, he reflected. No Italian had that lunatic bulldog propensity to absorb pain and carry on until they got you.

Ernst examined the Vickers with fresh interest. He raised the feeder lever and removed the ammunition drum. The chamber and barrel were filthy, he found, his expression turning more sour. What could you expect? This wasn't Solingen.

Grunting, he drew in his stomach and pulled out his shirt. He ripped off a shirttail. He couldn't do much for the barrel, but he cleaned the breech and as many parts as he could. Stretching awkwardly over the wooden coin chest on his lap, he reached under the rear lip of the fuselage and found two ammunition drums clipped to their brackets. One felt light. He checked it: empty. *"Idioten!"* he yelled as he tossed it over the side. He inserted the heavy loaded drum.

Flying below them, the three aircraft appeared to be on a different course, heading more westerly, perhaps for Addis with bombs. *Luftpost,* Ernst's father used to call that. Then the planes came around, like lean-waisted corsairs tacking when they spotted a fat merchantman sailing low in the water. He thought of the Ethiopian colors painted on the tail of his own aircraft, an invitation to attack.

Fear grew like a tumor in his belly. Though the hunters appeared to have only a slight advantage in speed, Ernst watched helplessly as the distance gradually closed. Ephraim was nowhere near the Potez's ceiling, but from his own difficult breathing Ernst guessed they were at about fifteen thousand. Feeling giddy in the cold thin air, he raised the glasses as the pursuers came closer.

The lead aircraft filled the circular image of his lenses. He stopped breathing. His worst fear. Fiats, single seaters. That meant twin forward machine guns. He prayed the planes weren't the new CR-32's. "Couldn't be, or I'd be in flames already," he muttered nervously into the wind. Ernst looked down. The farther south they got, the more distant from the battlefront, and the closer to Kenya. He twisted in his seat to look ahead. Still no sign of the lakes.

The hounds were on them in ten minutes. When they were only a few thousand feet back and still a bit below, Ernst dropped the glasses and followed the lead aircraft through the sights of the Vickers. The gun was stiff on its mount. With one forefinger he collected the grease that still soiled the binoculars. He spread this at the point of the gun mount and pivoted the weapon. Better than nothing. A worse problem was that the horizontal stabilizer of the Potez denied him a full swing at depressed targets. He didn't want to shoot away part of his own plane.

On the other hand, he calculated, his own weapon would carry farther from its greater height. He also had another advantage: he'd be the only shooter in the fight who didn't have to fly at the same time. He turned and got Ephraim's attention, gesturing with both hands, telling him what to do. The black man looked back and nodded repeatedly, his eyes behind his goggles widening with fear.

Ernst raised his glasses for the last time. He made out the face of the Italian squadron leader, lean-cheeked, with a trim grey mustache and grey hair emerging from his flight cap. The leather collar of the pilot's coat was raised against the cold wind.

Abruptly the Potez dropped engine speed. Her nose fell. Ernst's stomach rose as the plane plunged. He stared upwards as one Italian wingman approached directly over him. Unable to shoot at the French plane with its guns mounted rigidly forward, the Fiat flew straight on.

Ernst pulled the trigger. The Vickers bucked and smoked. He saw bullets open the soft belly of the Fiat like a hyena ripping the stomach of a running calf.

The Potez levelled off. The sky before Ernst was empty. Exhilarated, he turned his head to look forward. The wounded Fiat was dropping in a trail of black smoke.

"Perhaps this fly boy game isn't so bad after all," Ernst muttered. In the distance he saw a lake, nearly round, small as a saucer from the air, slate-grey against the uneven browns of the high bush. He prayed it was part of the Rift chain, probably Lake Zwai.

The surviving Fiats had overflown the Potez and were turning in a wide arc. Their wings angled sharply as they made their turn. Meeting them dead on would be hopeless: the *Katzlmacher* would be firing forward with four machine guns, and he wouldn't be able to shoot his tail gun until they'd passed. "By then you'll be dead." Again his stomach hardened like a stone. He glanced at his feet. He should have put on his chute. Looking back, Ernst saw the long scalloped elevators of the Potez tilt upwards to maximum pitch. The engine whined faster. Slowly the aircraft rose. Ephraim must be trying to climb before diving a second time.

The Fiats had turned too soon. Before their turn was complete, the Potez would be past them. Frightened, with too much time to think, Ernst checked his ammunition drum and spat to one side. The Fiats turned more sharply to come in line behind the Potez. Probably just out of his range, but worth a try at the instant they would be broadside and before they could fire themselves. Never having faced one, the Italians might underestimate the Vickers' range.

The Fiats completed their turn, flying wing to wing. Ernst waited until he faced the Fascist rondel on the fuselage of the inside plane. He fired high in a long arc. The Italian plane shuddered as the bullets swept away two struts that connected her port wings. The lower wing flapped down and the plane sharpened its turn. The port wings dipped more and more as the aircraft fell into a spiral. Before Ernst could enjoy the moment, though, he saw the remaining Fiat coming into line directly behind him. Panicked, Ernst realized he could not fire without shooting away his own tail. His Italian pursuer would not have this problem.

The Fiat closed. It was the grey-haired Italian. The first bullets flew past the Potez. Then one chipped the upper starboard wingtip.

The Potez dived, but Ernst knew this maneuver would not work again. He tried to fire, but the Vickers was empty. As he expected, the Fiat instantly dived with them. He saw its guns firing as it followed closer and closer on their tail. Ernst groped near his feet, desperate to find another ammunition drum.

A line of bullets cut through the fuselage just below Ernst's gun mount. He heard each one: *chop chop chop.* Splinters flew. One hit just above his goggles. Instantly blood covered his left lens. More splinters, then a bullet struck the wooden chest on his lap. He screamed as the force of a maul pounded his chest.

Oily smoke enveloped him. Coughing, he heard the engine fail, then stop. Probably a severed fuel line, he thought. Realizing it was hopeless, he suddenly felt strangely relaxed, certain he would die. At least the Italian would leave them now: pilot chivalry required not firing on a crashing aircraft.

Yet he saw the Fiat screaming after them, the pilot facing him, as if across a dinner table, closer and closer. The Fiat's machine guns sparkled through the smoke. Something struck his right foot.

The wounded Potez flattened her dive and dipped sharply to the left, the Italian fighter tight on her tail as she continued down. His head sideways, Ernst saw rocks and scrub trees rush towards him. The bastard was still firing. For an instant Ernst saw a sheet of water. The Potez slammed down and sank as he lost consciousness.

— 20 —

"Would've killed a white man. Look at that hip and groin," said Dr. Fergus to Gwenn, stripping off his tight wet rubber gloves as he looked up.

"That should hold him together for a bit," he said almost cheerily, his eyes red through his spectacles. "Don't know how they do it. Take wounds that should stop them on the spot, then hobble for miles through the mountains and wait in line for us to try to put them back together." He dropped the gloves into a murky enamel basin and shook his head before collapsing onto a medical chest at the edge of the tent. "Is this the sort of thing you saw in the war?"

"More or less, Malcolm," said Gwenn wearily. "But these men seem more accepting, their bodies more tolerant. I don't know, they seem to take pain better."

After relocating northwest of Harar, knowing the battle was advancing towards them, the ambulance team had arranged its vehicles in a laager beside a stream in a long valley. The sixteen trucks and ambulances were formed in a tight square. A canvas red cross, thirty feet square, was set on the ground in the center to ensure protection from air attacks. The two surgical tents were pitched in opposite corners of the square, each with a red cross on its roof.

Nearly two hundred baggage mules, small black pack animals purchased in Harar, were picketed between the laager and the stream. These had arrived in camp a day after the trucks. They carried food and the medical supplies that had been removed from the lorries to make place for some of the critical casualties.

At first the camp received a trickle of wounded, mostly privileged cases, officers and tribal leaders brought in by truck and muleback. Then came the foot soldiers, hardy uncomplaining men of the African mountains.

The field hospital was overwhelmed on the third day. When Gwenn awoke in the early morning, after a few hours' rest in one of the ambulances, she became aware of a buzzing droning sound as if rising from some swarm of creatures. She moved, crouching, to the back of the ambulance and opened the door, peering into the early light rising in the eastern sky.

"Oh, God," she said.

The bed of the valley was thick with slowly moving men. A sea of casualties was flooding towards them. She pulled on her low white boots and jumped down, stumbling to the main surgery tent. She heard the grating progress of a saw on bone as she entered. Probably a femur. Oil lamps swung from a cable slung along the roof of the tent.

The old Scot was back at work. Six nurses and orderlies, women and men, Europeans and North Africans, toiled beside him around the two operating tables. A thrill shot through Gwenn as she saw them. Thank God she was here. In the first two days, orderlies had been doing the work of fully trained nurses, and nurses were doing the work of doctors. She herself had completed operations, most of them successfully, that in Cairo required two experienced surgeons. There was no time for anxiety or self-doubt or protocol.

Dr. Fergus looked up, his old eyes bright. He straightened his back and stretched his shoulders and spoke to her in his soft deep voice.

"They need you in the other tent, lass. Today you're a surgeon."

All day they worked. In the mad rush Gwenn forgot herself. Her training and years of observation were part of her as she swabbed and cut and extracted and stitched, sometimes giving up too late. The crowds of wounded grew and swarmed and murmured outside the tents. At first two nurses sought to select patients from the mass of wounded, and set aside those lightly or mortally injured. But soon the doctors found that survival and mortality were not so easily discernable among these barefoot Abyssinians, and the throngs of wounded grew restive and angry at what seemed arbitrary choices. So they began to take them as they came and measured care in time dispensed.

As the day progressed, helpers seemed to appear as if by gift. A few stretcher bearers stayed on inside to assist the victims on and off the tables. They continued, learning quickly, helping silently, removing bodies, wiping off tables, emptying buckets, holding down patients, bearing water from the stream, washing bandages and instruments, disposing of discarded arms and legs.

After the first few hours, or perhaps five or six, Gwenn grew dizzy. The smells of the tent were thick in her lungs. No longer was she merely looking down at each wound. She herself was now inside one immense wounded body. The blood and the slippery damaged organs rose around her like gory prison walls.

Her hands trembled and grew useless. She leaned her head on her fore-arms, almost collapsing across the messy table before her. Finally a nurse brought Dr. Fergus to her.

"Here, lass," Malcolm said, as always younger and more vigorous when he was operating, "come with me now." Helping her to a corner of the tent, he forced her to eat bits of his tinned Dundee shortbread and drink two cups of strong sugary tea with her soiled hands.

"Now you'll be better, Gwennie," he said, using an endearment she had not enjoyed since her early days with Anton.

Suddenly famished, she washed her face and hands in a bucket and de-voured four hard-boiled eggs. Then she stepped to the door of the tent to breathe.

Wounded men lay and stood in jagged lines as far as she could see. Hundreds, perhaps a thousand, more, a valley of wounded. Some, at the front, pressed forward hopefully when they saw her, nodding and waving and calling out, leaning on their comrades, eager, confident they would be helped more than they could ever be.

By the river, clusters of men, and a few women, stretched on the ground beside fires, eating *enjara,* drinking from gourds and bowls, examining wounds. Here and there plumed spears, the rallying pennants of tribal leaders, were planted in the ground. One man, near her, the stump of his left leg bound with knots of darkened cotton, sat cleaning a long ancient rifle with dedicated concentration. Close to the stream, mangy camp dogs, lean and feral, fought over a scattering of human limbs.

At the sight, Gwenn put one hand to her mouth, unable to breathe. Then she rubbed her face with both hands and gazed across the valley and squared her shoulders. Nodding vaguely towards the men nearby, she turned and reentered the tent.

It was the most rewarding day of her life.

For three days and nights it continued, interrupted by pauses to eat and drink, and by a few hours of collapse as the doctors and nurses toiled in turn. Worst was the ceaseless ocean-like murmuring of the pained throngs sur-rounding the tents and camp. Some supplies were already alarmingly de-pleted, particularly bandages, gut and anesthetics.

Resting for a few hours in the cab of an ambulance, unable to sleep, Gwenn wondered what more the war could bring.

Thrashing madly like a beast in a snare, unaware of where he was, Ernst von Decken fought the weight that pinned him in his watery confinement. One leg ignored him as he struggled to rise and escape the sunken aircraft. Choking on a mouthful of water, he gripped the wooden chest in his lap and heaved it from the cockpit. He kicked down violently with his left leg, twisting his body to free himself. Turning in the water, he faced the front of the Potez. He kicked once more. His left foot struck the shoulder of the motionless body in the pilot's seat.

He jerked back his leg and frantically stroked upwards with both arms. Desperate for air, his lungs boiling, he glided past the upper wing as he rose through the filmy water. A plume of blood trailed behind him.

Finally he broke the surface. Dazzled by the sun, his lungs exploding, he gasped and spat while his arms flailed in spastic splashes.

Gulping air, he cast his head back on the still water and blinked repeatedly at the blue of the sky. A calm exhaustion overtook him. His lungs and heart steadied. He was aware that his clothes and boots were hanging heavily in the fresh water. The binoculars were tangled about his neck. His legs were stiff as logs, so he paddled slowly with both arms.

After a time, his mind resumed control. He was thirty or forty yards from what appeared to be an island in the lake. He breast-stroked towards the shore of the island, aiming for an inverted reed canoe. Some yards off, one foot struck something beneath the water. Crocodile? He flinched and paddled frantically. Then he felt it again: land. He took a few more strokes, swimming in between a scattering of green and tan reeds.

He stopped and tried to stand in the shallows. A paroxysm of pain chopped through him like an axe. He cried out and stared down at his feet.

"Oh, my God!" He vomited and collapsed on the gritty grey sand of the beach.

First von Decken smelled smoke and broiling fish. As if from a great distance he heard the slow chanting of many male voices. His leg throbbing, he opened his eyes but could not see. Blearily he stared into the darkness before finally turning his head towards the smoke.

He made out a fire set between three long stone benches. One seemed to be cut directly from the rocky hillside, carved just enough to turn nature to man's use.

Ernst found himself lying between the wooden shafts of a leather litter. A roll of white cotton cloth was under his head. An aching pain throbbed through his body from his right foot.

He rose on his elbows and squinted down through the shadows to his feet. His boots were on the ground beside him. The binoculars rested on the litter at his side. At least these primitives weren't thieves.

He lifted the right boot. Still soggy, it had been sliced open from tongue to toe. He smelled the stink of drying sweat and blood and cast the boot aside. He stared towards his feet. They were covered in a white cloth, badly stained.

Growing afraid, Ernst tried to move his toes. The left ones wiggled freely. The right he could not feel. Alarmed, he reached along his leg with his right hand. Just below the knee he felt a tight band of knotted leather: a tourniquet.

"Kristiyani?" A low firm voice spoke behind him.

Ernst turned his head. He saw two black men in off-white robes. He could not discern their faces in the darkness. Perhaps a dozen others stood behind them, still as tree trunks.

"Kristiyani?"

"*Ja, ja,* yes, Christian," he said loudly. If they were Christians, they must have drink, he thought, feeling waves of pain assault him.

"Talla, talla," Ernst said, hoping for local barley beer, or perhaps some sweet honey wine, the Ethiopian mead. *"Tajj? Tajj?"*

One of the two men knelt beside him and shook his head. The tall lean man set an oil lamp on the ground beside Ernst's litter. A silver Coptic cross hung from a chain about his neck. His bright eyes examined Ernst's face. The man wore a grey cotton cloak over his shoulders, pinned at his chest with a clasp in the shape of a cross. His leather slippers had raised pointed tips. A rosary was wrapped around one wrist. The ivory beads dangled between his fingers. A tight white skullcap was low on his lined forehead. He wore a beard of small white curls. He pointed at his chest and spoke. "Theodorus. *Szzwo man nau?*"

"Von Decken," Ernst grunted. The man must be some sort of priest, or, worse, a monk. At least they must have water. Ernst tried to remember. *"Weha, weha?"*

The second monk passed him a bowl of water, and Ernst gulped it down.

"Petros," the man said, gesturing at himself and accepting back the bowl.

Theodorus removed the covering from Ernst's legs. *"Szr krfu."* He shook his head and crossed himself and replaced the cloth. Ernst feared what this might mean.

Petros returned with a woven platter containing round flat-bread and a whole grilled fish. Their odors mingled as Petros presented the food. *"Enjara, asa."*

Ernst ripped off a piece of the hot bread and stuffed it in his mouth.

Theodorus made a sound of protest and seized back the platter.

"Damn you!" Ernst cried, pain cutting him as he tried to move.

Ignoring him, Theodorus bent and blessed the food before returning it.

Grace? thought Ernst. It was worse than a *Gymnasium.* Where did these savages think they were?

He lifted the striped large-eyed fish in a folded piece of enjara and tore at its flesh with his teeth. He spat out the larger bones and ate swiftly as the two men stood and watched him. He finished, a clean job of it. As Petros took the plate, Ernst shifted his position on the litter. He screamed despite himself.

"*Inglesi?*" said Petros, touching Ernst's shoulder with concern. "I speak Inglish!"

"*Ja, ja,*" said Ernst. "I speak English."

"We monks," said Petros. "Theodorus, abbot."

Theodorus came to Ernst with a warm drink in a wooden cup. "*Qwalqwal.*" Ernst suspiciously eyed the small dark seeds floating on the thick milky liquid. Perhaps this was what he needed. His leg throbbed like a churning piston. Ernst drained the cup and lay back and closed his eyes. He gripped the wooden shafts with both hands to fight off the pain. Soon even he would begin to pray. What about my silver? he wondered hazily as dizziness overcame him. Like distant murmuring surf he heard the voices of many monks at prayer.

Whenever he woke up, the night was clear and cold and bright with stars, but his leg was baking in an oven. Twice he thought he heard himself cry as he awoke. Each time a monk came to him from the shadows and held a cup to his eager lips. Sometimes half awake, groggy with pain and drink, his mind kept turning to the last time he had fled across Africa.

He thought of General von Lettow-Vorbeck, cut off for years from his country's support, like Hannibal in Italy, with the Rhodesians and Indians harrying him on one flank, Kenya's King's African Rifles hounding him on the other, and the damned Britishers themselves, slow and more heavily armed, ridden with fever but dogged as terriers, relentlessly pursuing him across four countries. Outnumbered ten or more to one, the German commander was never defeated. Unpaid for four years, his men of the *Schutztruppe,* mostly *schwartzes,* followed him to the end, bitterly laying down their arms only after the Kaiser himself had handed his sword to the British four thousand miles away. Ernst groaned at the thought as oblivion overtook him once again.

Dawn was worse. The potion wore off, and his pain increased with the light. Ernst von Decken had never cried for anyone else, and he was not going to cry for himself. He set the strap of the field glasses in his teeth and felt his eyes flood.

He forced himself to concentrate as he watched the first rays strike the top of the stony hill behind the camp fire. Gradually the light brightened the spiny cactus arms of two candelabra trees before bringing life to the immense folded upper leaves of a wild banana tree, each one bent over and floppy like the ears of an aged elephant. The candelabra, he guessed, had yielded the milky juice that was the basis of last night's drink. Then he saw the light pick out the yellow flowers of a *kosso,* and define the patterned veins in the leaves of a frankincense tree.

He turned and saw a group of eight round huts laid out in the pattern of a cross. Each conical thatched roof was meticulously finished and perfectly circular. Wooden crosses crowned all but the center one. In Tigre, he had inquired about the curious varied ways the Abyssinians topped their dwellings. As he watched, the rising light struck a shiny round object atop the central hut: an ostrich egg, symbolizing the protection of the Holy Spirit. The egg gleamed orange like the center of a candle flame.

At that moment Ernst realized that the bloody rag had fallen from his legs. Below the tourniquet, his right leg was dark and swollen, the flesh raised with the soft puffy look of rotting fruit. Would he ever again walk like a man?

"Petros!" he yelled.

Von Decken had seen enough in the Great War to know when a man was finished. Each morning they had left men clustered near the trail, Germans and *askaris,* some dead and barely covered, others still living and armed, not to kill the Africans or British, but to fight off lion and hyena.

He raised himself on one elbow. For the first time he saw his foot. It was a shattered pulpy mass, split in two from the fork of the big toe to the base of the ankle, cloven like the hoof of a goat.

"Petros!"

Ernst remembered assisting at a field hospital after the battle of Tanga, the first and greatest German victory of their four-year war. Wet to his elbows, the gaunt doctor had looked up with hollow eyes, shaking his head. "There are more bones in two feet than in the rest of the human body," the surgeon muttered hopelessly.

Ernst sniffed and detected a thick odor in the breeze. It was not yet the stink of infection and rot and gangrene, but he knew that would not be long. This was a sweeter muskier smell. It reminded him of sex. He lay back and closed his eyes. Spittle ran down the binocular strap as he bit through the leather.

"Zndet adarh," said Theodorus, who then spoke more quietly to Petros.

"*Guten Tag,* Theo," said the German. He'd best treat these people as if they were civilized, although instinctively he feared their priestcraft.

"Theodorus says you have the foot of the devil, cloven," said Petros quietly, "and that it cannot be."

The abbot crouched and studied Ernst's foot more closely. He spoke again, but his words were not explained. He handed Ernst a bowl of water, then a small plate of mashed pumpkin. Ernst drank but could not eat.

Theodorus left him and walked to the rocky hillside, followed by a file of eight or nine monks. Fifteen or twenty more waited near an outdoor stone altar draped with a white cloth. Ernst heard chanting in Amharic. Morning service, he imagined. Why didn't the moralizing bastards do something for his pain?

Theodorus returned accompanied by a short heavily-built young monk. Five others stood nearby. All deferred to Theodorus. One monk, possibly a farmer of the community, carried a thick-bladed panga in his belt, a weapon suitable for chopping sugercane or cutting reeds. The bright edge appeared clean and newly sharpened. Another monk crouched nearby, working on a fire.

"Johan," Theodorus said, *"yañña doktar."* The young man smiled modestly. A leather strap hung over his shoulder. Slivers of some shiny metal were imbedded along its center. A thick dowel of dark wood, perhaps two feet long and thinner in the center, was tucked into his rope waistband.

"What are you going to do?" Ernst asked with fear, his leg twitching.

Theodorus spoke and the monks began to moan, almost to chant.

Petros leaned down towards him and spoke slowly.

"We must kill this foot of the devil."

"Nein!" Ernst screamed, trying to sit up. But Petros and Johan restrained him.

"Dear God!" he cried.

A monk stepped forward and handed a bucket of filmy water to Johan, who poured it slowly over Ernst's right leg and foot. Then Johan sat on the ground by the end of the litter and studied the damaged foot before exchanging glances with the abbot.

A tall monk handed Ernst a drink similar to that of the evening before, but with a thicker bitter taste.

"Drink." Theodorus encouraged him to drain the deep cup. Ernst felt himself grow giddy. The monk refilled the cup. Ernst closed his eyes and drank again.

"Szr!" The abbot spoke sharply. *"Bande!"*

The five monks stepped forward and seized Ernst by his legs and shoulders. Johan slipped the metal-lined leather belt under Ernst's lower right calf, then edged it down until it rested just below the gory ankle bone. The sharp silvery shards faced inwards towards the joint. Gently Johan closed the belt and fashioned a sturdy loop above the top of the foot. He then passed the dowel through the loop. The monk with the panga stood beside him. Johan twisted the dowel twice, hand over hand.

Ernst trembled and cried as the band bit into him. The German heaved and struggled while Theodorus and the other monks held him down.

Johan turned the dowel further. Ernst screamed and bit through his tongue. For an instant he stared up and caught the abbot's shining eye. He saw approval, as if Theodorus found virtue in his suffering: the agony was good for him.

"Bastard!" Ernst screamed.

Blood ran from the corners of von Decken's mouth. Petros slipped a leather bit between his teeth. The leather and metal band narrowed and tightened around his ankle, burying itself in the pulpy mess of swollen flesh and shattered bone.

Ernst lost consciousness as Johan leaned his heavy shoulders into the work.

He awoke for an instant when the monk with the panga sharpened it noisily on a flat stone. Then the man passed it through the flames and examined the edge. Sunlight sparkled from the blade as the abbot touched it with his silver cross.

The monks tightened their grip on Ernst as every nerve and sense he possessed became acutely conscious. He felt the blade before it touched him.

Johan sliced and sawed through his Achilles tendon. Ernst heard the cutting of his own flesh like so much gristle at a butcher's. He smelled a burning brand nearby and spat the bloody leather pad from his mouth.

"God!" he cried. Still the panga sawed. Over his own screams, he heard the resistance in the core of his ankle where the bones were tightly joined. Once more Ernst cried out and struggled briefly, his face wet with blood and mucus, tears and sweat. A monk held the brand closer. Johan tightened the dowel and Ernst lost consciousness as his foot fell away and he smelled his flesh burn like pork.

— 21 —

"The men want to know when the air force is going to use the gas, Colonel," said Captain Uzielli loudly as he wiped his tin plate with a thick piece of bread. "The fighting's getting worse every day. Especially for small units fighting on their own. A lot of *bambinos* are dying out there in the mountains for nothing."

Grimaldi bristled, offended that this *Bersaglieri* had used the accepted informality of the campaign mess table to challenge him with this indiscreet question.

"First, Captain, they are dying for Italy. Second, there is no gas. The Duce himself has said so," Grimaldi stated in a voice that could be heard the length of the table. Continuing, he was pleased to see both Mussolini boys look up from their minestrone as he used their father's name.

"And if there were gas, Captain, your words would be a violation of military security."

"Everyone knows it's stored right over there, sir," persisted Uzielli, chewing as he spoke, his mouth never closed. "Half these sloggers are here to guard it."

"And to be fair to the captain," said an air force intelligence major, flown in for the day to brief the base on the course of the war, "we all know three of your Capronis are being fitted as we speak to test aerial spraying with those nozzles under the wings. You can see them working on it just over there." The officer turned and gestured to one side of the open structure.

"That's one reason you've been so short of bombers here." Rising to begin the briefing, the officer could not avoid Colonel Grimaldi's eye. "But the colonel is correct, of course. Your knowledge of this must never leave this base."

The major approached the new maps mounted on the wall, drawing his swagger stick from his boot and slapping it against one palm. Grimaldi was aware the man hadn't even piloted his own plane when he arrived.

"As you know, gentlemen, so far things have gone well, especially from the air. Marshal Badoglio is advancing relentlessly along the royal road from Aksum to Addis Ababa. Already advance units have swept past Makalle, here." The major slapped the map with his stick. He hesitated briefly when he caught the eye of the Madonna of Loretto, the patroness of all Italian airmen, whose dolorous portrait was secured to the wall beside the map.

"From Italian Somaliland to the south, Marshal Graziani, based in Mogadishu, has now started the second front. With one nasty exception, very small losses. His motorized columns are crossing the desert of the Ogaden towards Harar, advancing from oasis to oasis, supported from the rear by the Division of Fascists Raised Abroad."

An officer snickered. The major paused and looked around before continuing.

"Like Caesar's legions in the mountain campaign against the Helvetians," the man declaimed, "our divisions are climbing into the highlands, the most magnificent on the continent. Everywhere local forces are assisting us, settling old scores and selling their services as they help carve up the body of their neighbor. The way some Alpine tribes helped Hannibal, you'll recall, when that African invaded Italy. On the northern front the Eritreans assist us in the mountains; to the south the Somali *shifta,* organized into *bandas,* share our struggle in the desert."

Rumored to be a history professor from the University of Pisa, the major was at home with his own lecture. Grimaldi, on the contrary, was anxious to fly his reconnaissance mission, and he prayed the man would not take an academic hour. No doubt this man was flitting from base to base, repeating his story like an old woman gossiping from shop to shop.

"The rotten Abyssininan kingdom is breaking apart, revealing its natural fault lines like a gem under the jeweller's hammer: Shoans and Tigreans, princes and priests, Muslims and Christians, slaves and masters. Courageous enough, but poorly trained and equipped, her soldiers have been able to resist only by massing in great numbers. Then they must face the modern weapons the Duce has provided us: machine guns and artillery and tanks, and, most of all, aircraft. Whenever the battle has been in doubt, I am proud to report, the *Regia Aeronautica* has destroyed them from the sky, bombing and machine gunning without interference." The major paused for an informal comment. "One pilot has told me that from the air it is even better than Libya, more like a hunting party than a war."

Enzo had to agree with that. Never would air power have such a clean campaign: no resistance from the air, perfect weather, ineffective ground fire. In Europe the next war would not be like this. He wondered if the Japanese had been as lucky in Manchuria. But here on the ground, he knew, there had been serious losses.

"Recently, however, as our lines extend deeper into Africa from the coasts, as our forces disperse, the war is getting harder. The more successful the advance, the more this geography becomes our enemy, and the larger grows the responsibility of the air force. The Abyssinian armies are moving more by night. Some of their men are no longer intimidated by tanks, and our road-building crews cannot keep up with the advance." The major paused to acknowledge a question from the table.

"We've heard some regiments've been chopped up, sir, or lost in the mountains, and the prisoners tortured, even crucified."

"And what about Lieutenant Minnetti?" another pilot called out loudly down the table. "After he crashed, they beheaded him in the cattle market in Daggahbur, the same town he'd just bombed and strafed." Several men murmured support for the speaker.

The major chose to answer the first man's question.

"A very few units, mostly native troops, Eritrean, and one battalion from Libya, have been overrun when they have not maintained formation. And at Anale, here, one squadron of tanks, unable to turn on a narrow mountain trail, lost and without infantry, was trapped and overrun by hordes of savages clambering over them like ants. Trouble was the tanks' own machine guns are fixed, you understand, capable of only a limited traverse, fifteen degrees, so they couldn't do much to help themelves." The major paused, knowing he had every man's attention. One of his duties was to stiffen the men and discourage surrender.

"The men left alive, the ones not butchered or castrated, were captured and shown off to foreign journalists in a royal garden in the capital like bears in a zoo. They fetched one tank all the way to Addis for the show." The major drew breath and took a step towards the mess table before continuing in a lower voice.

"This brings me to the delicate matter raised by the captain here," said the officer to his students, pointing at Uzielli with his stick. "Victory must come swiftly. Our country is not rich. War is costly. We must finish the job before the world turns on us. Back at home, roaring crowds gather every night around Marconis in the cafés and the piazzas to listen to *Il Duce* report your victories, and to demand vengeance and justice in Africa. But in unfriendly jealous capitals they work for our defeat. Already we've been fighting for nearly a month."

Listening impatiently, Enzo wondered where this professor had been doing his fighting. Probably in the officers' brothels in Asmara and Massawa. The girls were said to be magnificent, indeed some connoisseurs said the finest in the world, though overworked and somewhat passive. Knowing what was coming, Grimaldi watched the faces of the listeners as the major continued.

"To win swiftly, we must use our secret weapon. This afternoon, after Colonel Grimaldi's reconaissance identifies a target, some of you will test it." A slight commotion interrupted the major as several men stirred uncomfortably at the long mess table.

"This decision," he said more slowly, looking around the table, "has been made in Rome, at the highest levels. If this weapon works, and it will, Italy must deny its use while employing it without restraint. On this single fact the war could turn. Questions?"

Enzo already had supported the army's request for permission to test the effectiveness of poison gas, proscribed after the horrors of the Great War. In that war, the Germans had done the necessary homework, successively testing chlorine, phosgene and mustard gases over the trenches of their enemies. Today, the *Regia Aeronautica* would be testing, in bomb canisters, a cousin of the mustard gas first used in 1917. It was said to be more "persistent" than earlier gases, heavier, better able to hold together at ground level. It was Grimaldi's job to report on its effectiveness.

"Questions?"

"If Geneva learns we're using gas, won't they embargo the oil and close the Canal? If they do that, how will four hundred thousand of us survive in the mountains of Africa without petrol?" asked the Blackshirt liaison officer.

"Not to mention another hundred thousand laborers and farmers already here or on the way," added a pilot. "Even the road work has to be done by Italians. These Abbos are useless."

"What good will our new roads and lorries and tanks and planes be without oil?" exclaimed the Blackshirt. "The League's already voted for other economic sanctions against us."

"Precisely, precisely," said the intelligence officer. "So far the League of Nations has not embargoed oil and coal and steel, and we've made up for the other sanctions by increasing imports from Germany and the United States. Now the League must be spared the proof that would embarrass it into further, more serious action. Suspicions and accusations are one thing. The complaints of the Abyssinians will mean nothing."

He looked over the men and lowered his voice.

"To the League's diplomats in Geneva, the most accomplished cynics of their generation, Emperor Haile Selassie of Abyssinia is just a little black man in a dark suit and English shoes. No, no, only real evidence, the firsthand testimony of Europeans, will lead to an embargo by the League."

"But foreigners are all over the country!" protested the Blackshirt. "Missionaries, ivory hunters, journalists, these so-called Red Cross teams who're serving the enemy, Swedish or English, Belgian or Egyptian or whatever. What do we do about them?"

"We are soldiers," said the major. "Any dangerous witnesses must be treated like enemies at war, eliminated."

One young officer raised his hand. Massimo something. Grimaldi tried to recall the name, some old military family, possibly even titled.

"Sir," said the pilot, his face tight and pale, his voice on edge, "can't we win without using this weapon? Our country promised never to use gas in another war. You said the campaign is going well." A different type of silence seized the room. Then one or two others murmured support as the young man continued. "My own father was blinded by yperite in 1918. Then it took him six years to cough himself to death."

The major slapped his stick nervously against his palm and for a moment did not speak.

"Young man," intervened Colonel Grimaldi, rising, signalling to the waiting Paolo with one hand, rotating his forefinger like a propeller, "we are all soldiers. A weapon is a weapon. What is a whiff of gas compared to the agonies of a burned pilot who survives after his plane goes down in flames?"

There was no reply. Enzo sensed the mood of the table shifting against the protesting officer. He raised his voice.

"Have you seen a brother pilot burned alive?" Enzo paused. "With his face and half his body covered in blisters, his gloves burned into his hands, the fabric of his charred helmet coming away with the blackened skin and flesh of his face?"

Some men sat stiff and silent. Others grunted approval as Grimaldi continued.

"This is a war, Lieutenant, not a debate. You and I will obey orders."

The meeting dispersed as Enzo walked to his fighter. Part of him respected the young officer's sentiments, but what did it matter which way a man died?

"Did you hear any of that, Paolo?" asked Grimaldi as he drew on his goggles and prepared to climb into the Fiat.

"Too much, sir," complained his mechanic in a tone the colonel had not heard before. Had the old man taken an interest in the dispute?

Enzo reflected on other matters while he headed towards the front, relieved to be flying on his own. Despite how they had left things, he missed the English girl and hoped she would be safe. Where was she now? He undid one button of his leather coat and removed her photograph from a pocket, careful to hold it low in his lap where it would not catch the wind. He kissed the photo and returned it to his pocket.

But how could Gwenn care for these Abyssinians she had never seen? Deserting her sons in Cairo, interrupting her own education, even abandoning him? Perhaps that was it. Leaving with the Red Cross was a convenient way to escape his house and his bed. He had felt it as soon as her rough beggar of a husband appeared in Cairo. Those small discreet withdrawals that marked a lover's flight. Touches not given, words not spoken, finally absences and that first dreadful shrinking back, the slight recoiling that neither could avoid recognizing for what it was, a dark snake lying on the white sheet between them. Enzo craved the chance to give the Englishman what he owed him.

He thought of the Potez he had downed in the lake. Last week he had learned it was loaded with silver, which the army was determined to recover. No wonder the poor devil hadn't been able to maneuver with a load like that. But that gunner knew his trade. Had to be a white man. Any day Enzo expected to be ordered to guide the *Bersaglieri* to the wreck.

Grimaldi looked down and watched the scouts of the *Valpusteria Alpini* toiling up the jagged walls of the next escarpment. On the plateau he saw masses of men, Abyssinians, clouds of them in dusty white, more than he had ever seen in one concentration, moving towards the rim of the escarpment. He wondered if the *Alpini* knew what awaited them. He was tempted to turn back and dive but saw that he was short of petrol. He banked and returned to base.

As he taxied in, he was surprised not to see Paolo waving him in at the end of the strip. Instead he noticed a knot of twenty or more men gathered at the open door of the warehouse that held the poison gas. Others were busy around the Capronis, loading canisters and checking the aircraft.

"Some of the men don't want to take the gas canisters, Colonel," said Bruno Mussolini breathlessly, rushing to Grimaldi as he left his aircraft. "They're asking for bombs instead."

"I'll take charge of this, Lieutenant," said Enzo reassuringly, at once appreciating the importance of the moment. "Stand by, you'll see. You can't let these things go. Every man must do his duty."

The men by the warehouse became silent as Grimaldi strode up to them. Not all saluted. Deliberately Enzo unbuttoned his flight coat and unstrapped the holster of his Beretta. He trusted Paolo had kept his pistol in order.

"Which of you is the senior officer?" demanded Grimaldi.

"I've been asked to speak for some of the men, sir," said young Massimo respectfully in a quiet tense voice.

"Do so briefly, Lieutenant," said Grimaldi, "remembering that you are an Italian officer and at war."

"We're asking for bombs, sir, not the gas. We'll fly as many missions as you like, Colonel, as low as you like," the pilot said carefully. *"Il Duce* himself has promised publically that Italy will not use gas."

"And the rest of you?" Grimaldi said to the gathered men, soldiers, ground crew, one signalman. For an instant he recalled the warning words of Marshal Balbo. "All this may not help your career, Colonel, but if you fail, it will destroy it." Enzo was aware of Lieutenant Mussolini watching and listening from a distance, trying to stay a bit removed.

"We've refused to help with the gas, Colonel Grimaldi," said Paolo, speaking from the back in that throaty voice Enzo knew so well.

Astounded by this personal betrayal, Enzo recalled that Paolo himself had been gased as a young soldier in the Great War. But he knew it was time to make an example. The young pilot, Grimaldi thought, was too valuable, and who was to know what influence Massimo's family might possess? The men parted as the colonel, his jaw set, walked towards his old mechanic, then paused and spoke.

"At this moment, thousands of Italian soldiers are depending on each of you to do your duty." Grimaldi's voice was hard and loud. The men held in a circle around him. "I have just seen a battalion of *Alpini* being overrun by a horde of black savages, thousands of them. This weapon will save Italian lives, and even the lives of Abyssinians if it helps end the war. You will service those bombers at once and load and drop the gas."

"We can't do that, sir," said Paolo slowly as other men nodded and muttered and stepped away from the old veteran. "Everything else we will do."

Grimaldi drew his Beretta. Without word or hesitation he fired three rapid shots into the left side of Paolo's chest.

Several men screamed and fell back as the small bullets struck. For a moment Paolo remained standing, facing Enzo, rocking back, then towards him. Sighing, gargling deep in his lungs, he put both hands to his chest. Bubbly blood spread over his fingers. Too late, the signalman held out his arms to support him. Paolo stumbled forward one step, reaching out to his colonel, his open bloody hands sliding down Enzo's boots as he collapsed on the dusty ground.

"I will not have treason." Grimaldi stepped back and holstered his pistol. "Do your duty, gentlemen." He turned and walked to the line of Capronis. The silent men followed him.

Enzo was back in his Fiat in one hour. He missed Paolo at takeoff, but did not regret what he had done. He was aloft, circling slowly, watching the giant box-like bombers gather in formation as he prepared to lead them to the escarpment.

Enzo was certain what he would recommend in his report on the gas. He smiled at what Gwenn would think of that. Were she still his, that alone would end their liaison. Her innocence always surprised him. For a woman who knew war and medicine and loss, she was absurdly devoid of cynicism, of what his mother called *"la rilassatezza morale."*

Below, the army of Shoa was massing to defend the highlands. Drawing some distant ground fire, Enzo dropped down and banked along the rim of the escarpment, searching for the *Alpini.* He found them laagered in an arc around a jagged bowl-shaped outcropping edged with thorn bush and low trees, like an immense eagle's nest set on a cliff. Another battalion or two appeared to have joined the *Alpini,* whether regulars or Blackshirts he could not be certain, but after ascending the mountain tracks they must be without the heavy equipment, the artillery and tanks that their predicament required.

Scattered white-robed bodies, riderless animals, and a few skirmishers appeared to separate the Italian force from the approaching masses of Ethiopians. The more orderly Abyssinian units wore khaki. They were better equipped, no doubt, and probably part of the Emperor's Guard, his household troops trained by those perfidious Belgian mercenaries. Nearby Grimaldi saw hundreds of cloaked men on horseback. Their mounts pranced and capered as the aircraft approached. Behind them swarmed the provincial foot soldiers of Abyssinia, thousands of men in grey *gallabiyyahs* advancing in clusters across the rocky thorny slopes and broad brown fields of the plateau.

Enzo freed the lock on his trigger guard. He felt the tight rush of excitement in his stomach. He was tempted to dive, but it was not his turn. First he would have to assess the work of the bombers, and the gas. Then he must see that any European witnesses were bombed or machine-gunned and driven from the front. Beneath him the African soldiers began to run, not yet in panic, but making for the trees that lined a stream.

The nine Capronis, flying slowly in a long V, descending another thousand feet, looked like giant geese coming in to settle on a lake. Their gas would burn and blind, but it would not carry far. It was essential to drop it in the thick of the Abyssinians, well away from friendly soldiers, though the gas would soon disperse. Fortunately, it would settle naturally in the lower land along the stream where the Ethiopians were sheltering.

Enzo saw the first long cylinders tumble from the lead bomber, Vittorio Mussolini's aircraft. Premature, spinning end over end like great grey sausages, the canisters struck the ground and burst open in front of the advancing troops. Ignorant, the men pressed forward into the invisible clouds of gas.

The other Capronis, in position as they sailed forward, were directly over the concentrations. Cylinders burst among the Ethiopians. The bombers flew on towards the majestic mountain fortress of Amba Alagi, the scene of great historic sieges. Enzo dived and turned in a tight circle.

The hilly mountain plain had become a chaos of horses and men fleeing in all directions. Few soldiers had fallen, but weapons and equipment littered the ground. Enzo imagined he could hear the screams of the burned men and beasts. He saw soldiers stagger and collapse. Others rolled on the ground.

He recalled accounts of the first use of gas in the Great War. Habituated to machine guns and wire and mines, shelling and rats and mud, the men on the ground had been surprised by the smell of mustard as the faint clouds of gas settled into the trenches and shell holes, burning the skin, searing the lungs, blinding their eyes like drops of molten metal. But in that war, he realized as he watched the Capronis diminish in the sky, the troops had time to adjust to each new weapon and to match it with their own: airplanes, tanks and gas. Today these Abyssinians would meet all three for the first time.

Excited, Enzo dived and felt the buck of the Fiat's machine guns.

"Dammit, Malcolm, do you know what they're doing?" Gwenn screamed to Dr. Fergus from the entrance to the tent. Breathless from dashing across the open laager, she was too angry to cry, but she ached with rage as if she herself were wounded.

"What's that, Doctor?" He looked up from his work as two black orderlies dragged off the body that lay before him.

"The Italians are using poison gas!"

"How do you know?" Fergus asked urgently.

"I've seen these wounds before. It's probably yperite, the mustard gas they first used at Passchendale." Or Ypres, she thought, as the French used to call it. During three battles at that village, the British lost four hundred thousand men. By the end it hardly mattered who lived and who was dead.

"They just carried a man into the other tent," Gwenn added, thinking with horror of the twitching body she had seen lifted onto the operating table on a stretch of canvas. This case was different from the rest of the day's work. The others were the classic wounds of warfare: the results of moving metal meeting bone and flesh, the thousand artfully-invented traumas that bullets and bayonets, shrapnel and explosives imposed on the human body. But not this man.

"He looks like he's been dipped in boiling oil," she said. "Come and see." They hurried to the other tent.

Every inch of the Abyssinian's exposed skin was bubbling and blistering as if seared on a spit. Hands, forearms, neck and face were a single massive burn.

"It's hopeless," she said, hanging back from the table in despair, thinking of the long intense pain every burn victim suffers. "There'll be thousands, tens of thousands."

Gwenn rubbed her perspiring face on her sleeve, forgetting the gory condition of her surgical robe. She smelled the drying blood. Suddenly she felt incredibly tired, weak, keenly aware she was no longer the girl who had gone forth from Wales in 1915 to serve as a Volunteer Ambulance Driver in France and Belgium.

As Malcolm examined the body that lay trembling between them, Gwenn looked away. In 1918, when it ended, she had prayed never to see such wounds and agony again. She saw already that the "war to end all wars" had been for nothing.

"It's endless," she said quietly. "The League's useless. Even these horrific weapons haven't been put aside."

Malcolm did not reply but set to work, bathing the African's face, examining his eyes, forcing open the lids and wiping away the filmy fluid that leaked from them. He stretched a band of damp folded gauze across the man's eyes and knotted it neatly behind one ear. Before continuing, Malcolm looked across at Gwenn and smiled, no sign of exhaustion or disgust in his eyes.

Gwenn tucked a lock of hair into her white cap and looked down at the Abyssinian. The worst cases had inhaled too much gas. Their lungs were seared. Few survived. This man seemed lucky. Probably blind, but he was breathing well. In time, deep ulcers might replace his burns and blisters.

She selected a scissor and slit open the grey cotton robe of the black warrior. The rest of his slender body seemed to be spared, save a raised border of injured skin near the exposed parts. Second degree burns were spread unevenly beneath the edges of the garment.

"That's all we can do for now," said Malcolm a bit later. "I'd best return to the other tent."

Gwenn turned to a basin to wash her hands as another wounded man was carried in. Her eyes lost focus. She felt dizziness overtake her. Even the sound coming through the canvas walls seemed to be changing. The beast outside was stirring. The droning moan had changed to something more shrill. It was the sound of terror, of many men screaming in fear and panic.

She shook her head and stepped to the door of the tent, looking out between a lorry and an ambulance to the mass of wounded. They were scrambling about in desperation, pointing to the sky. Then she heard another sound, trembling and echoing up the valley, the engines of aircraft flying low. Mules and horses snorted and bolted through the crowds. What could planes be doing here?

Gwenn heard rifle fire rise from the riverbank as the first three planes came in. Mesmerized, she walked outside and watched as if observing some distant spectacle. Three tan biplanes, strangely beautiful, advanced in a perfect V formation, their machine guns sparkling like fireflies.

Could this be Lorenzo? she wondered instantly. She recalled sensing the pleasure he found from flying in wartime. A chill anger hardened within her as she stood and watched.

Between the ambulance laager and the stream, she saw rows of bullets cut lines through the men like the tines of giant rakes. Small bombs, possibly grenades, tumbled from the aircraft. The valley became a howling chaos of unimaginable frenzy. Horrified, outraged, she realized that their work was for nothing. By assembling the victims, the field hospital was causing more suffering, not less.

Two more flights followed the first. As the planes came in, Gwenn discerned the colors and rondels of Fascist Italy.

She ran for the operating tent. She saw two lines of bullets strike an ambulance and continue on across the red cross in the open square. Jets of dust rose from the neat holes that stitched across the large flag. Two Egyptian nurses ran towards her. The open truck next to the ambulance, loaded with petrol tins, took similar hits, then exploded as a bomb burst beside it. The nurses vanished in the flash. An orderly stumbled past her, his hair on fire.

As she reached the tent, Gwenn saw burning gasoline splash the roof and one side of the other surgical tent. Flames enfolded it like the walls of an oven. She hesitated and watched orderlies and nurses and patients dash and stumble from the burning canvas entrance. Finally Malcolm staggered out, one shoulder of his smock smoldering, a naked black man across his arms.

Gwenn ran to him as he fell. The wounded patient struggled feebly where Malcolm dropped him. Lying on his back on the stony ground, his chest pumping blood, the man moved his arms and legs like a crab. Malcolm tried to get up as she came to him. His hands were bloody as he struggled to his knees and reached for her assistance. Above, the third flight came in. Terrified at last, she heard the guns chasing and crackling behind her. The ground beside her exploded. She felt blows to her shoulder and face as she collapsed.

— 22 —

"How exciting to have our big hunter on his back again," said an American voice. "It's been such a long time."

Anton turned his head and squinted at the long slender legs from between the front wheels of the Oldsmobile. They seemed more tan and fit than they had only a fortnight ago. But neither the voice nor the shapely calves told him which twin it was.

"Pass me the big spanner, Kimathi," he said, already in a foul mood. "This damn thing's coming apart." He looked up at the battered axle and springs and pan and wiped some oil from his jaw. Diwani worked on his back beside Anton, spreading cooking grease with his fingers.

"And tell Lapsam to sort out the food and leave a box of tins behind," Anton added to Kimathi.

"Oh, and miss, you and your sister, please prepare to chuck out one more case, the biggest one this time. We have to lighten up the lorry. Better leave some of that photographic stuff as well. Won't be much time for toys, you know."

"My Bell and Howell is not a toy," Harriet snapped. "It's for professionals. Brand new, sixteen millimeter. They're using them to make newsreels. And stop calling us 'miss.' We have names, Mr. Rider."

"You make the choices," said Anton, pleased he had piqued her. "Just leave that big case behind, if you please. This is a safari, not the *Queen Mary.*"

"I'll tell Berny to toss out some of her old junk," said Harriet sulkily. "And Charlie's hopelessly overloaded with all that artsy rubbish. But I've hardly got a stitch left since we bargained with those people for this silly truck." She kicked hard against the sole of one of Anton's boots. "What sort of safari do you call this?"

"You're quite right. Actually, it's a war. Should be even more exciting for you. No extra charge." He watched her ankles turn as she stamped one foot. "Better hop to it and do it now, please. We're off at the crack tomorrow."

"Couldn't you have gotten us a better truck?"

"If you'd spared us your magnifying mirror and a few other goodies," he added only half under his breath, "we could've traded for a proper lorry instead of this useless American fall-about." He grunted as he turned the spanner.

"Allo!" called a different foreign voice from the other side of the cab. Anton turned his head in the dust and saw a pair of very tall, well-shined black boots. "Good afternoon."

"Why, good afternoon to you, sir," he heard Harriet reply to the stranger in her huskiest voice.

Anton wrenched the spanner several times more and started to crawl out as the man's voice continued in stiff clear English. Some sort of Scandinavian, probably Swedish from the singsong, Anton reckoned, recalling a previous princely client. Always slightly annoyed when uninvited strangers surprised him in his own camp, Anton stood and faced the man, stepping between him and Harriet.

"Anton Rider," he said, gripping the officer's hand harder than the man was accustomed to. "This is my client, Miss Mills, and this is Kimathi, our head man."

"Captain Larsen," said the handsome blond officer, ignoring Kimathi while he grinned boyishly over Anton's shoulder at Harriet. "Royal Swedish Advisory Mission." Then he looked down at his right hand, now stained with dark oily grease.

"Welcome to Africa, Major." Anton turned and handed the spanner to Kimathi with a nod and a smile. He reached through the window of the truck and wiped his hands on a rag before withdrawing his .375 from the cab.

"Captain," the officer corrected. Slender and graceful in his movements, even taller than Anton, perhaps twenty-four or twenty-five, the confident young man stirred in Anton a mixture of irritation and reluctant envy. The soldier's eyes brightened and stared over Anton's shoulder as the second twin approached.

"The *Dejazmatch,* our Ethiopian commander Ras Timoun, commands me to invite you and your safari clients to join his excellency for dinner when the sun falls."

"Thank you," said Harriet, deferring the introduction of her sister, "we'd love . . ."

"You'll have to excuse us tonight, Captain," Anton interrupted, aware of Harriet's annoyance. He had no wish to become entangled with the Abyssinian army and its problems.

"Actually, we thought we'd be eating early this evening, in just a few minutes. Cook's got the stew on now." Anton drew a dented cigarette tin from a pocket of his shorts. He flipped it open with his thumb and offered one to the soldier.

Harriet sensed tension between the two men, and she tried again. "Perhaps we could . . ." she began.

"My clients've had the devil of a long day," said Anton, giving her a stern look, "and tomorrow we're up at dawn to press on south."

Ignoring the cigarettes, the captain straightened and spoke deliberately as if addressing a platoon of untrained native levies.

"You will take this as more than an invitation, Monsieur Reader . . ." His eyes shifted to the well-cared-for rifle the older man carried in his other hand.

"Rider." Anton held in his anger. He'd met these young military advisers before, mostly Belgians and Swedes, and a few froggies. Spoiled by accelerated promotion and a degree of authority they would never have at home, not to mention servants and luxury and influence beyond their dreams in Europe, they soon became used to having their way. And in Abyssinia, as in Somalia, the women were uncommonly lovely and accessible. No doubt this young warrior had enjoyed more than his share.

"The Ras and his army may today be in retreat, Mr. Rider, but you and I are still guests in the kingdom of Abyssinia." The Swede drew a stiff leather whip from his right boot. "You may be on holiday, but this nation is at war."

When had Sweden's soldiers last fought a war? Anton almost asked. Flogging weapons to the locals and dressing up in the capital were all very well. Perhaps this campaign would show what sort of soldiering these dandies were made for.

"Didn't we see you chaps drilling your boys before cocktails in the capital?" Anton said in a neutral voice.

The captain pointed to his right with the whip.

"We have four thousand armed men camped in the next valley, directly on your route. The entire province is under military authority," the young officer continued, slapping one boot with the switch and looking at Anton for submission.

"You will require a letter of transit to move your camp and animals."

Anton hesitated before replying.

"Will you be making your stand here?" He knew he shouldn't say it. "You may find bullying civilians is sharper work than fighting the Italians."

The captain's neck swelled in his tall blue-grey collar. The boyish face darkened.

"I will send an escort to lead you to the Ras's war tent. You will bring your passports and a manifest of your weapons and ammunition. And, I can inform you, you may not receive permission to travel with your armament." He clicked his heels and bowed his chin to the ladies before turning and walking off.

"Maybe you should've been a soldier," said Harriet to Anton, not without some admiration. "Come on, Berny, we'd better vamp up for the party, and you have to throw out your things."

These American girls were made for this sort of thing, Anton realized two hours later when the twins appeared for dinner. They knew how to get things done, or at least how to get what they wanted.

Shimmering like lightning bugs in slinky lamé dresses, Harriet and Bernadette pretended to ignore the captain as they courted Ras Timoun, clucking and ooing over the old rogue. Clearly, the twins understood their mission: securing permission from the *Dejazmatch* for the safari to travel south in the morning.

"What a lovely jewelled sword!" exclaimed Bernadette, clapping her hands and looking into the eyes of the Ras, a heavy, very dark, grizzled man with a brocade vest hanging over a loose embroidered shirt secured at the waist with a European military belt.

The Ras smiled at the young woman.

"This sword was given by the Emperor Menelik to my father as he was dying after the battle of Adowa. With this I will take the head of the Benito."

"What a perfect idea," Bernadette said. "And what is your map made from, parchment, isn't it?"

"It is the skin of a very young lamb." The man turned it over and displayed the old Amharic calendar that was painted on the back. On the map, each Abyssinian province was illustrated with primitive colored figures, lions for the Ogaden, coffee plants and gazelle for the Arussi district, a fat hippopotamus for the Boran territory.

"Here now are the Italians, with the dogs who follow their camps, coming towards us through these valleys." The Ethiopian drew Bernadette closer while he traced the routes of his enemies with long gnarled fingers. "But when they come to the next valley, they will be in the cave of the lion," said the hawk-nosed warrior, and Anton guessed he was one.

"Please allow us to present a few trifles as gifts for your camp," said Anton grandly, spreading his hands as Laboso appeared at one edge of the great open tent, followed by three camp boys bearing boxes. At least it was a useful way to lighten the lorry's load. This was the sort of drill, Anton thought, at which his friend Olivio excelled. He tried to proceed as might the dwarf himself.

"Here are tinned delicacies we bring to you from Paris and from London, Excellency, some fashionable garments for your wives, a forged axe from the United States of America, certain other modest offerings." Anton saw annoyance, even scorn rise in Captain Larsen's face, but he knew what he was about. He, not this boy, was the old Africa hand.

The *Dejazmatch* nodded at the tribute, then looked at the boxes one by one, spilling their contents out onto the carpet before turning several over with the toe of his slipper. Tins of foie gras and truffles, cherries and capers, stewed plums and water biscuits rolled beneath his foot. But only the lace underclothes, high-heeled shoes and black silk stockings seemed to divert his attention.

"No guns?" the old Ras asked.

"Had we expected this special evening, we would have presented more," said Harriet, seeking to capture the man's attention. "What beautiful guns you have, though."

On a carpet behind the *Dejazmatch* rested his personal weapons: an old Mauser with a new chromiumed bolt, an Enfield resting on a canvas scabbard bound with leather and bright brocaded bands worked with gold thread, and a Czechoslovak machine gun. Nearby rested a tangle of bandoliers and a .32 revolver in a fawn leather holster.

The Ras noticed Anton's interest in the weapons and invited him to examine them.

"Obersdorf Arsenal, 1913," said Anton, inspecting the stamp on the Mauser. He swung out the bolt and gazed along the bore. The German weapon was shot out, the grooves of the rifling thinned near the muzzle. It was a rare infirmity, probably from misuse. He scowled and the Ras nodded in agreement

"But this is very nice work," said Anton, admiring the Enfield, customized as a sporting rifle. The shortened barrel was stamped with the mark of a Birmingham gunsmith. The walnut stock was elaborately carved and checkered. Anton lifted the machine gun with effort, interested in the gas-driven weapon, particularly by the curling twist of the cooling ribs that ran along its barrel.

"Mitrailleuse," the commander said, stepping over and taking the heavy gun from Anton's hands with no sign of exertion. He pointed with pride to a word engraved on the barrel. "Brno!" he exclaimed. "Brno!"

The Abyssinian stripped the automatic weapon down to a collection of springs and guides and pawls, aware he held the attention of his guests. He reassembled the machine gun with remarkable speed, then lifted it easily to his shoulder, swinging it through high arcs with his left hand as he shot down imaginary Italian aircraft. *"Tat! Tat! Tat!"* he said.

"My goodness!" said Bernadette, doing her share.

Laughing loudly, the *Dejazmatch* set down the gun and smiled at his female guests. He unsheathed his long curved sword. The silver-trimmed hilt was made from the polished hoof of a bullock. Near the hilt the balanced blade was thick and dull. It grew sharper with the curve, slightly hollow, silver-edged and razor-fine as it neared the tip. The Ras lifted a mandarin with his left hand and tossed it up repeatedly. Then he smiled at Bernadette and handed her the mandarin. She looked him in the eye and threw the mandarin in the air. The blade whistled above her hand and split the fruit in two. The Ras bowed and offered one piece to each of the women on the tip of his sword.

Charlie, seated nearby on a pile of cushions, wasn't doing too badly either. His portrait of the Abyssinian commander was coming along handsomely. Glancing at the flattering sketch, Anton was impressed. Charlie seemed to have a useful gift for toadying with pencil and charcoal. The Ras's magnificent war tent and his grey stallion made a brave background for his noble countenance. Gone were the smallpox pits on the cheeks, the creases and scowl lines that surrounded the leader's eyes and mouth. Intelligence and courage flashed from the penetrating eyes set between a tall forehead and prominent cheekbones.

"Well done, Charlie. Splendid," said Anton very quietly. "It's the head of a young prince, a black Alexander."

Following the Ras's invitation, they moved out to a row of cushions set on carpets by a fire before the broad tent. An immense copper drum, shaped like a giant tambourine, was suspended in a wood and leather frame nearby. The ground sloped away behind the fire. Several tall spears were set in the earth, apparently marking the limits of the *Dejazmatch*'s private camp. Beyond lay scores of fires. The sound of many men, the twanging of stringed instruments, and the odors of camels, mules and horses rose towards them. To one side three men butchered a cow. Its throat slit, the long gory dewlap hanging loose, the animal collapsed on its knees as if at prayer. Scarcely had the body touched the earth before long strips of flesh were cut from its flanks and tossed into waiting bowls and paniers.

A white-robed slave approached the party, bowing as he presented a tray with six silver goblets. This African did not have the slender aquiline features of most Ethiopians. Probably the victim of a slave raid in his youth, Anton guessed, somewhere to the south or west. Perhaps Dinka or Azande, very far from home. The man's status was marked by the coarse black iron bracelet around his right wrist, from which dangled a single link of heavy chain. A second slave followed with a pitcher.

Captain Larsen took the last cup and stood, striking and elegant in his high-waisted trousers and sky-blue dress tunic, prepared for a ball at the Royal Palace in Stockholm. He removed his peaked blue cap. Parted in the middle in neat lines, his slick blond hair shone. Annoyed, Anton was aware that both twins were giving the officer their full attention even before the young man spoke.

"To His Imperial Highness Haile Selassie, Emperor of the Abyssinians, King of Kings, Negus Negesti, Lion of Judah, and to victory over his enemies!" They all drank the *tajj,* following the Ras as he drained his cup.

"Mmm, it's lovely." Bernadette licked her foam-covered lips as her goblet was refilled with the rich mead. "Is it very strong?" she whispered to the Swede innocently, touching his wrist with red-tipped fingers.

"One gets used to it." The captain laughed, smiling at her with sparkling eyes. The silver of his Abyssinian decoration, the Star of Solomon, twinkled in the firelight. "Would you prefer arrack? They make it from those coconut palms."

"I'm sure my sister's fiancé would try that, if they have some," Harriet interrupted, trying to edge Bernie out of the race. "Wouldn't you, Charlie?"

"Can't hurt," Charlie said, strengthening the Ras's chin with a stroke of charcoal. "I'll explode if I overdo it with this other stuff."

Anton glanced at the portrait again. Just the thing, the man-of-destiny look.

"If the chap fights as well as he looks on paper," he whispered to Harriet, "the Eyeties're finished already."

Servants presented *enjara,* hot and round as pancakes, with shavings of onions mixed into the millet. An immense bowl of warm raw beef was passed among the guests, the meat swimming in its own warm juice, each piece large as a salmon. Platters of fava beans and stewed squash were set before them.

The *Dejazmatch* assisted Bernie, picking through the fresh meat with swift black fingers, thrusting his right hand into the blood to his wrist. He raised a heavy dark organ, not the heart, perhaps half of the animal's liver, and slapped it loudly with his free hand. Anton saw Berny flinch. The Ras released the slippery cut back into the bowl and grunted as he found something more pleasing. Not a drop spilled when he twisted the slab of meat like a wine bottle as he removed it from the bowl. He gripped it with a piece of *enjara* and handed it to his guest. The captain attempted a similar courtesy for Harriet, but blood soiled the cuff of his tunic.

Damn fine sports, Anton thought as the girls exchanged glances and nibbled the moist protruding ends of the beef.

The Ras clapped his hands and servants appeared with richly sugared fruit to complete the meal. When they were finished, Charlie rose and presented his portrait to their host.

"Larsen," said the Ras, well pleased, snapping his fingers, "prepare a paper of passage for my guests."

After numerous attempts to take their leave, finally Anton and his clients were guided to the edge of the encampment by the *Dejazmatch* himself. Many figures moved back into the shadows of fires as they proceeded across the rough ground escorted by four torchbearers. Stopping at last, the Ras bowed to the ladies and presented the document to Charles. "With this permit you will travel in safety through my mountains."

Better start early, Anton reminded himself the next morning, lying alone under canvas in the darkness. His mouth was dry as the Ogaden. His temples throbbed with arrack and *tajj.* His belly was bloated and hard with raw meat, swollen like a python after devouring a kid. Worse, he was annoyed by his own jealousy, still bitter and resentful after hearing Harriet and the Swede giggling as the young officer had staggered from her tent only an hour before. Another reason to get this safari underway. Anton realized he had grown spoiled. He was not used to sharing the favors of his camp.

Anton stepped naked from his tent into the darkness. He gazed up while he relieved himself. The stars were losing their full brightness as dawn opened. He bent over the enamel basin that rested on a bamboo frame beside his tent. He held his breath and lowered his face into the cold water. He trembled and the muscles of his stomach tightened when he raised his head and the chilling drops streamed down his body. He did the same twice more, spitting and gargling before he slapped soap on his face and worked quickly with his straight razor. Then he wiped his face and stared at the sky over the top of the towel. The seven points of Phoenix dimmed as the first light softened the sky. He wondered where Gwenn was, and whether she found moments to think of him.

He dressed and walked to the boys' fire. Only Kimathi sat awake, a coarse blanket wrapped about his ears. He stood and nodded as Anton tossed him a packet of Senior Service. Anton knelt, lifted a glowing branch and lit their cigarettes.

"Here's the drill, Kimathi." He kicked the stubs of the sticks into the coals. "Get the boys up smartly. We'll make a fast start with no breakfast, just tea and biscuits for the clients while we pack the animals and load that wretched Olds."

"Ndio, Tlaga."

Anton shoved the big black kettle into the coals with the toe of his boot. He checked the pocket of his shorts for the letter of transit. "Then it's straight through the Abyssinian camp and on south towards Zwai, the first Rift lake, before that old *Dejazmatch* has second thoughts about letting us pass." He pulled out the letter of transit, signed by the Swede and marked with the stamp of Ras Timoun. With this, no man could stop them.

His sleeping men stirred as Anton finished his smoke. Laboso kicked one or two, clicking his tongue and giving orders as he prowled the camp with his knobkerry.

"Morning *chai*!" announced Lapsam a few minutes later as he served dark morning tea with tinned cream and crystalized brown sugar to the clients in their tents. Anton followed immediately behind him, clapping his hands and urging haste.

"Morning, Charlie. Up and out. No time for a shave. Want to get clear of the soldier boys."

Already the sky was brighter. In the far distance, like a bothersome mosquito, Anton heard the buzzing of a light plane. Probably an Italian scout on recce. It was time to move on and get clear of this lot.

Nearby, the *saises* were watering the horses and mules in pairs. The animals snuffled and stamped their feet while they waited their turns. Lapsam organized his chests while other men set the wooden pack frames on the backs of the mules and balanced their loads. Bales of horse fodder and sacks of feed were packed onto the kneeling camels as Kimathi stalked from man to man urging speed and checking their work.

Not bad, Anton thought, as he climbed into the Olds. Fifty-five minutes from start to saddle. Each morning it should get better. He was pleased the old truck had no driver's door. Warming up, it rattled and trembled beneath him. The blinking American engine was trying to shake free from its mounting. Anton put his Holland in its scabbard on the floor beside him. Then he turned and looked back at Harriet through the glassless window at the rear of the cab.

Harriet, in a good mood, sat on a folded tent in the rear of the lorry, fiddling with her Bell & Howell.

"Don't forget!" she called to Anton imperiously. "Don't bounce the truck. I'm going to film our safari column and that beautiful Abyssinian camp."

She opened a square yellow cardboard box, removed a new roll from the tin canister inside it, and set the film into the figure-eight-shaped housing of the heavy movie camera. She raised the hinged silver handle that lay flat against the side of the camera, then turned the handle clockwise again and again, winding tight the driving mechanism, preparing it for filming.

"Ready, *Tlaga,*" Kimathi said, resting a foot on the running board and gripping his pony's chin strap with one hand. Behind the truck in a tight line were ten more horses, eighteen camels and a gang of mules. Most of Anton's men, nearly twenty altogether, carried spears and swords or pangas.

"Keep them in close order while we pick our way through," said Anton to Kimathi, concerned about their passage through the unruly Abyssinian camp to the far end of the valley. He leaned out of the lorry and waved at old Haqim. Ugly as ever, blessedly unable to converse with the rest of the boys, the Nubian would follow last to discourage stragglers or pursuit.

"Hang on," Anton yelled at Harriet as he put the truck in gear.

Warmed by the expresso and grappa, Enzo Grimaldi screwed the cap onto his thermos. He considered the performance of the Capronis the day before. Neither bombs nor gas had the dependable deadly effect of artillery and machine guns against massed infantry, but together they had served to devastate and disperse the enemy's formations. During a long and difficult campaign, every weapon would make a contribution, but to terrify an uneducated enemy into prompt submission, there was a certain magic horror that made an invisible gas particularly effective. Once an enemy was on the run, there was no substitute for low-level bombing and aerial machine guns. Uneasy, unable to avoid the thought, he wondered if Gwenn could have been at the Red Cross camp he had attacked the day before.

He looked to both sides and raised a thumb to his wingmen. Far to their left the unarmed scout plane, a nimble cloud-grey Breda-25, originally built as a trainer, dipped one wing and turned back for base. Enzo regretted he could not hear the chatter of its two hundred horsepower Alfa Lynx engine. His own Fiat, with twice the power, droned on steadily. This would be the sort of day Enzo enjoyed. With luck, they would save many Italian lives.

Amused, he thought of the excitement at the base the previous evening. The Mussolini boys, more at home, becoming airmen, were relishing their evenings at the officers' mess, drinking Campari with their brother pilots and telling war stories to eager journalists.

"What was the bombing like at Adowa?" asked the writer from the *Corriere Della Sera.* "They can't get enough of this at home, you know, Lieutenant Mussolini."

"*Miracolo*!" said Bruno again, his account perfected, his right hand floating above the bar like a Caproni. "Our bombs burst among the Africans like blossoming red roses."

"Can't say it's all been so easy," said the mildly drunk military correspondent of the Vatican's *Osservatore.* "Over in Wollo they shot down a Fiat and impaled the pilot without his head." Enzo smiled as he recalled how this useful report had dispelled any mawkish humanitarianism that might have lingered among the stunned airmen.

Now the rising sun was at his tail. The nine Capronis, their pilots getting used to Africa, were fifteen hundred feet above him and perhaps a mile behind, flying in three tight V's. Enzo was proud of the young aviators. They no longer flew too high, dropping bombs and gas uselessly at the first crack of ground fire. The weapons, too, were improving. Instead of a few heavier bombs that were ineffective unless dropped perfectly on target, now each Caproni often carried five hundred two-pound bombs, a more forgiving and effective load.

Sometimes Enzo marvelled at this war: the new energy of Europe's greatest civilization, reborn on campaign in Africa, each smooth-paced engine manufactured by the craftsmen of Milan, every machine gun properly rifled and greased by the hands of artisans in Turin, every canister of gas lovingly charged by the scientists at home, all turned to use by Italy's boys in this jagged wilderness. Mercifully Haile Selassie, this Ras Tafari, this so-called King of Kings, was no Hannibal.

This morning six Capronis carried the conventional heavy sausage-shaped tanks of mustard gas. The last three would be conducting an experiment: testing the new aerial sprayers that had been mounted under their wings. Inside these noisy bombers, dubbed *docce volanti,* "flying douches," by their air crews, the bombardiers would be manning the pumps to eject the gas from the metal nipples.

The job of Enzo's squadron of CR-20's was twofold: to suppress ground fire so the Capronis could come in low and slow enough to maximize the effects of the mustard gas, and to assess the effectiveness of the gas after the attack.

The Fiats dropped to seven hundred feet, then lower still. The congested valley lay just ahead of them. Remarkable that these Abbos hadn't yet learned to disperse, Enzo thought with disgust. Behind the CR-20's, the Capronis had dropped to about fifteen hundred, safely above effective rifle fire.

Enzo felt excitement tighten his stomach when he saw the armed camp in the valley below turn from dawn lassitude to desperate panic. He crossed himself. His senses tingled as men leapt up and burst from their tents. A few, and he admired them, were already firing into the air as the Fiats came in.

He began using his guns when he flew over the stream at the mouth of the valley. Hundreds of men rose up before him as if from the ground itself. Many fell before the machine guns of the Fiats. As he flew up the valley, it seemed to Enzo that his own aircraft was moving incredibly slowly, although he must be doing eighty or more. Yet the action below appeared swift and frantic.

Concerned by his limited supply of ammunition, Enzo searched for targets that would make a difference: modern weapons, leadership, spirited defense, European witnesses. Just ahead, near the center of the valley, were two lorries mounting pairs of machine guns or light anti-aircraft guns, probably Swiss Oerlikons. A khaki tent and a pole carrying the blue and yellow flag of Sweden stood between the two trucks. A European dashed from the tent as Grimaldi approached.

Shirtless, pale as milk among the sea of black figures, the white man scrambled onto a truck and turned his guns towards the attacking aircraft. Enzo heard the *pop-pop pop-pop* of the Oerlikons and felt a buffeting shock. "*Dannazione!*" he said, fearful of these modern guns, his stomach knotted. He returned fire as he closed. The bullets reached the tall Swede and climbed his chest to his shoulders like a pair of red suspenders.

Grimaldi was so low, perhaps a hundred and twenty feet or less, that he made out the man's blond hair and sky-blue trousers as the soldier fell. Pleased with his shooting, Enzo watched the truck explode as bullets struck the ammunition cases and gas tanks. To both sides men and animals were falling to the guns of Enzo's wingmen. Some were cut down as they tried to flee across the stream.

On the hillside to his right, level with his own flight, Enzo saw a cluster of large Abyssinian tents. He would get these on his second pass. Below him, amidst a chaos of plunging animals, too late for him to use his guns, he spotted a single open truck seeking to escape at the far end of the valley.

Enzo climbed and banked to his left, beginning a long circle that would enable him to come in behind the Capronis for a second pass. His wingmen followed him in tight formation. The starboard CR-20 trailed light smoke from one wing. Her pilot gave Colonel Grimaldi a thumbs-up.

Following the nine Capronis, Enzo saw the first two flights of bombers dump their tanks of gas. The barrel-like metal vessels tumbled in the air like toy cigars. The drop was perfect. The containers fell in the thick of the men and mules and camels. Some burst into fragments on impact, others bounced and split when they hit softer ground.

Directly behind Enzo, flying dangerously low, the three *doccie volanti* came in down the valley. Blessedly, there was no wind. Enzo had checked the camp's flags and pennants on his first run. He could not discern the clouds of gas that should be emerging from beneath the wings. Only the reactions of the victims could tell him what must be happening.

He checked his gasoline gauge and reminded himself to concentrate on his mission. He banked and made for the tents of the enemy commander. He saw an Abyssinian striking a metal gong set beside the highest tent, no doubt trying to rally this rabble of an army. Enzo fired his guns. Two lines of bullets stitched through the tent. For an instant Enzo was sightless, dazzled by the rising sun reflected off the copper of the giant drum. The machine gun bullets crossed the drummer's body and sent the gong hurtling.

A plume of oily smoke blinded Enzo. The port Caproni was on fire, her bow engine a torch of flame and thick black smoke. The pilot tried to climb, but the plane would not respond. Like a duck settling on a lake, her nose rose and her tail dropped. Before she sank past the far end of the valley, Enzo detected beneath her the fleeing truck, moving slowly. He himself was now so low that he could make out a figure sitting in the back of the vehicle with some black object raised before its face. As he passed overhead, Enzo realized it was not a weapon. He wondered what it was.

Ahead of him, in the next narrow valley, the tail of the dying Caproni finally touched the ground. For an instant the great aircraft rose, as if bouncing, struggling to rise like a wounded animal. Then the tail struck again, scraping along the ground before it struck a massive boulder. The flaming plane flipped and crashed on its back. Disturbed, but relieved that neither Lieutenant Mussolini was aboard, Enzo climbed above the smoke.

Once again, his ammunition expended, his petrol low, Enzo and his port wingman flew low over the Abyssinian camp. The wounded CR-20 had already flown for home, escorted by the second wingman.

The poison gas had done its work. Beneath him, men were tearing off their clothes, clawing their chests, rolling on the ground. Enzo Grimaldi imagined he could hear their screams. Wounded mules and horses limped and dragged themselves about. Weapons and baggage and equipment littered the valley floor. Scores of burned men had thrown themselves into the river. There they thrashed among the dead. Others, blinded, stumbled amidst the carnage of the camp. Both machine-gun lorries were destroyed. The great tents were aflame. Only the downed smoking Caproni in the next valley made an ugly sight, its belly up, the two lines of exposed gas nozzles pointing up like teats on a dead sow. There was no sign of her crew.

Near the Caproni stood the truck he had seen fleeing, apparently broken down at the edge of a rocky outcrop. Enzo passed overhead. He stared down in horror.

What Colonel Grimaldi saw could cost Italy the war.

A woman, a European, stood on the back of the truck, a large black camera before her face as she filmed the downed gas-spraying bomber. Enzo checked his guns. Empty. At that instant a shot struck the fuselage beside him. Splinters brushed his thigh. Frightened, he glanced back. A white man in shorts stood straight and still among the rocks, steady, calm as a duck hunter, following Enzo's flight with a raised rifle. A second shot nicked Enzo's propeller as he climbed hurriedly and turned for base.

— 23 —

Ernst von Decken felt the fat soft-bodied creature struggle like a fetus within his cupped palms. The webbed feet braced for leverage, forcing its head upward against his fingers as the lids blinked to protect the prominent bulbous eyes. Perhaps smelling its fate, the frog urinated on his hand.

It was feeding time at the island monastery in Lake Zwai, the hour for Ernst to perform the chore that had been his for more than a week.

Beside Ernst's litter a hungry civet cat scrambled to face him. It growled with a low-pitched cough, arching its back like a house cat as it turned in the long narrow rattan cage. Four feet nose to tip, heavily built, the black-and-white nocturnal carnivore scratched the wooden bars with vicious strokes of its short claws.

"*Frühstück,* Klaus." The big man made a kissing sound as he sat forward on the edge of the litter and extended his hands to the cage. *"Ein grosser Frosch,* Klausie." For a moment he was distracted by the tingling of the right foot that was no longer his. He shifted his leg and ignored the dense, almost nauseating, sweet odor that came from the anus of the imprisoned cat.

"Jag Meil!" Ernst spread his fingers. Free at last, the frog leapt forward between the bars. Before it touched the bottom of the cage, the civet slapped it with one paw, cutting open the frog's flank. The amphibian fell onto the row of dried reeds that formed the bottom of the cage.

Holding its broad head low to the ground, the cat studied the trembling frog without moving. The shaggy black stripe of the civet's dorsal mane rose with excitement and stood straight up above its arched spine. Its eyes narrowed and shone like small hot lamps inside the black band of the mask that crossed its face. Ernst felt the angry feral intensity of the cat's imprisoned instinct, the pent frustration of the hunter, concentrated and focused by the cruelty of confinement. He himself longed to be free from this island.

Bleeding fluids, the frog sprang for the last time.

The cat caught the amphibian in the air. The green head swelled when the civet squeezed the frog's body between its front paws. The cat's black nose twitched as it raised the frog close to its face. It devoured the head of the frog, then dropped the leaking body to the floor of the cage. Its long whiskers and pointed white muzzle now shiny red, the civet toyed with the twitching body, nipping and nibbling as it pushed the oozing remains about the floor. The cage, suspended above the ground from a pole stretched between two wooden forks set into the earth, rocked from the agitation.

Ernst groaned as he turned on his litter. He reached into a wide-mouthed clay gourd and lifted out the next morsels of the cats' breakfast: a thick brown slug and two snails. Knowing the snails would be more patient, more shy and withdrawn within the cornucopia-shaped walls of their elegant white fortresses, he tossed the shrivelling slug into the cage.

"*Grosswild,* Hansel!"

It was Ernst's daily duty to collect the oily musk that ran from their scent glands into the membrane-like pouches near the anus of the cats. In the dense bush and thick savannah that these creatures favored, the musk, looking like rancid butter, was used to mark their territory and deter rivals. But here on the island the precious fluid was collected in stone jars, then taken to market by Theodorus himself, to be sold and bartered for tools and bolts of cloth, and medicines for the lepers dwelling on a nearby island. Only the abbot ever saw the money.

These anal drippings would become the essence for the costliest perfumes, furnishing a thousand ladies of Africa and Europe with the magic for seduction. For many an aging tart, Ernst reckoned, these anal glands were the veritable fountain of youth. Generations of children would be in his debt.

Hansel, an elderly slower civet, ten or more years old, less generous with its musk, switched its bushy striped tail from side to side and advanced like a matador with short precise steps. The cat gazed down at the compacted rounded body and licked the slug with its thin pink tongue. Turning its head to the side to employ its few remaining sharp rear teeth, the old civet spread its black lips and bit the juicy gastropod in two.

Omniverous as bears, the cats were habituated to a varied diet. Their chosen treat seemed to be birds' eggs, particularly when the chicks, fully formed but soft and downy, were about to emerge. Several days before, Ernst and Petros had watched one civet for an hour. The vigorous young cat, Helmut, Ernst's favorite, held a shiny egret's egg between its paws, waiting for the baby bird to appear.

Patient as a banker, its head low to the ground, the civet assisted the baby egret as the dewy bird cracked its veined grey shell and struggled to come forth. Twitching fluffy white wings, unable to stand on its long black legs, but for a time astonishingly durable, the infant lurched and tumbled about the cage while Helmut batted it around like a shuttlecock. Gasping, the egret opened its stumpy yellow bill. *"Kwark, kwark."* Like a domestic cat rubbing affectionately against its master's leg, the civet rubbed its neck and shoulders against the thin downy body of the exhausted bird. Eventually the cat pinned the panting baby on its back and opened the bird's belly wtih one slow stroke of a paw. That evening Helmut mated like a bull.

Ernst's six charges recently had been short of meat. Brother Petros had furnished insufficient rats and snakes. Scholars of scent, the monks had taught Ernst that a civet's diet affected the odor of its glands, and the volume and value of its perfume: too many lizards or scorpions, and the musk grew bitter; too many berries or batoka plums, and the oil became too thin. He was learning to balance the menu with the care of a *chef de clinique* at Baden-Baden.

Annoyed when Brother Theodorus had obliged him to adopt this chore, Ernst had come to take pleasure in this introduction to the day. Immobilized, waiting for his charred stump to heel, he was tired of lying restless on the litter, carving his crutch, devising schemes for the recovery and transport of his silver. Just his luck, he thought. Why couldn't they be nuns instead of monks? Only the civets and his language lessons amused him.

As for Theo, the busy abbot had no tolerance for idleness. He was appreciative of all Ernst did, but held back the *tajj* when his patient grew lazy. The German cat keeper had liberated one of Theo's monks for other duties.

Ernst, however, had grown uneasy, as he detected in the island abbot a relentless spirit of dominance, an appetite for control reminiscent of his Prussian cousins.

Theodorus enriched his days with a thousand tiny tyrannies. No doubt he would regard the loss of any subject as a diminution of his empire. Ernst became certain that the white-bearded despot would resent his departure, and perhaps seek to impede his flight rather than assist it. But perhaps he could buy off the old rascal with a few silver coins. The man thought himself a Christian; thirty pieces of silver should do. Or would the sight of Maria Theresa's metal breasts increase Theo's appetite, make his juices run, until, like the popes, he would grasp for more and more?

At least, if things grew nasty, von Decken was confident the abbot would not be his superior when it came to violence.

Ernst watched the old civet tormenting a snail. His mind turned to the pilot who had cost him his foot, and perhaps his silver. He thought of the bullets pursuing him into the water as the Italian violated the aviator's code, firing on Ernst's aircraft after it was diving in flames. Von Decken recalled the ethic of duelling he had learned as a student in Heidelberg: one cut to your enemy's face, and you put up your sword. Perhaps one day he would teach this Italian how to fence.

This afternoon, Ernst decided, after his musk gathering was done, he would offer to assist with the fishing, having indicated to Theo that this was his highest skill. Once he had access to the canoes, how distant could his freedom be?

Ernst had put two green locusts in his shirt pocket. With luck, the grasshoppers would still be alive when needed. They would provide the bait to justify his boastings. In another pocket he had hidden a long string fashioned from cotten ripped from various rags and garments. Using this string he would lower a stone into the lake to determine the depth of his Potez treasure craft.

The monks did not swim and rarely washed. But von Decken himself, stronger after another week, made a practice of bathing daily in the shallow water among the reeds on the south side of the island, where the water was heavy with filmy deposits of alum and other minerals. There were no crocodiles here and the Potez lay sixty feet offshore.

He often lay naked on his back, bracing his hands on the soft bottom while he paddled his legs. This exercise and the styptic quality of the lake water seemed to advance the healing of his stump. Each day Ernst felt stronger and more restless. Even his belly was less impressive. Occasionally he shared crumbs of *enjara* with the knob-billed ducks.

Von Decken wondered how the ladies, especially Harriet, would like him with one foot. A few might even take to it. Most women, of course, would rather count his silver than his toes. As he considered this, he heard a lonely sound, a faint creaking whistle from the reeds to his left. A large duck sailed into view. Again the drake's mating call sighed across the water. Two feet long, with copper-green wings and tail feathers over a white stomach, and a speckled head crowned by a narrow dark crest, the magnificent bird suffered one deformity, the mark of his breed: a large fleshy knob bunched like a goiter between his eyes. No wonder he swam alone.

Ernst flicked some breadcrumbs into the reeds. A second smaller duck, with similar coloring but without a knob, floated into view, skimming the surface with her wide bill as she scooped up a scrap of bread. The drake paddled forward, puffing out his white chest feathers, raising and ruffling his wings until the sun caught the shine of his copper. Glittering like a Teutonic knight, the bird glided towards the approaching female.

What had drawn her? Had it been the call, or the bread? Ernst recalled his father's one French expression: *Chaque chameau trouve un autre chameau.* And the French should know, the old German always added.

Occasionally, when winds gusted up, a fine grey ash stirred and rose like a monster from the bottom of the lake. It filled the water with a cloud, a reminder of the Rift's volcanic past. Ernst knew the great valley in which these lakes sat was the earth's greatest exposed *Gräben,* a steep-sided depression between two faults, shaped like a grave and formed by violent movements of the plates of the earth's crust. Vast reaches of Abyssinia were covered by fertile volcanic ash, and much of it had washed into these lakes. To see beneath the water, he must wait for a day of perfect calm.

Whenever Ernst went fishing, Theo, disliking the water, watched him from the shore, sometimes squatting for hours with his silver crucifix in hand, only returning to the settlement when he saw Ernst poling home. At first the frowning priest had trusted Ernst only with a pole, forcing the German to fish like a heron, or another of the long-legged waders that gathered food in the shallow water amongst the reeds and lily pads. But soon the abbot took pleasure from Ernst's catches, waiting for his supper, sniffing the air as Brother Josef broiled the bream with wild onion grass and herbs.

This morning Theodorus watched Ernst perform the awkward task of entering his *tanqwa* without capsizing or filling the low-lying craft with water. The exercise was delicate enough for a graceful Abyssinian waterman, let alone for a heavy German with one foot. Often Ernst's crutch stuck in the sand under water when he planted it for stability before lowering himself into the narrow pointed vessel made from papyrus reeds. After several days Ernst had learned to leave the crutch where he set it, to offer him a secure disembarkation on his return.

The abbot followed him into the shallows, wetting his robe, and passed von Decken a long paddle once Ernst was in the reed canoe. Like a yellow-billed stork or a pink-backed pelican, he would now be able to fish the deep water and go where he pleased. Ernst was careful to return with his finest catch. He had learned to snap the back of each locust before setting the hook through it, so that the grasshopper would move just enough to attract the fish but not enough to alarm them.

For the first time he was able to paddle farther out, sixty or seventy yards from shore. Paddling back, lying on his side, towing a line, he studied the water with his back to the sun.

Breathless with concentration, excited as if opening his own grave, Ernst finally saw it: a great grey cross far beneath him, nearly fifty feet across. As the clouds moved overhead, the broad wings appeared to wave and flutter in the moving shadows like a giant skate or manta. His aircraft and his fortune. Ernst paddled backwards a few strokes in the calm water until he was directly over the Potez.

He drew the weighted cord from his pocket and lowered it slowly over the side until the line grew slack. He tied a knot and pulled in the line hand over hand. The cord back in the boat, he measured the length of wet line that ended at the knot: twenty-five feet, perhaps a bit less.

After dinner Ernst took the abbot aside.

"Asa, tru, dahna asa," Theo said, honoring the fish, placing one hand on Ernst's shoulder as he spoke. He asked Ernst to follow him as he went to say a prayer with a delinquent monk imprisoned in the punishment cell, a narrow cave-like chamber cut into the rocky hillside. An ornate Coptic cross was carved into a niche in the rear wall, still part of the living rock that had been cut away to reveal it. The cross, Theodorus had explained, had always been there, prepared by God, waiting in the stone for someone to discover it.

Nine or ten monks acknowledged the abbot as he passed them sitting by their fires.

Brother Markus, one of the younger monks, had been placed in the cell on Ernst's fifth day on the island. Once he was inside, four sturdy poles had been set into fitted recesses carved into the upper face of the entrance. Baskets of damp mud were packed around the bottoms of the poles. In the morning the mud was dry, and the poles were firmly set. Ernst saw Theo checking the work, pulling on each pole in turn.

The reason for Brother Markus's incarceration was not clear. Ernst thought it might be the reward for some transgression in daily conduct, perhaps disobedience, stealing food, or insufficient meditation. At other times, when Markus's brothers prayed with him on their knees beside the cell, he wondered if instead this was merely another sacrament, some routine atonement, taken by the monks in turn, akin to flagellation, the wilderness, or kneeling on sharp stones at the stages of the cross. Whatever the cause, Ernst detected the abbot's satisfaction in observing the caged brother.

Markus occasionally earned appreciation by providing bats for the civets. He trapped them in the corners of the cell as night ended, snaring them in the skirt of his robe and breaking one wing at the elbow to prevent their flight. Holding them by their pointed ears, Markus would proudly pass the bats through the bars to Ernst while the tiny folded creatures chirped shrilly. Had any civets ever dined so well? Ernst wondered. What musk could rival his?

Markus knelt when Ernst and the abbot approached. He extended his cupped hands between the bars as if awaiting a holy wafer. Theo passed him the heads of three fish between a piece of folded *enjara*. Ernst knew the monk was allowed a small bowl of water every other day, provided he did not implore, or drink too eagerly.

After delivering the food and sharing a swift prayer, the abbot walked to the stone bench near the hillside. Ernst hobbled after him and sat down.

Von Decken, not knowing the word in Amharic, leaned over and drew a picture of his aircraft in the dust. Then he raised two fingers. *"And,"* he said, "two," pointing at himself and also indicating a second man. He tried to make clear that the second man was dead, drowned in the plane. The abbot rubbed his tight white curls and nodded.

Ernst picked up his crutch, leaning forward and striking the ground as if he were shovelling. He pointed to the ground and steepled his hands in prayer. This dead Christian must be buried.

Theodorus understood. "With Christ," he said.

The next morning, all three canoes were made ready. Each reed canoe could carry only one or two men. Brother Petros was in charge of the expedition. In his canoe was a heavy rope. Bound to one end was a leather line prepared by Ernst. The line was tied in the form of a harness with two loops. Ernst removed his clothes and hobbled with his crutch into the shallows, careful to exaggerate his incapacity.

The abbot stood on the shore with his arms folded as the three craft paddled from the island. Ernst's binoculars hung on the abbot's chest.

Feigning ignorance, Ernst led the *tanqwas* in a search. The calm water reflected the movement of the scattered clouds.

"Na!" Petros called out after a time, excitement in his voice. *"Na!"*

Ernst and the third boatman, Gregoreyos, paddled to him. Below was the shadow of the aircraft. Petros held one side of Ernst's boat while the German slipped over the other into the water. Ernst was aware of Theo and other monks watching intently from the shore. Feeling fresh and strong and free in the water, he took a long breath and dived.

The lake was not as clear as it seemed. Sunlight sparkled off tiny bits of mineral sediment that hung in the water like fragments of a filament. Ernst breast-stroked deeper. Finally he reached the upper wing. He gripped it with both hands, feeling the fine layer of grit that had already gathered to begin the plane's burial. His hands led him along the edge until he came to the deep notch in the wing above the cockpit. His eyes smarting from the sediment, Ernst strained to see through the dark shadow beneath the wing.

He groped downwards and felt the back of the pilot's seat. Reaching into the darkness, his right hand found Ephraim's head, still protected by the flight helmet and goggles. First, he would try to recover the dead man's sidearm.

Upside down, his face almost touching the pilot's, Ernst reached for Ephraim's belt buckle. His hand slipped into the pilot's shirt. For an instant he had the sensation that Ephraim's body was strangely yielding, open, as if unformed. Suddenly something moved violently, lashing Ernst's arm as an animal thrashed to escape the confinement of the dead man's shirt.

An immense eel, thick and blunt-headed, emerged from inside Ephraim's belly. Bits of lung and a coil of intestines drifted from the creature's open mouth. Corkscrewing like a giant worm, the speckled snake-like fish slid upwards along Ernst's body, biting him in the shoulder as it rose. Underwater, it felt more like a blow than a penetrating wound. Ernst kicked and stroked upwards.

Pain tore his shoulder as Ernst broke the surface, striking a canoe with his head. He gasped and threw both arms over the side of the *tanqwa* as Petros steadied it. Ernst retched and vomited into the canoe. When the spasm had subsided, he bathed his face and examined the two small puncture wounds in his shoulder. Nothing serious, unless it drew the crocodiles.

He must dive again. So far he had accomplished nothing. He glanced towards shore and saw Theodorus watching through the field glasses. Ernst was certain the old priest valued the silver more than he did his guest.

The German dived and swam toward the bottom with slow strokes. He gripped the side of the cockpit and steadied himself. He removed Ephraim's pistol belt before rising to the surface. Taking breaths of fresh air, he set the belt around his waist and dived again with the rope and leather harness looped over his shoulder.

He forced Ephraim's arms through the two loops and tightened the harness about the pilot's shoulders. Then he inspected the door of the cargo hold. Bent inwards, it was jammed shut. Ernst braced his good leg against the side of the aircraft and struggled without success to wrench open the door. He would need some tool to force it.

Back in his *tanqwa,* Ernst watched as Petros hauled in the remains. Ephraim's helmeted body broke the surface, its arms extended like a crucifix. Amused, Ernst appreciated the horror with which the two boatmen received the corpse. The monks struggled to heave the body into Petros's canoe. For a moment the torn corpse hung over the edge of the boat, legs inside, the face still under water as the *tanqwa* dipped precariously to one side. Then they removed the harness and jammed the body facedown between Petros's legs.

Their *tanqwas* side by side, Ernst saw Petros raise his bare feet to avoid the small white fresh-water crabs that scuttled out from the dead man's trouser cuffs, helmet and shirt collar. The active long-legged creatures burrowed between the reeds in the bottom of the boat. The civets would love them, Ernst reckoned.

With a casualness intended to shock the monks, he reached into Petros's canoe and raised Ephraim's head while he removed the flight goggles. The pilot had no eyes. The crabs had eaten them from the inside. Naked save for the gun belt, von Decken rinsed the glasses and hung them about his own neck. They might be useful when he dived.

His next dive, Ernst promised himself, would set him free.

— 24 —

"It's ours, Daddy!" Clove said, standing by her father's table with Tariq just behind her. The Nubian held three silver film tins by a belted strap. "A little old, but you'll love it. It's Douglas Fairbanks, *The Thief of Baghdad.*"

Stealing a glance at Clove's breasts, a bar boy at the next table wiped an ash tray and cleared away the pigeon droppings for which the terrace of the hotel was renowned. A bird lover, the girl glanced up at the fat grey birds roosting in the ironwork trim that hung above the café. Far above, she spied a black-shouldered kite, its forked tail spread wide, its slender blunt wings slightly bent while it glided over the street and terrace.

"Wonderful, my treasure," said the dwarf, proud of his child. If there were a single reason to wish for more prosperity and a longer life, she stood before him now. Despite himself, with Dr. Hänger's imminent diagnosis already tightening his heart, he studied his daughter's face and form for symptoms of his own affliction.

"Next we're going to buy *Reaching for the Moon,*" Clove said, hoping her father would invite her to join him for an ice. He smiled at her but did not reply.

"Why do they always give you the best table?" she asked, looking up to see the kite suspended for an instant at the bottom of its dive, transforming from plunge to ascent. Soft pale feathers from the baby pigeon fluttered in its talons as the raptor rose from the fretwork of a terrace lamp, its pale yellow bill shining, its large red eyes glaring.

"At Shepheard's they understand these matters," said the dwarf, touching his daughter's shoulder, recovering her attention, though he, too, admired the way these desert birds found their place in the frantic city. Lacking the deathly speed of falcons, or the strength and size of eagles, these discriminating predators lived by their wits, scavenging and dining with taste, selective in their residence. The dwarf was pleased that he and his daughter could share this small diversion without the need to speak of it. What understanding could they not share as she grew older?

"I am waiting for Dr. Hänger, child."

"Will he be coming home with us?" she asked, seeking to share his concern.

"No." Olivio shook his head, wishing he did not have to see the man at all. He had tried to keep from Clove the cause of the doctor's visit to Cairo but the girl was too intelligent, and too sensitive to him, not to be aware. She was the only person with whom he had been almost always honest, even sometimes candid.

"Today he is meeting me here to provide his diagnosis," the dwarf added, hoping she did not sense his anxiety.

"Of course, Daddy," she said with lightness in her voice. "I hope you'll be home for tea. Don't forget we're having Denby's birthday party." Clove kissed her father's cheek and with evident confidence walked across the terrace to the steps. Tariq nodded to his master and followed her closely.

The dwarf watched the two depart, certain that only his eye, and perhaps Dr. Hänger's, could discern the very slight distortion in her gait.

The German physician, Olivio had learned, was always punctual, but never early. The dwarf, however, was concerned lest he himself make an awkward entrance on this fashionable stage. Dreading being jostled or demeaned by some clumsy mountainous stranger, he always arrived first to prepare and dominate his setting.

This morning, guided past the giant potted palms to table number two by the bowing *chef du terrasse* himself, Olivio Fonseca Alavedo was early. Table one, set in the corner of the back row of the terrace café, was always vacant in case Prince Farûq should appear for a sweet.

The *chef du terasse,* a man whose favor defined status among the most elegant Cairenes, kept a long and precise ledger in his mind. Anticipating his small client, not wishing to embarrass him with the arrangements, he had prepared the dwarf's rattan chair by adding two fitted brocade cushions and had himself set a discreet stool at its foot. Vigilant, jealous of their sectors, table captains in long white robes, dark sashes and matching tarbushes stood watching with folded arms against the wall of the hotel.

It was not yet eleven, too early in the morning for the elegant mistresses and costly courtesans who later would bring energy to the café. A few European men were taking coffee and reading newspapers and starting an early cigar. Several tables of travellers waited for their guides to collect them and escort them to Giza or Saqqâra or the bazaars. Like a canary in its cage, the grand piano was still covered in a nighttime canvas shroud. Shoeshine boys and donkey carts waited along the street below. Altogether, it was the only café that Olivio conceded was a rival to his own.

While he waited, Olivio turned his eye to *The Egyptian Gazette.* He had grown accustomed to his morning reading with Lord Penfold, and he thought of their friends adrift in the wilds of Abyssinia. Daily the little man became more concerned about his stewardship. His own future had become theirs. Now both men, and perhaps Gwenn, too, were relying on him to turn their paltry pounds into fortunes. It was not yet impossible, he reflected, but steadily it grew more difficult. The path was strewn with villainy, greed and intrigue. He had never expected that he himself might be lacking in such resources.

Penfold Partners Estates now held properties that straddled the route of the proposed new irrigation canal at Wadi al-Sum. More than that, under different names, they held hectares scattered here and there at hopeful sites along the flanks of the Nile valley. Whenever buyers appeared for one of these properties, Olivio's agents traced them to determine whether the interest arose from a party with access to the ministry's plans for irrigation. If so, the dwarf pursued the scent like a ferret in a maze of tunnels, deeper and deeper, undeterred by darkness and complexity as he hounded down each red-eyed mole. In this and other ways he followed his enemy's schemes and redirected and refined his own. Soon he would identify this powerful secret rival for the properties and water that he coveted.

ITALIAN AIR FORCE MACHINE GUNS EMPEROR'S ROYAL GUARD. GRAZIANI ADVANCES ON SOUTHERN FRONT, he read without concern, searching only for matters that affected his own interests. THOUSANDS FLEE ADDIS. HARAR UNDER SIEGE. NATIONS JOIN PROTEST. What nonsense this would all be if his friends were not there. If the League of Nations didn't care, why should he?

FRENCH CONFER WITH HERR HITLER. HMS Agamemnon JOINS MEDITERRANEAN FLEET. He skipped the pages of sporting news that always mesmerized his lordship: regimental polo and county cricket. What schoolboys the English were. He turned the page. More nonsense. 200,000 STARVING IN ILLINOIS. RELIEF DEPOTS CLOSED. DEMONSTRATORS PETITION STATE LEGISLATURE. His interest sharpened when he turned to the Exchanges and the Cotton Bourse. COTTON FUTURES SOAR. CROPS SHORT IN RUSSIA. DROUGHT IN INDIA. Perhaps there was still hope for a decent man. He must pray for flood and drought in these distant lands.

"Guten Morgen, Herr Alavedo." August Hänger stood before his table and bowed his head. His body remained erect while he saluted his patient. The physician always insisted on a few words of German, just to confirm the terrain was his.

"And to you, Doctor." The dwarf extended his hand. "Your color has improved in Cairo," said Olivio, pleased to be the first to comment on the other's condition.

The German's dark clothes were still tight and immaculate, almost brittle with the sharpness of their creases, but he himself seemed looser, more vigorous. Egypt had been kind to his arthritis. No doubt he would be hungry after such a night. Olivio turned his head and caught the captain's eye. The Egyptian whispered an order to a table boy.

"I to the point at once will come." Hänger rested a black leather folder on the zinc tabletop. He smiled once with the brevity and mechanical perfection of a camera's diaphragm. Olivio's research had disclosed that among Hänger's colleagues this habit or technique had earned him the *nom de guerre* of "Dr. Leica."

The physician opened the folder and exposed one sheet of paper. Six little figures filled the pages, each with its arms and legs extended like a cutout doll. Small neat notations in black ink surrounded each figure like a cage: measurements in centimeters, annotations in German, citations to texts on dwarfism, here and there a double underline for emphasis. Studying the diagrams upside down, Olivio was surprised to notice one correction to the notes. Hänger resumed.

"Your feet, your spine, your joints, everywhere there is already damage." The German stabbed each figure with the point of his table knife as he detailed the dwarf's deformities. "Everywhere there is damage."

For once Olivio felt himself not in control. A chill passed through him. Soon this man would store him on a shelf, floating in a bottle of formaldehyde, his one eye forever open.

"The first thing to understand is that we all are dying. All of us." Hänger smiled fraternally and tapped the sheet with the knife, then closed the folder.

"Once full growth is achieved, life is decay." The doctor, his almost black eyes magnified through his rectangular glasses, looked at Olivio as he might an amoeba on a slide under a lens: with interest, even intensity, but not with sympathy.

"We are all dying, one day at a time." Still holding Olivio's gaze, he gestured towards the terrace and street with the back of one hand, hesitating when his fingertips pointed towards the crowds passing below. "Some, to be sure, faster and more painfully than others."

Olivio did not respond. Before them the tables of the grand café began to fill with fashionable guests.

"You, in your way, are exceptional. Most little people of your sort, and *medizinische Wissenschaft* does not know of many, by thirty or forty years they perish, their organs and architecture and bodily functioning hopelessly misshapen and worn by the distortions of their bodies. Hopeless. Their spines, their joints, their livers and lungs and hearts all insupportably warped and abused. That is why I believe we can learn so much from studying the little people."

Olivio sought to suppress the sense of offense, of insult that was rising in his gorge. Where did Germany find such doctors? Were there more like him?

Hänger looked up at the arriving *suffragi.* He watched the servant carefully and hastened to complete his point while he tucked a linen napkin into his high stiff white collar. Like the dwarf, the doctor was habituated to controlling the details of life around him.

"Each one, forgive this, *Mein Herr,* each one, even you, is a precious laboratory."

The waiter set before the doctor a glass of warm boiled water and the flesh of a Nile perch, cleaned from the bone and rearranged on the plate in the shape of a smaller fish. The water was pink from the three spoonfuls of vinegar that had been stirred into it, the day's first weapon in his battle with arthritis. The German leaned forward. His high hooked nose hung over the table like a chimney over a fireplace as he widened his nostrils and smelled the fish. Two small plates of braised turnips and shredded red cabbage were set beside it.

Olivio saw that his physician was not pleased. Something was missing. He studied the table. Of course.

"Ver is my lemon?" Hänger spoke in a low exasperated voice without looking at the waiter.

The dwarf raised one hand. A captain hurried over. Olivio spoke two words.

The coffee boy, a handsome, very black Nubian youth in a long white robe and white turban, bowed and presented a plate of quartered lemons, each segment wrapped in knotted gauze to inhibit splashing and contain the seeds.

The doctor nodded. "Ah." The tension left him and he resumed speaking while he squeezed the lemons into his drink.

"You are what a superstitious person, a religious person, so to say, would call a miracle. You appear to have lived, and still live, with the intensity of most little people, as if you know you have no time. This is why those like you are so reckless, so driven, so excessive sexually, if I may zo say. We know this. It is fatalism, no?" The doctor hesitated and examined the round end of the handsome gherkin that was lanced on his fork. "Ah!"

The dwarf gave no reply. He felt smaller, reduced.

"But you, no fatalism. You care about tomorrow." Dr. Hänger wiped cream from his wide narrow lips before taking the pickle.

"In many ways your body, or your will, has resisted the erosion of which I speak. You have attained one half a century. I congratulate you."

Olivio Alavedo understood flattery. The doctor was thinking of his fee, in all its elements. Already he had enhanced the physician's life, expanding it the way a feast might swell the belly of a starving man, using his organs as they had not been tested before, the stresses of satiety replacing those of starvation. Olivio expected not thanks but extended service. Hänger's ivory statue was not yet complete. One dwarf was still missing.

Olivio smelled the odor of a silent belch. He recalled what Lord Penfold said of educated Germans: "They're the opposite of oysters, you know, smooth on the outside, coarse on the inside."

The man chewed the pickle before speaking again. "Your body is crying for an end. Think of it as a damaged creature trapped inside you who wishes to escape." He paused and stared across the table. The dwarf did not blink.

"Ahead is pain, debility, faster *und* faster, *immer schneller.* Your decline will be interesting. You must learn to step back and study it with fascination."

"What can I do?" Olivio said in a cool distant voice. He was determined to control his demeanor. "What can you do?"

"We have the three choices. First, you can do nothing, or almost nothing. Continue on as best you can, always a bit worse, for two, three years."

Olivio nodded and held up two small fingers.

"Two, a program of surgery, a campaign, one battle after another. You would take the war to the enemy. *Angriefen!* Painful, yes, expensive, very, but interesting and at some stages helpful. Zürich would be the battleground. There we have everything: scalpels and saws from Sölingen, filaments and gut from Basel, student nurses from Heidelberg, everything what you want." The German stared at his four plates, empty save for several slices of turnip that he now gathered together. Before carving and eating them, he tapped on the table with the handle of his knife, directing his host's attention downward.

"Everything requires a foundation, even a dwarf. We take apart these arches and rebuild the feet, one by one in case it does not go so well. One or two of the worst toes will go. No thing lasts forever. We work up, up. Knees, hips, so forth *und* so forth, always creating better balance and proportion." The physician made short precise motions with his knife as he spoke.

"In time August Hänger gives to you some of what God did not. I cannot make you bigger, but I can make you better. Straighten the shoulders, clean and trim the scapulas. The back, even the spine."

The doctor's voice rose. Even at the extremes of lust and passion, it had been reported, when another man's heart would either stop or burst, August Hänger made no exclamation, revealed himself with no sound, except an occasional "Ah!" Now he leaned forward and removed his spectacles.

"We open the spine!" The black eyes, smaller now, almost smiled. He was promising Olivio a gift. "Then, on your tolerance for pain it depends. The extent of the surgeries will be determined by yourself."

Feeling doom seize him by the throat, Olivio held up three fingers. But he spoke with no concern in his voice. "Third?"

"Aggressive therapy. Less painful, less effective, but it would delay the enemy, perhaps for a time even roll him back. I speak not only of deep massage, very deep, but of something more. You would be stretched and kneaded and splayed out, bent and flexed with the tension of a cross-bow. Where now you are stiff and so tight, you would become loose-jointed as a *junger Hund.* But the work would be constant and hard, like a great boxer, yes? Max Schmeling training for a championship fight that might never come." He folded his napkin and stared down at the dwarf.

"And if you ever stopped my program, your body would close tight like a bear trap." Hänger clapped his hands together.

"Could I do this here in Cairo?"

"With my help, perhaps yes. But we would need to bring in a specialist, someone strong who understands what the body must be forced to do. Someone who will extend your body beyond itself. An expert, one who would not listen to your cries. The best is in Zürich."

"Who is he?"

"At the clinic we call her *Knöchel,* 'Knuckles.' In four days here she can be."

The four presented a curious sight, even by the standards of the cluttered back alleys of Khan al-Khalili. Old men looked up from their coffee and sweepers leaned on their brooms as the dwarf's party passed through the narrow passages of the vast labyrinthine market. Only the most bold and avaricious stall keepers failed to temper their importuning cries when Tariq shouldered past them

"Make way, make way," the Nubian urged in a loud deep voice as he led his master past the spice shops to the leather bazaar.

Adam Penfold and Knuckles Koch followed behind them. His walking stick in his right hand, Penfold had offered his left arm to the Swiss nurse when she entered the market at his side. She had accepted it, not demurely but firmly, and now employed it to force the Englishman along at her own pace. From time to time, distracted by some display or solicitation, Penfold sought to wander down an alley of ancient weapons or to stand sniffing over the copper scales of a tobacco vendor. But each time Knuckles led him smartly forward by the arm she gripped.

In the two days since the nurse's arrival in Cairo, Olivio had come to anticipate her first treatment with an unusual mixture of dread and enthusiastic curiosity, sentiments as contrasting as the two parts of her body.

"Before on you I begin," she had said, "we must prepare everything and make you special shoes."

As he and Tariq searched for the appropriate stall, Olivio recalled her alarming hands: square and hard as shovels. The coarse thick fingers were all the same length. The blunt thumbs appeared to have no joints. He feared she would crack him apart the way a hungry diner snaps off the claws of a lobster.

"Her hands," Dr. Hänger had enthused, "are from Zilesia. Her people are miners, you zee." The dwarf speculated what these instruments might do to him.

"Here, master," said Tariq, pausing before a stall and staring down at two old men who toiled at a cobbler's workbench. "These brothers are the finest leather-smiths in Cairo. With a needle and gut they can stitch up a skin and make the beast walk once more." To either side, gathered close together like the drawn curtains in a theater, hung uncut skins of cured leather: calves and kids, snakes and crocodiles.

"May I serve you, *effendi?*" inquired one brother, setting down his awl and standing stiffly. The other craftsman rose and began to prepare coffee for the new clients.

Olivio nodded, then turned to watch the approach of his friend and Knuckles.

The woman's legs were so confusing. Not just long and slender, but with fine ankles, shapely but not overly muscled calves, and long promising thighs with that faint hollow along the bone that suggested an alarming fitness. Legs to break a man's heart, or his back. Even the feet, so unlike his own, were gracefully arched, long toed, perfectly proportioned.

But from the hips north, Knuckles Koch was a fearsome creature. The hips joined front and back like two halves of an apple. From there her body rose like a barrel: belly, breasts, and shoulders inseparable, all thick, firm and tightly meshed. Her short neck, stout and surprisingly soft, like that of an older and heavier woman, supported an exceptionally round head carpeted in short straight dark hair. The pale flesh that is an adornment to so many ladies provided on her an alarming pallor, as if she were a creature that never saw light.

"How splendid," said Penfold, arriving with her at the leather stall. "Wonder if these chaps have any Russia?" Releasing his arm, Knuckles unbuckled her shoulder bag and removed a notebook.

"Russia, my lord?" protested the dwarf, keen to procure what was needed and escape this frightful bazaar. "We are in Egypt." He watched Knuckles turn to two pages of detailed drawings of curious sandals and footwear with long ankle straps. For once, he had little patience for his lordship's distractions. On another page he glimpsed with horror the diagram of a back brace.

"Russia's not a place, you see," explained Penfold patiently. "It's a type of leather, really, tanned with birch-bark oil on the fleshy side. Makes the best shoes, you know." The Englishman looked up, squinting with his mouth open, and pinched the shiny tail of a long crocodile skin. "Lasts forever." He gazed down at his own shoes. "Old Box never uses anything else."

The dwarf stared up at his friend with astonishment. Tariq wiped the top of a stool with the sleeve of his robe before Olivio sat down. One of the Egyptians knelt, removed the little man's slippers and spread a piece of paper before him. Penfold was careful not to stare at his friend's naked feet. Knuckles tore the two sheets from her notebook and handed them to the cobbler.

Olivio stood on the paper and folded his arms. The cobbler outlined his misshapen feet with a stub of charcoal before using a tape to measure around the ball of each foot and around each arch and ankle. Then the man gently replaced Olivio's slippers.

"My master requires these sandals at once," said Tariq, removing a money bag from inside his *gallabiyyah.*

"In two days," said the man.

Tariq bent forward and rested one hand on the older man's shoulder near his neck. "I will return for them tonight," he said.

The cobbler nodded. "Tonight," the man said before bowing to Olivio Alavedo. "Which leather do you require, *effendi?*"

"Russia, of course." The dwarf turned to leave.

Ten days later, suspended upside-down in his Koch sling, his feet secure in their tiny ankle sandals, Olivio swung back and forth in the breeze like a sleeping bat.

As his body stretched and moved, he wiggled his toes and reflected on the latest sketches he had procured from a French engineer who had been competing for the irrigation scheme. After intervention by the palace, the Italian bids for the sluice gates had been accepted, despite the excessively light design of the hinges and flow screws that opened and closed the gates. Seeking new value for their lost work, the French engineers had not scrupled to sell their plans and maps. For the dwarf it was not bad news: the first gates were assigned to the canal planned for Wadi al-Sum.

A flush of blood filled Olivio's head. His circulation had improved. Sometimes these sessions left him feeling hungry and aroused, eager as a boy.

"The first two centimeters, less than one inch," Dr. Hänger had said reassuringly the first day, holding up two fingers, "that is the easy piece. A little here, a little there, it is more straightening than stretching, fighting half a century of gravity, zimply your natural height regaining, like making a schoolboy stand up straight, your height of ten, of fifteen years before. We use this period to accustom you to our methods. Some of it you will even enjoy, others less so. For a time you will see the zoft zide of *Knöchel,* then it will be more interesting. She must become less indulgent, shall we say, more Swiss, perhaps even more German. You understand me?"

Like a fat man on a scale, Olivio's mornings now began with measurements. Instead of relaxing during the night-time, his body was contracting at night, recovering its regular, more compact form. Whether with callipers, tape or rod, the numbers were taken in centimeters. But the dwarf was accustomed to thinking of himself in inches, almost forty-four of them, and the doctor's sole dispensation had been to discuss him in those terms.

The elements of his body had been treated one by one, then together, then separately. For days, each arm and leg, toe and finger, was massaged, soaked in scalding seltzer and eucalyptus baths, swaddled in steaming camphor towels, and pulled and stretched like a ball of dough being rolled into a long loaf, stretched until he felt his joints had separated. During this period, Knuckles set up her station at the downstream end of the hold beneath the Cataract Café, near the foot of the sphinx. The work table, the scarecrow frame, the elastic harness, were secured, respectively, to floor, wall and ceiling. The dwarf wondered what they would do with his spine.

At first it had all seemed to work.

Knowing his time was nearly up, dreading the next treatment, Olivio began to swing more slowly. It was time for Knuckles's cherry, the test and the reward for each session in the ankle sling. His feet each day slightly closer to the ceiling, he was to stretch down and pick one cherry from the floor, using only his teeth.

He watched her legs as Knuckles strode to him, dangling a cherry by its stem. She seized the swinging dwarf by the belt of his white training shorts and held him till he steadied. She took his wrists and thrust his thumbs into the belt to keep his arms from hanging down. She lowered him until his face was just above the wooden floor, then placed the cherry on the plank under his head and set him swinging.

Olivio arched his neck and back so that his mouth would be close to the floor. The first day, less limber, the crown of his bald head had grazed the plank. A long splinter had pierced his scalp like a knitting needle through a sweater, eliciting a scolding from the nurse. She had forced his face between her lumpy breasts, pinning his round head beneath her chin while she worked the splinter free with both hands.

His face red as the cherry, he spread his lips as he swung down. The sphinx flashed past his head. Olivio grazed the cherry with his thick pointed tongue. He missed again, distracted by his fear of her impatience. It would be easier if he had two eyes. For an instant the dwarf recalled the burning red eyes of the kite when it dived for the pigeon on the terrace at Shepheard's. He flexed his knees and swung once more, arching his back, graceful as a swan. He soared with the small fruit between his lips.

"Gut!" Knuckles clasped the little man to her with one arm as she released his sandal straps with the other hand. She gave him a crushing squeeze of approval. The nurse had learned what her rich patient enjoyed.

Olivio's legs were pressed against the hell of her bosom, but his upper body and face were in heaven, between her legs, his second brief reward. He stroked one of her ankles with each hand and covered the left calf with nibbling wet kisses. Knuckles wore no stockings or undergarments when she worked.

His nostrils twitched and widened. His nose, always acute, warned him of her rising scent. He ran his hands up inside her white skirt as far as he dared, enjoying the mystery of the exploration and the baby-smooth skin of the inner thighs, knowing she was now juicy as a bruised peach, but terrified lest he arouse her fully and provoke the upper body to participate in the pleasures of the lower. For an instant he was tempted to slip his left hand higher and invade her with his magic fingers, but he dreaded the explosive consequences. What was a gentleman to do? Even her skin seemed to cover two different creatures, coarsening as it rose, red and mottled where it emerged from her sleeves and collar. He wondered where precisely it was that her two parts became one.

Pretending to ignore his attentions but flushing at the throat and cheeks, Knuckles righted the dwarf and carried him to the table under one arm like a sack of meal. As they passed a porthole Olivio spat the cherry pit into the Nile.

— 25 —

"The Italians were using poison gas back there, weren't they?" Bernadette repeated, still outraged.

"I told you I'm not certain, miss, but it looked that way." Anton raised his head from the hinged hood that was braced against an acacia branch above the exhausted engine of the Olds. Diwani's bare legs stuck out from beneath the vehicle.

"Of course it was gas," she persisted angrily. "What else could've burned and blinded all those poor people we passed in those two valleys? I've read what gas was like in the World War. And what about that crashed airplane Harry filmed with those strange nozzles under the wings?"

"Whatever the Italians were using, Miss Mills, and I hope it wasn't gas, the important thing is that we keep this safari moving," Anton said calmly. He had learned never to show anxiety or alarm to a client. "If it was gas, we're just fortunate it dissipates so quickly."

"How can they be such cowards?" Harriet said, joining in at last. "Using poison gas from airplanes against barefoot spearmen?"

Not about to defend the Italians, Anton reached into the cab and wiped his face and hands on a rag.

"The others are all waiting for you," he said to Bernadette. "Please. Catch up with them. Kimathi's in charge and most of the chaps are armed. We can only take three in this truck. If we can't start it, we'll catch up to you in the next camp as soon as we can."

"See you later, Berny," said Harriet carelessly as her sister set off on foot after the others.

After another two hours' work, the engine turned over and idled noisily.

Like every vehicle from Cairo to Cape Town, the lorry was old and overused and overloaded. Her oil was gritty as sandpaper. She was rugged enough, but the rear axle was badly mauled, the hydraulic brakes were thirsty for fluid, and the eighty-four horsepower were all working at different tempos. Six cans of petrol were lashed to the outsides of the wooden planks that formed the box body of the truck. Anton had no idea what they would do for fuel when these were gone.

"Best get started while she still sounds friendly," Anton said as Harriet climbed in beside him and Diwani made a place for himself in the back. For a while they drove in silence while Anton concentrated on the bumpy track that headed southwest, noting the fresh blazes and rock markers that Kimathi had left along the way. He reckoned they were lucky to be escaping from the war this easily. Getting through the Abyssinian camp hadn't been a clean job. They'd lost three men, too much equipment and half a dozen mules and horses to the Italian aircraft. Anton knew he'd nicked the fighter but was sorry he hadn't done a better job of it.

"I hope you know how to use those long legs, miss," he said as he felt the Olds tremble and resist when he shifted into second.

"What do you think they're for?" Harriet turned one foot on its fine ankle.

"You're going to need them," he continued. "It's another seven hundred miles to the Kenya border, and this old girl's not going to make it."

Diwani banged twice on the wall of the cab behind Anton's head. Harriet, seated close beside him, fussing with the camera on her lap, put one hand on Anton's bare leg as she turned to look back. She must know he was still sulking about the Swede. For an instant her eyes caught his. They were beginning to know each other. Her nails scratched him lightly with a familiar suggestion. Every woman had her ways.

"I think some vehicle's coming up behind us. There's a lot of dust." She left her warm hand on the edge of Anton's shorts, moving it gently, idly, as if unaware of what she was doing. "Could be another truck."

Alarmed that it might be Italian, Anton concentrated on the track ahead. His .375 lay in its scabbard behind his heels. He had slipped five cartridges into the pouches on his shirt. Whoever was behind them, it probably wasn't the Italian army, at least not yet, though the Swede had said some reconnaissance columns had turned up long before they'd been expected. On the floor of the narrow valley before him, he saw a wide stream crossing the track. The banks and riverbed appeared soft and spongy between the rocks. Goats and camels were drinking and defecating here and there. Better gain some speed, he told himself.

"Best put the camera in its case," he said without looking at Harriet, knowing she resented any suggestion of incompetence.

"I was." Harriet gripped the dented dashboard as the Olds gathered speed downhill. He slipped into neutral to save the gears and fuel.

The Oldsmobile hurtled down. Anton jinxed left and right, trying to keep at least one front wheel on firm ground as he wrenched the steering wheel to avoid rocks and gullies and bushes while they plunged down to the river. Ahead he saw Africans scattered along the riverbank. As they came to the water, finding no clear track as wide as the truck, he chose a patch of stone rather than mud.

He went into second just before the Olds met the wet rock with her left front wheel. Out of control, she skidded forward, spinning, leading with her right side. Small stones popped from her wheels as the truck skimmed into the river. Water splashed up from the sides like breaking waves. Anton heard a woman scream as she ran to a child. For an instant he thought the truck would roll. Too late, he pressed the gas pedal and recovered some control, trying to steer out of the riverbed before they lost headway. The side of the truck banged against high rocks set into the far bank. Diwani was hurled from the bed of the vehicle. Anton lifted his foot, then gave it more gas. The rear wheels spun and dug in.

Anton turned off the engine. For a moment the Olds continued to shake and cough like an old man in the morning. The driver's doorway was tight against the rocks. He turned and looked at Harriet.

"Sorry. You all right?" he said. Her eyes were bright. Dear Lord, he realized, she was having fun.

"You drive like my sister." Harriet jumped down into a few inches of water. "Is your friend okay?"

Anton followed her, rifle in hand. They helped Diwani to his feet. A crowd of Abyssinians was gathering and calling and chattering. Young herd boys were collecting their animals, slapping them with long staffs and spears and clucking with their tongues. Women abandoned laundry on the stones and walked towards them with long strides. Men appeared on both banks. Some carried rifles or spears. Anton lay his rifle on the seat of the truck. He waved and smiled to the Abyssinians. He climbed onto the back of the truck and opened a sack of yams.

"They're all so beautiful," Harriet said, reaching for the Bell & Howell, amazed by the easy elegance of these Abyssinian men. All were lean and very dark, with hollow cheeks, strong aquiline noses and hair tight to their skulls. Some held the long hems of their robes over one arm as they walked. The women wore their hair in neat tight rows. Several had silver bracelets and worn Maria Theresa dollars hanging from their necks on black cords.

"Here it comes!" Harriet said.

Anton looked back, one hand on his rifle. A heavy lorry was descending slowly towards them. At the last moment it chose a different route and accelerated before it came to the water. The Bedford crossed the river without difficulty. As it passed, Anton noticed a dusty red crescent painted on the driver's door. An enormous red cross was centered on the torn grey canvas covering the metal ribs which arched over the bed of the heavy truck. Anton's stomach tightened.

The Bedford stopped on the bank above them. Steam rose from the hood.

An elderly European in a blood-stained medical smock stepped down from the cab. Two soldiers emerged from the other door, Abyssinians outfitted in the khaki of the European-trained units. One wore a pistol on a Sam Browne belt.

"Tenáy!" Anton saluted the soldiers with authority.

They stiffened and returned the gesture. *"Abati!"*

The white man stared at Anton and Harriet.

"Can I help?" he called out in a gentle Scottish accent, his voice weary and tense.

"If you're carrying spares for an Olds." Anton climbed the bank and held out his hand. He saw horror and exhaustion in the man's eyes. Both the Scotsman's hands were crusted with blood and dust. One of his shoulders was bandaged.

"Anton Rider. I'm on safari with some American clients. Seem to have got caught up in this wretched war." Harriet joined them and shook hands. "This is Harriet Mills, and Diwani."

"Malcolm Fergus. Chief surgeon. How do you do? Excuse my hand. The planes interrupted my work. This is what's left of our Egyptian Red Cross team. Eyeties bombed us to bits. These two soldiers insisted on joining me along the way. Not bad chaps."

"Egyptian Red Cross?" Anton stopped breathing. "Are you the only one left?"

"Almost. Got a pair inside there." Fergus gestured at the truck. "I just patched 'em up in a hurry on the road, a half-dead orderly and one wounded nurse, or I should say surgeon, and a fine one she would've been . . ."

The doctor's speech slowed, almost stopping, as the recognition of Anton's name finally penetrated his exhaustion. "They're tied down in the back . . ."

Anton dashed to the rear of the truck. He raised the canvas flap and climbed in between the two strapped stretchers.

"Doctor!" he shouted.

Most of Gwenn's face was covered with a broad bandage. She was unconscious. The cloth was dark with blood where it crossed her left eye and temple. Her throat and left shoulder were roughly bandaged. Cuts covered her arms and lower legs.

Anton knelt beside her. He brushed back her tawny matted hair and touched her forehead with one hand. Her skin was cool but damp. He thought her beautiful, but so thin and pale. He noticed the deep shadow under her right eye and the new lines near her mouth. He knew she was alive, but he put one ear to her chest to hear her heart. Keeping his head lightly on her breast, he took her right hand in his. Tears lined his filthy face.

At length Anton raised his head and wiped his eyes, thinking how much Gwenn's courage always cost her. He kissed her cheek and tasted the salt of her sweat. Still kneeling, he looked back over the gate of the truck. Three faces looked up at him through the parted canvas without speaking, Dr. Fergus and Diwani and Harriet.

"How will she do, Doctor?" His voice surprised him as he collected himself, realizing for how many people he was now responsible, and how hard the rest of the safari would be.

"She should live, but there are things I must do as soon as we make camp. Is she . . ."

"She is my wife."

Harriet stared at him and stepped aside. Her lips tightened. After a moment she turned back and spoke. "Can I help, Doctor?"

" 'Fraid not, not just now," Fergus replied. "Have you any medical supplies?" he said to Anton.

"Nothing on the lorry, but we've a muleload up ahead with my safari." Anton jumped down, his mind clearing as he took charge.

"Tell your soldiers to have these people push us onto the bank. Then we'll carry on and catch up with our safari. By now they should be all set up in camp, somewhere near Lake Zwai." He glanced back at the truck. "Come on. Off we go."

Anton sat on the cracked running board of the Bedford cleaning his old Colt in the near darkness. Two camp fires and the glow from the big tent diminished the brightness of the stars. He drew an oily rag through each of the six chambers. He smelled the fires and the sizzling wild onions without his usual anticipation. He was worried that Gwenn had not woken up. He spun the cylinder, comforted by the smooth clicking of the mechanism. He thought of his long-dead friend whose .45 this had been. "Do you need a handgun in Carolina?" the American's story had begun. "Son, you may not need it the first year, and you may not need it the second," the old-timer replied. "But when you need it, you'll need it mighty bad."

Anton tried not to stare at the tent. He must review their situation and make plans. Including his clients and staff, he had twenty people to look after besides Gwenn. They had over six hundred rough miles to go just to get to the border, without adequate transport, weapons, food or supplies.

Even if there were no further problems with the Italians, it would be hard enough. He wiped each bullet and reloaded the revolver.

Soon Laboso and Diwani should be back from their recce. With luck they'd have spotted some game, or, if there was a God, come across a village with spare petrol or transport. They would have to abandon the Red Cross truck. The Bedford was heavier and thirstier than the Oldsmobile, and even more wounded. If the Olds died, or the petrol ran out, they'd need more horses, mules or camels. Here in the interior their paper currency was useless. Somehow they'd have to manage.

The worst problem was Gwenn, and part of it was his fault. "If I'd done better," he raged at himself, "none of this would've happened."

Now she was in the tent, on her back on the folding dinner table, naked, her wounds open in the amber light of three gas lamps. Dr. Fergus had warned him how things might go, and thought it best for him not to help. She had a fractured collarbone, bomb fragments in her shoulder and damage to her face. The poor orderly had died before they could move him from the truck, his chest cut up with shrapnel, drowned in his own blood, his lungs pulpy and gory as an uncooked blood pudding. They'd buried him under a few stones by the side of the track. The two Abyssinian soldiers had argued over his boots.

Fergus must be almost finished, Anton reckoned. The twins had been assisting him for over two hours. Twice Harriet had appeared at the entrance to the tent, declining his assistance. Businesslike, she asked for boiled water and clean bandages. The old bandages, washed, were drying on sticks by a fire.

Harriet had avoided Anton's eyes as she wiped her forehead and spoke in a low calm voice. He wondered what she thought of it all, and how much she understood. With an uncomfortable instant of recognition, he realized that she reminded him a bit of Gwenn when they'd first met: lovely and competent and spirited, optimistic in difficulty, and very nearly complete on her own. All Harriet lacked was the testing experience of hardship and suffering. Some women emerged worn and bitter; others, like Gwenn, still lovely and wise and appreciative.

Anton saw Bernadette and Harriet step from the tent. Their sleeves and shirtfronts were stained with the blood of his wife. Harriet glanced towards the camp fire, then followed her sister for a wash and change. Anton thought she had been crying.

He walked to the tent, dreading what he would learn.

Fergus met him. The doctor collapsed onto a log and rubbed his face. One of the boys poured water over his hands. Anton restrained himself while the doctor washed.

"How is she, Doctor?" He handed Fergus a whisky.

"Weak. She needs rest and care. Can't be moved. Collarbone has to set. May still be bits of shrapnel in her shoulder. She was bleeding too much for any more digging, and the chloroform was finished. Surprised the girl had that much blood in her." Fergus dried his hands and face.

"I did the best I could with the stitches, but she may never look quite the same." Fergus's red eyes looked up at Anton over the towel. "I've been doing too much doctoring for an old man. Couldn't've managed this last one without those twins of yours. Good hands."

"May I see her?" Anton thought he saw Dr. Fergus trying to conceal the trembling of his hand as he drank.

"Be quiet when you go in," the doctor said. "Leave one lamp on a bit, so she won't be frightened when she wakes."

The camp grew silent while Anton sat on a chest by the cot. The plate Lapsam had brought him rested untouched on the small camp table beside him. The lamp burned out and he sat on in the darkness, holding his wife's hand. When the night chilled he lit another lamp and with careful hands covered Gwenn with a second blanket.

Half asleep, bending forward as he dozed and twitched, he was not certain if the voice was hers.

"I knew it was you," Gwenn whispered distantly.

He kissed her hand. "Would you like some water?" he said quietly, worried when he saw her slowly raising one hand to her bandaged face. "Best not to move your head or touch your face, Fergus said. You have a bandage there and on your shoulder. But he says you'll be fine."

He put one hand under the folded blanket on which her head rested and raised it so she could drink from the cup he held to her lips.

She sipped, then collapsed exhausted as he lowered her head.

"What happened to the hospital camp?" she said in a thin voice.

He hesitated but knew better than to lie to her.

"The doctor said it was destroyed. My safari met up with you this morning, in one of your trucks."

"Oh, God, all those people." Gwenn turned her face aside.

"We're on our way south, home to Kenya, but Fergus says you can't be moved for a bit."

For a time neither spoke.

"Did he tell you what the Italians are doing?" she said haltingly.

"No," he said, not caring now about the cursed war. "But we've seen a bit of it."

"They're using poison gas, from airplanes. The Abyssinians have no masks. It's worse than last time." Suddenly she bit her lip and suppressed a groan, then continued weakly. "What will it be like if there's another war after this one? What could be worse than this?" She groaned again. "Some-one's going to have to stop them."

"Is the pain bad?" Anton reached for the pills in the dim light. "Fergus gave me something you can take."

Gwenn nodded without speaking and he raised her head. For a long time she lay silently, her eyes closed. Knowing she was awake, but sensing she was retreating to her privacy, he did not take her hand.

"I hope the boys are all right," she said suddenly, trying to turn her head towards Anton, slowly raising her right hand. "I left them with Olivio, at the villa."

"I'm sure they're fine," he said, taking her hand in both of his and rubbing it gently when he found it cool. "You're the one we have to worry about."

— 26 —

Improvisation was the richest lesson of campaigning in the bush with von Lettow-Vorbeck. Nineteen-eighteen seemed a hundred years away, but Ernst von Decken could still picture the general. By the end, his toenails removed so the cook could cut out the burrowing insects, the old soldier's feet had been too infected and swollen to wear boots. He had squinted with his wounded eyes, one slashed by elephant grass, the other infected, as he bent forward on his folding camp chair by the fire, cutting and stitching his own sandals from bits of bushbuck hide. The ragtag army of Germans, Arabs and *askaris* had made aerial masts out of bicycle spokes, and bread from rice and wild grains. In Tanganyika they chewed leather when they were hungry. In Mozambique they sucked pebbles when they were thirsty. In Kenya, in flight after raiding the British railway, the men drank their own urine and the blood of birds.

The medical side had been the worst. Unsupplied, famished, always on the run, the men understood that a moderate wound meant death. Even minor wounds became grave. Morphia, antiseptics, rest were unknown. Abandoned in groups on the trail, some wounded died at their own hands. Others were captured or taken by animals. German surgeons, trained in Stuttgart and Düsseldorf, picked herbs in the forest and mixed potions and poultices like witch doctors. Bandages were unwrapped from the dead, rinsed in muddy pools and returned to the living. Finally the *askaris* and camp followers had taken to chewing strips of bark, softening it until it was pliable and could be used to bind wounds.

Ernst had learned in a good school. Now he sat on the monks' stone pew with his bad leg outstretched. His right shoulder leaned against the wall of raw rock from which the seat was carved. Theodorus, quite a medicine man himself, sat at the other end of the bench fingering his silver cross.

"Careful, you old witch!" Ernst gave the abbot a hard smile. "You'll find it's dangerous to hurt a German." Alone too much, he had come to enjoy talking to himself, and sometimes to the monks even when he knew they could not comprehend.

Gibbering in Amharic, the abbot unwrapped the cotton bandage with gentle care. Ernst closed his eyes and tightened his lips as if in pain.

"I know your interest is drawn from a deeper well than kindness," said Ernst. The abbot, he reckoned, wished to learn the true condition of his guest, to determine Ernst's limitations, to assess his capacity for flight or mischief.

The stump was looking rather handsome today. Ernst winced as the monk set it down. The end of the shank bone was recessed in a dimple of puckered flesh, some of it an angry shiny red, but most of it smoothly scarred. The wound was closed, but still fragile and vulnerable. Ernst had seen its like before, and considered himself fortunate. Now he must wait for the protective leathery callus to build and harden. Secretly, he had fashioned a shielding cup of civet hide to protect the stump. It had perforations at the top to allow for a drawstring to hold it tight around the ankle, like the throat of a leather purse filled with silver coins. The cup hung from a thong under his shirt.

Theodorus pointed at the lake and wagged a finger in reproach. "You must stay away from the water," he seemed to be saying in Amharic.

Both men were aware that the present situation would not last. The previous morning, innocent as a hummingbird, an aircraft had droned towards them from the east, flying at two or three thousand feet. As soon as he heard it, the abbot had called in all the monks, gathering them under the deepest trees where they would not be seen. Changing direction when it came to the lake, the airplane had continued on to the south, taking the line of the other Rift lakes. Ernst had watched intently, fearing the shadow of his Potez could be spotted from the air, a ghostly cross beneath the filmy water.

In twenty minutes the plane had returned, lower, perhaps five or six hundred feet. Ernst was waiting with his field glasses. He followed it between the branches. It was a single-engined biplane, with upper wings longer than the lower, Italian, the same class of fighter that had shot him down, possibly even the same aircraft.

"It's that bastard," Ernst said aloud. "No one else knows where I crashed."

The small plane banked and returned, lower still, slower. It almost hovered over the lake, the port wing tipped low to allow the pilot to study the water. Circling to return home, it passed over once again and gained altitude and speed, as if the airman had learned what he sought.

It was time to raise the silver, von Decken thought grimly. And he would need help.

"Come here, dear abbot," said Ernst to Theodorus, beckoning with his forefinger. The German unbuttoned a hip pocket of his battered cut-off khaki trousers. He removed several crumpled bills and a few coins. One was a Maria Theresa dollar. He placed the five coins in a row beside his leg. Theodorus examined the coins with a new brightness in his dark brown eyes. Then he drew a dab of waxy ointment from a horn phial that hung at his waist. Ernst recognized the scent of civet mixed with some herb.

The German tapped the five coins. Then he made the sound of an aircraft engine, pointing to himself and to the lake. His opened hand dove as if an airplane crashing. The abbot nodded and applied a smear of ointment to Ernst's stump.

Ernst pointed to the silver dollar and to the lake. The abbot nodded again.

"Many, many. *Brzu! Brzu!*" Ernst held his left hand high above the ground, then pointed back to the dollar. Theo rubbed in the salve with unusual gentleness. The holy man understood: they would need him. None of the monks could swim.

Von Decken gestured towards the aircraft and the silver. He pushed one coin closer to the abbot and pulled back the other four. Theodorus shook his head and drew a second coin towards himself.

How priestly, Ernst thought, recalling the village clerics in Germany assisting the wretched crones up the stone steps, preparing to extract the final *pfennig* from the poorest peasant widow.

Ernst hesitated and covered the second coin with his hand, then nodded and held out his hand. The black abbot took the white hand in both of his. The division was agreed. Theodorus stood and gathered the younger monks around him. Later Ernst realized the old abbot had retained the two silver dollars in his fist.

By evening the raft was ready. She consisted of two crossed layers of rough logs and heavy branches, bound with coarse sisal bands and decked with two layers of buoyant reeds. Waiting in the shallows, one corner rode lower in the water.

"Not bad, boys," Ernst grunted, examining the work. Concerned about the weight of the chests, he pressed down on the raft with both hands. It seemed adequate to the task.

The moon, nearly full, rose above them like a yellow lantern. They would try working at night, lest a returning aircraft catch them at their labor.

A pale blue light glowed just above the surface of the lake. The flat sheet of water reflected each star and planet. Ernst stood to one side, watching the abbot lead his monks in prayer at the edge of the water. "I did not expect my silver to be blessed," he muttered.

"We help you," called Brother Petros excitedly, sitting cross-legged on the raft, two long coiled ropes before him. Four other monks slipped two pointed reed canoes into the water. They climbed in and began to paddle, drawing the heavy raft after them.

Barefoot, Ernst entered the third *tanqwa.* He gestured for Theo to join him, knowing the man detested the water. The abbot, stern, shook his head and rubbed his cross between his fingers.

Ernst paddled towards the Potez. His strokes barely disturbed the water, leaving tiny whirlpools as he withdrew the fan-shaped blade. He stopped paddling and coasted out, knowing the location of the gravesite as well as he knew the teeth in his mouth. When he got there, he back-paddled one stroke and the craft turned about. He shipped the paddle and took the pilot's goggles from his shirt pocket. He dipped them in the water and cleaned them as best he could. He slipped on the goggles and set them over his eyes. Earlier, he had waterproofed the split-lens goggles by filling their ventilation slots with beeswax.

The canoes and raft glided towards him in the moonlight like vessels in a torchlit Viking funeral. Theodorus stared out from the shore, as still and erect in his grey robe as the stone monoliths of his culture.

Ernst secured his *tanqwa* to the raft. He removed his shirt and rolled over the side into the water. The lake seemed strangely warm in the cool night air.

"Pass me the rope, Petros, the rope."

"Yes, rope," said the friendly monk, passing him an end. Ernst tied it about his waist with a loose knot. Then he removed a large flat stone from the floor of his canoe. He gathered his breath and dived with the stone in his left hand.

The familiar shadow welcomed him in the near darkness as he breast-stroked toward it. He felt the gathered sediment as his free hand led him along the upper port wing. He drew himself down by a strut to the lower wing, then followed that to the fuselage, barely able to discern forms and shadows in the moody gloom. He dreaded finding another eel.

The door of the cargo hold was still jammed. Ernst slammed the stone into the dent at its center. Groping with his left hand, he insinuated the thin edge of the stone between the door and the jamb. Levering with all his force, bubbles escaping from his lips, he popped open the door.

Excited but short of air, Ernst reached in and touched the first wooden chest. He untied the rope and set it in the doorway of the hold. Dizzy, he pulled the chest onto the rope but could not do more. His lungs ached as he kicked for the surface.

After he broke the water, he opened his mouth and gazed up Five black faces stared down at him. The moon shone over their heads. Disappointed, four monks spoke all at once. Where were the coins? the greedy devils must be asking. Only one monk seemed concerned for him.

"I help you." Petros leaned out and offered Ernst a hand up to the raft. Gruffly Ernst declined. For a moment he hung on the edge, his arms folded under his chin. Then he dived, the second rope about his waist. The monks would haul the ropes up when they tightened.

He belted the first rope around the chest that held it pinned. He secured the second rope so that it crossed the first. Then he tipped the chest out of the doorway. It settled onto the powdery floor of the lake, then began to rise as he did. When he kicked, his stump struck the edge of a wing. Stunned with pain, Ernst gasped and swallowed water.

Panicking, stroking desperately, he reached for the surface through the endless water. Finally he clutched the raft, breathing in swift deep gulps.

"I take you here," said Petros, helping him up. Retching and spitting, Ernst lay on the reeds of the raft. He removed his goggles. His eyes wept as he tried not to scream. He had not attached his leather cup. With his pistol and field glasses secured inside it, the cup was hidden inside the hollow pointed prow of his *tanqwa.* He had dried and cleaned the weapon and each cartridge but had found no opportunity to test it.

The other monks hauled the chest to the surface and clumsily set it on the raft amidst a tangle of ropes. One corner of the raft settled lower. Observing the monks struggling with the simple task, it occurred to Ernst that these were men of habit, not enterprise, each one confined by Theodorus to his own strict function. Although his leg throbbed, Ernst felt better as his body recovered and he saw his first chest safely aboard. Nodding encouragement, he watched Petros prepare the ropes for another lift.

Ernst finally sat up. Reluctantly, he looked down, certain that his stump had opened. Blood was leaking through the reeds. If only the Italians had given him a few more days to heal.

While he gathered himself, two monks gestured at him with impatience. Angry, Ernst drew on his goggles. Nine chests to go, plus one on the bed of the lake. He grabbed a rope and dived. The moon was higher and smaller now, not quite as bright. A thin plume of blood followed him down.

He found his skill with chest and rope increased with every dive. Even so, exhaustion and perhaps loss of blood were gaining on him as he worked. Deeper in the hold, the remaining chests were becoming more difficult to extract. He knew he must hoard some strength, and show the monks even more weakness than he felt. His stump was alternately numb and throbbing.

His head and upper body inside the long narrow space, toiling in complete darkness, Ernst was struggling to drag out the fifth chest when he felt a tickling sensation in his stump. He froze. Some creature, perhaps more than one, drawn by his blood, nipped and nibbled at his open wound. He felt a rush of pain as his flesh was taken. He kicked violently, cutting his forehead on the rim of the hatch as he freed himself. A long eel slid along his belly as he rose, frightened and revolted by the touch.

"Help me, Petros," he gasped when he reached the raft. The young monk seized him beneath the arms and dragged him aboard. For a few minutes Ernst lay gasping on the raft, knowing he must go down again.

"Lie here on the edge, Petros, with your head out over the water," he said, placing one arm across Petros's shoulder. "We will try to raise two chests each time I dive."

"Yes, yes," the monk said, lying on his belly.

"Take a rope in each hand, then pull up when you feel me tug on the cords. Have your brothers help you."

Twice it worked. He dived again and found the chest he had dumped onto the lake bed after the crash. He placed the next chest on it and rose for air. Descending, feeling stronger, Ernst lashed the two chests together and tugged on the ropes. Thinking he had sufficient air to extract the last case from the hold, he reached into the compartment.

An eel brushed his naked leg and touched his stump. The wide flat mouth buried itself in his wound. "Not again!" he thought desperately. Ernst seized the snake-like fish in both hands.

Twisting and thrashing, all muscle, the animal lashed his face with its finned tail as it fought him. Starved for air, Ernst started to rise, the eel still in his grip. As he rose a struggling black mass sank past him. He realized at once what it must have been: a man, Petros, tangled up with the ropes and chests, being dragged down by the weight of the silver.

Breaking the surface, Ernst flung the eel into a canoe between the feet of a monk. The man screamed and drew a knife. Other monks were fussing with the ends of the ropes. One man was trying to prize open a chest. Ernst cuffed the offending monk and directed them all to haul on the cords. They pulled at the ropes, without effect.

"Bleude Mönche!" Ernst yelled. Then he inhaled and dived.

Darker now, and thickened by agitated sediment rising from the lake floor, the water concealed Petros and his burden. Blindly Ernst followed one rope down, hand over hand. He found the cable looped around a blade of the Potez's propeller. Ernst freed it and continued down. Still unable to see, he groped about until he touched Petros's head. The ropes were coiled about the man's neck and one wrist, binding him to the two heavy chests. Desperately Ernst sought to free him, feeling the slick body turning slowly in the water as he struggled. Frustrated, needing air, he rose again and clutched the edge of the canoe.

"Give me your knife," he hollered at the monk with the weapon. Shrinking back, the wounded eel writhing between his feet, the man looked at the German without speaking. Ernst grabbed the man's right wrist and took the knife from his hand. Diving again, he freed Petros and rose to the raft with the body in his arms. The monks, still hauling on the ropes, had raised one of the last two chests. The other must have been lost when he cut the cord. Ernst counted the ten crates piled on the raft. He had done it.

Moaning and praying aloud, the monks awkwardly lifted their lifeless brother from the lake. Overweighted, the raft was now entirely under water. Only the chests and the face and feet of Petros appeared above the surface. The monks crossed themselves and knelt on the sunken reeds, wailing and crying out to Theodorus, invisible now in the deepening night.

"Tatanakkaka!" the voice of the abbot roared from the shore. *"Na!"* Clumsy in their wet robes, the four monks scrambled for their canoes. Two had left their paddles on the raft, Ernst saw with satisfaction. He seized a paddle from one man and flung it far into the lake. Without canoes the monks would be stranded on the island.

One monk raised the remaining paddle to strike the German. But Ernst wrenched it from the man's hand and twice stabbed it down through the floor of the canoe. Water rushed in and the small vessel began to list and settle in the lake. Ernst swung the paddle at the heads of the monks and heard the voice of Theodorus raging from the shore. Screaming, the monks struggled to distance themselves from the raft. Two hung onto their sunken *tanqwa.* The others paddled frantically with their hands.

Kneeling on the raft, Ernst lifted Petros's body in his arms and hesitated for a moment.

"*Auf Wiedersehen,* brother," he said, lowering the body into the water. He climbed into his canoe. Freed of the weight of the monks, the raft rose until the reed deck was level with the lake. Exhausted but exhilarated, Ernst paddled for the mainland, slowly towing the raft behind him.

— 27 —

The Macchi float plane circled Lake Zwai at three thousand feet. Substantially faster than the three Capronis he was guiding in, it had a top speed of nearly a hundred and sixty. When the sun was behind him, Colonel Grimaldi could discern the ghostly grey cross of the Potez beneath the water. He was confident she was not too deep for trained divers.

To extend his aircraft's range, Enzo had flown from the forward base at Geblilu, a town of the high bush, not the coast. It was Sparta, not Rome. The small luxuries, the civilizing details that fifty years of Italian occupation had brought to Eritrea were absent in the Ethiopian province of Wollo. Supplies were precious. Trucks and supply flights carried oil instead of chianti, carburetors and spark plugs instead of wheels of Parmigiano.

The airstrip itself was a graded section of the ancient unpaved road that ran on to Adigala and Dire Dawa. The crude strip had been punishing on the light wheels that served the Macchi in addition to her pontoons. Geblilu's old fort, once the bastion of the Mad Mullah, had been levelled by twenty tons of bombs. Aircraft fuel and bombs were now stored within its broken walls. The next base, at Adigala, would bring Harar and the Abyssinian wells and defences to the south and west well within the range of the Italian fighters. Like camps of legionnaires in the wilderness of Gaul and Iberia, these bases would provide support and strongpoints for the advance of Roman civilization.

Enzo did not look forward to working with the arrogant Captain Uzielli and the *Bersaglieri,* but knew he would be obliged to. Both his missions required it. Though it was less important, the general had taken a personal interest in the silver, doubtless realizing Rome would never believe it had been stolen by strangers. As to the photography, his instructions were clear: "Destroy the film and bury the photographer. Our nation is at war."

Both targets were still well beyond Italian lines. The front itself was fluid and uncertain. The invading armies were being absorbed by the immense wild geography of the Ethiopian plateau. Even as the armies advanced, Abyssinian irregulars prowled the country behind them like packs of hyenas. For this mission, an airborne operation was the only way. Now Enzo would learn how well these *Bersaglieri* really jumped and ran.

The *Regia Aeronautica,* however, was already supporting over three hundred thousand men on two fronts. Desperately short of transports, the air corps could spare but three Capronis for this operation. The bombers contained little space for human cargo. With each aircraft capable of carrying only eleven hundred extra pounds, that limited Enzo to thirteen men and two inflatable boats for the first day of the mission. Tomorrow the Capronis would return with fifteen more paratroopers. After they'd secured the silver, he could call in more men if necessary to dispose of the photographer in the truck.

Three of the thirteen men jumping today were neither paratroopers nor *Bersaglieri.* Two were navy recruits from the base at Massawa, men with a new specialty, divers in training for the next European war, probably against the British, when they would be needed to sabotage in port the enemy capital ships that the Italian navy would not be able to fight at sea. The third man, their interpreter, was a patriotic overweight restaurateur from Mogadishu whose father had been chef at the Italian embassy in Addis. Enzo was looking forward to his cooking in camp. Amazing what utility people could have in wartime, he reflected. All three would be jumping for the first time.

He saw the lead jumpers crouching in the open hatches as the three bombers came past in line. The first five men leapt in tight formation. The pale grey silk chutes strained and filled as they opened, ballooning outward between their seams. Below them the rocky brown plain spread endlessly towards the distant crags and cliffs of the great plateau, interrupted by the shimmering brightness of the lake and the scattered boulders and stands of euphorbia and palms and cactus. The men swung and floated down, manipulating the shrouds, rolling as they landed neatly in the rocky field west of the lake. Four men fell from the next plane, a trifle late. A crewman shoved the packaged boat out after them. Lighter than the heavily laden men, uncontrolled in its descent, the boat carried farther on its parachute, drifting almost to the edge of the water.

The third planeload fell farther still. The last two men pitched down a jagged hillside beyond the field. The second boat followed them. One of the last men, his chute opening late, struggled to untangle his harness as he came down too fast. Enzo saw him slam down on his back among the rocks, then lie motionless beside his crumpled chute. Too bad it wasn't Uzielli. Free of their parachutes, the troopers from the lead Caproni were already assembled in a tight group around the captain.

Although he knew he should wait for the *Bersaglieri* to secure the lakeshore, Enzo was impatient and prepared to land. He checked his petrol reserve and altitude. A snapshot of his English girl was fixed to the instrument panel with black tape. Good luck, he hoped. He had selected his landing path with care, mindful of the changing wind and the need for a secure berth for the Macchi. He would come in low over the barren northern tip of the lake, avoiding the island set near the western side, and then taxi into a thickly wooded cove at the narrow southern end. That should give him a calm place to tie up and load as much silver as she would carry. Then he could either fly back for the rest or leave it with the *Bersaglieri* until the paratroops linked up with the advancing army.

Heavier than his CR-20, but also powered by a twelve-cylinder Fiat engine and similarly armed with two 8mm machine guns, the graceful flying boat turned into the wind. With a broad balsa-wood bow and a small pointed pontoon under each double wing, the Macchi always floated high in the water and tended to dance or skip if the surface was choppy. The four-hundred-twenty horsepower engine was mounted under the back of the upper wing. The propeller faced backwards, thereby centering the weight and thrust instead of carrying them in her nose like land-based fighters. Conscious that Uzielli and the *Bersaglieri* would be watching, he adroitly cut his revolutions to the edge of stall. The Macchi floated down like an angel.

The smooth sheet of water cracked like a mirror and sparkled when the flying boat touched it. The airplane skipped once like a flat stone, then settled, skimming forward lightly. The resistance of the water rapidly braked the slender aircraft as the engine speed dropped to idle. The Macchi glided in through the reeds that lined the shore of the cove, and Grimaldi cut the motor, well pleased with his demonstration.

Enzo laid his jacket and flying helmet on the pilot seat. He checked his Beretta, reassured by the smooth action of the slide. He climbed out onto the wingplate, gripping a strut with one hand as the Macchi continued to ease forward among the reeds. In the other hand he held a rope. He felt a jarring bump as the nose grounded. He dropped into the shallow water and tied the rope to the tail ring. He turned the plane about until it faced out across the lake. When in a strange village, his grandfather had written in his diary, one must always prepare one's departure.

Enzo Grimaldi grasped the rope and waded ashore through the dense thicket of roots and bushes. His boots were heavy and awkward in the silty bottom. Must not let Uzielli see you stumble, he thought.

He could not see the loaded raft concealed among the reeds fifty yards to his left. Rocks had been piled on the raft until it settled onto the lake bottom. Reeds and vines congested the water above her.

From the swampy thicket nearby an old soldier studied Lorenzo Grimaldi through binoculars, recognizing his enemy by his grey mustache. This was the man who had cost him his foot, Ernst von Decken realized with satisfaction. He looked forward to settling the account.

Colonel Grimaldi wiped the toes of his boots on his trousers and straightened his shoulders before he emerged from the patch of forest that rose at the water's edge. The aircraft was secured to the trunk of a tree behind him. Ignoring the soldiers assembling nearby, he made his way slowly along the lakeshore, waiting for Captain Uzielli to come to him.

Enzo had been obliged to instruct the captain not to permit his men to treat the interpreter and the navy divers with disdain. Without the divers, the mission was doomed. Uzielli, hot-blooded, alarmed Enzo with his urgent thirst to avenge the mutilation of a young *Bersaglieri* scout captured by the Abbos earlier in the campaign.

"They found the *bambino* on a hillside overlooking a mountain trail," he'd heard Uzielli growl to his men, "naked, nailed to a rough cross like Jesus Christ himself." Before continuing, Uzielli had drawn a bent rusty nail from a pocket of his tunic and held it out to his men on the square palm of his left hand. "The first man we capture is going to eat those three nails."

Equipped in the latest tan and khaki green colonial uniform now being field tested in Africa, the paratroopers had insisted on one element of their traditional splendor. Each man had jumped with his wide-brimmed black leather hat fastened to his pack by its chin strap. Now the men were removing the black and green feathered cockades from inside their shirts and securing the rooster feathers to the right sides of their hats.

"You two collect that man who crashed among the rocks," ordered Uzielli as he inspected his troopers one by one. The two soldiers moved off at the loping *Bersaglieri* trot. Two other men were assisting a comrade who had broken a leg on the jump. "The rest of you make camp over there."

Enzo paused by the lake with his hands clasped behind his back. In another few minutes the two divers approached. One, a wrinkled sponge fisherman from Taormina, was not a young man, but it was said he could sound longer and deeper than a whale. The other, a boy, was light-haired, broad and solid, reminding Enzo of the northern hill peasants at home. The two set down one of the boats and saluted.

"Are you a Lombard?" Enzo said to the young diver.

"From Casteggio, sir." The boy grinned.

"Good lad." Enzo, enjoying the accent, smiled and clapped him on the shoulder. "When you get home, drink a bottle of Barbacarlo with your girl and tell her of today's adventure. Now get the boats ready."

"Capitano!" Enzo called loudly without looking at the officer. "If you please!"

Uzielli strode to him and saluted brusquely. Two *Bersaglieri* hurried over with the body of the interpreter slung between them. Trying to conceal their exertion, the men set down the heavy corpse at their captain's feet. Like a cat presenting a dead bird to its master, Enzo thought.

"Check his pockets for anything useful and bury him here." Uzielli looked down at the civilian's body with distaste. "No need to go too deep." Colonel Grimaldi saw the pale band of skin on the dead man's suntanned wrist.

"As soon as the first boat's ready, Captain, take four men and paddle to the island. I saw some movement from the air. Don't put up with any nonsense from the Abyssinians. I want this lake secure."

"Of course, sir," said Uzielli sharply.

"First," said Grimaldi "have your men remove their boots so they do not tear the rubber boat."

Uzielli stared at the colonel with visible resentment.

"And your own boots as well," said Grimaldi, "unless you all want to swim back. Meanwhile I'll take the divers in the second boat and check the wreck. Have one man guard my plane."

Trying to recall the breed of dog Uzielli reminded him of, the colonel paused and spoke again, gesturing towards the dead man while he looked the stocky officer in the eye.

"That interpreter was a volunteer, Captain. Get his wristwatch back from your men and collect his personal things for his family."

"Yes, sir," grunted Uzielli.

In thirty minutes, Grimaldi's boat was uncrated and ready. The thick black rubber was pumped full of air. The double paddles were assembled. The two divers slipped the craft into the shallow water and looked to Grimaldi for instructions.

"Put that straw and those wooden slats from the boat's packaging into the bottom of the boat so it won't be torn by the crates," Enzo said. "Then we'll go out for a look at the Potez."

Ernst von Decken held the field glasses to his eyes. The dried grey mud of the lake bank streaked his face and beard. His torso and head were sheltered in the hollow arching root structure of an aged mimosa that rose from the swampy edge of the bank. In the rainy season, when the ground was soft, the steep roots would brace the tree like the buttresses of the cathedral in Heidelberg. Now, with the rains over and the dry season underway, they were sucking nourishment from below the lake. For Ernst's purposes, the cavity of the tree fitted him better than a coffin. He was seated comfortably in the mud and silt. His legs extended into the water. His pistol lay in a cleft of the roots.

Ernst adjusted the lenses and peered out through the tangle of branches and vines that concealed his upper body. He watched the pilot seat himself on a rock and remove his boots and socks. He studied the officer's face. Not a young man, but handsome in a southern, Latin way, confident, a man who knew who he was. This Italian owed Ernst one right foot. "And now you're after my silver," Ernst mumbled.

Two men, in different uniforms from the others, were pumping the second boat with air. Already an officer and four soldiers were out on the lake. Three of the men carried short rifles across their backs. The fourth cradled a light machine gun in his lap. Crowded, they paddled slowly towards the island in the first boat.

When the second boat was inflated, the two men held it while the pilot clambered in. One tossed in a rope. Stripped to the waist, the two unarmed men climbed in carrying paddles. The pilot, Ernst noticed, wore a sidearm.

That left four active soldiers behind in camp with one wounded paratrooper. One man, armed, walked towards the aircraft. Two others began to dig with short pack shovels. Hard work, Ernst knew. Never had he seen a grave in Africa that was deep enough.

If he was forced to fight, he reckoned, this could be the best time. The small Italian force was divided into three groups. Plus, he doubted that the abbot and Markus and Johan and the other monks would get on well with these soldiers.

Ernst watched the lone *Bersaglieri* make his way towards the moored aircraft. The German turned his head slowly and reached for his pistol. A slender snake was there before him, coiling slowly into two perfect circles in the cool shadow just beside the grip of the weapon. Flat-headed, greyish at both ends, but with soft green and brown diamonds marking its body, the serpent moved leisurely, like a long train coming into a station. Probably poisonous, but almost certainly not mortal. Birds' eggs, frogs and snails would be its diet. Ernst wondered how his civets were faring without him.

Unsure of the weapon, and preferring stealth, Ernst left his pistol to the snake and leaned tight into the tree. He heard branches snap as the soldier, a smallish slender man, entered the thicket. The young *Bersaglieri* slipped and stumbled as he came to the mooring line near von Decken. A city boy, Ernst thought with satisfaction.

The soldier unslung his rifle and sat, resting his back against a sycamore. He played with the rope with one hand, idly drawing the plane towards him. After a time the Italian drew a cigarette from his shirt pocket. The smoke drifted towards Ernst. The German closed his eyes and gulped enviously. The two men shared the tobacco. When the cigarette was finished, the Italian stood and unbuttoned his trousers. He took a few steps towards Ernst's tree, preparing to relieve himself into the water.

A gunshot sounded from the island. The Italians must have lost patience with Theodorus, Ernst guessed. He turned his eyes to the lake and saw a diver clamber back into the second vessel. At once the pilot's boat began to make its way towards the island. At the same time the soldier near Ernst turned to face the sound. Losing his footing, he stumbled into the water just beside Ernst.

A brief burst of automatic fire came from the island. The *Bersaglieri* near Ernst slipped deeper into the water. *"Porca Madonna!"* he cursed. One foot entangled, he bent and grasped a root to steady himself. Seeing his chance, von Decken rose and threw himself onto the man's back. Together they fell forward into the lake.

Ernst forced the soldier's head below the water with one hand, tightening the heavy leather chinstrap about the man's throat with the other. The Italian twisted and thrashed. His body heaved up in the water, but he was unable to raise his head. Ernst was too heavy for him. One good drink and he would be lost.

Astride him like a horse, Ernst loosened the strap and felt the man gasp and open his lungs under water. He tightened the strap again with a sharp twist and forced the head lower with his other hand. The man struggled, but it was over. In his final violent wrenching, though, he slammed Ernst's stump against a root. Blinded with pain, Ernst toppled from the man's back. Inches away, he saw the face rise, eyes staring, mouth open as water ran from it, like a child gargling medicine. Ernst grabbed the man by the ears and forced his head down until he was still. Far away, he heard two more shots.

For a few moments von Decken reclined, gasping in his cranny. His stump was bleeding and throbbing. He wondered how many *Bersaglieri* had been strangled with their own chinstraps. He slipped back into the water and stripped the Italian's body before jamming the corpse beneath some roots under the water.

"Watch out for crocodiles," he said quietly to the dead man, reminded of how those beasts preserved their victims under sunken logs until the meat was ripe enough to eat.

He climbed out of the lake and examined the abandoned carbine with interest. Well cared for, it was a 6.5mm magazine-fed bolt-action Carcano, celebrated for the unusual accelerating pattern of the grooves of its rifling, which increased the spin and accuracy of the bullets. He recognized the advanced short-barrelled version of the classic 1892 model. The bolt and magazine, after all, were derived from the German Mannlicher. Ernst stripped and changed into the wet Italian uniform. "Tight but rather heroic," he said with pleasure.

He leaned against his mimosa and through its sheltering feathery leaves watched the three *Bersaglieri* standing with their weapons on the open lakeshore, staring towards the island. He spat into the water and frowned. He must dispose of these three while they were alone.

Well behind the three soldiers, the crippled trooper sat up, leaning on his hands. One soldier stepped aside and set his rifle against a rock before lifting a pair of field glasses to his eyes. Ernst raised the carbine and shot one of the armed men in the chest. Without looking up he swung the rifle, flicked the bolt and fired again. A second *Bersaglieri* fell. The man with field glasses threw himself down, searching for the source of the shot.

Ernst reloaded and set the leather hat on his head to deceive the soldier. He must act before the other Italians, alarmed by the shooting, hurried back from the island. The sun was behind him. For an instant the Italian might not see his beard and missing foot. Ernst hobbled into the open and waved at the *Bersaglieri.*

"Ma che succede?" the soldier called out to Ernst as he stood up. Then, his face instantly changing, he bent quickly and grabbed for his rifle. Ernst fired twice. The man fell on his belly across the weapon.

Pivoting, Ernst saw both boats setting out from the island. He thought he made out one of the monks seated in the pilot's craft. In minutes eight armed men would be after him. Perhaps he could use the Macchi's machine guns on them before they got back to shore. His stump aching, Ernst dropped the carbine and entered the water.

He swam to the float plane and dragged himself into the cockpit. He saw a small photograph taped to the instrument panel, but had not time to examine it. Ernst flicked off the safety and unlocked the twin machine guns from their fixed firing position. He checked the limited angles of traverse and depression available. With luck the black boats would just cross his line of fire.

The German looked down and, with a jolt, saw blood gathering on the floor of the Macchi as he waited. He bent and tightened the strap on his leather cup. The wind rose a bit and the plane drifted a few degrees to starboard. It was time to see if he was still as good as he thought.

The boat with the young officer came first. Ernst swung the guns ahead of it so he could traverse back through it and catch the second boat in the same sweep before it altered course.

Twisting awkwardly from the frantic uneven paddling, the lead boat approached his gunsight. *"Großwild!"* Ernst pulled the trigger in a long burst and swung the guns slowly as he tried to fire across both vessels.

The first boat appeared to explode in the lake. He was certain the three men in front must be dead. But then the plane shifted in the water as he fired, not allowing him to bring the guns properly to bear.

"Verdamt!" he screamed in frustration, still shooting. He saw the second boat burst. A paddle shattered in the air. The front soldier appeared to be injured. The others swam frantically. Ernst counted five men moving in the water, swimming back towards the island. Only the pilot, he guessed, was still armed. He recalled the aviator diving after him as his Potez went down. Ernst gritted his teeth and sprayed two lines of bullets through the water. One man leapt from the lake like a fish as the bullets crossed his back.

"That's it," Ernst said. "Now let's see what sort of welcome you get from your friends the monks."

Before rising, he caught sight of the photograph taped to the instrument panel. A slender woman with fine long legs, her face partly shadowed by a straw hat, stood in the desert by the Sphinx. Astonished, he peeled away the black tape and placed the picture in his shirt pocket. What was a photo of Rider's wife doing in this plane? he wondered, struck by the coincidence. It must be her Italian lover who had shot him down.

Von Decken rose on his good leg and left the cockpit. It was time to inconvenience his enemy and give him a crash of his own. Gripping the struts, Ernst knelt on the after-fuselage and relieved himself into the gas tank. He lowered himself into the water. He gathered silt from the lake bed and dropped several handfuls into the tank before hopping ashore.

His left shoulder bleeding from a long superficial cut, Colonel Grimaldi dragged himself forward through the thick reeds towards the island. Who had fired from the Macchi? Could one of the *Bersaglieri* have gone berserk?

To his right Enzo heard cries and the sounds of violence. The young diver had reached shore before him. After what that brute Uzielli had done to the monks they had found on the island, no sort of revenge would be surprising. Already, in the first weeks of the campaign, Italian intelligence had identified the clergy of the Ethiopian church as a powerful force at the center of Abyssinian resistance. With both sides haunted by memories of the campaign of 1896, a pattern of atrocities and reprisals had come easily. If the Roman church had defended herself with violence and brilliant cruelty through many centuries, how could one expect these black Copts not to do the same?

Enzo moved slowly on his belly in the shallow water. He parted the reeds with one hand.

An elderly monk, wounded, sat slouched with his back to a crude stone monument. His lined black face was gaunt with pain and exhaustion. The silver cross that hung from his neck glittered against the dark red that stained his robe from the waist down. He must be carrying one of Uzielli's bullets, Enzo judged. Nevertheless, the white-haired priest held a large rock between his hands. Two young monks dragged the unconscious diver to his side, like an offering. The older monk seemed to be their leader.

Slowly the abbot raised the rock and brought it down on the temple of the boy from Casteggio. His own teeth snapping together, Enzo heard the crack of bone. The abbot's hands rested on the boy's cheek with the bloody stone between them. The body did not move. Moving the stone to his lap, the old monk seized the Italian boy by the hair and turned his damaged head so that the other cheek was up. With great effort the abbot lifted the stone and struck again.

Enraged, Grimaldi drew his Beretta beneath the water. There was a commotion from the shore nearby, and two monks ran to join their brethren. Enzo held the pistol in both hands and aimed through the reeds at the seated abbot. He squeezed the trigger. The weapon would not fire. He checked the slide and tried again with no success. He raised his head and saw two *Bersaglieri* being beaten and subdued as they stumbled ashore. One, Captain Uzielli, seemed already injured but resisted with his knife before he was clubbed to the ground and bound. A third soldier, perhaps more fortunate, lay facedown in the water.

Patience, Enzo told himself. He sank lower and drew himself backwards through the water. Although painful, the shoulder wound, praise the Blessed Mother, was superficial. He began to swim towards a distant part of the island.

Once ashore he would rest for a bit before scouting out the situation on the island. At nightfall he would swim back to the Macchi and learn who had fired on him from the plane. By this time tomorrow the Capronis should be back with the rest of the *Bersaglieri* paratroopers. Then they would collect their debts.

Using the short bayonet of the soldier he had drowned, Ernst von Decken carved himself a crutch from a heavy branch. Already he had looted the *Bersaglieri* camp of medical supplies and food and ammunition. The wounded trooper, raving with pain, had offered no resistance. Ernst shouldered one of the Italian rifles and began to hobble away from Lake Zwai, a small sack of coins in his haversack. Twenty years before, General von Lettow had trained his officers always to leave while flight was still possible. Now the afternoon was cooling. It was time to march.

In three hours, after many pauses, he had made perhaps three or four miles. The track that led past the Rift lakes could not be more than a few miles due west. It should be the route recommended to him by Rider. It was nearly dark. With luck he'd find some sort of transport and return to the lake for the silver and carry it on south to Kenya.

Ernst followed every depression in the land, unable to climb or descend without slipping and falling, exhausted by each stumble. In Africa the terrain was never as flat and easy as it appeared from a distance. But after a few hundred yards he had learned the swinging stride used by the best of the walking wounded during the *Weltkrieg*. As he struggled along, Ernst realized he must be the first German to be engaged in this new African campaign. The last he'd heard, Chancellor Hitler had been opposed to the anticipated Italian adventure in Abyssinia, not wishing to provoke the other powers into rearmament.

Soon his armpit was troubling him more than the stump. Even bound with the stained shirt of a dead *Bersaglieri,* the head of the makeshift crutch cut his armpit with every step. Finally, near the top of a small eminence, he rested his rifle between a cluster of rocks. It was time to rest and review his plans. He unstrapped the rucksack and removed a packet of hard cheese and Italian sausage. He laid out his other supplies: canteen, ammunition belt, field glasses, knife, silver. Thank God for the cigarettes. He sat against a flat rock with his back to the setting sun.

The last light was just visible on the far edge of Lake Zwai. He thought he detected movement on the lake's surface. A dark shadow was crossing it. Alarmed, Ernst raised his glasses.

In another few minutes the float plane was turning about at the end of the lake. The Macchi paused, then adjusted its path to take advantage of the wind. Her propeller became a blur. The plane sailed across the lake and rose smoothly near the stand of mimosas. Cracking a smile, Ernst wondered how long she would stay aloft. He watched the Macchi climb, still flying west northwest. Then she turned in a broad arc and soared with the sun glinting on her tail.

Somewhere short of two thousand feet she ceased to climb. Ernst adjusted the glasses and climbed onto a rock and stood watching. He stopped breathing, waiting for the moment. The plane was losing altitude. Another minute and he made out the two individual blades of her propeller. Then they blurred and the aircraft recovered speed. "How could that be?" Ernst groaned and spat. The engine stalled again and died.

Tottering, yet erect on his good leg, he watched the plane fall. Gracefully, almost with the ease of a glider, the Macchi floated down, her engine weight providing perfect balance, her double wings utilizing every breath of wind. At length she landed roughly in the bush, her pontoons ripped away by the rocks, her left wings higher, the lower right wing bent back against an ant hill. This devil could fly.

Not quite satisfied, Ernst lowered the glasses and limped down. He cut off the butt of the sausage with the bayonet. He licked the coarse salami, relishing the slick greasiness and the grit of the peppercorns. He drank from the canteeen, then cut a thick slice of sausage. While he ate, night fell with that suddenness peculiar to Africa. He lit a cigarette and closed his eyes. A growling rumble echoed up the hillside. Ernst reached for his carbine and lowered his head to the ground, the better to hear the distant roar.

— 28 —

Ernst von Decken awoke when a sharp pain jabbed his heart. Thinking he'd been shot, he gasped and looked up into the dawn light. The tip of his crutch was jammed into the center of his chest. A big black man in shorts and a European shirt leaned forcefully on the stick, pinning him down like a beetle on a pin. Ernst seized the crutch in one hand and tried to twist himself aside. The man kicked him violently in the ribs and pressed down.

Ernst choked and wheezed and observed the man with more care. This was not the usual slender graceful Abyssinian. Heavyset, powerfully built, with an open broad face, he must be from the south, a proper Bantu, perhaps Ngoni or even Kikuyu.

"Jambo!" Ernst tried a smile. He pointed to his stump.

The pressure on the crutch relaxed. Ernst was relieved by the man's reaction. Waiting for an opportunity, he coughed, exaggeratedly heaving his chest up and down. The weight on the stick lessened.

With the fury of a badger, Ernst struck the crutch from the side with his right arm. The black man lost the support of the stick, stumbled and fell forward. As the big African collapsed across Ernst, the German rolled on his side and reached for the rifle, conscious of the other's weight and strength. The man's feet struck Ernst's head when the African struggled to rise. Ernst grabbed the barrel of the rifle and swung the heavy weapon like a scythe as the man rose to a crouch.

The rifle stock slapped the black man across the side of the head. The bolt slammed against his cheekbone. He collapsed, unconscious.

"My turn," Ernst said. He removed the man's belt and strapped his wrists tightly together behind his back. Then he turned him on his side. The

African's right temple and cheek were swollen and bleeding. Ernst sat on a rock facing his prisoner. Hungry, he ate a bit of sausage and smoked a cigarette as the light rose.

When his smoke was finished, Ernst leaned over and struck the man hard across the unbloodied side of his face. The eyes blinked and focused.

"Jambo," von Decken said again.

The big man struggled and sat up on his haunches. His face was closed and sullen.

Ernst was glad the fellow was bound. He reminded the German of the *askaris* he had campaigned with during the war. The best had been Manyemwesis. He knew the type: dangerous, dependable. Then, in the burgeoning light, von Decken noticed the three initials stitched on the pocket of the African's faded green shirt: "A.R.S." Anton Rider Safaris. He laughed aloud. *"Mein Engländer!"*

Sitting on a rock with a mug of tea while he planned the day's march, Anton heard a commotion and excited voices from the edge of camp. "*Bwana Mzee*!" Hoping all was well, he holstered the Colt and strode over.

The cook and camp boys were gathered in a cluster. The two Abyssinian soldiers stood to one side, lean-faced and uneasy, rifles in hand. Kimathi stood before them, his brow angry, his hands bound behind his back, his left eye almost shut from a large swelling on his cheekbone. Haqim pushed through the gathering. He moved to free Kimathi but hesitated before the levelled rifle held by a filthy bearded white man leaning on a crutch and wearing a ragged Italian uniform.

"Ernst!" said Anton, astonished and pleased to see his friend, but instantly aware that yet another problem had joined his camp. He felt just the slightest resistance when he lifted the weapon from Ernst's hand.

"We'll have this cleaned for you," Anton said reassuringly. Glancing down at the rifle, he was shocked to see that his friend had no right foot.

"What happened to your foot?" Anton said, handing the rifle to the gunbearer.

"I sold it for some silver." Ernst looked around the camp. "Give me a drink, *Engländer.*" By now he had remembered that the American girl was on this safari.

"You must learn to take care of yourself when your bwana isn't with you," said Anton to Kimathi while he freed the African's hands.

"I will," said Kimathi, angry and embarrassed by his capture. He rubbed his wrists and stared over Anton's shoulder at von Decken. "We have far to go."

Anton looked at the Kikuyu's swollen cheekbone. "My friend hasn't improved your black face, Kimathi. Better have Fergus take a look at it. Could use a stitch or two, a little white man's medicine."

"I will clean my own face, *Tlaga,*" said Kimathi, almost smiling.

"Time you had a drink." Anton led Ernst to the big fire. They sat on a chest and a camp chair.

Ernst gulped his first whisky. "I have a snapshot for you." He passed Anton the small photograph of Gwenn.

Anton stared at the picture. "Where did you get this?"

"In the cockpit of an Italian float plane. Back on Lake Zwai."

"Grimaldi," Anton said at once, jealous, filled with a surge of hate. One of these Italian planes, Grimaldi or not, had wounded his wife. Anger stiffened him, making his fingers wooden around his whisky glass.

"We have much to do." Ernst drank slowly, gauging his friend's reaction. After a moment he slapped Anton's knee. "My silver is waiting for us, boy," the German said. "A few miles on, in the lake. We'd better hurry, before our Italian friend comes back for it."

Tempted by the opportunity this might present for taking revenge on Grimaldi, Anton did not reply. Then he saw Bernadette and Harriet step from the tent. Harriet, though helpful, had been more distant since Gwenn had joined the camp. Indistinguishable, the twins turned towards the men at the fire.

"*Guten Abend, meine Engelen*!" cried Ernst, leaning forward and staring into the darkness at the girls, then speaking aside more quietly to Anton. "Angels!"

"They are not angels."

"How do you tell them apart?"

"Look for the one who doesn't have an engagement ring. Or just call them 'miss.' "

Ernst peered towards the twins.

"How do you do it? Where do you always find them?" Ernst snorted and shook his head. "Perhaps I should shave and borrow your best shirt for supper. I'll bet they've never dined in the bush with a proper German gentleman."

"Who has?" said Anton, still in the throes of planning a just revenge for Grimaldi.

The twins rushed to von Decken and embraced him. Anton saw the shock in Harriet's face when she realized the German had lost his foot. After an instant's hesitation, she took his arm closely and walked with him to the fire.

"Tell me what happened," she said as they sat down together.

A few moments later, Fergus and Charlie joined them. Malcolm introduced himself and took the bottle from Ernst. He tried not to notice the man's stump.

"Are you a surgeon, Doctor?" the German asked, holding out his hand for the whisky.

"I am," the doctor said with resignation. "Can I help you?"

"I'll go and wash, Doctor." Ernst stood. "Then Captain von Decken will present himself for examination by you and the ladies."

"Before you waste time on this German," said Anton, "please take a look at Kimathi, Doc. We're going to need him."

Anton went to the cook fire and poured a cup of tea from the big kettle. He spooned in a lot of sugar and stirred in the remaining milk from their last tin before walking to Gwenn's tent. He wanted to tell her that Grimaldi was near, that he would make the Italian pay for her suffering, but he knew she was too weak, and that it would only be his own indulgence, to make himself feel better, not her.

"You'll spill," she said in a weak voice when he tried to hold the cup to her lips. She took the tin cup and leaned forward as best she could.

Hastily he bolstered the blanket under her head. "Would you like me to read to you while they're making dinner?" He turned up the oil lamp. "I brought *Oliver*."

"Yes, please." Her voice brightened. "Just start wherever you are."

"Near the beginning," he said. He opened the ammunition chest and took out the book and found his place.

> *'That child that was half-baptized Oliver Twist, is nine year old to-day,' said the beadle. 'Notwithstanding the most superlative, and, I must say, supernat'ral exertions on the part of this parish, we have never been able to discover who is his father, or what his mother's name.'*

Gwenn began to smile, then stopped, thinking of Anton's own anonymous father. She sipped her tea slowly while Anton read.

> *'How comes he to have any name at all, then?' asked Mrs. Mann. 'I inwented it,' said the beadle with great pride. 'We name our fondlings in alphabetical order. The last was a S, -Swubble, I named him. This was a T, -Twist, I named him. The next one as comes will be Unwin.'*

Gwenn closed her eyes and slowly fell asleep while Anton continued in a low voice, pausing occasionally to look at her. After a time he closed the book and gently tucked in the edges of her blanket.

When Anton stepped from the tent he stood and looked about the camp, the war and their flight forgotten for the moment. The fires glowed and sparked against the deep starry blue-black of the night. The bare branches of an old banyan stood out like gibbets or the arms of an abandoned windmill. He heard laughter and chatter against the night sounds of the surrounding bush, reminding him of a thousand safari nights.

Like a sea captain, Anton was sometimes proud of the way his crew worked together. So far, the elements of a safari were well suited to the emergencies they'd faced. The mechanic, the laundry boy, the cook, the gunbearer, the *saises*, all had risen to the urgent demands of their flight. The food was still well prepared, the staff respectful, the camp clean.

A few shortcuts, of course, were beginning to show. The food was simpler; no more tinned fruit and puddings. They had discarded all save three tents: a low one-man fly tent, a small double for the twins, and the dining tent that was now the surgery. The shower canvas and the latrine tent had been bartered for two goats. His clients, for once, understood. At least Americans were adaptable.

The older goat, less able to keep up with their animals, was in the stew they now ate from the enamelled tin plates. Lapsam served Anton a large plateful as soon as he sat down with the others. The table, scrubbed down with sand and water after the surgery, was set between the fire and two giant palms.

"Mmm, remarkable, really, your English peasant stew." Ernst spoke with his mouth full. He was nearly clean shaven.

"We don't have peasants in England," Anton said. "You must be thinking of Bavaria." Indeed, he had rarely seen Ernst so neat. His thick silvery hair was parted in the center and smoothed down.

Ernst tapped his plate with his knife to request another helping. He watched carefully while he was being served, pointing to bits of meat he wanted, then leaned across Charles and addressed Harriet.

"Camping like this reminds me of the war," the German said.

"The war?" Harriet asked. Charlie rose from his place and settled a few yards away to sketch the scene.

"The last one, the Great War." Ernst moved to the empty seat beside Harriet. "In Tanganyika, German East Africa. We Germans fought the world, you know, Indians, Aussies, *Schwartzes*, Britishers." He picked a thick bone from his plate and sucked out the marrow. "I'll show you my scars if you like," he said quietly.

"Before you start on that war, you old Hun, we'd better talk about this one," Anton interrupted. Although his interest in Harriet had died the instant Gwenn appeared, he couldn't help being annoyed that she'd so easily switched to this German.

"Join me for a cigar." Anton rose. "They're in the lorry."

"Wait for me, treasure," the German whispered loudly to Harriet. "I just have to help this boy for a minute." Grumbling, he limped after Anton to the Oldsmobile. Charlie reappeared and sat on the ground by the fire with a sketch pad.

"This is our chance, boy." Ernst rested on a running board and accepted the matches from Anton. "Our silver's waiting in the lake, but it won't be there long. We must get it now, tonight."

"We could certainly use some silver to buy our way south," Anton said, not betraying his other interest in the matter. "Tell me the problems."

The two men talked and smoked. Then Anton checked the truck and gave orders to his men.

Dimmed with dried mud, the single headlight barely illuminated the rough track as they bumped along southeast towards the lake. Anton drove, Ernst beside him pointing the way and asking annoying questions about Harriet. Kimathi and Haqim and Anton's number two gunbearer, Clarence, a dependable man, were in the back. All were armed. Haqim, inexperienced with firearms, carried a short-barrelled twelve-gauge shotgun, Anton's stopper.

He slowed as he saw the black sheen of Lake Zwai spread before them.

"Careful, *Engländer.* Safer to do the last bit without the light."

Anton stopped and spoke to Kimathi. They drove forward slowly in the starlight. Kimathi tapped on the roof to indicate when to go left or right.

The ground near the tip of the lake was soft and spongy. "That's as far as she'll go." Anton shut down the engine. Then he switched the truck back on and turned it around, preparing for a swift departure.

Hobbling, Ernst led them to the stand of mimosa. They made out the glow of a fire on the island in the lake.

"What's on that island?" Anton whispered, concerned that Ernst had not told him all he should.

"Some black monks, perhaps a few wounded Wops. And my right foot." Ernst stumbled and cursed when his stump struck a root.

"Where are the Italians?" Anton asked anxiously, thinking of Grimaldi.

"Don't worry," Ernst said. "If they were nearby you'd see their fires. Just slip down into the water there, boy, and you should find my raft."

Anton laid his gunbelt on the bank. He clutched a vine to steady himself as he entered the water. He had a slimy musty sense of rotting vegetation and still water.

"Bit deeper," Ernst said encouragingly from the bank. "To your left."

Something large moved in the water against Anton's leg. "Steady," he reminded himself. "It's not fast and violent enough for a croc." He drew the knife from his sheath and stepped forward. The creature stayed with him, pressed against his naked legs below his shorts. Unnerved by its persistence,

Anton stabbed into the water with his knife. The blade stuck fast, anchored to something heavy and immobile.

Wary, Anton reached into the water with his left hand. He bent lower and groped forward. He felt teeth, a nose, a man's face. He breathed sharply, then held his left hand against the naked chest as he wrenched his knife from the body. The dead face broke the surface. Water drained from its mouth before the body settled back.

"Must be my first Italian." Ernst peered down. "I said a few more feet to your left, *Dumköpf*!"

Anton felt the sodden body shifting away from him beneath the surface. He moved carefully through the water, bent over as he reached low with both hands. At last he felt the splintery edge of a wooden packing case, then more as his hands continued to explore. He felt heavy stones lying atop the chests.

"I found it," he said quietly, groping along the edge of the sunken raft. He gestured for Kimathi and Haqim to join him. He guided them to the raft and the three men began to remove the stones that weighed it down. Slowly the craft rose. The wooden slats of the top chests broke the surface.

"Just as I told you!" exclaimed Ernst to the men working below him.

Kimathi and Anton passed the crates up to Haqim and Clarence on the bank. When they were finished, they each made several trips back to the truck, stumbling frequently with the bulky weight. Ernst sat waiting for them in the cab, the shotgun in his lap as he counted the chests. "That's the ten!" he cried at last. Full of excitement, he rose and embraced Anton and clasped the Africans around the shoulders.

The rough noise of the igniting engine broke the night, then steadied as they drove slowly away with no lights.

They had gone less than a hundred yards when a single rifle shot cracked behind them, then two more. One of the Africans screamed and fell against the rear of the cab. Anton felt his own body tighten. Only one rifleman, by the sound of it, he thought, bending lower over the wheel.

Desperate not to be followed back to camp, thinking of Gwenn, Anton accelerated. The truck bounced violently. One more shot followed them.

"Probably your pilot friend," Ernst said. "He may've been the only one left." A shotgun blasted into the night when Kimathi fired from the rear of the truck.

The Oldsmobile bucked as they bashed over stones and through the thorn bushes. Anton considered going back and dealing with the shooter on his own. Night could be best, and it was dangerous to leave an enemy behind. Still, he had too many responsibilities in camp, and he wouldn't want Gwenn to think he'd gone back just to murder an Italian in the hope it was her lover.

There was a crashing sound near the side of the truck.

"What was that?" Anton slowed. "Did a chest fall off?"

"Only your dead boy. Haqim tossed him out," Ernst said. "Keep going."

Disturbed, sensing bad luck, Anton stopped the truck. He hurried back along the track until he found the body: Clarence. He knelt and raised Clarence's head between his hands and closed the eyes with his thumbs. For a moment he rested one open palm on the man's cheek. He lifted the body of the Kikuyu across his shoulders and carried him to the truck. Kimathi helped set the body in the lorry, pleased his friend had not been abandoned on the trail.

"He's been with me nine years," Anton said as he resumed driving, saddened by his responsibility for the man's death. Feeling bitter, he wondered how many more would be lost, and who would survive. He worried about Gwenn and when she could be moved. Delay was dangerous to the rest of them, but safer for her. He drove as fast as he dared by the light of the rising moon, thinking about Gwenn and his clients, forming a plan for their continued flight. He must find a way to be the hunter.

The mood in camp changed with the arrival of the silver. Anton tried to ignore it, leaving no guards on the truck, conducting the camp as usual. The Africans seemed to be avoiding it, keeping their distance when they walked past the vehicle. Ernst was proprietary, as if he was now a different, more substantial man. Even Charlie and Dr. Fergus seemed to be influenced by it, as if assuming a new responsibility. Only the women didn't care. Probably too rich, Anton guessed.

In the morning they held a service for Clarence. Anton cast the first spade. Clarence was buried deep, where the animals would not get him, with a mass of stones atop the grave. The entire camp stood by the grave as Anton and Dr. Fergus read from *The Book of Common Prayer.*

"I will lift up mine eyes unto the hills," Anton read, reminded of other services.

"Excuse me," said Ernst to Harriet after the service. "This damn leg gets awfully stiff if I don't use it, and this blasted crutch is cutting my arm off. Do you think you could help me take a little walk?"

"You seem to get around rather well," said Harriet with admiration, aware Berny was listening. "But I'd love to help you if I can," she added, moving closer to the German.

"Perhaps I could leave the stick here and just lean on your shoulder a bit," said Ernst, handing the crutch to Charlie and putting his arm around Harriet's shoulder. "Ah, that's better," he grunted as they started off. "You know, this reminds me of '17."

Although he knew everyone else was anxious to get underway, Anton spent much of the day in the tent with his wife. He sat beside her cot on a green metal ammunition box, studying his maps, holding her hand and keeping the flies from her wounds while she slept. Several times she woke up, blinking and tightening her eyes as if in pain, not altogether there, but aware of him, he was certain.

Fergus lay nearby, curled up in a bedroll, dead asleep, weak and exhausted as any patient after an operation. Anton had sent Diwani and one of the Abyssinian soldiers out scouting on patrol.

Once Gwenn woke up and turned her head towards Anton. "The rest of you must go on ahead," she said slowly.

"When you're a bit better, Gwennie, you and I will be travelling together," he said.

"But you must go on and look after your clients and tell everyone about the gas. The world has to know. It would change everything."

"Don't you remember that you always ran the farm, and I always run the safaris?" he said chidingly as she collapsed back onto the bed. "Besides, I think Fergus is in worse nick than you are." He wondered if she was strong enough to be stubborn.

"Supper, Bwana," Lapsam called from the entrance to the tent. At the announcement the doctor stirred and sat up. Anton returned the prayer book to the ammunition box, protecting it from moisture and insects. He glanced at his Dickens before closing the lid.

After dinner was the time to tell them of the plans, he had decided. Whisky, curried goat and potatoes would make a fine meal.

Hungry, but more appreciative each day, his clients gathered near the fire with Ernst and Fergus. The twins seemed to understand, to have a taste for it all, as if finally they had found something that engaged more than a little of their attention. In some ways, the safari was getting better as it grew harder. They were getting closer to Africa.

Ernst took a seat between the twins and addressed Bernadette cheerfully. "Have you been taking many photos, *Fraülein*?"

"A few, but my sister Harry's been wasting lots of cine film with her new Bell and Howell," Bernadette said.

"Good for her, miss," Ernst said, confused as he looked from one twin to the other. They had both washed and changed before dinner and now were dressed in identical dark green shirts and long pleated khaki shorts. Neither wore an engagement ring. "Wonderful, you Americans. Always the latest thing."

"Not just safari pictures." Harriet bristled at the patronage in Ernst's tone. "The war. I filmed the Italians bombing the Abyssinian camp, poison gas and all. Airplanes, everything. I can't wait to see it . . ."

"Gas!" Fergus leaned forward, all fatigue vanished. He turned to Harriet. "You have film of the Italians using poison gas?" Elation enlivened his face.

"That could bring in the League. The world's just waiting for proof. They'd close the Suez Canal to Italian shipping!"

"Yes," said Bernadette, catching his excitement. "Harry got it all from the back of the truck, the planes with the gas, everything. One plane was lying crashed on its back with its tummy in the air and the gas nozzles showing." She spoke more slowly as doubt came into her voice. "But the truck was bouncing all over and who knows what'll come out."

"That's why they're bombing our Red Cross teams, to get us away from the fighting, so there won't be any foreign witnesses to the gas attacks," Fergus said more quickly. "That's why Gwenn was wounded. If the Italians knew you had that film, they'd kill us all."

No one spoke. Anton heard the fire crackle. Both twins were riveted by the doctor's words. Thin and stiff as a gibbet, Malcolm Fergus stood and faced Anton with his back to the flames.

"We must get that film out. It could stop the war, save thousands of lives, tens of thousands." He paused, breathing quickly while he sucked in his pale hollow cheeks. "Nothing else matters."

"He's right," Bernadette heard herself say in the silence. She shivered and caught her sister's eye.

"You must do it," the doctor said to Anton, shaking slightly where he stood, his voice rising. "You'd be much faster on your own. They'd never catch you. The rest of us will manage. You should take the best horse and run for the Kenya border with the film."

"I can't do that," said Anton in a low steady voice, feeling all eyes turning on him. "Sorry, Doctor, but I cannot." No one else spoke.

Anton looked past Fergus into the greying fire. For the first time in his life, even the bush was not providing an escape. This damn war was becoming bigger than all of them.

— *29* —

Olivio Fonseca Alavedo had grown strangely attached to his Koch sling. When the devil in his back denied him sleep, or when he found an unusual need for reflection, he sometimes rose from the immense canopied bed that was his wife's. Rinsed and dressed, he would rouse Tariq or another servant to drive him to the Cataract Café. He preferred to employ the sling in darkness, the better to contemplate and scheme while his back stretched and the pain muted.

Tonight he had done his duty, and more, leaving Kina sated, he believed, and peaceful, sable and lush against the creamy linen sheets. What other woman supported such breasts? He always found her still more arousing when pregnant, her body alive, her breasts swelling and firming. Would the child she now carried, he thought fervently, be a handsome son to suckle at these temples?

Standing naked near the side of the bed with his eye in one hand, he gazed up at her in the dim light that touched her. He admired her resemblance, indeed her superiority, to the languid naked white ladies in the decadent Parisian paintings he had studied years ago while his wife shopped along the Faubourg, followed by the creeping Panhard bearing her parcels and hat boxes.

About to leave but unable to help himself, he returned to the bed, a replica of that presented by Ismail the Magnificent to the Empress Eugénie for her visit to Cairo in 1869. Olivio's nostrils, always acute, enjoyed the flooding scent of his wife's sex as he approached the altar of pleasure.

A flagon of palest green Algarve oil in hand, he climbed one of the round leather-sided Arabian cushions that surrounded the high bed. He pushed to one side the silk-covered dromedary saddle that still rested on one corner. He lowered himself beside his wife, his back brittle with torment. He oiled his fingers generously and took one long nipple in each of his small hands. He closed his eyes and kissed the dark pointed flesh, delving the depression at its tip with the point of his tongue, drawing on its secret richness.

Kina's body recognized the preliminary ceremony. She stirred and rolled towards him. For a moment the dwarf was nearly suffocated between her breasts. Gasping, he freed his head. The movement brought a flash of pain down his back. He abandoned his idea and climbed down. His spine was getting worse. He washed his eye and prepared to leave for the Café. The dwarf always enjoyed motoring at night.

"Return and call for me in the early morning," he instructed Tariq after they arrived at the Café.

"While I am driving Miss Clove to the zoo?" asked the Nubian as he gently helped his master down from the Daimler.

"Yes, perfect." The dawn drive would give the dwarf an opportunity for a private conversation with his favorite child. It was time that he reminded the girl of certain standards required of a young lady of family, notably denial and, failing that, discretion. This was not a lesson that Clove's mother had been trained to instill, having herself fallen to the dwarf at the age of thirteen.

Alone in the dim lamplight from the quay, Olivio stepped along the gangway to the boat, peering about the deck for the night watchman. The Nile was higher now as the rainwater arrived from Ethiopia and the Sudan, and the covered walkway sloped down at a more comfortable angle. The rising waters reminded him of his friends at peril in Abyssinia. For a moment that concern diverted him. Nonetheless the little man gripped the braided rope with care as he descended with small steps.

He spotted the night watchman dozing in a chair on deck with his head resting on a round café table. Like a hunter stalking in the bush, Olivio stepped quietly towards the idle rogue. He lifted the man's wooden staff above his head with both hands, intending to slam the heavy stick on the metal table near the watchman's ear. That, and the sight of the enraged visage of his master, should be enough to teach this dog obedience. Then the dwarf thought better of it, valuing his own privacy, and left the man in peace. This opportunity for discipline could be enjoyed later.

Olivio opened the door to the hold and adjusted a dim lamp at the top of the stair. He removed his *gallabiyyah* so it would not hang over his face when he was suspended upside down. In the absence of Knuckles, he had contrived his own method for positioning himself in the sling. He pushed the sphinx replica to a spot beneath the hanging harness, then used a stirrup to climb onto the statue. For a moment he rested in the old saddle. There were so many memories, some tender, others excessively energetic.

With the agility born of Dr. Hänger's therapies, the dwarf stood on his head and forearms on the shoulders of the sphinx. He felt at home. He slipped his right foot, then the left, into the sandal leathers. They tightened naturally and held him as he shifted his weight from his arms to his feet. Then he pushed the sphinx to one side. Hanging freely like a bat, gravity defied, he felt his body relax.

The dwarf had come to appreciate the sensation of identifying with bats. Disgusting to some, the vampire-faced chiropteras were not to him. So silent, small and subtle, these nocturnals hunted when no other creature could. Olivio folded his arms across his chest, swinging gently with the rocking of the boat until his eyes closed.

Olivio's heart jumped when a knock interrupted his wild dream about giant cotton worms crawling over Jamila and himself. At first he was uncertain to which world the noise belonged. Something bumped against the starboard side of the vessel. His mind sharpened. A log, refuse or a small boat? Instinct told him he was not alone.

He focused his hearing like a bat. Did he hear a foot tread on the deck above? Soft early light entered the portholes. He heard a splash in the water beside the boat. The dwarf's naked body trembled in the dawn damp. His sensitive nostrils flared as he smelled a peculiar oily odor.

Olivio flexed his knees and swung, extending his arms to reach for the saddled sphinx so that he might reposition it and climb down. As he stretched his arms, recognition cut into him like a headsman's axe.

He knew this evil smell, from fifteen years before: lamp oil. The thatch roof had been soaked in oil, sparked with a torch, and his cottage in Nanyuki had caught in flames.

Swinging too fast, reaching desperately, Olivio's right arm knocked over the sphinx. He heard the saddle fall beside it.

"Maldito seja!" he cursed. He was not surprised to smell the first wisp of smoke. Fear grew in him. The sound of running steps reached him from the deck above his head, followed by the scraping noises of a man clambering down the side of the boat.

The dwarf's eye stared at the nearest porthole, only a few feet from where he swung. The opening darkened when a face peered in. Olivio smelled a second strong odor wafting in from the window, akin to that of some vaguely familiar animal.

With the light behind the face, Olivio could not make out its features, but he felt the eyes that saw his nakedness. His head upside down, the dwarf returned the stare with defiance. The face pulled back. For an instant it was caught by the light that struck it from the east. The dwarf discerned a long thin dark lined face with large eyes. The crown of the head was as bald as his own. Again Olivio noticed the heavy odor.

"Who are you?" the dwarf called out as loudly as he could. There was no reply.

As the face descended he saw a diagonal dent that crossed the scalp. Then an oar pushed off from the side of the Café. The villain was gone.

Sniffing and coughing, terrified of being caught in a second conflagration, Olivio struggled to jackknife up in order to free his feet. The pain of his back and the rush of blood to his head blinded him when he compelled his body to bend. His hands gripped his left knee, then forced their way along his short calf to his ankle. Twisted painfully to one side, he gripped his ankle and held on while he gathered his strength. He felt his knobby spine would burst through the skin of his back. With his left hand he loosened the ankle strap as he attempted to shift all his weight to the other leg. He scrunched the tiny toes of his left foot into a ball and wiggled and twisted like an eel until the foot slipped free.

He gasped and coughed when his body collapsed to its full length, swinging wildly from the right sandal. He saw flames, strangely beautiful, brighten the far corner of the roof of the hold. Beams of light from the portholes pierced the thickening smoke like searchlights through a fog. Sick with dread and fear, he felt the heat from the burning starboard wall.

Still upside down, the dwarf struggled again, furious at his incapacity, but unable to reach his right foot. Gasping for air, thinking he heard new steps on the deck, he choked and grew dizzy from the smoke.

Tariq drove slowly along Shari al-Nil, occasionally stealing a glance at Miss Clove in the backseat of the Daimler. A pious Muslim, his own illicit interest disturbed him. He shook his head and breathed deeply. Had these schoolgirl pinafores been designed for this? He watched the child nibble a pastry and pick the flaky crumbs from her tight blouse and from the notebook in her lap.

From Tariq's right the rising sun cast long shadows of minarets and domes and thin crescents across the brightening surface of the Nile. As the car made the gentle turn around the tip of Garden City, he was alarmed to see black smoke swirling along the edge of the embankment.

"There's a fire!" cried Clove from the backseat, banging on the glass, fear, even pain in her rising voice. "Faster, Tariq, faster! My father's there!"

"Yes, miss," he replied, horrified, pressing the pedal. Her face nearly touching it, his master's daughter pounded on the glass behind him.

"Faster!" the girl screamed again.

Tariq arrived at the Cataract Café and braked with two wheels on the embankment. He hurled himself from the car leaving his door ajar. He bounded down the gangway. Sections of the deck planking danced with flame. Black smoke rose where small pools of oil were trapped against the gunwales. The door to the hold was smoldering.

"Daddy!" Clove screamed as she jumped from the car. She ran down the gangway and followed Tariq across the deck.

"Find my father!" she yelled as the giant Nubian rushed to the door that led below. She saw him lower one shoulder and break through it. A flash of heat and smoke burst out at him, and he recoiled.

As Clove caught up with him,Tariq dashed forward and descended. The girl hesitated, coughing, her eyes pouring tears.

She began to stumble down the steps, her school kerchief clasped over her mouth. As she reached the floor of the hold she was relieved to see Tariq freeing her father from a strange suspended harness. She saw him moving his arms and legs but could not hear his voice over the crackling of the fire and the disturbance made by Tariq as he ripped apart the hanging harness with one hand and clasped her naked father to his chest with the other.

There was only one thing she cared about besides her father: their collection of films stored in a locker under the stair in the giant tin canisters. Seeing him cared for, she struggled to open the warped wooden doors of the film cabinet. Already the wood was hot to the touch.

She was aware of the intense explosive flammability of the nitrate film, even of the necessity to keep each image moving during projection lest a few seconds of heat from the lamp ignite the entire film. The older they were, she had been warned, the more unstable and volatile. Occasionally old ones, ten years of age or more, were destroyed by spontaneous combustion when the gases formed by the deteriorating film were trapped inside the sealed cans.

"Our movies!" she screamed, bracing one foot against the left door and gripping the brass handle of the right door with both hands. It popped open.

The film locker was an oven. A rush of hot air escaped from the cabinet and gusted against her face. Flinching, she turned to the side and saw Tariq moving to the stair.

"Come, miss!" the Nubian called to her.

"Clove! Get out! Get out!" her father hollered as Tariq carried him past. Just before they reached the stair her father reached for her, barely touching her shoulder with his tiny fingers, trying to compel her to come with him.

"Clove! Clove!" the little man cried.

"I'm coming!" she yelled after him. Squinting through the smoke, the girl was unable to read the labels on the edges of the heavy canisters. She knew where her favorites were located on the top shelf. Her eyes tearing, she reached up and ran her fingers along the cans. The tins were so hot they nearly burned her hand.

Tariq hurried up the stair directly above the cabinet. Her father, his face dark, still hollering down at her, was swaddled in the skirt of the Nubian's *gallabiyyah.*

"Stop, Tariq. Get my daughter," she heard him cry as his feet kicked in desperation. A leather strap dangled from one ankle.

Her fingers ranged along the edges of the five tins that held *Captain Blood* and the six that contained *Flesh and the Devil,* Greta Garbo's romance that Clove was due to show the next evening. She knew she could not carry more than one movie, and she paused to make her decision.

At the far corner of the upper shelf her fingertips recognized her Douglas Fairbanks favorites. Older, dating from 1922 and 1924, these tins had a slightly different form, with narrow ridges that ran along the outer rims. She felt the heat rising at her back. She hesitated for an instant, coughing while she considered whether to save *The Thief of Baghdad* or *Robin Hood.*

The Fairbanks. She rose on her toes and reached up to pull towards her the seven canisters of *The Thief of Baghdad.* Her left side felt so hot she feared her pinafore would catch fire.

The first two tins came easily, and she set them at her feet. The next pair, though, seemed to be jammed. Leaping towards her, feeding on itself, she heard the fire crackle more fiercely as it sucked in air through the portholes and vented heat up the stairway.

Coughing, hardly able to see, Clove struggled to pull free the hot canisters. They rolled towards her at the edge of the shelf, slipping down as she attempted to catch them. The falling tins struck her breast, then crashed to the floor and exploded in a flash of flame. She screamed once in a long agonized cry.

Her father lay on his back on the inshore gunwale while Tariq slapped his face and pressed on his chest. He vomited copiously. Black mucus ran from his nostrils.

"We must go back for her!" Olivio demanded as he sat up amidst the swirling smoke. He leaned back against his hands, panting, gathering his energy to stand. Tariq leaned down and wiped his master's nose on his own sleeve. Then he lifted the protesting dwarf, ran up the smoldering gangplank and stretched Olivio on the backseat of the Daimler beside Clove's notebook.

"No!" screamed Olivio between retching coughs. "No! We must save her!"

Tariq left him and dashed back to the Café.

The dwarf lifted the monogrammed camel hair lap rug that hung from the braided cord stretching along the back of the front seat. Wrapping himself in the rug, he hobbled back down to the smoking deck. The rug trailed behind him like a bridal train. The wood of the deck scorched his bare feet and he took a step back onto the carpeted gangway. He felt useless. Never had the physical limitations that defined his life been so cruel.

"Save her!" the dwarf cried as he stumbled forward across the scorching deck. "Save her!"

He saw Tariq hesitate at the flaming entrance to the hold. Along the deck behind the Nubian, chairs and umbrellas burned and sparkled like Roman candles. Clove was somewhere in the hellish furnace below.

The rug covering his head like a hangman's hood, the dwarf came up behind his servant. Tariq took a pace forward and nearly fell into the hold when the doorstep collapsed under his foot. The massive black man held his arms before his face as the heat beat at him. Flames erupted into the air. The hold seemed to rise under the man's feet. Screaming, his *gallabiyyah* on fire, his lungs seared, Tariq collapsed to one side and fell over the far gunwale into the river.

Olivio heard the clang of fire engines as they roared up Shari al-Nil against the traffic.

"Clove! Clove!" he screamed. Tears poured down his blackened face. He held his breath and pressed forward, blinded, stumbling and falling full length with his head hanging down where the top step had been. He felt someone seize him from behind as he sobbed his child's name.

For two hours he watched the men fight the fire as the Cataract Café became a flaming mausoleum for his daughter. The English commander of Cairo's fire service, Captain Sanderson, an occasional guest at the Café, arrived to direct the fight himself. His face blackened, twice unable to penetrate the hold, the officer spoke to Olivio. Two bodies were recovered from the water: the night watchman, his neck slashed, his head nearly severed, and Tariq, unconscious but alive.

For a long time Captain Sanderson himself restrained the dwarf, clutching the twitching weeping little man to him as a mother would hold a crying child. "We will find the man responsible," the commander pledged without conviction.

Finally, Olivio sat shrouded in his blanket on the edge of the embankment, rocking slowly back and forth, staring at his boat while the fire burned on. The Cataract Café was magnificent even as it died.

On the roof above the bar Clove's pigeons were trapped in their smoldering cages. Fire flashed across the roof. The bars of the wooden cages brightened and lit like kindling. He saw the fat grey birds flutter and collapse in the smoky corners of their cells. Others, in the upper rack of cages, flapped about, their wings afire.

Olivio gazed into the morning sky as one pigeon escaped the burning bars and soared from its cage, rising above the Nile with the tip of one wing trailing smoke like the engine of a flying boat.

The last thing the dwarf would remember as he stared down from the stone embankment at the charred ruin of his boat settling into the river was the uncoiling rolls of nitrate film lashing and burning furiously under the water as they sank into the Nile.

— 30 —

Lorenzo Grimaldi was still waiting by the lake for the second flight of *Bersaglieri* to come in. Then he'd be able to free any surviving men on the island before carrying on with his objectives. Something significant must have delayed them. The problem would be the aircraft, not the men. There were never enough transports or bombers for the missions. Each Caproni was being flown to the hilt. He hoped the troopers would bring with them one or two Dubat trackers. Dark silent Somalis with bare feet harder than a tank tread, they could pursue to the death. They would be useful on the hunt.

After the Macchi had stalled and crashed, Grimaldi had spent the night sleeping as best he could under his flight coat on the hard uneven ground beside the aircraft. Before dark he had bound a bit of cloth around a stick and reached into the petrol tank. He stirred about with the stick in the bottom of the tank. When he withdrew it, the sticky rag was speckled and gritty with sand. Enzo was not surprised. He assumed the crash had been caused by the same man who'd fired from the plane at the boats.

He woke frequently during the night, cold and anxious, reviewing his situation, concerned lest he find himself alone in the bush, surrounded by enemies, starving and hunted.

Enzo was thinking more and more of his grandfather and the campaign of '96. He found himself getting closer to Africa than he had ever planned. He wondered if the old count had experienced the same sensation.

His grandfather would be astounded by the scale of the Italian expedition, by the cost of recovering his nation's honor. The northern front alone, stretching from Adowa to Makalle, was one hundred and fifty miles wide, a soldier's nightmare of sheer mountain gorges and wild twisting valleys. On that front, massing before Makalle, Italy had assembled three hundred and fifty cannon, over two thousand machine guns, nearly one hundred tanks, thirty-five thousand pack animals, ten thousand trucks and over one hundred thousand men, all under the protection of one hundred and seventy aircraft. What sacrifices had this campaign required at home? How had these Fascists mobilized such energy?

God help them all if Suez were closed and they were cast loose in Africa. He thought of Rome's enemy, the dreaded Hannibal, cut off in Italy when the galleys of Carthage were destroyed, winning the campaign in the field, but losing it at sea and at home.

A weird barking sound, high-pitched and harsh and quarrelsome, woke him shortly before first light. Troubled, he heard the noise dance about from place to place. He sat up with his back to the fuselage, his pistol in his lap, sipping the grainy dregs of cold coffee from his flight thermos.

What animals could be creating such clamor?

As the light brightened, he discerned an erect dark shape directly in the path of the rising sun. Its long shadow touched his feet. At first he thought it was a man, seated and somewhat shaggy, with a cape across his shoulders. Occasionally the figure rocked back and forth, as if at prayer. He was no more than forty yards away, facing Enzo with the morning sun warming his back. The rising light created a curious orange halo as it came up immediately behind the figure, but the face and body facing him were still in deep shadow. It reminded him of some saint depicted darkly in mosaics in a church at home, the image of the man surrounded by a golden aura or halo of extraordinary brightness.

The creature raised two long hairy arms, and Enzo saw sunlight passing between its curled fingers. The arms stretched far back. The round darkened face opened and yawned. The light caught its long yellow canines. The beast wore not a cape, but a mantle or mane of grey and brown hair that hung from his neck and shoulders almost to the ground. Enzo relaxed and lowered the Beretta. He was facing a monkey.

To Enzo's left, beyond the tail of the plane, two other baboons, somewhat smaller, a lighter greyish brown, but powerfully built and more active than the first, approached him, wary as skirmishers. The two younger animals scrambled over the ground on all fours, then paused and stood and stared before sidling forward with small bounds to left and right. They were barking and coughing, as if communicating with their fellows and summoning courage to advance and examine him.

Distracted by the primates, Grimaldi was surprised by the variety of their calls. When they turned and stood, he observed two bright red hairless triangles in the center of their chests. These must be gelada baboons, peculiar to the Abyssinian highlands, about which his fellow officers made such sordid racial jokes.

The older heavier animal stayed where he was, occasionally turning his head with short stiff movements. Others gathered behind him, youngsters and females, and one or two dark adult males of almost his size. All had prominent nostrils that extended forward well beyond their muzzles. Deep ridges ran under their eyes to the sides of their noses, giving even the younger monkeys an expression of tragedy. The larger baboons appeared to be about three feet at the shoulder when they rested on all fours. Many browsed and foraged among the herbaceous plants and clumps of tussock grass. Some sat on their haunches eating herbs and bulbs and roots with their hands. Others scratched themselves and picked at one another's pelts. Several infants suckled at their mothers' bright red breasts. As if testing Enzo, the two young forward males kept edging towards him, capering and darting closer, then recoiling a few feet.

Uneasy, irritated by these feints, Grimaldi rose and stretched. The monkeys became silent and watchful. Enzo took a small scissor and a metal-backed mirror from his flight kit. He set the mirror against a wing strut and trimmed his mustache. The two younger males withdrew a few paces and watched him. He slapped the last of the coffee onto his face and shaved.

Annoyed by the animals but fascinated, Enzo lifted the mirror and turned it into the rising sun until it reflected a dazzling rectangle of sunlight directly into the eyes of the big baboon. The animal barked angrily and brushed the knuckles of a hand across his dog-like muzzle, then stiffened and drew himself up, turning a bit to one side as Enzo continued to harass him with the blinding light. Now it was evident that his head was nearly black. His eyes and mouth were surrounded by a deeply wrinkled mask of grey and white hair. Long whiskers hung at the corners of his mouth. Two females approached and picked at his fur. The old male ignored them while they groomed him. A third female joined them. She fussed over the long tufted leonine tail that curled on the ground beside the patriarch. Tiring of this amusement, Colonel Grimaldi put away his mirror.

Preparing to relieve himself, feeling strangely embarrassed, he turned to one side and urinated. The monkeys stared at him and began to chatter. Steadily their number increased to a hundred or more.

Hungry and impatient, waiting for the sound of aircraft, he watched one party of juveniles knock a birds' nest from a thorn bush. The young baboons pursued the hopping fledglings, catching them and batting them about as the baby birds struggled to take wing. At length the largest of the group of monkeys held the birds by their twitching wings and ate the tiny bodies.

Grimaldi decided to walk the few miles to the *Bersaglieri* camp by the lake. There, at least, he would find food and a rifle. He tightened his light flight boots and began to walk.

The baboons that surrounded Enzo moved with him. The two young male scouts bounded on ahead. Others skipped along to both sides. The old leader grunted, as if complaining, then followed laboriously at a distance, sometimes advancing with a heavy hopping sideways motion. The females and young kept in the center of the troop. Several small infants hung from their mothers' bellies. Others, larger, perched on the backs of their dams.

Almost insolent, one of the larger darker males, formerly a companion of the leader, followed directly in Grimaldi's path. The big animal, perhaps four feet tall when he stood, chattered rapidly. His tone rose as if excited. A second male joined him. They followed Enzo more and more closely, as if challenging him, their manner more confident and aggressive than that of the two younger males.

When a large thorn stabbed through one boot, Enzo paused to remove it. Feeling vulnerable with his foot bare, he tried to concentrate as he removed the tip of the thorn from the ball of his foot with his pocketknife. As he fussed over it, he heard the animals noisily shifting about and gabbling nearby, closer and closer. When he looked up, the entire troop was swarming after him.

"Basta!" he yelled at them, growing nervous.

He had heard tales of male baboon pursuing women, particularly during their menstrual periods, drawn by the scent, but he had not expected this.

The Italian turned and faced the pursuing monkeys.

"Buongiorno!" he called out, drawing his Beretta and aiming it at the most aggressive male. For an instant the tall baboon hesitated and stared Enzo in the eye, his mouth open, his long teeth exposed. Grimaldi fired twice. The big male screamed like a child and leapt in the air. Then he collapsed on his side, coughing and sighing, both hands pressed against his lower stomach.

Grimaldi watched the other lead male bend over him and pick at his companion's wounds. The uninjured animal stood and trumpeted, rushing forward a few steps. His dark eyebrows rose, revealing an angry red triangle above each eye. Enzo raised his arm to shoot again. The baboon stopped advancing and jumped about in one spot. Then the animal sat on his haunches, rocking forwards and back, shaking and blinking as he stared at the Italian officer. The monkey rolled back his upper lip and displayed long yellow teeth and red gums, as if smiling, offering peace. Grimaldi hesitated, then decided not to waste the bullets.

As Enzo walked on, the troop gathered around the dying animal, first in near silence, then in a chaos of high-pitched barking and chattering. When he looked back, the creatures had arranged themselves in a settlement or camp. Enzo found himself feeling as if he had just experienced his first skirmish in the bush.

Nearing the lake, Grimaldi spotted the prone figure of the young soldier who had been injured in the jump. The supplies, not yet organized, were assembled near him in their drop containers.

"*Soldato*!" Enzo called to the crippled trooper, pleased to find a man to talk with after his bizarre encounter with the baboons. *"Soldato!"* There was no reply.

Before he reached the man, Enzo came upon the corpses of three other soldiers. Two had been shot once in the chest. The third man had been hit twice, the two wounds very close together.

"Fine shooting," he murmured. The man must be a hunter.

The bodies had been mauled and partly eaten during the night, not by a heavy animal like a lion or leopard, or even a hyena, he guessed, but by something smaller, perhaps a jackal or fox. Only the exposed flesh had been taken, mostly about the neck and shoulders. It was neatly done, reminding him of the fastidious picking of a well-bred house cat. Enzo found himself strangely undisturbed, as if here this was all to be expected.

The wounded soldier was also dead. Grimaldi knelt and turned him over. A single bullet had entered under the man's chin. His forehead and eyes were blown away. Black ants and a few large beetles, dark and shiny-shelled as scarabs, were at work around his head. A rifle was still clutched in the soldier's hands: suicide. Enzo closed his eyes and crossed himself, wondering how much the man had suffered. He dragged the three others over by their boots and lay the four men side by side. They were too many for him to bury in this rocky ground. Let the *Bersaglieri* dig their own graves, he thought, concerned mostly about the effect of the losses on his mission. Uzielli should have taken better care of his men.

Grimaldi did not want to spend another night on his own. If the new drop of paratroopers did not come by nightfall, he would swim back to the island and do what he could for the men there. Enzo decided to make a small camouflaged float to push before him, behind which he could conceal himself, and on which to keep the Beretta and a rifle dry. A carbine would serve well for the close rough work he expected on the island. He would pay back that wounded monk who had pounded the boy's head with a stone.

Enzo gathered the four rifles, cleaned them and examined each with care. Three were carbines, short-barrelled rifles well suited for light infantry. The fourth was a more refined weapon, an *Assassino,* the new sniper variant of the Carcano, with an extra long barrel for better range and accuracy. Now it was time to test it in the field. Enzo balanced the rifle in his hands before loading it and checking the scope. Then he sat and sipped rough red wine from a flask he had found on one of the dead. True *vino scarso,* it reminded him of the family wines the peasant households made for themselves. Still, he was grateful for it.

Soon it would be dark, and he realized he should distance himself from the bodies in case lion or hyena were attracted. He walked to the mimosa grove and began work on a small float. He tied the reeds and branches together with the bootlaces of two dead soldiers.

Suddenly his neck prickled. He froze. Something had been missing from the cockpit when he climbed aboard the Macchi for the unsuccessful takeoff: the snapshot of his English girl. Gwenn's photograph had been stolen, ripped from the control panel. There was only one other man who could be interested in the picture. He, too, had been bound for Ethiopia, and the bastard knew how to shoot. Whatever else he was not, Rider was probably a dangerous man in the bush. But if it was Rider, Enzo could not figure out what might have brought him to this lake.

When the float was completed, Enzo waited for darkness. With some distaste he entered the water at the edge of the grove, pushing before him the float on which rested his boots, carbine and Beretta. He prayed his movements would not attract crocodiles, of which he had an exceptional horror. The reeds extended farther out than he had realized. As he breast-stroked forward among them, he heard the sound of an engine echo across the still surface of Lake Zwai.

At first he thought it must be the Capronis. But surely they would not come at night. He paddled back among the thicker reeds. The sound clarified as it grew louder. It was a motor vehicle, perhaps a truck. He saw a single light bouncing slowly down a twisting trail towards the lake. He doubted that the vehicle could be Italian.

Enzo returned to the thicker vegetation just as the truck pulled up and turned around a short distance away. Up to his waist in water, he waded into a dense patch of reeds under the dark canopy of a mimosa branch. He held the float directly in front of his face. The weapons were still dry. He settled in place, one hand on the rifle. Several voices approached, speaking English and various African tongues.

The reeds and darkness denied him a clear view, but he was aware of several men entering the water nearby. There was splashing and groaning as they worked, moving things in and near the water. There seemed to be five or six men of different nationalities. He heard a European curse in a guttural accent, then the exclamation, *"Das Silber!"*

"Put the silver chests in the truck," a man said in English.

Enzo recognized the voice: Gwenn's husband, the hunter Anton Rider.

Grimaldi shifted the float and gripped the rifle. If he moved the bolt to chamber a round, they would hear him, and there were too many for him to fight. He waited until they were boarding the truck. Then he climbed stiffly from the water and scrambled barefoot through the brush with the rifle. The engine started. He raised the carbine and fired several times. A scream satisfied him that at least his first shot had scored.

Grimaldi realized that he had already lost control of the mission. Both his career and his life were in danger. The enemy had recovered the silver. The surviving *Bersaglieri* were somewhere on the island in the lake, and no reinforcements had arrived. He must save the *Bersaglieri* himself to have any chance of succeeding. As the crescent moon rose, he gripped the edge of the float with both hands and began to kick with his feet.

After a few moments Enzo heard a snarling, then an angry roaring from the shore behind him. Although he had never head it before, the sound was unmistakable. He ceased swimming and rested with his arms on the float, thinking of the lion he had shot from the air. The lake itself seemed to tremble with the roars that echoed across the water. A lion must be driving hyena from the bodies.

Enzo swam to the reverse side of the island, avoiding the shore where he had seen the monks beating his men. After the swim, he knelt amidst a cluster of stunted palms near the water, recovering his breath. He pulled on his boots and checked the rifle and pistol. He moved as silently as he could from tree to tree and bush to bush.

Enzo found a dark stone monument in a clearing before him, a shorter primitive version of Cleopatra's needle. Beyond that, past some bush and cactus, he saw the remains of a fire glowing in the darkness, but still no life or movement. Where, he wondered, were his men, and the monks?

Grimaldi crept around the edge of the clearing. A thick smell reached him, a mixture of long-dead meat and sweet muskiness. He heard a low snarling to his right, a subdued defensive growling. He grew still and stared. He made out a low cage suspended above the ground, then several more. Most were occupied by some mid-sized animal he could not identify. He crept on. The cat-like creatures shifted heavily in their cages as he passed.

He passed a larger cage near the end of the clearing, perhaps one designed for two animals, he thought. The breeding cage? But something different was inside it. Guessing it might be a man, he approached the cage with care.

It was indeed a man, naked, bent double like a closed hinge. His legs were extended forward on the floor of the cage. His head was forced low between his knees. His back was arched like a bow against the roof of the cage. Grimaldi crept closer. He heard moans and long slow gasps. The smell of the animals was thick around them. Enzo put his head near the foot of the cage and sought to identify the unconscious prisoner. He could tell only that the man was one of his.

He moved on, not wishing to cause a commotion, surprised by how well his eyes had adjusted to the darkness. In Africa he was using his ears and his nose and his eyes as he never had before.

Just then Grimaldi stumbled against a mound of fresh earth. He found himself embracing a stone cross as he fell, cracking one knee when he went down. Suppressing a cry, he crouched beside the cross and traced the headstone with one hand. He felt the arcs and extra angles. It was the Coptic cross of Ethiopia. There were two more beside it. Apart from the stones, the graves appeared fresh, even hasty. The mounds of earth yielded under his foot. Were these the monks killed by that fool Uzielli on his first visit to the island? He tried to imagine what revenge the monks might have exacted on Uzielli.

Farther along he saw a long low building, a crude shed or lodge. Firelight glowed dimly through cracks in the rough walls. There were no windows. He heard snores as he approached a broad open doorway at the far end.

Grimaldi knew he would have to kill the monks to save his men and himself. Enzo crossed himself before he stood. He leaned the rifle against the side of the doorway. He drew his Beretta, then hesitated. After all, these were Christian monks. He was an Italian officer. Colonel Grimaldi put the pistol back in his belt.

He stepped inside what seemed like Dante's dungeon. The chamber was suffocating: low and dark and smoke-filled. A strange sweet odor, perhaps drugs or incense, was thick in the air. A low fire glowed at the far end. The remains of some half-eaten animal lay nearby, probably a goat or dog. Crude baskets and bunches of rotting vegetables hung from poles that crossed the ceiling. A tangle of firewood was piled against one wall. Enzo's eyes were smarting.

Two white men lay naked, facedown near the fire. Their wrists were bound to their ankles behind their backs, so tightly that their shoulders and knees were off the ground. Seven or eight other figures, black monks cloaked in white, lay on mats scattered here and there. One man was sitting against a wall, his head on his chest, a shiny cross in his lap. Grimaldi thought he recognized the white-haired wounded monk or abbot who had crushed the skull of the boy from Casteggio. The blood of the abbot's belly wound had dried on his skirt like a stiff black apron.

Enzo drew the Beretta and crouched, the better to shoot any rising figure outlined against the firelight.

The monk nearest Enzo lifted his head. He screamed and began to rise.

Grimaldi fired twice. The man collapsed. Other monks leapt up and Enzo emptied his pistol into the confusion of struggling white robes. The noise of the shots was loud and sharp in the confined space. One monk fell. Two or three were wounded. Jamming the light Beretta into his belt, Enzo stepped back into the doorway and seized the carbine in both hands.

Once, twice, again and again, Grimaldi fired into the scrambling shadows. A din of pain and rage greeted the shots. The monks staggered towards the fire. Several lay still. Most were wounded.

Enzo saw the wounded white-haired monk watching him from his seated position by the wall. The abbot gripped his cross with both hands and rose to his feet. He leaned against the wall. The lower half of his robe was dark with blood. Rocking from side to side, the priest walked towards Grimaldi with slow uneven steps. He stopped two feet away and raised the silver cross. Fresh blood dripped from the hem of his robe. As Enzo hesitated, the abbot swung violently and struck the Italian officer in the face. Enzo felt a sharp brief pain when the bloody cross cut his cheekbone.

He stepped back as if fencing. He reversed the carbine and drove the butt into the abbot's wounded belly. The Ethiopian howled and staggered backwards. Nearby, an unwounded monk fell to his knees and clasped his hands and cried out.

"Devil!" Enzo yelled as he punched the abbot in the stomach again with the weapon. The old man screamed and collapsed into the fire.

Enzo turned aside and knocked over the kneeling monk with a slap of the rifle stock. Seeing no one threatening him, he knelt and freed the two Italians with his knife. One of them moved. The man's back was covered in hair, thick and black as the pelt of a bear. Startled, Grimaldi recognized Captain Uzielli when the soldier rolled onto his back and stared up. Enzo turned over the other man. He, too, was alive. Both soldiers had blood and some mark on their right cheeks. Cursing, Uzielli began to move his feet and rub his wrists and ankles.

The abbot struggled to his knees, the skirt of his robe on fire. He lifted a brand and hurled it at the three Italians. Sparks flying as it spun end over end, the flaming branch flew past and settled against the far wall. Flames rose in a scarlet curtain.

Coughing in the thick smoke, Enzo dragged the weaker Italian towards the door.

"Come on, Uzielli, on your feet!" Grimaldi yelled. The captain crawled unsteadily after him as fire flared along the wall.

Enzo stopped a few yards from the entrance. Neither of the two *Bersaglieri* could use his legs. Each had a wound branded on his cheek in the shape of a cross. There was no gratitude, he saw, in Uzielli's eyes. Of course there wouldn't be, he thought irritably.

"Use this," Grimaldi ordered, handing the rifle and a handful of cartridges to the kneeling captain before reloading his Beretta. Now he must free the soldier in the cage. Enzo looked up and saw smoke pouring from the doorway to the lodge. The first flames flickered through the roof. Two monks stepped out through the smoke. One, wounded, leaned on the shoulder of the other.

"Porcile!" Uzielli yelled hoarsely as he fired four times from his knees.

Clutching each other, the two monks fell together. Flames ran up the sides of the entrance, framing a smoldering figure standing in the doorway like a human lantern. The man's white hair was on fire. Grimaldi and Uzielli fired. The abbot cried out once and collapsed backwards into the flaming shed. He screamed out one word: *"Iyyasus!"*

— 31 —

It reminded Anton of the way things used to be. Gwenn was asleep in the tent. He was content, but uncertain how to behave with her. For the moment they were alone, save for the six mules and horses. It was his favorite sort of camp: lean, almost hidden, set beneath a stand of blue gums in an oxbow bend in the stream. And no clients. One could hear the water coursing.

Dr. Fergus had gone strolling by the stream, taking the line and lures and flies he had saved from the Red Cross truck. Perhaps he understood enough to leave the couple alone. Diwani and Laboso were hunting. All the rest had left three days before with the truck and the silver and most of the animals. Intrepid Harriet, he was certain, would be carrying her precious film herself.

If they didn't find fuel, the truck would be useless anyway, and it made an easy target from the air. But it would be hell moving the silver without it. The Americans, after all, had paid for the safari and he owed them a fast run for the border. Kimathi would hold the camp together, and Ernst would keep them moving. Ernst had assumed that he would be in charge, but Anton had made it clear to all that Kimathi was head man until he himself caught up. "You're our guest, Ernst. No need to work." Anton had smiled at his German friend, knowing his overbearing ways. "Kimathi speaks for me." In reply, Ernst had grunted disapprovingly.

They'd planned the first rendezvous for Bulbula, the village at the bottom of the next Rift lake, Langana. If things went well, Kimathi might come back for them with the truck. Otherwise it would be slow going with Gwenn. He wondered how long they had before the Italian army would be after them.

Anton walked to the stream with two canvas buckets. He stripped and sat in the cool water and washed himself and wrung out his shirt. His gun belt rested nearby on a flat rock. He lay on his back on the polished river stones with his eyes closed and let the water wash over his face. He rubbed the bump on his ribs where an old buff had hammered him in the forest of the Aberdares.

Anton pulled on his khaki shorts and returned to camp, emptying the buckets into the black pot set in the coals. While the water warmed and his shirt dried by the fire, he squeezed the last two lemons into a tin mug. He added a tot of whisky and a big spoonful of thick dark wild honey, the gift of the *apis mellifer,* the small active bees that yielded his favorite form of sugar. He took two long swallows of whisky from the bottle, filled the mug with hot water, stirred it and walked to the tent.

Gwenn lay with her unbandaged eye open. A cup of vivid yellow wildflowers was set in the dirt by her narrow cot. His Rigby, loaded, rested on the medicine chest. There was a fresh smaller dressing on the left side of Gwenn's face, and her left shoulder was in plaster. She had some color but was thinner than he had ever seen her. Her arms were slender pale tubes.

"Are you hungry?" he said, sitting on the ground by her cot and stirring the steaming grog.

"No," she said. "Thirsty."

"You doctors are always terrible patients." He fed her some grog with a wooden spoon so as not to burn her lips.

"I'm not a doctor."

"That's not what Fergus says. He told me he'd let you operate on him."

Pleased despite herself, very happy he was back, Gwenn smiled and drank another spoonful. "It's good." She helped him raise the cooling cup to her lips.

"What wonderful honey," she said, looking over the top of the mug at his bare chest and arms.

"Later you're going to eat some stew," Anton said firmly, aware of her noticing his body.

When she finished drinking, she smiled at him with a spark in her green eyes. She had the loveliest face he knew, her lips slightly puffy now but still shaped, her bones well defined, with character, yet feminine, smooth and rounded.

"How did you get these new scars?" she asked, touching one of the leopard marks on his shoulder. "They're still a little fiery and soft."

Despite her natural reserve, Gwenn found herself comparing lovers. Lorenzo's body wasn't bad, she thought, but it wasn't substantial enough. There was no definition to the muscles of his arms, and she'd never liked the white hair that covered his chest. Anton's body was even better than she'd remembered, long-muscled but knotty and hard.

Anton was beginning to be aroused by her attention. "A cat caught me in the Din Din, a black leopard."

"Too bad you didn't get proper care right away," she said lightly, thinking how at ease he was with all the hazards of the bush. Her fingertips dallied on the long parallel scars. "These're going to be thick and rubbery as a garden hose."

"I was lucky as it was," he said, trying to recall how long it had been since they last made love. "Wouldn't have made it without Kimathi."

"Will you wash me?" Gwenn placed one hand on his bare chest. "I can't stand being like this."

Anton drew back the sheet and the green camp blanket. She was naked. For a moment he felt incredibly awkward. He was amazed how unchanged she was, her figure still young and spare, almost girlish, the softening of childbirths countered by her active life on the farm, and her recent hardships.

He went outside to the fire and dipped his shirt in the pot. He wrung it out and reentered the tent with the shirt and soap and a bucket of water.

Her feet extended over the bottom of the cot. He bathed them slowly with warm soapy water. Then he rinsed them, bending each foot to stretch the tendons of her ankles, slowly squeezing and flexing the toes and arches back and forth in opposite directions like the two parts of a pepper grinder.

"You never did that before," she said softly, delighting in the moment before she wondered who had taught him.

"You were never injured," he said, recognizing the change in her voice. "This is part of your medical program."

He squeezed each foot tightly in the hot wet shirt. Giving in to the sensation, yielding to his touch, Gwenn moaned. She thought of the first time they had made love, on a hilltop north of the farm. Did her young husband still want her now? She wondered how much their ages really mattered. She was fortunate, she knew, in the youthfulness of her body, but she feared her injuries, especially to her face, would make her less attractive.

Anton admired her perfect slender legs as he sponged them with the shirt. Even the American girls did not have legs like these, with such long thighs and just enough muscle to shape the calves and diminish the ankles.

Her ribs had always been too evident, and they were more so now. The bones projected at the lower corner on each side. She still had a schoolgirl's skin and small high breasts, but the nipples were larger since she'd had the boys. He liked the change.

Uncertain what she wished, careful not to disturb the wounded shoulder, he gently washed her breasts, first with his hands until they firmed, then lightly with the shirt, wishing not to seem to linger, lest she think he was doing it for himself, yet carrying on long enough to give her pleasure. She closed her eyes and turned her head, pressing her right cheek to the pillow. He saw her bite her lower lip as she recognized his touch.

"Make love to me," she whispered. Her feet parted at the foot of the cot.

Anton went on his knees beside her and kissed her slowly between her legs, aware that his face was scratching her smooth upper thighs as he moved his head.

"What are you doing?" she murmured.

"Just a recce," he said quietly, looking up before he entered her with his tongue. Slowly he transferred her moisture upwards, leaving her repeatedly before licking her again. He loved her smell.

"You must keep still," he said after a time when her body trembled and her knees rocked gently from side to side. Confident now, relaxing, welcoming her surrender, he felt her place one hand on his neck, then run her fingers up through his hair against the back of his scalp.

"Keep still," he said again, raising his head.

"I'm the doctor," Gwenn murmured. "And mind the flowers. Oh."

She felt him touch her more slowly with a familiar expert intimacy, his tongue entering her until she was running wet, his thumb and long fingers penetrating her separately and pinching and rubbing her between them, then gently teasing her, pressing along her bone, until the petals of her flesh rose and trembled with each slight caress, then leaving her untouched for a moment, her body warm and waiting, eager for each new attention.

She knew he was teasing her, that he had not forgotten how she was. Long ago he had learned how to make her want him, but he seemed different now, perhaps more deliberate than hungry. Yet it was not the deliberation of an overly practiced man, as it sometimes seemed with Lorenzo, but rather the care of a man wanting to reestablish himself as a lover, to approach her again through her body.

Colonel Grimaldi watched the *Bersaglieri* fall like angels from the sky. Never had he thought the army could be such a welcome sight.

For three days he and Captain Uzielli had cared for the two disabled *Bersaglieri.* One of the men was now on his feet. They had paddled to the mainland two by two in the only undamaged reed canoe they had discovered on the island.

The private in the cage, who had injured a monk before he'd been subdued, might never walk again. His naked body had been so tightly folded into the cage that Enzo was unable to drag him free by pulling on his feet and arms. While Enzo removed the bamboo pins to free the gate at the foot of the cage, he had heard several shots behind him. Uzielli was finishing off the wounded monks and hunting down others who had escaped from a second hut.

"Captain," said Grimaldi when Uzielli, out of breath, joined him at the cage, "help me get this man out."

Uzielli reloaded his carbine and wiped his short bayonet on the grass before helping the colonel cut and wrench apart the bars to free the young trooper.

"This one won't be good for much," said Uzielli sourly as the man slowly unfolded on the ground. "Spine's done. Look at those bones in his back. They stand out like the knuckles on my fist."

Once ashore on the mainland, they found the four dead *Bersaglieri* scattered in a cluster of rock and thorn bush near the old camp.

"Looks like the lions had their fill of these *bambinos,* starting with their buttocks and thighs," said Uzielli, kneeling and examining the corpses one by one. "But they've all been shot, Colonel." He looked up at Grimaldi with dark mistrusting eyes. "Who did this? Who killed my men?"

Enzo saw that somehow this officer considered him responsible for these deaths.

"Must be the same man who fired at us from my plane," said Grimaldi. "We'll move the bodies over there," he added, pointing to a patch of less rocky ground. "Then you can start digging. Come on." He lifted each man under the arms while Uzielli took their feet and they lay the men neatly side by side.

Uzielli spent most of a day burying the four men in one deep grave. He did not expect or ask for the colonel's assistance. From time to time he stopped for a smoke, sitting on the the edge of the common grave with his legs dangling inside. He thought of the men he had lost in the pacification of Tripolitania and Cyrenaica: the ambush at the oasis of Al Jufrah, when a crumbling sandstone wall surrounding an irrigated palm garden turned into a line of gunfire as his thirsty men approached at dusk; the mutilated corpses of the garrison at Bir al-Harash, each naked savaged body carrying its own pattern of burns and cuts; and the decapitated Italian, the usual boy soldier, found in a broken-down truck on a track in the sand sea near Sarir, with his charred head set on the seat between his legs and the photos of his village and family still taped to the dashboard of the vehicle.

Uzielli was always famished in the field, and as he scraped and dug into the hard ground he grew hungrier. When other men thought of women, he often thought of food.

Pausing, wiping the sweat from his face with both hands, Uzielli concluded that right now he'd give two *Bersaglieri* for a fine *sanguinaccio* fresh from the butcher's steaming pot. When he was little, Arnaldo, the Sicilian butcher, had let him into the back of the shop to watch him make the blood sausages. Young Uzielli had stood in the corner on the sawdust with a calf's head between his feet and watched the butcher knot one end of a nice length of cow intestine.

"Don't stand there, boy," Arnaldo had yelled at him. "Stir the blood!" The butcher had pointed at the pot of seasoned pig's blood that stood warming on one corner of the stove. "If I see one clot in there, I'll make you drink it all and you'll turn into a hog."

Uzielli had reached into the pot to his elbow and stirred the blood slowly with his arm.

Then Arnaldo ordered him to lift up the pot and carefully pour the rich fluid into the gaping intestine as the butcher held its lips wide. Finally Arnaldo threw in a handful of extra salt and knotted up the top before lowering the bloated organ into a huge pot of boiling water. When Uzielli returned in the afternoon, the water was cooling and the coils of *sanguinaccio* were solid and hard and big around as a boa constrictor. The boy had plucked one out and run home with it so they could devour it still warm and alive from the pot.

Watching Uzielli dig, Enzo noted the dark scab of the cross that marked the captain's cheek. The usual cycle of atrocities was underway. Once again Enzo would be compelled to do his share. But even in Libya his countrymen had not used poison gas. He wondered if there was something about Africa that brought out the worst in Europeans when they fought here. On the Italian side, was there a mythology of African savagery that built a brutalizing fear, and was it partly that these dark enemies seemed a different breed of man?

In the end, of course, the reasons wouldn't matter. He had never received such rigorous unqualified orders. The films and the safari that took the motion pictures must be destroyed. Nothing else mattered: not the silver, not the *Bersaglieri* themselves, and certainly not the rules of war.

While the captain toiled with the shovel, Colonel Grimaldi paused near the feet of the dead men, matching each of theirs to his own.

Painted with gritty red dust, the captain stood at one end of the wide rocky grave, the short pack shovel in his hands. Watching the colonel, he stopped digging and wiped his face. He looked up angrily without speaking as Grimaldi opened a pen knife and cut a strip of cloth from a dead soldier's shirt. Then the air force officer bent and unlaced the field boots of one of Uzielli's late comrades. Enzo was aware of the captain staring at him, his eyeballs protuberant like those of a deep sea fish habituated to pressure and darkness.

"Colonel," called Uzielli, trying to control his voice, "you can't . . ."

"Dig deeper, Captain, or the lions'll be back." Grimaldi looked the soldier in the eye.

Uzielli wished he could give the colonel just one chop with his shovel, or even one good blow with the side of his hand. He thought of old Arnaldo taking a plump soft rabbit from its cage. Holding the twitching creature by its heavy hind legs, the butcher would strike the rabbit one mortal blow with the edge of his hand, just at the base of its furry long brown ears. *"Scutulare l'orecchi,"* Arnaldo used to call it, "shaking down the ears."

The colonel strolled to the lake with the boots and an empty bologna tin. He was beginning to enjoy the crisp air of the highlands. Aware that Uzielli was watching him, he cleaned the dirt and blood from the dead man's boots. He used the rag to polish them with grease from the tin, finishing the job just as the new paratroopers gathered on the ground a hundred yards away.

The fifteen new men included a lieutenant and one Dubat tracker, a small thin wrinkled black man who had just made his first jump when the paratroopers pushed him from the plane. Restless and reserved, he still seemed shaken by the experience. An ancient rifle, nearly as tall as the tracker himself, was strapped to his back. The man removed a turban that was knotted into the green sash around his waist and lowered his chin as he arranged it on his head with careful fingers.

"Colonnello!" said the new officer, saluting aggressively. "Lieutenant Calandro, at your orders, sir."

Grimaldi studied him carefully. A short open-faced balding officer, the lieutenant appeared to cultivate his resemblance to the Duce. Enzo knew the type. Fascist destiny was heavy on the young man's shoulders. The Duce's dream had given him a life.

Lieutenant Calandro, ignoring Uzielli, dressed his men for the colonel's inspection. Grimaldi reviewed them one by one, his hands clasped behind his back.

"Where'd you find this Dubat?" said Grimaldi as he examined the African's aged weapon. The thick barrel of the rifle was bound to the stock with bands of leather and metal.

"We borrowed him from one of our *bandas* that's been skirmishing with the Ethiopians in the Ogaden, sir," said Calandro eagerly. "They say he can track like a starving dog after a rabbit."

"Could be useful," said Grimaldi, noticing the Dubat's gnarled feet and rough leather sandals. "And do you bring news of our quarry, Lieutenant?"

"A pilot of your squadron, sir, one of your wingmen from the raid on the enemy encampment, has spotted the truck on which the photographer was mounted . . ."

"How far?" interrupted Grimaldi.

"Heading south, sir, below Lake Zwai."

"Did he destroy it?" asked the colonel. "Did he kill them?"

"No, sir. He was nearly out of fuel. Just managed to strafe the truck once.

Said he left it broken down and smoking at the edge of a stream. Doesn't know if he killed any of the . . ."

"Where?" Grimaldi wanted to know. "Precisely where was the truck?"

Not concealing his satisfaction, Lieutenant Calandro drew a map and an envelope from his pack and handed them to the colonel.

Enzo examined the map in silence and found a large penciled X marked across a river to the south. To one side, his wingman had written, *"Buona caccia, Colonnello!"*

"The pilot says he braved a storm of ground fire," said the lieutenant in a skeptical tone, shrugging his shoulders, evidently himself not impressed with the role of the *Regia Aeronautica.* "The army, however, is doing its best to send a small flying column in pursuit, sir. They should meet us here in two days with transport."

"What's the war news, Lieutenant?" Enzo said as he cut open the heavy envelope.

"Advancing on all fronts, sir! *Sempre avanti*!" Calandro said, echoing one of the Duce's slogans. Eager to report, he used both hands to assist his response. "But the savages gave us a beating at some pass in the mountains called Abbi Addi, where they surrounded our Eritreans and butchered the lot. We got them back near Amba Alagi. That's an old fortress in the moun. . ."

"I know where Amba Alagi is, Lieutenant. My grandfather was there," snapped Grimaldi impatiently. "Continue."

"The last of old Emperor Menelik's generals was there, Colonel, some ras or other, with ten thousand men. We gassed them all out of their defenses. Then hit them with the biggest aerial bombardment in history. Two hundred and fifty planes. Killed the old general and both his sons. They say his bodyguard carried him off the field on the same rhino skin shield he'd had at Adowa in 1896. Then our men fought on up to the crest and raised the flag of Savoy."

"Very good, Calandro. Anything else?"

"They say the worst problems've been in Geneva, sir. Talk about oil sanctions, but nothing's happened. They're all afraid of the *Il Duce.* The French and British proposed a peace plan, giving us most of what we hold now, in the Ogaden and Tigre, and some sort of economic protectorate over much of the rest, but giving Ethiopia an outlet to the Red Sea and some corridor or other . . ."

"And what happened?" interrupted Grimaldi anxiously, fearing the war might end without full victory.

"That black emperor turned the whole thing down, said it would destroy his country and betray the League. Big racket in Europe. I think the British foreign secretary resigned."

Enzo nodded and read his dispatch. "Your orders are unchanged: recover the silver and destroy the party of photographers. There must be no film and no witnesses. We are sending what support and transport we can, but the army is now fully engaged. We are conquering a country four times the size of Italy and the campaign grows harder day by day."

Sobered by a brief service to bury their brother *Bersaglieri,* the men camped quietly in the evening, posting sentries and chatting by two fires. Enzo noticed Lieutenant Calandro trying to avoid Uzielli, after making it clear to both senior officers that he had been ordered to report to the air force colonel rather than the captain. No doubt, thought Enzo as he fell asleep, Calandro knew more about Uzielli than he did.

They set off shortly after dawn following a breakfast of coffee, old pizza bread and salami. Orabi, the tracker, scorned the coffee and ate a handful of dried peas and his own *enjara* that he took from a small sack that hung from his neck by a leather cord.

"Uzielli, Calandro!" Grimaldi called. The two men hurried to him while the colonel folded his map. "We'll leave the trooper who hurt his ankle here in camp with this chap with the damaged back. The rest of us will go to the end of the lake and pick up the trail of the truck where I saw it leave with the silver. Uzielli, you and your men know the area, you're on point." Then he added the orders he knew Uzielli would resent. "Full packs, silent march, no running."

Enzo led the others to the end of the lake. From there they followed the track of the truck, at first an easy matter not requiring the skills of Orabi.

Impatient, annoyed with the orders, Captain Uzielli wished to break into the *Bersaglieri* trot, both to challenge Calandro's unit, and to test the colonel himself. Except for Grimaldi and Orabi, every man carried fifty pounds or more.

Uzielli signalled urgently from a hilltop. The column hurried forward.

An abandoned truck waited for them at an old campsite. Well laid out, the camp bore the signs of hasty departure. A pile of laundry rested on flat rocks by a stream. Several tent pegs remained in the ground. A few empty tins and bottles lay unburied near a small square garbage pit. One of the men went through the laundry and held some pieces in the air: two sheets, one still blood-stained, a towel, socks, and a woman's undergarment.

"Una vacca sanguinosa!" the *Bersaglieri* shouted. The other men laughed. A soldier brought the empty containers to Grimaldi and Calandro. Ovaltine, Chivers Lime Marmalade, Senior Service Cigarettes, Col. Truscott's Rangoon Chutney: all the disgusting leavings of an English camp, the British empire in its domestic detail. It reminded Enzo of the worst of Cairo.

A heavy Bedford, the battered lorry bore the markings of the Red Cross and the Red Crescent. At once angry and regretful, Enzo thought instantly of Gwenn Rider. This was the sort of mischief she had chosen over him, repaying generosity with disloyalty. She had made her choice. Whatever it cost her, it would not be his doing.

The Bedford's tank was empty. The radiator was cracked. The spark plugs had been removed. Two tires were slashed.

"Bastards wanted to make sure we had to walk," said Uzielli.

"What, are your men tired already?" asked Grimaldi. "Another day or two and we'll have our own trucks."

"We have a job to do, sir," said Uzielli. "Transport would help."

Orabi pointed at the treads of the tires and to the track they had been following. He shook his head and pointed south.

"Two vehicles," Grimaldi said. "The one we're following has gone on."

Enzo and Orabi and the two officers made a slow circle around the site. They found footprints and animal tracks heading west on a slightly different bearing than the truck. "They've split into two parties," Grimaldi said, wondering which one was Rider's. It would not surprise him if the English hunter was on foot.

"Calandro, you and your men come with me. The truck's easy enough to follow, and it can't have gotten far after being hit from the air."

Then the colonel walked over to Uzielli, satisfied after the experience with the monks that the captain had a taste for thorough housecleaning.

"Uzielli, you take four troopers and Orabi and follow the small party that separated from the vehicle on foot. You'll know what to do when you find them."

Diwani spotted them first: five men trotting steadily along the track he and Laboso had taken after they had left the bwana's camp. He tapped Laboso's shoulder and pointed. Instantly the two Africans dropped behind a line of rocks. Then they saw a sixth man.

A slim black man went before the others, crouching, touching the ground with one hand, and running on. A *shifta* tracker leading the white soldiers. The Dubat wore a wide white turban with one loose end that hung down along his right cheek. His chest was naked save for a folded green sash that crossed it diagonally beneath the strap of his rifle. His white culottes were gathered at his waist by a wide leather cartridge belt.

"Laboso," said Diwani, "run to camp and tell Rider." Slower on his feet, but a better shot, Diwani was confident what each of them could do. "I will hunt a bit, kill one or two, lead them off."

"You know which man to kill first?" said Laboso, smiling. "The one who thinks he is a tracker. Look at that filthy Dubat. He follows the track like a jackal, nose on the ground, eyes only seeing as far as he can smell."

"Run, you stupid Luo," said Diwani, nearly knocking Laboso down with a clap on one shoulder. "*Haraka*!"

Laboso left him. Knowing the route the Italians must take, Diwani made his way to a ford they would have to cross. He checked his rifle, an old double-barrelled .425, a Westley Richards, too much bullet for small game, designed to stop buffalo or rhinoceros, but a weapon he had carried for ten years or more. What it lacked in range, it gained in stopping power. He wedged himself between two acacias.

A typical Somali, Diwani thought, spotting the tracker first. These filthy *shiftas* were all the same.

The Dubat ran downhill, came to the stream and hesitated. He stared along the bank in both directions. Carefully he set down his long rifle. Then the man dropped to his knees and lowered his face to the water, drinking like a dog.

The bullet hit him where his spine met his neck. His body jumped, then settled in the shallow moving water. His head, almost severed, drifted a bit downstream with the pressure of the current.

At that moment the first Italian came over the hill, crouching. Diwani fired the second barrel and missed. As he reloaded, he heard the scream of orders in a strange language. The four other men followed. Moving swiftly, the five spread to the sides in a long line. Each man bent and freed himself of his pack as he ran forward searching for cover. Diwani saw the sunlight twinkle on their short fixed bayonets.

He turned and began to run. Two bullets ricocheted off the rocks beside him. Suddenly Diwani felt he was the hunted animal. He dashed on, pain sharp in his lungs. He was certain he would die. Bullets continued to chase him as his pursuers alternated firing and sprinting. He was astonished that these white men could match his speed. He remembered running with his age brothers as a boy. It was as if all the runs he had ever made were gathered together end on end and now, older, he was finishing the race at last. For the first time in the bush, he feared not an animal but men.

Diwani stopped by an acacia, stepped behind it, then turned and steadied his breathing. He fired twice. The leading Italian fell, belly shot. That left four. He knew he would not escape. But he had done his duty. His hands hurried but steady, he ejected the brass jackets of the empties and began to reload, confident Rider would avenge him.

A shot struck the acacia near Diwani's head. Splinters tore his eyes. Dropping the rifle, he clutched his face, overwhelmed by pain. Blood slicked his hands as he pulled a long sliver of wood from his right eye. He knew there were more. He staggered back. Two bullets struck his lower legs, breaking bone.

He collapsed on his side, unable to see, and the Italians fell on him.

Diwani grappled with the men, seizing one by the throat. A man clubbed his wounded legs with the butt of a rifle, but Diwani only tightened his grip. He felt the man grow limp as others fought to pry him loose. His thumbs met in the Italian's throat. He heard another man screaming orders. He held fast. A rifle was jammed into his stomach, the bayonet to the hilt. Another cut at his face. Diwani felt the world explode.

Hearing the distant shots, Laboso stopped on the rim of a rocky ridge. Looking back, squinting into the sharp sunlight, he thought he saw one of Diwani's pursuers go down. Turning to run on, Laboso knew he would not see the old Wakamba alive again. But it was a death the old hunter would have chosen. At the bottom of the next ravine, Laboso stumbled, catching his foot in a dead root. As he rose, he heard one further shot, not from the heavy hunting rifle, then no more.

"Six men!" Laboso gasped at last, collapsing onto his knees in camp. "Soldiers, Italians!"

Anton came forward and faced Laboso.

"Where's Diwani?" He gripped Laboso's shoulder. Dr. Fergus walked stiffly from Gwenn's tent and joined them.

"Diwani is home, bwana, called by *Ngai.* They must have killed him."

Anton closed his eyes, saddened. Another friend dead. "Tell me."

"I was to run here while Diwani lead them away. They had a Dubat dog, who thought himself a tracker." Laboso spat. "Diwani wished to kill him."

"Did he?"

"Of course, and one or two more." Laboso grinned. "He killed them for you, bwana. I saw from the next hill. Now I think their leader carries the gun of Diwani."

"Not for long." Anton's face was set, his eyes cold and fixed on Laboso's. "How far are they?"

"Three miles, perhaps four. But now they will be slow to find us." Laboso made a wrinkled smile. "Their Dubat cannot lead them."

Anton turned towards the Scottish surgeon. "Could Gwenn travel on a horse or mule, Doctor?"

"She's not ready, and if we have to move she'd do better on a stretcher." Fergus shook his head wearily. "But three of us won't get far carrying her. I need to be carried myself."

Anton knew he would have to stop the Italians before they found the encampment.

"Stay here with her, Fergus." Anton knelt and tightened his boots. He hated to carry more than a rifle. He'd walk cheerfully till he dropped, and accept the hunger and cold of travelling light, but he had no patience for packs. "Grab a rifle, Laboso. We'll show these Italians how we hunt in Africa."

Laboso stuffed a handful of dates in his mouth, loaded a rifle and followed Anton from the camp.

They found the Dubat first.

While Laboso collected the dead man's rifle and bracelets, Anton stood by the stream and searched for Diwani's likely shooting position, knowing it must have been a close shot with the Westley.

"Those trees, I reckon," Anton said, hurrying up the hill to the acacias where Diwani had made his stand. He found two empty .425's and turned to look down to the river, as his friend had done. "Fine shot," Anton said aloud, feeling his loss.

Laboso joined him and the two men took up the track of Diwani and his pursuers.

"Here, *Tlaga,*" said Laboso calmly several hundred yards later. "Diwani."

The slender African lay on his back, pinned to the ground by a bayonet through his eye socket, his body slit from groin to breastbone.

Anton knelt beside him, shaking with anger. "Five bullets," he said, hurling the bayonet into the bush. "The knife work was just for fun."

"Here is one he killed," called Laboso from fifty yards away.

"Looks like Diwani caught him in the belly with his four-two-five," said Anton, joining Laboso. "Messy, like opening a tin of plums with one of those bayonets. Then his own chaps must've ended it with something smaller to the head. You pick up the trail while I cover old Diwani."

Swiftly, Anton scraped out a depression in the ground, then said a prayer for his friend and covered the body with large stones. Finishing, heavy with sadness, he looked up and saw Laboso beckoning to him from a distant hillside.

"They are lost without the *shifta,*" whispered Laboso when Anton joined him. The African knelt and pointed between the branches of an acacia bush to three men who sat near a stream eating and examining their weapons while a fourth searched the distance with field glasses. "Their track has gone in circles. The one holding his neck has been helped along by the others."

"Better to wait for them than follow," said Anton after a time. "They'll tend to stay with the water, probably try to get back to their mates somewhere near Lake Zwai."

Crouching, he led Laboso down to a narrow *donga* and the two men ran silently along the winding sandy course of the depression, startling a covey of vulturine guinea fowl. *"Kak! Kak! Kak!"* the plump blue and grey birds cackled as they scuttled off into the scrub thornbush that covered the slopes.

After a mile or more the two men crawled out and moved forward until they came to the stream, finally lying in among a cluster of dwarf wild fig trees that overhung the bank. Just to their left a small clearing of grassy ground sloped gently down to the water.

They heard the soldiers before they saw them. Moving slowly, evidently arguing, the four Italians came into view as they followed the bank of the stream. Three carried packs and carbines and bayonets. One of these, the officer, Anton guessed, was armed also with a pistol. The fourth man, lightly injured, carried only a rifle.

Pointing to the clearing, yelling some instruction, the heavily built officer dropped his pack and rested his rifle against it. He and another man went to the water and knelt to fill their canteens.

"Drop your rifles!" Anton yelled, stepping out from the trees a few yards away. Laboso rushed to the stream and covered the two kneeling men.

Of the remaining pair, one Italian dropped his pack and carbine and threw up his hands. The injured man pretended to do likewise, before suddenly raising his rifle.

Anton fired one barrel and swung to cover the other standing man.

Struck in the chest by the heavy hunting bullet, the man Anton shot fell backwards as if punched. Although he was still kneeling, Uzielli seized upon the distraction. He went for his pistol but Laboso savagely clubbed the captain's arm with his rifle. Uzielli grunted with pain as his hand opened and the pistol fell into the water.

"Don't shoot!" said Uzielli. His eyes shifting about the scene, he raised both hands and stood.

"Tie their hands, Laboso," Anton said, controlling his anger at the false surrender. "I'll collect the weapons. Then it's time for a drink before we take them back to camp. We can use some porters." He gathered the carbines and bent to examine the dying man. The soldier's chest and mouth frothed with bubbling blood. Feeling some remorse, Anton put a pack under the man's head and opened a canteen.

"Tlaga!" Laboso screamed behind him.

Anton spun about to see Laboso grappling with one Italian by the stream. As Anton stood, the powerfully-built officer stepped towards him and swung at him with a bayonet, just missing Anton's chest. Instantly Anton's *choori* was in his hand. Uzielli closed with him and raised his arm to strike again. Hoping to disable the man without killing him, Anton sliced a shallow cut across the man's belly with the slender knife.

Uzielli cursed and dropped his bayonet when Anton crashed into him, knocking him onto his back in the rocky streambed. The two men rolled in the water. Anton heard one shot from shore. Surprised by the man's strength, now aware he was fighting for his life, Anton tried to use his knife again. Raging, both his own hands engaged, Uzielli seized Anton's wrist in his teeth like a bulldog. Unable to free his arm, Anton felt the man's teeth puncture his skin and sink into the tendons and muscles between the bones of his wrist. He felt a stab of pain and his knife fell onto the gravel of the streambed. Furious, Anton grabbed Uzielli's thick neck in both hands and forced his head beneath the water. Pressing his thumbs together, he sought to prize up the man's Adam's apple.

Spitting water, the Italian lay thrashing on his back on the river stones. He kicked up violently with both legs, lifting Anton's body from his own. His neck freed, staring madly, Uzielli rose to his knees in the water. Anton seized a heavy rock from the streambed. As Uzielli lunged at him, Anton swung the rock with both hands, smashing the *Bersaglieri* in the mouth. Anton heard the man's teeth crack. The soldier fell on his face in the water and Anton knelt to recover his knife.

"Dead?" called Laboso from the bank.

After the intensity of the fight, it seemed to Anton that Laboso's voice came from nowhere. Gasping, he shook his head in response, then bent to wash his face. His hands shaking, he scraped up some sand and scrubbed the puncture wound in his left wrist.

Laboso waded into the water and hauled out the heavy Italian officer by his belt. The man's face and feet dragged along the stones and gravel before Laboso dropped him on the grassy bank. Another soldier stood silently with his hands raised.

Anton gathered himself and looked around. Two Italians lay dead.

"We'll load up these other two bastards, then quick-march 'em back to camp," he said, all remorse gone as he opened Diwani's Westley Richards and looked at the sky through the barrels. At his feet, the officer began to stir and groan.

In an hour Anton smelled the cooking fire as he and Laboso approached camp with their two prisoners.

"What happened to the rest of them?" Dr. Fergus said. "I thought there were six."

The two Italians in dirty campaign shorts and battered black leather hats stood to one side, their wrists bound before them. Each carried an outsize pack on his back. Both men looked surly and exhausted. The bigger one, a captain with the hot black eyes of a wounded bear, had a long horizontal slash across his shirtfront and the mark of a cross on one cheek. Both his lips were cut and swollen, and four or five of his front teeth were broken or missing. His stubbled chin was black with dried blood. The lower flap of his shirt was stuck to the dried blood of the flesh wound

"Pretty chap," the doctor said. "Must've been quite a party. What about the others?"

"They didn't make it," Anton announced hurriedly. He handed two rifles to Laboso, who now wore a black leather, feathered hat tilted over one eye. "Diwani got two and a half of them. This captain seems to have finished off one wounded man himself instead of leaving him for the hyenas." Scowling, Anton gestured towards Uzielli with his thumb. "Laboso and I had to kill a couple to get their attention. That left this pair."

"What happened to this man's stomach?" said Fergus. "And he looks like he could use a dentist."

"After they surrendered, the captain pulled a knife when we were all about to take a drink. Probably an old Italian custom." Fortunately the gypsies had taught Anton how to use his own. "Patch 'em up a bit, Doc, but leave their arms free. They'll be on stretcher duty."

Anton walked to Gwenn's tent. At least he had done what he had to do with the Italians. Pausing, he turned back to Fergus and spoke again. "Please go through their packs and see what might be useful. You're acting quartermaster." Eager to see his wife, he raised one flap and entered the tent.

"Welcome home," Gwenn said as Anton knelt to kiss her. She raised one hand and touched his cheek with her fingers. "Looks like you found more trouble." Her voice seemed stronger.

"Not too bad, except for old Diwani," Anton said, trying to speak gently, aware he was still too intense after what had gone before. "We'll miss him. But we've got to move, and you must eat some dinner, Gwennie. This could be our last hot meal, and you're going to need your strength."

"Why are the prisoners barefoot?" Gwenn asked later, after her stretcher was set by the fire. She spoke from curiosity, not compassion. She was still incensed by the Italians' use of poison gas. Her eyes followed Anton as he bent and stirred the heart of the fire with a stick.

"Best way to keep white men from running off in Africa," he said, looking up at her. He was happy to see how relaxed she seemed. Her color had returned. She was the only woman in camp. "Laboso'll be sleeping with their boots."

Anton sat down cross-legged beside her and held her plate while Gwenn used her good arm to eat. He was pleased she was so keen on the macaroni, a gift of the Italian army. As the others talked, he considered how the camp fire chat was still about the day's adventures, only on this safari a day's fighting had replaced a day's hunting, and the adversaries were men, not animals.

"We seem to be in the middle of this war," he said suddenly, "and I reckon we might as well learn the rules."

— 32 —

Gnawing on a mango pit, Olivio Alavedo lay on his back in Victoria Hospital in a private room with a large window. It had been a long week. His legs were raised in traction, making him unable to ignore the church tower of St. Andrews that rose between his feet. He was tired of looking down on the Presbyterians.

Tariq was recovering rapidly in the crowded ward downstairs. Even the burns to his face had been largely contained by his immediate immersion in the Nile. Soon he would be on his feet, eager to hunt the man who had killed Clove. Tariq's suffering would fuel the chase.

Olivio listened to the drill-like pacing of the German deaconesses who patrolled the halls and wards of this Protestant hospital. No doubt Dr. Hänger and Fräulein Koch found these women dependable assistants, but to the dwarf they provided no pleasure.

As the days passed and his body healed, Olivio recognized that Hänger was using the fire as an opportunity to ensnare his patient in a program that the dwarf had been avoiding: incarceration in a hospital where the German specialist could employ the instruments of more traditional spinal therapy. The doctor was even threatening him with a back brace, one of the final torments of achondroplasia. Then indeed he would be a prisoner, bearing his own steel cage, like a beggar's monkey with a ball and chain. One day he would pay back the medical man for these impertinences. He was right to have spurned Zürich.

The dwarf put aside the mango pit and, like a bug under a slide, looked up into the face of August Hänger. Habituated to the study of suffering, the German doctor squinted down at him with expressionless eyes.

"No more burns, zank God. No more *wildes Fleisch,*" Hänger said to Knuckles Koch. "But the back! The back is vorse. Like all these little people."

The nurse wrote in a black notebook as the physician updated his diagnosis and instructions. In recent days, Knuckles had displeased her patient. To his annoyance, she was occasionally closeting herself in the adjoining room. There some Egyptian lordling, a cousin of Prince Farûq, was finding costly satisfaction in her services. Was it possible that this spoiled fool was enjoying more than her legs? Doubtless a man of vile but simple-minded corruptions, the swarthy fellow had introduced the unspeakable standards of the Abdine Palace to the hospital. What could a gentleman expect of such people?

"The spinal canal, this is our battlefield," the doctor said, his tone something between resignation and enthusiasm as he made a diminishing circle with his thumb and forefinger.

"Instead of protecting the nerves that go down the spine, his canal is shrinking, so, so, compressing with age, pinching the ventral and dorsal nerves and encouraging constriction of the surrounding musculature, *und* further progressive distortions of the back." The physician squeezed his fist together.

Knuckles tightened the traction on his left leg. Olivio closed his eyes. Determined not to be the victim of his cure, the dwarf compelled himself to think of happier things: lust and revenge.

Dr. Hänger continued, addressing his nurse as if presenting a lecture at Heidelberg. In fact, Olivio feared, he was preparing his patient for the brutal regimen ahead.

To the extent of his ability, however, the doctor was not without sympathy.

"Spinal cord compression," Hänger explained, giving a quick smile, pointing towards the appropriate organs as he proceeded, "shortens the life due to respiratory, cardiac and neurological complications, not to mention painful but less terminal accompaniments in the joints, here and here, liver, spleen, elsewhere." He paused, his black eyes twinkling, and wagged both forefingers at his patient. "Some wicked dwarves challenge us physicians with a zymphony of complications."

"For dwarves suffering from Morquio's syndrome, forty years is generally the limit, for Hurler's syndrome, still less. But this one," he said to Knuckles, waving one hand dismissively at his patient, "is not a Hurler, no. They have little intelligence." The doctor had already explained that Pott's disease, and diastrophic and metatropic dwarfism, presented other clinical challenges.

"Is it a vunder so few of us are attracted to zis practice?" He shrugged his shoulders. "We do it for science."

Olivio considered if he would need to give Dr. Hänger the third dwarf of ancient ivory as a bribe to leave the hospital. The finest of the three images, apparently intended to depict the small figure at an older age, the third miniature depicted a man with legs and back more bowed, face still more lined and pained. How this German would love to pull the single thread to make the little creatures spin and dance! Would the physician make them dance in the same, or in opposite, dizzying directions?

The dwarf watched the specialist close his case and prepare to leave, removing and polishing his spectacles. August Hänger seemed unnatural without them. The two marks on the bridge of his nose awaited their return, deep and red as the hearths of a blacksmith. The physician replaced the eyeglasses and walked from the room as Knuckles held the door.

Left alone, Olivio tried not to let his thought drift to the fire, attempting instead to focus his mind on the future. Despising his helplessness, he had determined that his mind would do what his body could not: reach beyond the walls of the hospital to avenge his child.

But each night he cried. The loss of his daughter burned molten within him. On good nights he lay in the darkness and made plans for a grand service to honor his Clove's life. Afterwards he would host a reception for all Cairo. He would create for her a party to replace all those she would never have, combining into one celebration her birthdays, her coming-of-age and her wedding feast. All her favorite foods and treats would be served in abundance. Lying awake, his mouth sometimes watering with anticipation, he considered each dish and detail of what must be a triumphant display.

Tents would be erected in the back garden of his villa between the royal palms. For days his chefs would labor, preparing the canapés of Europe and the *mazzah* of the Levant, the small dishes served with drinks or as side plates in houses of fashion. Never would his guests have nibbled so well, and all of it from the bounty of his own fields, transported to town in the buses of the mourners from his villages: bean cakes and zucchini patties, the pulp of the young vegetable stirred frequently over a low fire until it achieved the dense ochre tones of a Goan roof tile; *beid mahshy,* his own fresh hens' eggs stuffed with black olives, pickles, onions and yoghurt; dry pastry fingers filled with parsley and skimmed cheese; pigeons filled to bursting with dried apricots; spinach *samosas* and fried sweet peppers and pickled limes and okra and turnips; a small school of cold stuffed sea bass; and, a favorite of his dead child, though rarely eaten outside one's house, *kibda nayya,* fresh raw calf's liver, pulpy and moist, cubed and marinated in mint juice and grated onions; and more dishes, twenty, thirty more, all steaming and aromatic. Carvers would stand behind their roasts like mighty janissaries, their blades singing while they sharpened them over the cold turkeys and *börek* and haunches of cold roast beef. Sipping Pommery, gossiping guests would wander past tables of decorated cakes and puddings and towers of spun sugar. To one side would be a platter of *tavuk gölesi,* so good for the hearts of old men, the tender white meat of Olivio's chickens pounded to a paste with egg whites, then cooked slowly and served cold, perhaps accompanying a platter of lady's thighs, the twice-cooked lamb roulades dripping with the thick lemon sauce into which Clove had loved to dip two fingers. Would this not be perfection? What jaded tongue would not be teased?

For special, knowing guests, there would be still more, a table offering the treasures of Goa itself: her cashew nectar, fontainhas; *oriste recha,* from the sea; and his own favorite chicken bathed in smooth rich coconut sauce, *murg xaccuti.*

The staff of the Café, desolate, unemployed since the holocaust, would cook and serve and carry as never before. Already several had visited him in the hospital, offering condolences for his child and their assistance towards the rebuilding of the boat. Two had even proffered their few shillings towards the reconstruction. He had accepted the gifts with gratitude. But money was not the need. Had he the heart for it?

There was a knock at his door, and Olivio acknowledged it.

"Bonjour, patron." A Frenchman entered the room with a light high step, bowing at the foot of the bed.

It was *Monsieur* Aristide, his daughters' art tutor, called now to a higher use than education. He was a talented affected man of few words. He rolled a white enamel medical trolley to the wall facing the window, careless of the pyramids of giant lemons and flawless mangoes that rested in a flat basket on the rolling cart, useful rewards for the hospital staff. One mango fell to the floor and rolled into the corner. The Frenchman made no effort to retrieve the fruit, now hopelessly bruised, the dwarf noticed with vexation.

Aristide rested his portfolio on the trolley and propped a tall leather folder against the wall before untying its cord. He exposed a charcoal portrait with the gravitas of a man drawing the curtain at an opera. Turning to observe the dwarf's reaction, he raised heavy black eyebrows, stroking his mustache and opening his mouth slightly as he awaited the ovation.

Olivio shook his head.

"Zut!" the man exclaimed under his breath as he tore the sheet in two and exhibited a second drawing. Again Olivio rejected his work. His lips tightening, the artist presented his final attempt.

"Aha," the dwarf murmured with enthusiasm, "only the eyes are wrong, *Monsieur* Aristide. His are larger, far larger." Olivio opened his own lids until his glass eye nearly popped free. "But the rest is him."

Aristide stroked his mustache with delight, then rubbed the paper with a large pink gum eraser. He swept aside the rubber crumbs with a fine brush and drew out a stick of charcoal, turning his back to the bed while he worked. He stopped and stared at the corrected portrait with his hands clasped before him. He made another stroke or two and then stood back and raised his eyebrows.

"Turn this face upside down," said the dwarf. The artist obeyed.

The eyes of the long lined face of the incendiary stared back at Olivio Alavedo from under the bald dented cranium.

Here was the butcher of his child.

"I congratulate you, *Monsieur,*" the dwarf said quietly. "You have just killed this man." Content at last, Olivio leaned back against his monogrammed pillows and spoke in a cheeerful voice.

"Prepare twenty more portraits exactly like it, one half the size. And take the envelope from that table. When his life is no longer his, you will receive another envelope."

Aristide withdrew and Olivio closed his eye as he thought of his adversaries. To them violence was indeed a weapon, but one too sharp to touch themselves. Shrewd but spoiled, with that lavish instinct for power and corruption peculiar to the Ottoman, they might be his equals in deception and in greed. But in revenge they were altar boys. These men had not studied at his school.

Once stirred, his mind would not allow him peace. He knew there must be something more. What did he know of this murderer that was not contained on the single page of the portrait?

One further thing: the high smell of some animal that had come and gone with the face at the porthole. What was that odor?

The dwarf closed his eyes and cast back his mind and sniffed to arouse the recollection. He dozed, snoring, his mind drifting to the afternoon he and his friends had visited his farms by *felucca* and by camel cart. He snorted and awoke as the thought aroused him. Camels! The villain had carried the stink of the humped beasts.

Four days later Tariq stood at the foot of his master's bed. His body appeared the same: dense and heavy-shouldered, but his impassive face, deeply lined about the sunken eyes, bore the marks of the pain he had endured, and, on the left side, the raised proud flesh of his burn scars. No doubt, Tariq, too, was now evaluating how well his master had recovered.

A powerful force struck the other side of the wall behind Olivio's head. Disgusted by what Knuckles must be doing with the wretch next door, he ignored the disturbance and fixed his eye on the wall behind Tariq. From the black-framed portrait hanging there, the dark eyes of the murderer stared back at him across the foot of his hospital bed. An experimental model of a back brace hung from a hook beside it, specially fashioned by an Italian craftsman in Alexandria. The broad leather straps and molded metal reminded the dwarf of the implements once used so successfully in the dungeons of the Inquisition. Would this device serve him as well?

"Your excellency?" said the Nubian, bowing his block-like head. "What must I do?"

"We have left our enemy in peace too long," said the dwarf.

"He will have no peace, master, once we know him."

Olivio lifted a thin canvas satchel from the table beside his bed. "Turn around, Tariq, and you will see him."

Tariq turned his back to the dwarf and stared at the hanging portrait as he might at a juicy shank of lamb. For a long moment Olivio respected Tariq's concentration, aware of his servant's affection for Clove. Observing him, noting the tight hunching of his shoulders, the pitching forward of the head, the dwarf reminded himself to restrain the Nubian at the end, lest the hound tear the fox to pieces. Tariq's vengeance must not eclipse his master's.

When the big man turned and faced him, Olivio spoke again.

"In this satchel you will find twenty more drawings like this one on the wall." Tariq nodded, and he continued. "You will carry this picture through Cairo, showing it everywhere as you would your own face. You will display these portraits in each coffee house and *suq* and slum, from the smoke-thick cafés of Bab al-Sha'riya to the mud brick hovels in the City of the Dead. From time to time we will do this work together."

He knew, however, that while Tariq pursued the perpetrator, the instrument, he himself must work to identify the organizer, the mind behind the act. One difficulty of the dwarf's labyrinthine dealings was the inevitable ruck of enemies that had suffered from each of his successes. How was he to select one serpent from such a swarming pit of vipers?

Fortunately, he was blessed with a nose for mischief, and it seemed to Olivio that the boat had been the target, not him. The fire had been intended as a warning, not a punishment. The crime was the work not of yesterday's enemy, but of tomorrow's. A conclusion that greatly narrowed the field. He rubbed the open lobe of one ear and considered which of his present schemes might have provoked such opposition. He was reluctant to recognize the direction in which suspicion led him.

Tariq hung the satchel across his chest by its leather cord. As he stepped to the door, there was a knock.

"Hullo there, Tariq, and good morning to you, Olivio," said Adam Penfold cheerily, entering the room with a bunch of yellow roses in one hand. "I picked these on the way. Thought you'd find 'em useful with the nurses."

"Thank you, thank you," said Olivio, eager for this opportunity to change the subject.

"Will you help me complete the arrangements for Clove's service?" he asked, anxious that each detail make his daughter proud, that elegant Cairo find no fault with this Alavedo rite. "And for the reception that will follow?"

"Of course," said Penfold, pained by the suffering of his friend. He bent with a groan to recover a mango that lay on the floor against the wall. "And Friday Tariq and I will come to collect you in the motor. Time you got up to your old mischief."

Restless after a few days at home, with no café to provide a refuge from his family, Olivio Alavedo called for Tariq to attend him on the terrace of the villa.

"How many drawings have you left?" asked the dwarf.

"Six, master." The Nubian slapped the satchel that hung at his side. "Most are being carried about the city by my cousins from the Sudd. They know, too, of the rank odor that marks this man."

"Have they found the scent?"

"Not yet, though each day they prowl the streets and *suqs.* When it grows dark they follow the rats and street sweepers who share Cairo's gutters at night."

"Remember, if he is found, the bounty is for capture and interrogation. Execution will be your master's gift."

"As you wish, master."

"Ah, Lord Penfold is here to join us," said the dwarf with a happier voice, painfully rising to his feet. "In a few moments, Tariq, we will join you as you dispense the remaining portraits."

"Evening, old boy," said Adam Penfold. "Any chance of a drink before we set off?"

"You shall have a drink, my lord, and your favorite *samosas,* bursting with dark French mushrooms and young peas, before we enter the night with Tariq. But first, I present you a modest gift." The dwarf took from the side of his chaise a black walking stick and handed it to his friend.

"Too kind! Too kind!" said Penfold. "And just the right height," he added, tapping it on the ground. At that moment he discovered a silver button near the top of the stick and pressed it. The shaft separated from the handle and Penfold drew the two apart. In his right hand was a slender blade, longer than a knife, yet shorter than a sword. "My goodness me!"

The little man smiled at his friend's pleasure, then frowned. "Cairo can be a dangerous city, my lord, especially where we may be going this night."

"Yes, I recall it can." Penfold remembered the battering he had taken near the Pyramids. "This should be just the thing." He bent his right knee, raised his left arm above his head and turned himself sideways.

"I believe you used to fence, my lord?"

"At school. Foils, you know." Penfold groaned as he shuffled forward with one quick step. "Sabres seemed so hearty, and epées too French and complicated." He straightened himself and replaced the blade, his face red.

They entered the car and drove along the great river as the sky darkened and Cairo brightened against the night.

"Remember the barbers," urged Olivio to his driver.

"*Aiwa*, master."

"The devil's head was shaved, smooth as a river stone," the dwarf explained in a quieter voice to Penfold.

For two hours, Penfold and Olivio sat in darkness in the backseat of the Rover, watching Tariq when he descended from the car and spoke to water carriers and food vendors, camel drivers and pedlers, often seeking out the Sudanese amongst them, frequently buying their attention with a silver coin, always waiting with particular patience when a street-side barber paused to consider the proffered portrait.

"Wouldn't it be best, really, to leave this sort of thing to the police?" asked Penfold at one stop, watching two street urchins approach the car.

"Alas, no, my lord," said his friend. "What I do not do will not be done."

The two youths, staying well clear of Tariq, pressed their hands and noses to a side window. *"Baqshîsh!"* one cried, tapping insolently on the glass. Both jumped back in horror when the dwarf leaned close to the window and removed one eye.

Wedged into one dirty lane barely wider than the car, with the torn canopies of decrepit stalls hanging above their vehicle, the two men watched Tariq squat on his heels to speak with an aged *rammal* who sat cross-legged on a palm mat. The turbanned soothsayer took the riyal Tariq offered him and kissed it before closing his eyes and speaking rapidly to the Sudanese. Sensing something worthy, the dwarf seized the braided cord before him and slowly pulled himself forward to the edge of his seat.

"He asks us to return in one hour and he will speak with me again," reported Tariq after Lord Penfold rolled down his window. "We spoke of camels and their scent."

"Perhaps we could find a gin somewhere while we're waiting for that old swami," said Penfold mournfully. "Why not the Mahroussa Bar, or old Groppi's?"

"Let us go back where you have left the other pictures," said Olivio to Tariq. "Indulge me, my lord."

"Here we must leave the car, master, if you wish to join me," said Tariq after a short drive. He paid a boy to watch the Rover and held the door for Penfold before assisting his master into the dusty street that ended near a narrow alleyway. Wearing a dark fez and his most simple grey *gallabiyyah,* the dwarf followed his servant with careful steps. For this chase, he had determined to put aside his avoidance of scenes and circumstances that he could not control. They followed the twisting alley beneath overhanging wooden balconies until they entered a small *midan.*

Tariq led them across the square to a low coffee house whose woodwork front was broken by three arches. Clouds of smoke drifted from the openings. With rare agility, the dwarf descended the two steps into the café. Before him men sat on mats along a low brick bench, sipping tea or drawing on the long stems of bubbling water pipes. He smelled the odor of hemp mixed with the strong tobacco that glowed in the bowls of some pipes. The din of backgammon and conversation ceased.

The dwarf was surprised to see that the row of faces was staring not at Lord Penfold or himself, but at Tariq. He knew they would despise the Nubian for his negritude, but respect him for his menace. As for himself, he had found that Egyptians viewed him graciously, without horror, the children even regarding him with open delight.

"May thy night be happy," said a waiter, bowing to Olivio. He prepared a small round table for the three men and set coffees and a wooden backgammon tray before them. The chatter resumed, but more quietly.

Tariq signalled to the fat proprietor who stood behind a narrow wooden counter, stacking coins and arranging a tray of sweetmeats. The soft-faced man appeared not to see the Nubian. Penfold cast the single pair of dice. In the Arab way, Olivio instantly snatched up the dice and rolled before Penfold had completed his play.

Tariq rose and approached the man while the game proceeded.

"As-salamu alaykum," Tariq said, resting his hands on the counter.

"The mercy and blessing of God," replied the host in a low wary voice. "Peace be with you."

"Where is the portrait I paid you to keep always on this counter?" demanded Tariq. Behind him, Penfold rolled and played, unable to keep pace, rather pleased he had brought his new cane. The dwarf, too, appeared to have eyes only for the game.

"Where is the picture?" repeated Tariq with anger.

"It is not here," whispered the proprietor with a shrug.

Tariq gripped each of the man's thin wrists in one massive black hand, holding them flat to the counter where the seated customers could not observe them.

"Where is my picture?" Tariq tightened and twisted until the man's palms were facing directly upwards.

"If you lie, I will crack your arms and crush your hands like the breast of a pigeon, *wallâhi.*"

"It is gone," gasped the man, rising to his toes and straining forward over the counter to reduce the torque that threatened to snap his forearms. "Burned."

"Who burned it?" Tariq drove his thick thumb into the inside of the man's right wrist until he could feel the long bone on either side. "On thy head, I ask you: who burned it?" He twisted more forcefully.

"I was not here." The man's face wrinkled tightly like a dried date as he struggled not to scream. "I was not here. It was at night. In the morning I found the ashes here on the counter where I kept it always as I watched the entrance."

The proprietor straightened like a loosed bow when Tariq released him. Then the black man drew another portrait from his satchel and turned to face the clients of the coffee house.

"I have money for the man who has seen this dog," he announced, holding up the drawing before each customer in turn. The pale raised scars on Tariq's face throbbed as he stared into the eyes of each man. None moved or spoke in the long silence.

Tariq slapped the picture against the front of the counter. With his other hand he took a knife from the countertop and stabbed it into the drawing, leaving the portrait pinned through its face for all to see.

"Double game, my lord," said Olivio to Penfold, taking his last piece from the board. "Your treat, I believe. I'd leave two piastres."

"That was jolly," said Penfold as he climbed into the Rover a few moments later.

"Our fish is rising to the hook," murmured the dwarf in the darkness. "The killer wishes to stop my servant's work."

Parked again near the spice vendors, Tariq turned off the engine and leaned back his head in response to his master's voice.

"Pay this soothsayer well," said the dwarf.

After a few moments, Tariq returned to the car and Penfold rolled down the window.

"What did he tell you?" said Olivio sharply.

"He said that camels are clean beasts, master, with a fair smell when healthy. For the odor of a camel to stink so and to linger, he explains, the beast must be dead, not alive. Therefor we must look where the camels are slain and butchered, at the abattoir, *al-Madbah.*"

The pigeons would have pleased her, Olivio thought the next day, gazing up into the gabled vault of the Basilique d'Héliopolis. Birds nested on the stone framing of the great rose window. Others fluttered and floated about the high stonework of the nave and chancel. White droppings bleached the flutings of the soaring pillars.

He was pleased that the church contained this life, a vitality that seemed to link Clove's service with his own childhood in Goa. Though not as baroque as Iberian colonial monuments, the basilica was nonetheless a proper church of Rome. Financed by a Belgian baron, designed by a Frenchman, it was supposed to be a quarter-size replica of the Hagia Sofia in Constantinople. Cairo's Anglican church, a stern instrument of empire as English as a stiff white collar or a line of polished bayonets, was suitably sterile. But the churches of his faith were alive, though not as alive in Cairo as Goa's cathedral had been in his youth. Why was the very air itself so different inside these temples, an atmosphere of its own, peculiarly sustaining, calming and cooler, yet always warm enough, as if it came from a different sky than the air outside?

In Goa's cathedral, babies had struggled under the pews while their mothers gossiped and received confession. Parakeets flew in and out of the sixteenth-century stone jungle. Old men in black passed their mornings leaning on malacca canes set between their knees. Lovers whispered and flirted. Priests intrigued and marketed the sacrements. Mongrels scratched themselves in doorways. Merchants bargained in the shadows by the poorbox. As a boy, he himself had hunted for lost coppers on the worn stone floor of the Cathedral of San Beatrice. However hot the Goan afternoon, however desperate the life outside, the accommodating sanctuary was always cool and dark and comforting. Whatever the sins of his church, whatever the greed and cruelty and intrigue that had nourished her, her other cathedrals were the same, he was certain, whether in Guadalajara or Oporto, Sao Paulo or Lourenço Marques.

Today the mother church would reward him for his loyal gifts. Thirty years of struggle would be affirmed by a service that would make his daughter proud. Great men would kneel and pray for Clove Fonseca Alavedo.

He thought of his natural grandfather, Dom Tiago de Castanheda y Fonseca, the late Archbishop of Goa himself. How proud that great shepherd would be!

A downy grey and white feather settled onto the black striped trouser of Olivio's morning suit. The dwarf left it where it lay and cast up his eye.

These wild grey birds were heavier than Clove's own sleek doves had been. Now, like his daughter, all were dead, burned alive or flown. Save one, perhaps.

Olivio wiped his eye with the back of one thumb and turned his head and gazed along the front pew at the five daughters who sat between his wife and him. All the girls wore black dresses and black mantillas. Only two, Cinnamon and Cayenne, were still shorter than he. Banging knees, nudging each other, they sat at the end near their mother. He admired Kina in her mourning dress and veil and long gloves. Her formidable maternity was apparent. His wife felt his look and turned towards him. He knew she was aware, without a sentiment of reproach, that Clove had been his favorite. Was Kina offering him a smile, as she often did, or did she still weep behind her veil? Although now she was sometimes a European lady, comfortable with the fashions of Paris and the courtesies of London, long ago he had taken her from a Kikuyu culture where women expected to carry many children and lose several.

He wondered if one day a son would sit beside him. He thought of all that he might teach his little boy. There would be many who could teach him virtue, even values. But who else could make such a lad truly wise, in the ways of life, great and small? To take a long view, to be subtle and discreet, to shorten your nails before you went to bed with a woman.

The dwarf was proud Lord Penfold was seated in his proper place just across the aisle, dignified as an old lion with a grizzled mane. His lordship sat tall and straight but stiff and dry, his friendship evident to all. As if hearing him, Penfold turned and nodded a friendly smile. He was saddened not so much for the lost girl, though he was that, but for his friend.

Olivio had learned that friendship was the one relationship at which the English excelled. They lacked the loose intuitions for romance, and the venom for vengeance, but for a school chum an Englishman would swim the Nile or walk the Sahara.

The places beside Lord Penfold, where his other true friends would have sat, were empty. Although he missed them, he knew that, in truth, both Anton and Miss Gwenn sat there now.

Like a stream that would become a torrent, like the River Nile itself, the dwarf heard the music begin and slowly swell. Soon the organ would shake the very stone. The music was not something he knew well, but he respected its interlocking German complexity, how it built the delicate into the powerful. That he understood. A man called Bach, Monsignor Lazaroni had promised him. The little man closed his eyes and let the organ carry him.

He would never, not for one day, forget Clove, but today was the last day he would cry tears. There was work to be done, and it must begin here at church. Here requiem and revenge would merge. He was confident the greater enemy he sought would attend to pray with him today. It was the way of the world. The man would be concerned lest his absence identify him.

Very well, thought the dwarf: today, church; tomorrow, the abattoir.

Seated at the front, there was not much Olivio now could do. But on the street outside, Tariq and his Nubians, armed with portraits, eager for the bounty on the head of the assassin, would be watching as they assisted mourners up the steps, looked after the cars, and pressed back the mendicants and the inevitable thronging Egyptians. Would the killer appear? Would the devil be drawn back to his dinner?

Monsieur Aristide, positioned to one side in the transept, would be sketching a face here and there, and preparing drawings for the painting of the service that soon would hang in Clove's old room. At the end, as the mourners filed out, before motoring to the villa for refreshments, each would sign the book as a mark of respect. For one man, the signature would be a mark of death.

Determined not to turn about in his seat, trying to imagine their faces and their garb, Olivio heard the mourners filling the pews behind him. The stone echoed what the music dimmed: the footfalls and the chatter of the living.

Tariq stood outside, on the top step of this foreign temple, watching his fellow Sudanese at work. Turbanned, sandalled, dark, taller than all but the most favored Egyptians, these Nubians were indeed the servants of Allah. Carriages and motorcars were drawing up to the basilica, directed by several policemen with batons and white gloves. Tariq recognized many of his master's friends and clients and associates. Two photographers flashed pictures as the mourners climbed the steps. One, known to many, represented a pictorial magazine popular in certain Cairene circles. The other, similarly equipped and also dressed in a frayed western suit made for someone else, had been retained by Mr. Alavedo. From time to time this photographer looked at Tariq for instruction. The churchgoers feigned annoyance as they passed the cameras, pretending not to pose as they hesitated ever so briefly, straightening and smiling before entering.

The automobiles, emptied, were lined in ranks in the paved yard beside the church. The dusty carts of the transported *fellahin* were parked in a nearby alley. Some of the uniformed drivers were taking coffee at a café in the side street across the square. A few slept in their seats. Others wiped their motor cars with cloths or dusters. Several Nubians kept street boys and vendors of drinks and nuts away from the parked cars.

In his pew, reminded of his physician by the pain in his back, Olivio wondered with a slight smile if Doctor Hänger would be seated with Jamila. Would discretion give way to desire?

He was confident all would be here: powerful members of the Muslim secular elite, the ministers and the functionaries, the ambassadors and bankers and the owners of great estates, the Copts and the British and the White Russians and Armenians, Greek cotton brokers from Alexandria, Italians from the Abdine Palace, his own *fournisseurs* and solicitors and accountants and servants and farm workers, even a few of the twisted little people he helped so freely but whom he hoped never to see. The dwarves would naturally sit to the rear and sides. Other places would be taken by the curious, and by the cadre of professional churchgoers who found a life in the christenings and marriages and deaths of others. Even so, it would not be possible to fill the cavernous basilica, but the impressive throng would make this ending complete.

What did they all think of him as they stared at the back of his round bald head? He sat as erect as his form allowed. Concerned lest his brace be apparent through the back of his tailcoat, due to the small bulges made by the buckles of the straps, he had left the monstrous harness at home. No doubt Knuckles would scold him. Even with the elevation of the brocade cushion that had awaited him, the crown of his lightly oiled head barely topped the back of the dark wooden pew.

Did the assembly see him as an oddity, a horror or amusement to whom some must defer but whom most found at best a distasteful curiosity? Or did a few perceive the cunning giant imprisoned within, the energy, the imagination, the sense of what matters, the hungry determination, perhaps even the cauldron of emotions?

Tariq, at the top of the steps, watched two elderly European ladies waiting to descend from a modest Hillman. Behind them a blue Bentley waited its turn. The magnificent machine bore the flag and license plate of an Undersecretary of the Ministry of Public Works. Impatient, the driver leaned forward out the window. The visor of his black cap shaded a long thin lined face. The man's large deep-set eyes squinted into the light.

Tariq stared at the driver, then nodded and the photographer snapped a photo as the Nubian turned and hurriedly entered the church.

"Master," whispered Tariq, bending low when he came to the front pew. "You have important guests."

Olivio crossed himself and rose reluctantly, intensely conscious of his height as he passed slowly up the center aisle, avoiding all eyes and acknowledgments as he kept his head downcast. At the top of the steps, he stood in the shadow by a secondary door.

The Bentley pulled forward and stopped. The driver adjusted the cap on his bald head. Tariq himself stepped down and opened the door before another Nubian could assist. Dignified, perfectly dressed *à l'Anglais,* tragedy and respect on his face, Musa Bey Halaib emerged slowly from his motorcar. He adjusted his red carnation while he waited for his wife and portly daughter to follow him.

"Your Excellency," Tariq said with a bow. Deliberately, he left the car door open as he escorted the Undersecretary to the steps. Grumbling, the tall lean-faced driver was obliged to step from the Bentley to close the rear door. Olivio stared down with a distant eye, his soul cold as death. He nodded. A flashbulb popped.

Chatting in French and English as they climbed the steps, Musa Bey Halaib and his family became caught up in the eager conviviality that delayed guests near the entrance. Olivio met them at the center door.

Bowing, he extended his hand to each of the women, noting that her jewelled bracelet was overly tight on Jasmine's plump wrist.

"Your presence is a gift to my family," the dwarf said gravely to the Bey, meaning his words, seeking without success to meet the eye of the Undersecretary. Then the little man turned and reentered the coolness of the basilica.

Olivio took his seat, his mind spinning. The long theater of the service unfolded as he knew it would. Ushers and pallbearers, cross and candle holders, choirboys and flag and incense bearers, all marched slowly to the music before the priests and Monsignor Lazaroni himself. The rich cleric paced his stride like a guardsman.

Finally the Eucharist made Olivio's daughter one with the Christian god. Clove had found peace. His enemies would not.

— 33 —

"You're the only one having an easy day of it, young man," complained Malcom Fergus as he clutched the hard wood-framed Abyssinian saddle with both hands and rocked from side to side.

"I'll try to make up for it, Doc," said Anton, watching the two Italian prisoners toil up the trail with Gwenn's stretcher slung between them.

He tried to calculate how Laboso might be doing, running on ahead, following the track of Ernst and the lorry, watching out for Italian paratroopers. Gwenn and Fergus were too weak for any futile travelling, and the Italian prisoners could carry her stretcher only a few miles at a time. Someone had to go ahead to find the way, keeping their route as short and safe as possible.

"How far do we have to go?" Fergus shifted his seat on the frayed red saddle blanket and tried to grip his mount without scraping the raw insides of his knees.

"Fifteen miles would be good today. If we're lucky, we'll get in sight of Lake Langana." Anton turned in the saddle to check the supply mules that straggled behind him on the lead rope. "For Africa, it's pretty easy going."

It was not hot in the high country. The sky was clear and bright. As they made their way south the acacia woodlands grew thinner and scarcer, and the high savannah was giving way to thorn bush and rock. The route was broken by jutting rocky outcrops and stands of euphorbia and thorn bush, but it was never impenetrable or truly precipitous.

"Ostrich!" Fergus pointed ahead with surprising interest.

"The birds always tell you what's coming." Anton noted the hard dry ground that rose before them, sprinkled with loose stones and pebbles.

Occasional patches of packed sand suggested what lay ahead to the southwest.

The column had skirted a lake and entered a stretch of dry country. The tree duck and black-headed heron and hadada ibis had been replaced by pygmy falcons and carmine bee-eaters. Now the spherical dwellings of colonies of masked weavers hung from branches. Anton watched one weaver hovering like a hummingbird before tucking in its yellow and olive wings and entering the spout-like entrance of its suspended residence. He wished he could make such a perfect home, or any home at all.

Uzielli was fed up with carrying the clumsy stretcher. Mario, carrying the front end, had the easier time of it. Unable to see the ground beneath it, Uzielli was forever stumbling. Annoyed, imagining himself alone with her, he stared down at the skinny English bitch who lay on the bouncing piece of canvas before him. Every now and then the woman tried to pull her torn skirt lower on her legs, but the uphill movement of the stretcher kept working it higher towards her thighs. Even bandaged and messed up, she looked like she'd be worth a few pokes.

Better than his own wife, Gina, anyway. Uzielli wondered what she was up to at home. Gina was getting old and fat for the usual mischief, but for such a woman there was always someone. At first she had complained when he went off soldiering. Then she had learned to wave good-bye with a smile, not a tear. Who knew which of the children were his? Did it matter? She was just an old *capra,* one of the yellow-toothed she-goats that foraged on the rocky hillsides in Sicily, scrounging about from weed to weed, taking whatever they could find. With enough silver, he could buy a café on the coast and find himself a fresh Gina. This time he'd find one that could cook. God, he was hungry.

Distracted, Uzielli stumbled yet again. Saving himself, lurching as he recovered his balance, for a moment the Italian lost his grip on the left shaft of the improvised bamboo and canvas stretcher.

Anton heard Gwenn cry out as she almost fell onto the rocky slope. Seeing what had happened, he dropped the lead rope and cantered to the front of the column. Trying to control his fury, he leapt from his horse and blocked Uzielli's way. He assumed the frog-eyed captain was aware she was a nurse, wounded by his countrymen while she was caring for the Ethiopians.

"Are we stopping?" said the Italian soldier without concern.

"It's all right, Anton," Gwenn said quickly, dreading his anger. "Nothing happened." She felt a jagged pain in her shoulder as she settled back.

Anton spoke slowly so the churlish officer would understand.

"If you fall and she is hurt, Captain, you will never get up."

Dismissing the man abruptly, Anton took water from a canteen and sponged Gwenn's face with his kerchief. "Would you like to stop?" he asked, careful to speak calmly.

"No," she said, smiling up at him. "I'm fine."

He was certain she was in pain. "We'll make camp soon," he said. "Then I'll go on ahead and try to catch up with the others and come back for you with the truck."

He reckoned the next lake and Bulbula weren't far off, and he planned to do a recce by moonlight, then come back to camp and get everyone up for a dawn start. Once they got Gwenn in the truck, things should go better.

In another hour, they found Laboso waiting in a hollow. Knowing it was them, he looked up casually from where he knelt by a stream, skinning a young reedbuck. A pile of firewood waited nearby.

"Start a small fire now, Laboso," Anton said at once. "I want it out before dark." Then he helped Malcolm from his horse and told the Italians where to set Gwenn down.

Anton stopped the prisoners as they hurried towards the stream after lowering Gwenn's stretcher.

"Shoes off," he said, hoping Uzielli would challenge him so he might teach the man another lesson. "Then unsaddle the horses and unload the mules. After you water them, you can have a drink."

He set up Gwenn's small tent while Laboso pulled some wild onions and roasted the meat on sticks. Before they ate, Anton cleaned his rifle and studied the map. When the sky began to darken, he rose and stamped out the fire, lest water make it smoke more. Even Gwenn ate hungrily as they all chewed the half-cooked meat in silence.

"Non c'è pane?" grumbled the second Italian as he tossed a bone into the ashes.

"Ma stai zitto, Mario," said Uzielli sharply.

Anton prepared to leave after supper. He went over to the two Italian prisoners who sat near the fire with their legs stretched before them and their hands tied behind their backs. He had not forgotten Uzielli's attempt to stab him after the captain had surrendered. The Italians had eaten as well as the rest of them, but they were surly and dissatisfied. Contemptuous of their civilian adversaries, both soldiers had the confident disrespectful attitude of men who expected to regain the upper hand.

"Up!" Anton clapped Uzielli hard on the shoulder. "On your feet. Over here."

The captain spat and stood, following Anton to a stout acacia at the edge of camp. Anton wrapped a pair of leather reins around the tree. He tied one rein to each of Uzielli's ankles, forcing the prisoner to spread his legs to either side of the trunk. Any excessive motion would force the Italian into the tree's spiny thorns. He tied Mario to a distant tree.

Fergus was already lying down, wrapped in his blanket, almost asleep, the fatigue showing in his face. The coals were dark. The mules and horses were hobbled.

Anton rested his rifle outside and bent to enter the low sleeping tent. Gwenn raised her good arm and touched his face before they kissed. Trying to put aside the urgency of the day, softening his demeanor, he sat beside her on the ground, took her hand, and rested his head lightly against hers. Her fingers traced the lines of his face. She must be thinking of the past, perhaps of the time they had lost, as he had been.

"I'll be back soon with the Olds," he said, rising.

"Don't get lost," she said lightly, although she was concerned at being left behind. "Malcolm and I don't want to get caught by the Italians. They know we saw victims of the gas."

"Don't worry," he said. "Italians're always late."

Anton kissed her cheek, tasting the salt of her tears on his lips.

He left the tent and checked the camp again. A low mournful hooting echoed from the acacias as he made his rounds. Laboso was on sentry in the near darkness at the edge of camp. At first Anton did not see him. After a long day in the field, the slender African stood leaning against a tree, the better to stay awake, one foot raised like a stork.

"Eyes sharp, Laboso," said Anton, knowing the man was exhausted. "I'm off." He put one hand on the skinner's shoulder and gave him a few cigarettes. "Watch those prisoners. They'll cut your scrawny black throat if you give 'em a chance."

"*Ndio*, bwana," Laboso grinned. "You are going on your own feet, like a black man?"

Anton declined the bait. "In this sort of country, I can make better time at night on foot," he said, "and we want the horses fresh tomorrow. If I'm not back by midday tomorrow, start on south without me." Laboso nodded.

The two men shared a smoke and watched the full moon rise through the bush behind the camp. Anton was pleased not to have to talk.

He saluted Laboso and set off carrying his rifle at the trail. A heavy-bodied bird with a large square head rose with him, probably a spotted eagle owl. For a moment the moon cast the bird's winged shadow along the path before him. He grinned, for it was a good omen to a gypsy. The bird continued its low silent flight. He reminded himself to move as quietly.

Anton was looking forward to being alone. Although this expedition had turned out differently, the worst part of being a safari hunter was the obligatory socializing and too many people in camp. At least, this safari had gained in excitement what it had lost in comfort.

He thought of his first day on his own in Africa as a lad of nineteen in Tanganyika, walking north from Dar-es-Salaam, passing the night in the open back of an abandoned lorry with *David Copperfield* to keep him company, tucked in a pocket of his corduroy jacket. He had studied the southern stars while he listened to the animals rustling in the bush around him.

Abyssinia was not as rich in game as East Africa. Perhaps it was the altitude and the thinner vegetation. The nights lacked some of the intense theater-like sense that as darkness falls the bush throbs to life, the predators stalking and the prey wary and light-footed.

He found himself less troubled than he should be by the wartime side of things, the Italians, the film, the safety of his clients and staff, the distance to Kenya, the need to hold things together and bring them all through it. That was the sort of on-the-ground physical effort with which he was comfortable, whether it all worked out or not. What worried him was Gwenn. Would she make it? How would they be together? What about their future and the boys? He prayed Olivio and Adam were prospering in Cairo, turning Anton's few guineas into a future.

Pushing harder, trotting where he could, he felt his body breathing and loosening as he found his pace. Twice he heard a leopard cough among some distant rocks. Probably hunting baboon. After two hours his path rose gently until it peaked on a small rocky plateau. With the moon directly above him, Anton sat on a rock to shake out his boots under the immense sparkling sky. For a moment he stopped breathing and stared at a blue-black Africa he had never seen before.

Lake Langana shone below him like a huge silver coin. Lake Shala, its sister lake, glistened in the moonlight to the west, almost meeting Langana. Behind them, a jagged black massif rose like dragon's teeth before falling away until it met the base of the escarpment that rimmed the horizon like a crenellated castle wall. Beyond these twin lakes, he knew, were three more of the Great Lakes of the Ethiopian portion of the Rift Valley. Between him and Langana the ground descended in a series of sloping rocky steps. One river crossed from east to west. Here and there darker patches indicated stands of trees and high bush, and possibly water. Perched on the high land at the far end of Langana he thought he made out the circular arrangement of thatched stone huts that should be Bulbula, hopefully the typical Rift Valley market town where chicken, spices and grains from the hills were bartered for the livestock, *ghee* and bars of rock salt of the valley floor.

Excited, Anton moved swiftly down to the river. Walking along the bank, searching for an easy ford, he came to a large grey shadow crouched at the water's edge. Like a wounded elephant collapsed on its front knees at the edge of a waterhole, the Oldsmobile's front wheels were set low in the soft bank at the edge of the stream. As he walked forward he heard a commotion in the bush behind it.

The passenger door was open. The raised hood rested on a stout branch. It was too dark to check the engine, but there were bullet holes in the bonnnet and he knew Ernst would never have walked if he could have driven. Four supply chests and a tangle of camp equipment were jumbled in the back of the truck. Some of that could be repacked onto the mules, Anton thought before climbing into the cab. The windscreen was cracked. Moonlight entered through two holes in the roof. Attacked from the air, he guessed, hoping no one had been hit. Having no vehicle would make everything harder, especially for Gwenn.

He stepped down and heard the grinding of bones and the scrambling and snapping of heavy animals, almost certainly hyena. He threw a stone and took a few steps towards them, his rifle held before him.

He saw a torn boot and some fragment of a leg among a scattering of large rocks. Nearby were the remains of one of the Abyssinian soldiers who had been with Dr. Fergus, apparently dug from a shallow grave by the five or six hyena who now snarled from the darkened bushes. Yelling loudly and throwing stones, Anton checked the grave and the nearby bushes but found no other bodies. The rest must have survived the air attack, he thought. He was relieved, confident that Ernst and Kimathi could lead the others on.

Finding no tracks along the bank, Anton entered the river. It was cold, reminding him of the numbing waters of the Aberdares. Wary of crocodile, for a time in over his waist, he splashed forward as quickly as he could. Slipping once, he climbed the far bank and bent to look for tracks. The ground was harder, and he was unable to detect any footprints in the moonlight. He followed the bank in both directions but found only a chaos of deep animal tracks where native cattle had come to water. He sat and lit a cigarette, then took the route he himself would have picked. He had chosen camp sites with Kimathi so many times that he knew he would find his friends.

It reassured her to hear faint noises in the camp, especially Malcolm's familiar snore and the occasional snuffling and stamping of the mules and horses. Nonetheless, Gwenn felt anxious and alone. Unable to sleep, she lay staring up in the darkened tent, wishing Anton had not left her. From time to time she dozed, then woke with her shoulder cramped and painful, to lie again waiting for daylight or the sound of his return.

Waking again, she heard a thump as something was lowered to the ground at the edge of camp, probably Anton setting down his pack. She longed for him to come to her.

The folds of the canvas parted behind her head. A patch of night sky glittered until a figure obscured it and entered the tent.

"Anton," she whispered, reaching up one hand to touch him.

But it was another hand she knew that took hers.

"*Amore,*" the familiar voice said.

She started to cry out, but the man's other hand covered her mouth.

"Keep still," Lorenzo said. "You know I won't hurt you." He lifted his hand from her mouth.

" 'Anton,' is it? Is your Englishman here?"

"Anton? You can see he's not here," Gwenn said. Her chest pounding, she tried to speak in a calm voice. "I was dreaming. You know I was asleep when you came in."

"You are injured?" he said, stroking her cheek. "Wounded?"

She flinched, turning her face from his touch before replying. "Your air force bombed us, the Red Cross hospital, killing everyone in camp . . ."

"You wanted to go to war," he interrupted, taking one of her hands again. "I told you not to come."

"Was it you?" she said, her fingers and body rigid, furious she was so weak, so trapped. "Did you bomb us, Lorenzo?" she asked accusingly with all her energy. "Did you? Was it you?"

"I'm a soldier, in the air force. You know that." He caressed her cheek and neck, excited to find her in his control.

"Soldier? Butchering wounded people and nurses and doctors? You're a soldier? Is that what you are?" she said, chilled by his stroking fingers.

"I do my duty." He moved his free hand slowly up her other arm, starting to caress her. "I do what I must. You should be proud of what we've done. *Il Duce* has declared the end of slavery in Abyssinia."

She forced herself to ignore his touch. "Did you kill all those wounded people?"

"Where are you hurt?"

She felt his hand rise along her neck and face until it came to the bandages.

"Right there. My neck, my face." She turned her head. "You did it, didn't you? You bombed our hospital."

He moved his hand back down to her good shoulder and along her side.

"Tell me the truth," she said angrily as he lowered his face. "Was it you?"

His mouth crushed her lips.

Gwenn twisted on her cot as Lorenzo sought to embrace her. He rested one hand on her breast and forced his face to hers. Fighting with her legs, she thrashed against him. Pain tore her shoulder.

"How dare you!" Fergus raised the canvas higher and looked in. The first light was rising behind him. "Leave her alone!"

Gwenn felt Enzo reach for the weapon at his belt.

"No! Lorenzo!" she screamed. She was dazzled by the flash and roar when his pistol went off near her head.

"God!" Fergus cried. He collapsed on top of her.

Gwenn screamed from the pain. As the shock subsided, she felt the doctor's warm blood moistening her sheet.

"Help him, Lorenzo!" she cried. "Please, tell me he's not dead."

"*Capitano*!" Colonel Grimaldi called when he retreated from the tent. Uzielli was kneeling by the stream washing his face and picking at the long scab on his belly. A dead African lay in the shadows behind him, his head crushed, a bloody stone nearby.

"*Pronto*!" Grimaldi yelled, gesturing at Dr. Fergus. "Drag this Englishman to the edge of camp before the old bastard bleeds to death. Before he's gone, we must learn if they have any cinema film or stolen silver and which way they're going. Quickly. Have one of the men who speaks English question him."

"Do you want to keep him alive?" asked Uzielli, buttoning his shirt while he approached the tent.

"Do what you have to do, Captain, anything," said Grimaldi quietly, "but not too much noise. I don't want the girl to hear him. Do you understand?"

Responsive now, Uzielli saluted and ordered two *Bersaglieri* to follow him with the doctor. As he passed the camp fire he drew a smoldering log from the coals.

"This will make you sit up," Uzielli said slyly to the doctor, who groaned and protested feebly while he was carried past the fire.

Enzo bent and entered Gwenn's tent, pleased she was so nearly helpless.

"*Amore,*" he said gently. Receiving no response, he crouched by her cot and reached under her sheet with one hand, stroking her rigid body.

"Leave me alone!" she protested. He ignored her feeble efforts to push his hand away.

An hour later, roughly satisfied, Grimaldi knelt by the fire studying a map. His men sat nearby cleaning their weapons and eating. He felt fortunate that Gwenn had not heard the doctor's screams. She was being uncooperative enough without being able to accuse him of torturing a wounded man. Uzielli came over and saluted.

"*Capitano*?"

"The old man has died, Colonel," Uzielli said in a low voice, kneeling and wiping his hands against the gritty sand. "He was not so difficult. There's nothing like a little fire up the backside."

"What did you learn?"

"They are perhaps ten or twelve, lightly armed, with two women, Americans. They have many cases of silver . . ."

"What of the film?" Grimaldi interrupted.

"Yes, Colonel. Seems they have cine pictures of the gas attack, victims, a poison gas bomber on the ground." Uzielli shrugged. *"Tutto."*

It was Grimaldi's worst fear. He felt his stomach knot. His body went cold. "Have the men get three hours' sleep. Then we leave the girl at the lake with your wounded soldier and two men while we go after them." Enzo's own future would depend on it.

"May I make a suggestion, sir?"

Colonel Grimaldi was surprised by the man's initiative. He nodded as he listened, liking what he heard, especially considering Uzielli's reputation for exterminating elusive rebels. It was time to wait, and to let his enemies find each other.

Not wishing to startle the safari camp, Anton slowed his rapid breathing and squatted on the ground near Birru, the Ethiopian sentry. The soldier's Belgian rifle lay across his lap. His back against a blue gum tree, the man slept with his head to one side.

Anton pursed his lips and fluttered his tongue, giving the lilting dawn song of a tropical boubou. There was no answer to the call. As the sky brightened Anton could see the shadows of the sleeping camp. On either side a canvas was stretched across a rope tied between a pair of trees, creating two low makeshift tents, one probably home to Charlie and Bernadette, the other to Harriet. He gave the boubou call once more. The Abyssinian stirred but did not waken.

From directly behind them the lilting call was answered. Anton turned slowly and saw Kimathi kneeling twenty feet behind him, rifle in hand, grinning as he whistled again.

"My bwana must be more careful in the bush," said Kimathi.

Anton smiled back, knowing how hard it was to catch Kimathi off guard. "Any sign of the Italians?" he asked, settling down on a rocky ledge a bit further from camp.

"Not yet," Kimathi said. "Except for the plane that attacked our truck. So they know about where we are. Got one of our Abbos. The man couldn't keep his head down."

"Hyena got him next." Anton nodded. "How're we set for food and animals?"

"For silver, these people will sell everything." Kimathi rubbed a thumb and two fingers together. "In Bulbula we bought eggs and meat and beans and six more pack animals. Could've bought some girls as well," Kimathi said regretfully. "But there is one surprise for you, *Tlaga.*"

The two men walked back to the camp and built up the fire before the others rose. Famished, Anton put a bucket of water on the fire. Finding half of a wild pig hanging from a rope tied to a branch, he cut off a handful of fat and dropped it into a pan set on the coals. He carved tenderloins from the carcass and slid them into the sizzling fat. He used a fork to stir some eggs in a cup and waited for the pork to cook.

"Anton!" said Charles warmly, yawning and stretching after he crept out from one of the tent canvases with Bernadette. "How's Gwenn doing?"

"Little stronger, thanks." Anton handed each of them a tin plate. "But travelling by stretcher's nearly harder on her than walking. I'm hoping she'll be able to ride a bit today."

Grunting, Ernst von Decken emerged from the other canvas, talking to someone over his shoulder. The German tucked one of Anton's safari shirts into his belt.

"Engländer!" Ernst grinned and sat down on a case of silver. He secured the leather cup to the bottom of his stump before sniffing repeatedly and looking up at Anton. "You are stealing my swine!"

"I see you put paid to my Olds," Anton replied. He threw two handfuls of coffee into the boiling water and watched the dark grains dance in the bubbles.

A second figure stirred under Ernst's canvas. Harriet crawled out from it and stood beside the German. The small yellow box of film hung from a leather cord about her neck.

"Ooo, it's cold!" She smiled at Anton without embarrassment and pulled on a sweater. "Welcome home, bwana. We missed you." Shameless, she kissed him on the cheek. "How is your wife?"

Anton tried not to reveal his annoyance. He dropped two eggshells into the coffee.

"Better, thank you," he said distantly, reminding himself he was speaking to a client. "A couple of the boys and I must go back for her at once. If the Italians didn't follow you lot, they must have followed us." He stirred the coffee with a long stick and watched the grains settle. "I'll take Haqim and your well-rested sentry." He poured the coffee. "Give 'em a kick, Kimathi, we're off in ten."

"Why doesn't coffee taste like this at home?" Harriet asked as she passed her mug to Ernst. Knowing he shouldn't be, Anton found himself irritated by this small familiarity as he listened to the German drink.

"Do your best with these." Anton gave the cup of eggs a final stir before handing it to Harriet.

"Ndio, bwana." She crouched on her heels and poured the eggs into a pan. "You like them soft, don't you?" she said, looking up at Ernst.

"Yes, *Liebling,* of course."

"I want this camp packed up and set to march by midday," Anton said a few moments later, tightening his boots. "Meantime, take everything useful from the truck and buy some food in Bulbula and a few more animals. Some camels would be helpful, better than mules if the country gets dry. This German invalid will be on sentry till I get back." He poked von Decken hard with the egg fork, then handed it to Harriet. "Try to remember your soldiering days, Ernst. The chase is on."

— 34 —

Moving swiftly in the cool morning air, refreshed by a sturdy breakfast, Anton and the two Africans headed back to the old camp to recover Gwenn and Dr. Fergus. Anton was disappointed that the Ethiopian soldier, a lean Shoan now wearing high Italian military boots, was not more adept in the bush. It turned out Birru was the son of a storekeeper in Ankober. Impatient, Anton was annoyed to hear the man stumbling after him. Even Haqim, after years in Cairo, snapped fewer branches and shuffled fewer stones.

By the time they neared the camp, the sun was high and they were thirsty. Still a bit downstream, they approached the river that passed the camp. Squatting to drink, Anton saw a giant molerat emerge from its burrow on the other side of the stream. The rushing water must have covered the sound of his arrival, Anton thought as he crouched and watched, waiting for Haqim and Birru to catch up.

The giant rodent lifted its blunt digger's nose and peered around before walking to the water. As it passed an anthill a rufous dog-like creature leapt from hiding with the speed of a cobra and seized the rat by the neck. The hunter's bright red coat and thick black tail shone in the sun as it shook the rat violently and kept its teeth buried in the neck of its prey.

Anton recognized the predator as a female Semien fox, a creature peculiar to Abyssinia, something between a jackal and a wolf. When the molerat was still, the fox dropped it and wiped its own long narrow muzzle and sticky whiskers with neat strokes of its front paws. Then the fox gave a high-pitched scream, *"weeah-weeah."* Anton saw two red cubs come forward cautiously from a thicket several yards away. He held up a hand for silence as his companions approached, but it was no use.

"Are we almost there?" asked Birru, blundering forward.

"Yeep-yeep," the female barked in alarm. She snatched up the rat and ran to her young, chasing them before her. The three vanished into the thicket.

Haqim joined them and they walked on. Shortly before the camp Anton hesitated. A chill touched him and he raised one hand to stop his comrades. Gwenn's tent was just visible past the blue gum tree. His instinct warned him that something was wrong. Birru ignored Anton's gesture and walked on, calling out "*Tenáy*!" in greeting. "*Tenáy*!"

Two rifles fired and Birru fell. Anton dropped behind some rocks. Haqim disappeared into the bush to the left. Birru, evidently belly shot, lay where he'd fallen, crying and moaning. The Ethiopian moved one hand along the stock of his rifle. Dirt and splinters of rock leapt from the ground beside him. Struck again, Birru lay still.

Haqim's hunting rifle fired twice, its roar distinct from the thin popping crack of the Italian military rifles. Figures moved through the thick bush between Anton and the tent. Fearful of hitting Gwenn, Anton did not shoot. If the Italians had come, he dreaded what he would find.

He heard the sounds of several men running away through the thicket across the stream. Haqim whistled to him twice from the camp, the signal for "game on the way." Anton rose to one knee.

A black campaign hat moved among the branches, finally stopping and turning some fifty or sixty yards from Anton. The rear guard, he guessed, looking back for pursuit before running on. Anton watched the arched dark feathers of the Italian hat bob and flutter like the tail of a rooster. When he was certain this soldier was the last, he raised his rifle and fired. He heard the bullet strike and saw a commotion among the branches. He fired again, a trifle lower. He waited but heard only the occasional sounds of a party of men retreating in the distance.

Anton rose and walked to the body of the Abyssinian. Anton grimaced as he collected Birru's rifle and walked to the tent. Haqim was searching the camp, having suffered a light flesh wound on one arm.

Anton saw a sheet of paper resting on his metal chest near the fire. It was held in place by a stone. It was an old envelope, addressed to an Italian soldier. Someone had unfolded it and spread it open to create a piece of writing paper. Anton turned it over and read the message.

Signore Rider

In the event you make it back to your camp, I have an arrangement to propose to you.

You will give me the cine camera and film carried by your safari party, together with the silver belonging to my government that was stolen by the German brigand who travels with you.

You have the word of an Italian officer that I will then return to you your wife, if she wishes it. She requires medical attention.

Captain Uzielli will return to this camp tomorrow morning, under a flag of truce, to receive your reply and to discuss arrangements.

With my compliments,

Col. Lorenzo Grimaldi

Anton went rigid. His wife was once again with Grimaldi? He looked up to see Haqim approaching with a body in his arms, wrapped in a soiled camp blanket. Haqim set the stiff figure down at Anton's feet and unwrapped the blanket.

Anton's fury at the Italian was displaced by disgust at the gory sight. He put one hand to his mouth as his gorge rose. He clenched the paper in his other hand.

The thin pale body of Dr. Fergus lay naked on its face. Burn marks and clotted blood covered most of the backs of his legs. The area around his anus was ripped and charred as if he had been spitted on a flaming poker.

"Is this how these white soldiers fight an old man?" said Haqim with contempt.

Enraged by the murder and kidnapping, feeling responsible, Anton knelt and covered Gwenn's dead friend. More horrified by Fergus's suffering than by his actual wounds, he went to the stream and washed his face in the fresh swift water and started to think what he should do. Then he walked about the camp until he found a shovel. Suddenly a better scheme occurred to him. He hesitated, then left the tool where it was.

He was not a soldier, he reminded himself, he was a hunter.

"Put the doctor's body back, Haqim, exactly where you found it, in the way you found it." Aware of the Muslim preference for immediate burial, he sensed Haqim's surprise and distaste at the instructions. "Put the body back, Haqim." Then, wanting time to think, he went back to the stream and stripped and lay flat on the stones as the cold water coursed over him.

He felt his spirit harden. He was not concerned about the film footage of the war, or about the silver, or even about whether hyenas would devour the corpse of the good doctor. For the first time in his years as a professional hunter, his clients would not come first.

"Haqim," Anton said as he cleaned his rifle. "You will go now, back to the safari. They will understand that you speak for me. Tell them to load everything onto the animals and to start at once for Kenya, making first for Lake Abaya. I will meet them there. If I do not come by four days from today, they must all go on again."

Surprised, Haqim hesitated before accepting the order. *"Saywa, effendi."*

"Then you must return here and meet me at that fallen tree downstream. We'll bury Dr. Fergus after you get back. And bring me a box of .375's. Be careful. I will need you."

Eager to get started and return, Haqim nodded and left.

Anton rose with his rifle in one hand, Colonel Grimaldi's note in the other. Then he had a new idea. He approached the metal chest near the dead fire. Carefully he unfolded the envelope into the form in which he had found it. He placed it exactly where it had been, with the same stone on top of it. He walked backwards into the adjoining patch of forest, sweeping his fresh footprints with a branch as he retreated.

Unaware that the altered bird song already had been his harbinger, an Italian soldier moved warily about the edge of Anton's camp. The man had the durable fitness of an athletic peasant, but not the easy silent movement of a forester or hunter. Once, walking up from the stream, his mountain boots sloshing with water, two guinea fowl scampering before him, he passed so close that Anton, recognizing him, smelled the odors of old sweat and tobacco. No doubt Uzielli had been searching for signs of ambush and was now awaiting Anton's response to his colonel's written message.

The *Bersaglieri* crouched under a dead wild fig tree at the edge of the clearing. Hatless, bearing no pack, he held his carbine across his knees. Behind him, the dark bark of the tree trunk was lightened and polished smooth by the rubbing of some short antelope, probably an itchy duiker or bushbuck. The soldier rested and waited for Anton as the light brightened.

Lying comfortably in a narrow trench scraped out between two dense thornbushes, with excavated dirt and light branches camouflaging his body, Anton watched with satisfaction. Haqim was hidden at the other side of the camp. With the patience of a hunter, Anton waited to follow the *Bersaglieri* back to the Italian camp. He was pleased that Grimaldi had chosen Uzielli for this mission.

Anton shifted the old gypsy dagger in his fingers and recalled the Romany legend that if one placed a thorn bush atop a grave the dead would not rise. It was at such times, when he had eased silently back into the land, that Anton contemplated the youthful education that had prepared him for Africa.

He watched the soldier settle in and thought of the games he and his gypsy mates had played about their camps as boys: creeping through the woods, silent as hedgehogs, throwing scraps to the mongrels to deter their high-pitched barking, waiting for a song or tambourine to cover their final advance. Excluded from certain rituals because he was not himself a Romany, it was in forest craft that Anton had become a leader.

He remembered the balancing of urgency and patience as each lad sought to be the first to shelter under the chief's *vardo* without being spotted when he entered camp to sneak beneath the narrow carved wagon. Trained for a lifetime of flight and poaching, stealth and sleight of hand, the youths were prepared for this sport as other boys were for cricket or football. Instead of classes dedicated to Horace and Euclid, their studies had been knife throwing, palm reading, and, in Anton's case, come-one-come-all fair ground boxing.

Best of all were the nights after the lads had discovered another gypsy camp nearby, perhaps that of a tribe with different roots, from the Danube or the Pyrenees or Moldavia, but sheltered now in a copse at the edge of some unwelcoming village in Dorset or Northumberland or Suffolk. Then the boys played at war.

They would bind *diklos* over their faces before stalking low to the ground like cats, making their way to the other camp. Then they would wait impatiently for the fires to die before testing their art as gypsies, celebrating their tribal craft as they sought to steal from this rival camp of thieves. A tinsmith's tool pack, a cracked *cithara,* or perhaps a trained performing goat were among the finest prizes. But best of all was every gypsy coper's favorite: a horse, to draw a wagon, to trade or to mount like a cavalier. Only once had Anton himself attempted this. As a result, his prominent nose had been broken for the second time. Caught and beaten, prudence and timing had been his lessons.

One night, on a bluff near the sea in Cornwall, Anton had lain outside another camp on such a mission. Rather than attempt theft, however, he had been stupefied by an unexpected spectacle. He had watched the *ursuari,* the bear trainers, at the peculiar trade said to be the specialty of Romanies from the mountains of Serbia, descendants of the Zapari gypsies from Turkey.

A shaggy young animal, trussed and with his jaw stretched wide by a wooden peg, had his teeth wrenched out with a blacksmith's pincers. The beast's howls tore the camp. Shackles were then fitted to the bear's front legs. A heavy collar was set about his neck. The animal lay twitching with pain and rage and terror.

Nearby the gypsy smith heated a sheet of metal over some coals. Untied, the young bear stumbled like a puppy when he rose. Guided and controlled by chains, the animal was led to the hot sheet. Blood dripped from his wet muzzle and sizzled like pig fat on the edge of the metal pan. Waiting close by were two short dark old men in red skull caps, corduroy britches and tattered silver-buttoned waistcoats. One carried a long staff, the other bore a goatskin drum on his hip.

The staff began to wave and the drum to beat. Children scampered over from the busy camp to watch. The bear's front feet were dragged forward onto the glowing sheet.

His front paws scorched, the young bear howled and reared on his hind legs. A tug on his collar and he fell back onto his wounded forepaws as the drum beat again. Long-haired boys and girls in kerchiefs laughed and clapped as the stick rose and fell in time with the bear's high-stepped dancing. Sickened, Anton smelled the searing flesh of the animal's velvety black pads. Plantigrade, like men, bears were used to walking on the full soles of their feet, using heel and toe. The old drummer tapped his foot merrily and nodded with the music. The bear cried like a child as his antic shadows were cast beyond the caravans deep into the forest. Anton had slipped behind a tree and vomited.

He knew that thereafter the enslaved toothless creature would stand and dance whenever he saw the staff and heard the drum.

As if hearing the end of the tale, Captain Uzielli yawned and rose to his feet in the shadow of the fig tree. Anton studied the soldier as he would a buck or rhino before selecting the best trophy for a client. Already the man was more comfortable in the bush than most Europeans ever became. He seemed unafraid to be alone. As he ambled about the camp, Uzielli's powerful legs revealed their thick thighs and knotty calves beneath his dark tan shorts. His carbine hung easily in one hand.

The Italian walked to the low tent that Gwenn and Anton had shared. He emerged with Anton's small metal locker. He knelt and spilled its contents at his feet, tossing Anton's book onto the dead fire. Anton watched the man draw the six tent stakes from the ground and roll the canvas itself into a tight bundle with the cords and stakes inside it. The Italian looked towards the body of Dr. Fergus, then walked over and kicked the stiff half-naked corpse with his boot, turning it face up with his left toe. Hot with rage, restraining himself because of Gwenn, Anton watched the man unbutton his shorts and relieve himself on the body.

Finally Uzielli stepped to the rock on which rested the ransom note from Colonel Grimaldi to Anton. Anton guessed that the soldier was bewildered as he stared at the stone that still held the paper in place. The captain lifted the letter and folded it into the pocket of his shirt. The rolled tent under one arm, he glanced carefully around the camp, scratching his balding scalp and gripping his carbine in his right hand as he walked away, soon breaking into the *Bersaglieri* trot.

Anton waited until he could no longer hear the running soldier. Then he rolled free of his shelter, lifted his rifle and twice clicked his tongue before stepping forward and kneeling by the body of Malcolm Fergus.

Haqim joined him from the far side of the camp.

"Please bury our friend well." Anton handed Haqim the shovel. "Then follow me quietly to the camp of the Italian soldiers. You will find my trail."

Haqim nodded and set to work, relieved that his master was not a barbarian.

His thoughts full of how Gwenn had been in the tent, Anton went to the fire and lifted *Oliver* from the coals. He dusted the ashes from the cover with his *diklo* and slipped the book into a pocket of his bush jacket. He rinsed the bandana in the stream, wiped his face and knotted the red cloth around his neck. Now he was set to track. Intent but relaxed, as he ran he considered what he must do. Should he be a gentleman like Adam Penfold, or effective like Olivio the dwarf?

With Gwenn as their prisoner, he could not fight a group of heavily armed men. Even if he freed her, travelling on foot, with Gwenn injured, they could never outrun the soldiers. To escape with her, he must use Grimaldi against his own men. He must force Grimaldi to help their escape.

Anton tracked the *Bersaglieri* for nearly an hour. He kept his distance, his body taut with concentration. Finally he halted when he heard the sounds of a camp some distance ahead in the bush.

Tempted to seize Uzielli once the soldier had led him within sight of the small Italian base, but fearful of creating a disturbance, Anton knelt behind a fist of boulders and watched the man trot into camp.

He chose a secure hide and settled in with his field glasses. The captain stopped amidst a knot of men near a pole that held a small Italian flag. As Anton watched, two men set up the tent that Uzielli had carried back. Colonel Grimaldi stepped forward and took Captain Uzielli to one side. Anton tensed when he saw his rival. He scanned the camp carefully, searching for Gwenn. There she was, sitting near a stretcher at the far side of the camp. His wife's back was turned to him. Her head was resting on her knees. Grimaldi walked over to Gwenn and assisted her to the tent, ignoring her efforts to shake off his arm. Anton was relieved to see her resisting the man. Determined to save her, he breathed deeply and forced himself to banish anger from his thinking.

By midday he had learned the habits of the camp. There was another officer besides Uzielli, and a medic with a Red Cross band around one sleeve. The nineteen men displayed better discipline and organization than Italy's ribald detractors in Cairo had led Anton to expect. Weapons, fires, food and sentries were neatly arranged. Whether this was to the colonel's credit, or was simply the mark of a superior regiment, he could not be certain, but he was interested to see that the troopers obeyed orders, for his scheme depended on their discipline. He noted that the refuse and the latrine were set well away from camp, some forty or fifty yards from Anton's rocks, perhaps halfway between him and the base. Their only failure seemed to be the empty-handed return of a two-man hunting party in the afternoon. Blessedly devoid of bushcraft, the young *Bersaglieri* hunters were received with a chorus of derision from their fellows.

Haqim appeared among the sheltering rocks as the shadows lengthened. He and Anton spoke quietly. Famished, Anton shared the Nubian's dried meat and dates while they waited for darkness.

At nightfall Anton took a new position behind the bushes that screened the Italian latrine. The soldiers walked unarmed from camp by ones and twos, joking and spitting as they used the facility. During one quiet interval, when the fires dimmed and only the two sentries seemed to be awake, Anton crept closer. He heard Gwenn give a scream of protest from the low tent where Grimaldi must have joined her. Anton clenched his rifle and forced himself to lie quietly. Once or twice more she cried out. Trembling, the sounds cutting him, Anton contained his anger as if he were packing grains of gunpowder into a brass-bound cartridge. After a time Anton crept back and again lay still by the latrine. Haqim lay beside him like a boulder.

Anton rested beside the Sudanese for several hours. Finally an exchange of words startled him. He heard Grimaldi snapping at an inattentive sentry as he made his way towards the sanitation trench. Anton could see the armed soldier follow the officer and stand nearby with his back turned.

Anton tapped Haqim's shoulder and together they rose like a single shadow.

Grimaldi stood and pulled up his trousers. There was a heavy grunt a few feet away. Anton grasped Enzo around the neck and pricked his knife through the skin behind his right ear.

"Silence," Anton whispered harshly. Thrilled to have Grimaldi in his hands, thinking of Gwenn's suffering, he was tempted to bury his knife to the hilt when the man struggled to free himself.

Grimaldi wheezed as Anton tightened his grasp, waiting for the man to weaken. The Italian continued to struggle and attempt to wrench his body free. Impressed by the tenacity of the older man's resistance, Anton warned himself not to underestimate the officer. Haqim walked silently past them back to the rocks, a large figure in his arms. Restraining himself from useless violence, Anton forced the colonel to follow them.

In a few moments both Italians lay on their bellies on the rocky ground between the boulders. Their hands were secured behind their backs with their bootlaces. A sock was stuffed into each of their mouths. Haqim knelt between the two men, holding up each of their heads by a fistful of hair, like a pair of oxen in a yoke. Anton was aware of the first light brightening the bush.

"I notice, Colonel, that in Africa you do not honor the rules of war when you fight civilians." Anton held his knife near Grimaldi's face. "You have bombed hospitals. You have maimed my wife. You have tortured and killed Dr. Fergus." He studied the impassive grey-haired man before continuing. If he were to save Gwenn and the others, he knew the officer must be broken down, his vanity and arrogance pierced. Without Grimaldi's assistance he could not free Gween and secure the cooperation of the *Bersaglieri* in their flight. The only alternative was to kill Grimaldi and every Italian in the camp.

"My friend Haqim and I accept your lesson. We will fight as you do." He saw Grimaldi trying to disregard the stone-faced man who held his head. "Now I will free your mouth and you will utter only whispers." He removed the filthy sock from the Italian's mouth with the tip of his *choori.* As if by accident he made a deep razor-fine cut along the officer's upper lip with the movement.

"You and I must work out how you will free my wife and ensure our escape from your men," Anton said.

Enzo coughed and spat, not aware he had been cut. Blood ran down over his teeth.

"Gwenn and I are lovers again," the Italian said eagerly, glancing down and seeing his own blood. He paused, startled, unable to raise a hand to his mouth, and spat again before continuing. "She will never go with you."

"You did not listen to me, Colonel." Anton nodded at Haqim. "You are going to free my wife and ensure our escape from your men."

The Nubian smashed the other soldier's face down into the ground and instantly jerked it violently backwards.

"No, Haqim!" Anton exclaimed, too late, as the thick neck broke with the crack of a heavy branch snapping. Enzo struggled at the sound. The *Bersaglieri*'s body twitched and lay still. Haqim released the dead man's head, then turned it on one cheek to face Grimaldi with its broken nose and open eyes.

Anton heard Enzo gasp, then cough and swallow before speaking in a different, less confident voice.

"That man was trained to die, a peasant in uniform." Enzo spoke slowly, collecting himself. "You cannot do the same to me. And if you did, then what would stop my men from killing you both?"

"You and I will now arrange how to free my wife and assist our escape." Annoyed by the man's resistance but almost pleased by what it might compel him to do, Anton moved the knife closer to his prisoner's face. He was not surprised that the soldier's death had not been sufficient. But if Grimaldi's defiance succeeded, Gwenn and his clients and he were all lost. He thought of the dancing bear. He smelled its scorching feet.

"You will order two men, unarmed, to carry my wife here on a stretcher, but first to bring here all seventeen pairs of your soldiers' boots and four canteens and two knapsacks of food and medical supplies."

"Ridiculous, Rider," Enzo said with deliberation. His teeth shone with blood. He cleared his throat, casting back his head as far as he could and speaking carefully with contempt.

"You are a failure, Englishman. Just another useless colonial gentleman, or something like one, and you will fail in this, too."

"I may not be the sort of Englishman you think."

With a swift movement Anton pricked the ridge of Grimaldi's left cheekbone with the point of his *choori.*

The Italian's face twitched with pain. "Gwenn would never forgive you, gypsy boy, if you hurt m . . ." Enzo's face grew red as Anton stuffed the sock back into his mouth. Haqim leaned one knee in the center of the Italian's back and put his free hand on the officer's neck, still gripping the man's hair with his other hand. He looked to Anton for direction.

Anton hesitated, certain Gwenn would hate him for this, but knowing that to save her, he must risk losing her.

Anton stabbed the knife tip through the lower lid of Grimaldi's left eye and flicked the eyeball from its socket. Like an oyster without its shell, the eye settled in the dust between them.

Enzo's body shook violently under the weight of Haqim, trembling and sweating despite the dawn cold. Blood ran down the colonel's left cheek into his mustache. A small bulb of ocular muscle and the white end of the optic nerve twitched between the two edges of the sunken slit of the lower eyelid. There was a long silence before Anton spoke again.

"This will be a long dark day, Colonel, particularly if you lose them both."

Thinking of Gwenn's injured face and what it would mean to the boys and him if she died, Anton found himself facing the Italian with detachment, as if he were skinning an animal, or had come upon a hyena crippled by a snare.

"What a shame Dr. Fergus is not with us to look after your wounds. It will be difficult for you to bomb hospitals if you are blind." Anton set the tip of his knife just beneath Grimaldi's other eye. "Now will you help to free my wife and assist our escape?"

The Italian nodded twice.

Addressing the kneeling Nubian, Anton said, "Time to start a fire, please, Haqim, while Colonel Grimaldi and I go to his camp to give some orders."

Anton grabbed Grimaldi by his knotted wrists and dragged the Italian to his feet. Together they walked towards the *Bersaglieri* camp until the colonel's voice could be clearly heard as he ordered his men to carry out Anton's instructions. Then Anton returned Grimaldi to Haqim's care. The Nubian seized the colonel roughly.

Anxious, trying not to appear nervous, Anton worried whether his plan would work. Half an hour later, he stood alone in the open near the latrine without his rifle. He watched two Italians walk towards him from the camp. Stepping carefully among the stones and thorns, the barefoot soldiers were carrying Gwenn on a stretcher. He saw her raise her head when she realized it was he. Anton sought not to be distracted by the sight of her.

The other fifteen troopers lay in the camp on their stomachs, facing away from Anton some distance from their stacked but empty weapons. With only one two-shot rifle to cover them, Anton had been obliged to rely on Colonel Grimaldi's authority to control the *Bersaglieri.* He judged that an attempt to leave them disarmed in the middle of Ethiopia might have provoked an uncontrollable rebellion.

Anton recognized the forward stretcher bearer as his former prisoner, Mario. Bound, his shirt knotted around his head, Grimaldi was back behind the rocks. Thick dark smoke rose from a fire nearby where the *Bersaglieris'* boots were burning.

Anton watched Mario and raised both his own hands above the level of his shoulders. The backs of his hands faced the advancing Italians. The fingers of his right hand were bent back towards his wrist.

Gwenn lifted her head off the stretcher. "He has a pistol behind his back!" she called.

Mario dropped the foot of the stretcher and reached behind him.

In a fluid motion Anton flung down his right arm. The *choori* flew from his sleeve.

The knife entered the base of Mario's neck. For an instant there was no blood. Below his Adam's apple, the hilt rested flat against the skin of Mario's throat like a gypsy wedding necklace.

Haqim fired from thirty yards. The heavy hunting slug hit the second stretcher bearer in the nose and split his face. Blood and bone and tissue splashed over Gwenn as the head of the stretcher struck the ground.

Anton reached Mario as the Italian stood rocking on his feet, one hand going to his throat, the other still gripping the pistol.

Anton grabbed the Beretta with his right hand and twisted out the knife with his left. He fired two warning shots over the heads of the prone but stirring *Bersaglieri,* then stuffed the weapons into his belt.

Mario collapsed forward onto his knees as if called suddenly to prayer, gargling blood. Haqim rushed forward in his new boots and helped Anton lift the stretcher.

The two men carried her past the boulders that concealed the trussed and seated body of the colonel. Grimaldi groaned loudy just as Gwenn was carried by the rocks. Finally Anton and Haqim set down the stretcher. Anton turned to walk back, the Beretta in his hand.

"Don't!" Gwenn called back to him. Unable to see Lorenzo, she feared what Anton might do. "Please, don't. Anton!"

Rider faced his prisoner. He knew better than to leave a vengeful and wounded enemy with fifteen trained men at his disposal, especially a man like Colonel Grimaldi. He thought of what the man had done to Malcolm Fergus and what he would do now if opportunity permitted. Anton cocked the pistol and let Grimaldi listen to the silence in his gag and blindfold.

"Anton, no," the clear voice called, stronger as she sat up in the stretcher and put her feet to one side and began to stand.

"Think of the boys!" She gripped Haqim's arm and took one step back towards the boulders. "Remember how much Lorenzo did for them when you were not with me and I was alone with nothing."

Anton tried not to listen. He watched Grimaldi tremble as the man tried to retain some dignity and sit up straight against the rock.

Violence and death were part of Anton's experience, but this would be his first defenceless man, his first murder. But if they were to escape, he knew he must do it. They were on foot, with hundreds of miles before them. Grimaldi would pursue them like no one else.

"Especially Denby, our son," she called to Anton, still not close enough to see Lorenzo. She raised her voice and spoke slowly.

"Anton, the boys would have been hungry and ragged and unschooled without him. Please, you can't . . ."

"Do you believe he did it for the boys?" Anton replied, turning back to speak to her. Finally he lowered the Beretta, not for the boys, but to keep her. He must not do something that she could never forgive.

He stepped over to Grimaldi and ripped off the gag and blindfold.

"Do I have your parole, Colonel, that if I leave you alive, you and your men will not pursue us?"

"You have nothing." Grimaldi spoke quietly through black lips. "*Niente.*" He blinked and looked up at his captor. A little blood leaked down his left cheek.

Exhausted, unable to hear their words, Gwenn sank back onto the stretcher. Hating it all, dreading further violence, she understood but feared Anton's anger. In any case, she knew the Italian medic would look after Lorenzo once they left.

Anton knelt close to the colonel, hesitating, wanting to kill him, trying to balance their safety against Gwenn's sense of what sort of man her husband should be.

"If I see you again, Grimaldi, I will kill you," he said evenly, putting the weapon in his pocket. "You have my word as an Englishman."

Enzo tried to spit into the dust but instead only drooled spittle on his chin. His chest trembling, he leaned back against the rock and closed his eye. Anton looked down at him for the last time.

Then Anton and Haqim, rifles and packs on their backs, lifted the stretcher and set off for the hills and lakes to the south. Anton felt the Nubian's disgust at his weakness.

"Aren't you tired?" Gwenn said many hours later, sitting against a log near the small river while Haqim scouted downstream and Anton cleaned the rifles and the Beretta. The water divided into two streams a short distance below them. She had loved being alone with him like this, or almost alone, but now she was not sure. So much had happened. For the moment she could not bear to be touched by any man. "You two've been carrying me for miles."

"Yes, a bit tired," Anton conceded, leaning back towards her. "We've done ten or twelve miles. But we've still a way to go." He was concerned the Italians would be after them already. He knew they would pay a price for letting Grimaldi live.

She was aware of him turning his head and looking up at her with a boy's eyes as she rose.

"I'm going back to that pool to bathe." Gwenn was desperate to wash herself. "I feel filthy."

"Gwenn," Anton said, "I must ask you something."

She stopped and stiffened, certain what it would be.

"Did you make love with him?"

"No," she said, turning back, resentful but almost relieved by the question, wanting Anton not to doubt her, to understand how it had been. She realized she had forgotten how straightforward Anton was.

"I was so weak. He forced me, raped me, really. Once in our old camp, once in theirs." Angry at both men, she paused and looked at this one.

"You were going to kill him, weren't you?" she said, challenge in her voice, knowing she should not start this.

"Perhaps. Probably. I really don't know." His voice hardened."Would you expect me to leave a wounded leopard or hyena by our camp?"

"Lorenzo is not an animal," Gwenn continued, aware she was provoking him.

"You just told me he raped you. What about Malcolm? Did you ask him what he did to Malcolm? Look what his bombing did to you. What about the gas?"

"I'm talking about you, not about him. I don't want you to be that sort of man. Can't you understand that? There're certain things decent people just don't do, like using gas and bombing hospitals. What will the world be like if everyone behaves like that? Imagine the next war!" She paused, looking at him, searching his eyes as if trying to find out who he was.

"Tell me what you did to him back there."

Anton hesitated, determined to be honest but not to lose her.

"Tell me."

"I took out his eye to save your life."

"How, how could you? You just can't do that. You make me guilty, too. Don't you see? It's like bombing the hospital, and all the rest of it . . ."

"I did it for you, for all of us, and for Malcolm and the others . . ."

"Did you have another reason, Anton? Something else?"

"If I hadn't done it, you wouldn't be free now."

"It wasn't worth it," she said, recognizing the horror of her words, trying to hurt him. Still, her time with Lorenzo was not a secret, and had to be resolved, both with Anton and herself. She spoke quietly.

"Did you do it because you were jealous?"

"No." He paused, withdrawing. Reluctantly he too sensed what this argument was about. "He was our enemy. He would've killed us both, as well as our friends. Now he still might. How do you think that would be for the boys?"

"Then why didn't you kill him if you thought he was so dangerous?"

"Because you asked me not to."

She knew he was telling the truth, and she knew where he felt weak.

"How could you ever have killed him when you know what he did for the children while you were doing nothing?"

"I told you he did not do that for the boys."

"The 'why' doesn't matter. I was desperate when we got to Cairo," she said, relieved to be releasing old resentment, feeling liberated by the candor. "I was alone. Can't you understand that?"

"Perhaps you have some other reason."

Gwenn turned aside, her lower lip trembling. "None that you would understand." She began walking towards the stream.

"Didn't you ever love him?" he called after her.

She turned and faced him, shouting. "Did you love all those women you've been with?"

"Did I ever have another woman in the same tent with our children?" Certain he'd stung her, he continued. "Did he always force you? Or was it always the money?"

Gwenn turned her back and walked away, trying to control the agitation of her body. At the river she knelt and cupped cold water to her face. Her hands were shaking. Then she sat on a rock with her face in her hands. Why were they both making it so hard?

Before bathing Gwenn stood and stretched her tightened back, relieved that her shoulder was less stiff and painful when she moved. When she returned, she was not surprised to hear Anton speak to her in his quiet detached manner, as if he were telling a client about the next day's plans. They both knew they had to stop all this and carry on and do the best they could.

"After we eat," he said, "Haqim will help me carry you on down the west fork of this river. Then he'll leave us after dark and double back here and make a fire and then follow the other stream to the next lake, straight along the route for Kenya, leaving traces of his path. If the Italians follow at all, they should follow him. You and I will be well off the route, and we'll camp somewhere safe until you're stronger."

Gwenn hoped it would be that easy, praying she had seen the last of Lorenzo. Confused by her emotions and Anton's bitterness, she wondered if she had been avoiding the truth in what he'd said.

— 35 —

"Not much cheery news from Abyssinia, I fear," said Adam Penfold, hoping to distract his friend from the brooding thoughts that gripped the little man. "Seems occasionally these black chaps manage to isolate a small unit or two and have some sport. But mostly the Eyeties've got 'em on the run, taking one big town after another. Axum, Goba, what not. Just won a nasty battle at some spot called Makalle. Africans massed and kept coming on into heavy fire. Machine guns, cannon, tanks, the lot. Fearful losses, but the Emperor says they're fighting on. Photo right here of him manning the ack-acks himself." Penfold folded the *Gazette* and held it up, but failed to draw a response from Olivio. So he continued.

"Tough little nut, this Selassie. They claim he brought down an Italian fighter. Neither side's wasting time with prisoners. Says here Italy denies using gas. They wouldn't dare, mind you."

"I pray our friends are staying well clear," said the dwarf absently.

The two men were sitting on the deck of the shabby houseboat. The craft had been bought and towed to the old quay of the Cataract Café, thereby preserving mooring rights and providing Olivio with a temporary flagship. The little man wore a broad black armband on his left sleeve. Sitting in a fan-shaped rattan chair, almost lost among his cushions, the dwarf looked older and wearier than Penfold had ever seen him. A leather portfolio lay on the ivory-inlaid table before him.

From time to time one of the divers, Greeks recruited from Suez, crawled up a rope ladder onto the deck of the boat in his underdrawers. Dripping water, slick as an ocean eel, his smooth deep chest pumping, their leader placed objects retrieved from the sunken vessel on mats arrayed near the dwarf. A small alabaster sphinx rested on the table beside the portfolio. Deaf, the head diver had learned to respond to the artful gestures of his employer.

"Trouble is, the whole world's carrying on about this invasion, even the Yanks, but nobody's doing much about it, just a lot of chat-chat," Penfold continued. "We're doing the best, really. Building up the Royal Navy in the Mediterranean, battleships cruising off Port Saïd, threatening oil sanctions, calling for another meeting of the League . . ."

"No one cares about the smoke," said the dwarf, "unless his own house is in flames." He noticed Tariq approaching along the deck with fresh coffee.

"Excellency," said Tariq, bowing to his sagacious master, watching him pass sketches of a new floating café to the English lord. "One question keeps me troubled."

Olivio Alavedo nodded without looking at his servant.

"Why did they burn the boat when no one knew you would be there?"

"To make me afraid," said the dwarf. "To make me desist from my business," he added, knowing he finally had Lord Penfold's attention. "To make me sell, instead of buy. They thought fear would be cheaper than money."

Tariq rarely laughed aloud, but this made him do so.

"It is fear they seek?" he said. "That we can help them find, *effendi*!"

"Yes. Fear." The little man raised his head and looked at the Nubian. For the first time since the death of his daughter, Tariq recognized the old brightness in his master's grey eye.

"Before you give us your report, Tariq, let me show you another view," said the dwarf. He opened the portfolio and arranged two portraits side by side near the sphinx. He turned the likenesses to meet first Lord Penfold's, then Tariq's gaze. One was *Monsieur* Aristide's drawing of the killer; the other, remarkably similar, a blurry photograph of the chauffeur of the Undersecretary of Public Works taken at the funeral of Clove Alavedo.

"Remarkable," said Penfold. "Your Frenchie got him best, but it's the same chap, all right."

"What have you learned, Tariq, what have you learned?" said the dwarf, sitting forward as if a good meal had just been set before him. "Who is this thin-faced man?"

"We are getting closer, master. The God-less one comes from Upper Egypt, the village of Armant, a town celebrated for its hired killers as other villages are known for their vegetables or craftsmen. This man they call 'Razorhead,' after the carrion-eating fish peculiar to the Red Sea," said Tariq, proud of his report. "They say he is a fine hand with a knife."

"What brought the wretched chap to Cairo?" asked Penfold, finding himself drawn into the pursuit.

"He fled here from Port Saïd. There he crushed three stevedores under a load of coal in the hold of a steamship," said Tariq.

"You don't say," said the Englishman. "Messy work."

"Yes, *effendi.* They found the bodies when the ship stopped in Cape Town, almost entirely devoured by rats."

"Shouldn't be so hard to find the fellow if he's working for that Undersecretary what-not," Penfold said.

"Alas, my lord, he was only a temporary chauffeur on the day we saw him at the basilique. It seems his work for Musa Bey is more private and keeps him from the light," explained Olivio with patience. "Now, Tariq, tell us where the trail leads."

"When time allows, this Razorhead drives an old taxi, a stolen Renault, that he shares with a partner. Most nights he passes in the room of two very young prostitutes . . ."

"Where is this dwelling?" interrupted the dwarf, barely breathing, relishing the notion of surprising the killer during his enviable pleasure.

Tariq hesitated, savoring the detail. "He sleeps with the camels, master, among the dead camels." The Nubian tapped one side of his nose before continuing.

"I am told this room is somewhere in an alley near *al-Madbah,* the abattoir, master. There the dense odor of camels, living and dead, is said to fill the air like grains in a sandstorm. Even the fresh laundry that waves above the alleys smells of camel."

The sound of cabinet-makers laboring belowdecks intruded on their conversation.

"We must find this Razorhead before he flees again," said the dwarf. "It is time for me to rejoin the chase," he continued, determined to be in at the kill. "Where will we take up the scent?"

"Near the abattoir there is an eating-place, Birzani's, attended daily by my uncle, Tawfiq Abd al-Hadi, and the other butchers. They are rich men and can take their ease."

"Yes, yes, of course," said the dwarf, as if acknowledging this distinction.

"Across from this place is a café where the drivers of taxis come to drink tea and throw dice. In time, every driver comes to Birzani's or to this café across the square, for there a market is made in stolen and forged licenses and other papers of their trade."

"Tomorrow," said Olivio brightly, "we will go hunting. I only wish Mr. Anton were here to join us."

Early the next morning the three men abandoned the Rover and slowly made their way through the narrow alleys towards Slaughterhouse Square. The Nubian walked ahead to clear the way, save where some ditch or barrier of mud or refuse prevented his small master from advancing. Then he turned and bowed and lifted Olivio Alavedo over the obstruction with gentle respect. Penfold waited patiently for each such diversion, catching his breath, deploring the condition of his shoes. Mongrel dogs and children squabbled under the dusty hanging laundry, running about barefoot amidst old garbage, trenches of waste and crowded chicken coops. As the Englishman resumed his advance, he gripped his new black cane in one hand. The dwarf held the other.

Over time, like a medieval town expanding around a rising cathedral, a dependent village had grown around the abattoir, one of Cairo's many cities within the city. It was a community of twisting alleyways and thin two-story houses of crumbling red and grey brick, in some ways a district like so many others. The overhanging wooden window grills of the second floors almost met above their heads. The drooping structures seemed to warn each other against collapse, nearly touching across the narrow streets.

They passed small coffee-houses, restaurant counters and open markets that provided some relief. Sandal makers and tobacconists, leather merchants and butchers were opening for business, removing wooden shutters and sweeping dirt and rubbish from place to place as they prepared to labor and trade in narrow shops wedged between the slanting walls. Women cloaked in long black *malayas* paused to chatter and bargain, peering under their headscarves as they examined pieces of cloth and fruit, occasionally interrupting their talk to watch the three men pass.

"This is Birzani's, master," said Tariq, spreading his hands to welcome them to one corner of the square. He wiped two wooden chairs and held one for Olivio at a rickety table set outside the open window counter of beaten nickel. Behind it, an old man in a felt skull-cap was serving his clients on the street.

"They seem to keep busy," said Penfold, enjoying himself. A shapely woman concealed in a scarf and cloak appeared at the edge of the window. She paid with a coin and accepted several fresh hot rounds of *aysh baladi* filled with stewed fava beans mashed with oil, lemon, onions and garlic.

"Some mornings there is a quiet interval between the time the last prostitutes go home and the first butchers start their predawn work," said Tariq. "But Birzani's kitchen is never cold. These women, of course, do not sit or linger, or go inside, and are not offered plates, but buy their food across the counter, as you see."

"You may sit with us, Tariq," said the dwarf.

Soon, as the butchers left, the first cart and taxi drivers arrived and took turns sniffing the uncovered tin pans and *dammassas.* Each thin-necked gourd-shaped stewing pot contained and concentrated its own aroma like a snifter or a tight-mouthed bottle of perfume. Outside, small grey donkeys twitched their nostrils and lowered their heads to the piles of bright green *birsiim* that their owners had dropped into the gutters. The men used long wooden ladels to fill their white enamel plates at the counter of the open kitchen. With their fingers they sprinkled cumin and chopped parsley onto their selections. Then they paid with half-piastre coins and leaned against the walls inside and out as they sipped and ate and chatted with their mates before returning to their cabs and donkey carts.

"Might have a bit of that meself," said Penfold, boyishly hungry. "What's that one there?"

"The common dish of Egyptians, my lord," said the dwarf. Excited by the chase, he pinched one of his open ear lobes while he tried to respond with interest. "*Fuul*, broad beans mashed with olive oil, salt and lemon, simmered overnight and flavored with crushed garlic and cumin."

"Sabâh al-khayr," said the proprietor, presenting his three clients with small glasses of mint tea.

"God grant you a good morning," replied Tariq, introducing Olivio and Penfold to old man Birzani.

Penfold watched the steam rise from the small glasses in the early morning chill. Before he could drink, a gust of wind dispersed the aromas of the tea and the dishes simmering inside the restaurant. The tall stone building where the camels were butchered and the two brick structures dedicated to slaughtering bulls and lesser beasts were nearly a hundred yards away. But the rush of air brought with it the dense stink of old remains and of other animals freshly dead. The desert wind carried through the barred windows of the great stone barn, along the brick passages that led from it, past the holding stalls and the piles of new skins, over the wooden platforms stacked with camel heads and the long tables covered in pulpy livers and white-membraned sinewy meat and innards and hocks and humps, and across the square to the restaurant.

In the open yard that was the center of the square, a few camels waited quietly, their left forelegs tied up, hobbled at the knee. Penfold knew the animals were driven north to Cairo in herds gathered from upper Egypt and the Sudan. Only the camels distinguished this district from so many others, he thought, watching his friend glance about at this new place with a sharp wary eye. At the desert camps outside Cairo, the camels were gathered around the men. Here, the people had collected around the animals that supported and fed and clothed them.

"Why're those poor camels all marked up like that?" said Penfold, referring to the lines of red chalk that stood out on the rough patchy hide of their necks and humps and quarters. The sight reminded him of how he himself must look during a fitting while his tailor marked his suit with chalk.

"To identify the owners of their various parts," said the dwarf, thinking of Dr. Hänger's notations of his own condition.

Penfold sipped his tea, impressed with how Tariq was managing this adventure for his friend. This morning the Nubian was dressed in a short shabby *gallabiyyah* and the heavy black rubber boots of a cutter from al-Madbah. His personal *sakiina* rested against the wall beside him near the open window counter. A thick curved knife the length and weight of a short sabre, it was the badge of a cutter's work.

"Handsome outfit, Tariq," said Lord Penfold, tapping his shoes together to shake loose the clinging filth of the alleys.

"Kattar khayrak." Tariq bowed his head.

"That's quite a knife," Penfold added.

"As custom requires, my lord," explained the dwarf with satisfaction, pleased to be passing on what he himself had learned earlier that morning. "The body of the blade was not cleaned after the last slaughter, lest that portend there would be no more camels to carve. That clear bright edge, of course, has been sharpened clean by one of those jolly camel boys throwing stones at the dogs over there, apprentices, you understand, who earn their way by looking after the knives and hatchets and hooks and chains that make this abattoir the envy of North Africa. *Al Häwïya,* the boys call it proudly, in Islam the 'lowest hell.' " Pleased with his authority, the dwarf wiggled back in his seat, feeling more properly in control.

Tariq nodded respectfully while his master talked, then spoke quietly as they watched a dark heavily-built man enter Birzani's kitchen to select his food. Wearing a white skullcap and carrying a long-handled hatchet in his waistband, the man wore a stained goat-skin apron.

"This great man is my uncle, Tawfiq Abd al-Hadi," said Tariq. "Hadi is a gut man, known to all for his ability to disembowel even the biggest camel in three minutes or less."

"You don't say," observed Penfold dryly.

"Yes," said Tariq, eagerly recounting his uncle's trade to his master and his friend. The apron, he said, was the uniform of the senior butchers who directed the cutting of the valuable joints, brisket and lesser cuts that gave the dead animals their value. Every part of the beast had its use, not least the feet, which were carried off in baskets to be made into that Cairene favorite, camel's foot soup.

Tawfiq Abd al-Hadi stood by the counter, aggressively eating his round bread and lentils.

"Your uncle eats with his left hand," said Olivio, noting this violation of Arab custom and good manners.

"For him, this is permissible," said Tariq. "He eats so because of the loss of three right fingers." Some years earlier, it seemed, Hadi's own son had accidentally severed his father's fingers. The young man had winched up a camel carcass with Hadi's hand still inside the chain and the short slippery blade of his intestine cutter gripped in his fingers. The men of the abattoir were not squeamish, but one had vomited when he saw the fingers slide down Hadi's arm and disappear, lost in the deep swamp of gore and ordure and intestinal waste that served as the floor of the abattoir.

Tawfiq Abd al-Hadi's position at the slaughterhouse entailed little exertion and kept his own table well laden each evening with the gamy stringy flesh, so that his body now filled out his immense white *gallabiyyah* like beans in a tight sack of coffee. Slowly the flesh of the humped animals had been transferred to his own frame. Even his back was massive, arched and thickly weighted as if a hump had been pressed down across it.

"Seems a solid sort of chap," said Penfold. "Wouldn't want 'im going after my camel."

"Uncle," said Tariq, rising and greeting his father's brother with respect, but recalling Olivio's injunction against the use of names. "These are my worthy friends, who search for this evil man. They are the sponsors of a great reward."

Tawfiq Abd al-Hadi bowed and wiped his hands one against the other. "God preserve thee, and thee," he said, acknowledging each stranger.

"How do you do, Mr. Hadi?" said Lord Penfold, rising with a smile.

"This reward, Uncle, is greater than the national lottery, and more certain," said Tariq with rare eagerness. "With it a man could buy a well-watered farm in the Fayûm, a choice young wife, or even a new motorcar."

"God is great!" said Hadi. "May I invite your friends across the square for coffee and a pastry?"

The four men crossed the square to the low open coffee-house set a bit below the level of the street itself. Hadi secured a favored table in an inside corner and ordered for them all. Close beside them, men sat on short three-legged stools and shared water pipes and conversation, slowly sipping coffee, colored fruit drinks and liquorice juice from slender half-filled glasses.

"I am advised," said Hadi after they had been served, "that the employer of this man you seek is a rich and powerful dignitary."

"There are many rich men in Cairo," said the dwarf, watching Penfold drip two drops of sugar syrup on his lapel while he ate his baklava. "And many kinds of power."

"They say this man is a pasha in the government, with influence as far as the Nile runs." Hadi's glass was lost in his great fist. "Each year, on his birthday, this pasha provides to his office staff and household servants a feast of choice camel flesh procured from our abattoir. Soon this day will be here again."

As if hearing none of this, Penfold picked raisins from a pastry finger, his striped tie hanging forward against the platter until it collected a dusting of ground cinnamon and finely crushed nuts.

"We will not forget the kindness of our friends," said the dwarf, promise rich in his voice, staring Hadi in the eye, "as we have not forgotten the crimes of our enemies." He rose, leaning on Tariq's arm.

The words reminded Tariq of Miss Clove, laughing as she leaned forward to chat with him from the back seat of the Daimler.

"Thank you for your generosity," said the dwarf graciously to Hadi. "I trust your nephew to find the man we seek."

This year, Tariq determined, for this birthday feast, it might serve Allah, and others, to deliver to the household of the Undersecretary a different dish than the meat of the desert, but one similarly prepared.

"You have been searching for me, black man." The voice spoke in the Italianate Arabic of Port Saïd.

Sloshing through the ordure of the passageway in his rubber boots, Tariq turned slowly to the right to face his unseen enemy. The menace was welcome. His master was safe. Deterred by the swampy path, the dwarf had stopped with the Englishman at the beginning of the passage.

In the dim early light Tariq was unable to see clearly into the shadows of the animal pen where the speaker waited. The Nubian did not yet reach for the long camel knife that hung at his belt. He knew that if he could prolong this scene his cousins and the other abattoir workers would shortly be following him down the mud brick alley that led to the slaughterhouse. He turned and heard the movement of several men in the stalls to either side.

"Is that you, Razorhead?" Tariq took two steps into the pen, determined to trap the man in his own snare. He thought of the boat fire and his burns and Miss Clove and felt the rage heating his blood like molten metal. "Is that you, killer of children?"

"Children, dogs, unclean Nubians, whatever God requires." A slender figure in a black *gallabiyyah* moved towards Tariq from the shadow beneath the broken plank roof that covered the far end of the stall. The man held up a paper between his hands. The voice grew angry. "Do you know this picture?"

Tariq squinted and made out one of the Frenchman's drawings he had been distributing in the markets and slums of Cairo. The man held the image directly beneath his own head. The large black eyes shone with fury from the same thin lined face. An identical dent crossed the same shaved scalp.

"Do you know this picture?"

The paper trembled, then ripped when the man began to scream.

Tariq did not reply. He had done his job.

"You have made me the hunted instead of the hunter!"

Tariq heard the rush of feet. He spun to his left as three men attacked him. He threw his back against the rough red bricks, drawing and scything with his *sakiina*. The long knife slashed across the belly of one man and caught the arm of another.

Swinging the dripping knife back and forth in front of him, Tariq kept the surviving attackers at bay. He felt comfortable, excited. If his older brother Haqim were beside him, all would be perfect. He glanced up when he heard movement on the wall behind his head.

A dark figure crouched like a monkey in the darkness above him. The man lowered his arms and smashed a brick into Tariq's head just behind one ear.

Tariq awoke when a sharp pain caught him between the legs. He opened his eyes and saw a man's boot crash into his crotch. He screamed twice, hoping desperately to be heard. He had no idea where he was. Razorhead kicked him and he screamed again. The killer bent and lifted the filthy torn portrait from the ground. He crumpled it and stuffed it into Tariq's mouth.

They were in a blacksmith's shop made from the same mud brick walls as the holding pens of the slaughterhouse. A big-bellied light-skinned man in a leather apron sat on a stool beside a charcoal fire in which glowed the tools of his trade. He pedalled an immense leather bellows with one sandalled foot.

Agitated with pain, his face covered with sweat, the assailant whose arm Tariq had slashed stood wrapping his wounded arm in a cloth torn from the hem of his own robe. Three other men leaned against a wall.

Seated on the ground with his legs before him, chained to a post in the center of the small space, Tariq sniffed and smelled the bloody wastes of the abattoir. They could not have come far. He recalled seeing several smiths who served the drovers who brought the camel herds to Cairo's slaughter-house.

"Now you will tell us where this infidel midget you serve will be each night and day this week," Razorhead said before nodding to the wounded man. "But I know that first we must teach you to be honest. I see your burns have almost healed. Perhaps we can help them stay alive."

The paper lodged deep in his mouth, Tariq did not speak.

The wounded man stepped to the fire, one side of his robe dark with blood. He touched the handles of one or two implements with his short thick fingers before selecting a set of heavy tongs. The broad lips of the tool shone red and gold when he lifted it from the furnace of the coals. The man turned to face Tariq, his mouth open and his single united eyebrow twitching with expectation.

Fear replaced Tariq's anger as the man flourished the fiery instrument before his face.

"We will first give you a mark to match my own. Then you, too, will be easy for your enemies to find." Razorhead caressed the uneven dent that crossed his own bald head. "Work slowly, Rashid. Let it arch down towards his right eye, like this."

Tariq felt the heat of the tongs when Rashid swung them above his head, the movement awkward due to the weakness of the man's left arm.

"Be careful!" Razorhead raised his voice. "If you do this wrong, you will have to start again."

"This Sudanese pig has injured me." Rashid looked around at Razorhead before lowering the instrument. "May I first do something for myself?"

"Not too much."

Rashid seized Tariq's left ear with the glowing lips of the tool.

Tariq's body rose and twisted against the post. He smelled the sizzle of his own flesh before the full pain seared through him. The wet paper burst from his mouth and his screams tore the early morning air.

"Al-Hadi!" he cried out within his shouts of pain. When he opened his eyes he saw Rashid stepping back, shock and delight in the man's face. A bit of Tariq's flesh still smoked where it had been torn away and was stuck between the tips of the tongs.

His eyebrow jumping, Rashid gestured towards Tariq's right ear with the instrument and looked to Razorhead for approval.

"Later." Razorhead crouched by Tariq and spoke in a calm satisfied voice. "Now, tell me, where will your master be each day? I have work to do with him."

At that moment there was a slight disturbance near the entrance.

Tariq turned his head and saw Lord Penfold stumble into the rough chamber, saving himself with his stick when he was pushed from behind by an Egyptian who followed him. Behind that man came another, nearly as big and dark as Tariq himself. Gripped like a troublesome bundle under that man's right arm was a struggling figure: Olivio Alavedo. Kicking and clawing to no avail, the small man made no sound, but his face was scarlet.

"Now we have no need to question this black pig," cried Razorhead. "Soon you may kill him, Rashid!" he said, stepping towards the dwarf.

Razorhead seized Olivio by his sash and collar and dropped him roughly on a pile of charcoal.

"Stop that!" cried Lord Penfold, struggling to reach his friend. He was pushed back violently against the brick wall.

"There is something under his clothes," said Razorhead, reaching down for the dwarf as Olivio scrambled painfully to find his footing amidst the tumbling charcoal.

Razorhead grabbed the little man's collar and ripped open his *gallabiyyah* until it hung about his waist like a shabby skirt.

Olivio fell facedown onto the charcoal, then stood. Partly concealed by the insulting armor of the metal and leather harness that bound his back, the dwarf's small blackened body trembled with anger. His round head red as blood, the dwarf faced his enemies with clenched fists in the glowing light of the blacksmith's fire.

In the shadows against the wall, catching his friend's eye, Penfold slipped his sword from the cane.

"Seize the midget, Abbud," ordered Razorhead to one of his men. "And bring him to the fire. We will see if he enjoys the flames as much as his daughter."

The smith pumped the bellows while Abbud moved to obey.

Olivio threw a handful of charcoal dust in Abbud's eyes when the man snatched for him.

"My eyes!" cried Abbud, twisting sharply away from the dwarf as Penfold lunged towards the man. Moving with surprising speed, sideways like a fencer, his right knee bent as far as he could, his bad leg stretched and dragging behind him, his left arm extended straight back, Penfold thrust forward with his sword arm as the two men met.

Charging forward, Razorhead clubbed Penfold across the shoulders with a wooden stool as the tip of the sword emerged through Abbud's back. Penfold collapsed, senseless, losing his grip after the short sword pulled free of Abbud's body.

The dwarf reached for the weapon as the blacksmith came for him and Rashid raised the tongs to Tariq's face.

The sounds of a violent brawl intervened from the alley beyond the open doorway.

The immense figure of Tawfiq Abd al-Hadi filled the entrance. A white cloth had been bound around his usual skullcap to form a large turban. Beneath it throbbed his black countenance. Hatchet in hand, the Nubian camel butcher stepped to the first man he could reach. A gang of gut men, skinners, entrail wrappers, knife boys, bone cleaners, all his brothers of the abattoir, swarmed in behind him. Each man carried the tool of his craft.

For an instant Rashid and Hadi faced each other in silence beside the bellows as each recognized what the other was about.

"Welcome to *al-Madbah,*" said Hadi in a voice like stone. "But you are foolish to abuse my nephew and my friends."

Rashid swung the smoking tongs. Their reflected glow sparkled in the eyes of the massive Nubian. Yet they never landed.

Adept after forty years with a heavy blade, Hadi parried the tongs and swung the hatchet as if trimming the limbs from a camel. With one stroke he took off Rashid's good arm at the shoulder joint. The tongs fell from Rashid's left hand as Hadi swung once more and severed the other arm.

His open shoulders bleeding like fountains, Tariq's torturer fell across his feet.

Hadi's fellows were not idle. Hurled back into his own fire, the smith was left to die with his molten poker in his navel. He had forgotten the code of the greatest slaughterhouse in Egypt: it was the abattoir that ruled the dependent world that spread outwards. Another man, groaning and retching, knelt with his face to the ground and his hands held to his open belly.

"Save that one!" Hadi yelled, lest a young kinsman act hastily with Razorhead.

Wrapped in a dirty cloak, erect and proud as a Roman senator, his face and hands black, Olivio stood by the entrance with Penfold and took the names of the men who had saved them.

"Lord Penfold and I will wait in the motorcar," the dwarf said to Tariq. "Finish this in your own way, Tariq. But let your brother be your inspiration."

Olivio wiped the blood and dirt from Penfold's sword on his own torn garments, then handed the weapon back to his friend with a small bow.

"You saved my life once again," said the dwarf with respect. "Your lordship fences like Douglas Fairbanks."

Watching the dwarf and Penfold set out for their car with an escort of three men, Tariq recalled his master's power and benevolence in securing Haqim's freedom and flight and his distant employment.

"Razorhead will not be needing this now, my lord," said Olivio, pausing as they walked. He handed Penfold the gold English watch Tariq had found in the killer's possession. Exhausted, Penfold wound the half-hunter with shaking fingers and held it to his ear, sad to hear no tick.

"Never really cared much about the time, anyway," the old Englishman said, leaning on his walking stick while he wiped his shoes against his torn cuffs.

Behind him, he heard the powerful voice of Hadi calling to his companions. *"Al Häwïya!"* Hadi led his party to the abattoir with Tariq and Razorhead in their midst.

The smells of the slaughterhouse rose to meet the early rays of the sun. The light penetrated the openings of the walls that alternated with the high stones of the abattoir barn several feet below the edge of the roof line. The echoing call of a muezzin carried through the apertures.

Bright dawn sunlight glinted from the moist chains that turned on the creaking metal wheels set on steel rods that crossed the ceiling. Thirty feet below, men and boys, deep in gore and offal, set about their morning duties, pretending to ignore the unusual finer work underway in one corner of the vast barn.

Tariq, not a professional, sat on a barrel with a wet cloth bound about his injured head. His skull throbbing, he watched his uncle's team sharpen their tools before finishing their work. When this ceremony was completed, perhaps his generous master would present him to the German physician.

Raised off the ground by chains attached to massive hooks set beneath their ribs, camel after camel would shortly be splayed, gutted, skinned and quartered. Only their heads and upper necks would not be flayed. Even the short curved tails would be peeled, until the entire hanging carcasses were ghostly white in their neat membranes, only stained here and there by pale patches of filmy red. The swollen sacks of the stomachs, ribbed like the seamed sections of an opulent bolster, would be removed entire. The feet and heads would be collected to one side.

A single live camel, still with shock, its flanks and joints marked with buyer's chalk, stood alone in another corner waiting its turn, barely breathing, watching the dismemberment of its desert brethren with huge unblinking eyes.

Today a different creature would share this ancient procedure.

Suspended upside-down by two ankle chains straining in opposite directions, Razorhead's body seemed too small for the artifacts that promised to engage him. His wrists bound together, he twisted to raise his body and free his face from the swampy floor so that he might find air. The smooth-shaven dented crown of his head was soiled with camel waste. He attempted to clear a bowl-shaped space in front of his mouth and nose with his hands, but the brown syrupy mass and fragments of decomposung organs flooded back.

Razorhead tried to blink away specks of offal from his eyes while he watched a young boy wade eagerly towards him. A long brown head cloth was bound beneath the youth's chin, one tasselled end swinging before his chest as he leaned forward into his work, hauling a large gory hook over his shoulder with both hands. The ceiling chain dragged behind the hook as the wheel whirred above him. A skinner waded behind the youth towards Razorhead, pausing every few steps to sharpen his blade against a leather strop that swung from his waist.

Before the next two prayer hours passed, Tariq himself would deliver to the villa of Musa Bey Halaib the fresh meat for the annual birthday feast to be celebrated by the household of the Undersecretary.

This was the sort of thing the Ministry of Public Works did well. Ceremonial openings were more eagerly attended than Gazira polo or the opera. Olivio wondered if it had always been so in Egypt. Had Imhotep, four and a half thousand years before, unveiled the step pyramid at Saqqâra with a panoply of priests and captive lions and capering dwarves and tumblers, Nubians and giraffes from the ends of empire? Were the Great Sphinx and Abu Simbel first presented with the drama that attended the opening of the Canal and the dam at Aswan, all scenes from the endless theater of the River Nile?

Today, too, the magic was in the water. This important new canal would bring the richness of the Delta into another corner of the Western Desert. The opening of the four gates in the dam would permit and control the further dispersal of the waters that now flooded too heavily from Upper Egypt.

"Splendid, really," said Adam Penfold to the dwarf, the two men splendid themselves in striped trousers and cutaways. "Just think, will you, what this'll mean for the fishermen and those poor farming villages," he said thoughtfully, "and I suppose some taxes for the government and a few more luxuries for the palace, of course. Ah, well . . ."

"For us, my lord," said Olivio hurriedly, annoyed by this distant line of thought, "it should mean an end to debt and to risk." And perhaps some bounty for himself, he thought, and dowries for his daughters and a gentleman's life for his lordship. "And we must think of Miss Gwenn and Mr. Anton, and their future." He recalled that these very waters had their source in Abyssinia and wished his absent friends were here to share the drama of this moment.

Prince Farûq himself was unable to attend. He was detained on his way home, it was whispered, at Cap d'Antibes by a precocious child dancer of the Ballets Russes de Monte Carlo. But his father's ministers were here. They sat gossiping and receiving on the wooden stage atop the dam, inclining their tarbushes and homburgs to the ambassadors of the nations whose engineers and companies had played a part, or wished they had, and to the governor of the province, his fief enhanced, and to the Delta mayors and grand merchants, and even to the land owners, great and small. A green-and-white-striped canopy crowned the platform, protecting the notables from the light of the sun.

"Who're that lot over there?" said Penfold, referring to a roped section beside the stage containing a crowded swarm of *fellahin.* "Probably poor farmers or the wretched chaps as've done all the work, shouldn't doubt."

"Of course," said the dwarf, thinking them fortunate to be included. "Laborers engaged on the project and the dependents of the owners of the new estates."

A line of Special Police separated the *fellahin* from the grandstand. The officers were Egyptians, but were armed and uniformed in colonial khaki drill and gleaming leather boots and belts. Olivio scrutinized them with care, failing to find among them his adversary Captain Thabet, now reduced to a lieutenant.

At the other side of the platform, the regimental band of the Scots Guards played "The British Grenadier," reminding the gathering that although Egypt was no longer occupied by Britain, she still lived with the protection of that distant island. "From Hector and Lysander, and such great men as these," the dwarf hummed to himself as he reviewed the meticulous protocol of the seating and Penfold tapped his stick in time to the stirring royal march.

Anchored to the rocky desert shore at both ends, the dam at the mouth of the canal was a small version of the Great Barrage that, for forty-five years, had controlled the Nile's flow to a width of nearly a mile. Stone pillars rose from the water, separating and framing each of the four vertical iron sluice gates. The pillars were connected to each other by arches. These in turn supported a broad causeway, wide enough to accommodate a pedestrian pavement, a road for public traffic, and an elevated narrow gauge rail track. Along this raised track travelled a small flatbed car mounted with two winches that lowered and raised the black gates that held back the river from the canal. At either end of the dam rose a fortress-like structure with crenellated ramparts and two-storied slender towers. The larger castle contained the machinery and counterweights that controlled the swing bridge which could be turned to give passage to vessels too large to pass beneath the arches.

This morning the green crescent and stars of Egypt flew from every tower and pier and from the Nile cruisers and feluccas tied to date palms along the riverbank upstream. Fields of rice sparkled behind the palms like platters of emeralds. A soft steady wind whistled through the sugarcane that rose like a yellow and gold screen behind the low watered rice.

"Isn't that your precious Frenchie sketching over there?" asked Penfold, gazing towards the high rocky bank where one end of the canal dam met the shore. *Monsieur* Aristide sat on a folding chair under the yellow blossoms of a golden shower tree with his easel before him and a brush set in his teeth. Barefoot children scrabbled like chickens in the dust beside him, gathering the long black sausage-shaped pods that had fallen from the tree in the night. An old women, her head covered with a *tarha,* sat on the ground nearby, a basket between her feet while she waited for the urchins to fill it with the seedy purgative fruit.

"That is he, my lord," said Olivio. The artist was recording this dramatic moment, with Olivio Fonseca Alavedo prominent at its center. The dwarf prayed Penfold would not consider this indulgence an excess of vanity.

Cotton bunting skirted the wooden platform centered above the four new gates. At each corner of the platform the flags of England and France joined those of Egypt, in tribute to the engineers and the banks that had built the work.

The river boiled against the new iron gates, waiting for the Undersecretary of Public Works personally to turn the first winch and raise the first gate. The Minister himself, too old and frail for this manly labor, had instead prepared an address, presenting in unheard whispers the thanks of all Egypt to God and to the *Banque de Suez et Indo-Chine.* Rejecting assistance, the Minister shuffled back to his chair in his long black *stambouline,* the collarless frock coat a reminder to all of the dignity of the Ottomans.

Two heavy black chains, forged in Glasgow, rose like dark sea serpents from the water. One end of each chain was attached to one of two massive hooks fixed on top of the vertical plate that formed the gate. The other ends of the chains were wrapped around the drums of the two winches on the rail car now positioned above the gate. The vertical black iron plate, like the others, was perhaps eight feet tall and eighteen feet wide.

Musa Bey Halaib, attended by appreciative murmurs from the seated dignitaries, walked proudly along the front of the platform to the steps that would take him down to the rail car. A red carnation was set in his buttonhole. Olivio observed Musa Bey Halaib pause to salute his cousin and confederate, Abd al-Azim Pasha, the Royal Chamberlain. Passing Olivio, the Undersecretary acknowledged his friend with a generous smile.

The dwarf nodded. There was no expression in his grey eye. Tariq stood behind his master's chair near the edge of the platform.

The Bey gave no sign that on his birthday, belatedly advised as to the unusual meat that had lain on his plate, evidently finding Razorhead indigestible, he had vomited across the banquet table at his villa.

"Sorry your Kina couldn't be with us," said Penfold to his friend, "but with the nipper coming she's better off in hospital, what?"

The dwarf crossed himself. "It could be any moment," he said, wondering again whether this infant would be a boy. Would it be an ordinary healthy child, or would it be small and exceptional, like him? God forgive him, he was not certain which he wished.

Olivio glanced down at the swirling Nile and recalled the body of Clove being recovered from the sunken wreck of the Cataract Café, and the sight of the motion picture film still thrashing and burning while it sank through the dark water. If only his vengeance could be complete, he vowed silently, he would thank God for any sort of child.

The Undersecretary mounted the iron steps of the flatbed with the assistance of one of the Nubian winch men. He set his soft hands on the handle of the nearest winch. Another Nubian, a cousin of Tariq and Haqim, leaned into the second winch, taking most of the weight of the rising plate, so that the official's winch carried only the burden of its chain. Two assistants waited to jam steel chocks into the gears of the drums and freeze the gate at the top of its ascent.

As the gate rose, the water rushed towards the only opening in the dam, rising in swift curls to either side of the cavity before marrying and plunging down through the arch in a foaming chute. The audience leaned forward as the first irrigation water rushed beneath them into the new canal. Voices heightened in appreciation of the moment. The plate rose and the winch car tilted to one side along its length, concentrating its weight on its four upstream wheels as it took the strain of the plate and the surge of the Nile against it.

One hand still on the handle of his winch, Musa Bey Halaib was beginning to sweat from exertion. His tight worsted waistcoat was pumping in and out like the breast of an excited fat bird as he turned to acknowledge his audience. All eyes on him, the rear rows of the crowd stood as the assembly joined in applause. Seated in the front rank, Olivio clapped his small hands and watched the Nubian on the second winch. He observed that handle begin to turn more slowly, then hesitate altogether as the man eased his grip. The winch man opened his hands and the handle turned in reverse, gaining speed with each revolution.

The entire weight of the plate slammed down on the Bey's winch. The handle spun from his grasp. Astonished, his right arm extended, he stopped still as a mannequin while the metal handle turned faster and faster, breaking his wrist as it whipped around again. The iron plate fell freely as both winches turned ever faster in reverse, the spinning handles impossible to arrest.

The end of the Bey's chain broke free of the drum. Its coils crashed together in the air with the crack of a cannon shot.

Lashing like a snake, the chain struck the Undersecretary across the upper legs, nearly severing both limbs. It swept him from the cart and disappeared with him over the edge of the dam into the water. Screams shrilled from the audience as the crowd panicked and abandoned the platform.

Through the turmoil Tariq walked slowly down the steps. His master sat erect on a cushion in his arms.

Two Nubian winch men rushed to the lip of the dam and stared down. The others struggled to regain control of the handles. They lowered the gate to calm the rush of the water.

Only Musa Bey Halaib's feet, still snarled in the chain, were visible in the churning eddy near the surface. Head-first, his neck broken, almost decapitated, his body was caught part-way through the arch, jammed between the sharp edge of the lowered plate and the stone floor of the gate. The water flooded past around him, rushing on its way to irrigate the dwarf's vast new estates.

In the press at the bottom of the steps, Olivio found himself face to face with the Chamberlain himself, Abd al-Azim Pasha. In the chaotic throng, the official was unable to find his driver. Dignity slipping from him, the Pasha turned his head anxiously from side to side like a bird searching for seeds.

Olivio craned forward from the sanctuary of Tariq's arms and addressed the Chamberlain.

"If you will permit me, Pasha." There was now so much to discuss. It might be time for accommodation. "May I have the honor of offering you a lift to town in my motorcar?"

Startled by the sight of the little man in his cutaway and tarbush bowing at him from the arms of the massive Nubian, Abd al-Azim recoiled and hesitated, his mouth slightly open.

"My Daimler is just there," Olivio Alavedo added as a hurrying diplomat jostled the Chamberlain.

"Ah," said the Pasha nervously, gripping his watch chain, "yes, yes. That would be most kind of you." He paused, recovering himself with dignity. "Most kind."

— 36 —

"I said stop the animals!" Ernst von Decken roared as Kimathi led the first camel to the bank of the rushing stream. "Stop!"

Mules, horses and camels ganged together and milled about as Kimathi stopped the column and Ernst caught up from the rear. Some of the animals lowered their heads and began to drink, slipping and sliding on the steep rocky riverbank.

"We must go on," Kimathi said in a hard voice, his face set and expressionless. "Mr. Rider told me to go as far as we can south from the Italians." He handed the lead to the short camel driver who waited beside him. "We cross now."

"It's too deep here," Ernst snapped, annoyed to be explaining himself to a black man who had never soldiered."Some of these mules might not make it. We lose one and I've lost over a hundred pounds of silver."

"We must get the river between us and the Italians if they come in lorries," said Kimathi, aware of the men waiting to be led.

"Then unload the chests and have the men carry them across one by one," said Ernst loudly as Charlie and Harriet and Bernadette dismounted and came closer, walking stiffly beside their horses.

"Soon it will be dark." Kimathi pointed at the sun growing cooler and larger and redder as it dipped to the horizon. He nodded to the small man beside him, who shortened the camel's lead and stepped to the riverbank.

Ernst pushed the camel driver hard in the chest. Taken by surprise, the man dropped the lead and fell on his back on the rocks.

"Now, hold on there," said Charlie. Ignored by the two men who faced each other, he gave the fallen man a hand. The camel lowered its head and fluttered its large lips above the water before it stretched its neck down and began to drink in long steady gulps.

Kimathi picked up the animal's lead and turned towards the water.

Ernst drew his pistol and struck the African's arm with the barrel. "Stop!" he yelled.

Kimathi, fists clenched, turned back and faced von Decken.

"I am taking Bwana Rider's safari across the river," he said. As if to show the matter was concluded, he paused and yelled an order to the men leading the mules laden with silver. They loosed their grips on the animals' halters and lead ropes.

"You take your silver where you wish," Kimathi said harshly. Behind him, the unattended silver mules stumbled forward to drink at the stream.

"Gentlemen," said Harriet, putting one hand on Ernst's arm, "don't be so stupid. Let's find out where it's shallowest, then lead the mules across one by one. We could put two men at their head." She took her small horse by the bridle and walked with it into the water, coaxing and talking to the mount while she edged carefully along the bank to a rough ford. She stumbled, plunging into a hole and getting wet to her waist. Then she waded to the far bank and mounted without looking back. By that time Bernadette and Kimathi were already in the river. Ernst watched with his fists on his hips.

They camped that night on a grey ledge two miles downstream. Supper finished, they sat idly listening to the rush of water below them. Pack canvases were slung over ropes tied between trees to make informal shelters for the Europeans. Kimathi strode about the camp, checking the picket ropes and sentries.

"Keep the fires low," he said quietly, "like Abyssinian shepherds." The twins sat side by side while the men smoked nearby.

"I hope Anton and his wife are managing all right," said Bernadette, her wet clothes steaming where they rested on branches near the fire. She gazed across the coals with mischief in her eyes. "Don't you miss your hunter, Harry?"

"Anton Rider's a married man," said Harriet demurely. "Besides, he and that wife of his seem to be getting on now, don't you think?"

"You know better than that, Harry. Right now they don't have much choice, well, except for you, I suppose . . ."

"Ssh! Not so loud! Ernst's trying to listen."

"How could those two ever get on?" Bernadette continued in a quiet voice.

"I suppose Gwenn's just too old for him," said Harriet with satisfaction.

"Maybe, but that's not it," Bernadette said with certainty, aware that for once her sister was listening. "She's not like us, she takes herself so seriously. She's a hopeless career girl, with children and no money. She needs schools and a job, or a rich man. But Anton wants to live like this. The tougher things get, the more he's at home. He's worse than that German."

"What's wrong with Ernst?" Harriet said quickly, crossing her arms.

"Well nothing, I suppose, if you like that sort of thing . . ."

"Berny . . ."

"You're not thinking of bringing him home to Lexington, are you?"

"And why not?" snapped Harriet.

"I suppose it might be rather fun, like turning a mustang loose in a field of thoroughbred fillies. When you get tired of him, you could rent him out to some of those frustrated old ladies at the club. Maybe a raffle. He'd get their attention."

"Why are you always so filthy minded?" Harriet wagged a finger at her sister.

"You know, sis, you and Ernst could probably work things out, for a while anyway. You both just want to have a good time. But those other two, they love each other madly, and it's hopeless. They're just not well suited." Bernadette shrugged and shook her head, wondering how much her sister cared. "Anyway, if Anton was here now, there wouldn't have been such a fuss back there at the river."

"I thought everything went very well," said Harriet archly, raising her voice and looking at Ernst in the dim firelight, knowing she still had to show him she was not repelled by his stump. "Everyone needs someone to tell him what to do."

"I must tell you, Ernst, I find it easier," said Charlie, approaching the fire with the German, "always to do what the twins tell me."

"What if they're wrong?" said Ernst in a loud voice, still gruff and surly but forgetting the stiffness in his leg as he smoked and drank whisky from a mug. He sat on the ground next to Harriet and stretched out his leg with a curse. "What if they're wrong? They're always wrong."

"Even then. It still works out better," Charlie said, grinning when Bernadette patted his hand. "Never fails. You'll learn."

"Hmph," grunted von Decken, drinking. "None of you care about my silver."

"Silver isn't everything. You'll see," Harriet said in a private voice, kneeling in the dust by Ernst and taking the mug from his hand. "And you needed a bath." She was surprised to find that the terror of their flight had made her more interested in mischief, not less.

"You'd care about those mules if that was your family's farm lashed to their backs," said Ernst, resenting the confidence of these rich women.

"Will you forgive me," Harriet said in a still softer tone, pointing to a canvas shelter, "if I take you over there and show you how we look after a horse with a bad leg in Kentucky?"

"Where I come from, we shoot them," said Ernst, smiling a bit, relaxing despite himself.

"We begin with a rubdown, a sort of massage, starting with the hock and gaskin," said Harriet, turning her head to wave at her departing sister. "Night, Berny. Behave yourself."

"Don't stay up too late," answered Bernadette's voice from the shadows.

"We better do what your sister tells us," Ernst grumbled, gripping Harriet's shoulder as he rose.

She stood and he put his heavy arm across her shoulders and together they hobbled to the makeshift tent.

"What's a gaskin?" the German asked, lying on his back in the darkness.

"It's the part between the stifle and the hock," Harriet said as she unbuttoned him and struggled to pull off his boot and trousers. "Right here," she added, biting him fiercely.

Aware several of the men were watching him, Colonel Grimaldi was careful not to flinch when the medic washed and dressed his wound again. Thank God for hydrogen peroxide. Without antiseptic, what white man could survive in Africa? Every thorn cut was prone to festering, let alone an injury like this, or the even more brutal wounds of war. A remarkably clean wound, the medic had said of this one. Trained to provide temporary relief for the lightly wounded, the young man was already hardened to mutilations and field amputations.

One soldier was still at work, seated on the ground near Grimaldi. The son of a cobbler from Taormina, the man was proceeding under the glaring patriotic eyes of Captain Uzielli, more aggressive than ever since the Englishman had humiliated them. A traditional *Bersaglieri* hymn had softened the bush while the three troopers killed by the Englishman and his monster had been buried quickly the first evening.

"The men are still angry, Colonel," said Uzielli, squatting on his heels near his commander, curious to see how much pain he revealed. "They blame Mario's death and their lost boots on the woman."

"You are responsible for seeing that they obey my orders," said Enzo brusquely. "Pass me that map." He tried to remember where before he had seen that beast Haqim who held him down while Rider mutilated him. Cairo? Had the ape not worked for Gwenn's friend, that vile midget, possibly guarding the ramp to the Cataract Café? The one-eyed midget, he thought, raising one hand to his own face.

The *Bersaglieri* cobbler, with two soldiers serving as apprentices, had nearly completed his assignment: outfitting six men with footwear adequate for several days' march. Fortunately, one soldier had defied regulations by jumping with a pair of light boots in his rucksack. These now waited beside the colonel's feet. They would be tight but serviceable. Shoes and sandals for the other six men of the pursuit team were being made from the sturdiest bits of canvas and leather, cut from packs, belts and even the *Bersaglieri* hats themselves. Motivated by the killing of their comrades, all fifteen men had volunteered. Grimaldi had chosen the six with care. Umberto, a trooper from the Italian Alps, would serve as tracker. Once a mountaineer and professional hunting guide, he had spent his youth tracking wild sheep along the sheer spiny peaks of the Dolomites.

Enzo heard it first.

"Quiet!" he ordered. It was an engine, an aircraft, coming in from the east. He stood at once, before the medic had finished, the bandage not yet secured around his head. He turned and faced east and cupped one ear.

The men saw the colonel's movement and turned to stare with him.

"A CR-20," he declared just before the Fiat first appeared. "She can't be carrying much."

The men stood and waved and cheered together, as if Italy herself were again beneath their feet.

The biplane came in low, dipping her wings. The pilot waved one gloved hand and stared down through his goggles. Unless they'd made new forward airfields, Enzo knew the plane could not tarry long. Fuel would be short.

Even from the ground the colonel was able to detect the grinding hardship of war in Africa: dents in the fuselage, bullet holes in the lower starboard wing, a makeshift landing carriage. Nor did the engine sound as smooth and steady as it should. Even the machines were tired. No wonder she wasn't going to stop. Had war been easier when Caesar's legions fought in Africa?

Turning, coming in now from the west, the pilot crossed the camp again, tossing out two small packages as he flew on to the east and home.

Two men ran in their stocking feet to recover the parcels as Enzo instructed the medic to complete his work.

"*Colonnello*!" Uzielli saluted and handed him the dispatch case. The other soldier remained behind, picking up a carton of cigarettes and scraping together the precious ground coffee that leaked from a tear in the canvas bag that had fallen with the satchel, a gift from one airman to another. Uzielli stood near Grimaldi, the man's curiosity palpable.

"That'll be all, Captain." The colonel ignored the circle of staring eyes while he unbuckled the straps and removed the thick military envelope from the dispatch case. He tossed the sturdy leather case to the cobbler and opened the single sheet. He saw the other soldier returning to camp, carefully holding the torn sack to prevent further loss.

"Distribute the cigarettes and boil some water and make coffee for the men," Enzo said. "Use it all. Once we start, there'll be no time."

"*Subito*!" said Uzielli, passing on the order. He was eager to take up the chase, and keen to see how the colonel would behave when he found his woman with the Englishman.

Initialled by Marshal Graziani himself, the message was brief: Despite occasionally fierce resistance, the campaign was moving forward, but Addis Ababa was still a distant target and the countryside remained hostile as the armies advanced. Soon half a million Italians would be in the field in Africa. Every day the Italian forces were more dispersed and more at risk. The League was about to meet in Geneva to debate the conflict. The emperor of Abyssinia was to address the conference to appeal for assistance in the war against Italy. If confirmed, the use of gas could lead to economic sanctions against Italy herself, not just to the closing of the Suez Canal. Accordingly, Rome insisted on the destruction of the film and the film party. Recovery of the silver was less important. A reconnaissance squadron of the *Frontieri Alpini* with five trucks was racing to meet Colonel Grimaldi and provide mobility for his *Bersaglieri.* They would be guided to him by the *Regia Aeronautica,* who would also search ahead for the film safari. The eyes of the Duce and of the Grand Council of Fascism were upon Colonel Grimaldi and his men.

Enzo did not need the spur. He brought his map case from his tent and called over Captain Uzielli. He spread out the creased map of Africa Orientale Italiana.

"While the track is still fresh," said the colonel, "six troopers and I will begin the pursuit on foot. If we capture the Englishman and the woman, they will lead us to the safari and the film. Meanwhile, Captain, you and the other seven men will wait for the trucks." Enzo was pleased at the disappointment in the captain's face. "At least one truck must follow my marked track to recover my party. With the other four trucks, you will pursue the safari as soon as the aircraft have located it."

"Perfect," said Anton, dropping his heavy pack while he waited for Gwenn to catch up. "We'll make camp here under the ledge." He cupped his hands and washed his face in the spring that worked its way down from a fissure in the basalt. "This spring's just right this time of year, enough to feed that pool but not enough to drain down to the valley and attract cattle or farming."

"That must be Lake Shala." Gwenn stood beside him in a cleft of the rocky escarpment. Without thinking, she rested one hand on his shoulder.

For a moment Anton stood quietly, appreciating her touch. Then he announced, "Klipspringer, fresh tracks." He knelt by the delicate heart-shaped prints that the tiny rock antelope had left by the side of the pool. "Might be a useful sentry."

Anton, she knew, had spent a lifetime selecting camp sites, and even on safari he favored hidden spots and sheltered corners. If they were not on the run, how perfect this would be. She admired his concentration, the way he traced the sharp footprint with his fingertips and dropped dust in the air to check the wind and crushed a dark pellet of spoor in his palm to assess its moisture and freshness. Feeling stronger, her shoulder wound beginning to itch, Gwenn sat down and stretched and loosened her boots while she watched Anton check the binding where he had lashed his gypsy knife to the tip of a stretcher pole.

"I'm off to find some supper," Anton said, spear in hand as he rose beside the pool. "Best to do it without any shooting. You might start a fire after a bit." He touched her cheek with his hand. "You know what to do with these," he said, leaving her with the pistol and rifle.

Gwenn watched him disappear among the rocks. Holding the smooth stock of the old .375 reminded her of early evenings in the hills above their farm, hunting for fresh meat to keep the Africans content when Anton was absent on safari, as he always was. Now she was hungry, and hoped he would return with something good. She rubbed her tired feet and removed the dressing from the wound on her face. Unable to see her reflection clearly in the pool, she washed her face in the water and traced the wound along her jawline with her fingertips, praying it would not be too disfiguring.

The first day's flight had been harder than she was prepared for. The bitter words by the stream had made it harder still. Why was it sometimes easier to say the cruel words than the loving ones? After a long and complicated time there were always enough of both to choose from, like a shelf of old spice bottles in a well-used kitchen. She wished she were better at it.

After eating, Anton and Haqim had walked for hours, carrying her south along the streambed in the shallow water, occasionally slipping on the river stones, sometimes dropping into a sinkhole or patch of soft sandy mud as they progressed by moonlight.

Even carried in the litter by Haqim and Anton, Gwenn took a battering that seemed to loosen the fusing bones in her shoulder. She had to grip the shafts and adjust her muscles with every shift and stumble of the route. On the easier stretches she dozed off, sometimes moving her hand to touch Anton's where he held the stretcher, gently trying to erase what they had said. At first he did not respond, hiding inside himself the way he often did, requiring her to reassure him with more small signals of affection.

Several times they had interrupted animals drinking at the river, though never a cat, thank God. There was no sign of crocodiles. Once she fell off the stretcher into the water, not injuring herself but leaving her shivering as they struggled on, and determined to begin walking on her own.

After Haqim had left them, she and Anton camped by the river until the early morning.

Anton seemed not to sleep at all, sitting by her quietly with his rifle across his knees. She wondered what he thought. Stirring once at night, she had found her hand in his. When she awoke, he was still at her side with his jacket covering her.

All morning they had climbed slowly into the western rise of the Rift Valley, pausing frequently as they distanced themselves from the traditional path that passed north and south along the lakes. Where it was flat, or nearly so, she walked on her own, past the euphorbia candelabra trees and the thornbushes and the hard red anthills. When it was steep or difficult, Anton assisted her. She had forgotten how strong he was, how natural in the bush. She loved the tan of his forearms and his smell and the feeling of his muscles through his shirt. For him it all seemed no effort, like a farmer strolling his fields, or an artist mixing paints with his palette knife. It reminded her why he could only be the way he was.

Gwenn stopped dreaming and picked up the field glasses he had left beside her. She scanned down the ridged ravine, first missing him, finally spotting him, flat on his stomach behind a bush, several yards from a small muddy pool. The cord of his snare was wrapped about his left hand, its loop patient at the water's edge. His battered brown bush hat was the color of the dust. She refocused and studied Anton's broad shoulders, his long bronzed legs, his stillness. Would Denby be like him?

She gazed down at her husband, seeing him at his best. From this distance he looked just the same, the same strong young boy she'd met on the boat to Mombasa, staring at her with those clear blue eyes as she'd left him for the first time and gone ashore in the plunging surf boat. Even if they did not end up together, she knew she could never love another man as she loved him. She wondered if he was still angry at her, still so obsessed with her relationship with Lorenzo.

Suddenly Anton was up, spear in one hand, taut cord in the other, dashing forward as a young wild pig thrashed and squealed and sought to scrabble away on the end of the line. A few yards ahead three other pigs made off, two youngsters first, the heavy sow behind, slick and shiny black from her roll in the mud, herding them on after a brief look at the lost offspring behind her. Gwenn watched the pigs disappear into the bush, trotting fast in line with neat small steps, their tails straight in the air like the lances of cavalrymen on parade.

The piglet was already dead. Carrying the animal by its rear trotters, Anton was cautious as he made his way home. She could feel his concentration from where she watched. Leaving no footprints, the slaughter scene swept with a thorn branch, he hurried back to her up the gorge, careful to take the rockiest route. She realized he must be more concerned about being tracked than he had let her believe.

Gwenn put down the binoculars and started to build a fire under the ledge from the pile of dry wood selected by Anton for its pale minimal smoke. Knowing how he valued it, she lifted *Oliver Twist* from a stone and gently tore out one end sheet, taking care not to rip it under the stitching. She filled the page with dry grass, crumpled it together and set it amidst the smallest branches. The flames caught. The white smoke puffed and dispersed broadly along the ceiling of the ledge.

Proud, feeling younger and as alive as she had ever been, Gwenn stood by the pool with her arms folded and waited for her husband to appear around the rocks. It reminded her of how they used to be, camping in the Aberdares, hearing the trees snap as the giant tuskers moved gracefully around them, like whales in the ocean.

Anton walked towards her and dropped the pig by the fire. He grinned at her, pleased and proud as a schoolboy poacher.

"I'm starving," she said, watching him free his knife from the pole and sharpen it before swiftly cleaning and spitting the young pig. "He looks beautiful. While you get him ready, I think I'll wash before it gets too cold." She turned her back and undressed and slipped into the shallow chilly pool after drawing water for the billy can.

Anton set the ends of the wooden spits onto rocks beside the coals. The smell of the roasting pork made the juices gather in her mouth. She knew the pork would take forever, even the way Anton had quartered it. She did not think she could wait.

"May I join you, Mrs. Rider?" He stripped and splashed in, barely covered, and they sat face to face in the pool by the ledge, like twins in a nursery tub, her small breasts tight with the cold of the water. Anton scrubbed their feet with sand, kneading and kissing her toes when he had finished. Getting out quickly, he shook himself like a dog while Gwenn pulled on her soiled clothes.

It had always been their favorite time of day, when the warmth of the afternoon lingered and the freshness of the evening had not yet turned cold. It was the hour for verandahs and drinks and a smoke. Instead they would share pork chops.

A bit warmer today, the African sun was retreating defiantly, opening and bleeding below them like a squashed blood orange on the jagged western horizon. And the night would be as beautiful. Only at sea, she thought, was darkness ever so bright and rich as it was in Africa.

"When it's nearly ready," Gwenn said, rubbing her hands, "I'll start the macaroni." Half shivering, half burning, she sat on a shelf of stone that had broken off and fallen from the ledge above the fire. She looked at Anton where he squatted on the other side of the low flames. Seeming distant and preoccupied, from time to time he turned the cooking sticks or threw on a handful of wild onion grass. Drops of fat flared and sizzled when they dripped onto the coals. She nudged the small billy closer to the fire and waited for it to boil so she could throw in the last handful of the pasta. Then she looked up and saw his open blue eyes regarding her as if for the first time. It made her feel young.

"The cutlets must be almost done," he said when she dropped in the macaroni.

They ate quickly, seated side by side on the canvas taken from the stretcher, passing his *choori* back and forth. As Gwenn lifted the meat to her mouth, she tried not to think of how the knife had been used.

When he was finished, Anton sat close behind her, one leg tight on either side, and put his arms around her. She felt content and safe. For the moment, they were giving each other what they needed

"I miss the boys," she said after a time, leaning back against him, relaxing.

"I always miss them," he said, careful not to put resentment in his voice.

"I know," she said, putting her hands over his, reluctant to disturb the present with the future, but needing to.

"Where could we all live if things worked out?" she asked, hoping her question would not spoil the moment. It was just the sort of test she knew he could never pass. She glanced up at him warmly, letting him know it was a question, not a challenge.

"I'm not sure," he said slowly, his hands stiffening slightly under hers. "We know the farm can't work, at least these days, and the safari game isn't much better now." She squeezed his fingers gently to encourage him, knowing he was doing his best.

"But my share of the silver should help," he continued. "And if Olivio's schemes work out, I could do very well from that. So maybe Cairo'd be better for a time . . ."

"Then I could finish my studies and become a doctor," she interrupted, annoyed he hadn't thought of her life, too. But at least things sounded possible, if they were lucky.

"Perhaps you could give shooting lessons," she said, knowing he'd hate it. "Teach diplomats and rich Cairenes how to slaughter birds in the Fayûm."

"There's always something," he said. He himself had been thinking of the card games and gambling by the pyramids, but he knew it was a life he could not stand for long.

"But the boys would love Kenya," he said carelessly. "It would be just their sort of life."

"No," she said, shaking her head, the difficulties clear again. "No, Anton, there's no future for them in the way you live. Don't you see?" She hesitated, certain he had no answer, hoping she could explain without losing what they had together now. "The world's changing. If there's another war, like Olivio says, or if this Depression just goes on, our old life may never be the same. The boys need school, and university. They must be able to choose and make their way." She paused again, feeling his sadness, and squeezed his arm before continuing.

"Please understand. I love you, but we can't let the boys live like you."

He closed his eyes for a moment and pressed his face into her hair, fearing that it would not work between them, knowing he could never love this way again. Then he drew back his head from hers, sadness filling him.

"They'll be who they are," he said evenly, aware that he might never have his family.

Suddenly he held up one hand, listening closely, his body growing rigid.

"Just the wind," he said after a moment. Gwenn felt his body relax again, but not completely.

"Would you read to me?" she said, moving and resting her head on Anton's lap. Sad, too, but wishing to make the most of these moments, she thought of her sons as he lifted the book and blew dust from the familiar pages. How they would enjoy spending such a time with him.

Anton reached for the book, still wanting to be as close to her as he could. He wrinkled his brow as he searched for his place in the low light of the dying flames.

"Chapter Eleven," he said slowly, reading the headnote. " 'Oliver Twist and his grandfather. Oliver gets kidnapped.' "

While he began to read, Anton's fingers opened her shirt buttons. At first she lay still, afraid he found her too thin and pale and injured. She trembled when his hand crossed one nipple and gently traced the line of her collarbone while he spoke Oliver's words.

Do let me return the books, if you please, sir. I'll run all the way.

"His grandfather reminds me of Adam," Gwenn interrupted, reaching up and opening Anton's shirt. Her fingers paused on the knob of his old broken ribs.

"Shh," Anton scolded, repeating Oliver's entreaty to his as-yet-undiscovered grandfather.

Gwenn could see Oliver's open honest face looking up eagerly as Anton read the lad's words, holding the book high to receive the falling light.

I won't be ten minutes, sir!

Anton's other hand was inside her shirt, warming her breast, holding her nipple between his fingers without moving. Gwenn felt at once relaxed and excited, her body eager for the intimacy of the evening.

She knew that Oliver, kidnapped, would not come home. A chill brushed her.

Anton set the book down beside them and lowered his head to kiss her cheek while he held her with both arms.

"Your face is greasy," she said, watching him close his eyes when she kissed the corners of his mouth. She kissed him again and like a cat licked clean his lips and chin.

Soon they were naked on the canvas near the coals.

"It would be best for the patient if you lay on your back," she said.

Anton lay back on his shirt and looked up at her. "I love you," he said after a moment.

Not wishing to echo a reply, she did not speak, but she hoped he knew the truth.

Before lowering herself onto him, she lay flat on his hard body and kissed him with soft slow lips. Then she knelt above him while his hands squeezed her tight cheeks and pressed her down.

"Open your eyes," she said, arching her back and reaching down behind her as she adjusted herself. Her stomach and breasts tightened when a cold breeze cut under the ledge and brushed her body, prickling her with goose bumps. Gwenn looked down into his eyes and saw something move against the darkening sky.

She glanced up and saw the klipspringer on its tiptoed hooves, standing in profile on the next cliff, lean and delicate and alone, its face seemingly turned to them but its countenance not visible, the short straight pointed horns and the large flared ears outlined against the blue-black sky as a thin moon rose beside it.

— 37 —

"I told you girls to leave that blasted camera," said Ernst as he stood beside the pile of abandoned baggage and supervised the reloading of the animals. "We're not taking anything but weapons, food and silver."

"No, the camera's Harriet's, and we won't leave it," said Bernadette defiantly, cramming the heavy black case into one of the canvas mule packs.

"This is our safari, not yours, Mr. von Decken. The camera's more important than your bit of old silver." She looked Ernst in the eye, impressed with her own words as she continued. "You heard Dr. Fergus. What Harry's doing with that camera could end this stupid war. Look what Malcolm and Gwenn have contributed already. It's about time the rest of us did something useful."

"Speak for yourself," said Ernst angrily, tired of arguing with kaffirs and women. "You already have the damned film," he added. "That's enough to get us all killed. You don't need the camera." He hopped one step towards her.

"Berny, perhaps he's right this time," said Harriet earnestly. She was seated on a rock, using her face kit for the last time. As she pinched her lips together and smoothed her lipstick, she turned to look at her sister. "For God's sake, let's leave the camera, Berny. And all that extra film, too. It just might fool the Italians. Open those other film boxes and canisters and make it look as if it's all been used. They'll have no way of knowing which is which."

"That won't fool them," Bernadette said hotly. "You remember what Dr. Fergus said. We're witnesses. The Italians won't feel safe until they've killed us all."

"You're right," said Charlie to Bernadette as he added his easel and paint box to the pile between the abandoned tents.

Bernadette lifted out the camera and strode over to her sister. "Whose side are you on?" she hissed privately at Harriet, throwing the case down onto the rocky ground beside her.

"I'm proud of what we're doing," Harriet said, looking up, not wanting to choose between Ernst and her sister. "But we have to get away. Look, Berny, bringing out the evidence will make a difference, but we're not going to get away if we're carrying all this stuff." She paused, opening her eyes wide. "Imagine what they'll say when we get back, all the reporters and the Pathé newsreels. What'll everyone say?" Excited, she stood up with three slim volumes of Karl Jung in one hand.

"No you don't, Harry," said Bernadette. "He stays, too." She snatched the books and pitched them near the remains of the dead mule that had been shot and stewed after it fell crippled.

"Thanks, Berny," said Harriet sarcastically. She pocketed her small enamel compact. "Let's leave the rest of our cosmetics for the Italians."

"Fine, but give me that film of the crashed Italian airplane." Bernadette knelt and recovered a flat leather purse. "I want to make sure it's safe."

Harriet reached into a saddlebag and handed the small tin canister to her sister. Bernadette squeezed it into the purse and slipped the purse inside the back of her own shirt.

"Let's go," snapped Ernst, shouldering his rifle and drawing his knife. "You girls aren't flirting at a garden party in Kentucky, or quarreling at some café in Paris. *Schnell*!"

Harriet saw Berny's lips narrow like razors, the way they always did when she was thwarted. She was about to bitch back when Ernst spoke once more with the finality of a vault door swinging shut.

"German officers do not debate." Impassively he turned to the tents and slashed each one with several long cuts.

Harriet had never seen her sister so suppressed. Of course, Berny was right about the silver, but that wasn't the point. To Ernst von Decken the spoiled aggressive intelligence of a rich American woman might as well be the babble of an African girl washing rags on stones by the stream. Maybe he could give lessons to the boys in Lexington.

Ernst mounted his pony and grabbed the lead rope of the first camel. The rest of the safari fell into line. Charlie was the last to mount up, climbing wearily into the hard saddle as if he'd already finished a long day's ride. Instead of growing stronger and more fit on this trip, Charlie seemed to be getting weaker, exhausted whenever they dismounted and in the mornings looking as if he hadn't slept a minute. Yet he always sketched, unfolding scraps of paper from the pockets of his bush jacket, sharpening his pencils with Ernst's knife while the rest of them made camp. And Harriet thought his work was getting better, more spare, each stroke more defining and suggestive, character in each face and landscape.

Why were there no men like Ernst and Anton at home? Harriet wondered as they picked their way along a narrow path that wound around the edge of a ridge. Here and there the trail had slipped away down the side of the drop, leaving small chutes of sand and chipped stone. At home, she thought, the gentlemen weren't tough and the hard-bitten ones weren't gents. No doubt there were some as rugged, probably cowboys and miners and lumberjacks. They were men a girl might take to bed, but not to dinner. They lacked the worldly manner of these colonial Europeans. She glanced at the solid figure riding ahead.

All the same, she doubted if Ernst von Decken could manage as well in Kentucky as she could in Africa. He'd be bored after a bit, and perhaps a trifle rough in his comfortable way, and too unimpressed with what Americans thought of as society to follow its ways and dress. Yet she was certain there were things he would get accustomed to, especially her body and her money. This brought a smile to her lips. Of course, his natural laziness would help. Perhaps if she bought back his family's plantation in Tanganyika, he might begin to see things her way.

Harriet thought about the silver. Might it be best if Ernst had no money of his own?

He was a leathery old devil, and he liked everything his way, especially sex, but she was learning how to get around him. He hadn't had a proper bath in the weeks since they'd met, and he never shaved until she asked him to, after the inside of her thighs were scraped and scratched like the floor of a breeding stall. And sometimes she was sore long after they had finished.

Tonight, she supposed, without tents, there'd be no chance for mischief. She didn't care what Berny saw or knew, but poor Charlie was always such a prude, and God only knew what these Africans would think if she and Ernst messed about in the moonlight.

Harriet looked ahead and saw Ernst's horse stumble with its right foreleg. A large rock shifted and bounded down the cliff. Dust rose from a line of smaller stones that slid after it. Even with no stirrup on the plunging side, her German stayed on with ease as the horse's right shoulder dropped down and recovered. He was adapting to one foot better than most men would to a new pair of boots.

Hungry and exhausted after fifteen hours of walking, talking to himself with loneliness, Haqim knelt by the ashes of the fire. He was hardened to many things, but not to infirmity. Whenever he paused on the trail in this forsaken land, the swollen ankle he had twisted two hours ago tightened up until he could barely stand.

The signs of a hasty one-night camp were all about him. His master's safari was not what it once had been.

Barefoot, he set down the Italian carbine and ran his fingers through the smooth grey ashes, detecting warmth but not heat. A goat or lamb shank rested in the dead coals. The safari must have gone on that morning. If not for this ankle, he would have caught up with them tomorrow.

Haqim removed the European boots that hung about his neck by their laces and glanced at the sky to determine the direction of the failing light as he limped down to the stream and washed his hands, wrists, upper arms and head.

The big Nubian completed his ablutions and returned to the campsite. He unwrapped the black sash that bound the tattered baggy trousers about his waist. He snapped the sash in the air to clean it and aligned it in the proper direction, folded twice, on the hard ground. Then he stood and knelt and prostrated himself repeatedly in prayer, compensating generously for the omitted devotions of the long day.

Rising, refreshed, he lifted the bone from the fire, dusted it and gnawed the scraps around the knuckle of the joint while he thought about what he was meant to do. He must not disappoint his brother, Tariq.

Haqim took a scrap of stale flatbread and his last handfuls of dates from his waist bag. He knelt by the stream and drank from his right hand before devouring them. Then he sat on a rock and ate slowly with his bad leg hanging in the cold running water. While he chewed the final crumbs, his mind wandered to his last woman, an unimaginative but patient five-piastre whore in a cheap stall behind Khan al-Khalili. Young enough, perhaps fifteen, she had smooth mottled tan and brown skin like the shell of a handsome turtle.

He lifted his head, catching a sound above the running of the water. Like the rush of demons he heard the distant angry hum of motor trucks. He hobbled back to the fire and recovered his rifle. If these were the enemy, he must delay them. He hesitated, trying to determine along which bank of the river the vehicles were coming.

He limped across the river just in time and knelt behind a candelabra tree. It would be difficult shooting in the failing light, and he was not yet skillful with guns, though Mr. Anton had congratulated him on his fine shot after he hit the Italian *afrangi* in the face. He was still more comfortable with honest close work, going at it man-to-man with his hands.

Used to a lifetime on the run but weary of the isolation, Haqim had found pleasure in the friendly well-fed safari life arranged for him by the dwarf of Cairo. Now it seemed his old hard life had returned. He knew how these

Italians would deal with him after what he and the *Inglizi* had done at their camp.

He felt hunted and alone and threatened, angry that he was being hounded once again.

Haqim stared across the river as the first truck entered the clearing. He cursed his usual stupidity when he saw he had forgotten his sash and his Italian boots.

Three large trucks pulled up in line. One had a gun mounted behind the driver's cab. The men, about fifteen, jabbered like monkeys while they climbed down and pissed and went to the river to drink. He recognized one or two from the camp where he had shot the soldier. Some still had no shoes or boots. A soldier picked up the abandoned pair of boots and called out to a comrade. A small black man was with them, a slave Somali, he assumed. This unclean man picked up Haqim's sash and smelled it.

One driver lifted the hinged bonnet above an engine and began to work with his tools. Other men took out food and bits of canvas to prepare a camp. Haqim wondered what to do. He watched the Somali scout carefully around the edge of the camp. Always there was trouble. If only he could reach the man with his hands.

Twisting the black cloth in his fingers, the Somali stared at the ground where the boots had been found. Then he walked down to the river, moving slowly in the near darkness. He stopped at the edge of the stream, staring across in Haqim's direction. He made the sharp clucking signal of a bush hunter, then pointed straight before him, turning his head and trying to get the attention of the soldiers behind him. With such a man tracking him, Haqim was certain any flight would be useless.

Haqim raised the unfamiliar Italian weapon, losing a moment as he struggled with the safety before he pulled the trigger. The shot echoed across the water.

Struck low in the stomach, the Somali screamed and staggered backwards. The soldiers grabbed for their weapons and abandoned the open center of the camp.

Haqim stayed where he was, knowing he could not make it far. He fired twice more without effect. He saw several Italians dash from the camp and begin to cross the river downstream. Another approached the water up-stream.

Haqim rose and limped hurriedly to the river with Allah on his lips. Several soldiers fired. A shot struck his left arm. He struggled across, firing as he scrambled up the opposite bank. Only the darkness protected him. He clubbed the kneeling Somali in the head with the butt of the rifle as he passed. Another bullet hit him in the side. Shots came at him from all sides as he crossed the center of the camp.

Haqim fell, hit in both legs. He crawled and staggered to the truck with the raised hood. He pulled himself up by the edge of the vehicle and repeatedly smashed his empty rifle into the engine and the ignition.

"Black bastard!" a soldier shouted.

A pistol was jammed into his side. Screaming when it fired, Haqim turned and seized the soldier who held the weapon. The man fired again as Haqim bent the Italian's head over the metal edge of the engine compartment. The suspended bonnet slammed down, trapping his arms and the man's head beneath the hood. Haqim held on to the struggling figure, grinding the screaming soldier's face against the hot steel machinery. Finally a powerful man grabbed him from behind.

Haqim forced the resisting head downwards with his last strength. He heard the screams stop and the neck snap as he collapsed with the Italian still clasped in his arms like a lover.

"They're still scouting the base of the hills," Anton said quietly without lowering the field glasses. Peering out under the rim of the ridge, he caught the reflection of binoculars as one of the Italians scanned the heights. The observer appeared not to hesitate as he surveyed the crest on which Gwenn and Anton were sheltered.

The *Bersaglieri* must have left the usual route south and followed their trail west from the river, but lost it when they came to the rocky elevation where Gwenn and Anton had begun to climb.

"At least one of them must be an experienced tracker," Anton added, "though it looks like all seven are Europeans."

On his own, he might manage in a running fight, killing one or two by surprise, using the nights and covering many miles each day until he caught up with the safari. But never had Anton been less alone. Despite the hard words they had exchanged, for the last few days he had felt closer to Gwenn than at any time since their marriage.

Their alternatives were limited: they could surrender, they could run, they could fight, or they could wait quietly, hiding where they were until the Italians moved on. Water was plentiful, but food was a problem. He hated to think of Gwenn not having enough to eat. She was already so much stronger after a few days in this camp, her cheeks less thin, her eyes bright, the stitched wound along the edge of her chin healing in a thin clean line.

One hand on his shoulder, she sat beside him under the ledge, waiting for her turn with the field glasses. Concerned that one of the soldiers was kneeling beside the mud pool where he had killed the pig, wishing he had taken more time to clean up the ground, Anton watched a bit longer, then passed the binoculars to Gwenn and lifted the map.

"Oh, no," she said, her voice different. "I see a line of dust. There's a vehicle coming, and two of the soldiers are running down the hill and waving at it." She passed the glasses to Anton. "Bad news."

Anton watched for several moments. The open wooden-sided army truck, a Fiat 633 with solid tires, pulled up at the edge of the valley. The *Bersaglieri* gathered around it, lifting out supplies while the driver jumped down, removed his dark goggles and relieved himself by a bush. A heavy-bellied man in shorts and long socks, he returned to the truck and saluted when another Italian strode over.

This must be Grimaldi, now wearing a *Bersaglieri* hat himself. The lorry carried three other men, one of them an African, and a machine gun mounted on a platform behind the cab. The long-barrelled weapon was covered in a canvas shroud. Heavy spare tires and twenty-liter cans of fuel were lashed along the sides. Some military insignia, obscured by dust, was painted on the driver's door.

"No," Anton finally replied. "Good news. That's our new truck. In that, we can catch up with our safari."

He was concerned, however, by the arrival of the African. He was probably a tracker, another of the hireling Dubat *shiftas.* If such a man saw the mudhole, they might be followed and discovered before he had a chance to steal the vehicle.

It must be done tonight.

Anton lowered the glasses and took Gwenn's hand as he looked at her.

"Time's up," he said.

"Do we have to leave?"

"We have to steal that truck before the tracker finds us," he explained, reassured to see sadness in her eyes. "I'm off to do a recce. I'll be back shortly after dark." He stood and checked his pistol. "Be ready to leave when I get back, and prepare a large fire but don't light it. We'll be using two fires as diversions."

Gwenn nodded and said nothing. He loves all this, she thought. He should have been a soldier.

An hour later, armed with the pistol, he lay fifty yards past the Italian camp, concerned about the rising moon. A broad canvas had been stretched out from the edge of the truck's siding to two posts set among piles of rocks. Most of the men were gathered beneath this shelter. One or two went back and forth to the fire where their rations were cooking. Anton watched the driver fill the Fiat's gas tank from the heavy cans. Grimaldi stood at one corner of the canvas, speaking to the African and another man carrying a carbine. The two men left the colonel, disappearing into the darkness towards the hills on the far side of the camp. Concerned about Gwenn, Anton wished he were close enough to follow the pair. He saw Grimaldi, a patch over one eye, walk to the fire with a map in his hand.

Anton slowly backed away farther and farther up the rocky slope behind him. Finally he was able to turn and climb swiftly onto the knobby boulder-strewn plateau of ancient lava. There he would prepare a fire. Once the flames were visible, he would have Gwenn light another one. Then she could descend to meet him on the far side of their ridge.

Returning from his reconnaissance, he found Gwenn calm and ready, the campsite stripped, everything packed, a fire set.

"I've laid a second fire on the escarpment past their camp," he said, blackening his face with ashes. "That should draw most of them off. As soon as you see that one burning, light yours." Concerned about her sense of mercy, not her skill or courage, he spoke again while he cleaned the Beretta. "A couple of soldiers are already scouting about in these hills somewhere nearby. I'm leaving you the Holland. If they come for you, shoot first. Don't hesitate. Shoot."

"Good luck," she said. "I hope the others've got away. It's the film that counts."

Knowing better than to argue, Anton kissed her and left.

Gwenn knelt by the unlit fire with the waxed matches in her hand. The double-barrelled .375 rested on the knapsack beside her. She tightened her boots and watched for Anton's signal. It pained her to leave this place, but God help them both if Lorenzo captured them. She remembered Anton's words about the danger of leaving him alive: "Would you expect me to leave a wounded leopard or hyena?" Now she knew they had.

She glanced up at the slender gibbous moon and saw the klipspringer again, outlined on the nearby cliff. It reminded her of the evening before, and Anton. She recalled their long lovemaking in the moonglimmer.

"May I have my body back?" she had said gently with a smile when at last they fell away from each other.

Suddenly the klipspringer started, rising in the air as if shot from beneath. Its legs still rigid, it landed neatly on a rock below, then sprang twice more and vanished.

Gwenn lay down at once and set the rifle before her. Grateful for the warning, she felt her stomach tightening with fear.

She saw a light flicker on the plateau past the Italian camp. Anton had started the main diversion. Now it was her turn. Her hands trembling, Gwenn rose and struck a match and dropped it into the dry grass at the center of the fire.

What was that? She heard a rock fall on the slope just below. The tracker? she wondered with alarm.

She gathered the knapsack and rifle and distanced herself from the rising fire. Some thirty or forty yards away, she crouched behind the rim of the ridge. Before she could begin her descent, two armed men appeared at the fire, a young *Bersaglieri* she recognized, and a gaunt-faced African with a rope belting his grey cotton robe. Her body stiffened while she watched them.

Gwenn knew what she must do. It was her turn to kill. Best to start with the tracker, she thought, remembering Anton's apprehension about the man.

The African studied the terrain by the growing light of the flames. His back to her, he moved with his head low and his right hand gliding just above the ground with the fingers spread as if he were receiving sensations directly from the earth. She rested the heavy Holland on the knapsack and tried not to hesitate.

Gwenn fired the first barrel. Struck in the center of his back, the African fell across the fire with his rifle in one hand. Feeling strangely remote, surprised by her own steadiness, swiftly she moved her finger to the rear trigger.

The soldier threw himself down as Gwenn fired the left barrel. Apparently struck in the hip, the Italian lay screaming by the fire as Gwenn scrambled down the rocky route she and Anton had selected for this moment. The young man's cries followed her down the hillside, upsetting her with his pain.

Anton hurried down from the plateau. The flames rising behind him, he stayed well distant from the natural route between the Italian camp and the fire he had lit. He heard two shots echo along the rocks. He recognized his .375. Was Gwenn all right? His fear for her consumed him as he sheltered behind a kopje and watched the soldiers organize and disburse. He couldn't go to her yet, not until he had the truck.

Grimaldi divided the men into two parties of four each. Leaving the driver behind, the colonel himself led one group towards Anton's plateau. The remaining *Bersaglieri* trotted into the darkness towards Gwenn's fire. Anton prayed she would be all right.

Anxious, but relieved to have heard no shots but hers, he waited until the Italian camp was quiet. Then he stole into the valley, circling behind the camp around the far side of the lorry. He lost sight of the driver when the heavy man walked to his own side of the truck and sat on the running board. Crawling towards the lorry, hurried by a dangerous sense of urgency he would never tolerate when hunting, Anton could see the soldier's boots and socks under the vehicle against the glow of the fire.

Anton knelt by the side of the truck, forcing himself to wait for a better moment. As he drew his *choori* from his belt, he smelled the man's strong cigarette. At length the driver stood and opened the door. He climbed into the lorry and grunted as he slid under the wheel to the seat next to Anton's door.

Coughing, the Italian flicked his smoke outside and opened the glove compartment. Anton smelled the coarse wine when the man pulled the cork from the straw-covered bottle with his teeth and spat it onto the floor. Let him drink, Anton said to himself, let him drink. The driver cast back his head and closed his eyes and chugged. Anton rose slowly from his crouch. His knife entered the man's neck below the ear and in one motion sliced forward above his Adam's apple until it emerged under his chin.

Anton opened the door and yanked out the body. The blood and wine spilled darkly over the driver's heavy belly. Calmly, untroubled by the killing, Anton took the packet of cigarettes from the driver's pocket. He recorked the wine, climbed in and closed the door. Red wine and blood dripped down the windscreen.

The Fiat started without fuss. He looked towards the escarpment but saw no sign of the scouting parties returning. Driving slowly, though burning with impatience, he left the lamps off as long as possible, finally lighting them when he came to the base of the hills.

Immediately he heard men shouting in Italian. They must have found the first abandoned fire and been hurrying back to camp. He heard the fast crack of 6.5mm repeating military rifles. Several shots struck the lorry before it turned the rocky corner at the base of the escarpment. Two split the door beside Anton. He yelled in fierce pain when he felt something punch him hard in the left side.

Anton drove slowly over the bumpy ground. Pain numbed his side as he approached the group of boulders where he and Gwenn had agreed to meet. Dizziness was taking hold of him as he arrived at the rendezvous. Feeling a wave of nausea, he stopped with the engine running. Twice he flicked the lights, then turned them off. Almost collapsing, he stretched across to open the far door, then leaned one hand on the seat beside him. He felt the Italian's blood, now joined by his own, thick and wet and slippery on the seat.

He switched on the lights. Two Gwenns stood directly in their beam, rifles and knapsacks in hand. He blinked and saw her run to the off door and jump in.

Gwenn slammed the door and gripped the seat as Anton shifted into first and the truck bounced forward.

"What happened?" she cried, raising her wet bloody hands from the seat and squinting at him in the darkness.

"Are you all right?" she asked, touching his waist and shoulder.

"We just have to get away," he mumbled, shaking his head to steady himself while he followed the lights into the night.

— 38 —

"One for Denby," Gwenn said, drawing the curved surgical needle high until the thread of gut was tight and the torn skin was pulled together. She hooked the needle through Anton's skin again. "One stitch for Wellie. One for Olivio. Two for Ginger and Clove. One for Haqim."

She knew Anton would pretend there was no pain, and he did, at first acting as if the half bottle of *grappa* had rendered him insensible. But now his clenched knuckles were white as young ivory. Why were men still boys when they were brave, and babies when they cried?

"One for Adam. One for Ernst. One more for Olivio." The line grew shorter as she stitched the long flesh wound. Except for the bleeding, his injury was more messy than dangerous. She was proud of the efficient way she had removed from his side the nearly spent bullet and the nasty splinters of the truck's door. She hoped she'd got them all.

"One for Kimathi. Another for Malcolm. I'm afraid we don't have enough friends. There, finished."

She set down the bloody needle and lifted a roll of gauze from the Italian medical chest bolted into the back of the lorry.

"Thank God you're a nurse, I mean a doctor," he said in a husky voice while she belted his waist with the gauze.

"I'm neither one." Gwenn paused to split the ends of the bandage with her teeth. "Though I mean to be. But this time you're the patient. Keep still." She knotted the ends. "Perhaps now you'll be more sympathetic to your wife's work."

"I'd rather bleed to death," he said tartly. His dirty unshaven face was running with sweat. Frustrated by his injury, he lay on a makeshift pallet in the back of the four-cylinder Fiat.

She jumped down and rinsed her hands and face in the brackish water of a murky pool. The truck was parked beneath the thin overlapping branches of two acacias. If they were spotted from the air, hopefully they would be taken for Italian. She rinsed Anton's torn shirt and rubbed it in the sand, then climbed back into the truck.

"You've so many scars." She stroked his bare shoulder with her fingertips before sitting beside him on a spare Pirelli. She wiped his face with the cool shirt and raised his head more comfortably against the platform of the machine gun mount. "At least this one will be mine." Perhaps we can be lovers, she thought, if not man and wife.

"We won't be alone here for long," Anton said in a stronger voice, looking over the side of the truck at a cluster of gnarled moss-covered trees nearby. "Ethiopians love to chew on those red *miraa* leaves. It's like *gat*. Makes 'em feel good. I could use a few myself."

"Try one of these instead." Gwenn removed a crumpled cigarette from the crude wrapper of the *Aurora Senza Filtros,* wanting to prevent Anton from reopening the wound by raising his left arm. A long fragment of black tobacco stuck to her lower lip after she lit the Italian cigarette and placed it in his mouth. The thin paper was crumpled in at both ends of the cigarette.

Anton grimaced after taking a deep puff.

"Hate to think where these Eyeties sweep up this stuff." He looked at Gwenn's mouth and caught her eye before plucking the tobacco from her lip with his right hand.

"Still, that driver chap did his best for us. Where's that wine he didn't finish?" Anton moved two fingers along her lower lip. She kissed them as they passed.

"Right here." She passed the bottle to him. "Where do you think we are?"

"Good two days' march from Grimaldi's mob, and about a day's drive from where the safari should be." He watched her eyes flicker at his mention of the name.

"Anton, look." Gwenn stood up, alarmed to see dust rising in the distance. "Someone's coming." She raised the field glasses while Anton groped for his rifle. "Oh, it's only two boys with some sheep or goats." She rested on the tire and shared the last of the wine.

"They're getting closer," she said after a time, lifting her hand from Anton's leg and watching the two shepherd boys approach with a herd of tan and white goats. The quick-stepping animals had slender elegant necks, long pointed faces and pendulous tear-shaped ears.

"They're so handsome," she said with interest.

"The goats?"

"No, Anton, these Ethiopian boys."

The boys threw stones at their skinny charges to keep them together and jabbed the animals mercilessly with long staffs. One youth carried a curved knife at his hip. Dressed in thick cotton robes with the hoods cast back over their shoulders, chewing and spitting as they advanced, both boys had large dark eyes, aquiline faces and shiny red lips.

"My, my!" she said softly. "Look at the tall one."

"Behave yourself. You're a married woman with two children." Stiff in his medical girdle, Anton tried to pull himself up by gripping the gun platform.

"Buckle on that Beretta and pass me the Holland. There'll be a village here any minute and it's best if they know we're both armed."

"Don't move like that!" Though annoyed with his foolishness, she did as he suggested with the weapons. "I'll get you up if it's necessary."

"Will you?" He raised his eyebrows. "Take a silver dollar from my shorts and buy us one of those kids."

She reached into Anton's pocket and dallied for a moment, teasing him a bit too much before jumping down from the lorry.

For one thaler the boys sold and killed and skinned a fine brown kid with an injured leg. First the youths went directly to the *miraa* trees, picking the red leaves of the young shoots. Some of these they began to chew while they slaughtered the animal. Others they wrapped together in scraps of old banana leaves and stuffed into the leather sacks that hung from their waists.

Before leaving, the boys gave Gwenn a handful of the leaves in exchange for two cigarettes.

"Field medicine," she said, somewhat concerned, but passing the leaves to Anton. Prolonged chewing of the stimulating leaves was said to provide euphoria and excitement, while reducing pain, fatigue and sexual interest.

Gwenn started a fire when the shepherds moved off. She was surprised they were leaving and that the inevitable crowd of Abyssinians had not materialized to join them. The boys must be driving the herd to fresh water. She handed the bottle of grappa to Anton, noticing the red stain on his lips. While she spitted the kid's joints and smaller cuts she wondered if she should do for her patient what he had done for her in the tent. She recalled Malcolm Fergus remarking that sex could be the best medicine. It had certainly helped with her. She hoped Anton would be able to lie still while she did her duty.

"Alto lā!" yelled Captain Uzielli, gripping the machine gun mount. He squinted through his dark goggles across the bouncing cab of the Fiat to the hard tan and grey landscape before him. His wide face and prominent ears

were coated with brown dust under the campaign hat that was pulled low on his forehead. The broad scar on his left cheek stood out darkly beside his nose. He had come to prefer these vast ravines and escarpments and cool high ridges to the parching sands of Libya.

"Alto lā!" He banged his fist twice on the roof of the cab, furious at the unresponsive driver, a typical idiot of the *Frontieri Alpini.* The driver braked the six-wheeler on the rim of a rocky eminence that rose like a stack of dishes, each plate a bit smaller than the one below it. Uzielli sensed they were getting closer, and he wanted an opportunity to spot the enemy first, before the colonel joined them.

A narrow steep gorge ran directly before him. The corrugated shelved rock dropped one hundred fifty feet or more to a snake-thin twisting valley. He saw patches of green cultivation at the bottom and wondered how the sunlight ever reached them. Small figures and animals stood out in the valley like toys. Here and there the ravine looked as if a man could jump across it.

Uzielli blew the thick grit from his field glasses and wiped the lenses before scanning along the opposing edge of the ravine to the distant descending plain that led on south past the next lake. Removing his goggles, he set the binoculars into the dust-free circles around his eyes. As he adjusted the lenses he was annoyed to hear the other truck approaching. A swirl of dust enveloped him and he heard the scratchy dry voice of Colonel Grimaldi.

"Pass me those glasses, Captain," ordered the colonel, stepping down from the second truck, a three-ton Bianchi designed to hold twenty men but now carrying only fifteen *Alpini* and *Bersaglieri.* Lieutenant Calandro passed a water bottle to the colonel. Grimaldi rinsed his mouth and spat before drinking.

Reluctantly, Uzielli handed Grimaldi the binoculars, astounded again at the incompetence of this officer who had lost his eye and his men's boots to a small party of civilians. The eye was of no account, but to a soldier in the mountains boots were more precious than water. Obviously a typical flyboy of the *Regia Aeronautica.* What did they care for foot soldiers?

"And check the vehicles, Uzielli, while I see where we're going." Grimaldi spoke without looking at the captain. "We can't afford to lose another machine." One of the *Alpini* was examining the Bianchi's tires.

Three trucks had been lost already, one to that bastard Englishman. The first of the five brought by the *Alpini* had collapsed near the rendezvous at the *Bersaglieri* camp, a main spring gone and the transmission reduced to two working gears. Uzielli would have preferred just three good vehicles of the same type, but that wasn't the army. Another truck, already suffering engine trouble, had been battered by that mad black beast in the abandoned camp. Uzielli had left two *Alpini* working on that one. If they could get it back in order, they were to drive it on and rendezvous at Lake Chamo. If they could not, they would probably never be seen again. At least the surviving vehicles now had sufficient gas and oil and a few spares.

Enzo Grimaldi climbed onto the first truck and leaned his elbows on the canvas-covered machine gun. He scanned the edge of the far side of the gorge. He saw no movement. Systematically quartering the more distant view, he spotted a line of dust and a straggling column of mules, horses and a few camels moving south along the far escarpment.

"Some Abyssinian traders," Enzo announced too quickly. Then he saw something glint in the clear light. He focused again and studied the column. A reflected sparkle met his eye. "No," said the colonel without taking the glasses from his face, "Europeans."

Uzielli felt the grip in his belly that always caught him when it was time for action. He strode to the edge of the gorge and stared across without blinking, searching for the best route to the enemy. This was why headquarters had chosen him for this run. He had a gift for hunting, but he was best working on his own, particularly if silver was to be the only reward.

Grimaldi saw a mounted man in European bush clothes stop his horse and study the Italian trucks through his own pair of binoculars. The colonel was pleased to observe that the man was a cripple. He was missing one foot. That should make things easier. Several other Europeans checked their mounts as they came up to the man with the glasses. One or two could be women. After a few moments they resumed their march along a route where no motor vehicle could follow, pressing on faster to the south in a tighter line. Enzo counted five mules tied nose to tail, each with a wooden case strapped to either side of its pack harness. The silver?

"Uzielli," said the colonel, looking down at the *Bersaglieri,* "here's the opportunity you've been waiting for. Take ten men and light packs and the new sniper rifle. You can have all the water and your pick of the boots." Grimaldi jumped down and handed Uzielli the glasses.

"Yes, sir," said Uzielli, pleased with the assignment even if he was contemptuous of the colonel's avoidance of the hard duty.

"And don't stop till you've got them all. I'll take the trucks and block the route to Lake Stefanie where they'd have to come down from that escarpment and cross the open country."

"Take off your boots," said Uzielli to the *Alpini* with the largest feet. "Now!" he yelled at the startled soldier. The man hesitated and looked briefly at his sergeant as Uzielli stepped towards him. Hurriedly the man bent and began to loosen his boots.

"Sir," protested the sergeant, "my men need their boots, we've . . ."

"The ones who come with me can keep theirs," said Uzielli, selecting five

Alpini as Grimaldi turned away. "You and you, take 'em off now." The captain sat on a rock and removed his own pinched boots, taken earlier from one of the soldiers killed by the huge black man at the camp.

"Calandro," said Grimaldi, walking to the cab of the lead truck. "Load up the rest of the men. I want you on the machine gun."

The lieutenant climbed up and unlashed the canvas that covered the gun. He shoved a long magazine of soft-lead long-nosed 8mm rounds into the Breda. Grimaldi took the wheel himself, bashing along between the thorn bushes and large loose rocks as he searched for an end to the ravine. With luck, he could still be in at the finish.

"It's all so stupid," said Bernadette crossly, twisting in the saddle to stare across the gorge at the pursuing vehicles. "Imagine being chased across Abyssinia by a bunch of Wops! What on earth do these Italians want in the middle of Africa?"

Von Decken looked carefully at the young American woman before he spoke.

"Think of it as their California, miss."

Harriet started to reply but caught herself and changed her mind.

Ernst swung his right leg up and rested it across the thin shoulders of his Ethiopian pony. He hooked the braided leather reins around his right knee, annoyed by the tingling that seemed to come from his missing foot. His hands free, Ernst adjusted the old Zeiss glasses and studied the enemy vehicles. Both bore the marks of hard service in the bush. One truck had a motorbicycle lashed to the back. He counted about fifteen men, perhaps two or three more dressed like officers, and one mounted machine gun. Two men were on their knees with spanners, changing a tire on the rear vehicle.

"Praise God for the thorns of Africa," the German muttered.

Ernst von Decken moved the glasses to study the route the enemy must take. He thought of the lessons of another chase many years ago. He had not survived four years on the run in East Africa by fighting battles he could not win. Violence had its place, even courage, but evasion and deception were steadier companions on a long march. He was getting too old for these games, he realized, though perhaps not yet for others.

"Water, Bwana?" asked Harriet, standing beside his horse with her reins in one hand.

He looked down and smiled as his twin held up a canteen. Harriet rested her other hand on his hip and looked up at him with reddened but twinkling eyes, her hair bound in a tight dusty kerchief. Ernst did not think himself a modest man, but he was surprised how this American girl had taken to him, and to this life.

"If you two *Rotkopfen* are still hunting for adventure," he said cheerfully, "I think you're going to find it. Your admirers are getting closer."

"I've always liked Italians," Harriet said, as if talking to herself. "They're so romantic. Where do you think Anton's going to meet us?"

"He'll find us." The German passed Harriet the canteen and wiped his mouth with the back of his hand.

"I've learned never to worry about your English gypsy."

Ernst rubbed his eyes, tired from another day of dust and squinting into the bright sun. Before opening them he saw von Lettow's face looking up with his left eye, the right one cut by elephant grass, as he folded his maps and gathered his lean officers about him by the fire, addressing each by name. Nearby the tattered black eagle of imperial Germany snapped in the night breeze on its bamboo flagstaff and the famished *askaris* squatted by their fires waiting for the thin mealie porridge to warm. *"Meine Kamaraden,"* the general would say in his clear strong voice, never revealing fatigue, "we will make *Afrika* their enemy. The land will do the fighting for us."

That was the idea. Ernst must lead his silver mules where these Fiats could never venture. Did these *Spagettifresseren* think to defeat a captain of the *Schutztruppe*? He scratched his leg and counted the other animals as they caught up and gathered on the small plateau.

Ten mules, six horses and four camels made a strange parade, but so far it was working. As the days varied, depending on the water and the terrain and the grazing or browsing, the different animals fared better or worse. The horses were too dependent on water. The moody camels disliked swaying along the narrow rough tracks that edged the shelves of the ridges. The mules, taking turns with carrying the silver, were having the hardest duty, their flanks and bellies lined and pitted with sores from the ropes and cinches, but they seemed the toughest.

"I hope all these animals will find enough to eat up there," said Harriet, surveying the land before them.

"They won't," said Ernst, "but we'll eat the ones that look the hungriest."

Horrified, she watched Chesterfield, the youngest and her favorite camel, nibbling thoughtfully at a thorny broad-eared cactus with his wide lewd lips. He seemed to be favoring one leg. Harriet had come to think of camels almost as she would of horses.

Ernst looked across the ravine and saw the big truck charge on ahead. The other vehicle followed. Ernst tracked them with his binoculars. Then he looked back and spotted a group of men they had left behind. He counted eleven, and watched as they began to pick their way down the far side of the gorge towards him. He was disturbed by their determination.

"What're we going to do?" Harriet asked. "Where is my wild Hun going to lead us?"

"We will teach them what it is to walk," Ernst said. "Mount up, *meine Kätzchen*, we must climb."

Five hours later, Harriet looked up and watched Ernst's horse pick its way along the cliff edge of a higher terrace on the escarpment. Horse and rider stood out against the sky, rocking from side to side. Her lover was leaning forward as the pony climbed, the reins high over the horse's neck to permit the animal's head to weave and bob as it found its way. He didn't ride the way one did in Kentucky, but it seemed to work. One of the Abyssinians was scouting ahead of him, his mule having an easier time with its lighter burden.

"These lakes are like pearls on a necklace." Bernadette pointed to a large oval sheet of water that shimmered in the wide depression opening below them to the southwest. "That's got to be Lake Chamo." Her pony nipped Harriet's as they jostled together on the narrow path. "We've already passed Awasa and Abaya."

"Just one to go till we're safely into Kenya," said Harriet hopefully. Still, she was certain it would be a long tough scramble, particularly as Ernst was now selecting the hardest route instead of the easiest. "Lake Stefanie. Anton said it straddles the border, and we can buy boats and paddle right across."

Harriet raised both hands to her eyes and watched the screen of dust that followed the Italian trucks.

Ernst whistled sharply.

Harriet looked up and saw him pointing with his right arm. He never seemed to hesitate. The Ethiopian in the lead rode down to show the rest of them the way, his skinny mule slipping and sliding with its head low. The safari gathered itself again. Everyone tightened their own girth before remounting. The mule boys led their animals by the head as they climbed again. Before them waited the vast rocky ocean of the Abyssinian massif, an endless retreat of buttes and ravines, ridges and terraced escarpments, the compacted age lines of the earth as deep and harsh and revealing as the dark weather-carved face of an old sailor.

If anyone grew tired, they only had to look through the glasses and pick out the Italian trucks weaving among the ravines and gorges to the west as they sought a way to intercept the safari. One soldier stood on the machine gun mount, pointing ahead. Others gripped the wooden sides of the bouncing trucks, reminding her of hounds on the leash as they waited to join the hunt on foot. The trucks seemed to be working their way closer. From time to time, the safari could spot the small band of soldiers who were pursuing them on foot.

"Those're the bastards I'm worried about," Ernst said to Harriet when he paused to tighten his girth.

Two hours later von Decken stopped his exhausted horse and the safari gathered around him on a small plateau. A cool wind was blowing from the north, swirling tight spirals of hard dust that danced across the plateau before leaping off into the void like suicides.

"Kimathi," said Ernst sharply, drawing his pistol. "Have Lapsam make his fire here." Von Decken hobbled over to a thin mule that stood with one leg raised. "The rest of you gather firewood."

"Lapsam will make the fire over there, Bwana, near all that wood," said Kimathi calmly.

Ignoring him, Ernst shot the weak mule behind the ear and left it for the Africans to skin and butcher.

"No!" protested Bernadette, too late.

"Can't be helped, Berny," said Harriet, not unkindly, as she loosened her boots. "Wonder what the Italians thought of all our clothes and things."

"Probably wear them in the evening around the fire," replied her sister.

Harriet noticed Charlie sitting wearily on a rock, pulling up one trouser leg with both hands to examine something under his knee. Bernadette walked over and sat close to him on the ground, smoking while she craned her head to see what he had found.

"Another camel tick," Bernadette said. Anton had warned them these ticks could cause fever and temporary blindness. "This one's big as a grape." Harriet admired the way her sister went after it. No longer squeamish, Berny puffed hard on her cigarette, then pressed the glowing end against the tick and wiped Charlie's bloody leg with some sand while he bit his lip.

Harriet looked back at Ernst and wondered what he was thinking. Perhaps he would do in Lexington, after all. What did it matter what some of her friends would think? The ones who understood would be jealous.

Ernst stood facing north, leaning against a ledge, studying their pursuers before the light fell. Waiting for dinner, he held his heavy binoculars to his eyes. He was losing his belly, just when she was getting used to it.

"I still make eleven," he said. "The trucks have gone on along the valley. These other boys are coming straight up after us. They're travelling light."

"I wish Anton was here," Bernadette said to Charlie. "He'd know what to do."

Harriet hoped her German hadn't heard. She watched him hobble over to the cook and give some instructions.

"Why do you always have to bark at the Africans?" Harriet said when Ernst passed by, annoyed that he treated them with none of Anton Rider's easy humor or respect. Somehow, they didn't seem to mind. But it wouldn't do with the Negroes in Kentucky.

"You think you're still in the army," she added when Ernst did not reply. "You're so German."

"Thank you." Ernst paused and looked down at her. "Our blacks were always free. Yours spent two hundred years in chains."

She'd have to change Ernst a bit if he came home with her. But not too much, she thought, noticing his powerful shoulders and the strong lines in his face. It should be fun, trying to bend an oak. She tried to remember what Jung wrote about people really changing.

"Build up that fire so it keeps going after we move on," von Decken said sharply to Lapsam as he dropped his crutch behind him and sat down on a rock.

"Aren't we camping here?" Charlie said, the dread of further effort in his voice.

Busy removing the leather cup from his stump and shaking out the dirt and grit, Ernst spoke without looking at the American.

"Not unless you want to have breakfast with Mussolini."

"How much further to the border?" said Bernadette.

"Lake Stefanie might be another seventy miles," said Ernst, "if we could go dead straight. Then it's about another twenty till the lake crosses the Kenya border."

Harriet had learned that Ernst hated to be questioned. His accent always grew harsher when he was annoyed.

Harriet picked up his crutch and sat behind him. She made a thick pad from a bit of tan cloth she had cut from one of her skirts. She bound the pad to the top of his crutch with some fishing line she had found in a pack. Without saying anything, she put the crutch back where she had found it and went and sat beside her sister.

"After we finish chewing on that mule, we'll do another three or four hours while those Eyeties chase this fire." Ernst said. "There'll be moon enough and we'll lead the animals."

"Why don't we go on in the morning?" Charlie complained. "They can't catch us if we're mounted."

"In this country, a man with two good legs can cover more miles than a horse, unless you get down on the flat and gallop from time to time," Ernst said with surprising patience. "And we have to walk. When these mules trot, the packs keep shifting and the harnesses break." Sometimes Ernst seemed to like Charlie, or perhaps he just felt sorry for him. Whatever the reason, Harriet found he had an annoying willingness to discuss decisions with Charlie, but not with the twins.

"Why don't we leave the silver?" Charlie said.

"Why don't we leave the film?" said Ernst. "Who cares if the Eyeties and these *Schwartzes* kill each other, or what they use to do it?"

"No," Bernadette and Harriet said together, accepting tin plates of rice and gravy and charred meat.

"What's in this gravy, Lapsam?" Harriet smiled, pushing the meat to the side of her plate.

"Onions and mule marrow, miss. Bits of pieces." Lapsam pointed at Chesterfield. The young long-necked ruminant stood on three legs, one forefoot balanced delicately on the front curve of its toe. "Tomorrow camel meat."

After dinner Ernst rose and slung his rifle across his back. He picked up his crutch, nodding and grunting after he examined it. Then he turned away and hobbled swiftly along the ridge that zigzagged to the southwest. The camp rose and followed him, everyone else leading an animal.

— 39 —

Surprised by how little they had gained on the civilians in the last three days, Captain Uzielli sat on a rock and tightened his boots. He watched his men file past along the ledge. The *Frontieri Alpini* and his five *Bersaglieri* still held themselves a bit apart, each group bunching together on the trail and making their own fire in the evening.

The *Bersaglieri* had not shown as much dash as he'd expected, probably because they'd lost a few comrades. One, a sullen lad with the heavy accent of Brindisi, dumb as a sausage, was fussing with his feet. He still wore some rubbish made in the *Bersaglieri* camp, more like sandals than shoes or boots, but he'd probably spent his first eighteen years barefoot in the streets at home. Soon he'd be barefoot again.

Uzielli worried how the men would do when the time came for the rough work that lay ahead, not the fighting but the murdering. Fortunately, two of the *Bersaglieri* had been with him in Libya. They understood what it was to campaign in Africa. He called to one now. The man was preoccupied, cleaning his new sniper rifle, the *Assassino.*

"That should help finish the job, Umberto," said Uzielli. "Should've been over already," he added, "what with hand-picked mountain troops pursuing women and a cripple." He was annoyed with himself for not bringing more food and water bottles, but he had expected to rendezvous with the trucks, and already the chase had gone on longer than planned. At least the rivalry between his men had kept the traditional army complaining to a minimum.

The first two days had been easier, with the troops well nourished and the climbing gradual. The younger soldiers had laughed while they ransacked their quarry's abandoned gear, joking as they opened the French perfumes and American rouge jars and lipsticks. The experienced men had searched without success for something more useful or rewarding. The captain himself had been most interested in the boxes of heavy shells, English .375's and .450's. His adversaries must be well armed for civilians, and there must be someone familiar enough with soldiering to know the Italians couldn't use such ammunition.

"Rhino-stoppers," Uzielli called them, hating to think what a .450 slug would do to one of these *bambinos.*

Today they were thirsty, each man allowed only a few sips from the canteens every two hours. There was no sign of the trucks on the flat far below, and they lacked a native guide to help them find water in the hills. Last night they'd feasted on the remains of a half-eaten camel abandoned by the safari under a pile of sand. They'd driven off the vultures and gone at it like an Easter lamb, but it was dry stringy chewy meat that made them thirsty and hung in a man's belly all night like a stone.

Uzielli scanned with his binoculars as his men sat down nearby. One or two removed their boots to get rid of stones or check their sores and blisters. Their quarry was high above them, moving slowly as they led their animals along a narrow cliff-side trail.

The Italians had been gaining for the last few hours, occasionally cutting a corner on the zigzag path that wound up and down and up from one ridge to the next. On a straight course, they were probably no more than three or four miles back, but it was perhaps twice that on the route they had to follow. Uzielli adjusted the lenses as his men stared up at the steep rise above them. The wind had risen and a fine stone-hard dust was driving into his face, reminding him of the sand seas that had claimed so many men in Libya.

Watching the enemy day after day, he had begun to identify each one as a hunter might a particular stag or ram in the mountains at home. Even their animals were now familiar to him. The safari was down to eight mules, and two of these seemed to be limping. The last in line was carrying two of the chests. The crippled man was again leading the march.

Uzielli saw one of the women take a rifle from the saddle scabbard of the bony pony she was leading. She passed her reins to one of the six Africans and turned to face the rear of the column. She knelt and shouldered the weapon. After a moment he heard a shot echo along the rock walls.

The last mule went down on its forelegs as if clubbed in the head, then struggled to rise before rolling to one side and pitching over the edge of the cliff.

Astonished, Uzielli and his men watched the animal crash down, twisting its body and kicking long thin legs as it fell, twice diving end over end. The two chests smashed and burst open when the animal came to rest with its twitching black body wedged against a boulder on the side of the trail far below.

Uzielli directed his glasses back to the column and observed a commotion as the crippled man struggled back along the narrow path, striking the animals with a crutch as he pushed past them and approached the woman with the rifle. He brandished his crutch as he faced her. She appeared to ignore him, returning her rifle to its holster and again taking her horse by the head. After a time the column moved on as the man on crutches raised binoculars to his eyes and stared down at the mule and the broken chests. Understanding his sentiments, the Italian officer focused on the same scene. He saw the sunlight dance on a pile of silver.

Uzielli's men rose to their feet without any command. He himself retied his boots and set off at their head. "Stay back!" he yelled at several men who, for once, pressed him from behind. "Remember who you are!"

As if arriving at an oasis or a brothel, the men cheered and ran past Uzielli as they approached the dead animal several hours later. By the time he reached them they had laid down their weapons and stuffed their pockets with silver. Others had opened their packs and were removing spare rounds and rations and medical kits to make space for the Maria Theresa coins that glinted before them. On the hillside just above, a *Bersaglieri* and one *Alpini* were brawling over a sack of thalers caught in a depression in the slope.

"Attenzione!" Uzielli hollered with rage. He drew his Beretta. "*Attenzione*!"

The men near him scrambled to their feet. He fired one shot into the ground amongst them. The round cracked and whistled as it ricocheted away. The other men by the mule stood and snapped their heels together.

"Empty your pockets and packs, all of you. These coins belong to Italy." The old soldier knew who the army would hold responsible if the silver was stolen a second time. "Put all the silver in your packs," he said to three *Bersaglieri.* "We're going to count every coin. And the rest of you take what was in their packs."

Slowly the surly men began to gather the coins on the rocky dry ground beside the dead mule. Uzielli looked up and saw the two soldiers still fighting on the slope above them. The *Bersaglieri* slammed the *Alpini* in the chest with a heavy stone and rose to his knees holding his black leather hat. Captain Uzielli raised the Beretta and fired.

The *Bersaglieri* rocked forward facing down the hill. The hat tipped in his hands. Silver thalers poured from the side of the hat. Uzielli fired again. The soldier crashed down on his face among the rocks.

"Get his boots and canteen," the captain said to the boy from Brindisi, wanting to get back to the chase. "*Presto*!"

"Subito, Capitano, subito!"

It was time, Uzielli saw, for a new tactic. Ten men would always be delayed by the slowest of the group. Better to do this in the classic way of the Bersgalieri scouts: send the fastest man ahead. Uzielli would send the mountain boy, Umberto, armed with their one longer-range weapon, the *Assassino*.

Harriet handed the glasses back to Ernst, knowing he was still angry about the lost silver, although it had served its purpose and delayed the enemy. She didn't have to say anything. Her mother had taught her that every divorce began with the words, "I told you so." From now on she wouldn't disagree with Ernst, she'd just do what she wanted.

"You were right, Harry," said Bernadette instead. "The Italians are shooting each other over a bit of the silver. Amazing how dumb men can be."

They were approaching a basin in the ridge that sheltered a long shallow sheet of water. The animals had quickened their pace, hurrying on towards the pool, confirming Jung's observation that conduct changes when something is desired, although the personality itself remains the same. So Harriet thought as she washed the dust from her face.

"This *Jäger* could be trouble," Ernst said, and Harriet guessed that this time he was right. One of the Italians had left his comrades and gone off on a route of his own, no longer following their own zigzag trail south.

"That one looks like a hunter," the German muttered.

A second report came a bit later. "He's not carrying a short carbine like the rest," Ernst leaned heavily on her shoulder, his glasses still trained to the north. "It's got a long barrel and a scope. Must have better range."

"Sort of like an old Kentucky Long Rifle," replied Harriet, worried. "Our hunting rifles aren't much use over two or three hundred yards," she added, knowing that their heavier weight of lead was designed for even closer work than the short Italian carbines.

Trotting slowly, as Harriet imagined the Indians used to do, the Italian was following an easier lower route that ran parallel to theirs. In time, of course, they would have to descend to lower flatter ground to get to the lake. She remembered reading in Fenimore Cooper how a pack of pursuing Indians would sprint alone in turn, one man after another dashing on after the last collapsed until their prey was finally exhausted.

Now this hunter had actually gone past them on the lower course. He continued on, doubtless planning to climb after a time and head them off.

"If he climbs above us," Ernst called back, "the bastard'll pick us off from a safe distance."

Harriet watched the Italian disappear around a jagged spine of stone that rose like a buttress against the base of the escarpment before them.

"Zu Pferd!" Ernst exclaimed, increasingly concerned about the danger. "Keep moving."

Refreshed by the water they'd found during the afternoon, they pushed hard until sunset, finally making a hurried camp in an angle of two ledges before slaughtering the weakest mule. Even Charlie had nearly gotten over his distaste for killing and eating their mounts. So far their walking menu had served them well.

"Mules are the worst meat," said Bernadette crossly as Lapsam set to work. "Why don't we eat another camel?"

"We need the rest of the camels and horses, *Fräulein,*" Ernst said as if addressing a child, "for the final push through the bush that leads to Lake Stefanie and the border. It's flat and sandy."

"Only the French love to eat horses," said Berny, ignoring him and repeating a point she made every day.

"What would you expect?" Harriet said, knowing the best way to discourage repetition was to repeat the response. "They don't read *Black Beauty* when they're little." She enjoyed seeing her sister roll her eyes.

Bernadette passed her cigarette to Charlie and rested one hand on her fiancé's shoulder, looking down to see what he was sketching on the small pad in his lap. They sat side by side on a flat shelf of rock and smelled the grilling strips of muscle.

Charlie rose and moved to the fire, sitting cross-legged to face them as he drew the twins by firelight. Harriet thought he looked so thin with the shadows on his face. Lapsam crouched nearby, turning the mule meat in the flames.

A rifle shot cracked in the near-darkness, echoing off the rock wall beside them. Several voices yelled, and the animals jerked and strained at their leads and hobbles.

Harriet knew it was Charlie's bullet.

"Charlie!" Bernadette screamed as his body slumped after the impact.

Her fiancé lay moaning on his back with one shoulder in the fire. A flame danced across his sketch-pad.

Lapsam reached him first, pulling him to one side as Bernadette and Harriet ran to him. The African helped them drag Charlie into the lee of the rock shelf before they withdrew into the shadows.

Ernst crouched with his rifle facing the gunfire. No second shot came. The *Jäger* did not reveal himself.

Too shocked to weep, Bernadette knelt with Charlie's head on her lap. His lips bubbled with blood. Bent low, Ernst came over to them.

"Lung shot," Ernst said evenly. He handed Harriet his rifle and opened Charlie's shirt with careful fingers. The pale chest was drenched. Blood oozed from a small hole between his ribs. Harriet crept along the edge of the shelf and returned with the medical kit.

A second gunshot split the night. Lapsam screamed, then crawled slowly towards them and collapsed on his side, both hands bloody where he held his stomach. His dark eyes were large as he moaned and gargled with his mouth open.

"We can't stay here," Ernst said as one of the camels fell to another bullet. Lying on its side a few yards away, the animal breathed in and out in great high-pitched groans.

"How can we move them like this?" Breathless with fear and shock, Harriet stared at Lapsam and then at Charlie, uncertain how to dress their wounds with the small gauze pads Bernadette lifted from the kit. "Look how they're bleeding." Just then a rock splintered above her head, and she flinched.

"We can't move Charlie and Lapsam without killing them." Ernst held two pads against the wound in Charlie's chest. His own hand was soon dark and wet.

"Their only hope is if we leave them here, so an Italian medic will look after them. Sooner the better for both of them." Ernst paused. He looked at Harriet's face and his voice softened. "The trucks are the only way. If we stay with them and hold off the Italians, they're both bound to die."

He limped into the darkness, calling to the Africans to help him reload the animals behind an outcrop in the ledge.

"Ernst's right, Berny," Harriet whispered, one arm around Bernadette's shoulder, the other hand cupping her sister's cheek. "You and I can't save them. We can't. They need medical help and a vehicle."

"I'm staying with Charlie." Bernadette wiped his face with the tail of her shirt when his mouth bubbled red again. Then she reached into the back of her shirt and removed the leather purse containing the film. "The Italians won't dare kill an American woman."

True enough, thought Harriet, hesitating. "Then I'm staying, too," she said firmly.

"No. Someone has to go on so they'll know they can't kill Charlie and me without word getting out. It's safer for all of us if you go now." Bernadette held Harriet's face between her hands and looked her in the eye.

"And someone has to get that film out. You've got to do it, Harry. Please. You must. It's more important than we are." Bernadette leaned over and hugged her sister. "Go on, hurry. Help Ernst get ready. You can't do anything here. Go on, Harry, and take this." She handed her sister the purse. "The sooner you leave the better."

Harriet put the purse inside her own shirt. Then she knelt by Lapsam and closed his eyes before taking a white shirt from her pack and hanging it from a stick near the fire. At least that should stop any further shooting.

In fifteen minutes the animals were packed and Harriet knelt by her sister, hugging her.

"Hurry up, Harry, they'll leave without you," Bernadette said, kissing her sister's cheek before releasing her. "Go, right now. Don't make it harder. Please." Harriet nodded and hugged her again. Both twins parted without crying.

Ernst was waiting for her behind the rocks with two horses.

Harriet took her horse's reins. She felt thin and cold, trying not to think she might never see her sister again.

"I'm sorry," Ernst said, squeezing her hand as they set off, but getting no reply. As they hurried after the rest of the safari, he considered who should stay behind to slow the Italians.

There was only one man left he could trust for the job: that devil Kimathi. Ernst knew the African's eyes and legs were getting old, but he remembered Anton Rider's words. "He's steady as a two-ton anchor," Rider had told Ernst. "When you check your back he's always there."

At dawn, once he'd cleaned out the camp, that *Jäger* would be after them again. Someone had to stop him. It was the sort of job Ernst would've enjoyed doing on his own when he was younger, but he had to keep this safari moving and he himself was now too slow to be able to catch up if he stayed behind.

They left Kimathi in a cleft above the trail with the double .450 and a handful of dried dates and a tin cup filled with water.

For several hours the safari continued on by the light of the stars and moon, finally finding safety behind the spiny rampart of a long winding ridge as they turned back a bit towards the east and the glimmering pan of Lake Chamo.

"We'll stop here." Ernst threw down his crutch, groaning at the painful sore under his arm. Behind him was the low mouth of one of the volcanic caves formed millions of year before when lava had flowed and cooled in distinct layers. Some, he'd heard, ran on for miles.

"No camp or fire," he called out in a loud whisper, troubled as he looked at Harriet, "just an hour's rest and some of that rice." He'd miss the cook. Now they were down to two camels, six mules and the horses. There were only three Africans left, unless Kimathi made it back.

"I should never have left her," Harriet said quietly, seated by herself, leaning against the volcanic rock with her head back and her eyes closed.

"There was nothing you could do," said Ernst, trying to speak gently, "nothing any of us could do. They need transport and a doctor. Only the Italians can help them."

Three shrill shots echoed towards them along the side of the ridge, the sounds paced at intervals precise as buttons on a tunic.

"Is that from the camp?" Harriet leapt to her feet.

"Must be that sniper signalling to the other Italians," Ernst said easily. "Should help to get the medic to them sooner." He held out one hand towards Harriet, knowing she would not take it. She looked as if she had been shot herself. "We'd best keep moving."

Trembling, Harriet stood and folded her arms across her chest with her fists clenched. She turned and stared back to the north. Her body began to rock.

Ernst gripped her shoulders from behind, feeling her slender frame shrink and stiffen. He squeezed her shoulders.

"Come," he said in a quiet firm voice, remembering how they often had left wounded men behind to be cared for by the British. "It'll slow the enemy down," von Lettow used to say, ordering older weapons with a few rounds to be left with the men. But of course these three had not been left for British troops.

For an hour they made their way slowly along the edge of the ridge as the morning warmed. Once Ernst thought he saw a line of dust among some thorn trees far below. The Italian trucks, or a dust devil?

Two heavy shots, almost sounding as one, boomed and rolled distantly along the rock behind them.

"Kimathi!" Ernst called loudly to the small column behind him. "God bless him!"

Harriet, chilled, did not respond. All she knew was that she had left her sister to the killers.

— 40 —

"These things are always a little messy, Rosario," said Captain Uzielli to the sturdy *Alpini* as he watched two or three vultures spiral down. He noticed the slender angled wings and diamond-shaped tails of the large birds and wondered what he and his men would find when they got to the ledge. Perhaps these were the bearded vultures said to drop bones from great heights in order to fracture them and expose the marrow.

An arc of birds backed away angrily on the rocky ground as the soldiers approached the bodies near the dead fire. Leaping backwards, whistling querulously, they flapped their long grey wings in the dust. Red-beaked but not yet heavy-bodied or sated, the orange-bellied birds retreated step by step with their bristly black beards trembling in the wind, relinquishing their prizes for the moment.

The vultures had done their worst, opening the belly wound of the heavy African. A strip of wrinkled intestine hung from one bird's beak like the uneven links of a homemade *salsiccia.* Uzielli glanced up and saw other vultures descending perhaps a mile ahead.

"My God," said one young *Alpini* as he watched the impatient birds hopping about irritably while they waited to return to their meal. Two soldiers crossed themselves.

"Why are you city boys so squeamish?" Uzielli lit a cigarette. "Soon you'll be sorry Umberto didn't get a couple more of them."

Uzielli remembered the neighboring farmer bringing the live lamb into his grandmother's kitchen for Easter. She'd pinch its shoulders and ribs, then squeeze the upper rear legs in her fists until the animal squealed. "Thin," the old lady always said, "and don't mess my floor." The farmer straddled the animal and held a bucket beneath its neck with one hand while he stabbed a thin knife into its throat with the other. Thirty minutes later the animal was drained, skinned and eviscerated and the floor was clean.

Uzielli looked around the camp.

Only the woman had died of a single shot.

"Bit of a waste," Uzielli said, admiring the long slim legs and figure. He rested one hand on her neck, slipping it down to her shoulder just inside her shirt, feeling her cool temperature and the smoothness of her skin.

"Wonder what this *capelli rossi* was like alive," said one of the men.

"Too bad she's not still warm," said Rosario with a laugh.

"These two men were first wounded from a distance," said Uzielli. "Then Umberto finished them when he got here. Just five bullets for the three of them. Couldn't have done better myself."

He crouched on his heels and unbuttoned the pockets of the European's bush jacket and went through his things. Disturbed to find an American passport, he pocketed it together with a wad of dollars and a sketch of two identical women. One was the dead girl, her full lips in a circle as she smoked. Uzielli knelt and spat into his right hand, using the moisture to remove the woman's gold ring without having to mutilate her.

As he and the other eight men left the camp, one *Bersaglieri* lingered behind, unlacing the boots of the white man.

Further down the trail, Umberto was an even uglier sight but served to harden the men's resolve.

"Bastards. Looks like they opened his chest with a shovel," said a soldier, kneeling by the body. "And the sniper rifle's missing."

"Two heavy caliber bullets from close range," said Uzielli, staring down. He glanced around, then climbed up into the crevasse that overlooked the site. He knelt in the hard rock dust and picked up two spent cartridges.

"Porci Inglesi," the captain exclaimed. "An elephant gun. Do they think we're animals?" He had never seen such a wound from a rifle bullet. "Kynoch .450 Nitro Express" was stamped on the round rim of each copper casing. He put one in his pocket. It would make a useful whistle.

"Cover his body with stones," he said to two *Alpini* since the men carried no shovel. "Quickly. Then catch up with us fast as you can."

Travelling more cautiously, Uzielli and the others continued along the trail. Scanning with his glasses, he was relieved to see two of the trucks in the far distance below. Finally the trap was closing.

"Never thought I'd be so excited to see a *Schwartze,*" said Ernst von Decken, resting on a rock as he watched Kimathi run up to them.

Breathing hard, parched, the deep wrinkles of his face etched deeper with exhaustion, Kimathi appeared with a rifle in each hand.

Ernst whistled as he took the long-barrelled Carcano from the old tracker's hand. "Cartridges?" he said to Kimathi as the man gulped water from a canteen. "*Risasi?*"

"*Ndio,* Bwana," the African said slowly as if reassuring an impatient child. "*Ndio.*" Then he emptied a leather pouch of long sharp-pointed 6.5's into the German's cupped hands.

"Not a bad job, you filthy old dog," said von Decken grudgingly. "With this I might be able to hold them off while we make a dash across the lower country to Lake Stefanie."

The telescopic sight would make the weapon less practical at under fifty yards, or with a rapidly moving target, but he was hoping he wouldn't have to use it at close range. Small black leather cups protected the lenses at either end of the instrument. They reminded him of his stump cup.

In half an hour they were ready to start the descent. Both camels were packed with silver. The weakest mule was killed and abandoned, save for the two hindquarters, which were lashed to the pack frame of one of its resisting fellows.

The escarpment split into a broadening cleft near the bottom of the ridge, then opened onto the rocky plateau of the great massif that contained the lake. At the bottom, keeping close to the wall of the escarpment, Ernst mounted his horse and turned back to watch the safari collect itself before riding off. Underfoot the ground was deep and yielding, covered with fine pale grey igneous dust or ash, akin to powdery pulverized pumice.

Von Decken scanned the heights and the exposed turns of their precipitous path. He saw nothing of their pursuers but knew they would not be long. Here and there the dark mouths of volcanic caves or tunnels broke the rock wall. The greatest highlands on the continent were beginning their staged descent to a different Africa. Like the Rhine or the Channel or Gibraltar, this was one of the natural geological breaks that defined nations and set men at war.

While Ernst watched for the Italians, he drew the *Assassino* from his saddle scabbard and examined the telescopic sight, concerned that he had not yet had an opportunity to zero in the range. He looked forward to trying his new weapon on its countrymen.

Harriet was the last to mount. Gaunt, silent, she hunched her shoulders as if cold and alone.

"I'm going back," she said suddenly, turning her horse's head. "I know Berny's been hurt. She needs me."

"No," Ernst said harshly. "Whatever's happened, you can't help her." He leaned across and seized her horse's halter. Things would be hard enough if they kept going, he thought impatiently. Lightly armed, in the open, with camels and horses instead of trucks, he doubted any of them would make it.

"Let go of my horse!" She struck his arm with her crop. "How dare you!"

Determined to stop her, Ernst kicked his mount and both animals began to move. "You'll be killed if you go back!" he yelled. "Don't be stupid."

"I don't care," Harriet screamed, feeling they were all lost anyway. She swung again, hitting him across the face as he forced her horse to follow close beside him. "Let me go!"

"Don't make me tie your hands." Ernst wrenched the leather crop from her hand. "Can't you understand we're in the middle of a war?" He slapped her horse with the crop and both animals began trotting along the base of the escarpment.

He pulled up after a few minutes and waited for the rest of the safari to catch up before heading into the more open country. Harriet was calmer. Soon Ernst became aware of a different sound. Above the snorting animals and the pounding of hooves he heard the unmistakable growl of engines approaching around the rocks behind him.

If they bolted for the lake, he realized, they'd be caught in the open by the trucks and cut down by the mounted machine gun.

Von Decken turned and flogged his horse.

"A cave's our best chance." Ernst galloped back, leading Harriet and the others towards the entrance of the largest cave. Perhaps seventy or eighty yards from the cave they passed a giant fig tree that sheltered a small spring. The thirsty animals resisted as they were hurriedly led past the water towards the cave.

"Don't let them stop," Ernst ordered. "Get them into the cave."

Bats retreated into the narrowing black void when Ernst led his horse inside. Nervous in the cool darkness, disliking the jagged lava floor and rough low ceiling, the horses and mules clustered tightly in the wide mouth of the cave.

"The camels're too tall!" yelled the camel boy, unable to move the animals back.

"Leave them in front," Ernst told him. The boy whacked their knees and both beasts folded to the ground, blocking the entrance.

Ernst knelt behind a camel with the long Carcano in his hands. Kimathi and Harriet joined him with the hunting rifles as the first truck appeared

"At least here we have a chance," Ernst said as Harriet knelt beside him and rested one hand on his shoulder. "Check your rifles," he added to them both.

"Thank you, Bwana," the old tracker growled sarcastically before grinning at Harriet.

They watched the dusty Bianchi lurch to a stop by the fig tree. Both doors opened. There were no men in the back. The driver and a barefoot soldier flung themselves on their knees by the small pool. The barefoot man flattened his hands on the powdery bank and lowered his face and drank from the water like an animal. Ernst removed the leather cups from the telescopic sight and chambered a 6.5. The Italians would spot them any moment.

Stripping off his sun goggles, the driver cupped his hands and opened his mouth when he splashed his face. Ernst focused the scope until he could see the Italian's eyes and teeth. The soldier's face was tired, unshaven and dusty. The man licked his lips and again lowered his hands to the water. He began to raise the water to his face. Through the telescope Ernst saw the soldier's eyes shift when he spotted the mass of deep fresh animal tracks that led from the fig tree to the cave. The driver leapt to his feet and dashed to his truck as a Fiat six-wheeler nosed around the rocks. One man was driving and another leaned on a mounted machine gun. Just what we need to escape in, Ernst thought.

The first driver reached into his truck and lifted a carbine from the seat. Ernst's sniper round caught him in the spine. The barefoot Italian screamed and ran behind the truck. Ernst swung the Carcano to cover the Fiat as it arrived in a fury of pale dust.

"Damn!" Harriet snapped after firing high at the moving truck. Kimathi's first bullet blew apart the windscreen like a spray of mist. Ernst turned his head and nodded at the African. The truck banged to a stop against the fig tree. Ernst heard gunfire come from the hill above them as he fired twice at the struggling machine gunner, missing as he tried to aim through the telescope.

"Verflucht!" he cursed.

Clouds of dust puffed into the air as a line of heavier bullets chattered towards them, finally hitting a kneeling camel in the belly and back. A chest of silver split open. Harriet threw herself against the jagged wall of the cave. She felt the tin film canister crack inside her shirt when her back struck the rock. Ernst flung himself to one side as blood flew from the dying camel and the Italian gunner traversed the mouth of the cave.

Blinded by dust and blood, deafened by the firing and the rock-splintering ricochets inside the cave, Harriet held her second shot, crouching as she moved to one edge of the entrance. Bleeding at the neck, a horse lay kicking on its side towards the rear of the cave.

Kimathi stood behind the second camel and raised the .450. The beast moved its head and caught a heavy slug intended for the gunner. The Kikuyu blinked and wiped the mess from his face with one arm, then broke the gun to reload. As he closed the double rifle, three bullets ripped across his chest.

Slammed against the side of the cave, the big African leaned for a moment against the rough stone. *"Tlaga!"* he called as the gun fell from his hand. Blood ran from his lips. He struggled to rise. Then his body slid down against the wall. He sat there gasping with the gun resting on his legs and his fingers spread across his chest as the blood covered his hands.

For a moment there was silence save for the moaning of Kimathi and the dying animals.

Ernst watched Harriet kneel beside Kimathi, wiping his face and forcing away his hands to examine his wounds. He knew the man was finished.

The German removed the telescopic sight from his weapon and squinted into the light. He saw two Italians still alive, the machine gunner and another who hollered to the troops apparently hurrying down the hillside to join the trucks.

Behind them, the last African crouched among the surviving mules and horses. Ernst fired at a running soldier and missed.

"Can't help him," Ernst said to Harriet without turning his head to look at Kimathi.

"Don't worry, you're right," Harriet said with anger, thinking how upset Anton would be. "Kimathi's dead." Her cheeks were wet with tears. Her hands were slick with blood. She removed Kimathi's rifle before taking him by the shoulders and shifting him so that his body lay flat. Then she closed his eyes and crossed his hands on his belly.

"Check your rifle," said Ernst impatiently after Harriet wiped her hands on the sandy floor of the cave. "We must grab one of those trucks before the other soldiers get here."

"Which truck?" she said, having had the same idea.

"The six-wheeler. Then we won't have to stop if we get a bad tire," he said, studying the vehicle. It appeared big enough to carry them and all the silver.

Harriet reloaded and knelt beside Ernst. Her forehead had been cut by a stone splinter. Concerned, Ernst touched her brow with two fingers.

"One of us must go for the truck while the other fires at the gunner." He was reaching for his crutch, hoping he would be fast enough, when she stayed his arm.

"You won't make it," she said. "You can't run. I'll do it while you cover me." He looked at Harriet while she calmly retied her boots. When she had finished, she spoke again. "I'll drive out the last four horses and mules and run behind them while you shoot."

He was impressed with the offer, but was still doubtful. "Can you drive that thing?" he asked, checking his rifle while Harriet gathered the animals near the mouth of the cave.

"Can you shoot?" she snapped, tense and frightened but feeling anger replacing the sadness that filled her. Taking a deep breath, Harriet prepared to sprint. She moved forward and crouched between the bodies of the camels.

"Too late," Ernst said flatly. "They're here. Must be the others who were following us on foot."

Three soldiers appeared near the oasis and ran to the trucks. Ernst fired and hit one as the man climbed over the side of the Fiat to replace the wounded machine gunner. Two more appeared, firing, then two more. An officer seemed to be gathering the men behind the vehicles.

Von Decken refitted the scope to his rifle. Harriet sat against the wall reloading the .450. The other hunting rifle was ready by her side. For the first time in her life she felt scared and alone. She was thinking of Bernadette, certain her sister had been hurt or killed. Then she tightened her lips. She had to carry on. Berny would want her to fight.

Ernst cleaned both lenses and focused on the machine gun. The gunner lay in the bed of the truck, his hands moving on an ammunition box. The man's weapon was turned at an angle to the cave. Ernst examined the Breda end-to-end, from the long metal-strapped wooden stock to the wide perforated cooling barrel at the muzzle. He set down the sniper rifle.

"Give me the Holland."

Curious as to what he had in mind, the question in her eyes, Harriet passed him the heavy double rifle.

"Let's hope Rider keeps this English toy well sighted." Ernst wiped his sweaty hands on his trousers before resting his elbows on a silver chest still lashed to the back of a dead camel. "That machine gun's more dangerous than the Italians." The German closed his left eye and allowed for the drop, aiming a trifle above the rectangular metal plate where the magazine clip fed into the gun. Ernst squeezed the front trigger of the hunting rifle.

The bullet struck like the clash of cymbals. The machine gun swung wildly on its pivot mount. Ernst hesitated until it steadied, then fired again. The heavy gun fell between the mount and the cab of the truck. Harriet cheered and exchanged glances with Ernst. Several Italians returned fire. Harriet responded. One soldier abruptly stopped firing.

"Now we should be all right until it's dark." Ernst wiped his face on a sleeve. "There must be seven or eight left. I'll get one or two more while they're gulping their macaroni. Then we'll break out on the horses." He paused and spat the dust from his mouth before giving her his hard grin. "With a little silver for our old age."

"And the film," Harriet said, determined now to carry it out in order to avenge her sister, not to help the Abyssinians. She wondered if her Berny had already died for it.

Harriet checked the animals one by one, tightening the girths and adjusting the balance of the packs on the overloaded mules. Why was she risking her life for Ernst's silver? she asked herself. It meant nothing to her, of course, but to him it meant his old life in Tanganyika. And after what they'd both been through for it, she was beginning to care about that herself.

"When the firing starts," Ernst whispered, resting a rough hand on her cheek, "ride out fast as you can, *Liebchen*. Pick me up at the edge of those rocks. Another two or three hundred yards and there's a small ravine. That should slow the trucks." He hesitated and squeezed her to him for a moment, feeling the leather purse inside the back of her shirt. Her damn film was going to get them both killed.

He parted Harriet's shirt and kissed her between her breasts, scratching her roughly with his beard, fiercely sucking her left breast into his mouth before releasing her. Then he crawled out into the darkness with his crutch. Trembling, conscious of how much she had come to enjoy his rough touch, she watched Ernst avoid the moonlight as he stayed within the deep shadow of the stone ridge that rose above their cave.

After he left her, Harriet gave a handful of silver to the camel boy.

"Off you go," she said. "Shoo." The thrilled youth slipped silently into the night. For twenty minutes she stood with the horses and mules, stroking and calming them, knowing the nervous animals sensed her expectation. Feeling the soft noses of the ponies reminded her of sneaking down to the stables at night as girls to lie on the baled straw and stare in wonder at a wobbly new foal, so close they could smell its freshness, daring each other to touch it.

Surprised the Italians had not yet attacked the cave, Harriet saw firelight flickering in the shelter behind the trucks and occasionally heard voices from their camp.

One shot came from the far side of the spring to her right. Ernst. She was learning to recognize and distinguish gunfire. A man screamed. Rifles fired. Someone tried to kick out the camp fire. Almost too scared to breathe, forcing herself to be steady, Harriet led her mare to the mouth of the cave and climbed into the saddle. Gripping the lead ropes, lying Indian-style on her horse's neck the way she and Berny used to play games as girls, she kicked the mare and burst out of the cave around the dead camels.

Certain a faster pace would jar loose the silver chests, Harriet slowed to a fast walk and circled far out into the darkness around the spring and the Italian camp. Her stomach hard with fear, she prayed for Ernst as she listened to the intermittent firing and heard an engine start. She rode beyond the shadow of the escarpment and suddenly entered the moonlight. Harriet shifted to a trot as a pair of headlights flooded the bowl of land around the fig tree. She heard the engine of the damaged truck turning and grinding when it failed to catch.

The first truck began to move, its lights illuminating successive sections of the hillside as it turned to get around the spring. Harriet cantered towards the rocks, restraining her horse so the two mules could keep up on their tight leads. Straight ahead of her, almost in line with the base of the escarpment, she saw two tiny pricks of light. Then they were drowned by the flood of light behind her as the pursuing truck came in line with her flight. She saw a muzzle flash from the last cluster of boulders before her: Ernst. She made directly for the rocks as firing came from the truck behind her.

Ernst continued firing as the truck closed. One headlight went out. She reached the rocks and Ernst stood, rocking on one crutch as he struggled to secure his lathered horse behind a boulder.

"I'll hold him!" cried Harriet, trying to seize his prancing animal by the halter. Ernst abandoned his crutch. Hopping on one foot, he grabbed the horse's mane and reins in one hand, holding his rifle with the other. "Another truck!" she screamed as the pair of lights grew closer.

Ernst got his foot in the stirrup and climbed on. A mule screamed and went down, splitting one of the chests as the animal fell against a rock. Entangled in the leads and reins, Harriet tried to release the correct rope.

"We'd be away," she yelled, "if it weren't for your damned silver!"

The pursuing truck pulled up directly beside them. Ernst struggled to reload as his horse moved under him. Four men stood in the back of the truck with rifles.

"Drop your guns!" a voice screamed in Italian. "Get off your horses!"

The driver and another soldier jumped down and seized the reins of both horses. Ernst tried to club one man with his rifle but was pulled from his horse, cursing in German, still fighting and struggling as he was slammed to the ground on his back. Harriet saw his leather cup ripped off. His stump was open and bleeding.

Shaking, Harriet dismounted and surrendered her weapon. Even disarmed and crippled, bleeding from the face, Ernst's raw savageness frightened the young Italians who covered him. Panting with his mouth open, glaring at the soldier who prodded him with the barrel of a carbine, the German stood leaning on her with his arm around her shoulder. She felt his body tremble as he restrained himself.

Harriet and Ernst were forced against a boulder. They stood blinded in the glare of the headlights. The light was reflected off the tall rocks and illuminated the truck itself. Harriet felt Ernst tap the film under her shirt. Was he asking her to surrender it, to make it her decision? She did not quite understand the rough accent when one of the Italians spoke.

"Should I kill them, *Capitano?*" Rosario grabbed a handful of coins from the broken chest. "The black must have told them we killed the others in that camp."

"Not yet," said Uzielli. "There are questions I must ask them."

Understanding the Italian, Ernst prepared to make a choice about the film. If the Italians found it, they would certainly kill their prisoners. Would they kill them if they did not find it, or torture them to find it?

"Throw that *cagna* up here," Uzielli said, still standing in the back of the truck. The first rule of these things was to separate the victims and use the weakest against the strongest. He lowered his Beretta and shot the struggling mule twice in the head. A soldier grabbed Harriet. Uzielli stared at her and remembered the dead woman just like her whom he had touched in the camp.

"I am an American citizen," Harriet Mills said in a loud slow clear voice, first in English, then in her schoolgirl Italian. "Is Italy at war with the United States?"

"You have made yourselves combatants," Uzielli said as the soldier pulled her to the side of the truck by the wrist. "You are fighting on Italian soil."

With no one to lean on, Ernst fell back against the boulder, trying to appear unthreatening. He must find some opportunity.

"You have killed Italian soldiers," Captain Uzielli continued, kneeling inside the truck. He pointed his pistol at von Decken. "And if that gimping Kraut's an American, I'm the nigger Queen of Sheba."

Uzielli reached out and ripped the scarf from Harriet's head, tearing out strands of hair. He noticed the subdued redness of her hair.

"I've seen you before." He took the drawing of the two women from his tunic and unfolded it. He studied Harriet for a moment before pressing it into her hand. "Looks like it's not too late for the boys to enjoy you, after all."

Uzielli chuckled loudly while she studied the sketch of Bernadette and herself. Harriet looked up at him with horror and anger in her face.

"You killed my sister!" she raged, trying to reach up and strike him. "Didn't you? You killed my sister!"

"Where is the cinema film?" Uzielli reached down from the truck. Brushing aside her flailing arm, he cupped Harriet's cheek with his left hand. She felt as if some strange animal had seized her.

Looking on with hard eyes, holding himself back, Ernst knew better than to waste indignation. He thought he heard an engine in the distance, or was it just this one idling? His own truck running, the Italian officer would not be able to hear another vehicle until it was close.

Uzielli pinched Harriet's cheek hard between his fingers. Finally hearing the approaching truck, he became even more determined to secure the film before Colonel Grimaldi could join them and take charge.

"Where is the damn film?" Uzielli said, uncontrolled anger in his voice.

Lowering his face close to hers, he squeezed and twisted her flesh as if turning the lid of a stubborn jar.

Harriet screamed but did not speak. It would take more than this to make her do what this greaseball wanted. She prayed Ernst would not try to intervene.

Uzielli twisted her skin until she felt her eye would pop out. He spoke slowly so the American woman would understand.

"I thought we already killed you," he said to her. He moved his fingers to her nipple and seized it violently through her shirt, almost pulling her off her feet as he wrenched upwards. Clawing at his hand, cutting deep scratches into his wrist, Harriet shrieked at the blinding pain.

"Stop it!" Ernst yelled. Despite himself, he began to move forward, until a soldier raised his carbine.

"I'm getting a little old for this sort of thing," Uzielli said, flinching as he clenched and turned his fist, still holding her, "but these boys haven't had a woman in months, unless you count those monkeys in Massawa, and you've killed several of their comrades." Uzielli lowered his face to Harriet's until she smelled the stink of his breath. "Maybe you'll be more cooperative after you've had a little attention. Women usually talk more after sex."

The captain turned to the stocky *Alpini* who was heaving a silver chest into the truck.

"Rosario, you romantic bastard, you go first. But wipe yourself before you touch her. I may change my mind myself."

"The film's under her shirt," Ernst said, certain they would find it anyway, and hoping to distract the soldier nearest him and seize the man's weapon. He'd been sure the Italians would get around to this, and he knew he wouldn't be able to stand idly while they raped her. Inevitably he'd do something stupid and get them both killed.

"*Capitano, una macchina*!" Rosario exclaimed. "*Una Fiat*!"

Captain Uzielli squinted into the arriving headlights from the back of his own truck. This must be that damned Grimaldi in the repaired vehicle. The pistol still in one hand, Uzielli released Harriet with a push and waved a salute. She collapsed by the side of the truck, thinking what she could do now to save the film.

A Fiat pulled up in the darkness fifteen yards away. Uzielli saw a man standing by the mounted machine gun. He wore no uniform. A woman was at the wheel.

Something was wrong, Uzielli realized instantly. He raised his Beretta. "*Fuoco*!" he yelled to his men.

Ernst fell to the ground as the soldiers swung their rifles.

Anton Rider fired the bucking machine gun in a long burst, sweeping the other truck from cab to tail, then back again more slowly, pausing before reversing to kill one of the *Alpini* who had already dismounted. Silver coins fell from Rosario's fingers as he died.

The remaining soldier threw down his carbine.

Anton hesitated before the next burst, swinging the smoking gun from left to right.

"Stop!" Gwenn screamed at him, leaning up out of the window. "Stop shooting! They're all dead."

"No," said Ernst. "One's still moving in that truck."

Anton jumped down and looked into the bed of the other Fiat. Wounded in the arm and twice in the side, Uzielli lay in the back between two dead troopers. Recognizing him at once, Anton picked up the man's Beretta and threw it to Ernst.

"At last, *Engländer,* at last!" Ernst roared as he held out one arm, supporting himself on Harriet with the other. "Late, as usual, of course!"

Anton and Gwenn hurried to them.

"Where're your sister and Charlie?" Anton said to Harriet after they had hugged.

"We had to leave them after Charlie was wounded . . ."

"I'll go back for them," Anton said at once.

"*Nein.* Useless." Von Decken shook his head. *"Zwecklos."*

Harriet turned her head to stare at Ernst. He averted his eyes, nervously checking the slide and magazine of the automatic.

Finally Ernst told her. "You were right." Kicking the dead soldier who lay near the silver chest, he spoke in a low voice. "This man just said this bunch killed them."

Harriet shivered and freed herself from Ernst's arm. Then she walked slowly away from the others and stood with her back to them, staring up at the escarpment.

The German hopped two steps to the first truck with the pistol in his belt, trying to prevent his bare stump from dragging in the dirt. "These boys don't take prisoners. *Verbrecherin,* not soldiers."

The Italian captain struggled to sit up. Ernst reached into the truck, grabbed Uzielli by the shirt and went through the Italian's pockets. He put the money in his own pocket and handed Bernadette's gold ring and passport to Gwenn. He turned back to the truck and opened one of the Italian's knapsacks lying in the bed of the lorry. "My silver!"

Then von Decken drew and cocked the Beretta.

"No!" Gwenn said. "Don't!"

"Why not?" Ernst said with mild curiosity.

"He's wounded. You can't just kill him like that."

"If you insist."

As Gwenn reached for his arm, von Decken placed the pistol near Uzielli's right ankle and fired. *"Kätzlmacher!"* He turned and shot the other soldier in the leg. Both Italians screamed.

"I hope you find this more civilized, Doctor." Ernst picked up his crutch and flung it on the bed of the truck with the knapsacks. Grunting as he lifted in his bad leg, he took a seat in the front and slammed the door.

For a moment no one spoke. Gwenn clutched the ring and passport, then walked over and put her arm around Harriet's shoulders. The American girl stiffened, trying to gather herself.

"There was nothing you could have done," Gwenn said gently.

Anton lifted the sobbing *Bersaglieri* and set him in the back of the truck beside Uzielli. The Italian captain cursed him.

"Where's old Kimathi, and the others?" Anton said.

"Dead." Harriet bent to retrieve the cup for Ernst's stump. "Back there, by the spring, and the rest are all dead or gone."

"Dead?" Anton said. "Kimathi, too?" When no one answered, he spoke again.

"We'll bury Kimathi," he said quickly, thinking also of Laboso and Lapsam. "Then we'll get some water and load the silver and supplies into the best lorry and make for the border." He dropped one of the bodies over the side of the truck. "We'll leave the wounded Italians at the spring."

"Help me with these two," Gwenn said to Harriet as she started over to the wounded soldiers. "How could Ernst shoot those wounded men?"

"Don't be silly, Gwennie," Harriet said with annoyance. "Where do you think we are? Those trash killed Berny and Charlie. They were going to rape me. Those two would've come after us later if Ernst hadn't hurt them."

Gwenn gave Harriet her sister's ring and tossed the passports in the cab.

"We have to hurry." Anton dropped the second dead man from the bed of the vehicle. "One more lake to go. This morning we spotted another Italian lorry in the distance. It had a motorbike mounted on the back."

— 41 —

The Goliath heron opened its long straight bill, then clacked it together as if stifling a yawn.

The bird stood among the green and tan reeds on long black legs. Nearly as tall as Anton, it straightened its pink neck and regarded his dugout with perfectly round yellow eyes. The dark centers always reminded him of sunflowers.

"Ernst!" Anton yelled from the long wooden canoe. "Ernst! Hurry up!" The German did not respond. Certain that Grimaldi must still be after them, and concerned about the other Fiat he and Gwenn had spotted two days before, Anton was keen to get started across Lake Stefanie.

"He's almost finished," Harriet called from the shore through cupped hands.

Gwenn, exhausted, dozed in the bow. Behind her, Anton's old Merkel rested between them on a single chest of silver. Anton looked through the reeds to the shore. There a crowd of Ethiopians swarmed over the abandoned Fiat, its petrol tank empty. Goats sheltered in the shade of the lorry. Two women struggled to remove the driver's seat from its frame. Others knelt by the shore rinsing out the gasoline tins. A gang of boys tussled in the bed of the truck while all around them men worked to dismantle the wooden planks that formed the sides. A little girl in a spotless white robe saw Anton watching and waved one hand demurely.

Two clusters of round reed huts with conical thatched roofs stood on the lakeshore. Each structure was trimmed with plaited fronds and crowned by a pointed top supporting a carved Coptic cross. Both groups of huts were surrounded by a shoulder-high palisade with one open gate through which goats and humpbacked cattle and children in long robes wandered in and out.

Gwenn opened her eyes and splashed her face with lake water. Feeling stronger, she stepped from the canoe and watched a young woman walking towards them along the edge of the lake. Layers of small red beads covered her neck from shoulder to chin. A long black catfish balanced on a cloth set on her head. The tail of the fish hung before her face.

On the shore near the truck von Decken struggled with the silver, supervising two well-paid Ethiopians, determined not to leave one coin behind. They had used a dozen poles to attach an additional smaller dugout to either side of Ernst's canoe, like pontoons or the secondary hulls of catamarans, set three or four feet from the central canoe to allow space for paddling. Ernst had piled chests of silver into the three dugouts until all the vessels lay low and heavy, even in the salty buoyant water of Lake Stefanie. The silver from the broken chests he had thrown loose into the bottom of Anton's canoe. "That's your share," he said to his friend. Even that would help, thought Anton, but not enough.

While they all worked, an Ethiopian came to them along the shore, carrying a young boy wrapped in a bloody cloak. The man set down the unconscious child beside them. Gwenn opened the boy's garment. Both of his thin thighs were serrated with deep puncture wounds.

"Crocodile," Anton said, noting the space between each wound. "Biggest crocs in Africa are hereabouts or in the Sudd." He hurried back to the truck for the medical chest.

Gwenn cleaned and dressed the wounds as best she could. She marvelled again at the durability of Africans. By the time she finished, a cluster of Abyssinians was waiting for help: families thin and feverish with malaria, an old man suffering from bilharzia, another with vacant milky-blue eyes, glossy-blind as marbles, two brothers with identical spinal deformities, an old woman afflicted by some parasite Gwenn could not identify.

Feeling useful but inadequate, Gwenn realized she could not wait to get back to medical school and complete her training. Her efforts reminded her of Kenya and her weekly clinics at the farm. For a doctor, there was nowhere like Africa. Everyone needed you. Each physician was his own hospital.

While she examined the Africans and did what was possible with the Italian medical chest, she heard Ernst hammering away on the boat. Harriet was helping bind the poles together with the wire, cord, engine belts and clamps that Anton had stripped from the truck. Gwenn was aware of a leper with swollen grey legs and puffy short fingers crouching at a distance. The noseless man shielded his rheumy eyes with a banana leaf as he watched her work, doubtless knowing she could do nothing for him.

"Ernst! We're leaving," Gwenn heard Anton holler. Her work finished, her shoulder aching, she climbed into the canoe and picked up a heart-shaped paddle. The lake was low. Mosquitoes swarmed in the shallow pools among the floating green leaves and yellow-centered blue petals of the water lillies. Concerned to see fresh blood staining the left side of Anton's shirt as he worked, she watched him check the balance of the canoe and shift the load.

Long muddy sandbars ran parallel to the shore, spotted here and there with heron and hadada ibis and the spoor of hippopotamus. It appeared that in places they would have to drag the canoes across the bars to find deeper water. On an island to the south she saw a party of red-billed ducks waddle ashore.

Gwenn could not believe that Kenya waited at the end of the lake. For the first time she felt she might be going home. She prayed Lorenzo wasn't close. Even without the film, she knew he would keep after them.

Only after Anton had pushed off and begun to paddle did Ernst finally climb into his canoe. Gwenn looked back and saw Harriet fit his crutch into one of the side dugouts. She knew how Harriet must miss her sister. When this was over she would begin to ache. Gwenn watched the American wade in deeper, sinking to her knees as she pushed the three boats through the soft grey sand. Gwenn heard Ernst's voice grumbling as he gave Harriet advice and instructions. Gwenn smiled and touched Anton's hand.

For several hours they struggled forward. Regretting that she was unable to paddle herself, Gwenn had not believed canoing could be so arduous.

"With the rains over," Anton said, waving a hand to encompass the lake ahead of them, "Stefanie's not so much one lake as a series of swampy puddles surrounding muddy islands and these spongy sandbars."

They had to unload the canoes twice before dragging them across the small islands, leaving only the carpet of silver sliding about in the first dugout. Warily, they used the hippopotamus paths that cut through the tall reeds and fronds that covered much of the islands. Each time, Anton went first, then hurried back for a second load. His shirt dark and slick with blood, he refused to stop and let Gwenn dress his wound.

Occasionally they came across fresh hippo prints and the dark droppings of crocodile. Wherever it was soft or sandy, Ernst was useless. His crutch and stump sank in, making him barely able to look after himself.

"Take two rifles, Ernst, and nothing else. We'll do your work," Anton finally told him on the second island, keen to push on. "But no shooting, we're still too close to shore. No need to attract attention."

Harriet was astounded to see her German accept an order without complaint.

Ernst crossed the third island and sat on a rock by the water, watching a black openbill stork prying snails and molluscs from the mud with its long pincer-shaped bill. As Anton and Harriet made a trip back across the island to reload the dugouts, he followed a flight of Egyptian geese with the Holland, not shooting but leading them and clicking his tongue like a boy.

A few yards ahead of Anton, Harriet screamed and dropped the end of the chest she was dragging through the sand.

Anton ran forward, crossing a fresh snaking trail made by a crocodile's tail. He passed a shallow depression in the dry sand amidst the reeds. There in the small basin was an exposed nest. He glanced down and saw several baby crocs hatching in the pit, their long fingers pushing aside fragments of ivory-colored shells as they clawed their way to life, piping shrilly.

As he reached Gwenn, a female crocodile ran past her with astonishing speed. The creature's long jaw was slightly agape as it scrambled down a croc chute that led to the water near Ernst. Three infant hatchlings were visible inside the protection of the animal's jaws. Their long thin bodies were tumbled together on the floor of her mouth within the crib formed by their mother's uneven protruding teeth.

Her spine and black upper body as jagged as Abyssinia, the broad-snouted amphibian switched her tail violently when Ernst shot her in the head as she passed him and plunged into the lake.

"Must be eight or ten feet long," said Harriet, pale and trembling.

"Actually, just a baby herself," Anton observed, lifting the abandoned chest, concerned about the noise of the shot.

Harriet climbed unsteadily into the bow of Ernst's dugout and sat clutching her shoulders while Anton finished loading the boats. It was the first time Anton had seen the American girl incapacitated by fear. Everyone, he knew, had their different terrors.

To the west a long wide sandbar still separated them from the center of the lake. From time to time they saw or heard hippos blowing and breaching in the deeper water on the far side of the bar.

For three or four hours more they paddled and poled and portaged in sight of shore, travelling more and more painfully as fatigue slowed them. To their right the water glimmered golden while the sun dropped. The falling light caught the metallic green wings of a lone ibis as the bird's call crossed the water. *"Hah, dah, dah."*

"Should we stop for the night?" Gwenn suggested. She could see Harriet was near collapse.

"No." Anton guided the first canoe between two sandy islands. "One or two more hours and this water's British." He reached forward and touched Gwenn's shoulder.

She put her hand on his.

Anton heard the report as the bullet struck.

Splinters flew near the bow of Ernst's canoe. Harriet cried out and covered her face. A spout of water poured into the dugout.

"We're lucky the sun's in the bastard's eyes," Anton said as he raised his Merkel. "Must be Grimaldi." No one else was left to pursue them. He wondered if Gwenn understood.

Anton thought of his dead friends, and of the man who had started all this. He wished he could abandon his companions and swim ashore through the reeds and teach this Italian a final lesson. Staring ahead, he sought to imagine where he would position himself if he were the hunter. Only the islands provided shooting platforms to cover the lake from shore to shore.

The Merkel was longer-barrelled than the Holland, but not up to military range. Anton tried to lower himself in the boat as he squinted ahead along the shore to a spit of land that entered the water perhaps two hundred yards before them. A figure moved there behind some obstacle, perhaps a log or old canoe. Too far.

"Lie down, Gwenn," Anton said as he lifted his paddle.

"Ernst! Pin him down with the Carcano while I paddle closer!" he yelled, wanting to get the Italian within range of his heavy double rifle. "Gwenn, lie down! "

Ernst fired steadily as Anton's canoe moved forward. In reply, two bullets struck the water between the canoes. When he was close enough, Anton lifted the Merkel and set his elbows on his knees. He aimed high and fired both barrels. Chips of wood jumped near his target. As he reloaded, a bullet struck Ernst's canoe. "Bastard," Anton muttered. Raising the tips of his barrels very slightly as he fired, trusting the old trick would give him extra range, Anton squeezed the front trigger. The man disappeared from sight. There was no further gunfire.

"Maybe we'll lose him if we keep going," Gwenn said.

They came to a channel in the sandbar and paddled through it towards the sun into deeper water.

Anton heard a shrill light engine cough and start up on the east bank, paralleling them in the distance as they glided south in the setting sun. "Reckon that's the motorbike that was lashed to their truck," Anton said. They all began to paddle faster. Patches of thick reeds occasionally obliged them to force their way forward with the poles.

Emerging into a broad reach of clear water, Anton looked ahead to a chain of muddy islands that nearly crossed the lake from shore to shore. He raised his glasses and made out the motorbike lying on the edge of the east bank. Scanning across the lake, he saw Grimaldi wading knee deep from one island to another. The Italian officer carried a rifle in one hand. He swung his arms in a hooking motion as he forced his way forward.

Anton watched Grimaldi stagger up the shore of the center island. Steering the canoe towards a passage to the left, he saw the muddy silt sucking at the Italian's boots while the man made his way step by step through the thick short reeds. Here and there Anton discerned the shadows of logs or dark debris scattered among the water growth that covered the low island.

The floor of the canoes brushed the tall bottom grass that rose wave-like from the lakebed. While Ernst paddled with powerful strokes, Harriet used his hat to empty the canoe as the water rose inside it.

Suddenly a dome of water erupted three feet to Anton's right. A hippopotamus exploded to the surface like a breaching whale as the canoe passed.

"Anton!" Gwenn screamed. He lifted the Merkel and turned to face back, squinting into the sun when the hippo struck Ernst's dugout.

Anton fired both barrels. In the difficult light, he was certain he had hit the animal twice, but not mortally. The hippo's immense head rose from the water with the bow of the canoe across it. The great jaws opened like a portcullis. Water poured out between the tusk-like yellow canines. The side dugouts snapped free and rolled over as the poles were broken by the violence and the unsupported weight of the silver. In the water, Ernst clung to his own overturned canoe, his rifle in one hand. Harriet swam towards Anton, crawling with smooth strokes despite the drag of her boots and clothes.

Bleeding from one ear, open-mouthed, the wounded bull hippo rushed for Harriet with the force and noise of a locomotive.

"Anton, stop him!" Gwenn yelled. He reloaded with his last bullets and fired again. At the close range, they heard the slap of impact as both bullets struck the hippopotamus above one eye. The huge animal slid forward in the water with its mouth closed and its small protruding red eyes open and shining, almost touching Harriet with its round flank as her hands gripped the side of the canoe next to Anton.

"Careful," he said, seeing the fear in her wide eyes as she caught her breath. "You'll overturn us." He leaned forward and lifted the chest of silver that sat between Gwenn and him.

"Here, we can't afford to be weighed down with this," he said, dropping the crate over the side. Only a few yards away in the lake, Ernst screamed when the chest hit the water and sank.

"Lean that way, Gwenn," Anton said. "More." He hauled Harriet over the side, feeling the soaked film purse under her shirt. At the same moment he noticed the small splinters lodged in her left cheek. She sloshed down in the middle of the dugout on the bed of silver coins.

"Damn it!" said Harriet, spitting water, "the film must be ruined." She reached into her shirt and removed the purse. She held it upside down. Green lake water and a few grains of sand poured from it before she pulled out the canister. The tin container was dented and split open with a wide crack across the top of the lid. The round edges were bent open. For a few seconds, Harriet held the canister in her shaking hands, struggling unsuccessfully to force the broken lid back on. While she struggled, water leaked out and more light entered the tin.

"Useless!" Harriet cried, stuffing the canister back inside the purse. "I've ruined it." She closed her eyes as Gwenn twisted around in the narrow vessel to comfort her.

"Don't worry," Gwenn said, putting one hand on Harriet's shoulder, knowing her own words were false, fearing Harriet felt her sister had died for nothing. "Perhaps the film will be all right. And we can still tell everyone what we saw."

"Berny! Berny!" Harriet cried, sobbing and rocking backwards and forwards in the canoe. "I'm sorry!"

"Ernst," Anton said, pausing to confirm that the engine was still following them on shore, "you're too heavy to get in. Give me that rifle and then hang onto the stern."

"Blast you," Ernst snarled at Anton, spitting after he swam over and clutched one side of the canoe. His face was red.

"You stupid English bastard." He handed Anton the dripping weapon and gasped while he caught his breath. "That was the last chest. I've risked my life for that silver. It's already cost me a foot."

"My own silver's in the bottom of this canoe," Anton said. "Mark where we are with something on the shore. Then you can come back and find yours," Anton added to his friend in a calm voice. "And shout if you see a croc." Anton chuckled when the German cursed again. "Or if you touch one with your good foot."

Anton began to paddle while the body of the hippopotamus sank into the darkening water behind them. By the time its gasses made the body rise again, they should be either safe or dead, he thought.

They continued on, slowly approaching within rifle range of the center island. If he were Grimaldi, that's where he'd be waiting for them, lying prone among the reeds.

The sun now barely brushed the water, striking only the taller reeds, occasional hillocks on the shore and whatever else broke the watery horizon.

"Keep paddling until I tell you both to lie flat." Anton passed his paddle to Harriet and lifted the Carcano. He opened the rifle, dried the chamber and the last bullet with his diklo, and reloaded. He spotted movement on the island and raised the rifle. "Get down!" Fully conscious that his one shot had to count, he breathed in and closed his left eye.

Before he could fire, the Italian stood erect on the island, then collapsed to one knee. A single terrible scream cut the silence of the lake.

Spreading its broad black wings, its chestnut belly bright in the rays of the falling sun, a fish eagle rose slowly from a dead acacia atop the island. The bird's wild gull-like call echoed across the water. Its thick yellow claws were empty.

Closer now, Anton saw Grimaldi struggling to lower his rifle and aim at something in the reeds that had him by one leg.

"A crocodile!" Gwenn cried in horror.

Grimaldi fired twice, apparently without effect. His body, limping, was being jerked about, denying him a well-aimed shot. With each struggling step, drawn by the crocodile that manacled him, he seemed to be getting closer to the water. From here and there, through the cover of the water growth, movement came towards him. Long dark shapes switched their tails from side to side as they hurried to get their share. Anton saw one immense broad beast, perhaps fifteen feet long, lying unmoving just at the water's edge, its body partly covered by the lapping lake.

"Shoot the crocodile!" Gwenn screamed.

With Harriet paddling frantically, the canoe slowly approached the channel to the island's left.

"Rider," yelled Ernst from the stern. "Shoot that devil while he's standing!"

Anton raised the rifle and hesitated, knowing Grimaldi deserved his fate but feeling bound to help. He knew what he would want if he were the Italian.

Grimaldi fell full length near the shore as a second smaller crocodile reached him.

The Italian's rifle fired again, then fell from his hands as he rose screaming to both knees. His face was mottled in sandy mud. His eye patch had been torn away.

"Lorenzo!" Gwenn called in an agonized voice. "Help him, Anton! Shoot the crocodile!"

With only one shot, Anton knew he could not save Grimaldi even if he wished to, and he knew Gwenn would never forgive him if he did not try.

Four or five crocodiles bit and snapped at the struggling figure. The enormous reptile on the shore rose onto its short legs and swung its head. With astonishing speed it turned and lunged into the fray, knocking aside smaller rivals with swinging thrusts of its immense jaws. Its broad scaly tail slapped the edge of the water as it seized the man about the waist, like a fish in the beak of a heron.

The great reptile lifted Grimaldi off the ground, shaking him violently from side to side as it sought to force the first crocodile to release his leg. The smaller animal hung on, flung this way and that, its dangling front feet looking pale and small like a child's hands.

Anton shouldered the Carcano as the canoe entered the channel. He thought of Gwenn before he closed his eye and aimed. Just as well to let the crocs give the bastard what he deserves, he thought, though it went against all his instincts after a lifetime in the bush.

Drawing itself backwards with its hind legs, the giant amphibian retreated into the lake through a patch of water lilies, its tail thrashing from side to side and the human creature still struggling in its jaws.

"Shoot the crocodile!" Gwenn yelled.

Knowing the small bullet would be useless, Anton aimed his last shot between the scaly ridges behind the crocodile's eyes.

Enzo flailed with his arms and legs, his body scraping along the bank while the smaller reptiles closed around it as the grinding jaws dragged him into the water. His terrible cry carried across the lake.

Adjusting his aim at the last instant, Anton fired and shot Grimaldi in the chest. The crocodile dived with the dead man in its jaws.

Gwenn collapsed forward on her knees, her head in her arms while the canoe swept past the island.

"Faster, Rider," urged Ernst, spitting water. "Paddle, damn you! They'll be after me next."

Anton lifted his paddle and looked up.

On the shore, he saw a man standing in shorts, a tall African, armed, and four more in uniform. Each man wore a fez and long dark socks and khaki shorts and a dark blue sweater. Kenya's King's African Rifles. In the background stood a small stockade with a flag.

A torn Union Jack waved in the setting sun.

— 42 —

"At last," said the dwarf, smiling at Lord Penfold under the umbrella set on the unfinished stern of the new Cataract Café. The beginnings of the upper shell of the poopdeck rose around them like the bars of a bird cage. "They've finally understood."

"How's that?" said Penfold, squinting at the *Gazette* through his spectacles with watery blue eyes. "Says here the Eyeties've about wrapped it all up down there in Ethiopia. Nothing left but a few mountain redoubts. Emperor's hiding in a cave. Shouldn't be surprised if one day our chaps'll have to go down and sort 'em out. Africa's no place for Italians, really."

"My lord . . ."

"Not much good news about," continued the Englishman as Tariq presented his gin. "Ah, thank you. Headlines no better than yesterday's: SUICIDES ON WALL STREET. BLACKSHIRTS RALLY IN VIENNA BY TORCHLIGHT. CIVIL WAR IN SPAIN. ITALIANS CLEAN UP ADDIS. MASS EXECUTIONS BY MACHINE GUNS." Penfold folded the paper and sipped his gin before continuing.

"Says Mussolini's boys've been murdering Abyssinian priests and Red Cross wounded. The foreign Red Cross teams are leaving, complaining about being bombed. More on this gas business. Eyeties still deny it. The locals call it 'burning rain.' Burns the skin right off their faces. Even burns the mouths of the pack mules when the poor things eat the poisoned grass."

"My lord," tried Olivio again, gnawing at a mango pit.

"Sorry, old boy." Penfold folded the paper and set it on the small table between them. "Understood what?"

"About how to finish this craft we're sitting on," said the little man, slightly exasperated. "You see, working from Maître Aristide's drawings, my naval architect, an Alexandrine Greek *de bonne famille,* has finally designed the new café in harmony with my desires," said Olivio, determined to engage his friend in his own satisfaction. Thanks to the lavish new blessings of the Nile, expense was beneath concern. What's more, the dwarf smelled a far larger war, and with conflict the price of cotton and sugar could only rise.

"She'll be a caravel, you see," he added, leaning to one side and looking down at what rested near his chair. Soon the ship would boast the squared stern and high narrow poop, the broad bows, and even the masts of the most daring and graceful of all ships, a Portuguese caravel.

"Of course, she'll be twice the length of Vasco da Gama's, and she'll never sail from Lisbon to Goa." Olivio smiled, enjoying his jest. Only the square lateen sails would be missing when the new Cataract Café opened, though her slender forked pennants would be flying in the desert wind, one bearing the Egyptian name of the vessel herself. She was to be a caraval designed for love and profit. Belowdecks he would provide corruptions to charm even the most jaded Egyptian official.

"What'll she be called?" said Penfold.

"Qurunfil," said the dwarf. "Clove."

"How very splendid!" cried Adam Penfold with true delight.

"All Cairo will vie and beg and bribe for tables in the bow and forecastle." The dwarf spread his hands and fingers, his eye sparkling as he continued.

"I can see the guests pressing forward down the gangways, keen as boarding parties. Can you not sniff now, my lord, and smell the moist stuffed pigeons and the smoky grilled kebabs, and your own favorites, the baking *samosas*?"

Olivio looked along his ship and saw already the elegant lunches and teas, the teeming bar in the enclosed poop, the last dancers, lovers, gliding alone under the Nile moon, and the private theatricals unfolding under the gaze of the sphinx in the mysterious shadows of the hold below.

"And one other thing, your lordship," he said more quietly, thinking of the child he had lost. "On deck there will be motion pictures in the springtime."

Relishing the bustle and sawing and hammering raging inside the hull below, the little man turned his round head to watch a messenger clamber up the ramp towards him. The dwarf's face did not reveal the rush of pain the movement caused him in his back. Elegant in the tan livery of Suez Cable & Wireless, the boy carried the monogrammed leather pouch of the telegram delivery service. Without looking down, Olivio lowered an arm and rocked the rattan cradle that rested in the shade close to his side.

He gave the bowing courier a sixpence. Never willing to display anxiety, the dwarf set down the cable atop the *Gazette.* After a patient moment, he opened the pale blue envelope and peeked at the cable as he unfolded the message from Mombasa.

> MY DEAR OLIVIO
> GWENN SAILING FOR SUEZ MONDAY WITH VON DECKEN AND HARRIET MILLS. THEY INTEND MARRYING AT YOUR CAFE. PLEASE CABLE YOUR NEWS. GIVE OUR LOVE TO WELLIE AND DENBY. HAQIM AND KIMATHI AND BERNADETTE AND CHARLES KILLED BY ITALIANS. GWENN HURT BUT RECOVERING AND SENDS HER LOVE. I'M OFF TO NAIROBI AND THEN UP COUNTRY. WILL SEE YOU ALL IN CAIRO WHEN I CAN. TELL CLOVE TO SAVE A GOOD FILM. AS EVER
>
> ANTON

Olivio could no longer see the words. He groaned and cried out once. His body trembled, then shook with sobs. He gave himself up to it, heaving and weeping like a child. For all of them, his daughter, his friends, himself. Adam Penfold leaned forward and touched both his arms, then took the message from the little man's hand. For a time the two friends were silent.

The dwarf felt something seize his little finger and grip it and suck it as if kissing. He inclined his head and smiled down through his tears at his exceptionally small son.

— *A Note About the Book* —

I have taken several liberties of date and geography in *A Café on the Nile.* The first use of poison gas by the Italian forces took place on December 23, 1935, not in October or November of that year, as implied in this novel. Lake island monasteries do exist in Ethiopia, but not in Lake Zwai. The semien fox generally lives in a more northeasterly habitat than that indicated in this book. Gelada baboons favor somewhat more precipitous terrain than that described here. The Din Din forest, however, does harbor melanistic animals.

The slaughter of Christian monks did not take place at Lake Zwai, but instead occurred at the monastery of Debre Libanos northeast of Addis Ababa. There two hundred and ninety-seven monks and one hundred and twenty-nine young deacons were shot by Italian forces in May, 1937 on the instructions of Marshall Rodolfo Graziani, the Viceroy of *Africa Orientale Italiana,* following an attempt on the Viceroy's life by Abyssinian partisans. When I climbed the mountainous hillside behind Debre Lebanos on Coptic Christmas Day, 1994 I found the skulls of the murdered monks still preserved in piles on a rocky shelf above the monastery.

The terms "Abyssinia" and "Ethiopia" have been effectively interchangeable for generations, although in the 1930s "Abyssinia" was generally in favor. Almost unique among the fifty nations of Africa (the other exception being Liberia), Ethiopia was never in its history a European colony. Never complete, the Italian occupation ended in 1941 when Abyssinia was liberated by British troops under Major Orde Wingate. My own father spent time there during that period while on a combined parliamentary and military mission for the British government. It is generally agreed that two blessings of the six-year Italian occupation were the remarkable advance in road building and the virtual elimination of slavery. Abyssinia had been the last country in Africa to practise formal slavery on a widespread basis. Today slavery exists in the Sudan on a limited basis.

The "Grandpa" referred to in the author's dedication was in fact my American grandmother, there depicted at Giza, who insisted on that appellation for herself after my infant sister once called her by that name when she was confused while trying to describe a bronze bust of my paternal grandfather during a stay at his house in London. Though kindly, Grandpa was not a lady easy to dissuade, having become a lawyer in 1907, led suffragette parades, managed a corporation, toured Russia by train in 1927, ran for the U.S. Congress twice during the 1930s and, at the age of eighty, addressed the Republican National Convention in Chicago in 1952, so we continued to call her by that name until her death at ninety-six.

B.B.